THE TIGH

THE ENEMY

Desmond Bagley was born in 1923 in Kendal, Westmorland, and brought up in Blackpool. He began his working life, aged 14, in the printing industry and then did a variety of jobs until going into an aircraft factory at the start of the Second World War.

When the war ended, he decided to travel to southern Africa, going overland through Europe and the Sahara. He worked en route, reaching South Africa in 1951.

Bagley became a freelance journalist in Johannesburg and wrote his first published novel, *The Golden Keel*, in 1962. In 1964 he returned to England and lived in Totnes, Devon, for twelve years. He and his wife Joan then moved to Guernsey in the Channel Islands. Here he found the ideal place for combining his writing and his other interests, which included computers, mathematics, military history, and entertaining friends from all over the world.

Desmond Bagley died in April 1983, having become one of the world's top-selling authors, with his 16 books – two of them published after his death – translated into more than 30 languages.

'I've read all Bagley's books and he's marvellous, the best.' ALISTAIR MACLEAN

By the same author

Flyaway AND *Windfall*

The Golden Keel AND *The Vivero Letter*

High Citadel AND *Landslide*

Running Blind AND *The Freedom Trap*

The Snow Tiger AND *Night of Error*

The Spoilers AND *Juggernaut*

Wyatt's Hurricane AND *Bahama Crisis*

DESMOND BAGLEY

The Tightrope Men

AND

The Enemy

HARPER

HARPER
an imprint of HarperCollins*Publishers*
77-85 Fulham Palace Road
Hammersmith, London W6 8JB
www.harpercollins.co.uk

This omnibus edition 2009
1

The Tightrope Men first published in Great Britain by Collins 1973
The Enemy first published in Great Britain by Collins 1977
'*Desmond Bagley*' press release first published by Collins 1973

Desmond Bagley asserts the moral right to
be identified as the author of these works

ISBN 978 0 00 730475 2

Printed and bound in Great Britain by
Clays Ltd, St Ives plc

CONTENTS

THE TIGHTROPE MEN

To Ray Poynton and all his team.

Fons et Origo,

He the one and I the other.

You may reasonably expect a man to walk a tightrope safely for ten minutes; it would be unreasonable to do so without accident for two hundred years. *Bertrand Russell*

ONE

Giles Denison lay asleep. He lay on his back with his right arm held hooked across his forehead with the hand lightly clenched into a fist, giving him a curiously defensive appearance as of one who wards off a blow. His breathing was even and shallow but it deepened a little as he came into consciousness in that everyday miracle of the reintegration of the psyche after the little death of sleep.

There was a movement of eyes behind closed lids and he sighed, bringing his arm down and turning over on to his side to snuggle deeper into the bedclothes. After a few moments the eyelids flickered and drew back and he stared uncomprehendingly at the blank wall next to the bed. He sighed again, filling his lungs with air, and then leisurely drew forth his arm and looked at his wristwatch.

It was exactly twelve o'clock.

He frowned and shook the watch, then held it to his ear. A steady tick told him it was working and another glance at the dial showed the sweep second hand jerking smoothly on its circular course.

Suddenly – convulsively – he sat up in bed and stared at the watch. It was not the time – midday or midnight – that now perturbed him, but the realization that this was not his watch. He normally wore a fifteen-year-old Omega, a present from his father on his twenty-first birthday, but this was a sleek Patek Philippe, gleaming gold, with a plain leather strap instead of the flexible metal band he was accustomed to.

A furrow creased his forehead as he stroked the dial of the watch with his forefinger and then, as he raised his eyes to look about the room, he received another shock. He had never been in the room before.

He became aware that his heart thumped in his chest and he raised his hand to feel the coolness of silk against his fingers. He looked down and saw the pyjamas. Habitually he slept peeled to the skin; pyjamas constricted him and he had once said that he never saw the sense in getting dressed to go to bed.

Denison was still half asleep and his first impulse was to he down and wait for the dream to be over so that he could wake up again in his own bed, but a pressing necessity of nature was suddenly upon him and he had to go to the bathroom. He shook his head irritably and threw aside the bedclothes – not the sheets and blankets to which he was accustomed but one of those new-fangled quilt objects which fashion had recently imported from the Continent.

He swung his legs out of the bed and sat up, looking down at the pyjamas again. *I'm in hospital,* he thought suddenly; *I must have had an accident.* Recollection told him otherwise. He had gone to bed in his own flat in Hampstead in the normal way, after perhaps a couple of drinks too many the previous evening. Those extra couple of drinks had become a habit after Beth died.

His fingers caressed the softness of the silk. Not a hospital, he decided; these were not National Health issue – not with an embroidered monogram on the pocket. He twisted his head to see the letters but the embroidery was complex and the monogram upside down and he could not make it out.

He stood up and looked about the room and knew immediately he was in a hotel. There were expensive-looking suitcases and in no other place but a hotel room could you find special racks on which to put them. He walked three paces and stroked the fine-grained leather which had hardly a scuff mark. The initials on the side of the suitcase were plain and unmonogrammed – H.F.M.

His head throbbed with the beginning of a headache – the legacy of those extra couple of drinks – and his mouth was parched. He glanced around the room and noted the unrumpled companion bed, the jacket hanging tidily on the back of a chair and the scatter of personal possessions on the dressing-table. He was about to cross to the dressing-table when the pressure in his bladder became intolerable and he knew he had to find a bathroom.

He turned and stumbled into the small hall off the bedroom. One side was panelled in wood and he swung a door open to find a wardrobe full of hung clothes. He turned again and found a door on the other side which opened into darkness. He fumbled for a switch, found it, and light sprang up in a white-tiled bathroom.

While he was relieving himself his mind worried about the electric switch, wondering what was strange about it, and then he realized that it was reversed – an upward movement to turn on the light instead of the more normal down pressure.

He flushed the toilet and turned to the hand basin seeking water. Two glasses stood on a shelf, wrapped in translucent paper. He took one down, ripped off the paper and, filling it with water from the green-topped tap, he drank thirstily. Up to this moment he had been awake for, perhaps, three minutes.

He put down the glass and rubbed his left eye which was sore. Then he looked into the mirror above the basin and, for the first time in his life, experienced sheer terror.

TWO

When Alice went through the Looking Glass the flowers talked to her and she evinced nothing but a mild surprise; but a psychologist once observed, 'If a flower spoke to a man, that man would know terror.'

So it was with Giles Denison. After seeing the impossible in the bathroom mirror he turned and vomited into the toilet bowl, but his laboured retchings brought up nothing but a thin mucus. Panting with his efforts, he looked into the mirror again – and reason left him.

When he became self-aware he found himself prone on the bed, his hands shaped into claws which dug into the pillow. A single sentence was drumming through his mind with mechanical persistence. *'I am Giles Denison! I* am *Giles Denison! I* AM *Giles Denison! I am* GILES DENISON!'

Presently his heavy breathing quieted and he was able to think beyond that reiterated statement of identity. With his head sideways on the pillow he spoke aloud, gathering reassurance from the familiar sound of his own voice. In a slurred tone which gradually became firmer he said, 'I am Giles Denison. I am thirty-six years old. I went to bed last night in my own home. I was a bit cut, that's true, but not so drunk as to be incapable. I *remember* going to bed – it was just after midnight.'

He frowned, then said, 'I've been hammering the bottle a bit lately, but I'm *not* an alcoholic – so this isn't the DTs. Then what is it?' His left hand moved up to stroke his cheek. 'What the hell is *this*?'

He arose slowly and sat on the edge of the bed, screwing up his nerve to go back into the bathroom as he knew he must. When he stood up he found his whole body trembling and he waited a while until the fit had passed. Then he walked with slow paces into the bathroom to face again the stranger in the mirror.

The face that looked back at him was older – he judged the man to be in his mid-forties. Giles Denison had worn a moustache and a neatly clipped beard – the stranger was clean shaven. Giles Denison had a full head of hair – the stranger's hair receded at the temples. Denison had no distinguishing marks as called for in passport descriptions – the stranger had an old scar on the left side of his face which passed from the temple across the cheekbone to the corner of the mouth; the left eyelid drooped, whether as a result of the scar or not it was impossible to say. There was also a small portwine birthmark on the angle of the right jaw.

If that had been all perhaps Denison would not have been so frightened, but the fact was that the face was *different*. Denison had been proud in a non-committal way of his aquiline good looks. Aquiline was the last word to describe the face of the stranger. The face was pudgy, the nose a round, featureless blob, and there was an incipient but perceptible double chin.

Denison opened his mouth to look at the stranger's teeth and caught the flash of a gold capping on a back molar. He closed both his mouth and his eyes and stood there for a while because the trembling had begun again. When he opened his eyes he kept them averted from the mirror and looked down at his hands which were gripping the edge of the basin. They were different, too; the skin looked older and the nails were shortened to the quick as though the stranger bit them. There was another old cicatrice on the back of the right thumb, and the backs of the forefinger and middle finger were stained with nicotine.

Denison did not smoke.

He turned blindly from the mirror and went back into the bedroom where he sat on the edge of the bed and stared at the blank wall. His mind threatened to retreat to the mere insistence of identity and yammered at him, 'I AM GILES DENISON!' and the trembling began again, but with an effort of will he dragged himself back from the edge of that mental precipice and forced himself to think as coherently as he could.

Presently he stood up and went to the window because the street noises forced themselves on his attention in an odd way. He heard an impossible sound, a sound that brought back memories of his childhood. He drew back the curtain and looked into the street to find its origin.

The tramcar was passing just below with the accompanying clangour of a past era of transport. Beyond it, in a dazzle of bright sunshine, were gardens and a bandstand and an array of bright umbrellas over tables where people sat eating and drinking. Beyond the gardens was another street filled with moving traffic.

Another tramcar passed and Denison caught a glimpse of the destination board. It made no sense to him because it seemed to be in a foreign language. There was something else odd about the tramcar and his eyes narrowed as he saw there were two single-deck coaches coupled together. He looked across the street at the fascia boards of the shops and found the words totally meaningless.

His head was aching worse than ever so he dropped the curtain to avoid the bright wash of sunlight and turned into the dimness of the room. He crossed to the dressing-table and looked down at the scatter of objects – a cigarette case, apparently of gold, a smoothly modelled cigarette lighter, a wallet and a note-case, and a handful of loose change.

Denison sat down, switched on the table lamp, and picked up one of the silver coins. The head depicted in profile was that of a fleshy man with a prow of a nose; there was something of the air of a Roman emperor about him. The wording was simple: OLAV.V.R. Denison turned the coin over to find a prancing horse and the inscription: I KRONE. NORGE.

Norway!

Denison began to feel his mind spin again and he bent forward as a sudden stomach cramp hit him. He laid down the coin and held his head in his hands until he felt better. Not a lot better, but marginally so.

When he had recovered enough he took the wallet and went through the pockets quickly, tossing the contents into a heap on the table top. The wallet emptied, he put it aside after noting its fine quality and began to examine the papers. There was an English driving licence in the name of Harold Feltham Meyrick of Lippscott House, near Brackley, Buckinghamshire. Hair prickled at the nape of Denison's neck as he looked at the signature. It was in his own handwriting. It was not his name but it was his penmanship – of that he was certain.

He stretched out his hand and took a pen, one of a matched set of fountain pen and ballpoint. He looked around for something on which to write, saw nothing, and opened the drawer in front of him where he found a folder containing writing paper and envelopes. He paused for a moment when he saw the letter heading – HOTEL CONTINENTAL, STORTINGS GATA, OSLO.

His hand trembled as the pen approached the paper but he scribbled his signature firmly enough – Giles Denison. He looked at the familiar loops and curlicues and felt immeasurably better, then he wrote another signature – H. F.

Meyrick. He took the driving licence and compared it with what he had just written. It confirmed what he already knew; the signature in the driving licence was in his own handwriting.

So were the signatures in a fat book of Cook's traveller's cheques. He counted the cheques – nineteen of them at £50 each – £950 in all. If he was indeed Meyrick he was pretty well breeched. His headache grew worse.

There were a dozen engraved visiting cards with Meyrick's name and address and a fat sheaf of Norwegian currency in the note-case which he did not bother to count. He dropped it on to the desk and held his throbbing head in his hands. In spite of the fact that he had just woken up he felt tired and light-headed. He knew he was in danger of going into psychological retreat again; it would be so easy to curl up on the bed and reject this crazy, impossible thing that had happened to him, taking refuge in sleep with the hope that it would prove to be a dream and that when he woke he would be back in bed in his own flat in Hampstead, a thousand miles away.

He opened the drawer a fraction, put his fingers inside, and then smashed the drawer closed with the heel of his other hand. He gasped with the pain and when he drew his hand from the drawer there were flaring red marks on the backs of his fingers. The pain caused tears to come to his eyes and, as he nursed his hand, he knew this was too real to be a dream.

So if it was not a dream, what was it? He had gone to bed as one person and woken up, in another country, as another. But wait! That was not quite accurate. He had woken up knowing he was Giles Denison – the persona of – Harold Feltham Meyrick was all on the exterior – inside he was still Giles Denison.

He was about to pursue this line of thought when he had another spasm of stomach cramp and suddenly he realized why he felt so weak and tired. He was ravenously hungry. Painfully he stood up and went in to the bathroom where he stared down into the toilet bowl. He had been violently sick but his stomach had been so empty that there was hardly anything to be brought up but a thin, acid digestive juice. And yet the previous evening he had had a full meal. Surely there was something wrong there.

He went back into the bedroom and paused irresolutely by the telephone and then, with a sudden access of determination, picked it up. 'Give me room service,' he said. His voice was hoarse and strange in his own ears.

The telephone crackled. 'Room service,' it said in accented English.

'I'd like something to eat,' said Denison. He glanced at his watch – it was nearly two o'clock. 'A light lunch.'

'Open sandwiches?' suggested the telephone.

'Something like that,' said Denison. 'And a pot of coffee.'

'Yes, sir. The room number is . . .?'

Denison did not know. He looked around hastily and saw what must be the room key on a low coffee-table by the window. It was attached to about five pounds of brass on which a number was stamped. 'Three-sixty,' he said.

'Very good, sir.'

Denison was inspired. 'Can you send up a newspaper?'

'English or Norwegian, sir?'

'One of each.'

'*The Times*?'

'That and an equivalent local paper. And I may be in the bathroom when you come up – just leave everything on the table.'

'Very good, sir.'

Denison put down the telephone with a feeling of relief. He would have to face people some time but he did not feel eager to do so immediately. Certainly he would have to ask a lot of questions, but he wanted time to compose himself.

He could not help feeling there would be a lot of trip wires to avoid in the taking over of another personality.

He took the silk Paisley dressing-gown which he found draped over a chair and went into the bathroom, where he was coward enough to hang a towel over the mirror. After fumbling for a moment with unfamiliar plumbing, he drew a bath of hot water, then stripped off the pyjamas. He became aware of the sticking-plaster on his left arm and was about to take it off but he thought better of it, wondering if he really wanted to know what was underneath.

He got into the bath and soaked in the hot water, feeling the heat ease his suddenly aching limbs, and again, he drowsily wondered why he felt so tired after being up only two hours. Presently he heard the door of the suite open and there was a clatter of crockery. The door banged closed and everything was quiet again so he got out of the bath and began to rub himself down.

While sitting on the cork-topped stool he suddenly bent forward and examined his left shin. There was a blue-white scar there, about the size and shape of an orange pip. He remembered when that had happened; it was when he was eight years old and had fallen off his first bicycle.

He raised his head and laughed aloud, feeling much better. He had remembered that as Giles Denison and that little scar was a part of his body that did not belong to Mr Harold Blasted Feltham Bloody Meyrick.

THREE

The Norwegian idea of a light lunch was an enormous tray filled with a variety of edible goodies which Denison surveyed with satisfaction before plunging in. The discovery of the scar had cheered him immensely and had even emboldened him to shave Meyrick's face. Meyrick was old-fashioned enough to use a safety-razor and a silver-mounted badger-hair brush instead of an electric shaver and Denison had had some difficulty in guiding the blade over unfamiliar contours and had cut himself – or Meyrick – twice. And so, when he picked up the newspapers, his face was adorned with two bloody patches of toilet paper.

The London *Times* and the Norwegian *Aftenposten* both had the same date – July 9 – and Denison went very still, a piece of herring on rye bread poised in mid-air. His last memory as Giles Denison had been going to bed just after midnight on July 1 – no, it would be July 2 if it was after midnight.

Somewhere he had lost a week.

He put his hand to his arm and felt the sticking-plaster. Someone had been doing things to him. He did not know who and he did not know why but, by God, he was going to find out and someone was going to pay dearly. While shaving he had examined his face closely. The scar on his left cheek was there all right, the remnant of an old wound, but it did not feel like a scar when he touched it. Still, no matter how hard he rubbed it would not come off, so it was not merely an example of clever theatrical make-up. The same applied to the birthmark on the right jaw.

There was something else odd about his nose and his cheeks and that double chin. They had a rubbery feel about them. Not ever having had any excess fat on his body he did not know whether this was normal or not. And, again, Meyrick's face had grown a little stubble of hair which he had shaved off, but the bald temples were smooth which meant that whoever had lifted his hairline had not done it by shaving.

The only part of his face Denison recognized were his eyes – those had not changed; they were still the same grey-green eyes he had seen every morning in the mirror. But the expression was different because of the droop of the left eyelid. There was a slight soreness in the outer corner of that eye which aroused his suspicions but he could see nothing but a tiny inflamed spot which could have been natural.

As he ate voraciously he glanced through *The Times*. The world still seemed to be wobbling on its political axis as unsteadily as ever and nothing had changed, so he tossed the newspaper aside and gave himself up to thought over a steaming cup of black coffee. What could be the motive for spiriting a man from his own bed, transforming him bodily, giving him a new personality and dumping him in a luxury hotel in the capital of Norway?

No answer.

The meal had invigorated him and he felt like moving and not sitting. He did not yet feel up to encountering people so he compromised by going through Meyrick's possessions. He opened the wardrobe and in one of the drawers, underneath a pile of underwear, he found a large travelling wallet. Taking it to the dressing-table he unzipped it and went through the contents.

The first thing to catch his eyes was a British passport. He opened it to find the description of the holder was filled out in his own handwriting as was Meyrick's signature underneath. The face that looked out of the photograph on the opposite page was that of Meyrick, who was described as a civil servant. Whoever had thought up this lark had been thorough about it.

He flipped through the pages and found only one stamped entry and his brow wrinkled as he studied it. *Sverige*? Would that be Sweden? If so he had arrived at a place called Arlanda in Sweden on a date he could not tell because the stamping was blurred. Turning to the back of the passport he found that the sum of £1,500 had been issued a month earlier. Since the maximum travel allowance for a tourist was £300 it would seem that H. F. Meyrick was operating on a businessman's allowance.

At the bottom of a pocket in the wallet he found an American Express credit card, complete with the ubiquitous fake signature. He looked at it pensively, flicking it with his fingernail. With this he could draw money or traveller's cheques anywhere; he could use it to buy an airline ticket to Australia if he felt the urge to emigrate suddenly. It represented complete and unlicensed freedom unless and until someone put a stopper on it at head office.

He transferred it to the small personal wallet along with the driving licence. It would be better to keep that little bit of plastic available in case of need.

Meyrick had an extensive wardrobe; casual clothing, lounge suits and even a dinner-jacket with accessories. Denison investigated a small box and found it contained personal jewellery – studs, tiepins and a couple of rings – and he realized he probably held a thousand pounds' worth of gold in his hand. The Patek Philippe watch on his wrist would cost £500 if it cost a penny. H. F. Meyrick was a wealthy man, so what kind of a civil servant did that make him?

Denison decided to get dressed. It was a sunny day so he chose casual trousers and a sports coat. The clothing fitted him as though made to measure. He looked at himself in the full-length mirror built into the wardrobe door, studiously ignoring the face on top of the body, and thought crazily that it, too, had probably been made to measure. The world began to spin again, but he remembered the small scar on his shin that belonged to Denison and that helped him to recover.

He put his personal possessions into his pockets and headed for the door, key in hand. As the door swung open a card which had been hung on the outer handle fell to the floor. He picked it up and read: VENNLIGST IKKE FORSTYRR – PLEASE DO NOT DISTURB. He was thoughtful as he hung it on the hook inside the door before locking the room; he would give a lot to know who had hung out that sign.

He went down in the lift with a couple of American blue-rinsed matrons who chattered to each other in a mid-West twang. 'Say, have you been out to Vigeland Park? All those statues – I didn't know where to look.' The lift stopped and the doors slid open with a soft hiss, and the American ladies bustled out intent on sightseeing.

Denison followed them diffidently into the hotel lobby and stood by the lifts for a while, trying to get his bearings, doing his best to appear nonchalantly casual while he took in the scene.

'Mr Meyrick . . . Mr Meyrick, sir!'

He turned his head and saw the porter at the desk smiling at him. Licking lips that had suddenly gone dry he walked over. 'Yes?'

'Would you mind signing this, sir? The check for the meal in your room. Just a formality.'

Denison looked at the proffered pen and laid down the room key. He took the pen and scribbled firmly 'H. F. Meyrick' and pushed the slip across the counter. The porter was hanging the key on the rack but he turned and spoke to Denison before he could slip away. 'The night porter put your car away, sir. Here is the key.'

He held out a key with a tag on it and Denison extended his hand to take it. He glanced at the tag and saw the name, Hertz, and a car number. He cleared his throat. 'Thank you.'

'You sound as though you have a cold coming on,' said the porter.

Denison took a chance. 'Why do you think that?'

'Your voice sounds different.'

'Yes, I do feel a bit chesty,' said Denison.

The porter smiled. 'Too much night air, perhaps.'

Denison took another chance. 'What time *did* I get in last night?'

'This morning, sir. The night porter said it was about three o'clock.' The porter offered Denison a man-of-the-world smile. 'I wasn't surprised when you slept in this morning.'

No, thought Denison; *but I was!* He was growing bolder as he gained confidence. 'Can you tell me something? I was having a discussion with a friend about how long I've been here in Oslo and, for the life of me, I can't remember the exact day I booked in here. Could you check it for me?'

'Certainly, sir.' The porter moved away and began to run through cards in a file. Denison looked at the car key. It was thoughtful of Hertz to put the car number on the tag; he might even be able to recognize it when he saw it. It was also thoughtful of the night porter to put the car away – but where the hell had he put it?

The porter returned. 'You checked in on the eighteenth of June, sir. Exactly three weeks ago.'

The butterflies in Denison's stomach collided. 'Thank you,' he said mechanically, and moved away from the desk and across the lobby. An arrow pointed the direction to the bar and he glanced sideways and saw a dark, cool cavern with a few drinkers, solitary or in couples. It looked quiet and he desperately wanted to think, so he went in.

When the barman came up, he said, 'A beer, please.'

'Export, sir?'

Denison nodded absently. *June 18.* He had reckoned he had lost a week so how the devil could he have booked into the Hotel Continental in Oslo three weeks earlier? How the hell could he have been in two places at the same time?

The barman returned, poured the beer into a glass, and went away. Denison tried to figure where he had been on June 18 and found it difficult. Three weeks was a long time. *Where were you at 6.17 on the evening of June 18?* No wonder people found it difficult to establish alibis. He found it extraordinarily difficult to focus his thoughts; they flicked about, skittering here and there wildly out of control. *When did you last see your father?* Nuts!

A vagrant thought popped to the surface of his consciousness. *Edinburgh!* He had been to Edinburgh On the 17th and the 18th he had taken off as a reward for hard work. There had been a leisurely morning and he had played golf in the afternoon; he had gone to the cinema in the evening and had dined late in Soho, getting back to Hampstead fairly late.

He – as Giles Denison – had dined in Soho at about the same time as he – as Harold Feltham Meyrick – had dined in Oslo. Where was the sense of that?

He was aware that he was looking at bubbles rising in amber liquid and that he had not touched his beer. He lifted the glass and drank; it was cold and refreshing.

He had two things going for him – two things that kept him sane. One – Giles Denison's scar on H. F. Meyrick's shin – and two – the change in the timbre of Meyrick's voice as recognized by the hotel porter. And what did that imply? Obviously that there were *two* Meyricks; one who had booked in on June 18, and another – himself – who had just been planted. Never mind why and never mind how. Just accept the fact that it was done.

He drank some more beer and rested his chin in his hand, feeling the unaccustomed flab of his jowl. He had lost a week of his life. Could so much plastic surgery be done in a week? He added that to the list of things to be checked on.

And what to do? He could go to the British Embassy and tell his story. Mentally he ran through the scenario.

'What can we do for you, Mr Meyrick?'

'Well the fact is I'm not Meyrick – whoever he is. My name is Giles Denison and I've been kidnapped from London, my face changed, and dumped into an Oslo hotel with a hell of a lot of money and an unlimited credit account. Can you help me?'

'Certainly, Mr Meyrick. Miss Smith, will you ring for a doctor?'

'My God!' said Denison aloud. 'I'd end up in the loony-bin.'

The barman cocked his head and came over. 'You wish something, sir?'

'Just to pay,' said Denison, finishing his beer.

He paid from the loose change in his pocket and left the bar. In the lobby he spotted a sign saying GARAGE, so he went through a door and down a flight of stairs to emerge into a basement car park. He checked the number on the Hertz key and walked along the first row of cars. It was right at the end – a big black Mercedes. He unlocked the door.

The first thing he saw was the doll on the driver's seat, a most curious object made of crudely carved wood and rope. The body was formed of rope twisted into a spiral and coming out in the form of a tail. His feet were but roughly indicated and the head was a round knob with a peg nose. The eyes and a mouth twisted to one side had been inked on to the wood, and the hair was of rope teased out into separate strands. It was a strange and somehow repulsive little figure.

He picked it up and discovered a piece of paper underneath it. He unfolded the deckle-edged note-paper and read the scrawled handwriting: *Your Drammen Dolly awaits you at Spiraltoppen. Early morning, July 10.*

He frowned. July 10 was next day, but where was Spiraltoppen and who – or what – was a Drammen Dolly? He looked at the ugly little doll. It had been lying on the driver's seat as though it had been deliberately left for him to find. He tossed it in his hand a couple of times and then thrust it into his pocket. It made an unsightly bulge, but what did he care? It was not his jacket. The note he put into his wallet.

The car was almost new, with just over 500 kilometres on the clock. He found a sheaf of papers relating to the car hire; it had been rented five days earlier, a fact which was singularly devoid of informative content. There was nothing else to be found.

He got out of the car, locked it, and left the garage by the car entrance, emerging on to a street behind the hotel. It was a little bewildering for him; the traffic drove on the wrong side of the road, the street and shop signs were indecipherable and his command of Norwegian was minimal, being restricted to one word – *skal* – which, while being useful in a cheery sort of way, was not going to be of much use for the more practical things of life.

What he needed was information and he found it on the corner of the street in the form of a bookshop. He went inside and found an array of maps from which he selected a map of central Oslo, one of Greater Oslo, and a motoring map of Southern Norway. To these he added a guide to the city and paid out of the slab of Norwegian currency in Meyrick's wallet. He made a mental note to count that money as soon as he had privacy.

He left the shop intending to go back to the hotel where he could study the maps and orient himself. He paused on the pavement and rubbernecked at the corner of a building where one would normally expect to find a street name – and there it was – *Roald Amundsens Gata*.

'Harry!'

He turned to go in the direction of the hotel but paused as he felt a hand on his arm. 'Harry Meyrick!' There was a note of anger in the voice. She was a green-eyed redhead of about thirty and she was flying alarm flags – her lips were compressed and pink spots glowed in her cheeks. 'I'm not used to being stood up,' she said. 'Where were you this morning?'

Momentarily he was nonplussed but remembered in time what the hotel porter had thought about his voice. 'I wasn't feeling well,' he managed to get out. 'I was in bed.'

'There's a thing called a telephone,' she said angrily. 'Alexander Graham Bell invented it – remember?'

'I was knocked out by sleeping pills,' he protested. With a small portion of his mind he noted that this was probably a true statement. 'Perhaps I overdid it.'

Her expression changed. 'You do sound a bit glued-up,' she admitted. 'Maybe I'll forgive you.' There was a faint American undertone to her English. 'It will cost you a drink, darling.'

'In the hotel?' he suggested.

'It's too nice a day to be inside. We'll go into the *Studenterlunden*.' She waved her arm past a passing articulated tramcar towards the gay umbrellas in the gardens on the other side of the street.

Denison felt trapped as he escorted her across the street, but he also realized that if he was to learn anything about

Meyrick then this was too good a chance to pass up. He had once been accosted in the street by a woman who obviously knew him but he did not have the faintest idea of who she was. There is a point of no return in that type of conversation after which one cannot, in decency, admit ignorance. On that occasion Denison had fumbled it, had suffered half an hour of devious conversation, and they had parted amicably without him finding out who she was. He still did not know. Grimly he thought that it was good practice for today's exercise.

As they crossed the street she said, 'I saw Jack Kidder this morning. He was asking about you.'

'How is he?'

She laughed. 'Fine, as always. You know Jack.'

'Of course,' said Denison deadpan. 'Good old Jack.'

They went into the outdoor café and found an empty table with difficulty. Under other circumstances Denison would have found it pleasant to have a drink with a pretty woman in surroundings like this, but his mind was beleaguered by his present problems. They sat down and he put his parcel of maps on the table.

One of them slipped out of the packet and his main problem prodded at it with a well-manicured forefinger. 'What are these?'

'Maps,' said Denison succinctly.

'Maps of where?'

'Of the city.'

'Oslo!' She seemed amused. 'Why do you want maps of Oslo? Isn't it your boast that you know Oslo better than London?'

'They're for a friend.'

Denison chalked up a mental note. *Meyrick knows Oslo well; probably a frequent visitor. Steer clear of local conditions or gossip. Might run into more problems like this.*

'Oh!' She appeared to lose interest.

Denison realized he was faced with a peculiar difficulty. He did not know this woman's name and, as people do not commonly refer to themselves by name in conversation, he did not see how he was going to get it, short of somehow prying into her handbag and looking for identification.

'Give me a cigarette, darling,' she said.

He patted his pockets and found he had left the cigarette case and lighter in the room. Not being a smoker it had not occurred to him to put them in his pocket along with the rest of Meyrick's personal gear. 'I'm sorry,' he said. 'I don't have any with me.'

'My!' she said. 'Don't tell me the great Professor Meyrick has stopped smoking. Now I *will* believe in cancer.'

Professor!

He used the pretext of illness again. 'The one I tried this morning tasted like straw. Maybe I will stop smoking.' He held his hand over the table. 'Look at those nicotine stains. Imagine what my lungs must be like.'

She shook her head in mock sorrow. 'It's like pulling down a national monument. To imagine Harry Meyrick without a cigarette is like trying to imagine Paris without the Eiffel Tower.'

A Nordic waitress came to the table; she looked rather like Jeanette MacDonald dressed for an appearance in *White Horse Inn*. Denison raised his eyebrows at his companion. 'What will you have?'

'The usual,' she said indifferently, delving into her handbag.

He took refuge in a paroxysm of coughing pulling out his handkerchief and only emerging when he heard her giving the order. He waited until the waitress left before putting away the handkerchief. The woman opposite him said, 'Harry, that's a really bad cough. I'm not surprised you're thinking of giving up the cancer sticks. Are you feeling all right, darling? Maybe you'd be better off in bed, after all.'

'I'm all right,' he said.

'Are you sure?' she asked solicitously.

'Perfectly sure.'

'Spoken like the old Professor Meyrick,' she said mockingly. 'Always sure of everything.'

'Don't call me Professor,' he said testily. It was a safe enough thing to say regardless of whether Meyrick was really a professor or whether she was pulling his leg in a heavy-handed manner. The British have never been keen on the over-use of professional titles. And it might provoke her into dropping useful information.

All he got was a light and inconsequential, 'When on the Continent do as the Continentals do.'

He went on the attack. 'I don't like it.'

'You're so British, Harry.' He thought he detected a cutting edge to her voice. 'But then, of course, you would be.'

'What do you mean by that?'

'Oh, come off it. There's nobody more British than an outsider who has bored his way in. Where were you born, Harry? Somewhere in Mittel Europa?' She suddenly looked a little ashamed. 'I'm sorry; I shouldn't have said that. I'm being bitchy, but you're behaving a bit oddly, too.'

'The effect of the pills. Barbiturates have never agreed with me. I have a headache.'

She opened her handbag. 'I have aspirin.'

The waitress, Valkyrie-like, bore down on them. Denison looked at the bottles on the tray, and said, 'I doubt if aspirin goes with beer.' That was the last thing he would have thought of as 'the usual'; she did not look the beery type.

She shrugged and closed the bag with a click. 'Please yourself.'

The waitress put down two glasses, two bottles of beer and a packet of cigarettes, said something rapid and incomprehensible, and waited expectantly. Denison took out his wallet and selected a 100-kroner note. Surely two beers and a packet of cigarettes could not cost more than a hundred kroner. My God, he did not even know the value of the currency! This was like walking through a minefield blindfolded.

He was relieved when the waitress made no comment but made change from a leather bag concealed under her apron. He laid the money on the table intending to check it surreptitiously. The redhead said, 'You've no need to buy my cigarettes, Harry.'

He smiled at her. 'Be my guest,' he said, and stretched out his hand to pour her beer.

'You've given it up yourself but you're quite prepared to pay for other people's poison.' She laughed. 'Not a very moral attitude.'

'I'm not a moral philosopher,' he said, hoping it was true.

'No, you're not,' she agreed. 'I've always wondered where you stood in that general direction. What would you call yourself, Harry? Atheist? Agnostic? Humanist?'

At last he was getting something of the quality of Meyrick. Those were questions but they were leading questions, and he was quite prepared to discuss philosophy with her – a nice safe subject. 'Not an atheist,' he said. 'It's always seemed to me that to believe in the non-existence of something is somewhat harder than to believe in its existence. I'd put myself down as an agnostic – one of the "don't know" majority. And that doesn't conflict with humanism.'

He fingered the notes and coins on the table, counted them mentally, subtracted the price of two beers based on what he had paid for a beer in the hotel, and arrived at the price of a packet of cigarettes. Roughly, that is. He had an idea that the price of a beer in a luxury hotel would be far higher than in an open-air café.

'I went to church last Sunday,' she said pensively. 'To the English church – you know – the one on Møllergata.' He nodded as though he did know. 'I didn't get much out of it. I think next time I'll try the American church.' She frowned. 'Where is the American church, Harry?'

He had to say *something*, so he took a chance. 'Isn't it near the Embassy?'

Her brow cleared. 'Of course. Between Bygdøy Alle and Drammens Veien. It's funny, isn't it? The American church being practically next door to the British Embassy. You'd expect it to be near the American Embassy.'

He gulped. 'Yes, you would,' he said, and forbore to mention that that was what he had meant. Even a quasi-theological conversation was strewn with pitfalls. He had to get out of this before he really dropped a clanger.

And an alarming suspicion had just sprung to mind, fully armed and spiky. Whoever had planted him in that hotel room and provided him with money and the means to provide all the necessities of life – and a lot of the luxuries, too – was unlikely to leave him unobserved. Someone would be keeping tabs on him, otherwise the whole operation was a nonsense. Could it be this redhead who apparently had qualms about her immortal soul? What could be better than to plant someone right next to him for closer observation?

She opened the packet of cigarettes and offered him one. 'You're sure you won't?'

He shook his head. 'Quite sure.'

'It must be marvellous to have will power.'

He wanted peace and not this continuous exploration of a maze where every corner turned could be more dangerous than the last. He started to cough again, and dragged his handkerchief from his pocket. 'I'm sorry,' he said in a muffled voice. 'I think you're right; I'd be better off in bed. Do you mind if I leave you?'

'Of course not.' Her voice was filled with concern. 'Do you want a doctor?'

'That's not necessary,' he said. 'I'll be all right tomorrow – I know how these turns take me.' He stood up and she also rose. 'Don't bother to come with me. The hotel is only across the road.'

He picked up the packet and thrust the maps back into it, and put the handkerchief into his pocket. She looked down at his feet. 'You've dropped something,' she said, and stooped to pick it up. 'Why, it's a Spiralen Doll.'

'A what?' he asked incautiously. It must have been pulled from his pocket when he took out the handkerchief.

She regarded him oddly. 'You pointed these out at the Spiralen when we were there last week. You laughed at them and called them tourist junk. Don't you remember?'

'Of course,' he said. 'It's just this damned headache.'

She laughed. 'I didn't expect to see you carrying one. You didn't buy this when we were there – where did you get it?'

He told the truth. 'I found it in the car I hired.'

'You can't trust anyone to do a good job these days,' she said, smiling. 'Those cars are supposed to be cleaned and checked.' She held it out. 'Do you want it?'

'I may be a bit light-headed,' he said, 'but I think I do.' He took it from her. 'I'll be going now.'

'Have a hot toddy and a good night's sleep,' she advised. 'And ring me as soon as you're better.'

That would be difficult, to say the least, with neither telephone number nor name. 'Why don't you give me a ring tomorrow,' he said. 'I think I'll be well enough to have dinner. I promise not to stand you up again.'

'I'll ring you tomorrow afternoon.'

'Promise,' he insisted, not wanting to lose her.

'Promise.'

He put the rope doll into his pocket and left her with a wave, and went out of the garden, across the road and into the hotel, feeling relieved that he was well out of a difficult situation. *Information,* he thought, as he walked across the hotel lobby; *that's what I need – I'm hamstrung without it.*

He paused at the porter's desk and the porter looked up with a quick smile. 'Your key, sir?' He swung around and unhooked it.

On impulse Denison held out the doll. 'What's that?'

The porter's smile broadened. 'That's a Spiralen Doll, sir.'

'Where does it come from?'

'From the Spiralen, sir – in Drammen. If you're interested, I have a pamphlet.'

'I'm very much interested,' said Denison.

The porter looked through papers on a shelf and came up with a leaflet printed in blue ink. 'You must be an engineer, sir.'

Denison did not know what the hell Meyrick was. 'It's in my general field of interest,' he said guardedly, took the key and the leaflet, and walked towards the lifts. He did not notice the man who had been hovering behind him and who regarded him speculatively until the lift door closed.

Once in his room Denison tossed the maps and the leaflet on to the dressing-table and picked up the telephone. 'I'd like to make a long distance call, please – to England.' He took out his wallet.

'What is the number, sir?'

'There's a little difficulty about that. I don't have a number – only an address.' He opened the wallet with one hand and extracted one of Meyrick's cards.

The telephonist was dubious. 'That may take some time, sir.'

'It doesn't matter – I'll be in my room for the rest of the day.'

'What is the address sir?'

Denison said clearly, 'Lippscott House, near Brackley, Buckinghamshire, England.' He repeated it three times to make sure it had got across.

'And the name?'

Denison opened his mouth and then closed it, having suddenly acquired a dazed look. He would appear to be a damned fool if he gave the name of Meyrick – no one in his right mind rings up himself, especially after having admitted he did not know his own telephone number. He swallowed, and said shortly, 'The name is not known.'

The telephone sighed in his ear. 'I'll do my best, sir.'

Denison put down the telephone and settled in a chair to find out about the Spiralen. The front of the leaflet was headed: DRAMMEN. There was an illustration of a Spiralen Doll which did not look any better for being printed in blue. The leaflet was in four languages.

The Spiralen was described as being 'a truly unique attraction, as well as a superb piece of engineering.' Apparently there had been a quarry at the foot of Bragernesasen, a hill near Drammen, which had become an eyesore until the City Fathers decided to do something about it. Instead of quarrying the face of the hill the operation had been extended into the interior.

A tunnel had been driven into the hill, thirty feet wide, fifteen feet high and a mile long. But not in a straight line. It turned back on itself six complete times in a spiral drilled into the mountain, climbing five hundred feet until it came out on top of Bragernesasen where the Spiraltoppen Restaurant was open all the year round. The views were said to be excellent.

Denison picked up the doll; its body was formed of six complete turns of rope. He grinned weakly.

Consultation of the maps revealed that Drammen was a small town forty kilometres west of Oslo. That would be a nice morning drive, and he could get back in the afternoon well in time for any call from the redhead. It was not much to go on, but it was all he had.

He spent the rest of the afternoon searching through Meyrick's possessions but found nothing that could be said to be a clue. He ordered dinner to be sent to his room because he suspected that the hotel restaurant might be full of unexploded human mines like the redhead he had met, and there was a limit to what he could get away with.

The telephone call came when he was half-way through dinner. There were clicks and crackles and a distant voice said, 'Dr Meyrick's residence.'

Doctor!

'I'd like to speak to Dr Meyrick.'

'I'm sorry, sir; but Dr Meyrick is not at home.'

'Have you any idea where I can find him?'

'He is out of the country at the moment, sir.'

'Oh! Have you any idea where?'

There was a pause. 'I believe he is travelling in Scandinavia, sir.'

This was not getting anywhere at all. 'Who am I speaking to?'

'This is Andrews – Dr Meyrick's personal servant. Would you like to leave a message, sir?'

'Do you recognize my voice, Andrews?' asked Denison.

A pause. 'It's a bad line.' Another pause. 'I don't believe in guessing games on the telephone, sir.'

'All right,' said Denison. 'When you see Dr Meyrick will you tell him that Giles Denison called, and I'll be getting in touch with him as soon as possible. Got that?'

'Giles Denison. Yes, Mr Denison.'

'When is Dr Meyrick expected home?'

'I really couldn't say, Mr Denison.'

'Thank you, Mr Andrews.'

Denison put down the telephone. He felt depressed.

FOUR

He slept poorly that night. His sleep was plagued with dreams which he did not remember clearly during the few times he was jerked into wakefulness but which he knew were full of monstrous and fearful figures which threatened him. In the early hours of the morning he fell into a heavy sleep which deadened senses and when he woke he felt heavy and listless.

He got up tiredly and twitched aside the window curtain to find that the weather had changed; the sky was a dull grey and the pavements were wet and a fine drizzle filled the air. The outdoor café in the gardens opposite would not be doing much business that day.

He rang down for breakfast and then had a shower, finishing with needle jets of cold water in an attempt to whip some enthusiasm into his suddenly heavy body and, to a degree, he succeeded. When the floor waitress came in with his breakfast he had dressed in trousers and white polo-necked sweater and was combing his hair before the bathroom mirror. Incredibly enough, he was whistling in spite of having Meyrick's face before him.

The food helped, too, although it was unfamiliar and a long way from an English breakfast. He rejected the raw, marinated herring and settled for a boiled egg, bread and marmalade and coffee. After breakfast he checked the weather again and then selected a jacket and a short topcoat from the wardrobe. He also found a thin, zippered leather satchel into which he put the maps and the Spiralen leaflet which had a street plan of Drammen on the back. Then he went down to the car. It was exactly nine o'clock.

It was not easy getting out of town. The car was bigger and more powerful than those he had been accustomed to driving and he had to keep to what was to him the wrong side of the road in a strange city in early rush-hour traffic. Three times he missed signs and took wrong turnings. The first time he did this he cruised on and got hopelessly lost and had to retrace his path laboriously. Thereafter when he missed a turn he reversed immediately so as not to lose his way again.

He was quite unaware of the man following him in the Swedish Volvo. Denison's erratic course across the city of Oslo was causing him a lot of trouble, especially when Denison did his quick and unexpected reversals. The man, whose name was Armstrong, swore freely and frequently, and his language became indescribable when the drizzle intensified into a downpour of heavy driving rain.

Denison eventually got out of the centre of the city and on to a six-lane highway, three lanes each way. The windscreen wipers had to work hard to cope with the rain, but it was better when he fiddled with a switch and discovered they had two speeds. Resolutely he stuck to the centre lane, reassured from time to time by the name DRAMMEN which appeared on overhead gantries.

To his left was the sea, the deeply penetrating arm of Oslofjord, but then the road veered away and headed inland. Presently the rain stopped, although no sun appeared, and he even began to enjoy himself, having got command of the unfamiliar car. And suddenly he was in Drammen, where he parked and studied the plan on the back of the leaflet.

hand plucked at his waist and he dropped into a crouch. Sun gleamed off the blade of the knife he held in his right hand. Denison ran full tilt at him and made as to break to the man's left – the safe side – but at the last minute he sold him the dummy and broke away on the knife side.

He nearly got through unscathed because the man bought it. But at the last moment he lashed out with the knife and Denison felt a hot pain across his flank. Yet he had got past and plunged along the trail with undiminished speed, hoping to God he would not trip over an exposed tree root. There is nothing like being chased by a man with a knife to put wings on the feet.

There were three of them. The big man he had laid out with a blow to the solar plexus would not be good for anything for at least two minutes and probably longer. That left the knifer and the other man who had chased him. Behind he heard cries but ahead he saw the roof of the restaurant just coming in sight over the rise.

His wind was going fast and he knew he could not keep up this sprint for long. He burst out into the car park and headed for his car, thankful there was now firm footing. A car door slammed and he risked a glance to the left and saw the man who had been reading the newspaper in the parked car beginning to run towards him.

He fumbled hastily for his car key and thanked God when it slipped smoothly into the lock. He dived behind the wheel and slammed the door with one hand while stabbing the key at the ignition lock with the other – this time he missed and had to fumble again. The man outside hammered on the window and then tugged at the door handle. Denison held the door closed with straining muscles and brought over his other hand quickly to snap down the door catch.

He had dropped the car key on the floor and groped for it. His lungs were hurting and he gasped for breath, and the pain in his side suddenly sharpened, but somewhere at the back of his mind cool logic told him that he was reasonably safe, that no one could get into a locked car before he took off – always provided he could find that damned key.

His fingers brushed against it and he grabbed it, brought it up, and rammed it into the ignition lock. Cool logic evaporated fast when he saw the man stand back and produce an automatic pistol. Denison frantically pumped his foot on the clutch, slammed into first gear, and took off in a tyre-burning squeal even before he had a finger on the wheel. The car weaved drunkenly across the car park then straightened out and dived into the Spiralen tunnel like a rabbit down a hole.

Denison's last glimpse of daylight in the rear-view mirror showed him the other car beginning to move with two doors open and his pursuers piling in. That would be the ferret after the rabbit.

It took him about ten seconds, after he hit the curve, to know he was going too fast. The gradient was one in ten and the curve radius only a hundred and fifteen feet, turning away to the right so that he was on the inside. His speed was such that centrifugal force tended to throw the car sideways over the centre line, and if anything was coming up he would surely hit it.

He could be compared to a man on a bobsled going down the Cresta Run – with some important differences. The Cresta Run is designed so that the walls can be climbed; here the walls were of jagged, untrimmed rock and one touch at speed would surely wreck the car. The Cresta Run does not have two-way traffic with a continuous blind corner a mile long, and the competitors are not pursued by men with guns – if they were, more records might be broken.

So Denison reluctantly eased his foot on the accelerator and risked a glance in his mirror. The driver of the car behind was more foolhardy than he and was not worrying about up-traffic. He was barrelling down the centre line and catching up fast. Denison fed more fuel to the engine, twisted the wheel and wondered if he could sustain a sideways drift a mile long.

The walls of the tunnel were a blur and the lights flicked by and he caught sight of an illuminated number 5. Four more circuits to go before the bottom. The car jolted and pitched suddenly and he fought the wheel which had taken on a life of its own. It did it again and he heard a nasty sound from the rear. He was being rammed. There was another sound as sheet metal ripped and the car slewed across the whole width of the tunnel.

He heard – and felt – the crunch as the rear off-side of the car slammed into the opposite wall, but Denison was not particularly worried about the property of the Hertz Company at that moment because he saw the dipped headlights of a vehicle coming up the Spiralen towards him. He juggled madly with wheel, clutch and accelerator and shot off to the other side of the tunnel again, scraping across the front of the tour bus that was coming up. There was a brief vignette of the driver of the bus, his mouth open and his eyes staring, and then he was gone.

The front fender scraped along the nearside tunnel wall in a shower of sparks and Denison wrenched the wheel over and nearly clipped the rear of the bus as it went by. He wobbled crazily from side to side of the tunnel for about a hundred and fifty yards before he had proper control, and it was only by the grace of God that the bus had not been the first in a procession of vehicles.

Level 2 passed in a flash and a flicker of light in Denison's eyes, reflected from the rear-view mirror, told him that the car behind had also avoided the bus and was catching up again. He increased speed again and the tyres protested noisily with a rending squeal; the whole of the

Spiralen would be filled with the stench of burning rubber.

Level 1. A brightness ahead warned of the approach of another vehicle and Denison tensed his muscles, but the tunnel straightened and he saw it was the daylight of the exit. He rammed down his foot and the car surged forward and came out of the tunnel like a shell from a gun. The fee-collector threw up his arms and jumped aside as the car shot past him. Denison screwed up his eyes against the sudden bright glare of sunlight and hurtled down the hill towards the main street of Drammen at top speed.

At the bottom of the hill he jammed on his brakes and wrenched the wheel sideways. The car heeled violently as it turned the corner and the tyres screamed again, leaving black rubber on the road. Then he literally stood on the brake pedal, rising in his seat, to avoid ploughing into a file of the good people of Drammen crossing the street at a traffic light. The car's nose sank and the rear came up as it juddered to a halt, just grazing the thigh of a policeman who stood in the middle of the road with his back to Denison.

The policeman turned, his face expressionless. Denison sagged back into his seat and twisted his head to look back along the road. He saw the pursuing car break the other way and head down the road at high speed out of Drammen.

The policeman knocked on the car window and Denison wound it down to be met by a blast of hot Norwegian. He shook his head, and said loudly, 'I have no Norwegian. Do you speak English?'

The policeman halted in mid-spate with his mouth open. He shut it firmly, took a deep breath, and said, 'What you think you do?'

Denison pointed back. 'It was those damn fools. I might have been killed.'

The policeman stood back and did a slow circumnavigation of the car, inspecting it carefully. Then he tapped on the window of the passenger side and Denison opened the door. The policeman got in. 'Drive!' he said.

When Denison pulled up outside the building marked POLISI and switched off the engine the policeman firmly took the car key from him and waved towards the door of the building. 'Inside!'

It was a long wait for Denison. He sat in a bare room under the cool eye of a Norwegian policeman, junior grade, and meditated on his story. If he told the truth then the question would arise: *Who would want to attack an Englishman called Meyrick?* That would naturally lead to: *Who is this Meyrick?* Denison did not think he could survive long under questions like that. It would all come out and the consensus of opinion would be that they had a right nut-case on their hands, and probably homicidal at that. They would have to be told something other than the strict truth.

He waited an hour and then the telephone rang. The young policeman answered briefly, put down the telephone, and said to Denison, 'Come!'

He was taken to an office where a senior policeman sat behind a desk. He picked up a pen and levelled it at a chair. 'Sit!'

Denison sat, wondering if the English conversation of the Norwegian police was limited to one word at a time. The officer poised his pen above a printed form. 'Name?'

'Meyrick,' said Denison. 'Harold Feltham Meyrick.'

'Nationality?'

'British.'

The officer extended his hand, palm upwards. 'Passport.' It was not a question.

Denison took out his passport and put it on the outstretched palm. The officer flicked through the pages, then put it down and stared at Denison with eyes like chips of granite. 'You drove through the streets of Drammen at an estimated speed of 140 kilometres an hour. I don't have to tell you that is in excess of the speed limit. You drove through the Spiralen at an unknown speed – certainly less than 140 kilometres otherwise we would have the distasteful task of scraping you off the walls. What is your explanation?'

Denison now knew what a Norwegian policeman sounded like in an extended speech in the English language, and he did not particularly relish it. The man's tone was scathing. He said, 'There was a car behind me. The driver was playing silly buggers.' The officer raised his eyebrows, and Denison said, 'I think they were teenage hooligans out to throw a scare into someone – you know how they are. They succeeded with me. They rammed me a couple of times and I had to go faster. It all led on from that.'

He stopped and the officer stared at him with hard, grey eyes but said nothing. Denison let the silence lengthen, then said slowly and clearly, 'I would like to get in touch with the British Embassy immediately.'

The officer lowered his eyes and consulted a typewritten form. 'The condition of the rear of your car is consistent with your story. There was another car. It has been found abandoned. The condition of the front of that car is also consistent with your story. The car we found had been stolen last night in Oslo.' He looked up. 'Do you want to make any changes in your statement?'

'No,' said Denison.

'Are you sure?'

'Quite sure.'

The officer stood up, the passport in his hand. 'Wait here.' He walked out.

Denison waited another hour before the officer came back. He said, 'An official from your Embassy is coming to be present while you prepare your written statement.'

'I see,' said Denison. 'What about my passport?'

'That will be handed to the Embassy official. Your car we will keep here for spectrographic tests of the paintwork. If there has been transfer of paint from one car to another it will tend to support your statement. In any event, the car cannot be driven in its present condition; both indicator lights are smashed – you would be breaking the law.'

Denison nodded. 'How long before the Embassy man gets here?'

'I cannot say. You may wait here.' The officer went away.

Denison waited for two hours. On complaining of hunger, food and coffee were brought to him on a tray. Otherwise he was left alone except for the doctor who came in to dress an abrasion on the left side of his forehead. He dimly remembered being struck by a tree branch on the chase along the trail, but did not correct the doctor who assumed it had occurred in the Spiralen. What with one thing and another, the left side of Meyrick's face was taking quite a beating; any photographs had better be of the right profile.

He said nothing about the wound in his side. While alone in the office he had checked it quickly. That knife must have been razor sharp; it had sliced through his topcoat, his jacket, the sweater and into his side, fortunately not deeply. The white sweater was red with blood but the wound, which appeared clean, had stopped bleeding although it hurt if he moved suddenly. He left it alone.

At last someone came – a dapper young man with a fresh face who advanced on Denison with an outstretched hand. 'Dr Meyrick – I'm George McCready, I've come to help you get out of this spot of trouble.'

Behind McCready came the police officer, who drew up another chair and they got down to the business of the written statement. The officer wanted it amplified much more than in Denison's bald, verbal statement so he obligingly told all that had happened from the moment he had entered the Spiralen tunnel on top of Bragernesasen. He had no need to lie about anything. His written statement was taken away and typed up in quadruplicate and he signed all four copies, McCready countersigning as witness.

McCready cocked his eye at the officer. 'I think that's all.'

The officer nodded. 'That's all – for the moment. Dr Meyrick may be required at another time. I trust he will be available.'

'Of course,' said McCready easily. He turned to Denison. 'Let's get you back to the hotel. You must be tired.'

They went out to McCready's car. As McCready drove out of Drammen Denison was preoccupied with a problem. How did McCready know to address him as 'Doctor'? The designation on his passport was just plain 'Mister'. He stirred and said, 'If we're going to the hotel I'd like to have my passport. I don't like to be separated from it.'

'You're not going to the hotel,' said McCready. 'That was for the benefit of the copper. I'm taking you to the Embassy. Carey flew in from London this morning and he wants to see you.' He laughed shortly. '*How* he wants to see you.'

Denison felt the water deepening. 'Carey,' he said in a neutral tone, hoping to stimulate conversation along those lines. McCready had dropped Carey's name casually as though Meyrick was supposed to know him. Who the devil was Carey?

McCready did not bite. 'That explanation of yours wasn't quite candid, was it?' He waited for a reaction but Denison kept his mouth shut. 'There's a witness – a waitress from the Spiraltoppen – who said something about a fight up there. It seems there was a man with a gun. The police are properly suspicious.'

When Denison would not be drawn McCready glanced sideways at him, and laughed. 'Never mind, you did the right thing under the circumstances. Never talk about guns to a copper – it makes them nervous. Mind you, the circumstances should never have arisen. Carey's bloody wild about that.' He sighed. 'I can't say that I blame him.'

It was gibberish to Denison and he judged that the less he said the better. He leaned back, favouring his injured side, and said, 'I'm tired.'

'Yes,' said McCready. 'I suppose you must be.'

FIVE

Denison was kept kicking his heels in an ante-room in the Embassy while McCready went off, presumably to report. After fifteen minutes he came back. 'This way, Dr Meyrick.'

Denison followed him along a corridor until McCready stopped and politely held open a door for him. 'You've already met Mr Carey, of course.'

The man sitting behind the desk could only be described as square. He was a big, chunky man with a square, head topped with close-cut grizzled grey hair. He was broad-chested and squared off at the shoulders, and his hands were big with blunt fingers. 'Come in, Dr Meyrick.' He nodded at McCready. 'All right, George; be about your business.'

McCready closed the door. 'Sit down, Doctor,' said Carey. It was an invitation, not a command. Denison sat in the chair on the other side of the desk and waited for a long time while Carey inspected him with an inscrutable face.

After a long time Carey sighed. 'Dr Meyrick, you were asked not to stray too far from your hotel and to keep strictly to central Oslo. If you wanted to go farther afield you were asked to let us know so that we could make the necessary arrangements. You see, our manpower isn't infinite.'

His voice rose. 'Maybe you shouldn't have been *asked*; maybe you should have been *told*.' He seemed to hold himself in with an effort, and lowered his voice again. 'So I fly in this morning to hear that you're missing, and then I'm told that you isolated yourself on a mountain top – for what reason only you know.'

He raised his hand to intercept interruption. Denison did not mind; he was not going to say anything, anyway.

'All right,' said Carey. 'I know the story you told the local coppers. It was a good improvisation and maybe they'll buy it and maybe they won't.' He put his hands flat on the desk. 'Now what really happened?'

'I was up there walking through the woods,' said Denison, 'when suddenly a man attacked me.'

'Description?'

'Tall. Broad. Not unlike you in build, but younger. He had black hair. His nose was broken. He had something in his hand – he was going to hit me with it. Some sort of cosh, I suppose.'

'So what did you do?'

'I laid him out,' said Denison.

'*You* laid him out,' said Carey in a flat voice. There was disbelief in his eye.

'I laid him out,' said Denison evenly. He paused. 'I was a useful boxer at one time.'

Carey frowned and drummed his fingers. 'Then what happened?'

'Another man was coming at me from behind, so I ran for it.'

'Wise man – some of the time, anyway. And . . .?'

'Another man intercepted me from the front.'

'Describe him.'

'Shortish – about five foot seven – with a rat-face and a long nose. Dressed in jeans and a blue jersey. He had a knife.'

'He had a knife, did he?' said Carey. 'So what did you do about that?'

'Well, the other chap was coming up behind fast – I didn't have much time to think – so I charged the joker with the knife and sold him the dummy at the last moment'

'You *what*?'

'I sold him the dummy. It's a rugby expression meaning . . .'

'I know what it means,' snapped Carey. 'I suppose you were a useful rugby player at one time, too.'

'That's right,' said Denison.

Carey bent his head and put his hand to his brow so that his face was hidden. He seemed to be suppressing some strong emotion. 'What happened next?' he asked in a muffled voice.

'By that time I'd got back to the car park – and there was another man.'

'Another man,' said Carey tiredly. 'Description.'

'Not much. I think he wore a grey suit He had a gun.'

'Escalating on you, weren't they?' said Carey. His voice was savage. 'So what did you do then?'

'I was in the car by the time I saw the gun and I got out of there fast and . . .'

'And did a Steve McQueen through the Spiralen, roared through Drammen like an express train and butted a copper in the arse.'

'Yes,' said Denison simply. 'That about wraps it up.'

'I should think it does,' said Carey. He was silent for a while, then he said, 'Regardless of the improbability of all this, I'd still like to know why you went to Drammen in the first place, and why you took the trouble to shake off any followers before leaving Oslo.'

'Shake off followers,' said Denison blankly. 'I didn't know I was being followed.'

'You know now. It was for your own protection. But my man says he's never seen such an expert job of shaking a tail in his life. You were up to all the tricks. You nearly succeeded twice, and you did succeed the third time.'

'I don't know what you're talking about,' said Denison. 'I lost my way a couple of times, that's all.'

Carey took a deep breath and looked at the ceiling. 'You lost your way,' he breathed. His voice became deep and solemn. 'Dr Meyrick: can you tell me why you lost your way when you know this area better than your own county of Buckinghamshire? You showed no signs of losing your way when you went to Drammen last week.'

Denison took the plunge. 'Perhaps it's because I'm not Dr Meyrick.'

Carey whispered, *'What did you say?'*

SIX

Denison told all of it.

When he had finished Carey's expression was a mixture of perturbation and harassment. He heard everything Denison had to say but made no comment; instead, he lifted the telephone, dialled a number, and said, 'George? Ask Ian to come in here for a minute.'

He came from behind the desk and patted Denison on the shoulder. 'I hope you don't mind waiting for a few minutes.' He strode away to intercept the man who had just come in and they held a whispered colloquy before Carey left the room.

He closed the door on the other side and stood for a moment in thought, then he shook his head irritably and went into McCready's office. McCready looked up, saw Carey's expression, and said, 'What's the matter?'

'Our boy has rolled clean off his tiny little rocker,' snapped Carey. 'That's what's the matter. He started off by telling cock-and-bull stories, but then it got worse – much worse.'

'What did he say?'

Carey told him – in gruesome detail.

Ten minutes later he said, 'Discounting a lot of balls about mysterious attackers, *something* happened up there on top of the Spiralen which knocked Meyrick off his perch.'

He rubbed his forehead. 'When they wish these eggheads on us you'd think they'd test them for mental stability. What we need now is an alienist.'

McCready suppressed a smile. 'Isn't that rather an old-fashioned term?'

Carey glared at him. 'Old-fashioned and accurate.' He stabbed his finger at the office wall. 'That . . . that *thing* in there isn't human any more. I tell you, my flesh crawled when I heard what he was saying.'

'There isn't a chance that he's right, is there?' asked McCready diffidently.

'No chance at all. I was facing Meyrick at the original briefing in London for two bloody days until I got to hate the sight of his fat face. It's Meyrick, all right.'

'There is one point that puzzles me,' said McCready. 'When I was with him at the police station in Drammen he didn't speak a word of Norwegian, and yet I understand he knows the language.'

'He speaks it fluently,' said Carey.

'And yet I'm told that his first words were to the effect that he spoke no Norwegian.'

'For God's sake!' said Carey. 'You know the man's history. He was born in Finland and lived there until he was seventeen, when he came to live here in Oslo. When he was twenty-four he moved to England where he's been ever since. That's twenty-two years. He didn't see a rugby ball until he arrived in England, and I've studied his dossier and know for a fact that he never boxed in his life.'

'Then it all fits in with his story that he's not Meyrick.' McCready paused for thought. 'There *was* a witness at Spiraltoppen who said she saw a gun.'

'A hysterical waitress,' sneered Carey. 'Wait a minute – did you tell Meyrick about that?'

'I did mention it.'

'It fits,' said Carey. 'You know, I wouldn't be surprised if the story Meyrick gave to the police wasn't the absolute truth. He was razzled by a few kids out for a joyride in a stolen car and the experience knocked him off his spindle.'

'And the gun?'

'You told him about the gun. He seized that and wove it into his fairy tale, and added a few other trimmings such as the knife and the cosh. I think that in the Spiralen he felt so bloody helpless that he's invented this story to retain what he thinks is his superiority. At the briefing I assessed him as an arrogant bastard, utterly convinced of his superiority to us lesser mortals. But he wasn't very superior in the Spiralen, was he?'

'Interesting theory,' said McCready. 'You'd make a good alienist – except for one thing. You lack empathy.'

'I can't stand the man,' said Carey bluntly. 'He's an overweening, overbearing, supercilious son-of-a-bitch who thinks the sun shines out of his arse. Mr Know-it-all in person and too bloody toplofty by half.' He shrugged. 'But I can't pick and choose the people I work with. It's not in my contract.'

'What did you say he called himself?'

'Giles Denison from Hampstead. Hampstead, for Christ's sake!'

'I'll be back in a minute,' said McCready. He left the room.

Carey loosened his tie with a jerk and sat biting his thumbnail. He looked up as McCready came back holding a book. 'What have you got there?'

'London telephone directory.'

'Give me that,' said Carey, and grabbed it. 'Let's see – Dennis, Dennis, Dennis . . . Dennison. There's a George and two plain Gs – neither in Hampstead.' He sat back, looking pleased.

McCready took the book and flipped the pages. After a minute he said, 'Denison, Giles . . . Hampstead. He spells it with one "n".'

'Oh, Christ!' said Carey, looking stricken. He recovered. 'Doesn't mean a thing. He picked the name of someone he knows. His daughter's boy-friend, perhaps.'

'Perhaps,' said McCready non-committally.

Carey drummed his fingers on the desk. 'I'll stake my life that this is Meyrick; anything else would be too ridiculous.' His fingers were suddenly stilled. 'Mrs Hansen,' he said. 'She's been closer to him than anybody. Did she have anything to say?'

'She reported last night that she'd met him. He'd broken a date with her in the morning and excused it by pleading illness. Said he'd been in bed all morning.'

'Had he?'

'Yes.'

'Did she notice anything about him – anything odd or unusual?'

'Only that he had a cold and that he'd stopped smoking. He said cigarettes tasted like straw.'

Carey, a pipe-smoker, grunted. 'They taste like straw to me without a cold. But he recognised her.'

'They had a drink and a conversation – about morals and religion, she said.'

'That does it,' said Carey. 'Meyrick is ready to pontificate about anything at the drop of a hat, whether he knows anything about it or not.' He rubbed his chin and said grudgingly, 'Trouble is, he usually talks sense – he has a good brain. No, this is Meyrick, and Meyrick is as flabby as a bladder of lard – that's why we have to coddle him on this operation. Do you really think that Meyrick could stand up against four men with guns and knives and coshes? The man could hardly break the skin on the top of a custard. He's gone out of his tiny, scientific mind and his tale of improbable violence is just to save his precious superiority, as I said before.'

'And what about the operation?'

'As far as Meyrick is concerned the operation is definitely off,' said Carey decisively. 'And, right now, I don't see how it can be done without him. I'll cable London to that effect as soon as I've had another talk with him.' He paused. 'You'd better come along, George. I'm going to need a witness on this one or else London will have me certified.'

They left the office and walked along the corridor. Outside the room where Meyrick was held Carey put his hand on McCready's arm. 'Hold yourself in, George. This might be rough.'

They found Meyrick still sitting at the desk in brooding silence, ignoring the man he knew only as Ian who sat opposite. Ian looked up at Carey and shrugged eloquently.

Carey stepped forward. 'Dr Meyrick, I'm sorry to . . .'

'My name is Denison. I told you that.' His voice was cold.

Carey softened his tone. 'All right, Mr Denison; if you prefer it that way. I really think you ought to see a doctor. I'm arranging for it.'

'And about time,' said Denison. 'This is hurting like hell.'

'What is?'

Denison was pulling his sweater from his trousers. 'This bloody knife wound. Look at it.'

Carey and McCready bent to look at the quarter-inch deep slash along Denison's side. It would, Carey estimated, take sixteen stitches to sew it up.

Their heads came up together and they looked at each other with a wild surmise.

SEVEN

Carey paced restlessly up and down McCready's office. His tie was awry and his hair would have been tousled had it not been so close-cropped because he kept running his hand through it. 'I still don't believe it,' he said. 'It's too bloody incredible.'

He swung on McCready. 'George, supposing you went to bed tonight, here in Oslo, and woke up tomorrow, say, in a New York hotel, wearing someone else's face. What would be your reaction?'

'I think I'd go crazy,' said McCready soberly. He smiled slightly. 'If I woke up with your face I would go crazy.'

Carey ignored the wisecrack. 'But Denison didn't go crazy,' he said meditatively. 'All things considered, he kept his cool remarkably well.'

'If he is Denison,' remarked McCready. 'He could be Meyrick and quite insane.'

Carey exploded into a rage. 'For God's sake! All along you've been arguing that he's Denison; now you turn around and say he could be Meyrick.'

McCready eyed him coolly. 'The role of devil's advocate suits me, don't you think?' He tapped the desk. 'Either way, the operation is shot to hell.'

Carey sat down heavily. 'You're right, of course. But if this is a man called Denison then there are a lot of questions to be answered. But first, what the devil do we do with him?'

'We can't keep him here,' said McCready. 'For the same reason we didn't keep Meyrick here. The Embassy is like a fishbowl.'

Carey cocked his head. 'He's been here for over two hours. That's about normal for a citizen being hauled over the coals for a serious driving offence. You suggest we send him back to the hotel?'

'Under surveillance.' McCready smiled. 'He says he has a date with a redhead for dinner.'

'Mrs Hansen,' said Carey. 'Does he know about her?'

'No.'

'Keep it that way. She's to stick close to him. Give her a briefing and ask her to guard him from interference. He could run into some odd situations. And talk to him like a Dutch uncle. Put the fear of God into him so that he stays in the hotel. I don't want him wandering around loose.'

Carey drew a sheet of paper towards him and scribbled on it. 'The next thing we want are doctors – tame ones who will ask the questions we want asked and no others. A plastic surgeon and – ' he smiled at McCready bleakly – 'and an alienist. The problem must be decided one way or the other.'

'We can't wait until they arrive,' said McCready.

'Agreed,' said Carey. 'We'll work on the assumption that a substitution has been made – that this man is Denison. We know when the substitution was made – in the early hours of yesterday morning. Denison was brought in – how?'

'On a stretcher – he must have been unconscious.'

'Right!' said Carey. 'A hospital patient in transit under the supervision of a trained nurse and probably a doctor. And they'd have taken a room on the same floor as

Meyrick. The switch was made and Meyrick taken out yesterday morning – probably in an ambulance at the back entrance of the hotel by arrangement with the management. Hotels don't like stretchers being paraded through the front lobby.'

'I'll get on to it,' said McCready. 'It might be an idea to check on all the people who booked in on the previous day, regardless of the floor they stayed on. I don't think this was a two man job.'

'I don't, either. And you check the comings and goings for the past week – somebody must have been watching Meyrick for a long time.'

'That's a hell of a big job,' objected McCready. 'Do we get the co-operation of the Norwegians?'

Carey pondered. 'At this time – no. We keep it under wraps.'

McCready's face took on a sad look at the thought of all the legwork he was going to have to do. Carey tilted his chair back. 'And then there's the other end to be checked – the London end. Why Giles Denison of Hampstead?' His chair came down with a thump. 'Hasn't it struck you that Denison has been very unforthcoming?'

McCready shrugged. 'I haven't talked to him all that much.'

'Well, look,' said Carey. 'Here we have this man in this bloody odd situation in which he finds himself. After recovering from the first shock, he not only manages to deceive Mrs Hansen as to his real identity but he has the wit to ring up Meyrick's home. But why only Meyrick? Why didn't he check back on himself?'

'How do you mean?'

Carey sighed. 'There's a man called Giles Denison missing from Hampstead. Surely he'd be missed by someone? Even if Denison is an unmarried orphan he must have friends – a job. Why didn't he ring back to reassure people that he was all right and still alive and now living it up in Oslo?'

'I hadn't thought of that,' admitted McCready. 'That's a pointer to his being Meyrick, after all. Suffering from delusions but unable to flesh them out properly.'

Carey gave a depressed nod. 'All I've had from him is that he's Giles Denison from Hampstead – nothing more.'

'Why not put it to him now?' suggested McCready.

Carey thought about it and shook his head. 'No, I'll leave that to the psychiatrist. If this is really Meyrick, the wrong sort of questions could push him over the edge entirely.' He pulled the note pad towards him again. 'We'll have someone check on Denison in Hampstead and find out the score.' He ripped off the sheet. 'Let's get cracking. I want those cables sent to London immediately – top priority and coded. I want those quacks here as fast as possible.'

EIGHT

Giles Denison stirred his coffee and smiled across the table at Diana Hansen. His smile was steady, which was remarkable because a thought had suddenly struck him like a bolt of lightning and left him with a churning stomach. Was the delectable Diana Hansen who faced him Meyrick's mistress?

The very thought put him into a dilemma. Should he make a pass or not? Whatever he did – or did not – do, he had a fifty per cent chance of being wrong. The uncertainty of it spoiled his evening which had so far been relaxing and pleasant.

He had been driven back to the hotel in an Embassy car after dire warnings from George McCready of what would happen to him if he did not obey instructions. 'You'll have realized by now that you've dropped right into the middle of something awkward,' said McCready. 'We're doing our best to sort it out but, for the next couple of days, you'd do well to stay in the hotel.' He drove it home by asking pointedly, 'How's your side feeling now?'

'Better,' said Denison. 'But I could have done with a doctor.' He had been strapped up by McCready, who had produced a first-aid box and displayed a competence which suggested he was no stranger to knife wounds.

'You'll get a doctor,' assured McCready. 'Tomorrow.'

'I have a dinner date,' said Denison. 'With that redhead I told you about. What should I do about that? If she goes on like she did yesterday I'm sure to put my foot in it.'

'I don't see why you should,' said McCready judiciously.

'For God's sake! I don't even know her name.'

McCready patted him on the shoulder, and said soothingly, 'You'll be all right.'

Denison was plaintive. 'It's all very well you wanting me to go on being Meyrick but surely you can tell me *something*. Who *is* Meyrick, for instance?'

'It will all be explained tomorrow,' said McCready, hoping that he was right. 'In the meantime, go back to the hotel like a good chap, and don't leave it until I call for you. Just have a quiet dinner with . . . with your redhead and then go to bed.'

Denison had a last try. 'Are you in Intelligence or something? A spy?'

But to that McCready made no answer.

So Denison was delivered to the hotel and he had not been in the room more than ten minutes when the telephone rang. He regarded it warily and let it ring several times before he put out his hand as though about to pick up a snake. 'Yes?' he said uncommunicatively.

'Diana here.'

'Who?' he asked cautiously.

'Diana Hansen, who else? We have a dinner date, remember? How are you?'

Again he caught the faint hint of America behind the English voice. 'Better,' he said, thinking it was convenient of her to announce her name.

'That's good,' she said warmly. 'Are you fit enough for dinner?'

'I think so.'

'Mmm,' she murmured doubtfully. 'But I still don't think you should go out; there's quite a cold wind. What about dinner in the hotel restaurant?'

Even more convenient; he had just been about to suggest that himself. In a more confident voice he said, 'That'll be fine.'

'Meet you in the bar at half past seven,' she said.

'All right.'

She rang off and he put down the telephone slowly. He hoped that McCready was right; that he could manage a sustained conversation with this woman in the guise of Meyrick. He sat in the armchair and winced as pain stabbed in his side. He held his breath until the pain eased and then relaxed and looked at his watch. Half past five. He had two hours before meeting the Hansen woman.

What a mess! What a stinking mess! Lost behind another man's face, he had apparently dropped into the middle of an intrigue which involved the British government. That man, Carey, had been damned patronizing about what had happened on top of the Spiralen and had not bothered to hide his disbelief. It had been that, more than anything else, that had driven Denison into disclosing who he was. It had certainly taken the smile off Carey's face.

But who was Carey? To begin with, he was obviously McCready's boss – but that did not get him very far because who was McCready? A tight little group in the British Embassy in Oslo dedicated to what? Trade relations? That did not sound likely.

Carey had made it clear that he had warned Meyrick not to move far from the hotel. Judging by what had happened on the Spiralen the warning was justified. But who the hell was Meyrick that he was so important? The man with the title of Doctor or perhaps Professor, and who was described on his passport as a civil servant.

Denison's head began to ache again. *Christ!* he thought; *I'll be bloody glad to get back to Hampstead, back to my job and the people I . . .*

The thought tailed off to a deadly emptiness and he felt his stomach lurch. A despairing wail rose in his mind – *God help me!* he cried silently as he realized his mind was a blank, that he did not know what his job was, that he could not put a name to a single friend or acquaintance, and that all he knew of himself was that he was Giles Denison and that he came from Hampstead.

Bile rose in his throat. He struggled to his feet and staggered to the bathroom where he was violently sick. Again there was that insistent beat in his mind: I AM GILES DENISON. But there was nothing more – no link with a past life.

He left the bathroom and lay on the bed, staring at the ceiling. *You must remember!* he commanded himself. *You must!* But there was nothing – just Giles Denison of Hampstead and a vague mind picture of a house in a half-forgotten memory.

Think!

The scar on his shin – he remembered that. He saw himself on the small child-size bicycle going down a hill too fast, and the inevitable tumble at the bottom – then the quick tears and the comfort of his mother. I remember that, he told himself in triumph.

What else? Beth – he remembered Beth who had been his wife, but she had died. How many years ago was it? Three years. And then there was the whisky, too much whisky. He remembered the whisky.

Denison lay on the bed and fought to extract memories from a suddenly recalcitrant mind. There was a slick sheen of sweat on his brow and his fists were clenched, the nails digging into his palms.

Something else he had remembered before. He had come back from Edinburgh on June 17, but what had he been doing there? Working, of course, but what was his work? Try as he might he could not penetrate the blank haze which cloaked his mind.

On June 18 he had played golf in the afternoon. With whom? Of course it was possible for a man to play a round of golf alone, and also to go to the cinema alone and to dine in Soho alone, but it was hardly likely that he would forget everything else. Where had he played golf? Which cinema did he go to? Which restaurant in Soho?

A blazing thought struck him, an illumination of the mind so clear that he knew certainly it was the truth. He cried aloud, 'But I've never played golf in my life!'

There was a whirling spiral of darkness in his mind and, mercifully, he slept.

NINE

Denison walked into the bar at a quarter to eight and saw the woman who called herself Diana Hansen sitting at a table. He walked over and said, 'Sorry I'm late.'

She smiled and said lightly, 'I was beginning to think I was being stood up again.'

He sat down. 'I fell asleep.'

'You look pale. Are you all right?'

'I'm fine.' There was a vague memory at the back of his mind which disturbed him; something had happened just before he had fallen asleep. He was reluctant to probe into it because he caught a hint of terror and madness which frightened him. He shivered.

'Cold?' Her voice was sympathetic.

'Nothing that a stiff drink won't cure.' He beckoned to a passing waiter, and raised his eyebrows at her.

'A dry Martini, please.'

He turned to the hovering waiter. 'A dry martini and . . . do you have a scotch malt?' Normally he bought the cheapest blend he could buy in the cut-price supermarkets but with Meyrick's finances behind him he could afford the best.

'Yes, sir. Glenfiddich?'

'That will do fine. Thank you.'

Diana Hansen said, 'Food may be better than drink. Have you eaten today?'

'Not much.' Just the meal in the police station at Drammen, taken for fuel rather than pleasure.

'You men!' she said with scorn. 'No better than children when left on your own. You'll feel better after dinner.'

He leaned back in his chair. 'Let's see – how long have we known each other, Diana?'

She smiled. 'Counting the days, Harry? Nearly three weeks.'

So he had met her in Oslo – or, rather, Meyrick had. 'I was just trying to find out how long it takes a woman to become maternal. Less than three weeks, I see.'

'Is that the scientific mind at work?'

'One aspect of it.' Could that mean anything? Was Dr Meyrick a scientist – a government boffin?

She looked across the room and a shadow seemed to darken her face momentarily. 'There's Jack Kidder and his wife.'

Denison paused before he turned round. 'Oh! Where?'

'Just coming in.' She put out her hand and covered his. 'Do you want to be bothered by them, darling? He's a bit of a bore, really.'

Denison looked at the tall, fleshy man who was escorting a petite woman. Jack Kidder was the name Diana Hansen had mentioned when he had bumped into her outside the bookshop. If she did not want to mix with the Kidders it was all right with him; he had enough to cope with already. He said, 'You're right. I don't think I could cope with a bore tonight.'

She laughed. 'Thanks for the compliment – hidden though it was. I'll put him off tactfully if he comes across.' She sighed theatrically. 'But if he says that damned slogan of his again I'll scream.'

'What's that?'

'You must have heard it. It's when he pulls off one of his dreadful jokes.' She burlesqued an American accent. '"You know me – Kidder by name and kidder by nature."'

'Jack was always the life and soul of the party,' said Denison drily.

'I don't know how Lucy puts up with him,' said Diana. 'If you can talk about a hen-pecked husband, can you refer to a cock-pecked wife?'

Denison grinned. 'It sounds rude.' Diana Hansen was making things easy for him. She had just given him a thumbnail sketch of the Kidders, including names and temperaments. It could not have been done better if done deliberately.

The waiter put the drinks on the table and Denison found he had a scotch on the rocks, a desecration of good malt. He did not feel like making a fuss about it so he raised his glass. *'Skal!'* He sipped the whisky and reflected that this was the first real drink he had had since his transformation into Meyrick.

The familiar taste bit at his tongue and somehow released a wave of memories which washed through him tumultuously, tantalizingly close to the surface of his mind. And with the memories, unrealized though they were, came the fear and the terror which set his heart thumping in his chest. Hastily he set down the glass, knowing he was close to panic.

Diana Hansen looked at his shaking fingers. 'What's the matter, Harry?'

Denison covered up. 'I don't think a drink is a good idea, after all. I've just remembered I'm stuffed full of pills.' He managed a smile. 'If you shook me I'd rattle. I don't think they'd mix with alcohol.'

She put down her glass. Then let's have dinner before the Kidders catch up with us.' She stood up and took her handbag from the table. Denison arose and they moved towards the entrance, but then she turned her head and murmured, Too late, I'm afraid.'

Kidder was also standing up, his big body blocking the way. 'Hey, Lucy, look who's here. It's Diana and Harry.'

'Hallo, Jack,' said Denison. 'Had a good day?'

'We've been up to Holmenkollen; you know – the big ski-jump you can see from all over the city. It's quite a thing when you get up to it close. Can you imagine, it's only used once a year?'

'I can't imagine,' said Denison blandly.

Lucy Kidder said, 'And we went to the Henie-Onstad Art Centre, too.'

'Yeah, modern art,' said Kidder disparagingly. 'Harry, can you make any sense out of Jackson Pollock?'

'Not much,' said Denison.

Kidder turned on his wife. 'Anyway, why the hell do we have to come to Norway to see an American artist?'

'But he's internationally famous, Jack. Aren't you proud of that?'

'I guess so,' he said gloomily. 'But the locals aren't much better. Take the guy with the name like a breakfast food.' Everyone looked at Kidder with blank faces and he snapped his fingers impatiently. 'You know who I mean – the local Scowegian we saw yesterday.'

Lucy Kidder sighed. 'Edvard Munch,' she said resignedly.

'That's the guy. Too gloomy for me even if you can see the people in his pictures,' said Kidder.

Diana cut in quickly. 'Harry's not been feeling too well lately. I'm taking him in to an early dinner and sending him right to bed.'

'Gee, I'm sorry to hear that,' said Kidder. He sounded sincere.

'There's a lot of this two-day flu about,' said his wife. 'And it can be nasty while it lasts. You look after yourself – hear?'

'I don't think it's too serious,' said Denison.

'But we'd better go in to dinner,' said Diana. 'Harry hasn't eaten a thing all day.'

'Sure,' said Kidder, standing aside. 'I hope you feel better real soon. You look after him, Diana.'

Over dinner they talked in generalities, much to Denison's relief, and he was able to hold his own without much effort. There was not a single thing to trouble him until the coffee was served and that startling thought about the possible relationship between Diana and Meyrick came into his head. He looked at her speculatively and wondered what to do. For all he knew, Meyrick was an old ram.

He held the smile on his face and stirred his coffee mechanically. A waiter came to the table. 'Mrs Hansen?'

Diana looked up. 'Yes.'

'A telephone call.'

'Thank you.' She looked at Denison apologetically. 'I told someone I'd be here. Do you mind?'

'Not at all.' She stood up and left the restaurant, going into the lobby. He watched her until she was out of sight and then stopped stirring his coffee and put the spoon in the saucer with a clink. Thoughtfully he looked at the handbag on the other side of the table.

Mrs Hansen! He could bear to know more about that. He stretched out his hand slowly and picked up the handbag, which was curiously heavy. Holding it on his lap, below the level of the table, he snapped open the catch and bent his head to look inside.

When Diana came back the bag was back in its place. She sat down, picked it up, and took out a packet of cigarettes. 'Still not smoking, Harry?'

He shook his head. 'They still taste foul.'

Soon thereafter he signed the bill and they left, parting in the lobby, he to go to bed and she to go to wherever she lived. He had decided against making a pass at Mrs Diana Hansen because it was most unlikely that Dr Harold Feltham Meyrick would be having an affaire with a woman who carried a gun – even if it was only a small gun.

TEN

The next day was boring. He obeyed instructions and stayed in the hotel waiting to hear from McCready. He breakfasted in his room and ordered English newspapers. Nothing had changed – the news was as bad as ever.

At mid-morning he left the room to allow the maid to clean up, and went down to the lobby where he saw the Kidders at the porter's desk. He hung back, taking an inordinate interest in a showcase full of Norwegian silver, while Kidder discussed in a loud voice the possibilities of different bus tours. Finally they left the hotel and he came out of cover.

He discovered that the bookshop on the corner of the street had a convenient entrance inside the hotel, so he bought a stack of English paperbacks and took them to his room. He read for the rest of the day, gutting the books, his mind in low gear. He had a curious reluctance to think about his present predicament and, once, when he put a book aside and tried to think coherently, his mind skittered about and he felt the unreasoning panic come over him. When he picked up the book again his head was aching.

At ten that night no contact had been made and he thought of ringing the Embassy and asking for McCready but the strange disinclination to thought had spread to action and he was irresolute. He looked at the telephone for a while, and then slowly undressed and went to bed.

He was almost asleep when there was a tap at his door. He sat up and listened and it came again, a discreet double knock. He switched on the light and put on Meyrick's bathrobe, then went to the door. It was McCready, who came in quickly and closed the door behind him. 'Ready for the doctor?' he asked.

Denison frowned. 'At this time of night?'

'Why not?' asked McCready lightly.

Denison sighed. It was just one more mystery to add to the others. He reached for his underwear and took off the bathrobe. McCready picked up the pyjamas which were lying neatly folded on top of the suitcase. 'You don't wear these?'

'Meyrick did.' Denison sat on the edge of the bed to put on his socks. 'I don't.'

'Oh!' McCready thoughtfully tugged at his ear.

When Denison picked up his jacket he turned to McCready. 'There's something you ought to know, I suppose. Diana Hansen carries . . .'

'Who?' asked McCready.

'The redhead I took to dinner – her name is Diana Hansen. She carries a gun.'

McCready went still. 'She does? How do you know?'

'I looked in her handbag.'

'Enterprising of you. I'll tell Carey – he'll be interested.' McCready took Denison by the arm. 'Let's go.'

McCready's car was in the garage and when he drove out into the street he turned left which Denison knew was away from the Embassy. 'Where are we going?'

'Not far,' said McCready. 'Five minutes. Possess your soul in patience.'

Within two minutes Denison was lost. The car twisted and turned in the strange streets until his sense of direction deserted him. Whether McCready was deliberately confusing him he did not know, but he thought it likely. Another possibility was that McCready was intent on shaking off any possible followers.

After a few minutes the car pulled up outside a large building which could have been a block of flats. They went inside and into a lift which took them to the fifth floor. McCready unlocked a door and motioned Denison inside. He found himself in a hall with doors on each side. McCready opened one of them, and said, 'This is Mr Iredale. He'll fix up your side for you.'

Iredale was a sallow, middle-aged man, balding and with deep grooves cut from the base of his nose to the corners of his mouth. He said pleasantly, 'Come in, Mr Denison; let me have a look at you.'

Denison heard the door close behind him and turned to find that McCready had already gone. He whirled around to confront Iredale. 'I thought I was being taken to a doctor.'

'I am a doctor,' said Iredale. 'I'm also a surgeon. We surgeons have a strange inverted snobbery – we're called "mister" and not "doctor". I've never known why. Take off your coat, Mr Denison, and let me see the damage.'

Denison hesitated and slowly took off his jacket and then his shirt. 'If you'll lie on the couch?' suggested Iredale, and opened a black bag which could only have been the property of a doctor. Somewhat reassured, Denison lay down.

Iredale snipped away the bandages with a small pair of scissors and examined the slash. 'Nasty,' he said. 'But clean. It will need a local anaesthetic. Are you allergic to anaesthetic, Mr Denison?'

'I don't know – I don't think so.'

'You'll just feel three small pricks – no more.' Iredale took out a hypodermic syringe and filled it from a small phial. 'Lie still.'

Denison felt the pricks, and Iredale said, 'While we're waiting for that to take effect you can sit up.' He took an ophthalmoscope from his bag. 'I'd just like to look at your eyes.' He flashed a light into Denison's right eye. 'Had any alcohol lately?'

'No.'

Iredale switched to the left eye upon which he spent more time. 'That seems to be all right,' he said.

'I was stabbed in the side, not hit on the head,' said Denison. 'I don't have concussion.'

Iredale put away the ophthalmoscope. 'So you have a little medical knowledge.' He put his hands to Denison's face and palpated the flesh under the chin. 'You know what they say about a little knowledge.' He stood up and looked down at the top of Denison's head, and then his fingers explored the hairline. 'Don't knock the experts, Mr Denison – they know what they're doing.'

'What sort of a doctor are you?' asked Denison suspiciously.

Iredale ignored that. 'Ever had scalp trouble? Dandruff, for instance?'

'No.'

'I see. Right.' He touched Denison's side. 'Feel anything?'

'It's numb but I can feel pressure.'

'Good,' said Iredale. 'I'm going to stitch the wound closed. You won't feel anything – but if you do then shout like hell.' He put on rubber gloves which he took out of a sealed plastic bag and then took some fine thread out of another small packet. 'I'd turn your head away,' he advised. 'Lie down.'

He worked on Denison's side for about fifteen minutes and Denison felt nothing but the pressure of his fingers. At last he said, 'All right, Mr Denison; I've finished.'

Denison sat up and looked at his side. The wound was neatly closed and held by a row of minute stitches. 'I've always been good at needlework,' said Iredale conversationally. 'When the stitches are out there'll be but a hairline. In a year you won't be able to see it.'

Denison said, 'This isn't a doctor's surgery. Who are you?'

Iredale packed his bag rapidly and stood up. 'There'll be another doctor to see you in a moment.' He walked to the door and closed it behind him.

There was something about the way the door closed that vaguely alarmed Denison. He stood up and walked to the door and found it locked. Frowning, he turned away and looked about the room. There was the settee on which he had been lying, a table, two armchairs and a bookcase against the wall. He went over to the bookcase to inspect it and tripped over a wire which threatened to topple a telephone from a small table. He rescued the telephone and then stood looking down at it.

Iredale walked along the corridor and into a room at the end. Carey glanced up at him expectantly, breaking off his conversation with McCready. Harding, the psychiatrist, sat in an armchair, his long legs outstretched and his fingertips pressed together. There was also another man whom Iredale did not know. Carey saw Iredale looking at him, and said, 'Ian Armstrong of my staff. Well?' He could not suppress his eagerness.

Iredale put down his case. 'He's not Meyrick.' He paused. 'Not unless Meyrick has had plastic surgery recently.'

Carey blew out his breath in a long gasp. 'Are you sure?'

'Of course I'm sure,' said Iredale, a little testily.

'That's it, then.' Carey looked across at Harding. 'It's your turn, Dr Harding. Try to get out of him as much as you can.'

Harding nodded and uncoiled himself from the chair. He walked out of the room without speaking. As the door closed Carey said, 'You understand that, to the best of our knowledge, this alteration was made in the space of a week – not more.' He took a thin, cardboard file from the table. 'We've just received a lengthy cable from London about Denison – and a photo came over the wire.' He took the photograph and handed it to Iredale. 'That's Denison as he was quite recently. It hardly seems possible.'

Iredale studied the photograph. 'Very interesting,' he commented.

'Could this thing be done in a week?' Carey persisted.

Iredale put down the photograph. 'As far as I could ascertain there was only one lesion,' he said precisely. 'That was at the outside corner of the left eyelid. A very small cut which was possibly held together by one stitch while it healed. It would certainly heal in a week although there might have been a residual soreness. I detected a minute inflammation.'

McCready said in disbelief, 'You mean that was the only cut that was made?'

'Yes,' said Iredale. 'The purpose was to draw down the left eyelid. Have you got that photograph of Meyrick?'

'Here,' said Carey.

Iredale put down his forefinger. 'There – you see? The eyelid was drawn down due to the skin contraction caused by this scar.' He paused and said sniffily, 'A bit of a butcher's job, if you ask me. That should never have happened.'

'It was a war wound when Meyrick was a boy,' said Carey. He tapped the photograph of Meyrick. 'But how the devil did they reproduce this scar on Denison without cutting?'

'That was very cleverly done,' said Iredale with sudden enthusiasm. 'As expert a job of tattooing as I've ever seen, as also was the birthmark on the right jaw.' He leaned back in his chair. 'In my field, of course, I come across a lot of tattooing but I specialize in removal rather than application.' He leaned forward again and traced a line on the photograph. 'The hairline was adjusted by depilation; nothing as crude as mere shaving and leaving the hair to grow out. I'm afraid Mr Denison has lost his hair permanently.'

'That's all very well,' said McCready, coming forward. He leaned over the table, comparing the two photographs. 'But just look at these two men. Denison is thin in the face, and he'd look thinner without the beard. Meyrick is fat-jowled. And look at the differences in the noses.'

'That was done by liquid silicone injection,' said Iredale. 'Some of my more light-minded colleagues aid film stars in their mammary development by the same means.' His tone was distasteful. 'I palpated his cheeks and felt it. It was quite unmistakable.'

'I'll be damned!' said Carey.

'You say that Denison lost a week of objective time?' asked Iredale.

'He said he'd lost a week out of his life – if that's what you mean.'

'Then I can hazard a guess as to how it was done,' said Iredale. 'He was drugged, of course, and kept unconscious for the whole week. I noticed a dressing on his left arm. I didn't investigate it, but that was where the intravenous drip feed was inserted to keep him alive.'

He paused, and Carey said in a fascinated voice, 'Go on!'

'The cut would be made at the corner of the eye, giving it a full week to heal. Any competent surgeon could do that in five minutes. Then I suppose they'd do the tattooing. Normally there'd be a residual soreness from that, but it would certainly clear up in a week. Everything else could be done at leisure.'

He picked up the two photographs. 'You see, the underlying bone structure of these two men, as far as the heads go, is remarkably similar. I rather think that if you had a photograph of Meyrick taken fifteen to twenty years ago he would look not unlike Denison or, rather, as Denison used to look. I take it that Meyrick has been used to expensive living?'

'He's rich enough,' said Carey.

'It shows on his face,' said Iredale, and tossed down the photographs. 'Denison, however, looks a shade undernourished.'

'Interesting you should say that,' said Carey, opening the folder. 'From what we have here it seems that Denison, if not an alcoholic, was on the verge. He'd just lost his job – fired for incompetence on June 24.'

Iredale nodded. 'Symptomatic. Alcoholics reject food – they get their calories from the booze.' He stood up. 'That's all I can do tonight, gentlemen. I should like to see Denison tomorrow with a view to restoring him to his former appearance, which won't be easy – that silicone polymer will be the devil to get out. Is there any more?'

'Nothing, Mr Iredale,' said Carey.

'Then if you'll excuse me, I'll go to bed. It's been a long day.'

'You know where your room is,' said Carey, and Iredale nodded and left the room.

Carey and McCready looked at each other in silence for some time, and then Carey stirred and said over his shoulder, 'What did you make of all that, Ian?'

'I'm damned if I know,' said Armstrong.

Carey grunted. 'I'm damned, too. I've been involved in some bizarre episodes in this game, but this takes the prize for looniness. Now we'll have to see what Harding comes up with, and I suspect he's going to be a long time. I think somebody had better make coffee. It's going to be a long night.'

Carey was right because more than two hours elapsed before Harding returned. His face was troubled, and he said abruptly, 'I don't think Denison should be left alone.'

'Ian!' said Carey.

Armstrong got up, and Harding said, 'If he wants to talk let him. Join in but steer clear of specifics. Stick to generalities. Understand?'

Armstrong nodded and went out. Harding sat down and Carey studied him. Finally Carey said, 'You look as though you could do with a drink, Doctor. Whisky?'

Harding nodded. 'Thanks.' He rubbed his. forehead. 'Denison is in a bad way.'

Carey poured two ounces of whisky into a glass. 'How?'

'He's been tampered with,' said Harding flatly.

Carey handed him the glass. 'His mind?'

Harding sank half the whisky and choked a little. He held out the glass. 'I'll have water in the other half. Yes. Someone has been bloody ruthless about it. He has a week missing, and whatever was done to him was done in that week.'

Carey frowned. 'Iredale suggested he'd been unconscious all that week.'

'It's not incompatible,' said Harding. 'He was probably kept in a mentally depressed state by drugs during the whole week.'

'Are you talking about brain-washing?' asked McCready sceptically.

'In a manner of speaking.' Harding accepted his refilled glass. 'Whoever did this to Denison had a problem. The ideal would have been to get Denison into such a condition that he thought he *was* Meyrick – but that couldn't be done.' Harding paused for consideration. 'At least, not in a week.'

'You mean the possibility of such a thing is there?' asked Carey incredulously.

'Oh, yes,' said Harding calmly. 'It could be done. But this crowd didn't have the time for that, so they had to go about it another way. As I see it, their problem was to put Denison in the hotel as Meyrick and to make sure he didn't fly off the handle. They didn't want him to take the next plane to London, for instance. So they *treated* him.' From Harding's mouth the emphasis was an obscenity.

'How?' said Carey.

'Do you know anything about hypnosis?'

McCready snorted and Harding, staring at him with suddenly flinty eyes, said coldly, 'No, it is *not* witchcraft, Mr McCready. Denison was kept in a drug-induced hypnogogic state for a long time, and in that period his psyche was deliberately broken down.' He made a suddenly disarming gesture. 'I suspect Denison was already neurotically inclined and no doubt there were many ready-made tools to hand – irrational fears, half-healed traumas and so on – to aid in the process.'

'What do you mean by neurotically inclined?' asked Carey.

'It's hard to say, but I suspect that he was already a disturbed man before this was done to him.'

'Off his head?' interjected McCready.

Harding gave him a look of dislike. 'No more than yourself, Mr McCready,' he said tartly. 'But I think something had happened which threw him off balance.'

'Something did happen,' said Carey. 'He lost his job.' He took a thin sheaf of papers from the file. 'I didn't have time to discuss this with you before, but this is what we have on Denison. There'll be more coming but this is what we've got now.'

Harding studied the typed sheets, reading slowly and carefully. He said, 'I wish I'd seen this before I went in to Denison; it would have saved a lot of trouble.'

'He was a film director for a small specialist outfit making documentary and advertising films,' said Carey. 'Apparently he went off the rails and cost the firm a packet of money. They thought his drinking had got out of hand, so they fired him.'

Harding shook his head. 'That wasn't what threw him off balance. The drinking must have been a symptom, not a cause.' He turned back a page. 'I see that his wife died three years ago. She must have been quite young. Have you any idea how she died?'

'Not yet,' said Carey. 'But I can find out.'

'It would be advisable. I wonder if it was about that time he started to drink heavily.'

'That isn't the present point at issue,' said Carey.

Harding's voice took on an edge. 'It is for me,' he said curtly. 'I have to treat the man.'

Carey's voice was soothing. 'I know, Doctor, and you shall have all the relevant information as soon as we get it ourselves. But my present interest is in what was done to Denison and how it was done.'

Harding was placated. 'Very well. Denison was literally dismantled. All he retained was a name and a location – and the location wasn't very exact. Giles Denison of Hampstead. They could, of course, have induced complete amnesia, but that wouldn't do because Denison had to substitute for Meyrick and he would need enough active personality to carry out the role. Why Denison had to act as Meyrick I don't know.'

'I have ideas on that,' said Carey. 'Go on, Doctor.'

'At the same time Denison must not retain too much personality, certainly not enough for him to reject the persona that had been thrust upon him. He had to be kept in a sort of limbo. There were some very strong blocks inserted into his mind to the effect that he should not question his origins. In addition, to confuse the issue, he has been given selective false memories. For instance, he distinctly remembers playing a game of golf, but at the same time he knows that he has never played a game of golf in his life. So he is a very confused man and this leads to a paralysis of the will, enough to make him stay in one place – a hotel in Oslo – while he tries to sort things out.'

McCready stirred restlessly. 'Is all this possible?'

'Quite possible. If I draw an imaginary square on the floor of this room I could hypnotize you into avoiding it by a post-hypnotic suggestion. You could spend the rest of your life coming in and out of this room but you would never walk on that imaginary square. More to the point, you would not be aware of the irrationality of your behaviour.'

McCready looked sceptical, and Harding said, 'I'm willing to give you a demonstration at any time.'

'No!' said McCready hurriedly. 'I believe you.'

Carey smiled grimly. 'Carry on, Doctor.'

'The mind is a self-stabilizing organism,' said Harding. 'If it wasn't we'd all go crazy. And to inquire is basic. When Denison did try to delve into his past life he encountered the blocks and was so shocked at the impossibility of what he found in his own mind that he took refuge in a fugue.' He saw the incomprehension on Carey's face, and said simply, 'He fell asleep. A typical hysterical symptom. He did it twice when he was talking to me. I let him sleep for a quarter of an hour each time, and when he woke up he'd forgotten the reason for it – wiped it out of his mind. It's a self-protective mechanism against insanity, and I rather think it's happened to him before.'

'I don't think I've got this straight,' said Carey. 'You're saying that Denison is half out of his mind and likely to fall asleep – or unconscious – at any time. How do you square that with the fact that he pulled the wool over one of my people's eyes very successfully, and that he encountered a very tricky situation which might have been the death of him and coped with it very well?'

'Oh, he's quite competent,' said Harding. 'It's only when he tries to question his own past that he faces the impossible and goes into a fugue. Judging by what you told me of the manner in which he was wounded I'd say that he's more competent than I would have expected under the circumstances.'

'He's bloody competent,' said McCready suddenly, and Carey turned to look at him. 'I haven't told you this, but he's tagged Mrs Hansen.'

'He's *what*?'

'He knows she carries a gun – he told me so. He said he thought I ought to know.'

Harding wore an I-told-you-so expression and Carey's face was a study in bafflement. 'Another thing,' said McCready. 'Alcoholic or not, he's on the wagon now. Mrs Hansen said he tried a whisky last night and he gave the impression that he'd swallowed prussic acid.'

'Interesting,' said Harding. 'The man's mind has been stirred like porridge. It would be remarkable if it has cured his alcoholism. However, I'm afraid the cure is much worse than the complaint. He'll have to be hospitalized, of course. I can make the arrangements for that.'

Carey stood up. 'Thank you, Dr Harding.'

Harding also arose. 'I'd like to see him again tomorrow. What's going to happen to him now?'

'I'll take good care of him,' said Carey smoothly.

'You'd better,' warned Harding. 'If he doesn't get skilled attention he's quite likely to go insane.' He yawned. 'Well, I'm off to bed.'

He left the room and Carey sat down again. He picked up the two photographs and brooded over them. McCready said, 'That's it, then; the whole thing's a bust. No Meyrick – no operation.'

Carey did not say anything, and McCready asked, 'What are you thinking?'

Carey said slowly, 'I'm thinking that, while we may not have Meyrick, we've got a bloody good substitute.'

McCready's jaw dropped. 'You mean you want to hang on to him? You heard what Harding just said – the man's likely to go crazy. It's not what I'd call ethical.'

'Don't talk to me about ethics,' said Carey harshly. 'I have a job to do.' He threw down the photographs. 'Iredale wants to give Denison his face back, and Harding wants to restore his past. If we let Harding at him tomorrow with his tricky bloody hypnotism then Denison is going to pick up his marbles and go home.'

He frowned and came to a decision. 'Take him back to the hotel,' he said abruptly.

'For Christ's sake!' said McCready. 'Do you know what you're doing?'

'I know,' said Carey. 'But just work this one out while you're taking Denison back. When the attempt was being made on Denison's life at the Spiralen who was being attacked – Denison or Meyrick?'

McCready opened his mouth slowly while his mind spun. Carey said, 'Denison must be watched. The guard on his room stays and I want somebody outside keeping an eye on his window. And I want that whole bloody hotel sewn up tight. Now get cracking.'

McCready dropped Denison off in the garage of the hotel. 'I won't come up,' he said. 'But I'll see you tomorrow.' He looked at his watch. 'Which is today. God, it's nearly five o'clock in the morning. You get to bed.'

They had both been silent during the short drive. Now Denison said, 'What was all that about? I understood the first doctor, but the second was a psychiatrist, wasn't he?'

McCready said, 'Carey will be seeing you tomorrow. He'll explain everything.' He paused, biting his lip. 'I promise you.'

'All right,' said Denison. 'I'm too tired to argue now. But Carey had better come up with something good.' He nodded to McCready and walked towards the stairs. He did not look back, but if he had and if he had been able to interpret the look in McCready's eyes he might have recognized compassion.

Denison opened the door leading into the hotel lobby and saw suitcases stacked into a pile. There was a peal of laughter from the group of early arrivals, a crowd of young people who adorned the lobby like butterflies. He walked towards the porter's desk and stood waiting while the overworked night porter did his best to deal with the rush.

At last, Denison caught his eye, and said, Three-sixty, please.'

'Yes, Mr Meyrick.' The porter unhooked the key.

Denison did not see the girl who stared at him in surprise, but heard the cool voice behind him saying, 'Daddy!' He turned leisurely and was suddenly and horrifyingly aware that the young woman was addressing him.

ELEVEN

It was greatly to Denison's credit that he did not panic. His first impulse was to step back and deny he was Meyrick – that it was a question of mistaken identity. Hard on that decision came the realization that it would not do; the night porter knew his name and was within earshot, and, in any case, a disclaimer in the hotel lobby was sure to create a fuss. He cancelled the impulse.

She was kissing him and he felt his own lips hard and unresponsive. Perhaps it was his lack of reaction that caused her to step back, the smile fading from her face. She said, 'I was hoping to find you here, but I hardly expected to run into you in the same hotel – and at five in the morning. What are you doing up so early – or so late?'

She was young – not much more than twenty – and had the clear eyes and clear skin of youth. Her eyes were grey and her mouth wide and generous, perhaps too wide for perfect beauty. To the untutored male eye she wore no make-up but perhaps that was a tribute to skill.

He swallowed. 'I was visiting a friend; the talk tended to go on a bit.'

'Oh.' She thrust her hands deep into the pockets of her motoring coat and turned her head to look at the harassed porter. 'It's going to take hours before I get my room. Can I freshen up in yours? I must look a sight.'

His mouth was dry and, for a moment, he could not speak. She looked at him curiously. 'You *are* staying here?' Then she laughed. 'Of course you are; you have the key in your hand.'

'I just have to make a telephone call,' he said, and stepped away slightly, disengaging himself.

'Why not from the room?'

'It's just as easy from down here.' He walked away to the public telephones, fumbling in his pocket for coins.

The public telephones were not in booths but were surrounded by large transparent plastic hoods which theoretically would keep conversations private. He was aware that the girl had followed him and was standing close by. He took out his wallet, extracted a slip of paper, and dialled the number. The ringing sound buzzed in his ear six times, and then a voice said, 'Yes?'

He kept his voice low. 'I want Carey.'

'You'll have to speak up. I can't hear you.'

He raised his voice a little. 'I want to talk to Carey.'

Doubtfully: 'I don't think that's possible. He's in bed.'

'I don't care if he's in his coffin. Get him up. This is Denison.'

There was a sharp intake of breath. 'Right!'

In a remarkably short time Carey came on the line. 'Denison?'

'It's trouble. Meyrick's . . .'

Carey cut in with a voice like gravel. 'How did you know to ring this number?'

'For God's sake! That can wait.'

'How did you know?' insisted Carey.

'There was a telephone in the room where I saw the doctors,' said Denison. 'I took the number off that.'

'Oh!' said Carey. Then, with grudging respect, 'Harding said you were competent; now I believe him. All right; what's your problem?'

'Meyrick's daughter has just pitched up at the hotel.'

The telephone blasted in his ear. *'What!'*

'What the hell am I to do?' said Denison desperately. 'I don't even know her bloody name.'

'Jesus H. Christ!' said Carey. 'Wait a minute.' There was a confused murmur and then Carey said, 'Her name is Lyn – L-Y-N.'

'Do you know anything else about her?'

'How the devil would I?' demanded Carey. 'Not off the top of my head.'

'Damn you!' said Denison violently. 'I have to talk to this girl. I must know something about her. She's my *daughter.*'

'Is she there now?'

Denison looked sideways through the plastic hood. 'She's standing within ten feet of me. I'm in the hotel lobby and I don't know how soundproof this canopy is. She wants to come to my room.'

'I'll do what I can,' said Carey. 'Hold on.'

'Make it quick.' Out of the corner of his eye he saw the girl walking towards him. He put his head around the edge of the hood, and said, 'I won't be a minute, Lyn. Is there anything you want to take up to the room?'

'Oh, yes; my little travelling bag. I'll go and get it.'

He watched her walk across the lobby with a bouncing stride, and felt the sweat break out on his forehead. Carey came back on the line. 'Margaret Lyn Meyrick – but she prefers Lyn – Meyrick's daughter by his first wife.'

Denison digested that, and said quickly, 'Is her mother still alive?'

'Yes – divorced and remarried.'

'Name?'

'Patricia Joan Metford – her husband is John Howard Metford; he's something in the City.'

'What about Meyrick's present wife?'

'There isn't one. Also divorced three years ago. Her name was Janet Meyrick, née Austin.'

'About the girl – what does she do? Her work? Her hobbies?'

'I don't know,' said Carey. 'All this stuff is from Meyrick's dossier. We didn't delve into the daughter.'

'You'd better get something fast,' said Denison. 'Look, Carey; I don't know why I'm doing this for you. My impulse right now is to blow the whole thing.'

'Don't do that,' said Carey quickly. 'I'll get as much information on the Meyrick girl as I can and I'll let you have it as soon as possible.'

'How?'

'I'll send it in a sealed envelope by special messenger; she doesn't have to know what's on the sheet of paper you're reading. And if things get too tough I'll find a way of separating her from you. But, Denison – don't blow your cover, whatever you do.'

There was a pleading quality in Carey's voice and Carey, in Denison's brief experience of him, was not a man who was used to pleading. Denison thought it a good opportunity to turn the screw. 'I've been given the fast run around by you ever since this . . . this indecent thing was done to me. Now I want an explanation – a full explanation – and it had better be good.' He was aware that his voice had risen and that he was in danger of becoming hysterical.

'You'll get your explanation today,' promised Carey. 'Now do your best to handle that girl.'

'I don't know if I can. It's one thing fooling a stranger and another to try it on a member of Meyrick's family.'

'We may be lucky,' said Carey. 'I don't think they were too close. I think she was brought up by her mother.'

Denison turned to face the lobby. 'I'll have to go now – the girl's coming.' He put down the telephone and heard a faint, squawking noise just before the connection was broken. It sounded as though Carey had said, 'Good luck!'

He walked away from the telephone as she approached. 'All finished.'

She fell into step with him. 'You looked as if you were having an argument.'

'Did I?'

'I know you're an argumentative type, but I wondered who you'd found to argue with at five o'clock in the morning in the middle of Oslo.'

They stopped in front of the lifts and Denison pressed the button. 'Where have you just come from?'

'Bergen. I hired a car and drove over. Most of yesterday and all night.' She sighed. 'I feel a bit pooped.'

He kept his voice neutral. 'Travelling alone?'

'Yes.' She smiled, and said, 'Wondering about a boyfriend?'

He nodded towards the thinning group in the lobby. 'I just thought you were with that lot.' The lift arrived and they stepped inside. 'No wonder you're tired if you did all that driving. What it is to be young.'

'Right now I feel as old as Methuselah,' she said glumly. 'It's the hunger that does it. I'll feel better after breakfast, I dare say.'

He risked a probe. 'How old are you, Lyn? I tend to lose track.'

'Yes, you do, don't you? You even forgot my twenty-first – or did you forget?' There was an unexpected bitterness in her voice. 'Any father who could do that . . .' She stopped and bit her lip. 'I'm sorry, Daddy. It's my birthday next week.'

'That's all right.' There was an undercurrent of antagonism Denison did not understand. He hesitated, and said, 'Anyway, you're old enough to stop calling me Daddy. What's wrong with Harry?'

She looked at him in surprise and then impulsively squeezed his hand.

They had arrived at the room door and he unlocked it. 'Bedroom straight ahead – bathroom to the left.'

She walked ahead of him into the bedroom and put down the travelling bag. 'The bathroom for me,' she said. 'I want to wash off some of the grime.' She opened the bag, picked out a couple of small articles, and disappeared into the bathroom.

He heard the sound of water as she turned on a tap and then he picked up the telephone. 'This is room three-sixty. If there are any messages for Meyrick – or anything at all – I want to know immediately.' He put down the telephone and looked contemplatively at the travelling bag.

The bathroom noises continued so he crossed the room quickly and looked into the bag. It was more neatly packed than he had expected which made it easier to search. He saw the blue cover of a British passport and took it out and turned the pages. It was Lyn Meyrick's birthday on July 21, and she would be twenty-two. Her occupation was given as teacher.

He put the passport back and took out a book of traveller's cheques. As he flicked through them he whistled softly; the Meyrick family did not believe in stinting themselves. There was a wallet fitted with acetate envelopes which contained credit cards and photographs. He had no time to examine these in detail because he thought she might come out of the bathroom at any moment.

He thrust back the wallet and zipped open a small interior pocket in the bag. It contained the key for a rented car and a bunch of smaller keys. As he zipped it closed he heard all sound cease in the bathroom and, when she emerged, he was standing by the armchair taking off his jacket.

'That's much better,' she said. She had taken off the motoring coat and, in lime green sweater and stretch pants, she looked very trim. 'When is the earliest I can order breakfast?'

He checked his watch. 'Not much before half past six, I think. Perhaps the night porter can rustle up sandwiches and coffee.'

She frowned and sat on the bed. 'No, I'll wait and have a proper breakfast.' Blinking her eyes, she said, 'I still feel as though I'm driving.'

'You shouldn't push so hard.'

'That isn't what you told me the last time we met.'

Denison did not know what to make of that, so he said neutrally. 'No.' The silence lengthened. 'How's your mother?' he asked.

'She's all right,' said Lyn indifferently. 'But, my God, he's such a bore.'

'In what way?'

'Well, he just sits in an office and makes money. Oh, I know you're rich, but you made money by making *things*. He just makes money.'

Denison presumed that 'he' was John Howard Metford who was 'something in the City'. 'Metford isn't such a bad chap,' he said.

'He's a bore,' she said definitely. 'And it isn't what you said about him last time.'

Denison decided against making gratuitous judgements. 'How did you know I was here?' he asked.

'I got it out of Andrews,' she said. 'When he told me you were in Scandinavia I knew you'd be here or in Helsinki.' She seemed suddenly nervous. 'Now I'm not sure I should have come.'

Denison realized he was standing over her. He sat in the armchair and, perhaps in response, she stretched out on the bed. 'Why not?' he asked.

'You can't be serious when you ask that.' Her voice was bitter. 'I still remember the flaming row we had two years ago – and when you didn't remember my twenty-first birthday I knew *you* hadn't forgotten. But, of course, you didn't forget my birthday – you never forget anything.'

He was getting into deep water. 'Two years is a long time,' he said platitudinously. He would have to learn how to speak like a politician – saying a lot and meaning nothing.

'You've changed,' she said. 'You're . . . you're milder.'

That would never do. 'I can still be acid when I want to be.' He smiled. 'Perhaps I'm just becoming older and, maybe, wiser.'

'You always were wise,' said Lyn. 'If only you weren't so bloody right *all* the time. Anyway, I wanted to tell you something to your face. I was disappointed when I found you weren't in England, so I rushed over here.' She hesitated. 'Give me a cigarette.'

'I've stopped smoking.'

She stared at him. 'You *have* changed.'

'Temporarily,' he said, and stretched out his hand to open a drawer in the dressing-table. He took out the gold cigarette case and the lighter and offered her a cigarette. 'I've had a bad head cold.'

She took a cigarette and he lit it. 'That never stopped you before.' She drew on the cigarette nervously and blew a plume of smoke. 'I suppose you're surprised I'm not smoking a joint.'

Denison suspected that he was encountering something of which hitherto he had only heard – the generation gap. He said, 'Stop talking nonsense, Lyn. What's on your mind?'

'Direct and to the point as usual. All right – I've taken my degree.'

She looked at him expectantly and he was aware that she had dropped a bombshell. How he was supposed to react to it he did not know, but the damned thing had better be defused carefully. However, taking a degree was usually a matter for congratulation, so he said, 'That's good news, Lyn.'

She regarded him warily. 'You mean it?'

'It's the best news I've heard for a long time.'

She seemed relieved. 'Mother thought it was silly. She said that with all the money I'm going to have why should I worry about working – especially with a lot of snotty-nosed East End kids. You know what she's like. And the Bore didn't care one way or another.' For a moment she sounded pathetic. 'Do you really mean it?'

'Of course I do.' He found he was really glad for her and that put sincerity into his voice.

'Oh, Daddy; I'm so glad!' She scrambled off the bed and went to her bag. 'Look what it says in here. I had to get a new passport, anyway.' She opened the passport and displayed it 'Occupation – teacher!' she said proudly.

He looked up. 'Was it a good degree?'

She made a wry face. 'Middling-good.' There was no smile on her face now. 'I suppose you think a Meyrick should have passed with honours.'

Mentally he damned Meyrick who, apparently, set a superhuman standard. This girl was set on a hair trigger and his slightest word could cause an explosion in which somebody would get hurt – probably Lyn. 'I'm very glad you've got your degree,' he said evenly. 'Where are you going to teach?'

The tension eased from her and she lay on the bed again. 'First I need experience,' she said seriously. 'General experience. Then I want to specialize. After that, if I'm going to have a lot of money I might as well put it to use.'

'How?'

'I'll have to know more about what I'm doing before I can tell you that.'

Denison wondered how this youthful idealism would stand up to the battering of the world. Still, a lot could be done with enthusiasm and money. He smiled, and said, 'You seem to have settled on a lifetime plan. Is there room in the programme for marriage and a family?'

'Of course; but he'll have to be the right man – he'll have to want what I want.' She shrugged. 'So far no one like that has come my way. The men at university could be divided into two classes; the stodges who are happy with the present system, and the idealists who aren't. The stodges are already working out their retirement pensions before they get a job and the idealists are so damned naive and impractical. Neither of them suit me.'

'Someone will come along who will,' predicted Denison.

'How can you be so sure?'

He laughed. 'How do you suppose the population explosion came about? Men and women usually get together somehow. It's in the nature of the animal.'

She put out her cigarette and lay back and closed her eyes. 'I'm prepared to wait.'

'My guess is that you won't have to wait long.' She did not respond and he regarded her intently. She had fallen asleep as readily as a puppy might, which was not surprising considering she had been up all night. So had he, but sleep was the last thing he could afford.

He put on his jacket and took the keys from the zippered compartment of her bag. In the lobby he saw two suitcases standing before the desk and, after checking to make sure they were Lyn's, he said to the porter, 'I'd like these taken to my daughter's room. What's the number?'

'Did she have a reservation, Mr Meyrick?'

'It's possible.'

The porter checked and took down a key. 'Room four-thirty. I'll take the bags up.'

In Lyn's room Denison tipped the porter and put the two cases on the bed as soon as the door closed. He took out the keys and unlocked them and searched them quickly, trying not to disturb the contents too much. There was little that was of value to him directly, but there were one or two items which cast a light on Lyn Meyrick. There was a photograph of himself – or, rather, of Harry Meyrick – in a leather case. The opposing frame was empty. In a corner of one suitcase was a small Teddy-bear, tattered with much childish loving and presumably retained as a mascot. In the other suitcase he found two textbooks, one on the theory and practice of teaching, the other on child psychology; both heavyweights, the pages sprinkled with diagrams and graphs.

He closed and locked the suitcases and put them on the rack, then went down to his own room. As the lift door opened on to the third floor he saw Armstrong just stepping out of the other lift. Armstrong held out an envelope. 'Mr Carey told me to give you this.'

Denison ripped open the envelope and scanned the sparse typescript on the single sheet. The only thing it told him that he had not learned already was that Lyn Meyrick's sport was gymnastics. 'Carey will have to do better than this,' he said curtly.

'We're doing the best we can,' said Armstrong. 'We'll get more later in the day when people have woken up in England.'

'Keep it coming,' said Denison. 'And don't forget to remind Carey that I'm still waiting for an explanation.'

'I'll tell him,' said Armstrong.

'Another thing,' said Denison. 'She said she'd find me either here in Oslo or in Helsinki in Finland. That baffled me until I realized I don't know a bloody thing about Meyrick. Carey mentioned a dossier on Meyrick – I want to see it.'

'I don't think that will be possible,' said Armstrong hesitantly. 'You're not cleared for security.'

Denison speared him with a cold eye. 'You bloody fool!' he said quietly. 'Right now *I* am your security – and don't forget to tell Carey that, too.' He walked past Armstrong and up the corridor to his room.

TWELVE

Carey walked past the Oslo City Hall in the warm mid-afternoon sunshine and inspected the statuary with a sardonic eye. Each figure represented a different trade and the whole, no doubt, was supposed to represent the Dignity of Labour. He concluded that the Oslo City Fathers must have been socialist at one time.

He sat on a bench and looked out over the harbour and Oslofjord. A ship slid quietly by – the ferry bound for Copenhagen – and there was a constant coming and going of smaller, local ferries bound for Bygdøy, Ingierstrand and other places on the fjord. Camera-hung tourists strolled by and a tour bus stopped, disgorging more of them.

McCready walked up and sat on the bench. Carey did not look at him but said dreamily, 'Once my job was easy – just simple eyeball stuff. That was back in the days when Joshua sent his spies into the land of Caanan. Then the bloody scientists got busy and ballsed the whole thing up.'

McCready said nothing; he had encountered Carey in this mood before and knew there was nothing to do but wait until Carey got it off his chest.

'Do you realize the state we've got ourselves into now?' asked Carey rhetorically. 'I think you're George McCready, but I could be wrong. What's more, *you* could think you're

George McCready and, if Harding is to be believed, still be wrong. How the hell am I supposed to cope with a situation like that?'

He disregarded McCready's opening mouth. 'The bloody boffins are lousing up the whole damned world,' he said violently, and pointed towards the line of statuary. 'Look at that crowd of working stiffs. There's not a trade represented there that isn't obsolete or obsolescent. Pretty soon they'll put up a statue of me; there'll be a plaque saying "Intelligence agent, Mark II" and my job'll be farmed out to a hot-shot computer. Where's Denison?'

'Asleep in the hotel.'

'And the girl?'

'Also asleep – in her own room.'

'If he's had five minutes' sleep that's five minutes more than I've had. Let's go and wake the poor bastard up. Mrs Hansen will join us at the hotel.'

He stood up, and McCready said, 'How much are you going to tell him?'

'As much as I have to and no more,' said Carey shortly. 'Which may be more than I want to tell him. He's already putting the screws on me through young Ian. He wants to see Meyrick's dossier.'

'You can't expect him to carry out an impersonation without knowing something of Meyrick,' said McCready reasonably.

'Why did that damned girl have to turn up?' grumbled Carey. 'As though we don't have enough trouble. I had a row with Harding this morning.'

'I'm not surprised.'

'George – I have no option. With Meyrick gone I have to use Denison. I'll play fair; I'll tell him the truth – maybe not all of it, but what I tell him will be true – and let him make up his own mind. And if he wants out that's my hard luck.'

McCready noticed the reservation and shook his head. The truth, in Carey's hands, could take on a chameleon-like quality. Denison did not stand a chance.

Carey said, 'Something Iredale told me gave me the shudders. This silicone stuff that was rammed into Denison's face is a polymer; it's injected in liquid form and then it hardens in the tissues to the consistency of fat – and it's permanent. If Denison wants to get his own face back it will be a major surgical operation – they'll have to take his face apart to scrape the stuff out.'

McCready grimaced. 'I take it that's a part of the truth you're not going to tell him.'

'That – and a few other titbits from Harding.' Carey stopped. 'Well, here's the hotel. Let's get it over with.'

Denison woke from a deep sleep to hear hammering on his door. He got up groggily, put on the bathrobe, and opened the door. Carey said, 'Sorry to waken you, but it's about time we had a talk.'

Denison blinked at him. 'Come in.' He turned and went into the bathroom, and Carey, McCready and Mrs Hansen walked through into the bedroom. When Denison reappeared he was wiping his face with a towel. He stared at Diana Hansen. 'I might have known.'

'You two know each other,' said Carey. 'Mrs Hansen was keeping tabs on Meyrick.' He drew back the curtain, letting sunlight spill into the room, and tossed an envelope on to the dressing-table. 'Some more stuff on the girl. We have quite a few people in England running about in circles on your behalf.'

'Not mine,' corrected Denison. 'Yours!' He put down the towel. 'Any moment from now she's going to start playing "Do you remember when?" No information you can give me will help in that sort of guessing game.'

'You'll just have to develop a bad memory,' said McCready.

'I need to know more about Meyrick,' insisted Denison.

'And I'm here to tell you.' Carey pulled the armchair forward. 'Sit down and get comfortable. This is going to take a while.' He sat in the other chair and pulled out a stubby pipe which he started to fill. McCready and Diana Hansen sat on the spare bed.

Carey struck a match and puffed at his pipe. 'Before we start on Meyrick you ought to know that we discovered how, and when, the switch was made. We figured how we'd do a thing like that ourselves and then checked on it. You were brought in on a stretcher on July 8 and put in room three-sixty-three, just across the corridor. Meyrick was probably knocked out by a Mickey Finn in his nightly Ovaltine or something like that, and the switch was made in the wee, small hours.'

'Meyrick was taken out next morning before you woke up,' said McCready. 'He was put into an ambulance, the hotel management co-operating, and driven to Pier Two at Vippetangen where he was put aboard a ship sailing to Copenhagen. Another ambulance was waiting there which took him God knows where.'

Carey said, 'If you'd contacted the Embassy as soon as it happened we'd have been able to work all that out so damned fast that *we* could have been waiting at Copenhagen.'

'For God's sake!' said Denison. 'Would you have believed me any the quicker? It took you long enough to check anyway with your doctor and your tame psychiatrist.'

'He's right,' said McCready.

'Do you think that's why it was done this way? To buy time?'

'Could be,' said McCready. 'It worked, didn't it?'

'Oh, it worked all right. What puzzles me is what happened at the Spiralen the next day.' Carey turned to Denison. 'Have you got the doll and the note?'

Denison opened a drawer and handed them to Carey. He unfolded the single deckle-edged sheet and read the note aloud. ' "Your Drammen Dolly awaits you at Spiraltoppen. Early morning. July 10." ' He lifted the paper and sniffed delicately. 'Scented, too. I thought that went out in the 1920s.'

Diana Hansen said, 'This is the first I've heard of a note. I know about the doll, but not the note.'

'It's what took Denison to the Spiralen,' said McCready.

'Could I see it?' said Diana, and Carey passed it to her. She read it and said pensively, 'It could have been . . .'

'What is it, Mrs Hansen?' said Carey sharply.

'Well, when Meyrick and I went to Drammen last week we lunched at the Spiraltoppen Restaurant.' She looked a little embarrassed. 'I had to go to the lavatory and I was away rather a long time. I had stomach trouble – some kind of diarrhoea.'

McCready grinned. 'Even Intelligence agents are human,' he said kindly.

'When I got back Meyrick was talking to a woman and they seemed to be getting on well together. When I came up she went away.'

'That's all?' asked Carey.

'That's all.'

He regarded her thoughtfully. 'I think there's something you're not telling us, Mrs Hansen.'

'Well, it's something about Meyrick. I was with him quite a lot during the last few weeks and he gave me the impression of being something of a womanizer – perhaps even a sexual athlete.'

A chuckle escaped from McCready. 'Did he proposition you?'

'He had as many arms as an octopus,' she said. 'I thought I wasn't going to last out this operation without being raped. I think he'd go for anything on two legs that wore skirts, with the possible exception of Scotsmen – and I wouldn't be too sure of that.'

'Well, well,' said Carey. 'How little we know of our fellow men.'

Denison said, 'He was divorced twice.'

'So you think this note was to set up an assignation.'

'Yes,' said Diana.

'But Meyrick wouldn't have fallen for that, no matter how horny he was,' said Carey. 'He was too intelligent a man. When you and he went to Drammen last week he checked with me according to instructions. Since you were going with him I gave him the okay.'

'Did Meyrick know Diana was working for you?' asked Denison.

Carey shook his head. 'No – we like to play loose. But Meyrick didn't find the note.' He pointed his pipe stem at Denison. 'You did – and you went to the Spiralen. Tell me, did the men who attacked you give the impression that they wanted to capture or to kill you?'

'I didn't stop to ask them,' said Denison acidly.

'Um,' said Carey, and lapsed into thought, his pipe working overtime. After a while he stirred, and said, 'All right, Mrs Hansen; I think that's all.'

She nodded briefly and left the room, and Carey glanced at McCready. 'I suppose we must tell him about Meyrick.'

McCready grinned. 'I don't see how you can get out of it.'

'I have to know,' said Denison, 'if I'm going to carry on with this impersonation.'

'I trust Mrs Hansen and she doesn't know,' said Carey. 'Not the whole story. I work on the "need to know" principle.' He sighed. 'I suppose you need to know, so here goes. The first thing to know about Meyrick is that he's a Finn.'

'With a name like that?'

'Oddly enough, it's his own name. In 1609 the English sent a diplomat to the court of Michael, the first Romanov Czar, to negotiate a trade treaty and to open up the fur trade. The courtiers of James I had to get their bloody ermine somewhere. The name of the diplomat was John Merick – or Meyrick – and he was highly philoprogenitive. He left by-blows all over the Baltic and Harry Meyrick is the end result of that.'

'It seems that Harry takes after his ancestor,' commented McCready.

Carey ignored him. 'Of course, Meyrick's name was a bit different in Finnish, but when he went to England he reverted to the family name. But that's by the way.' He laid down his pipe. 'More to the point, Meyrick is a Karelian Finn; to be pedantic, if he'd stayed at home in the town where he was born he'd now be a Russian. How good is your modern history?'

'Average I suppose,' said Denison.

'And that means bloody awful,' observed Carey. 'All right; in 1939 Russia attacked Finland and the Finns held them off in what was known as the Winter War. In 1941 Germany attacked Russia and the Finns thought it a good opportunity to have another go at the Russkies, which was a pity because that put them on the losing side. Still, it's difficult to see what else they could have done.

'At the end of this war, which the Finns know as the Continuation War, there was a peace treaty and the frontier was withdrawn. The old frontier was too close, to Leningrad, which had the Russians edgy. An artilleryman could stand in Finland and lob shells right into the middle of Leningrad, so the Russians took over the whole of the Karelian Isthmus, together with a few other bits and pieces. This put Meyrick's home town, Enso, on the Russian side, and the Russians renamed it Svetogorsk.'

Carey sucked on his pipe which had gone out. It gurgled unpleasantly. 'Am I making myself clear?'

'You're clear enough,' said Denison. 'But I want more than a history lesson.'

'We're getting there,' said Carey. 'Meyrick was seventeen at the end of the war. Finland was in a hell of a mess; all the Karelian Finns cleared out of the isthmus because they didn't want to live under the Russians and this put the pressure on the rest of Finland because there was nowhere for them to go. The Finns had to work so bloody hard producing the reparations the Russians demanded that there was no money or men or time left over to build housing. So they turned to the Swedes and asked calmly if they'd take 100,000 immigrants.' Carey snapped his fingers. 'Just like that – and the Swedes agreed.'

Denison said, 'Noble of them.'

Carey nodded. 'So young Meyrick went to Sweden. He didn't stay long because he came here, to Oslo, where he lived until he was twenty-four. Then he went to England. He was quite alone all this time – his family had been killed during the war – but as soon as he arrived in England he married his first wife. She had what he needed, which was money.'

'Who doesn't need money?' asked McCready cynically.

'We'll get on faster if you stop asking silly questions,' said Carey. 'The second thing you have to know about Meyrick is that he's a bright boy. He has a flair for invention, particularly in electronics, and he has something else which the run-of-the-mill inventor doesn't have – the ability to turn his inventions into money. The first Mrs Meyrick had a few thousand quid which was all he needed to get started. When they got divorced he'd turned her into a millionairess and he'd made as much for himself. And he went on making it.'

Carey struck a match and applied it to his pipe. 'By this time he was a big boy as well as a bright boy. He owned a couple of factories and was deep in defence contracts. There's a lot of his electronics in the Anglo-French Jaguar fighter as well as in Concorde. He also did some bits and pieces for the Chieftain main battle tank. He's now at the stage where he heads special committees on technical matters concerning defence, and the Prime Minister has pulled him into a Think Tank. He's a hell of a big boy but the man-in-the-street knows nothing about him. Got the picture?'

'I think so,' said Denison. 'But it doesn't help me a damn.'

Carey blew a plume of smoke into the air. 'I think Meyrick inherited his brains from his father, so let's take a look at the old boy.'

Denison sighed. 'Must we?'

'It's relevant,' said Carey flatly. 'Hannu Merikken was a physicist and, by all accounts, a good one. The way the story runs is that if he hadn't been killed during the war he'd have been in line for the Nobel Prize. The war put a stop to his immediate researches and he went to work for the Finnish government in Viipuri, which was then the second biggest city in Finland. But it's in Karelia and it's now a Russian city and the Russians call it Vyborg.' He looked at Denison's closed eyes, and said sharply, 'I trust I'm not boring you.'

'Go on,' said Denison. 'I'm just trying to sort out all these names.'

'Viipuri was pretty well smashed up during the war, including the laboratory Merikken was working in. So he got the hell out of there and went home to Enso which is about thirty miles north of Viipuri. He knew by this time that no one was going to stop the Russians and he wanted to see to the safety of his papers. He'd done a lot of work before the war which hadn't been published and he didn't want to lose it.'

'So what did he do?' asked Denison. He was becoming interested.

'He put all the papers into a metal trunk, sealed it, and buried it in the garden of his house. Young Harri Merikken – that's our Harry Meyrick – helped him. The next day Hannu Merikken, his wife and his younger son, were killed by the same bomb, and if Harri had been in the house at the same time he'd have been killed, too.'

'And the papers are important?' said Denison.

'They are,' said Carey soberly. 'Last year Meyrick was in Sweden and he bumped into a woman who had given him a temporary home when he'd been evacuated from Finland. She said she'd been rummaging about in the attic or whatever and had come across a box he'd left behind. She gave it to him. He opened it in his hotel that night and looked through it. Mostly he was amused by the things he found – the remnants of the enthusiasms of a seventeen-year-old. There were the schematics of a ham radio he'd designed – he was interested in electronics even then – some other drawings of a radio-controlled model aircraft, and things like that. But in the pages of an old radio magazine he found a paper in his father's handwriting, and that suddenly made the papers buried in Merikken's garden very important indeed.'

'What are they about?' asked Denison.

Carey ignored the question. 'At first, Meyrick didn't realize what he'd got hold of and he talked about it to a couple of scientists in Sweden. Then the penny dropped and he bolted back to England and began to talk to the right people – we're lucky he was big enough to know who to talk to. The people he talked to got interested and, as an end result of a lot of quiet confabulation, I was brought in.'

'The idea being to go and dig up the garden?'

'That's right. The only snag is that the garden is in Russia.' Carey knocked out his pipe in the ashtray. 'I have a couple of men scouting the Russian border right now. The idea was that as soon as they report, Meyrick and I would pop across and dig up the papers.'

McCready snapped his fingers. 'As easy as walking down Piccadilly.'

'But Meyrick was snatched,' said Carey. 'And you were substituted.'

'Yes,' said Denison heavily. 'Why me?'

'I don't think we need to go too deeply into that,' said Carey delicately. He did not want Denison to ruminate about his past life and go off into a fugue. 'I think it could have been anybody who looked enough like Meyrick to need the least possible surgery.'

There was a whole list of other qualifications – someone who would not be missed too easily, someone who had the right psychological make-up, someone very easily accessible. It had been a job which had been carefully set up in England and back in London there was a team of ten men sifting through the minutiae of Denison's life in the hope of coming up with a clue to his kidnapping. It was a pity that Denison could not be directly questioned but Harding was dead against it, and Carey had a need for Denison – he did not want an insane man on his hands.

'Which brings us to the next step,' said Carey. 'Someone – call them Crowd X – has pinched Meyrick, but they're not going to broadcast the fact. They don't know if we've tumbled to the substitution or not – and we're not going to tell them.' He looked steadily at Denison. 'Which is why we need your co-operation, Mr Denison.'

'In what way?' asked Denison cautiously.

'We want you to carry on being Meyrick, and we want you to go to Finland.'

Denison's jaw dropped. 'But that's impossible,' he said. 'I'd never get away with it. I can't speak Finnish.'

'You've got away with it up to now,' pointed out Carey. 'You fooled Mrs Hansen and you're doing very well with Meyrick's daughter. It's quite true what Harding said – you're very competent.'

'But the language! Meyrick speaks Finnish.'

'He speaks Finnish, Swedish, Norwegian and English fluently and idiomatically,' said Carey easily. 'His French passes but his Italian and Spanish aren't too hot.'

'Then how the hell can I get away with it?' demanded Denison. 'All I have is English and schoolboy French.'

'Take it easy. Let me tell you a story.' Carey began to fill his pipe again. 'At the end of the First World War quite a number of the British troops married French wives and stayed in France. A lot of them were given jobs by the War Graves Commission – looking after the war cemeteries. Twenty years after, there came another war and another British Expeditionary Force. The new young soldiers found that the old soldiers had completely lost their English – their mother tongue – and could speak only French.'

He struck a match. 'And that's what's going to happen to Meyrick. He hasn't been back to Finland since he was seventeen; I don't think it's unreasonable to suppose he'd lose the language.'

'But why do you want me? I can't lead you to the papers – only Meyrick can do that.'

Carey said, 'When this happened my first impulse was to abandon the operation, but then I started to think about it. Firstly, we don't know that Meyrick was snatched because of this operation – it might have been for a different reason. In that case the papers are reasonably safe. Secondly, it occurred to me that you could be a good distracting influence – we could use you to confuse the opposition as much as they've confused us. If you go to Finland as Meyrick they won't know what the hell to think. In the ensuing brouhaha we might get a chance at the papers. What do you think?'

'I think you're crazy,' said Denison.

Carey shrugged. 'Mine is a crazy profession – I've seen crazier ploys come off. Look at Major Martin – the man who never was.'

'He didn't have to stand up to questioning,' said Denison. 'The whole thing is bloody ridiculous.'

'You'd be paid, of course,' said Carey casually. 'Well paid, as a matter of fact. You'd also get a compensatory grant for the injuries that have been done to you, and Mr Ireland is ready and willing to bring you back to normality.'

'Dr Harding, too?'

'Dr Harding, too,' confirmed Carey. He wondered to what extent Denison knew his mental processes to be abnormal.

'Suppose I turn you down,' said Denison. 'Do I still get the services of Iredale and Harding?'

McCready tensed, wondering what Carey would say. Carey placidly blew a smoke ring. 'Of course.'

'So it's not a matter of blackmail,' said Denison.

The unshockable Carey arranged his features in an expression of shock. 'There is no question of blackmail,' he said stiffly.

'Why are Merikken's papers so important? What's in them?'

'I can't tell you that, Mr Denison,' said Carey deliberately.

'Can't or won't?'

Carey shrugged. 'All right, then – won't.'

'Then I'm turning you down,' said Denison.

Carey put down his pipe. 'This is a question of state security, Denison; and we work on the principle of "need to know". Mrs Hansen doesn't need to know. Ian Armstrong doesn't need to know. You don't need to know.'

'I've been kidnapped and stabbed,' said Denison. 'My face has been altered and my mind has been jiggered with.' He raised his hand. 'Oh, I know that – Harding got that much across – and I'm scared to the marrow about thinking of who I once was. Now you're asking me to go on with this charade, to go to Finland and put myself in danger again.' His voice was shaking. 'And when I ask why you have the gall to tell me I don't need to know.'

'I'm sorry,' said Carey.

'I don't care how sorry you are. You can book me on a flight to London.'

'Now who is using blackmail?' said Carey ironically.

'It's a reasonable request,' said McCready.

'I know it is, damn it!' Carey looked at Denison with cold eyes. 'If you breathe a word of what I'm going to tell you you'll be behind bars for the rest of your life. I'll see to that personally. Understand?'

Denison nodded. 'I've still got to know,' he said stubbornly.

Carey forced the words through reluctant lips. He said slowly, 'It seems that in 1937 or 1938 Hannu Merikken discovered a way of reflecting X-rays.'

Denison looked at him blankly. 'Is that all?'

'That's all,' said Carey curtly. He stood up and stretched.

'It isn't enough,' said Denison. 'What's so bloody important about that?'

'You've been told what you want to know. Be satisfied.'

'It isn't enough. I must know the significance.'

Carey sighed. 'All right, George; tell him.'

'I felt like that at first,' said McCready. 'Like you, I didn't see what all the fuss was about. Merikken was doing a bit of pure research when he came across this effect before the war and in those days there wasn't much use for it. All the uses of X-rays depended upon their penetrative power and who'd want to reflect them. So

Merikken filed it away as curious but useless and he didn't publish a paper on it.'

He grinned. 'The joke is that now every defence laboratory in the world is working out how to reflect X-rays, but no one has figured out a way to do it.'

'What happened to make it important?' asked Denison.

'The laser happened,' said Carey in a voice of iron.

'Do you know how a laser works?' When Denison shook his head, McCready said, 'Let's have a look at the very first laser as it was invented in 1960. It was a rod of synthetic ruby about four inches long and less than half an inch in diameter. One end was silvered to form a reflective surface, and the other end was half-silvered. Coiled around the rod was a spiral gas discharge lamp something like the flash used in photography. Got that?'

'All clear so far.'

'There's a lot more power in these electronic flashes than people imagine,' said McCready. 'For instance, an ordinary flash, as used by a professional photographer, develops about 4,000 horse power in the brief fraction of a second when the condensers discharge. The flash used in the early lasers was more powerful than that – let's call it 20,000 horse power. When the flash is used the light enters the ruby rod and something peculiar happens; the light goes up and down the rod, reflected from the silvered ends, and all the light photons are brought in step with each other. The boffins call that coherent light, unlike ordinary light where all the photons are out of step.

'Now, because the photons are in step the light pressure builds up. If you can imagine a crowd of men trying to batter down a door, they're more likely to succeed if they charge at once than if they try singly. The photons are all charging at once and they burst out of the half-silvered end of the rod as a pulse of light – and that light pulse has nearly all the 20,000 horse power of energy that was put into the rod.'

McCready grinned. 'The boffins had great fun with that. They discovered that it was possible to drill a hole through a razor blade at a range of six feet. At one time it was suggested that the power of a laser should be measured in Gillettes.'

'Stick to the point,' said Carey irritably.

'The military possibilities were easily seen,' said McCready. 'You could use a laser as a range-finder, for instance. Fire it at a target and measure the light bouncing back and you could tell the range to an inch. There were other uses – but there was one dispiriting fact. The laser used light and light can be stopped quite easily. It doesn't take much cloud to stop a beam of light, no matter how powerful it is.'

'But X-rays are different,' said Denison thoughtfully.

'Right! It's theoretically possible to make an X-ray laser, but for one snag. X-rays penetrate and don't reflect. No one has found a way of doing it except Merikken who did it before the war – and the working of a laser depends entirely upon multiple reflection.'

Denison rubbed his chin, feeling the flabbiness. Already he was becoming used to it. 'What would be the use of a gadget like that?'

'Take a missile coming in at umpteen thousand miles an hour and loaded with an atomic warhead. You've got to knock it down so you use another missile like the American Sprint. But you don't shoot your missile directly at the enemy missile – you aim it at where the enemy will be when your missile gets up there. That takes time to work out and a hell of a lot of computing power. With an X-ray laser you aim directly at the enemy missile because it operates with the speed of light – 186,000 miles a second – and you'd drill a hole right through it.'

'Balls,' said Carey. 'You'd cut the damned thing in two.'

'My God!' said Denison. That's a death ray.' He frowned. 'Could it be made powerful enough?'

'Lasers have come a long way since the first one,' said McCready soberly. 'They don't use the flash any more on the big ones – they pour in the power with a rocket engine. Already they're up to millions of horse power – but it's still ordinary light. With X-rays you could knock a satellite out of orbit from the ground.'

'Now do you understand the significance?' asked Carey. When Denison nodded, he said, 'So what are you going to do about it?'

There was a long silence while Denison thought. Carey stood up and went to the window where he looked across to the *Studenterlunden*, his fingers drumming on the window sill. McCready lay back on the bed with his hands behind his head, and inspected the ceiling closely.

Denison stirred and unclasped his fingers. He straightened in his chair and stretched his arms, then he sighed deeply. My name is Harry Meyrick,' he said.

THIRTEEN

Three days later Denison, descending for breakfast, bought a newspaper at the kiosk in the lobby and scanned it over coffee. Diana Hansen joined him, and said, 'What's new?'

He shrugged. 'The world is still going to hell in a hand-cart. Listen to this. Item one. Two more skyjackings, one successful and one not. In the *unsuccessful* one – God save the mark – two passengers were killed. Item two – pollution. A tanker collision in the Baltic and a fifteen mile oil slick is drifting on to Gotland; the Swedes are understandably acid. Item three. There are strikes in Britain, France and Italy, with consequent riots in London, Paris and Milan. Item four . . .' He raised his head. '. . . do you want me to go on?'

She sipped her coffee. 'You sound a bit acid yourself.'

'Just how would you feel in my circumstances?' he asked a little grimly.

Diana shrugged. 'Where's Lyn?'

'The young sleep late.'

'I have a feeling she's sharpening her claws, getting ready to scratch my eyes out,' said Diana meditatively. 'She's made one or two odd remarks lately.' She stretched over and patted Denison's hand. 'She thinks her daddy is getting into bad company.'

'How right the child is.'

'Child!' Diana raised her eyebrows. 'She's only eight years younger than I am. She's no child – she's a healthy young woman with all her wits about her – so watch your step.'

Denison put his head on one side. 'Of course!' he said, somewhat surprised. Privately he thought that Diana was drawing the longbow a bit. He put her age at thirty-two which probably meant she was thirty-four; that would give her twelve years on Lyn, not much less than the fourteen years he had himself.

'Carey wants to see you,' said Diana. 'If you leave the hotel, turn left and walk about three hundred yards, you'll come to a place where they're building a memorial or something. Be around there at ten o'clock.'

'All right,' said Denison.

'And here's your darling daughter.' Diana raised her voice. 'Good morning, Lyn.'

Denison turned and smiled appreciatively at Lyn's *chic* appearance. It's the money that makes the difference, he thought; the grand ideas of the rulers of the fashion world are apt to look tatty when filtered through the salary of a junior London typist. 'Did you have a good night?'

'Fine,' said Lyn lightly, and sat down. 'I didn't expect to see you at breakfast, Mrs Hansen.' She glanced sideways at Denison. 'Did you sleep in the hotel last night?'

'No, darling,' said Diana sweetly. 'I brought a message for your father.'

Lyn poured coffee. 'What are we doing today?'

'I have a business appointment this morning,' said Denison. 'Why don't you two go shopping?'

A shadow briefly crossed Lyn's face, but she said, 'All right.' Diana's answering smile was sickly in its sweetness.

Denison found Carey with his rump buttressed by a coping stone and his back to the Royal Palace. He looked up at Denison's approach and said brusquely, 'We're ready to move. Are you fit?'

Carey nodded. 'How are you getting on with the girl?'

'I'm tired of being Daddy,' said Denison bitterly. 'I'm only getting through by the skin of my teeth. She asks the damnedest questions.'

'What's she like?'

'A nice kid in danger of being spoiled rotten – but for one thing.'

'What's that?'

'Her parents were divorced and it's messed up her life. I'm beginning to realize what an unmitigated bastard Harry Meyrick is.' He paused. 'Or was.' He looked at Carey. 'Any news?'

Carey flapped his hand in negation. 'Tell me more.'

'Well, the mother is a rich bitch who ignores the girl. I don't think Lyn would care if she dropped dead tomorrow. But Lyn has always had a respect for her father; she doesn't like him but she respects him. She looks up to him like a . . . like a sort of God.' Denison rubbed his chin and said meditatively, 'I suppose people respect God, but do they really *like* him? Anyway, every time she tries to get near Meyrick he slaps her down hard. That's no way to bring up a daughter and it's been breaking her up.'

'I never did like his arrogance myself,' said Carey. 'It's the one thing that would have given you away in the end. You're not bloody-minded enough to be Meyrick.'

'Thank God for that,' said Denison.

'But you get on with her all right? As Meyrick?'

Denison nodded. 'So far – but no future guarantees.'

'I've been thinking about her,' said Carey. 'Suppose we took her to Finland – what would the opposition think?'

'For God's sake!' said Denison disgustedly.

'Think about it, man,' Carey urged. 'They'd check on her, and when they find out who she is they'd be bloody flummoxed. They might think that if you're good enough to deceive Meyrick's daughter you're good enough to deceive me.'

Denison was acid. 'That's not far short of the mark. I had to *tell* you who I was.'

'You can do it,' said Carey. 'It adds a bit of confusion, and there's nothing like confusion for creating opportunity. Right now we need all the luck we can create for ourselves. Will you ask her if she'll go with you to Helsinki tomorrow?'

Denison was troubled. 'It's all right for me,' he said. 'I'm going into this with my eyes open – but she's being conned. Will you guarantee her safety?'

'Of course I will. She'll be as safe as though she were in England.'

It was a long time before Denison made his decision. 'All right,' he said resignedly. 'I'll ask her.'

Carey slapped him lightly on the arm. 'Which brings us back to Meyrick's character. As you said – he's a right bastard. Bear that in mind when you're handling her.'

'You want her in Finland,' said Denison. 'I don't. If I really act like her father she's going to run and hide like she always has. Do you want that?'

'I can't say I do,' said Carey. 'But lean too far the other way and she'll know you're not Meyrick.'

Denison thought of the many ways in which he had hurt Lyn by his apparent forgetfulness. As in the case of her mascot, for instance; he had idly picked it up and asked what it was. 'But you *know,*' said Lyn in astonishment. He had incautiously shaken his head, and she burst out, 'But you *named* him.' There was a hurt look in her eyes. 'You called him Thread-Bear.'

He laughed sourly. 'Don't worry; I'm hurting her enough just by being myself.'

'It's settled then,' said Carey. 'You have an appointment at Helsinki University tomorrow afternoon with Professor Pentti Kääriänen. Your secretary arranged it.'

'Who the devil is he?'

'He was one of Hannu Merikken's assistants before the war. You are to introduce yourself as Merikken's son and pump him about what Merikken was doing in his laboratory from 1937 to 1939. I want to find out if there's been any other leakage about his X-ray researches.' He paused. 'Take the girl with you; it adds to your cover.'

'All right.' Denison gave Carey a level look. 'And her name is Lyn. She's not a bloody puppet; she's a human being.'

Carey's answering stare was equally unblinking. 'That's what I'm afraid of,' he said.

Carey watched Denison walk away and waited until he was joined by McCready. He sighed. 'Sometimes I have moments of quiet desperation.'

McCready suppressed a smile. 'What is it this time?'

'See those buildings over there?'

McCready looked across the road. 'That scrubby lot?'

'That's Victoria Terrace – there's a police station in there now. The authorities wanted to pull it down but the conservationists objected and won their case on architectural grounds.'

'I don't see the point.'

'Well, you see, it was Gestapo Headquarters during the war and it still smells to a lot of Norwegians.' He paused. 'I had a session in there once, with a man called Dieter Brun. Not a nice chap. He was killed towards the end of the war. Someone ran him down with a car.'

McCready was quiet because Carey rarely spoke of his past service. 'I've been running around Scandinavia for nearly forty years – Spitzbergen to the Danish-German border, Bergen to the Russo-Finnish border. I'll be sixty next month,' said Carey. 'And the bloody world hasn't changed, after all.' There was a note of quiet melancholy in his voice.

Next morning they all flew to Finland.

FOURTEEN

Lyn Meyrick was worried about her father, which was a new and unwanted experience. Her previous worries in that direction had always been for herself in relation to her father. To worry for her father was something new which gave her an odd feeling in the pit of her stomach.

She had been delighted when he suggested that she accompany him to Finland; a delight compounded by the fact that for the first time he was treating her like a grown-up person. He now asked her opinion and deferred to her wishes in a way he had never done before. Diffidently she had fallen in with his wish that she call him by his given name and she was becoming accustomed to it.

However, the delight had been qualified by the presence of Diana Hansen who somehow destroyed that adult feeling and made her feel young and gawky like a schoolgirl. The relationship between Diana and her father puzzled her. At first she had thought they were lovers and had been neither surprised nor shocked. Well, not *too* shocked. Her father was a man and not all that old, and her mother had not been reticent about the reasons for the divorce. And, yet, she had not thought that Diana Hansen would have been the type to appeal to her father and the relationship seemed oddly cold and almost businesslike.

And there were other things about him that were strange. He would become abstract and remote. This was nothing new because he had always had that ability to switch off in the middle of a conversation which made her feel as though he had dropped a barrier to cut her off. What was new was that he would snap out of these abstracted moments and smile at her in a way he never had before, which made her heart turn over. And he seemed deliberately to put himself out to please her.

And he was losing his memory, too. Not about anything big or important, but about minor things like . . . like Thread-Bear, for instance. How could a man forget a pun which had caused so much excitement in a little girl? If there was anything about her father that had annoyed her in the past it was his memory for detail – he usually remembered too much for her comfort. It was all very odd.

Anyway, she was glad he had invited her to go to the University to meet the man with the unpronounceable name. He had been hesitant about it, and she said, 'Why are you going?'

'It's just that I want to find out something about my father.'

'But that's my grandfather,' she said. 'Of course I'm coming.'

It seemed strange to have a grandfather called Hannu Merikken. She sat before the mirror and contemplated herself, making sure that all was in order. I'm not bad-looking, she thought, as she regarded the straight black eyebrows and the grey eyes. Mouth too big, of course. I'm no raving beauty, but I'll do.

She snatched up her bag and went to the door on the way to meet her father. Then she stopped in mid-pace and thought, *What am I thinking of? It's my father . . . not . . .* She shook the thought from her and opened the door.

* * *

Professor Kääriänen was a jolly, chubby-faced man of about sixty, not at all the dry professorial stick Lyn had imagined. He rose from his desk to greet Denison, and shot out a spate of Finnish. Denison held up his hand in protest: 'I'm sorry; I have no Finnish.'

Kääriänen raised his eyebrows and said in English, 'Remarkable!'

Denison shrugged. 'Is it? I left when I was seventeen. I suppose I spoke Finnish for fifteen years – and I haven't spoken it for nearly thirty.' He smiled. 'You might say my Finnish language muscle has atrophied.'

Kääriänen nodded understandably. 'Yes, yes; my own German was once quite fluent – but now?' He spread his hands. 'So you are Hannu Merikken's son.'

'Allow me to introduce my daughter, Lyn.'

Kääriänen came forward, his hands outstretched. 'And his granddaughter – a great honour. But sit down, please. Would you like coffee?'

'Thank you; that would be very nice.'

Kääriänen went to the door, spoke to the girl in the other office, and then came back. 'Your father was a great man, Dr . . . er . . . Meyrick.'

Denison nodded. 'That is my name now. I reverted to the old family name.'

The professor laughed. 'Ah, yes; I well remember Hannu telling me the story. He made it sound so romantic. And what are you doing here in Finland, Dr Meyrick?'

'I don't really know,' said Denison cautiously. 'Perhaps it's a need to get back to my origins. A delayed homesickness, if you like.'

'I understand,' said Kääriänen. 'And you want to know something about your father – that's why you've come to me?'

'I understand you worked with him – before the war.'

'I did, much to my own profit. Your father was not only a great research worker – he was also a great teacher. But I was not the only one. There were four of us, as I remember. You should remember that.'

'I was very young before the war,' said Denison defensively. 'Not even into my teens.'

'And you don't remember me,' said Kääriänen, his eyes twinkling. His hand patted his plump belly. 'I'm not surprised; I've changed quite a lot. But I remember you. You were a young rascal – you upset one of my experiments.'

Denison smiled. 'If guilty I plead sorrow.'

'Yes,' said Kääriänen reminiscently. 'There were four of us with your father in those days. We made a good team.' He frowned. 'You know; I think I am the only one left.' He ticked them off with his fingers. 'Olavi Koivisto joined the army and was killed. Liisa Linnankivi – she was also killed in the bombing of Viipuri; that was just before your father died, of course. Kaj Salojärvi survived the war; he died three years ago – cancer, poor fellow. Yes, there is only me left of the old team.'

'Did you all work together on the same projects?'

'Sometimes yes, sometimes no.' Kääriänen leaned forward. 'Sometimes we worked on our own projects with Hannu giving advice. As a scientist yourself, Dr Meyrick, you will understand the work of the laboratory.'

Denison nodded. 'What was the main trend of my father's thought in those days before the war?'

Kääriänen spread his hands. 'What else but the atom? We were *all* thinking about the atom. Those were the great pioneering days, you know; it was very exciting.' He paused, and added drily, 'Not long after that, of course, it became too exciting, but by that time no one in Finland had time to think about the atom.'

He clasped his hands across his belly. 'I well remember the time Hannu showed me a paper written by Meitner and

Frisch interpreting Hahn's experiments. The paper showed clearly that a chain reaction could take place and that the generation of atomic energy was clearly possible. We were all excited – you cannot imagine the excitement – and all our work was put aside to concentrate on this new thing.' He shrugged heavily. 'But that was 1939 – the year of the Winter War. No time for frivolities like atoms.' His tone was sardonic.

'What was my father working on when this happened?'

'Ah – here is the coffee,' said Kääriänen. He fussed about with the coffee, and offered small cakes to Lyn. 'And what do you do, young lady? Are you a scientist like your father and your grandfather?'

'I'm afraid not,' said Lyn politely. 'I'm a teacher.'

'We must have the teachers, too,' said Kääriänen. 'What was that you asked, Doctor?'

'I was wondering what my father was working on at the time he read the paper on atomic fission.'

'Ah, yes,' the professor said vaguely, and waved his hand a little helplessly. 'It was a long time ago, you know; so much has happened since – it is difficult to remember.' He picked up a cake and was about to bite into it when he said, 'I remember – it was something to do with some aspects of the properties of X-rays.'

'Did you work on that project?'

'No – that would be Liisa – or was it Olavi?'

'So you don't know the nature of the work he was doing?'

'No.' Kääriänen's face broke into a smile, and he shook with laughter. 'But, knowing your father, I can tell you it had no practical application. He was very proud of being a pure research physicist. We were all like that in those days – proud of being uncontaminated by the world.' He shook his head sadly. 'A pity we're not like that now.'

The next hour and a half was spent in reminiscences from Kääriänen interspersed with Denison's desperate ploys to fend off his inquiries into Meyrick's work. After allowing what he thought was a decent time he excused himself and he and Lyn took their leave of the professor with assurances that they would keep in professional contact.

They came out into Senate Square and made their way back to the hotel along Aleksanterinkatu, Helsinki's equivalent of Bond Street. Lyn was thoughtful and quiet, and Denison said, 'A penny for your thoughts.'

'I was just thinking,' she said. 'It seemed at one time as though you were pumping Professor Kääriänen.'

Did it, by God! thought Denison. *You're too bloody smart by half.* Aloud he said, 'I just wanted to know about my father, the work he did and so on.'

'You didn't give much back,' said Lyn tartly. 'Every time *he* asked a question you evaded it.'

'I had to,' said Denison. 'Most of my work is in defence. I can't babble about that in a foreign country.'

'Of course,' said Lyn colourlessly.

They were outside a jeweller's shop and Denison pointed. 'What do you think of that?'

She caught her breath. 'Oh, it's beautiful!'

It was a necklace – chunky, rough-hewn gold of an intricate and yet natural shape. He felt reckless and took her arm. 'Come on,' he said. 'Inside.'

The necklace cost him £215 of Meyrick's money which he paid by credit card. Apart from the fact that he thought that Meyrick ought to pay more attention to his daughter he thought it would take her mind off other things.

'Your birthday present,' he said.

Lyn was breathless with excitement. 'Oh, thank you, Da . . . Harry.' Impulsively she kissed him. 'But I have nothing to wear with it.'

'Then you'll have to buy something, won't you? Let's go back to the hotel.'

'Yes, let's.' She slipped her fingers into his. 'I have a surprise for you, too – at the hotel.'

'Oh? What is it?'

'Well, I thought that now you're back in Finland you ought to become reacquainted with the sauna.'

He laughed, and said cheerfully, 'I've never been to a sauna in my life.'

She stopped dead on the pavement and stared at him. 'But you must have. When you were a boy.'

'Oh, yes; I went then.' He cursed himself for the slip. Carey had given him books to read about Finland; language was one thing but there was a minimum any Finn would know, expatriate or not. The sauna definitely fitted into that category. 'I tend to regard my years in Finland as another life.' It was lame but it would have to do.

'It's about time you were reintroduced to the sauna,' she said firmly. 'I go often in London – it's great fun. I've booked for us both in the hotel sauna for six o'clock.'

'Great!' he said hollowly.

FIFTEEN

In the hotel he escaped to his room and rang the number he had been given. When Carey answered he gave a report on his interview with Kääriänen, and Carey said, 'So it all comes to this: Merikken *was* working on X-rays at the time but no one can remember exactly what he was doing. Those who would know are dead. That's encouraging.'

'Yes,' said Denison.

'You don't sound pleased,' said Carey.

'It's not that. I have something else on my mind.'

'Out with it.'

'Lyn has booked me in for the sauna this evening.'

'So?'

'She's booked us both in.'

'So?' There was a pause before Carey chuckled. 'My boy; I can see you have a wrong impression or an evil mind. This is not Hamburg nor is it the lower reaches of Soho; you're in Helsinki and the Finns are a decent people. I think you'll find there is one sauna for gentlemen and another for ladies.'

'Oh!' said Denison weakly. 'It's just that I don't know much about it. One gets the wrong impression.'

'Didn't you read the books I gave you?'

'I must have missed that one.'

'In any case, there's nothing wrong with a father joining his daughter in the sauna,' said Carey judicially. 'It may be done in your own home but not, I think, in an international hotel.' He paused. 'You'd better read up on it. Meyrick wouldn't have forgotten the sauna – no Finn would.'

'I'll do that.'

'Have fun,' said Carey, and rang off.

Denison put down the telephone and rummaged in his suitcase where he found a slim book on the sauna written for the benefit of English-speaking visitors to Finland. On studying it he was relieved to find that the sauna appeared to be little more than a Turkish bath in essence – with differences.

He turned back the pages and read the introduction. There was, apparently, one sauna for every six Finns which, he reflected, was probably a greater incidence than bathrooms in Britain. A clean people, the Finns – *mens sana in corpore sauna.* Stones were heated by birch logs or, in modern times, by electric elements. Humidity was introduced by *löyly* – tossing water on the stones. The booklet managed to convey an air of mystic ritual about what was essentially a prosaic activity, and Denison came to the conclusion that the sauna was the Finnish equivalent of the Japanese tea ceremony.

At quarter to six Lyn rang him. 'Are you ready?'

'Yes, of course.'

'I'll meet you afterwards in the swimming pool. Have you got your trunks?'

Denison mentally ran down a checklist of Meyrick's clothing. 'Yes.'

'At half past six, then.' She rang off.

He went up to the top floor of the hotel, found the sauna for men, and went into the change room where he took his time, taking his cue from the others who were there. He stripped and went into the ante-chamber to the sauna where he showered and then took a square of towelling from a pile and went into the sauna itself.

It was hot.

Out of the corner of his eye he saw a man lay his towel on a slatted, wooden bench and sit on it, so he followed suit. The wood beneath his feet was almost unbearably hot and sweat was already beginning to start from his skin. A man left the sauna and another took a bucket of water and sluiced it along the wood on which his feet were resting. Tendrils of steam arose but his feet were cooler.

Another man left the sauna and Denison turned and found a thermometer on the wall by his head. It registered 115 degrees. Not too bad, he thought; I can stand that. Then he looked again and saw that the thermometer was calibrated in degrees Celsius. Christ Almighty! Water *boils* at 100°C.

He blinked the sweat out of his eyes and turned his head to find that there was just himself and another man left – a broad-shouldered, deep-chested man, shaggy with hair. The man picked up a wooden dipper and filled it with water from a bucket. He paused with it in his hand, and said interrogatively, *'Löylyä?'*

Denison answered with one of the few Finnish words he had picked up. *'Kiitos.'*

The man tossed the dipperful of water on to the square tub of hot stones in the corner. A blast of heat hit Denison like a physical blow and he gasped involuntarily. The man shot a sudden spate of Finnish at him, and Denison shook his head. 'I'm sorry; I have no Finnish.'

'Ah; first time in Finland?'

'Yes,' said Denison, and added, 'since I was a boy.'

The man nodded. A sheen of sweat covered his hairy torso. He grinned. 'First time in sauna?'

Sweat dripped from Denison's nose. 'For a long time – many years.'

The man nodded and rose. He picked up the dipper again and, turning away from Denison, he filled it from the bucket, Denison gritted his teeth. Anything a bloody Finn can stand, I can; he thought.

With a casual flick of the wrist the man tossed the water on to the hot stones, then quickly went out of the sauna, slamming the door behind him. Again the wave of heat hit Denison, rising to an almost intolerable level so that he gasped and spluttered. A bloody practical joker – baiting a beginner!

He felt his head swim and tried to stand up but found that his legs had gone rubbery beneath him. He rolled off the top bench and tried to crawl to the door and felt the hot wood burning his hands. Darkness closed in on him and the last thing he saw was his own hand groping for the door handle before he collapsed and passed out.

He did not see the door open, nor did he feel himself being lifted up and carried out.

SIXTEEN

He awoke to darkness.

For a long time he just lay there, unable to think because of the throbbing pain in his head. Then his head cleared a little and he stirred and knew he was lying on a bed. When he moved he heard a metallic clinking noise. He moved again and became aware that he was naked, and a recollection of the sauna came back.

His first thought was that he had collapsed of heat prostration and had been taken to his own room, but when he lifted his hand that theory disintegrated quickly. There was a tug on both wrists and he felt cold metal, and when he twisted his hands around he heard that clinking sound again and felt the handcuffs.

He lay quiet for a while before he levered himself up on one elbow to stare into the blackness, then he swung his legs over the side of the bed and sat up. Tentatively he moved his feet apart; at least they were not manacled and he could walk. But walk where? He held his arms out before him and moved them sideways, first to the left and then to the right, until he encountered an object. It was flat with square edges and he concluded it was a bedside table. Exploring the top brought no joy; there was nothing on it.

Although his headache had eased he felt as weak as a kitten and he sat for a few moments to conserve his strength.

Whether his weakness was a natural result of the heat of the sauna was debatable. He reasoned that if the sauna did that to everyone then it would not be so popular in Finland. Apart from that, he had no idea of how long he had been unconscious. He felt his skin and found it cool and with no moisture.

After a while he stood up with his arms out in front of him and began to shuffle forward. He had gone only a few feet when he stubbed his toe on something and the pain was agonizing. 'Damn!' he said viciously, and stepped back until he felt the bed behind his legs. He sat down and nursed his foot.

A sound came from the other side of the room and he saw a patch of greyness, quickly obscured and vanishing. A light suddenly stabbed at him and he blinked and screwed up his eyes against the sudden glare. A voice said in accented English, 'So Dr Meyrick is awake – and up, too.'

Denison brought up his hands before his eyes. The voice said sharply, 'Don't move, Meyrick. Stay on the bed.' Then, more coolly, 'Do you know what this is?'

The lamp dipped a little so that he could see the vague outline of a man in back-reflected light. He saw the glint of metal in an out-thrust hand. 'Well?' said the voice impatiently. 'What is it, Meyrick?'

Denison's voice was hoarse. 'A pistol.' He cleared his throat. 'I'd like to know what the hell this is all about.'

The voice was amused. 'No doubt you would.' As Denison tried to sort out the accent the light played over him. 'I see you've hurt your side, Dr Meyrick. How did that happen?'

'A pack of maniacs attacked me in Norway. They seem to have the same breed in Finland, too.'

'Poor Dr Meyrick,' mocked the voice. 'You seem to be continually in trouble. Did you report it to the police?'

'Of course I did. What else would you expect me to do? And to the British Embassy in Oslo.' He remembered what Carey had said about Meyrick's bloody-mindedness, and added irascibly, 'Bloody incompetents – the lot of them.'

'Who did you see at the Embassy?'

'A man called McCready picked me up at the police station and took me to the Embassy. Look, I've had enough of this. I'm answering no more questions. None at all.'

The pistol moved languidly. 'Yes, you will. Did you meet Carey?'

'No.'

'You're a liar.'

'If you think you know the answers, why ask me the questions? I don't know anyone called Carey.'

A sigh came out of the darkness. 'Meyrick, I think you ought to know that we have your daughter.'

Denison tensed, but sat quietly. After a moment he said, 'Prove it.'

'Nothing easier.' The pistol withdrew slowly. 'Tape recorders are made conveniently small these days, are they not?' There was a click and a slight hissing noise in the darkness beyond the flashlight, then a man spoke:

'Now tell me; what's your father doing here in Finland?'

'He's on holiday.'

That was Lyn's clear voice. Denison recognized it in spite of the slight distortion which was far less than that of a telephone.

'Did he *tell you that?'*

'Who else would tell me?' She sounded amused.

'But he went to see Professor Kääriänen this afternoon. That sounds more like business than pleasure.'

'He wanted to find out something about his father – my grandfather.'

'What did he want to find out?'

There was a raw silence, then the man said, *'Come now, Miss Meyrick; nothing will happen, either to you or to your father, if you answer my questions. I assure you that you will be released unharmed.'*

A switch snapped and the voices stopped. From the darkness: 'You see, Dr Meyrick! Of course, I cannot guarantee the truthfulness of my friend regarding his last statement.'

The pistol reappeared, glinting in the light. 'Now, to return to Mr Carey – what did he have to say?'

'He hauled me over the coals for being in a road accident,' said Denison.

The voice sharpened. 'You can do better than that. Now, having put you and Carey together, I want to know just what you're doing here in Finland. I want it truthfully, and I want it quickly. And you'd better start thinking seriously of your daughter's health.' The gun jerked. 'Talk!'

Denison was never more conscious of the disadvantages of being naked; it took the pith out of a man. 'All right,' he said. 'We're here to see the Finnish government.'

'What about?'

'A defence project.'

'Who in the government?'

'Not really the government,' said Denison inventively. 'Someone in the army – in military intelligence.'

'The name?' When Denison was silent the gun jerked impatiently. 'The name, Meyrick.'

Denison was hastily trying to slap together a name that sounded even remotely Finnish. 'Saarinen.'

'He's an architect.'

'Not this one – this one's a colonel,' said Denison, hoping it was a rank in the Finnish army. He was listening intently but heard no sound other than an occasional rustle of clothing from the other side of the bright light.

'What's the project?'

'Electronic espionage – equipment for monitoring Russian broadcasts, especially on military wavelengths.'

There was a long silence. 'I suppose you know that this is already done.'

'Not the way I do it,' said Denison.

'All right; how do you do it? And let's not have me extract answers like pulling teeth or that girl of yours might have some of her teeth pulled.'

'I invented an automatic decoder,' said Denison. A barrier broke in his mind and a wave of panic and terror swept over him. He felt sweat trickle down his chest and then deliberately pushed the panic back where it had come from – but he retained the words that had come with it.

'It's a stochastic process,' he said, not even knowing what the word meant. 'A development of the Monte Carlo method. The Russian output is repeatedly sampled and put through a series of transformations at random. Each transformation is compared with a store held in a computer memory – if a match is made a tree branching takes place leading to a further set of transformations. There are a lot of dead ends and it needs a big, fast computer – very powerful.'

The sweat poured off him. He had not understood a word of what he had said.

'I got most of that,' said the voice, and Denison thought he detected a touch of awe. 'You invented this thing?'

'I developed the circuits and helped with the programming,' said Denison sullenly.

'There's one thing I don't understand – and this I really have to know. Why give it to the Finns?'

'We didn't,' said Denison. 'They gave it to us. They developed the basics. They didn't have the resources to follow up, so they gave it to us.'

'Professor Kääriänen?'

'Look,' said Denison. 'Let me hear that tape again.'

'Why?'

'I'm not saying another bloody word until I hear it,' said Denison stubbornly.

A pause. 'All right; here's a re-run.'

The gun vanished and there was a click.

'Now tell me; what's your father doing here in Finland?'

'He's on holiday.'

Denison strained his ears as he listened to the conversation and evaluated the voices. He raised his hands and slowly parted them so that the link of the handcuffs tightened.

'He wanted to find out something about his father – my grandfather.'

'What did he want to find out?' A pause. *'Come now, Miss Meyrick; nothing will happen, either to you or to your father, if you ans . . .'*

Denison lunged, moving fast. He had moved his legs under the bed, so that when he moved he was on the balls of his feet and utilizing the maximum thrust of his thighs. His hands were as wide apart as he could spread them and he rammed them forward as though to grab the man by the ears. The link between the handcuffs caught the man right across the larynx.

Both tape recorder and flashlight dropped to the floor; the flashlight rolled, sending grotesque shadows about the room, and the recorder babbled. Denison kept up his pressure on the man's throat and was aware of cloth as he pressed his hands to his opponent's face. In the shifting light he saw the glint of metal as the man raised the pistol from his pocket and he twisted his hand frantically and managed to grab the wrist as it came up.

With his left hand holding firmly on to his opponent's right wrist he thrust firmly so that the steel link cut into the man's throat. The gun was thus held close to the man's right ear, and when it went off with a blinding flare and a deafening explosion the man reeled away and dropped it.

Denison dived for it and came up again quickly. The door banged closed and the recorder chattered insanely. He made for the door and opened it, to find himself in a narrow corridor with another door at the end. As he ran for it he heard Diana Hansen say, from behind him, *'Lyn, if you take this attitude it will be the worse for you.'*

He heard the words but they made little sense and he had no time to evaluate them. He burst through the door and found himself in the brightly lit hotel corridor. There was no one to be seen, so he ran to the corner where the corridor turned and came to the lifts, and skidded to a halt in front of an astonished couple in evening dress. One lift was going down.

He made for the stairs, hearing a startled scream from behind him, and ran down two flights of stairs, causing quite a commotion as he emerged into the lobby yelling for the police and wearing nothing but a pair of handcuffs and an automatic pistol.

SEVENTEEN

'Incredible!' said Carey. His voice was dead as though he, himself, did not believe what he was saying, and the single word made no echo in the quiet room.

'That's what happened,' said Denison simply.

McCready stirred. 'It would seem that more than water was thrown on to the hot stones in the sauna.'

'Yes,' said Carey. 'I have heard that some Finns, in an experimental mood, have used koskenkorva as *löylyä.*'

'What's that?' asked Denison.

'A sort of Finnish vodka.' Carey put down his dead pipe. 'I dare say some smart chemist could come up with a vaporizing knock-out mixture. I accept that.' He frowned and shook his head. 'Could you repeat what you told this fellow about your bloody decoder?'

'It's engraved on my memory,' said Denison bitterly. 'I said, "It's a stochastic process – a development of the Monte Carlo method. The Russian output is repeatedly sampled and put through a series of transformations at random. Each transformation is compared with a store held in a computer memory – if a match is made a tree branching takes place leading to a further set of transformations. There are a lot of dead ends and it needs a big, fast computer – very powerful."'

'It would,' said Carey drily.

'I don't even know what stochastic means,' said Denison helplessly.

Carey took a smoker's compendium from his pocket and began to clean his pipe, making a dry scraping sound. 'I know what it means. A stochastic process has an element of probability in it. The Monte Carlo method was first devised as a means of predicting the rate of diffusion of uranium hexafluoride through a porous barrier – it's been put to other uses since.'

'But I don't know anything about that,' expostulated Denison.

'Apparently you do,' said Carey. 'If you thought you were talking gobbledegook you were wrong. It would make sense to a mathematician or a computer man. And you were right about something else; you'd need a bloody powerful computer to handle it – the transformations would run into millions for even a short message. In fact, I don't think there is that kind of a computer, unless the programming method is equally powerful.'

Denison developed the shakes. 'Was I a mathematician? Did I work on computers?' he whispered.

'No,' said Carey levelly. 'What did you think you were doing when you reeled off all that stuff?'

'I was spinning a yarn – I couldn't tell him why we were really here.'

McCready leaned forward. 'What did you feel like when you were spouting like that?'

'I was scared to death,' confessed Denison.

'Of the man?'

There was violence in Denison's headshake. 'Not of the man – of myself. What was in *me.*' His hands began to quiver again.

Carey caught McCready's eye and shook his head slightly; that line of questioning was too dangerous for

Denison. He said, 'We'll leave that for a moment and move on. You say this chap accepted you as Meyrick?'

'He didn't question it.'

'What made you go for him? That was a brave thing to do when he had a gun.'

'He wasn't holding the gun,' said Denison. 'He was holding the recorder. I suddenly tumbled to it that the recording was a fake. The threatening bit at the end had a different quality – a dead sound. All the other stuff was just ordinary conversation and could have happened quite naturally. It followed that this chap couldn't have Lyn, and that left me free to act.'

'Quite logical,' said Carey. 'And quite right.' There was a bemused look on his face as he muttered to himself, *'Competent!'*

McCready said, 'Lyn was in the hotel lounge yesterday afternoon and a chap sat at the table and began to pump her. Either the flower pot or the ashtray was bugged and the conversation recorded. Diana Hansen was around and caught on to what was happening and butted in, spoiling the game. Of course, she didn't know about the bug at the time.'

A look of comprehension came over Denison's face. 'I heard Diana's voice on the tape. She was threatening Lyn, too.'

McCready grinned. 'When this character was foiled he went away, and Diana and Lyn had a row. The bug was still there so that, too, was picked up on the tape. It seems that your daughter is trying to protect her father against the wiles of a wicked woman of the world.'

'Oh, no!' moaned Denison.

'You'll have to come the heavy father,' McCready advised.

'Does Lyn know what happened?'

Carey grunted and glanced at his watch. 'Six in the morning – she'll still be asleep. When you went missing I had Mrs Hansen tell her that the two of you were going on the town and you'd be late back. I didn't want her alarmed.'

'She's certain to find out,' said McCready. 'This is too good a story to suppress – the eminent Dr Meyrick capering in the lobby of the city's best hotel as naked as the day he was born and waving a gun. Impossible to keep out of the papers.'

'Why in hell did you do it?' demanded Carey. 'You were bawling for the police, too.'

'I thought I could catch the chap,' said Denison. 'When I didn't I thought of what Meyrick would have done – the real Meyrick. If an innocent man is threatened with a gun the first thing he does is to yell for the coppers. An innocent Meyrick would be bloody outraged – so I blew my top in the hotel lobby.'

'Still logical,' muttered Carey. He raised his voice. 'All right; the man in the sauna. Description?'

'He was hairy – he had a pelt like a bear.'

'I don't care if he was as hairy as Esau,' said Carey caustically. 'We can't go stripping the clothes off suspects to find how hairy they are. His face, man!'

'Brown eyes,' said Denison tiredly. 'Square face – a bit battered. Nose on one side. Dimple in chin.'

'That's the bloke who was quizzing Lyn Meyrick,' said McCready.

'The other man – the one with the gun.'

'I never saw him,' said Denison. 'The room was darkened and when I got my hands on him I found he was wearing some kind of a mask. But I . . .' He stopped on a doubtful note.

'Carry on,' said Carey encouragingly.

'He spoke English but with an accent.'

'What sort of accent?'

'I don't know,' said Denison desperately. 'Call it a generalized middle-European accent. The thing is that I think I've heard the voice before.'

At that, Carey proceeded to put Denison through the wringer. Fifteen minutes later Denison yelled, 'I tell you I don't know.' He put his head in his hands. 'I'm tired.'

Carey stood up. 'All right; you can go to bed. We'll let you sleep, but I can't answer for the local cops – they'll want to see you again. Got your story ready?'

'Just the truth.'

'I'd leave out that bit about the decoder you invented,' advised Carey. 'It's a bit too much.' He jerked his head at McCready. 'Come on, George.'

They left Denison to his bed. In the lift Carey passed his hand over his face. 'I didn't think this job would call for so many sleepless nights.'

'Let's find some coffee,' proposed McCready. 'There's sure to be an early morning place open by now.'

They left the hotel in silence and walked along Mannerheimintie. The street was quiet with only the occasional taxi and the odd cyclist on his way to an early start at work. Carey said suddenly, 'Denison worries me.'

'You mean that stuff he came out with?'

'What the hell else?' The corners of Carey's mouth turned down. 'And more – but principally that. A man like Meyrick might design just such a contraption – but where did Denison get it from?'

'I've been thinking about it,' said McCready. His voice was careful. 'Have you considered the possibility of a double shuffle?'

Carey broke stride. 'Speak plainly.'

'Well, here we have a man whom we think is Denison. His past is blocked out and every time he tries to probe it he breaks into a muck sweat. You saw that.'

'Well?'

'But supposing he really is Meyrick – also with the past blocked out – who only thinks he's Denison. Harding said it was possible. Then anything brought out of the past in an emergency would be pure Meyrick.'

Carey groaned. 'What a bloody roundabout to be on.' He shook his head decisively. 'That won't wear. Iredale said he wasn't Meyrick.'

'No, he didn't,' said McCready softly. 'I can quote his exact words. Iredale said, "He's not Meyrick – not unless Meyrick has had plastic surgery recently." '

Carey thought that out. 'Stop trying to confuse me. That would mean that the man we had in the hotel in Oslo for three weeks was *not* Meyrick – that the ringer was the other way round.'

He stopped dead on the pavement. 'Look, George; let's get one thing quite clear.' He stabbed a finger back at the hotel. 'That man there is *not* Meyrick. I *know* Meyrick – he fights with his tongue and uses sarcasm as a weapon, but if you put him in a real fight he'd collapse. Denison is a quiet-spoken, civil man who, in an emergency, seems to have the instincts of a born killer. He's the antithesis of Meyrick. Ram that into your mind and hold on to it fast.'

McCready shrugged. 'It leaves a lot to be explained.'

'It will be explained. I want Giles Denison sorted out once and for all back in London. I want his life sifted day by day and minute by minute, if necessary, to find out how he knows that mathematical jargon. And I want Harding brought here *tout de suite.*'

'He'll like that,' said McCready sardonically. 'I'll pass the word on.'

They walked for another hundred yards and McCready said, 'Denison is quite a boy. Who else would think of handcuffs as a weapon?' He chuckled. 'I think he's neither Meyrick nor Denison – I think he's Clark Kent.'

Carey's jaw dropped. 'And who the blazes is that?'

'Superman,' said McCready blandly.

EIGHTEEN

Denison slept, was interviewed by the police, and slept again. He got up at four, bathed and dressed, and went downstairs. Crossing the lobby he saw the receptionist stare at him, then turn and say something to the porter with a smile. Dr H. F. Meyrick was evidently the hotel celebrity.

He looked into the lounge, saw no one he knew, and then investigated the bar where he found Diana Hansen sitting at a table and reading a paperback. She looked up as he stood over her. 'I was wondering when you'd show.'

'I had to get some sleep. Yesterday was a bit wearing.' He sat down and picked up the ashtray to inspect its underside.

Diana laughed. 'No bugs – I checked.'

He put it down. 'Where's Lyn?'

'Out.' At his raised eyebrows she elaborated slightly. 'Sightseeing.'

A waiter came up. *'Mittö otatte?'*

'A olutta, olkaa hyvä,' said Denison. He looked at Diana. 'And you?'

'Nothing for me,' she said. 'Your Finnish is improving.'

'Only enough to order the necessities of life. Has Carey come to any conclusions about yesterday?'

'Carey isn't here,' she said. 'I'm to tell you to sit tight until he comes back.'

'Where is he?'

'He's gone to Sweden.'

'Sweden!' His eyes were blank. 'Why has he gone there?'

'He didn't tell me.' She stood up and picked up her book. 'Now that I've passed on the word I'll get about my business.' Her lips quirked. 'Don't take any wooden saunas.'

'Never again,' he said fervently. He bit his lip. 'But they might take another crack at me.'

'Not to worry,' she said. 'You're under Ian Armstrong's eye, and he's well named. He's sitting at the bar now. Don't acknowledge him – and don't move so fast he can't keep up with you.'

She went away as the waiter came up with his beer. He drank it moodily and ordered another bottle. Over at the bar Armstrong was making a single beer stretch a long way. Why Sweden? What could possibly have happened there to drag Carey away? No answer came.

He was half-way through the second bottle when Lyn entered the bar. She sat at his table and looked at his beer. 'You look dissipated.'

He grinned at her. 'I feel dissipated. I was up late.'

'So I'm told,' she said unsmilingly. 'I heard a strange story this morning – about you.'

He regarded her warily and decided to riposte. 'And I've heard something pretty odd about you. Why did you quarrel with Diana?'

Pink spots came into her cheeks. 'So she told you.'

'She didn't say anything about it,' said Denison truthfully.

Lyn flared up. 'Then who did if she didn't? We were alone.' She tugged viciously at the strap of her bag and looked down at the table. 'It doesn't feel nice to be ashamed of one's own father. I never really believed anything Mother said about you, but now I can see she was telling the truth.'

'Calm down,' he said. 'Have a drink. What will you have? A Coca-Cola?'

Her chin came up. 'A dry Martini.'

He signalled to the waiter, suppressing a smile, and gave the order. When the waiter had gone, she said, 'It was disgusting of you.'

'What's so disgusting about Diana Hansen?'

'You know what I mean. I've heard the jet set gets up to some queer things but, my God, I didn't expect it of you. Not my own father.' Her eyes were unnaturally bright.

'No, I don't know what you mean. What am I supposed to have done?' he asked plaintively.

A hurt look came into her eyes. 'I know you went out with that woman last night because she told me so. And I know how you came back, too. You must have been disgustingly drunk to do that. Did *she* have any clothes on? No wonder they had to send for the police.'

'Oh, my God!' said Denison, appalled. 'Lyn, it wasn't like that.'

'Then why is everyone talking about it? I heard it at breakfast this morning. There were some Americans at the next table – you ought to have heard them. It was . . . dirty!' She broke into tears.

Denison hastily looked about the bar and then put his hand on Lyn's. 'It wasn't like that; I'll tell you.'

So he told her, leaving out everything important which would only complicate the issue. He was interrupted once by the waiter bringing the Martini, and then he bore in again to finish his story.

She dabbed at her eyes with a small handkerchief and sniffed. 'A likely tale!'

'If you don't believe me, would you believe the police?' he said exasperatedly. 'They've been on my neck all morning.'

'Then why did Diana tell me you were going out with her?'

'It was the best thing she could have done,' said Denison. 'She didn't want you worried. And about your quarrel – I heard a bit of it on the tape.' He explained about that, and said, 'The police have the tape now.'

Lyn was horrified. 'You mean everyone is listening to that quarrel?'

'Everyone except me,' said Denison drily. 'Have your Martini.'

Something else occurred to her. 'But you might have been hurt – he might have *killed* you!'

'But he didn't – and all's well.'

'Who could it have been?'

'I suppose I'm a fairly important man in some respects,' said Denison tiredly. 'I told you yesterday that I don't babble about my work. Someone wanted information and took direct action.'

She straightened her shoulders and looked at him with shining eyes. 'And didn't get it.'

He brutally chopped the props from under the hero worship. 'As for Diana Hansen, there's nothing in it – not the way you think. But even if there were it's got nothing to do with you. You're behaving more like an affronted wife than a daughter.'

The glow died. Lyn hunched her shoulders a little and looked down at the Martini glass. Suddenly she picked it up and drained the contents at a swallow. It took her breath away and she choked a little before putting down the empty glass. Denison grinned. 'Does that make you feel better?'

'I'm sorry,' she said miserably.

'That's all right,' he said. 'No harm done. Let's go for a walk.' He signalled to the waiter and paid the bill and, as he got up from the table, he glanced over at the bar and saw Armstrong doing the same. It was comforting to have a bodyguard.

They left the bar and went into the lobby. As they approached the entrance a porter came in loaded with baggage, and a burly figure followed. 'Hey, Lucy; look who's here,' boomed a voice. 'It's Harry Meyrick.'

'Oh, hell!' said Denison, but there was no escape.

'Who is it?' asked Lyn.

'I'll introduce you,' said Denison grimly.

'Hi, Harry!' shouted Kidder, advancing across the lobby with outstretched hand. 'It's great to see you, it sure is.'

'Hallo, Jack,' said Denison without enthusiasm, and allowed his hand to be pulped.

'It's a small world,' said Kidder predictably. 'I was only saying that to Lucy the other day when we bumped into the Williamsons in Stockholm. You remember the Williamsons?'

'Of course,' said Denison.

'I guess we're all on the same Scandinavian round, eh? I wouldn't be surprised if the Williamsons don't turn up here, too. Wouldn't it be great if they did?'

'Great!' said Denison.

Lucy Kidder popped out from behind her husband. 'Why, Harry; how nice to see you. Did Jack tell you we saw the Williamsons in Stockholm?'

'Yes, he did.'

'It's a small world,' said Lucy Kidder.

'It sure is,' said Jack. 'If the Williamsons get here – and that nice friend of yours, Diana Hansen – we could get down to some poker. That gal is a mean player.'

Lyn said, 'Diana Hansen? Why, she's here.'

Surprise and pleasure beamed from Kidder's face. 'Now, isn't that just great? Maybe I'll be able to win some of my dough back, Lucy.'

'Lose it, more likely,' she said tartly. 'Jack really believes he can play poker.'

'Now then, Momma,' he said good-humouredly. 'Don't knock the old man.' He looked down at Lyn. 'And who's the little lady?'

'Excuse me,' said Denison. 'Jack Kidder – my daughter, Lyn – Lucy Kidder.'

They shook hands and Kidder said, 'You didn't tell me you had a daughter, Harry. You certainly didn't tell me you had a beautiful daughter. Where you been hiding her?'

'Lyn's been at University,' said Denison. 'She's now on vacation.'

Lucy said, 'I don't want to break things up, Jack, but I guess we gotta register. The desk clerk's waiting.'

'Sure,' said Kidder. 'I'll be seeing you around, Harry. Tell Diana to break out that deck of cards – we'll be playing poker.'

'I'll do that,' said Denison and, taking Lyn by the arm, he steered her out of the hotel. Under his breath he said, 'Over my dead body.'

'Who was that?' asked Lyn.

'The biggest bore from the North American continent,' said Denison. 'With his long-suffering wife.'

NINETEEN

Carey and McCready were being violently seasick. They clung to the rail of the small boat as it pitched in the summer gale which had blown up from the south and whistled up the narrow channel between the Swedish mainland and the island of Oland. There was but one significant difference between them – while Carey thought he was dying McCready *knew* he was dying.

They both felt better when they set foot ashore at Borgholm. There a car awaited them, and a police officer who introduced himself with a jerky bow as 'Hoglund, Olof.'

'I'm Carey and this is McCready.' The wind blew off the sea and riffled his short grey hair. 'Shall we get on with it?'

'Certainly. This way.' As Hoglund ushered them to the car he said, 'Your Mr Thornton arrived an hour ago.'

Carey stopped dead in his tracks. 'Has he, indeed?' He glanced sideways at McCready, and muttered, 'What the hell does he want?'

They were silent as they drove through the streets of Borgholm. It was not the time yet for talk; that would come later after they had seen what they had come to see. Carey's mind was busy with speculations arising from the presence of Thornton, and even if he wanted to discuss it with McCready he could not do so in the presence of Hoglund.

The car pulled up in front of a two-storey building and they went inside, Hoglund leading the way. He took them into a back room where there was a trestle table set up. On the table was a long shape covered with a white cloth. Behind the table stood a short young man with a neat vandyke beard, who wore a white coat. Hoglund introduced him as Dr Carlson. 'You already know Mr Thornton.'

Thornton was a tall, dark man of cadaverous features, smooth unlined skin and indecipherable expression. He was a young-looking sixty or an aged forty – it was hard to determine which and Thornton was not going to tell anybody. It was not his habit to tell anyone anything that did not concern him and he was chary of doing even that. He could have been Carey's boss but he was not; Carey was proud and pleased to be in another department.

He lifted yellowed, dyspeptic eyes as Carey and McCready entered the room. Carey nodded to him curtly, and turned to Carlson. 'Good afternoon, Doctor,' he said in a weary voice. He was very tired. 'May I see it?'

Carlson nodded without speaking and drew back the cloth. Carey loked down with an expressionless face and motioned for the cloth to be drawn back farther. 'This is how he was found?'

'The body has been cleaned externally,' said Carlson. 'It was covered with oil. And the manacles have been removed, of course.'

Carey nodded. 'Of course. There was no clothing?'

'The man was naked.'

McCready looked at Carey and raised his eyebrows. 'The same as . . .'

Carey was unaccountably clumsy. He turned and trod heavily on McCready's foot. 'Sorry, George.' He turned to Carlson. 'What was the cause of death, Doctor?'

Carlson frowned. 'That will have to await the autopsy,' he said cautiously. 'At the moment it is a question of whether he was drowned or poisoned.'

Thornton stepped forward. 'Did you say poisoned?' Carey analysed the tone of voice. In spite of Thornton's habitual flatness of expression he thought he detected a note of genuine surprise.

'I'll show you,' said Carlson. He opened the jaws of the corpse and took a long spatula and thrust it down the throat. McCready winced and turned away. Carlson withdrew the spatula and held it out. 'A scraping from the inside of the throat.'

Carey inspected the blackened end of the spatula. 'Oil?'

When Carlson nodded Thornton said, 'I don't think it really matters if he drowned in oil or if it poisoned him.' His attitude was relaxed.

'I agree,' said Hoglund. 'Do you make the identification, Mr Carey?'

Carey hesitated. 'At this moment – no.' He nodded at Thornton. 'What about you?'

'I've never seen the man before in my life,' said Thornton.

A grim expression settled on Carey's face. 'The body will have to be . . . preserved. Do you have facilities?'

'Not on Oland,' said Carlson.

'We can take it to the mainland as soon as Dr Carlson has completed the autopsy,' said Hoglund.

'No,' said Carey forcibly. 'I need a positive identification before the body is touched. That means the body must go to England or someone must come to Sweden. In any case, I want one of our own pathologists to assist at the autopsy.'

'This comes within our jurisdiction,' said Hoglund sharply.

Carey rubbed his eyes tiredly; the inside of his eyelids seemed to be covered in sand. This would have to be handled carefully considering the Swedish tradition of neutrality. He said slowly, 'As far as we are concerned this has now become a matter of State. I am going to push the question upstairs, and I suggest you also consult your superiors. Let our masters argue the question of jurisdiction, my friend; it will be safer for both of us.' As Hoglund considered the suggestion Carey added, 'In any case, the incident took place in international waters.'

'Perhaps that would be best,' said Hoglund. His manner was stiff. 'I will do as you suggest. Would you like to see the manacles?' When Carey nodded he strode to a shelf and took down a pair of handcuffs.

Carey examined them. 'British,' he commented. He handed them to Thornton. 'Wouldn't you think so?'

Thornton shrugged. 'It means little.' He turned to Hoglund. 'Is it established he did not come from the tanker?'

'The crew of the tanker are all accounted for,' said Hoglund. 'One man was killed but the body was recovered.' Carlson was replacing the sheet over the body as Hoglund gestured at it. 'This man probably came from the other boat. The captain of the tanker says it must have been running without lights.'

'He would say that,' said Carey cynically. 'He could be right, though. It has not been identified yet?'

'Not yet. No boat has been reported missing; no insurance claim has been made. We are making inquiries, naturally.' Hoglund frowned. 'Apart from the body there is the matter of the oil. It will cost a lot to clean the coasts of Gotland and someone must pay.'

'That's something I don't understand,' said McCready. 'If the oil is drifting on to Gotland how is it that the body turned up here on Oland? They are a long way apart.'

'The body was taken from the sea south of Gotland,' said Hoglund. 'But the ship was coming here.'

Carey cleared his throat. 'What have you got to go on in your inquiries?'

'Not a great deal. The captain of the tanker was not on the bridge at the time, and the boat sank within minutes. The captain estimated it as something between three hundred and four hundred tons. He derives this figure from the damage done to the bows of the tanker and its speed at the time of impact.'

'A small coaster,' said Carey thoughtfully. 'Or a biggish fisherman.'

Hoglund shrugged. 'We will soon find out.'

I wouldn't hold your breath, my friend, thought Carey. He turned to Carlson. 'There is no reflection on your ability as a pathologist, Dr Carlson. I hope you understand that. Will you begin preparations for the preservation of the body?'

Carlson looked warily at Hoglund, who nodded. 'I understand. I will do as you ask.'

'Then there's nothing more we can do here,' said Carey. 'Unless Mr Thornton has anything further to add.'

'Nothing,' said Thornton. 'I'll leave the details of the identification to you.'

They left the room. At the entrance of the building Carey paused to button up his coat, and turned to Thornton. 'Your arrival was unexpected. What brought you here?'

'I happened to be at the Embassy in Stockholm,' said Thornton easily. 'About another matter, of course. They're a bit short-handed so when this thing blew up I volunteered to come here and look after the British interest.'

Carey turned up his collar. 'How did you know there *was* a British interest?' he asked blandly.

Thornton was equally bland. 'The handcuffs, of course.' He nodded back towards the room they had come from. 'Who was he?'

'We'll know that when he's been identified.'

Thornton smiled. 'Your department has a vested interest in mysteries, I know – but you shouldn't let it become an obsession.' He pointed. 'Hoglund is waiting for you at the car.'

'Aren't you coming?'

'I came by helicopter,' said Thornton. 'Sorry I can't offer you a lift back, but I don't know where you came from, do I?' His smile was malicious.

Carey grunted and walked towards the car. Again there was silence in the car because Hoglund was there but, as they drew up to the quay side, Carey said abruptly, 'Was the British Embassy informed of the country of origin of those handcuffs?'

Hoglund furrowed his brow. 'I don't think so. Not by me.'

'I see. Thank you.'

The wind had moderated and the passage back to the mainland of Sweden was easier. Carey and McCready stayed on deck where it was possible to talk with some privacy. 'I didn't expect to see Thornton,' said McCready. 'What's he up to?'

'I don't know,' said Carey broodingly. 'He tried to spin me a yarn. Can you imagine a Whitehall mandarin like Thornton volunteering for an errand boy's job which any Embassy whippersnapper could do? The mind boggles.' He thumped the rail with his fist. 'Damn these interdepartmental rivalries! We're all supposed to be on the same side, but I spend more time guarding my back against people like Thornton than I do on my job.'

'Do you suppose he knows about the switch on Meyrick?'

'I don't know. According to what he said back there he doesn't even know Meyrick.' Carey looked down at the grey sea. 'Somebody's luck ran out.'

'Meyrick's certainly did.'

'I was thinking of the people who snatched him. They got him to Copenhagen and put him on a boat to take him . . . where? And the boat was run down by a tanker travelling westwards.'

'So it was probably going east,' said McCready. 'Suggestive – to say the least.'

'Let's not jump to any fast conclusions,' said Carey irritably.

'I agree,' said McCready. 'Especially let's not jump to the conclusion that this oil-poisoned stiff is Meyrick. We've been had before.'

Carey gave him a withering look, and said abruptly, 'I want Iredale present at the autopsy to check for any signs of plastic surgery. I want the fingerprints of the corpse taken and a check made at Meyrick's home for matching prints. For legal identification I suggest one of Meyrick's ex-wives.'

'What's wrong with his daughter?'

'I'm trying to work that one out,' said Carey with a sigh. 'If I can do it before we get to the plane then maybe I can get some sleep on the flight back to Helsinki.' He did not sound too sanguine.

TWENTY

Carey sat in the Café Hildén on Aleksanterinkatu and sank a beer while waiting for Harding. After twelve hours' sleep he felt refreshed and no longer as depressed as he had been. He knew his depression had been caused by tiredness. All the same, rested and clear-headed though he was, the coming decision was not going to be easy to make.

He saw Harding come around the corner so he held up his hand. When Harding came over, he asked, 'You've seen Denison?' On Harding's nod, he said, 'Have a beer.'

Harding sat down. 'That'll be welcome. I didn't think it got as hot as this in the frozen north.'

Carey went to the counter and returned with two more beers. 'What's the verdict?'

Harding had his head on one side, apparently watching the foam rise in his glass. 'Oddly enough, he's improved since I last saw him. He's better integrated. What are his drinking habits like now?'

Carey tapped the side of his glass. 'He just has the odd beer.'

'In an odd sort of way this experience might have been therapeutic for him.' Harding smiled wryly. 'Although I wouldn't recommend it as a well-judged treatment. Now that we know more of his past history I'm better equipped to assess his present state.' He took a notebook from his pocket. 'Denison was something of a car enthusiast and ran a Lotus Elan. Three years ago he was driving with his wife, there was an accident for which he was partly – and only partly – to blame, and his wife was killed. They had been married eighteen months. She was pregnant at the time.'

'That's bad,' said Carey.

'He took *all* the blame on himself,' said Harding. 'And one thing led to another. He began to drink heavily and was on the verge of alcoholism when he lost his job for incompetence.'

'That baffles me,' said Carey. 'Because he's bloody competent at what he's doing now.' He grinned. 'I'm thinking of offering him a permanent job.'

Harding sampled his beer. 'He can't remember his wife in any meaningful way because of what's been done to him. He remembers her and he remembers her death but it's as though it happened to someone else. Of course, that's just as it should be after three years. In a normal person the sharpness of grief is blunted by the passage of time and, in that respect, Denison is now normal.'

'I'm glad to hear it,' said Carey.

Harding gave him a sharp look. He mistrusted Carey's reasons for being glad. He said, 'Consequently he has lost his irrational guilt feelings and has no need to anaesthetize himself with booze. Hence the return to competency. I rather think that, with a little expert treatment, he can be made into a much better man than he was immediately prior to his kidnapping.'

'How long would that take?'

'Three to six months – that's just a guess.'

Carey shook his head. 'Too long; I want him now. Is he fit to carry on?'

Harding pondered for a moment. 'You know, I think he's actually enjoying himself right now. He likes the cut and thrust of this business – the opportunity to exercise his wits seems to be good for him.'

'So he's fit,' said Carey in satisfaction.

'I didn't say that,' said Harding testily. 'I'm not thinking of your damned operation – I'm thinking of Denison.' He thought for a while. 'The present pressures don't seem to worry him. I'd say the only danger is if his past is revealed to him in a traumatic manner.'

'That won't happen,' said Carey definitely. 'Not where I'm sending him.'

'All right,' said Harding. 'Then he's as fit as a man in his position can be – which isn't saying a hell of a lot.'

'Which brings me to another problem,' said Carey. 'Meyrick is dead.' He inspected that statement, found it wanting, and amended it. 'Probably dead. We have a body but once bitten, twice shy.'

'I see your difficulty,' said Harding with a half smile.

'I can't tell the girl her father's dead – not with Denison around. She'd blow up like a volcano and bang goes his cover as Meyrick – and I need him as Meyrick. The point is – do I tell Denison?'

'I wouldn't,' said Harding. 'Handling Lyn Meyrick is tricky enough for him as it is. If he knows her father is dead it might put him into a moral dilemma, assuming he's a moral man which I think he is.' He sighed. 'God knows we're not.'

'We represent the higher morality,' said Carey sardonically. 'The greatest good for the greatest number. I've always been a Benthamite at heart; it's the only way to keep my job bearable.' He drained his glass. 'That's it, then. Where is Denison now.'

'Sightseeing,' said Harding. 'He took his daughter to see the Sibelius Memorial.'

TWENTY-ONE

'It looks like an organ,' said Lyn judiciously. 'If it had a keyboard you could play it. A bit funny, that, come to think of it. Sibelius was an orchestra man, wasn't he?'

'I think so,' said Denison. He consulted his guide book. 'It weighs twenty-eight tons and was made by a woman. I suppose you could call it an early example of Women's Lib – the hand that rocks the cradle can also wield the welding torch. Let's sit and watch the passing parade.'

They sat on a bench and watched a tour group debark from a bus; transatlantic accents twanged the air. Denison saw Armstrong stroll along the path below the monument, then he lifted his eyes to look at the sea. The white sails of yachts dotted the deep blue which echoed the lighter blue of the cloudless sky. He wondered when Carey was going to make his move.

Lyn sighed comfortably. 'Isn't this beautiful? I didn't think Finland would be like this – it's more like the Mediterranean, like Ibiza. Remember when we went there?'

'Mmm,' said Denison neutrally.

Lyn laughed. 'That funny little hotel where there was no hot water and you couldn't have a hot bath. I've never heard you complain so angrily. What was the name of the owner – that little fat man?'

'I don't remember,' said Denison. That was safe enough; a man was not expected to remember every casual encounter.

'And then the seafood was bad and they took you off to hospital and pumped out your stomach.'

'I always had a delicate stomach,' said Denison. He pointed out to sea. 'I think they're racing out there.' He wanted to divert her mind to the present.

'Yes, they are,' she said. 'That reminds me – I suppose *Hesperia* is still laid up if you've not been sailing her this summer. The reason I ask is that if you're not going to sail her I'd like to. I sort of half promised Janice and Kitty – friends of mine – that we'd sail together.'

Denison was silent, not knowing what to say.

Lyn said, 'Don't be a spoilsport. Billy Brooks will put her in the water and I can rig her myself.'

'All right,' he said. 'But don't get into trouble. English waters aren't as calm as the Baltic. When are you intending going back?'

'I haven't made up my mind yet. I have to write to the girls and make plans, then I'll drop a line to Billy at the yard. You were going to get a new suit of sails two years ago – did you?'

'Yes.' He stood up quickly. 'Let's press on – it's quite late and I have to see someone at the hotel'

'All very mysterious,' she said. 'What's the sudden appointment?' She grinned at him. 'It sounds rather like Wilde's excuse – "I must decline your invitation owing to a subsequent engagement."'

Had he been as transparent as that? He forced a smile and said, 'It's just that I promised to have a drink before dinner with the Kidders, that's all.'

'Oh,' she said lightly. 'Then let's go. We mustn't keep the Kidders waiting.'

As they walked away Denison saw Armstrong rise from his bench and follow them. *What's the use of a bodyguard?* he thought. *The enemy is by my side and stabs with a sharp tongue.* More and more he was conscious of the injustice of the fraud he was perpetrating on Lyn Meyrick and he determined to see Carey and ask him to find a way of separation.

They got back to the hotel, and Lyn said, 'Do you mind if I come to your room?' She looked about the hotel lobby. 'There's something I want to talk to you about.'

'What?'

She pointed to the hotel entrance. 'Him, for one thing.' Denison looked around and saw Armstrong just coming in. 'He's been following us for the last two days.'

'He's supposed to,' said Denison. 'You might call him a bodyguard. If I go into the sauna again – which God forbid – he'll be in there with me.'

She said quietly, 'I think you'd better tell me what it's all about. There's a lot you're keeping from me. In your room?'

'All right,' he said resignedly. They went up in the lift with three other people and Denison used the time to sort out what he was going to tell her – no lies but withholding most of the truth. He decided that a lot could be hidden behind the Official Secrets Act.

He unlocked the door and followed her in. 'What do you want to know, Lyn?'

'There's a big secret, isn't there?' She sat on the bed.

'Which I can't tell,' he answered. 'It's part of my work. Somebody had a go at me the other day so the Embassy sent that young fellow – he's called Armstrong, incidentally – to look after me. That's all.'

'No more?'

'Nothing you're entitled to know, Lyn. I'm sorry.' He spread his hands. 'I'm bound by the Official Secrets Act.'

Her face was drawn. 'I'm sorry, too, because it isn't enough.'

'My God, I *can't* tell you anything more. If I tattle about what I'm doing they'll assume I'm a bad security risk.' He laughed shortly. 'I'd never be allowed into my own factories – and that's the best that could happen. At the worst I could go to prison.' He sat on the bed next to her. 'It isn't that I don't trust you, Lyn; it's that if you knew what I know you'd be vulnerable. I don't want to put you in danger.'

She was silent for a while. Her face was troubled and her fingers plucked at the coverlet. She moistened her lips. 'I've been worried.'

'I know you have, but there's nothing to worry about. It's over, and Armstrong will see that it doesn't happen again.'

'It's not that I've been worrying about.'

'What, then?'

'Me,' she said. 'And you – principally you. There's something wrong somewhere.'

Denison felt his stomach churn. He said, 'There's nothing wrong with me. It's your imagination.'

It was as though she had not heard him. 'Nothing big – the big things were all right. It's the little things. Thread-Bear, for instance; how could you have forgotten Thread-Bear? And then there are the Kidders.'

'What about the Kidders?'

'Two years ago you'd have cut a man like that down to size in five words.' She looked at him steadily. 'You've changed. You've changed too much.'

'For the better, I hope,' said Denison, fighting a valiant rearguard action.

'I'd say so.' There was a slight waver in her voice. 'You're not nearly as hard to get on with.'

'I'm sorry if I gave you a bad time in the past,' said Denison soberly. 'As I said before: perhaps as I grow older I grow wiser.'

'It confused me,' she said. 'And I'm no different from anyone else; I don't like being confused. And I had a crazy idea – it was so crazy I thought I must be losing my mind.'

Denison opened his mouth but she covered it with her hand. 'No, don't speak. Let me sort it out myself. I don't want to be confused again.'

She took her hand away, and Denison said quietly, 'Go on, Lyn.'

'I found myself having strange thoughts about you.' She swallowed. The kind of thoughts a girl shouldn't have about her own father, and I felt ashamed. You were so *different*, you see; not like my father at all – and the change was too much. I tried to see how you'd changed and the only conclusion I could come to was that suddenly you'd become human.'

'Thanks,' said Denison.

'There's a bit of my old daddy come back,' she said vehemently. 'Oh, you could use irony and sarcasm like knife blades.'

'No irony intended,' said Denison sincerely.

'Then I saw the other things like Thread-Bear and the Kidders and the fact that you've stopped smoking. Look at your hands now – no nicotine at all. Then I got this wild idea.'

Denison stood up. 'Lyn, I think we'd better stop this now,' he said coldly. 'You're becoming hysterical.'

'No, we won't stop,' she shouted, and stood to face him. 'You knew all the works of Sibelius backwards and sideways, and why wouldn't you? You're a Finn! But this morning you only *thought* his work was for the orchestra. And I don't know about you – we've been parted for many years – but I've never been to Ibiza in my life and, to the best of my knowledge, you've never been to hospital with food poisoning.'

Denison was appalled. 'Lyn!'

She was merciless. 'There is no yacht called *Hesperia*. You always said that sailing is the most inefficient means of locomotion known to man, and everyone knows that efficiency is your god. And Billy Brooks doesn't exist – I invented him. And you said you'd bought a suit of sails for a non-existent yacht.'

Her face was white and her eyes brimmed with tears and Denison knew she was deathly frightened. 'You *can't* be my father,' she whispered. 'You're *not* my father. *Who are you?'*

TWENTY-TWO

'Where the hell is Denison?' said Carey irritably.

McCready was soothing. 'He'll be along. He's not very late.'

Carey was on edge. 'He could have been jumped again.'

'It's you that's jumpy. Armstrong's looking after him.'

Carey said nothing. He bent his head to re-read the lengthy cable. Presently he said, 'Well, that's cleared up. It was a hell of a problem while it lasted.'

'What was?' asked Harding interestedly.

'When Denison was lifted from the sauna he came out with a string of mathematical stuff to confuse the opposition. He didn't know what it meant himself but it was the jargon Meyrick might have used.' He tossed the cable on to the table. 'We couldn't see how Denison could possibly have known it.'

Harding said, 'It must have come out of his past somewhere.'

'Precisely,' said Carey. 'But he didn't have that kind of past.'

'Of course not.' Harding wrinkled his brow. 'He was a film director.'

'Of a special kind,' said McCready. 'He made documentaries. We found he'd done a series of educational films on mathematics for the public relations department of one of the big computer firms. I suppose a film director must have a working knowledge of his subject although, judging by some of the movies I've seen, you wouldn't think so. Anyway, somebody talked to the computer people and we find that not only did he have a ready grasp but a keen interest. The films were largely in cartoon style and the subject was probability theory. He knew the jargon, all right.'

'But it gave me a shudder at the time,' said Carey. 'Mrs Hansen, ring the hotel and find what's keeping Denison.'

Diana Hansen got up and crossed the room. She was about to pick up the telephone when it rang shrilly. She put it to her ear, then beckoned to Carey. 'For you – it's Armstrong.'

Carey took the telephone. 'Ian, what's the hold-up?'

'I was in my room,' said Armstrong. 'I had my door open so I could see the door of Denison's room. About twenty minutes ago Miss Meyrick busted out of there fast so I went into the corridor to find what was happening. She grabbed me and said Denison had had some kind of attack. I went into the room and found him on the floor, out cold. He came round about five minutes ago.'

'Is he all right now?'

'He says he is.'

'Then you'd better bring him along here,' said Carey. 'I'll have Harding have a look at him.'

There was a pause. 'Miss Meyrick says she's coming, too.'

'Nothing doing,' said Carey. 'Ditch her.'

'I don't think you understand,' said Armstrong. 'When she spoke to me in the corridor she said *Denison* had had an attack – not Meyrick.'

Carey's eyebrows crawled up his forehead. 'She *knows*?'

'Apparently so.'

'Bring her along and don't take your eyes off the pair of them. And be discreet.' He put down the telephone. 'The girl has caught on – and your patient is coming home to roost, Harding. He's had another of his thingummy attacks.'

'A fugue,' said Harding. 'It must have been the Meyrick girl.'

'She called him Denison,' said Carey flatly.

They waited for twenty minutes in silence. Carey produced his pipe and filled it, and then smoked jerkily. Harding stretched out his long legs and contemplated the tips of his shoes with an all-consuming interest. His forehead was creased into a frown. Diana Hansen smoked cigarettes one after the other, stubbing each out half-way down its length. McCready paced back and forward, wearing a groove in the carpet.

There was a tap at the door and everyone jerked to attention. McCready opened it, letting in Lyn and Denison, with Armstrong close behind. Carey stared at Denison. 'Harding would like a word with you in the other room. Do you mind?'

'No,' said Denison quietly, and followed Harding.

When the door closed behind them Carey stood up and said to Lyn, 'Miss Meyrick, my name is Carey and I'm from the British Embassy here. This is Mr McCready. Mrs Hansen you already know, and you've already met Mr Armstrong.'

Lyn Meyrick's face was pale but two pink spots deepened in her cheeks when she saw Diana Hansen. Then she flung out her arm at the door through which Denison had gone. 'Who is that man? And where is my father?'

'Please sit down,' said Carey, and nodded to McCready who brought up a chair.

'I don't understand,' said Lyn. 'He said his name was Denison and he told me an unbelievable story . . .'

'. . . which happens to be true,' said Carey. 'I wish it wasn't so.'

Lyn's voice rose. 'Then what's happened to my father?'

Carey wagged his eyebrows at Diana Hansen who stood up and went close to Lyn. He said, 'Miss Meyrick, I'm sorry to tell you this . . .'

'He's dead, isn't he?'

Carey nodded. 'We believe it to be an accident. His body was recovered from the Baltic three days ago. There had been a collision between an oil tanker and another ship.'

'Then what this man, Denison, said is correct?'

'What did he tell you?'

They listened as Lyn spoke and finally Carey nodded. 'He seems to have given you all that's relevant.' He noted that Denison had not told her of the contents of Merikken's papers; he had just said they were important. 'I'm sorry about your father.'

'Yes,' she said coldly. 'I suppose you are.'

Carey thought that she found no difficulty in holding back her grief but that might be understandable in the circumstances. He said deliberately, 'Miss Meyrick; after Denison had told you his story did you try to probe into his past?'

'Why, yes; I wanted to know who he was – who he is.'

'You must never do that again,' said Carey solemnly. 'It could be most dangerous for him.'

She flared up. 'If only a quarter of what he told me is true, what you're doing to that man is despicable. He ought to have psychiatric treatment.'

'He's getting that now,' said Carey. 'Dr Harding is a psychiatrist. How did Denison give himself away?' She told him and he nodded. 'We couldn't hope to get away with it for ever,' he said philosophically. 'But I did hope for another day. I was going to separate you tomorrow.'

'My God!' she said. 'Who the hell do you think you are? We're not chess pieces.'

'Denison is a volunteer,' said Carey. 'It's his own choice.'

'Some choice!' she said cuttingly.

The door behind Carey opened. He swung around in his chair and saw Harding alone. 'Ian, go and sit with Denison.'

'It won't be necessary,' said Harding. 'He'll be out in a minute. I've just given him something to think about.'

'How is he?'

'He'll be all right.'

'Does he remember spilling the beans to Miss Meyrick?'

'Oh, yes,' said Harding. 'It's just that he can't remember what Miss Meyrick was asking him just before he passed out.' He looked at Lyn with interest. 'What was it?'

'I wanted to know who he was,' Lyn said.

He shook his head. 'Don't try that again. I think I'll have to have a talk with you, young lady.'

'Don't bother,' said Carey grimly. 'She's going back to England.'

Lyn inspected Harding with a cold eye. 'Are you a doctor?'

Harding paused as he lit a cigarette. 'Among other things.'

'I think you must have been confused when you took the oath,' she said. 'You took the hypocritic oath instead of the Hippocratic oath.' Harding coloured but before he could answer she had rounded on Carey. 'As for going to England, I most certainly am. A lot of people will be very interested in what I have to tell them.'

'Oh, I wouldn't try that,' said Carey quietly.

'Try to stop me,' she challenged.

Carey leaned back in his chair and glanced at McCready. 'It looks as though we'll have to keep her here, George. Arrange the necessary – booking her out of the hotel and so on.'

'And then what?' she asked. 'You can't keep me here for ever. I'll be back in England some time and I'll make sure the story gets around about what's been happening to this man. It will make interesting reading.'

McCready smiled. 'The papers won't print it. There's a thing called a "D" notice.'

She looked at him contemptuously. 'Do you think twenty universities full of students will take any account of your stupid "D" notices?' she asked in scorn.

'My God!' said McCready.'She's right. You know what students are like.'

'So what are you going to do?' she asked interestedly. 'Kill me?'

'They're going to do nothing,' said Denison from behind Carey. He closed the door behind him. 'Or they'll have to get themselves another boy.'

Carey did not turn round. He merely said, 'Draw up a chair, Denison. We have a problem to solve.'

Denison sat next to Carey. 'Coercion won't solve it.'

'So I'm finding out,' said Carey caustically. 'So maybe we'll try persuasion. What exactly is it you want, Miss Meyrick?'

She was suddenly nervous. 'I want you to stop whatever it is you're doing to . . . to him.' Her hand trembled as she pointed at Denison.

'We're not doing anything to him. He's a volunteer – and he'll confirm it.'

She flared. 'How can he be a volunteer when he doesn't know who he is? Any court of law would toss out that argument.'

'Careful,' said Harding suddenly, watching Denison.

'He needs help,' she pleaded.

'He's getting it,' said Carey, and indicated Harding.

'You already know what I think of that.'

'Tell me something,' said Carey. 'Why are you so agitated about Denison? He is, after all, a stranger.'

She looked down at the table. 'Not any more,' she said in a low voice. She raised her head and regarded Carey with clear eyes. 'And aren't we supposed to care for strangers? Have you never heard of the parable of the Good Samaritan, Mr Carey?'

Carey sighed, and said dispiritedly, 'See what you can do, Giles.'

Denison opened his mouth and then closed it again. It was the first time Carey had addressed him by his Christian name, as he normally did with Armstrong and McCready.

Was he now accepted as a member of the team, or was it just that the cunning old devil had decided to use psychology?

He looked across the table at the girl. 'I know what I'm doing, Lyn – and this operation is very important.'

'How can you know what you're doing?' she demanded. 'You're not competent to judge.'

'That's just what he is,' interjected Carey. 'Sorry, Giles; carry on.'

'That's not the point,' said Denison. 'It wasn't of my own free will that I was pitched into the middle of all this, but now that I'm in it I agree with Carey. If the operation is to be a success then I must continue to be Meyrick – to be your father. And that I'm going to do, regardless of what you think. I appreciate your concern, but this is too important for considerations like that.'

She was silent, biting her lip. She said, 'All right, Har . . . Giles. But on one condition.'

'What's that?'

'That I come with you – as Lyn Meyrick with her father.' There was a dead silence around the table. 'Well, isn't that what you wanted – for the masquerade to go on? You've used me unknowingly – now you can use me knowingly.'

Carey said softly, 'It might be dangerous.'

'So is having a father like Harry Meyrick,' she said bitterly. 'But that's my condition – take it or leave it.'

'Taken,' said Carey promptly.

'No!' said Denison simultaneously.

They stopped and looked at each other. 'She's stubborn,' said Carey. 'And she's got us by the short hairs. It's the answer.'

'Are you sure?' asked Denison. He might have been replying to Carey but he looked at Lyn.

'I'm sure,' she said.

'Well, that's it,' said Carey briskly. 'Now we can get on with the planning. Thank you, Dr Harding; I don't think we'll need you on this. I'll keep in touch with you.'

Harding stood up and nodded. He was walking to the door when Lyn said, 'No!' Her voice was sharp.

Harding stopped. 'No *what*?' said Carey exasperatedly.

'Dr Harding stays with Giles,' she said. 'The three of us stay together.'

'For Christ's sake!' said Carey, and a suppressed snort came from McCready.

Harding had a white smile, 'My dear Miss Meyrick; I'm hardly . . . I'm no . . . no . . .'

'No guman, like the rest of them probably are? Well, let me tell you something. You won't be worth a damn as a psychiatrist unless you stay with your patient.'

Harding flushed again. Carey said, 'Impossible!'

'What's so impossible about it?' Lyn looked at Harding speculatively. 'But I'm willing to leave it to the doctor – and his conscience, if he has one. What about it, Dr Harding?'

Harding rubbed his lean jaw. 'Insofar as it will help Denison I'm willing to stay. But I warn you – I'm no man of action.'

'That's it, then,' said Lyn, parodying Carey.

Carey looked at her helplessly, and McCready said, 'It might not be a bad idea if the doctor is willing, as he seems to be.'

Carey gave up. 'Sit down, Harding,' he said ungraciously.

As he picked up his briefcase Denison murmured, 'You did say by the short hairs, didn't you?'

Carey ignored him and opened the briefcase. 'I have reason to believe that quite a lot of people are interested in the movements of Dr Meyrick. We're going to give them some movements to watch.'

He spread out a large map of Finland. 'George will fly to Ivalo in Northern Lapland – ' his finger stabbed down – 'here. That's as far north as you can fly in Finland. There'll be a car waiting and he'll drive still farther north to this place up by the Norwegian border – *Kevon Tutkimusasema* – that's a station for the exploration of the Kevo Nature Preserve, the jumping off place, as you might call it.'

He looked up at McCready. 'Your job is to cover the party from the outside. You'll inspect Kevo Camp, make sure it's clean – and I don't mean in the hygienic sense – and you'll keep an eye on the party all the time it's up there. But you won't acknowledge it – you'll be a stranger. Understand?'

'Got it,' said McCready.

'Denison and Mrs Hansen – and now, of course, Miss Meyrick and Dr Harding – will travel by car from Helsinki. You will leave early tomorrow and it will take you two days to get to the camp at Kevo. George will already be there but you *don't* recognize him. He's your trump card should you get into trouble.' Carey's finger moved slightly south. 'You will then explore the Kevo Nature Park. It's rough country and you'll need packs and tents.' He wagged a finger at McCready. 'We'll need extra gear; see to it, George.'

'What's the point of all this?' asked Denison.

Carey straightened. 'From my reading of Meyrick's dossier and from what I know of his character he never did take an interest in natural history. Is that correct, Miss Meyrick?'

'He was a pure technologist,' she said. 'If he ever thought of natural history – which I doubt – it would be with contempt.'

'As I thought,' said Carey. 'So if Meyrick becomes interested now it will be out of character. The people who are watching him – as I am certain they are – will be mystified and will suspect an ulterior motive, which I will be careful to provide.' He tapped Denison's arm. 'You'll take some simple instruments – a theodolite and so on – and you'll act out a charade as though you're looking for something. Got the idea?'

'A red herring,' said Denison.

'Right. You'll spend three days at Kevo and then you'll move south to another Nature Park at Sompio. There you will put on the same act until you're recalled.'

'How will that be done?' asked McCready.

'There's a little village called Vuotso just outside. I'll send you a telegram to *poste restante* – "Come home, all is forgiven." It would be useful to have webbed feet at Sompio – it's very marshy.'

'Then there'll be wildfowl,' said Harding with sudden enthusiasm.

'Very likely,' said Carey uninterestedly.

'Let me get this straight,' said Denison. 'Meyrick is supposed to be looking for something – let's say buried – in a Nature Park, but he doesn't know which one. And all he has to go on are landmarks, hence the theodolite for measuring angles.'

'Just like in a treasure hunt,' said Lyn.

'Precisely,' said Carey. 'But the treasure doesn't exist – at least, not up there. I've even got a map for you. It's as phoney as hell but very impressive.'

Denison said, 'And what will you be doing while we're wandering all over the Arctic?'

Carey grinned. 'Young Ian and I will nip into Svetogorsk to dig up the loot while, hopefully, all eyes are on you.' He turned to Mrs Hansen. 'You're very quiet.'

She shrugged. 'What's there to say?'

'You'll be bodyguarding this lot from the inside. I had hoped you'd have but one person to worry about but, as you see, there are now three. Can you manage?'

'If they'll do as they're told.'

'They'd better,' said Carey. 'I'll give you something a bit bigger than the popgun you so incautiously let Denison see.' He looked about. 'Can anyone else here shoot?'

'I'm not bad with a shotgun,' said Harding.

'I doubt if a shotgun in a Nature Preserve would be appreciated,' said Carey ironically. 'But at least you'll know one end of a gun from the other. I'll let you have a pistol. What about you, Giles?'

Denison shrugged. 'I suppose I can pull the trigger and make the thing go bang.'

'That might be all that's needed.' Carey looked at Lyn, appeared to be about to say something, and changed his mind.

'Are you expecting shooting?' asked Harding. He looked worried.

'Let me put it this way,' said Carey. 'I don't know if there'll be shooting or not, but if there is, I hope you'll be on the receiving end and not me, because that's the object of this bloody exercise.' He put the map back into his brief-case. That's all. Early start tomorrow. George, I'd like a word with you before you go.'

The group at the table broke up. Denison went across to Lyn. 'Harding told me about your father. I'm sorry.'

'No need,' she said. 'I ought to feel sorry, too, but I can't.' She looked up at him. 'Carey said you are a stranger, but it's my father who was the stranger. I hadn't seen him for two years and when I thought I'd found him again, and he was different and nicer, I hadn't found him at all. So then I lost him again and it made no difference, after all. Don't you see what I mean?'

Denison followed this incoherent speech, and said, 'I think so.' He took her by the shoulders. 'I don't think you should come on this jaunt, Lyn.'

Her chin came up. 'I'm coming.'

He sighed. 'I hope you know what you've got yourself into.'

Carey filled his pipe. 'What do you think, George?'

'The girl's a bit of a handful.'

'Yes. Look after them as best you can.'

McCready leaned forward. 'It's you I'm worried about. I've been thinking about Meyrick. If the people who snatched him were the Russkies, and if he talked, you're in dead trouble. You're likely to find a reception committee awaiting you in Svetogorsk.'

Carey nodded. 'It's a calculated risk. There were no signs of physical coercion on Meyrick's body – burn marks or anything like that – and I doubt if he'd talk voluntarily. I don't think they had time to make him talk; they were too busy smuggling him around the Baltic. In any case, we don't know who snatched him.'

He struck a match. 'It's my back I'm worried about right now. I had a talk to Lyng last night on the Embassy scrambler. I told him that Thornton was nosing about. He said he'd do something about it.'

'What?'

Carey shrugged. 'They don't use guns in Whitehall but I believe they have weapons that are equally effective. It's no concern of yours, George; you won't have to worry about the Whitehall War until you get up to my level.'

'I'm not so worried about Whitehall as I am about Svetogorsk,' said McCready. 'I think it ought to be swapped around. Armstrong can go north and I'll come with you acioss the border.'

'He doesn't have the experience for what might happen up there. He's yet to be blooded, but he'll be all right with an old dog like me.'

'He'd be all right with me,' said McCready. 'He and I could cross the border and you could go north.'

'Sorry,' said Carey regretfully. 'But I'm pushing sixty and I don't have the puff for that wilderness lark. And I don't have the reflexes for the fast action you might get. The plan stands, George.' His voice took on a meditative note. 'This is likely to be my last field operation. I'd like it to be a good one.'

TWENTY-THREE

The car slowed as it came to the corner. Harding, who was driving, said, 'This might be the turn-off. Check it on the map, will you?'

Denison, in the back of the car, lifted the map from his knee. 'That's it; we've just passed Kaamanen. The Kevo Camp is eighty kilometres up this side road and there's damn-all else.' He checked his watch. 'We ought to arrive before eleven.'

Harding turned on to the side road and the car lurched and bumped. After a few minutes he said, 'Make that midnight. We're not going to move fast on this road.'

Diana laughed. 'The Finns are the only people who could coin a word like *kelirikko*. It's a word Humpty-Dumpty would be proud of.'

Harding notched down a gear. 'What does it mean?'

'It means, "the bad state of the roads after the spring thaw".'

'Much in little,' said Harding. 'There's one thing I'm glad of.'

'What's that?'

'This midnight sun. I'd hate to drive along here in the dark.'

Denison glanced at Lyn who sat by his side. She was apparently asleep. It had been two days of hard driving, very tiring, and he was looking forward to his bed. He wound the window down to clear the dust from the outside surface, then looked at the countryside covered with scrub birch. Something suddenly caught him in the pit of the stomach. *What the hell am I doing here? Hundreds of miles north of the Arctic Circle in the Finnish wilderness?* It seemed preposterously improbable.

They had left Helsinki very early the previous morning and headed north out of the heavily populated southern coastal rim. Then they had left the rich farmlands very quickly and entered a region of forests and lakes, of towering pine and spruce, of white-trunked, green-leaved birch and the ever-present blue waters.

They took it in turns driving in two-hour shifts and made good time, sleeping that night in Oulu. After Oulu the land changed. There were fewer lakes and the trees were not as tall. A birch that in the south towered a hundred feet now had hardly the strength to grow to twenty, and the lakes gave way to marshes. As they passed through Ivalo, where there was the northernmost airstrip, they encountered their first Lapps, garish in red and blue, but there were really very few people of any kind in this country. Denison, under the prodding of Carey, had done his homework on Finland and he knew that in this most remote area of the country, Inari Commune, there were fewer than 8,000 people in a province the size of Yorkshire.

And there would be fewer still around Kevo.

Diana stretched, and said, 'Stop at the top of the next rise, Doctor; I'll spell you.'

'I'm all right,' said Harding.

'Stop anyway.'

He drove up the hill and was about to pull up when Diana said, 'Just a few yards more – over the crest.' Harding obligingly let the car roll and then braked to a halt. 'That's fine,' she said, taking binoculars from a case. 'I won't be a minute.'

Denison watched her leave the car and then opened his own door. He followed her back along the road and then into a growth of stunted birches. When he caught up with her she was looking back the way they had come through the glasses. 'Anything in sight?'

'No,' she said curtly.

'You've done this every hour,' he said. 'And you've still seen nothing. Nobody's following us.'

'They might be ahead,' she said without taking the glasses from her eyes.

'How would anyone know where we were going?'

'There are ways and means.' She lowered the glasses and looked at him. 'You don't know much about this business.'

'No, I don't,' Denison said reflectively. 'What's a nice girl like you doing in it? You're American, aren't you?'

She slung the binocular strap over her shoulder. 'Canadian. And it's just a job.'

'Just a civil servant,' he said ironically. 'Like any nine-to-five typist in Whitehall.' He remembered the occupation given in Meyrick's passport. 'Or like Dr Meyrick.'

She faced him. 'Let's get one thing straight. From now on you do not refer to Meyrick in the third person – not even in private.' She tapped him on the chest with her forefinger. 'You are Harry Meyrick.'

'You've made your point, teacher.'

'I hope so.' She looked around. 'This seems a quiet spot. How long is it since you've seen anyone?'

He frowned. 'About an hour. Why?'

'I want to find out how much you lot know about guns. Target practice time.' As they went back to the car, she said, 'Go easy on Lyn Meyrick. She's a very confused girl.'

'I know,' said Denison. 'She has every reason to be confused.'

Diana looked at him sideways. 'Yes,' she agreed. 'You could call it confusion – of a sort. It's not easy to fall in love with a man who looks like the father you hate, but she's managed it.'

Denison stopped dead. 'Don't be idiotic.'

'Me!' She laughed. 'You do a bit of thinking and then figure who's the idiot around here.'

Harding pulled the car off the road and into the trees. Diana loaded a pistol from a packet of cartridges and set an empty beer can on a fallen tree trunk. 'All right; let's see who can do this.' Almost casually she lifted her arm and fired. The beer can jumped and spun away.

They took it in turns to fire three shots each. Denison missed every time, Harding hit the can once and Lyn, much to her own surprise, hit it twice. Diana said to Denison caustically, 'You were right; you can make the gun go bang.'

To Lyn she said, 'Not bad – but what would you be like shooting at a man instead of a beer can?'

'I . . . I don't know,' said Lyn nervously.

'What about you, Doctor?'

Harding hefted the gun in his hand. 'If I was being shot at I think I'd shoot back.'

'I suppose that's as much as I could expect,' said Diana resignedly. 'Let's go back to the car.'

She gave them each a pistol and watched them load. 'Don't forget to put on the safety catch. More important, don't forget to release it when you shoot. You'll put those in your bedrolls now. When we move off on foot tomorrow you'll need a more accessible place for them. Let's go.'

TWENTY-FOUR

Carey lit his pipe and said, 'Slow down.'

Armstrong eased his foot on the accelerator and hastily wound down his side window. He wished Carey would not smoke at all in the car or, at least, change his brand of horse manure.

'See that tower over there?' asked Carey. 'To the right.'

Armstrong looked past him. 'A water tower?' he hazarded.

Carey grunted in amusement. 'A Russian observation tower. That's Mother Russia.'

'We're *that* close to the frontier! It can't be more than a kilometre away.'

'That's right,' said Carey. 'You can turn round now; we'll go back to Imatra and book into the hotel.'

Armstrong came to a wide part of the road and slowed to a halt. As he turned the car, he said, 'Are there many of those towers around here?'

'All along the frontier. I suspect they're linked with electronic detection devices. The boys in those towers can record every footfall.' He looked at the spindly tower with a critical eye. 'The Russians have a suspicious nature – always trying to look over other people's walls. They're a funny crowd.'

Armstrong was silent, but his mind was busy with speculation. The trouble with Carey was that he was uncommunicative about his plans until the last moment, an idiosyncrasy apt to unnerve his subordinates. He wondered how they were going to cross the border.

He drove back into Imatra under Carey's direction and pulled up outside the entrance to the hotel. It was a big, rambling building constructed of stone with turrets and cupolas and towers. He thought it looked like a fairy tale castle as designed by Walt Disney had he been a more controlled artist. 'Some place!'

'The Valtionhotelli,' said Carey. 'Built at the turn of the century and genuine Art Nouveau. Come on.'

The hotel foyer was elaborately luxurious in an old-fashioned style. The stonework of the entrance was carved with grotesque mythological beasts and was panelled in dark wood. They registered and entered a lift accompanied by a porter carrying the bags.

The porter unlocked a door and stood back deferentially. Carey strode in, followed by Armstrong. He led the way along a wood-panelled corridor into a very large circular bedroom. 'I'll take the bed on the left,' he said as he tipped the porter.

Armstrong looked about him. 'Not bad. Not bad at all.'

'Nothing but the best for us civil servants,' said Carey. 'Let's go upstairs and have a drink.'

'There's an upstairs?'

They climbed a broad winding staircase leading off the corridor. Carey said, 'This hotel was built back in 1902 when Finland was still a part of Russia. The Finns will give you arguments that it was never a part of Russia, but facts are facts. Imatra was a playground for the St Petersburg aristocracy. The Czar stayed in the hotel – probably in this apartment.'

They emerged into another large circular room with windows all round. It was furnished with half a dozen easy-chairs and a long, low table of highly polished wood. A bear skin decorated the wall. Carey strode over to a built-in refrigerator while Armstrong looked through one of the windows. 'We must be at the top of the main tower.'

'That's right.' Carey pulled out a bottle. 'Skâne – that's Swedish; Linie – it's funny the Norwegians think that shipping their booze to Australia and back improves it. Koskenkorva – that's local. Stolichnaya – what the hell is that doing here? I call it damned unpatriotic. Ah, here's the beer.'

Armstrong turned and looked at the array of *snaps* bottles. 'Are we expected to be poured into Russia?'

Carey winked. 'The perquisites of the job. Besides, we might have to do a little entertaining.'

'Oh!' He held out field glasses he had found on a window ledge. 'Someone must have left these behind.'

Carey shook his head as he uncapped a beer bottle. 'Part of the room fittings. This apartment is where they bring the V.I.P.s to give them a little thrill.' He picked up a glass and joined Armstrong at the window. 'See those chimneys?'

Armstrong looked out of the window at the smoking factory chimneys. 'Yes?'

'That's Stalin's Finger,' said Carey. 'Svetogorsk!'

Armstrong put the binoculars to his eyes. The chimneys jumped closer and he could almost distinguish the separate bricks. 'My God!' he said. 'It's nearly part of Imatra.' He stared for a long time then slowly lowered the glasses. 'What did you say about Stalin?'

'Stalin's Finger – that's the local name. After the war the Russians wanted the frontier pushed back so there was the usual conference. Svetogorsk – or Enso, as it was then – is quite a nice little industrial town making paper. One of the Russians was drawing the revised frontier with a pen on the map but when he got to Enso he found that Stalin had put his finger in the way. He looked up at Stalin and Stalin smiled down on him, so he shrugged and drew the line around Stalin's finger. That put Enso in Russia.'

'The old bastard!' said Armstrong.

'Sit down and have a beer,' said Carey. 'I want to talk to you about procedure. I'll just nip down and get my briefcase.'

Armstrong took a beer from the refrigerator. When Carey came back he indicated the bear skin on the wall. 'Could that be a Russian bear with its hide nailed to the wall?'

'It could,' said Carey with a grim smile. 'That's part of what I want to talk to you about.' He put the briefcase on the table and sat down. 'As far as I'm concerned Svetogorsk is Svetogorsk – I'm a realist. But we'll be talking to some Finns and we'll refer to the town throughout as Enso. They're a mite sensitive about it.'

'I can understand that,' said Armstrong.

'You don't know the half of it,' said Carey flatly. 'This has been my stamping ground all the time I've been in the service, so listen to some words of wisdom from the old man. Back in 1835 a man called Lönnrot gathered together a lot of folk tales and issued them in verse form – that was the Kalevela, the Finnish national epic. It was the first major literary work the Finns ever had of their own, and it formed the basis of the new Finnish culture.'

'Interesting,' said Armstrong. 'But what the hell?'

'Just listen,' said Carey sharply. 'The heartland of the Kalevela is Karelia – which is now in Russia. The village of Kalevela itself is now Russian.' He rubbed the side of his nose. 'There's no exact English parallel, but it's as though the French had occupied Cornwall and Nottingharnshire and taken over all the King Arthur and Robin Hood legends. Of course, it runs deeper than that here, and some Finns are bitter about it.'

'They think the Russians pinched their national heritage?'

'Something like that.' Carey drained his glass. 'Now to politics. After the war President Paasikivi adopted a foreign policy that was new to Finland, and the idea was to remain strictly neutral, rather like Sweden. In actual practice it's a neutrality in favour of Russia – at all costs no offence must be given to Big Brother in the east. This is known as the Paasikivi Line, and it's followed by the current President, Kekkonen. It's like walking a tightrope but it's difficult to see what else Finland can do. They already have the example of what happened to Estonia and the other Baltic States.'

He got himself another beer. 'We're going to meet some Finns tonight who don't agree with the Paasikivi Line. They're Right Wingers and, personally, I'd call them bloody reactionaries, but they're the boys who are going to get us into Enso. If Kekkonen knew what we were doing here, what little hair he has left would turn white. He's getting on with the Russians reasonably well and he wants it to stay that way. He doesn't want any incident on the frontier that could cause a diplomatic breach and give Moscow an excuse for making demands. Neither do we – so to the Finns we meet tonight we talk softly, and when we're in Enso we walk softly.'

He fixed Armstrong with a firm eye. 'And if we're caught over there we've done it on our own hook – no Finns were involved. That's bloody important, so keep it in mind.'

'I understand,' said Armstrong soberly.

'Of course, the whole idea is *not* to get caught' Carey unzipped his briefcase. 'Here is a street plan of Enso, dated 1939.' He unfolded it and spread it on the table. His finger wandered over the surface and then went down. 'This is the house in which Hannu Merikken lived. He buried his box full of papers in the garden which is something under half an acre – but not much under,'

Armstrong bent his head over the plan. 'That's quite an area. How big is the box?'

'Meyrick described it as two feet by one-and-a-half by one.'

Armstrong did some mental, arithmetic. 'If we dug a hole at random the chances against hitting it would be over eight hundred to one.'

'We can do better than that,' said Carey. 'The original idea was to have Meyrick point out the spot – he was present when the box was buried. But after all these years his memory had slipped a few cogs.' He dipped into the briefcase again. 'All he could come up with was this.'

Armstrong examined the large scale plan which was drawn meticulously in Indian ink. Carey said, 'There are four trees and the box is buried under one of them but he couldn't remember which one.'

'At least that's cutting it down to a maximum of four holes.'

'1944 is a long time ago,' said Carey. 'Three of the trees are no longer there. Look at these.' He produced some photographs. 'These were taken by our Finnish friends about three weeks ago.' As Armstrong looked at them, Carey said, 'I had hoped that taking Meyrick back would jog his memory, but we don't have Meyrick any more, so what we're left with is half an acre of ground and one tree.' He peered over Armstrong's shoulder and pointed, 'I think that's the one, but I'm not sure.'

'So we dig,' said Armstrong. 'It will have to be done under cover of darkness.'

Carey stared at him. 'What darkness? I know we're not in the Arctic Circle, but even so, there's precious little darkness at this time of year. The most we'll get is a deep twilight.'

'Do we have to jump in now?' asked Armstrong. 'Why not wait until later in the year?'

Carey sighed. 'Apart from the fact that these papers are of overwhelming importance, there's one very good reason why we have to go in now.' He tapped the street plan. 'When Merikken was living in this house it was in a good class suburb. But Enso has been expanding, the area has become run-down, and it's due for redevelopment. The bulldozers will be moving in before the autumn. We've got to get in first.'

'A pity Meyrick didn't make his great discovery a year earlier,' commented Armstrong. 'Anyone living in the house?'

'Yes; a Russian called Kunayev – he's a foreman in one of the paper mills. A wife and three children; one cat – no dogs.'

'So we just go along and start to dig holes all over his garden in broad daylight. He's going to like that!' Armstrong tossed down the photograph. 'It's impossible!'

Carey was unperturbed. 'Nothing is impossible, my lad. To begin with, the papers are in a tin trunk. That's a misnomer – a tin trunk is made of sheet steel and I have a natty metal detector, small but efficient.'

'Like a mine detector?'

'Something like that, but smaller. Small enough for us to take over the border without much risk. I had it specially made up. According to Meyrick's dicey memory there's not much more than two feet of earth on top of the box. I've tested this gadget with a smaller box and even three feet under it gives a signal that blasts your eardrums.'

'So we get the signal and start to dig. What's Kunayev going to be doing while this is happening?'

Carey grinned. 'With a bit of luck he won't be there. The comrade will be toiling like a Stakhanovite in his bloody mill, reeling up the toilet paper, or whatever it is he does.'

'His wife will be there,' objected Armstrong. 'And his kids – and probably the next-door neighbours.'

'It won't matter. We'll take them all by the hand and lead them right up that bloody garden path.'

TWENTY-FIVE

The meeting with the Finns took place that night in a house on the outskirts of Imatra. 'There are three of them,' said Carey, as they drove towards the rendezvous. 'Lassi Virtanen and his son, Tarmo, and Heikki Huovinen.'

Armstrong giggled, perhaps more out of nervous tension than anything else. 'I never thought I'd meet the Son of Lassie.'

'If you have any more remarks like that left in your system bottle them up until this operation is over,' said Carey grittily. 'This particular crowd doesn't have a strong sense of humour. Old Virtanen was a fighter pilot during the war and he still reckons it's a bad thing the Germans lost. I still don't know which is topmost in him – the Nazi sympathizer or the Russian-hater – probably a fifty-fifty mixture of both. He's brought up his son in his own image. Huovinen is a shade more liberal, but still well to the right of Atilla the Hun. These are the tools we have to work with and I don't want them turning in my hand. Remember that.'

'I'll remember,' said Armstrong. He felt as though Carey had suddenly thrown a bucket of ice water over him. 'What's the scheme?'

'The Finns are expert paper makers,' said Carey. 'And the Russians are quite willing to take advantage of their expertise. They're building a new paper mill in Enso; all the machinery is Finnish and the installation is done by Finns, most of whom live in Imatra. They go over the border every day.'

A great light broke on Armstrong. 'And we go with them. How convenient.'

Carey grunted. 'Don't shout too soon. It won't be as easy as all that.' He pointed. 'There's the house.'

Armstrong drew the car to a halt. 'Do these three go over to Enso?'

'That's it.'

Armstrong thought for a moment. 'If the Virtanens hate the Russians so much why do they help them build paper factories?'

'They belong to a half-baked secret society – very right wing, of course. They fondly believe they're spying and preparing for *Der Tag.*' Carey shrugged. 'It's my belief they're at the end of their rope and the government is going to hang them with it. One of the troubles with the Paasikivi Line is keeping to the middle ground between right and left. The government can't crack down too hard on the communists because of Russian pressure, but who the hell cares what happens to a lot of neo-Nazis? They're only left loose as a makeweight on the other end of the political see-saw, but if they get out of line they get the chop. So let's use them while we can.'

Lassi Virtanen was a hard-faced man in his middle-fifties who walked with a limp. His son, Tarmo, was about thirty and did not look much like his father, he was fresh-faced and his eyes sparkled with excitement. Armstrong measured him carefully and thought he would be too excitable to be relied on for anything important. Heikki Huovinen was dark with a blue chin. To look respectable he would have to shave twice a day but, to Armstrong's eye, he seemed not to have shaved for two days.

They sat around a table on which there was an array of dishes, the open sandwiches of Scandinavia. There were also a dozen bottles of beer and two bottles of a colourless spirit. They sampled the herring and then the elder Virtanen filled small glasses with the spirit, and raised his glass slightly. '*Kippis!*' His arm went up and he threw the contents of his glass down his throat.

Armstrong took his cue from Carey and did the same. The fierce spirit bit the back of his throat and burned in his belly. Carey put down his empty glass. 'Not bad,' he said. 'Not bad at all' He spoke in Swedish for the benefit of Armstrong. Finding Finnish speakers for the Service was the very devil and it was fortunate that Swedish was the second language of Finland.

Tarmo Virtanen laughed. 'It's from the other side.'

'Their vodka is the only good thing about the Russians,' said Lassi Virtanen grudgingly. He refilled the glasses. 'Heikki is worried.'

'Oh!' Carey looked at Huovinen. 'What about?'

'It's not going to be easy,' said Huovinen.

'Of course it'll be easy,' said Lassi. 'Nothing to it.'

'It's all right for you,' said Huovinen. 'You won't be there. It's me who has to come up with all the explanations and excuses.' He turned to Carey. 'It can't be done for three days.'

'Why not?'

'You and your friend, here, are taking the place of the Virtanens – right? Well, the Virtanens have got work to do over there – I know, I'm their damned foreman. Tomorrow Lassi is working on the screening plates, but Tarmo hasn't much to do and he wouldn't be missed. The day after that Tarmo will be busy. The only time I can spare them both without too many questions being asked will be the day after, and even then I'll have to tell a hell of a lot of lies.'

Carey thought Huovinen was getting cold feet but not by any sign did he show it. He said, 'What about it, Lassi?'

'It's true enough – as far as it goes – but it doesn't have to be that way. Heikki, you could fix things so that no one works on the screens tomorrow. A little bit of sabotage?'

'Not with that Georgian bastard Dzotenidze, breathing down my neck,' said Huovinen heatedly.

'Who's he?' asked Carey.

'The Chief Engineer for the Russians. He'll be Chief Engineer of the mill when it gets working, and he wants everything right. He watches me like a hawk.'

'No sabotage,' said Carey flatly. 'I want things to go right, too.'

Huovinen nodded vigorously. 'In three days,' he said. 'Then I can conveniently lose the Virtanens.'

Carey said, 'We'll come here in the evening the day after tomorrow. We'll spend the night here and we'll leave in the morning just as the Virtanens would. Won't the rest of the crew be surprised at a couple of strangers joining it?'

'That's taken care of. They may be surprised, but they won't talk.' Huovinen drew himself up. 'They're Finns,' he said proudly. 'They're Karelians.'

'And you're a foreman.'

Huovinen smiled. 'That's got something to do with it, too.'

Carey regarded Lassi and Tarmo Virtanen. 'And you two will stay in the house that day and you won't go out. We don't want anyone asking questions about how in hell can you be in Imatra and Enso at the same time.'

Young Virtanen laughed and tapped the bottle of vodka. 'Leave us plenty of this and we won't go out.'

Carey frowned, and Lassi said, 'We'll stay in the house.'

'Very well. Did you get the clothing?'

'It's all here.'

Carey took two folded cards from his pocket. 'These are our passes – will you check them?'

Huovinen picked them up and studied them. He took out his own pass for comparison, then said. 'These are very good; very good, indeed. But they look new – they're too clean.'

'We'll dirty them,' said Carey.

Huovinen shrugged. 'It doesn't really matter. The frontier guards have got tired of looking at passes. You'll be all right.'

'I hope so,' said Carey drily.

Lassi Virtanen picked up his glass. 'That's settled. I don't know exactly what you're doing over there, Mr Englishman, but I know it will do *Ryssä* no good. *Kispps!*' He knocked back his vodka.

Carey and Armstrong both drank and immediately Virtanen replenished their glasses. Armstrong looked about the room and saw a photograph on the sideboard. He tipped his chair back to get a closer look and Lassi, following his gaze, laughed and got up. 'That's from the Continuation War,' he said. 'I had fire in my belly in those days.'

He passed the photograph over to Armstrong. It showed a much younger Lassi Virtanen standing next to a fighter aircraft decorated with the swastika insignia. 'My Messerschmitt,' said Virtanen proudly. 'I shot down six Russian bastards in that plane.'

'Did you?' said Armstrong politely.

'Those were the good days,' said Virtanen. 'But what an air force we had. Any aircraft that had been built anywhere in the world – we had it. American Brewsters and Curtis Hawks, British Blenheims and Gladiators, German Fokkers and Dorniers, Italian Fiats, French Morane-Saulniers – even Russian Polikarpovs. The Germans captured some of those in the Ukraine and sent them to us. Unreliable bastards they were, too. What a crazy, mixed-up air force we had – but we still held the Russians off until the end.'

He slapped his leg. 'I got mine in '44 – shot down near Räisälä and it took four of them to do it. That was behind the lines but I walked out with a bullet in my leg, dodging those dammed Russian patrols. Good days those were. Drink up!'

It was late before Carey and Armstrong were able to leave because they had to listen to a monologue from Virtanen about his war experiences, interspersed with glasses of vodka. But at last they got away. Armstrong got behind the wheel of the car and looked eloquently at Carey. 'I know,' said Carey heavily. 'Drunken and unreliable. I'm not surprised they're getting nowhere.'

'That man lives in the past,' said Armstrong.

'There's a lot like him in Finland – men who've never really lived since the war. Never mind the Virtanens – they're staying here. It's Huovinen we have to rely on to get to the other side.'

'He was packing the stuff away as though he wanted to start a drought in vodka,' said Armstrong dispiritedly.

'I know – but they're all we've got.' Carey took out his pipe. 'I wonder how McCready and company are doing up north. They can't be doing worse than we are.'

TWENTY-SIX

'I'm tired,' said Harding. 'But I don't think I'll sleep.'

Denison inspected the narrow patch of ground for stones before he unrolled his sleeping bag. He flicked an offender aside and said, 'Why not?'

'I can't get used to broad daylight in the middle of the night.'

Denison grinned. 'Why don't you prescribe yourself a sleeping pill?'

'I might do that.' Harding picked a blade of grass and chewed it. 'How are you sleeping these days?'

'Not bad.'

'Dream much?'

'Not that I can remember. Why?'

Harding smiled. 'I'm your resident head-watcher – appointed by that chit over there.' He nodded towards Lyn who was peering dubiously into a camp kettle.

Denison unrolled his sleeping bag and sat on it. 'What do you think of her?'

'Personally or professionally?'

'Maybe a bit of both.'

'She seems to be a well-balanced young woman.' There was amusement in Harding's voice. 'She certainly knew how to handle Carey – she caught him coming and going. And she jabbed me in a sore spot. She's very capable, I'd say.'

'She took her father's death pretty coolly.'

Harding threw away the blade of grass and lit a cigarette. 'She lived with her mother and stepfather and didn't have much to do with Meyrick apart from quarrelling. I'd say her attitude to her father's death was perfectly normal. She had other things to think about at the time.'

'Yes,' said Denison pensively.

'I don't think you need worry about Lyn Meyrick,' said Harding. 'She's used to making up her own mind – and the minds of others, come to that.'

Diana Hansen came down the hill looking trim and efficient in the neat shirt and the drab trousers which she wore tucked into the tops of field boots – a world removed from the cool sophisticate Denison had met in Oslo. She cast a look at Lyn and walked over to the two men. 'Time to do your bit with the theodolite, Giles.'

Denison scrambled to his feet. 'Are they still with us?'

'So I'm told,' said Diana. 'And there's another party. We're becoming popular. I'd go up on that ridge there – and stay in sight.'

'All right.' Denison took the theodolite out of its case, picked up the lightweight tripod, and walked up the hill in the direction Diana had indicated.

Harding smiled as he watched Denison's retreating figure. He thought that Lyn Meyrick would make up Denison's mind were she allowed to. From a psychiatric point of view it was most interesting – but he would have to have a word with the girl first. He got up and walked over to where Lyn was pumping the pressure stove.

Denison stopped on top of the ridge and set up the theodolite. He took the sheet of paper from his pocket, now much creased, and studied it before looking around at the view. This was the bit of fakery Carey had given him to make the deception look good. It had been written with a broad-nibbed pen – 'No ballpoints in 1944,' Carey had said –

and artificially aged. Across the top was scrawled the single word, *Luonnonpuisto* and below that was a rough sketch of three lines radiating from a single point with the angles carefully marked in degrees. At the end of each line was again a single word – *Järvi, Kukkula* and *Aukio* – going around clockwise. Lake, hill and gap.

'Not much to go on,' Carey had said. 'But it explains why you're wandering around nature preserves with a theodolite. If anyone wants to rob you of that bit of paper you can let him. Maybe we can start a trade in theodolites.'

Denison looked around. Below ran the thread of a small river, the Kevojoki, and in the distance was the blue water of a lake pent in a narrow valley. He bent his head and sighted the theodolite at the head of the lake. Every time he did this he had a curious sense of *déjà vu* as though he had been accustomed to doing this all his life. Had he been a surveyor?

He checked the reading on the bezel and sighted again on the hill across the valley and took another reading. He took a notebook from his pocket and worked out the angle between the lake and the hill, then he swept the horizon looking for a possible gap. All this nonsense had to look good because he knew he was under observation – Carey's red herring appeared to be swimming well.

It had been at lunchtime on the first day that Diana had said casually, 'We're being watched.'

'How do you know?' asked Denison. 'I've seen nobody.'

'McCready told me.'

McCready had not been in evidence at Kevo Camp and Denison had not seen him since Helsinki. 'Have you been talking to him? Where is he?'

Diana nodded across the lake. 'On the other side of the valley. He says that a party of three men is trailing us.'

Denison was sceptical. 'I suppose you have a walkie-talkie tucked away in your pack.'

She shook her head. 'Just this.' From the pocket of her anorak she took a small plate of stainless steel, three inches in diameter; it had a small hole in the middle. 'Heliograph,' she said. 'Simpler than radio and less detectable.'

He examined the double-sided mirror – that is what it amounted to – and said, 'How can you aim it?'

'I know where George McCready is now,' she said. 'He's just been signalling to me. If I want to answer I hold this up and sight on his position through the hole. Then I look at my own reflection and see a circle of light on my cheek where the sun comes through the hole. If I tilt the mirror so that the circle of light goes into the hole, then the mirror on the other side flashes light into George's eyes. From then on it's simply a matter of Morse code.'

Denison was about to experiment when she took the gadget from him. 'I told you we're being watched. I can get away with it by pretending to make up my face – you can't.'

'Has McCready any idea of who is watching us?'

She shrugged. 'He hasn't got near enough to find out. I think it's about time you started your act with the theodolite.'

So he had set up the theodolite and fiddled about checking angles, and had repeated the charade several times during the past two days.

Now he found what might, by a stretch of imagination, be called a gap and took the third reading. He calculated the angle, wrote it into his notebook, and put the notebook and the fake paper back into his pocket. He was dismantling the theodolite when Lyn came up the hill. 'Supper's ready.'

'Thanks,' he said. 'Hold this.' He gave her the theodolite. 'Did Diana say anything about another group following us?'

Lyn nodded. 'They're coming up from behind very fast, she says.'

'Where's the first group?'

'Gone on ahead.'

'We're like the meat in a sandwich,' Denison said gloomily. 'Unless it's all a product of Diana's imagination. I haven't seen anyone around – and I certainly haven't seen George McCready.'

'I saw him signalling this morning,' said Lyn. 'He was on the other side of the valley. I was standing next to Diana and saw the flash, too.'

Denison collapsed the tripod and they both set off down the hill. 'You and Harding have had your heads together lately. What do you find so interesting to talk about?'

She gave him a sideways glance. 'You,' she said quietly. 'I've been finding out about you; since I can't ask you I've been asking him.'

'Nothing bad, I hope.'

She smiled at him. 'Nothing bad.'

'That's a relief,' he said. 'What's for supper?'

'Bully beef stew.'

He sighed. 'I can't wait.'

TWENTY-SEVEN

McCready was desperately tired. He lay on a hillside in a grove of dwarf birch and watched the group of four men making their way up the valley on the other side of the river. He had had very little sleep in the last two days and his eyes were sore and gritty. He had long since come to the conclusion that it needed two men to do this job.

He lowered the binoculars and blinked, then rubbed his eyes before checking on the camp on the top of the bluff across the river. There was a new figure on the rock above the camp which looked like Denison. At three in the morning there was quite enough light to see; the sun had skimmed the horizon at midnight and was already high in the sky. It seemed that Diana had insisted that a watch be kept.

He shifted his elbows and checked on the higher reaches of the valley and his mouth tightened as he saw a movement. The three men of the first party were coming down, keeping close to the river. Earlier he had crossed the river to scout their camp and, although he had not got close enough to hear clearly what they had been talking about, he had heard enough to know they were not Finns. Their tones had Slavic cadences and he had seen that they were very lightly equipped with no tents or even sleeping bags.

He switched his attention to the group of four who were coming up the valley. The two groups could not see each other because of a bend in the river where the water swirled around the bluff. He judged that if both groups kept up the same pace they would meet under the bluff and just below Denison.

McCready frowned as he watched. If the first group was under-equipped the second was well-outfitted to the point of decadent luxury. He had watched them stop for a meal and had seen what seemed to be a collapsible barbecue. Two of the men carried coils of rope as though they might expect rock climbing. Maybe Finns, he had thought, but now he was not so certain; not even Finns made route marches at three a.m.

At the time he had first seen the second group he had been too far away to distinguish faces, but now the men were nearer and he had a better chance. As he waited patiently he pondered over the differences between the two parties and came to the conclusion that they were indeed quite separate. Two minutes, later he was sure of it when he saw the face of the leading man of the four.

It was Jack Kidder, the big loud-mouthed American who had cropped up in Oslo and, later, in Helsinki.

Whatever the first group had been speaking it had been neither Finnish nor English. It was reasonable to assume that not only were the two parties quite distinct but also that neither knew of the existence of the other. Even more interesting, they were going to run into each other within twenty minutes.

McCready put down the binoculars and twisted around to open the pack which lay beside him. He took out what appeared to be the stock of a rifle and slapped open the butt plate which was hinged. From inside the hollow glassfibre stock he took out a barrel and a breech action and, within thirty seconds, he had assembled the rifle.

He patted the stock affectionately. This was the Armalite AR-7, originally designed as a survival rifle for the American Air Force. It weighed less than three pounds and was guaranteed to float in water whether knocked down or ready to fire, but what made it suitable for his purpose was the fact that, stripped down, it measured less than seventeen inches in length and so could be smuggled about unobtrusively in a back pack.

He inserted a magazine containing eight rounds of long rifle and put another clip in his pocket, then he crawled backwards out of the grove of trees and began to make his way down to the river along a ravine he had previously chosen for the eventuality. He came out to the river's edge opposite the bluff and right on the bend of the river, and took shelter behind boulders which a long-gone glacier had left in its passage.

From his position on the outside bend of the river he could see both groups although neither, as yet, was aware of the other. He looked at the bluff and could not see Denison who was farther back up the hill. Nothing like adding confusion, he thought, as he raised the rifle to firing position.

As both groups were about to round the bend he fired, not at Kidder but just in front of him, and the sand spurted at Kidder's feet. Kidder yelled and rolled sideways and, as if by magic, all four men disappeared.

McCready did not see that sudden transformation of the scene; he had already turned and slammed another shot at the leading man of the trio which ricocheted off a rock by his head. The man ducked instinctively and went to ground fast, but not so fast that McCready did not see the pistol that suddenly appeared in his hand.

McCready withdrew into his niche like a tortoise drawing its head into its shell and waited to see what would happen next.

Denison heard the shot from below and jerked to attention. Even before he took the second quick pace back to the camp he heard the flat report of the second shot which echoed from the hill behind him. Then there was no sound but the thudding of his boots on the rock.

He stooped to Diana's sleeping bag and found her already awake. 'Someone's shooting.'

'I heard. Wake the others.'

He roused Lyn and then went to Harding who, in spite of his pessimism, was fast asleep. 'Wassamatter?' he said drowsily, but came awake with a jerk as two more shots broke the early morning silence. 'What the hell?'

Diana was gesturing vigorously. 'Over the ridge,' she called. 'Away from the river.'

Harding hastily thrust his feet into his boots and cursed freely. Denison ran over to Diana who was helping Lyn. 'What about the gear?'

'Leave it. Leave everything except your gun. Get moving.'

He hauled Lyn to her feet and they ran for it, up the hill and over the top of the ridge, a matter of some three hundred yards. There they waited, breathless, until Diana and Harding caught up. Three more shots were fired in rapid succession, and Denison said, 'It sounds like a bloody battle.'

'We've got to get lost,' said Diana. 'There's cover over there.'

They ran for it.

On the other side of the river, at the water's edge, McCready watched and smiled. As he had figured, neither of the groups had time to find out where the shots had come from. They had taken cover immediately in the manner of professionals, and now they were dodging about on each side of the bluff in skirmish lines, ready for defence or attack. Kidder, on the left, caught a glimpse of a man on the right, and fired. He missed but, in firing, he exposed himself and someone took a shot at him. Another miss.

Kidder pulled back and unslung his pack which was hampering him. As the others did the same McCready smiled. A typical battle situation was developing in miniature. Kidder, to improve mobility, was divesting himself of supplies, which might be a good idea considering he outnumbered the opposition – although he could not know that. But if he lost and was overrun and had to retreat then his supplies would be lost.

McCready patted his rifle again and withdrew, to worm himself up the ravine and back into his original position in the stand of stunted trees. On the way he heard three more shots fired. He picked up the glasses and studied the situation. Denison was gone from the rock and the camp was deserted, so it was likely that they had pulled back over the hill and gone to ground, which was the sensible thing to do.

He looked down at the river. The narrow strip of sand between the bluff and the water's edge was held at each end by two men, and both sides were engaged in a classic outflanking action. Kidder and another man were climbing the bluff on the left, obviously intending to come out on top. There they would have the advantage of height and dropping fire as well as greater numbers.

The only snag was that the opposition was doing the same with one man and he had got the idea first. McCready, enjoying his grandstand seat, watched their progress with interest and estimated that the deserted camp on top of the bluff would be the next battleground. If the single man on the right could get himself established on top of the bluff before Kidder and his friend arrived he would stand a good chance despite the two to one odds.

Meanwhile the holding action at the bottom of the bluff continued with a desultory exchange of shots more to indicate the presence of opposition than to press an attack. McCready stroked his rifle, and thought, *How to Start a War in One Easy Lesson.* He hoped no small nation got the idea – using atomic missiles instead of rifle bullets.

The man on the right made it to the top while Kidder and his man still had twenty yards to go. He came up slowly, looked at the deserted camp, and then ducked for cover behind a rock. Kidder came up to the top and also surveyed the camp from cover, then gestured to the other man to crawl farther along.

He shouted – a thin cry that came to McCready across the river – and they both broke into the open, running across the top of the bluff. The man in cover fired and Kidder's companion spun away and fell among the rocks. Kidder dropped into cover and simultaneously there was a renewed outburst of fire from the base of the bluff to which McCready transferred his attention.

There had been a casualty on the other side and from the way the man nursed his arm McCready judged it to be broken. He beard a confused and distant shouting; Kidder was worming his way among the rocks in the direction of his wounded friend, and suddenly the other man on the bluff broke away and retreated.

Within fifteen minutes both sides were retreating in opposite directions, Kidder's group going down-river, one man limping heavily with a bullet in his leg, and the others heading up-river. Honours were even in an inconclusive engagement, and McCready thought that neither party knew just exactly what had happened.

Diana Hansen waited an hour after the last shot before making a move, then she said, 'I'll go and see what's happening.'

'I'll come with you,' said Denison.

She hesitated. 'All right. I'll go to the left, you go to the right. We move alternately, one covering the other.' She looked back at the others. 'You two give us general cover. If anyone shoots at us you start banging away fast; it doesn't matter if you don't hit anything – just make a lot of noise.'

She went first and Denison watched her as she zigzagged forward up to the top of the ridge. Half-way up she stopped and waved him forward and he did his best to imitate what she had done. He flopped down when he was parallel with her and wondered how she had learned a trade like this.

She was on the move again and this time she got to the top of the ridge where she could look down on the camp. At her hand signal he also went forward and peered cautiously around a rock. The camp was deserted and nothing appeared to have been touched; he could even see a gleam from the open theodolite case where he had left it, forgetting to close the top.

She wriggled over to him. 'I'll go around to the left – you to the right – we'll come in on the camp from two sides. Don't be in too much of a hurry, and don't shoot at the first thing that moves – it might be me.'

He nodded. She was just going away when he took another look at the camp and saw a movement. He grabbed her ankle as he ducked back. 'Someone down there,' he whispered.

She turned. 'Where?'

'By the rock where we kept watch.'

After a while Diana said, 'I don't see anyone.'

'I saw it,' said Denison. 'A movement by that rock.'

Again they waited and watched until Diana said, 'Must have been your imagination.'

Denison sighed. 'I suppose so.' His hand suddenly tightened on hers. 'No – look! On the other side now.'

The figure of a man came over the edge of the bluff, paused a little wearily, and then walked slowly towards the camp. When he got there he stared about him and unslung his pack.

Diana clicked with her tongue. 'It's George McCready,' she said, and stood up.

McCready looked as though he was ready to drop on his feet. His clothing was soaked and his boots squelched when he walked. He saw them coming but made no move to advance. Instead he sat down and began to unlace his boots. 'That bloody river,' he said. 'That's the third time I've crossed it.'

'What was all the shooting?' demanded Diana.

McCready described what had happened. 'One crowd was American; I don't know who the others were. The language sounded vaguely Slav.'

'Russian?'

'Could be,' said McCready. 'I hope so. If they're chasing us up here there's a good chance they won't be on to Carey.' He wrung out his socks. 'When I'm sixty I'll be an arthritic cripple.'

'So you set them fighting each other,' said Denison. 'I don't know if that Was a good idea. They might think it was us, and next time they'll come shooting.'

McCready nodded. 'Now's the time to lose them. The best way of doing that is to cross the river and go back on the other side. That will give us the three days that Carey wanted us here.'

'But we don't want to lose them,' objected Diana. 'That isn't the object.'

'I know,' said McCready. 'But I'd like to get back to the cars and away while they're licking their wounds. We can leave plenty of signs to indicate where we've gone. They'll beat around here for a while – if we're lucky they'll have another shooting match – and then they'll follow. It's still gaining time for Carey and it's less risk for us.'

Diana thought about it. 'All right.'

McCready cocked his head on one side and regarded Denison. 'The leader of the American mob was your old pal, Kidder.'

'Kidder!' said Denison incredulously.

'I thought he turned up a bit too opportunely in Helsinki,' said Diana. 'But the man sounded such a fool I discounted him.'

'If it's any consolation, so did I,' said McCready. 'But you know what it means – our cousins of the CIA are muscling in.' He took a pair of dry socks from a plastic bag. 'Unless he's a renegade or a double agent. I fancy the CIA myself.' He looked up at Denison who was deep in thought. 'What's the matter with you? You look as though you've just been sandbagged.'

'For God's sake!' said Denison. 'It was *Kidder*!' He shook his head in a bewildered manner. 'The man who questioned me after I was knocked out in the sauna. I thought I recognized the voice but I couldn't place it because the American accent had gone.'

'Are you sure?' Diana's voice was sharp.

'I'm certain. I didn't associate the man with Kidder because we'd left him behind in Oslo. He hadn't appeared in Helsinki at that time. Is it important?'

'Could be,' said McCready. 'There's one bunch who knows you're *not* Meyrick – the crowd who snatched you from Hampstead. But the man who questioned you assumed you were Meyrick. If it was Kidder then the CIA weren't responsible for the resculpting of that unlovely face of yours. All these bits of jigsaw come in handy.'

'Dr Harding and Lyn will be wondering what happened to us,' said Diana.

Denison turned. 'I'll bring them back.' He started to walk up to the top of the ridge but then veered over to the rock where he had kept watch. Something niggled at the back of his mind – he wondered how McCready could have got from one side of the camp to the other. The first movement he had seen from the top of the ridge had been by the rock, but McCready had come up the other side from the river.

Denison walked around the rock keeping his eyes on the ground. When McCready had come up his boots had been wet – waterfilled – and he had left a line of damp footprints over a smooth rock outcrop. Here there was also an outcrop but no footprints. He went to the other side of the rock and out of sight of Diana and McCready.

Something struck him on the back of the head and he felt a blinding pain and was driven to his knees. His vision swam and there was a roaring in his ears. The second thump on the head he did not feel but plunged headlong into darkness.

TWENTY-EIGHT

The bus rocked as it rolled along the narrow country road in the early morning. It was cold and Carey drew his coat closer about him. Armstrong, next to him, looked out of the window at the tall observation tower. It was drawing nearer.

The bus was full of Finns, most of whom were quiet at that early pre-work hour. Two seats ahead of Carey, on the aisle, sat Huovinen. He turned his head and looked back; his eyes were expressionless but Carey thought he could detect worry. Huovinen had been drinking again the previous night and Carey hoped his hangover did not get in the way of his efficiency.

Brakes squealed as the bus drew to a halt and Carey craned his neck to look through the forward windows. A soldier in Finnish uniform walked up and exchanged a few words with the driver, then he smiled and waved the bus on. It jerked into motion again.

Carey took out his pipe and filled it with steady hands. He nudged Armstrong, and said in Swedish, 'Why don't you have a cigarette? Have you stopped smoking?'

Armstrong looked at him in surprise, then shrugged. If Carey wanted him to smoke a cigarette then he would smoke a cigarette. He felt in his pocket and took out a half-empty packet of Finnish cigarettes as the bus stopped again.

The bus drived leaned out of the cab and called to the advancing Russian soldier, *'Kolmekymmentäkuusi.'* The soldier nodded and climbed into the bus by way of the passenger door and surveyed the work party. He looked as though he was doing a head count.

Carey struck a match and lit his pipe, cupping his hands about the bowl and shrouding the lower part of his face. He seemed to be doing his best to make a smokescreen. Armstrong caught on fast and flicked on his cigarette lighter, guarding the flame with his hand as though the draught from up front was about to blow it out.

The Russian left the bus and waved it on and it lurched forward with a clash of gears and rolled past the frontier post. Armstrong averted his face from the window as the bus passed an officer, a square man with broad Slavic features. He felt a sudden tightening in his belly as he realized he was in Russia. He had been in Russia many times before, but not as an illegal entry – and that had been the subject of a discussion with Carey.

Armstrong had argued for going into Russia quite legitimately through Leningrad. 'Why do we have to be illegal about it?' he asked.

'Because we'd have to be illegal anyway,' said Carey. 'We couldn't get to Enso legally – the Russkies don't like foreigners wandering loose about their frontier areas. And they keep a watch on foreigners in Leningrad; if you're not back at the Europa Hotel they start looking for you. No, this is the best way. Over the border and back – short and sharp – without them even knowing we've been there.'

Black smoke streamed overhead from the factory chimneys as the bus trundled through Enso. It traversed the streets for some minutes and then went through a gateway and halted outside a very long, low building. The passengers gathered up their belongings and stood up. Carey looked at Huovinen who nodded, so he nudged

Armstrong and they got up and joined the file behind Huovinen.

They went into the building through an uncompleted wall and emerged into an immense hall. At first Armstrong could not take in what he was seeing; not only was the sight unfamiliar but he had to follow Huovenin who veered abruptly to the right and out of the main stream. He led them around the end of a great machine and stopped where there was no one in sight. He was sweating slightly. 'I should be getting twice what you're paying me,' he said.

'Take it easy,' counselled Carey. 'What now?'

'I have to be around for the next hour,' said Huovenin. 'Laying out the work and a fifteen-minute conference with Dzotenidze. I have to put up with that every morning.' He coughed and spat on the floor. 'I can't lead you out before then.'

'So we wait an hour,' said Carey. 'Where?'

Huovinen pointed. 'In the machine – where else?'

Carey turned and looked at the half-constructed machine. Designed for continuous paper-making it was over three hundred yards long and about fifty feet wide. 'Get in the middle of there and take your coats off,' said Huovinen. 'I'll bring you some tools in about ten minutes. If anyone looks in at you be tightening bolts or something.'

Carey looked up at a crane from which a big steel roller hung. 'Just see that you don't drop that on my head,' he said. 'And don't be longer than an hour. Come on, Ivan.'

Armstrong followed Carey as he climbed inside the machine. When he looked back Huovinen had gone. They found a place where there was headroom and Carey took off his coat and looked around. 'In this snug situation a British working man would be playing cards,' he said. 'I don't know about the Finns.'

Armstrong bent and peered through a tangle of complexity. 'They're working,' he reported.

Carey grunted. 'Then let's look busy even if we're not.'

Presently a man walked by and stooped. There was a clatter of metal on concrete and footsteps hastened away. 'The tools,' said Carey. 'Get them.'

Armstrong crawled out and came back with a selection of spanners and a hammer. Carey inspected them and tried a spanner on the nearest bolt. 'What we do now,' he announced, 'is to take off this girder and then put it back – and we keep on doing that until it's time to go.' He applied the spanner to a nut and heaved, then paused with a thoughtful look on his face. 'Just pop your head up there and see what happens when we remove this bit of iron. I don't want the whole bloody machine to collapse.'

An hour and a half later they were walking through the streets of Enso. Armstrong still wore his overalls and carried a spade over his shoulder, but Carey had removed his and was now more nattily dressed. He wore, he assured Armstrong, the regulation rig of a local water distribution inspector. In his hand he carried, quite openly, the metal detection gadget. To Armstrong's approval it had a metal plate attached to it which announced in Russian that it was manufactured by Sovelectro Laboratories of Dnepropetrovsk.

As they walked they talked – discreetly and in Russian. Armstrong noted the old-fashioned atmosphere of the streets of Enso. It was, he thought, occasioned by the Russian style of dress and he could be in the nineteen-thirties. He always had that feeling when he was in Russia. 'I nearly had a heart attack when that bloody man wanted to know where Virtanen was,' he said.

It had been a tricky moment. The Chief Engineer, Dzotenidze, had stood by the machine quite close to them while he interrogated Huovinen as to the whereabouts of Lassi Virtanen. 'Those screens aren't right,' he said in Russian. 'Virtanen isn't doing his work properly.'

An interpreter transmitted this to Huovinen, who said, 'Virtanen hasn't been feeling too well lately. An old war wound. In fact, he's not here today – he's at home in bed.'

Dzotenidze had been scathing but there was nothing he could do about it. 'See that he's back on the job as soon as possible,' he said, and stalked away.

Armstrong said, 'I could have stretched out my hand and touched him.'

'Huovinen could have come up with a better story,' said Carey grimly. 'What happens if that engineer checks back and finds that the bus came in with a full crew? Still, there's nothing we can do about it.'

They walked on for five minutes in silence. Armstrong said, 'How much farther?'

'Not far – just around the corner.' Carey tapped him on the arm. 'Now, Ivan, my lad; you're a common working man, so let your betters do the talking. If you have to talk you're slow and half-witted and as thick as two planks as befits a man who wields an idiot stick.' He indicated the spade.

'The heroic worker, in fact.'

'Precisely. And I'm the technician controlling the magic of modern science and haughty to boot.' They turned the corner. 'There's the house.' Carey regarded it critically. 'It looks pretty run-down.'

'That's why it's being demolished.'

'Just so.' Carey surveyed the street. 'We'll start on the outside just for the sake of appearances – right here in the street.' He took a pair of earphones from his pocket and plugged the lead wire into a socket on the metal detector. 'Do I look technical enough?'

'Quite sweet,' said Armstrong.

Carey snorted and switched on the detector, then adjusted a control. Holding the detector close to the ground like a vacuum cleaner he walked along the pavement. Armstrong leaned on his spade and looked on with an expression of boredom. Carey went for about fifty yards and then came back slowly. There was a worried look on his face. 'I'm getting quite a few readings. This street must be littered with metal.'

'Maybe you've struck gold,' suggested Armstrong.

Carey glared at him. 'I'm not being funny,' he snarled. 'I hope to hell the garden of that house isn't the same.'

'You're arousing interest,' said Armstrong. 'The curtain just twitched.'

'I'll give it another run,' said Carey. He went through his act again and paused in front of the house, then took a notebook from his pocket and scribbled in it.

Armstrong lounged after him just as a small boy came out of the house. 'What's he doing?'

'Looking for a water pipe,' said Armstrong.

'What's that thing?'

'The thing that tells him when he's found a water pipe,' said Armstrong patiently. 'A new invention.' He looked down at the boy. 'Is your father at home?'

'No, he's at work.' The boy looked at Carey who was peering over the garden fence. 'What's he doing now?'

'I don't know,' said Armstrong. 'He's the expert, not me. Is your mother at home?'

'She's doing the wash. Do you want to see her?'

Carey straightened up. 'I think it runs through here,' he called.

'Yes,' said Armstrong. 'I think we do want to see her. Run inside and tell her, will you?' The boy dashed into the house and Armstrong went up to Carey. 'Kunayev is at work; Mrs K. is doing the wash.'

'Right; let's get to it.' Carey walked up to the front door of the house just as it opened. A rather thin and tired-looking woman stepped out. 'This is the . . . er – ' Carey took out his notebook and checked the pages – 'the Kunayev household?'

'Yes, but my husband's not here.'

'Then you'll be Grazhdanke Kunayova?'

The woman was faintly alarmed. 'Yes?'

Carey beamed. 'Nothing to worry about, Grazhdanke Kunayova. This is merely a technicality concerning the forthcoming demolition of this area. You know about that?'

'Yes,' she said. 'I do.' The faint alarm turned to faint aggression. 'We're having to move just when I've redecorated the house.'

'I'm sorry about that,' said Carey. 'Well, under the ground there are a lot of pipes – gas, water, electricity and so on. My own concern is with the water pipes. When the demolition men come in there'll be bulldozers coming through here, and we don't want them breaking the water pipes or the whole area will turn into a quagmire.'

'Why don't you turn off the water before you start? she asked practically.

Carey was embarrassed. 'That's not as easy as it sounds, Grazhdanke Kunayova,' he said, hunting for a plausible answer. 'As you know, this is one of the older areas of Svetogorsk, built by the Finns just after the First World War. A lot of the records were destroyed twenty-five years ago and we don't even know where some of the pipes are, or even if they connect into our present water system.' He leaned forward and said confidentially, 'It's even possible that some of our water still comes from over the border – from Imatra.'

'You mean we get it free from the Finns?'

'I'm not concerned with the economics of it,' said Carey stiffly. 'I just have to find the pipes.'

She looked over Carey's shoulder at Armstrong who was leaning on his spade. 'And you want to come into the garden,' she said. 'Is he going to dig holes all over our garden?'

'Not at all,' said Carey reassuringly. He lifted the detector. 'I have this – a new invention that can trace pipes without digging. It might be necessary to dig a small hole if we find a junction, but I don't think it will happen.'

'Very well,' she said unwillingly. 'But try not to step on the flower beds. I know we're being pushed out of the house this year but the flowers are at their best just now, and my husband does try to make a nice display.'

'We'll try not to disturb the flowers,' said Carey. 'We'll just go around to the back.'

He jerked his head at Armstrong and they walked around the house followed by the small boy. Armstrong said in a low voice, 'We've got to get rid of the audience.'

'No trouble; just be boring.' Carey stopped as he rounded the corner of the house and saw the garden shed at the bottom of the garden; it was large and stoutly constructed of birch logs. 'That's not on the plan,' he said. 'I hope what we're looking for isn't under there.'

Armstrong stuck his spade upright in the soil at the edge of a flower bed, and Carey unfolded a plan of the garden. 'That's the remaining tree there,' he said. 'One of the four Meyrick picked out. I'll have a go at that first.' He donned the earphones, switched on the detector, and made a slow run up to the tree. He spent some time exploring the area about the tree, much hampered by the small boy, then called, 'Nothing here.'

'Perhaps the pipe runs down the middle,' said Armstrong.

'It's possible. I really think I'll have to search the whole area.'

Which he proceeded to do. For the benefit of the small boy every so often he would call out a number and Armstrong would dutifully record it on the plan. After half an hour of this the boy became bored and went away. Carey winked at Armstrong and carried on, and it took him well over an hour to search the garden thoroughly.

He glanced at his watch and went back to Armstrong. 'We have two possibilities. A strong reading – very strong – on the edge of the lawn there, and a weaker reading in the middle of that flower bed. I suggest we have a go at the lawn first.'

Armstrong looked past him. 'Mrs K. is coming.'

The woman was just coming out of the house. As she approached she said, 'Have you found anything?'

'We may have found a junction,' said Carey, and pointed. 'Just there. We'll have to dig – just a small hole, Grazhdanke Kunayova, you understand. And we'll be tidy and replace the turf.'

She looked down at the straggly lawn. 'I don't suppose it matters,' she said dispiritedly. 'My husband says the grass doesn't grow as well here as down south where we come from. Would you like something to eat?'

'We brought our own sandwiches,' said Carey gravely.

'I'll make you tea,' she said decisively, and went back to the house.

'Nice woman,' commented Carey. 'It's midday, when all good workers down tools for half an hour.'

They ate their sandwiches sitting on the lawn, and drank the glasses of lemon tea which the woman brought to them. She did not stay to make small talk, for which Carey was thankful. He bit into a sandwich and said meditatively, 'I suppose this is where Merikken and his family were killed – with the exception of young Harri.' He pointed to the house. 'That end looks newer than the rest.'

'Was there much bombing here?' asked Armstrong.

'My God; this place was in the front line for a time – the sky must have been full of bombers.'

Armstrong sipped the hot tea. 'How do we know the trunk is still here? Any keen gardener might have dug it up. What about Kunayev himself?'

'Let's not be depressing,' said Carey. 'It's time you started to dig. I'll give you a reading and then let you do the work, as befits my station in life.' He walked across the lawn, searched the area briefly with the detector, and stuck a pencil upright in the ground. 'That's it. Take out the turves neatly.'

So Armstrong began to dig. He laid the turves on one side and tried to put each spadeful of soil into as neat a heap as he could. Carey sat under the tree and watched him, drinking the last of his tea. Presently Armstrong called him over. 'How deep is this thing supposed to be?'

'About two feet.'

'I'm down two and a half and there's still nothing.'

'Carry on,' said Carey. 'Meyrick could have been in error.'

Armstrong carried on. After a while he said, 'I'm down another foot and still nothing.'

'Let's see what the gadget says.' Carey put on the earphones and lowered the detector into the hole. He switched on and hastily adjusted the gain. 'It's there,' he said. 'Must be a matter of inches. I've just had my ears pierced.'

'I'll go down a bit more,' said Armstrong. 'But it'll be difficult without enlarging the hole.' Again he drove the spade into the earth and hit something solid with a clunk. 'Got it!' He cleared as much as he could with the spade and then began to scrabble with his hands. After five minutes he looked up at Carey.

'You know what we've found?'

'What?'

Armstrong began to laugh. 'A water pipe.'

'Oh, for God's sake!' said Carey. 'Come out of that hole and let me see.' He replaced Armstrong in the hole and felt the rounded shape of the metal and the flange. He dug away more earth and exposed more metal, then he got out of the hole.

Armstrong was still chuckling, and Carey said, 'Fill in that hole and go gently. It's an unexploded bomb.'

Armstrong's laughter died away thinly.

'250 kilograms, I'd say,' said Carey. 'The equivalent of our wartime 500-pounder.'

TWENTY-NINE

They were grouped around Denison who lay prone on the ground. 'Don't move him,' warned Harding. 'I don't know what he'll have apart from concussion.' Very carefully he explored Denison's skull. 'He's certainly been hit hard.'

Diana looked at McCready. 'Who by?' McCready merely shrugged.

Harding's long fingers were going over Denison's torso. 'Let's turn him over – very gently.' They turned Denison over on to his back and Harding lifted one eyelid. The eye was rolled right back in the head, and Lyn gave an involuntary cry.

'Excuse me, Doctor,' said Diana, and her hand went to Denison's shirt pocket. She got up off her knees and jerked her head at McCready. They walked back to the middle of the camp. 'The plan and the notebook are gone,' she said. 'He carried them in the button-down pocket of his shirt. The button has been torn off and the pocket ripped. The question is by whom?'

'It wasn't the Yanks,' said McCready. 'I saw them well off down-river. And it wasn't the other mob, either; I'll stake everything on that.'

'Then who?'

McCready shook his head irritably. 'By God!' he said. 'There's someone around here cleverer than I am.'

'I'd better not comment on that,' said Diana tartly, 'You might get annoyed.'

'It doesn't really matter, of course,' said McCready. 'We were expecting it, anyway.'

'But we were expecting to use it to find out who the opposition is.' She tapped him on the chest. 'You know what this means. There are three separate groups after us.' She ticked them off on her fingers. 'The Americans; another crowd who is vaguely Slav – Russians, Poles, Bulgarians, Yugoslavs, take your pick – and now someone mysterious whom we haven't even seen.'

'It's what Carey was expecting, isn't it?'

'Yes, but it's worrying all the same. Let's see how Denison is.'

They went back to the rock where Lyn was saying worriedly, 'It is just concussion, isn't it?'

'I'm not too sure,' said Harding. 'Lyn, you'll find a black box in my pack about half-way down. Bring it, will you?'

Lyn ran off and McCready went down on his knees by Denison. 'What's wrong with him apart from a crack on the head?'

'His pulse is way down, and I'd like to take his blood pressure,' said Harding. 'But there's something else. Look at this.' He took Denison's arm by the wrist and lifted it up. When he let go the arm stayed there. He took the arm and bent it at the elbow, and again it stayed in the position into which he had put it.

McCready drew in his breath sharply. 'You can mould the man like modelling clay,' he said in wonder. 'What is it?'

'A form of catalepsy,' said Harding.

That did not mean much to McCready. 'Does it usually accompany concussion?'

'Not at all. It's the first time I've seen it induced by a knock on the head. This is most unusual.'

Lyn came back and held out the box to Harding. 'Is this what you wanted?'

He nodded briefly, took out an elastic bandage of a sphygmometer and bound it around Denison's arm. He pumped the rubber bulb, and said, 'His blood pressure is down, too.' He unwrapped the bandage. 'We'll carry him back and put him into a sleeping bag to keep him warm.'

'That means we don't move from here,' said McCready.

'We can't move him,' said Harding. 'Not until I can find out what's wrong with him, and that, I'm afraid, is mixed up with what's been done to him.'

A bleak expression came over McCready's face. If they stayed at the camp they'd be sitting ducks for the next crowd of international yobbos.

Lyn said, 'Is he conscious or unconscious, Doctor?'

'Oh, he's unconscious,' said Harding. 'Blanked out completely.

Harding was wrong.

Denison could hear every word but could not do a thing about it. When he tried to move he found that nothing happened, that he could not move a muscle. It was as though something had chopped all control from the brain. He had felt Harding moving his limbs and had tried to do something about it but he had no control whatever.

What he did have was a splitting headache.

He felt himself being lifted and carried and then put into a sleeping bag. After a few minutes he was lapped around in warmth. Someone had tucked the hood of the bag around his head so that sounds were muffled and he could not hear what was said very clearly. He wished they had not done that. He tried to speak, willing his tongue to move, but it lay flaccid in his mouth. He could not even move his vocal cords to make the slightest sound.

He heard a smatter of conversation . . . 'still breathing . . . automatic functions unimpaired . . . side . . . tongue out . . . choking . . .' That would be Harding.

Someone rolled him on to his side and he felt fingers inserted into his mouth and his tongue pulled forward.

After a little while he slept.

And dreamed.

In his dream he was standing on a hillside peering through the eyepiece of a theodolite. Gradually he became aware that the instrument was not a theodolite at all – it was a cine camera. He even knew the name of it – it was an Arriflex. And the small speck of blue lake in the distance became one of the blue eyes of a pretty girl.

He pulled back from the view finder of the camera and turned to Joe Staunton, the cameraman. 'Nice composition,' he said. 'We can shoot on that one.'

Great slabs of memory came slamming back into place with the clangour of iron doors.

'It's no good, Giles,' said Fortescue. 'It's becoming just that bit too much. You're costing us too much money. How the hell can you keep control when you're pissed half the time?' His contempt came over like a physical blow. 'Even when you're not drunk you're hung over.' Fortescue's voice boomed hollowly as though he was speaking in a cavern. 'You can't rely on the Old Pals Act any more. This is the end. You're out.'

Even in his dream Denison was aware of the wetness of tears on his cheeks.

He was driving a car, the familiar, long-since-smashed Lotus. Beth was beside him, her hair streaming in the wind.

'Faster!' she said. 'Faster!' His hand fell on the gear lever and he changed down to overtake a lorry, his foot going down on the accelerator.

The scooter shot, insect-like, from the side road right across his path. He swerved, and so did the lorry he was overtaking. Beth screamed and there was a rending, jangle of tearing metal and breaking glass and then nothing.

'Sorry about that,' said Staunton. 'This would have been a good one, but Fortescue won't have it. What will you do now?'

'Go home to Hampstead and get drunk,' said Denison.

Hampstead! An empty flat with no personality. Bare walls with little furniture and many empty whisky bottles.

And then . . . !

In his dream Denison screamed.

He stirred when he woke up and opened his eyes to find Lyn looking at him. He moistured his lips, and said 'Beth?'

Her eyes widened and she turned her head. 'Dr Harding! Dr Harding – he's . . . he's awake.' There was a break in her voice. When she turned back to him he was trying to get up. 'No,' she said. 'Lie quietly.' She pushed him back.

'I'm all right,' he said weakly.

Harding appeared. 'All right, Lyn; let me see him.' He bent over Denison. 'How are you feeling?'

'Not too bad,' said Denison. 'Hell of a headache, though.' He put up his hand and tenderly felt the back of his head. 'What happened?'

'Somebody hit you.'

Denison fumbled with his other hand inside the sleeping bag, groping for his shirt pocket. 'They got the plan.'

'It doesn't matter,' said Lyn. 'Giles, it doesn't matter.'

'I know.' He levered himself up on one elbow and accepted the pills Harding gave him and washed them down with water. 'I think I gave you a shock, Doctor.'

'You were aware?' asked Harding in surprise.

'Yes. Another thing – I've got my memory back.'

'All of it?'

Denison frowned. 'How would I know? I'm not sure.'

'We won't go into that now,' said Harding quickly. 'How do you feel physically?'

'If you let me stand up I'll tell you.' He got out of the sleeping bag and stood up, supported on Harding's arm. He swayed for a moment and then shook himself free and took three steps. 'I seem all right,' he said. 'Except for the headache.'

'The pills ought to clear that up,' said Harding. 'But if I were you I wouldn't be too energetic.'

'You're not me,' said Denison flatly. 'What time is it? And where are the others?'

'It's just after midday,' said Lyn. 'And they're scouting to see if anyone else is around. I think the doctor is right; you ought to take it easy.'

Denison walked to the edge of the bluff, thinking of the perturbation in McCready's voice when he discovered that, because of the attack on himself, the party was pinned down. 'I ought to be able to cross the river,' he said. 'That might be enough.'

THIRTY

Armstrong was digging another hole. He had filled in the first one and left Carey to replace the turf. Carey did his best but still the lawn in that place was bumpy and uneven and, in the circumstances, he did not feel like stamping it down too hard. He looked towards Armstrong who appeared to be systematically wrecking a flower bed. 'Found anything?'

'Not yet.' Armstrong pushed again with the spade, and then stooped quickly. 'Wait! I think there's some – ' before he finished the sentence Carey was by his side – 'thing here.'

'Let me see.' Carey put his hand down the hole and felt a flat surface. Flakes of something came away on his fingers and when he brought up his hand his fingerprints were brown. 'Rust!' he said. 'This is it. Careful with that spade.'

He looked back at the house and thought it was fortunate that Mrs K. had gone shopping and taken her son with her. A bit of good for a lot of bad. Earlier in the afternoon she had been out in the garden hanging out the weekly wash to dry, and then she had come over and chatted interminably about the iniquities of the planning authorities, the ridiculous prices in the shops and other matters dear to the housewifely heart. A lot of time had been wasted.

He said, 'If the trunk is corroded we might be able to rip open the top and take out the papers without making the hole any bigger.'

'I forgot my tin opener,' said Armstrong. 'But this might do.' He put his hand to the side of his leg and from the long pocket of the overalls designed to take a foot rule he extracted a sheathed knife. 'Bought it in Helsinki; thought it might come in handy.'

Carey grunted as he saw the design. He took the knife from the sheath and examined the broad blade and the simple wooden handle. 'The Yanks think Jim Bowie invented these,' he said. 'Don't ever try to tackle a Finn with one; they're better at it than you. And probably the Russians, too, in these parts. It'll do quite nicely.'

He cleared earth from the top of the trunk until about a square foot of rusty metal was showing, then he stabbed at it with the sharp point of the knife. The metal was rotten and the knife punched through with ridiculous ease. He enlarged the hole and bent up the metal into a tongue which he could hold in his fingers. He gripped it and pulled and there was a tearing sound.

Within five minutes he had made a hole in the trunk big enough to take his hand, and he groped inside and touched a hard square edge. His fingers curled around what felt like a book but when he tried to pull it out he found he was in the position of the monkey gripping the nut inside the bottle. The book was too big to come through the hole so he dropped it and concentrated on making the hole bigger.

At last he was able to get the book out. It was a school exercise book with hard covers and, when he flicked the pages, he saw mathematical symbols and lengthy equations in profusion. 'Jackpot!' he said exultantly.

The next thing out of the lucky dip was a roll of papers held by a rubber band. The rubber snapped at a touch but the papers, long rolled, held their curvature and he unrolled them with difficulty. The first pages were written in Finnish in a tight handwriting and the first mathematical equation came on the fourth page. From then on they were more frequent until the final pages were solid mathematics.

'How do we know what we're looking for?' asked Armstrong.

'We don't – we take the lot.' Carey dived into the hole again and groped about. Within ten minutes he had cleared the box which proved to be only half full but, even so, the books and papers made a big stack.

Carey took some folded paper bags from his pocket. 'Fill that hole; I'll take care of the loot.' He looked at his watch with worried eyes. 'We haven't much time.'

He filled three stout kraft-paper bags with documents and sealed them with sticky tape. Armstrong said, 'There's not enough earth to go back. It's filling the trunk.'

'I'll see to that,' said Carey. 'You nip along and fetch that wheelbarrow. You know where it's planted.'

'The empty house at the end of the street. I hope young Virtanen parked it in the right place.'

'You'll soon find out. Get going.' Carey began to fill in the hole and, as Armstrong had said, there was not enough earth, so he took more from other parts of the flower bed and took care not to pack it too tightly. It took him quite a while but when he had finished Armstrong had not yet returned.

He took the brown paper bags from where they had been lying among the long-stemmed flowers and hid them more securely in some shrubbery. His watch told him that time was running out; they had to get back to the paper mill and smuggle the papers aboard the bus. That had been arranged for but it would take time and there was little of that left.

Impatiently he went to the front gate and was relieved to see Armstrong trudging back with the wheelbarrow. 'What kept you?'

'The damn fool *hid* it,' said Armstrong savagely. 'What did you tell him to do?'

'To put it just inside the wall and out of sight.'

'He put the bloody thing in the cellar,' said Armstrong. 'I had to search the house to find it.'

'A misunderstanding – but we've got it. Come on.'

They put the documents into the wheelbarrow and covered the bags with dirty sacking. Armstrong put the spade and the detector on top and picked up the handles of the wheelbarrow. He was about to push off when he stopped. 'Someone's coming.'

Carey turned. A man was coming up the garden from the side of the house. His whole attitude was one of suspicion. 'What are you doing in my garden?'

Carey stepped forward. 'Grazhdaninu Kunayev?'

'Yes.'

Carey reeled out his story, then said, 'Your wife knows about it, of course. We've made very little disturbance.'

'You've been digging holes? Where?'

Carey pointed. 'There – on the lawn.' He refrained from drawing attention to the flower bed.

Kunayev walked over and prodded at the turf with his toe. 'You've been neat, I will say that.' He stamped hard with his foot, and Armstrong winced, thinking of the bomb below. 'Does this mean you'll be coming in earlier?'

Carey frowned. 'How do you mean?'

'With the bulldozers.'

'Not that I know of, comrade. That's not my department. I'm concerned only with water pipes.'

Kunayev looked at the house. 'I've liked living here; it's a good place. Now they want to pull it down and put up another damn factory. I ask you; is that right, comrade? Do you think it's right?'

Carey shrugged. 'Progress sometimes means sacrifice.'

'And I'm doing the sacrificing.' Kunayev snorted. 'I'm being transferred to the new housing development on the other side of town. A cheap, rotten, new house. Not like this house, comrade; those Finns knew how to build houses.'

'Meaning that Soviet workers don't?' asked Carey suavely.

'I didn't say that,' said Kunayev. He walked towards the wheelbarrow and picked up the detector. 'Is this your water diviner?'

Carey tightened his lips. 'Yes.'

'Like the mine detector I used during the war. I was at Stalingrad, comrade. Fourteen years old I was then.' He strolled towards the fence separating his garden from the one next door, still holding the detector. 'Boris Ivanevitch, are you there?'

'For Christ's sake!' whispered Armstrong. 'What do we do now?'

A woman called back. 'He's just going on duty,'

'Good afternoon, Irina Alexandrovna; ask him to come round here. I have something to show him.'

'Let's just leave,' urged Armstrong.

'We can't leave without that detector,' said Carey through his teeth. 'It would look too suspicious.'

Kunayev came back from the fence. He had put on the earphones. 'Seems to work just like a mine detector, too. Not as big and heavy, of course; but they're clever with their electronics these days.'

'It works on a different principle,' said Carey. 'But we've finished here, Grazhdaninu Kunayev; we must go about our work.'

'No great hurry, comrade,' said Kunayev carelessly. He walked over to the patch of relaid turf. 'You say you found your water pipe here?'

'A pipe junction,' said Carey, gritting his teeth.

Kunayev nicked a switch and walked back and forth several times. 'It works,' he said. 'I could find that junction blind-fold – see if I can't.' He closed his eyes and walked back and forward again. 'Am I there?'

'Right on the spot,' said Armstrong.

Kunayev opened his eyes and looked past them. 'Ah, Boris Ivanevitch,' he said. 'You'll be interested in this.'

Carey turned around and felt a sinking feeling in his stomach. Boris Ivanevitch was a policeman.

THIRTY-ONE

'The chief study here at Sompio is the ecology of wetland,' said Dr Matti Mannermaa. 'In northern Finland we have many marshes caused by the slow drying out of the shallow lakes. Sompio was chosen as a nature preserve because it not only has such a marsh but also has high ground of an altitude of over five hundred metres and a small part of Lake Lokka. Thus we have a varied habitat for many creatures, especially birds.'

'Very interesting,' said McCready, hoping the interest showed in his face. He was bored to death.

'I am an ornithologist, of course,' said Dr Mannermaa. 'My work here is similar to that done at your English research station at Slimbridge.'

'I've been there,' said Harding with enthusiasm.

'So have I,' said Dr Mannermaa. 'I spent many months there investigating British methods. We have adopted the rocket-driven net for use here. We ring a lot of birds for the study of migratory patterns.'

McCready indicated the rack of shotguns on the wall of Mannermaa's office. 'I see you shoot them, too.'

'We must,' said Mannermaa. 'We have a continuing study in pesticide residues in body fat. We break a lot of eggs, too, Mr McCready – to study the thickness of the shells. Decreasing shell thickness is mainly a problem with the raptors, of course.' He laughed. 'I am not a sentimentalist about birds; I like roast duck just as much as anyone else.'

'I'm a wildfowler,' said Harding. 'We get good shooting in Norfolk.'

'I hope you don't take a shotgun into Sompio,' said Mannermaa. There was a twinkle in his eye which belied the gravity of his voice. 'Well, now; let us look at the map and decide what is best for you to do.'

He stood up and went to a wall map. For a few minutes they discussed routes and possibilities. 'Here there is a hut,' said Mannermaa. 'On the edge of the marsh just below Nattaset – that's the mountain here. It's equipped with bunks and cooking facilities – rough living but better than tenting.'

'Most kind of you,' said McCready. 'Thank you very much.'

'A lot of our technical equipment is stored there. Please try not to disturb it.'

'We won't touch anything,' promised McCready. 'Thank you for everything, Dr Mannermaa.'

As they shook hands Mannermaa said, 'I hope your companions are successful in their shopping here. Vuotso is a small place and the range of choice may be restricted.'

'All we need are basic rations.'

'If you run out you'll find some tinned food in the hut,' said Mannermaa. 'You can pay for it when you get back.'

McCready and Harding left the office and emerged on to the main street of Vuotso. Harding said, 'Co-operative chap, isn't he? Those credentials Carey supplied must be really high-powered.'

'But we mustn't take a shotgun into Sompio,' said McCready. 'I wish we could take a machine-gun.'

'Do you think we'll be followed here?'

'It's a certainty – we left a trail like a bloody paper chase. Carey's plan is working and that's just fine for Carey, but I have a feeling that we're left holding the sticky end.' McCready sounded angry. 'It's all very well for him to set us up as targets but who likes being shot at? His plan that I should be an outside guard has already broken down. I have to sleep some time. It's too big a job for one man.'

'You'll be with us this time, then?'

McCready nodded. His brow was furrowed as he tried to cover all the angles. 'Another thing – how will Denison hold out?'

'He's got remarkable resilience,' said Harding. 'That crack on the head stirred things up and a lot of the blocks on his memory have been shaken loose. He's remembering more and more as time goes on, but he seems to have the ability to handle it.'

'What happens when he gets it all back? Does he crack up and go back on the bottle?' asked McCready sourly.

'I don't know. I tried him on whisky last night. He seems to have a positive aversion to it.'

McCready grunted. 'I hope he stays that way.'

In fact, Denison felt remarkably well. As they went on foot into the Sompio nature preserve he tried to analyse the reasons for his feeling of well-being and came to the conclusion that it was because of the absence of panic when he probed into the past. And then, of course, there was the immediate environment. He stopped and took a deep breath of the cool clean air and looked about him.

They were skirting the mountain called Nattaset and keeping to the high ground. Below there was a vista of the northern wilderness breathtaking in its beauty. Where there was firm ground the ever-present birches grew, but in between a multitude of islets there was a lacework intricacy of watercourses reflecting the blue of the sky, and in the distance an island-dotted lake shone like silver. Closer at hand white wreaths of last winter's snow lay all about.

Denison turned and saw McCready trailing about half a mile behind. He, too, appeared to have stopped and Denison thought he was doing a search with field glasses – and not just to look at the view. If beauty is in the eye of the beholder then, as far as McCready was concerned, this view would be bleak indeed. There were far too many places for a man – or even a regiment – to hide.

Denison hitched his pack to a more comfortable position and set off again, keeping up a fast pace so as to catch up with the others. He drew abreast of Lyn, and said, 'It's lucky no one took a crack at us when we were leaving Kevo. I was so woozy I wouldn't have been much help.'

Lyn looked at him worriedly. 'How are you feeling now?'

'Fine,' he said lightly. 'I feel a lot better now I can remember things. This morning I remembered the name of the man in the flat above mine; Paterson – a nice chap.'

'And you remember being a film director?'

'Yes.' He laughed. 'Don't run away with the idea that I was one of your big-time movie moguls – my stuff wasn't shown in the West End. I make educational films mostly.' He frowned. 'Or, at least, I did. I was fired from my job.'

'Don't worry about that, Giles,' she said quietly.

'I'm not worrying; I have more important things on my mind at the moment. All the same,' he said, looking into his past. 'I don't seem to have been a nice character.'

There was violence in her voice. 'Forget it!' she said crossly.

He glanced at her face in profile. 'You worry about me, don't you?' There was a tinge of wonder in his voice; it had been a long time since anyone had worried about what happened to him. All Fortescue had worried about was whether the job would get done – he hadn't given a damn about Denison himself.

'What do you expect me to do? Cheer when you get slugged on the head?' She walked on a few more paces. 'You should never have agreed to this mad scheme.'

'Carey talked me into it – he's a very persuasive man. But you talked yourself into it. Nobody asked you to come. Now why did you do that?'

She offered him a wan smile. 'You know, you're rather like Hamlet; you let yourself be pushed around.'

He grinned. 'Ah, the fair Ophelia.'

'Don't class me with that damned ninny,' she snapped. 'I'm not going to go mad in white satin. But I still think that if Hamlet had had someone to give him advice, to put some backbone into him, things would have turned out differently. As it was, all he had was that wet, Horatio.'

He felt suddenly depressed. 'Are you offering to supply backbone?'

'All I'm saying is that you mustn't depend on this gang of Whitehall thugs. Don't believe everything Carey tells you. He's in business for himself, not you.' She seemed angry.

He was silent for a while. 'You could be right,' he said at last. 'I have no illusions about this job. I know I was thrown into it involuntarily but I carried on of my own will and with my eyes open. I know I'm being used and I don't particularly like it. At the time when Carey put the proposition I was mixed up, to say the least, and I dare say Carey took advantage. I don't blame him for it – I was all he had.'

'But you're becoming better,' said Lyn. 'You'll be getting ready to make your own decisions.'

'We'll see,' said Denison thoughtfully. 'We'll see.' He hitched the pack on his back. 'When do we get to this hut?'

They pressed on late that night because Diana wanted to reach the hut. 'No point in staying in the open when we can have a roof over our heads,' she said. Travelling late was no problem; the light never left the sky and they were able to move as fast at midnight as at midday and they saw the hut at two in the morning.

It was built of birch logs and was bigger than they had expected. It was in the form of a letter 'H', wings having been added as was necessary. The living quarters were in the cross-bar of the 'H' and they were glad to divest themselves of the heavy packs. The two women began to prepare a meal and sent the men to get water.

Harding and Denison took buckets and went outside, and Harding stopped just outside the hut and looked across the marsh which seemed to consist of reeds and water for as far as the eye could see. 'Good wildfowling country,' he said appreciatively.

Denison slapped at his neck. 'Good mosquito country,' he grumbled.

'Don't worry; they're not malarial.'

'You mean I'm merely being eaten alive?' Denison slapped at himself again. 'Let's get the water.'

They went down to the water's edge and Harding inspected it critically. 'It looks all right; but we'd better boil it to make sure.' They filled the buckets and then Harding straightened. 'I wonder what that is.'

Denison followed the direction of his gaze and saw a low wooden hut on the water's edge about a hundred yards away. 'A sauna probably. The Finns like to have them on the edge of the water so they can jump right in. You won't catch me in there.'

'It doesn't look tall enough to be a sauna,' said Harding. 'The roof's too low. I think I'll take a look.'

'The girls will be screaming for water.'

'I won't be a minute.' Harding walked away following the shore line, and Denison shrugged. He picked up a full bucket and took it up to the main hut. Upon being told there was an insufficiency of water he went back for the other bucket. Harding called, 'Denison; look what I've found.'

Denison walked towards the little hut and thought Harding was probably right – the roof was so low that there would be barely sitting room in the hut, let alone standing room. He walked around it and found Harding squatting on his heels. 'What is it?'

'It's a gun punt,' said Harding. 'Haven't seen one for years.'

From this side Denison could see that the hut consisted of roof only and was merely a shelter over a flat boat which looked like an enlarged Eskimo kayak. 'So?'

Harding shook with laughter. 'Mannermaa told us not to bring a shotgun, and all the time he had this here. The old devil!'

Denison bent down beside Harding. 'I don't see what's funny.'

'You wouldn't. I bet the gun is up at the hut. I'll have to see if I can find it.' Harding pointed to the foredeck of the punt. 'Look there; that's where the breech ropes go.'

Denison looked at the two eyebolts – they told him nothing. 'You're not being very comprehensible.'

'I don't suppose I am. These things have gone out of fashion. There are a couple still in use on the east coast back at home, but I didn't expect to see one in Finland. You'll understand better when you see the gun, if I can find it.' Harding stood up. 'Let's go back.'

They went back to the hut, taking the second bucket of water. On the way they encountered McCready who was just coming in. He seemed tired and depressed. 'Not a sign of anyone,' he said. 'But that's not surprising.' He waved a hand at the marsh. 'How deep would you say that water is?'

'Not very deep,' said Harding. 'Not at the edges, anyway. Two or three feet, perhaps.'

McCready nodded. 'You could hide a bloody army in those reeds,' he said glumly. 'What's for supper?'

Denison smiled slightly. 'I'll lay you ten to one it's bully beef stew.'

'That's not very funny,' said McCready as he went into the hut.

* * *

After he had eaten McCready felt better. It had not been bully beef for once and, with his belly full, he felt sleepy. He glanced at the bunks in the corner of the room where Diana and Lyn were already asleep, huddled in their sleeping bags. 'Well, here we are – right in the middle of the bullseye,' he said. 'I suppose someone should keep watch.'

'You get some sleep,' said Denison. 'I'll toss with Harding as to who takes first watch.'

'Where is he?'

'Looking around for some kind of gun.'

McCready came alert. 'A gun?'

'Something to do with a boat he found. He's a wild-fowler, you know. He didn't make much sense.'

'Oh, a sporting gun.' McCready lost interest. He stretched for the coffee pot, refilled his cup and then produced a flask. He laced the coffee with whisky and offered the flask to Denison. 'Want some?'

'No, thanks.'

'Lost the taste for it?'

'Seems so.'

McCready put away the flask and sipped his coffee. 'You can keep watch from the hut,' he said. 'Take a turn outside once every half-hour and keep an eye on the hillside. Not that it matters but it would be nice to have warning of any-one coming.'

'They'll come?'

'If not today then tomorrow. We give them what they want and maybe they'll go away. Maybe.' He shrugged. 'I'm not getting killed for the sake of a scrap of paper that doesn't mean a damned thing. Anyway, we've got her to think about.' He nodded towards the bunk where Lyn lay asleep.

'Nice of you to be so considerate,' said Denison.

'Don't be so bloody snippy,' said McCready without rancour. 'We didn't ask her to come – she forced it.' He stretched. 'I'm going to bed.'

Denison picked up the binoculars. 'I'll do a check outside.'

He went out of the hut and looked around, studying the hillside through the glasses, especially in the direction from which they had come. There was nothing to be seen. Next he turned his attention to the marsh. A long way out there were dots on an open stretch of water which, through the glasses, proved to be birds. They were unmoving and apparently asleep. Too big to be ducks they were, perhaps, geese. Harding might know. Not that it made any difference.

After a while he went back into the hut, moving quietly so as not to wake anybody. Harding had just come back; he beckoned to Denison and said in a low voice, 'I've found it – and look!' He opened the palm of his hand and revealed a dozen small copper cylinders rather like .22 cartridge cases without the bullets.

'What are they?'

'Detonators,' said Harding. 'I can't find any powder, though. Come and have a look at the gun.'

'All right,' said Denison. It was something to do until he had to go outside again.

He went with Harding into a room at the side of the hut which was used as a store. Rolled up netting hung neatly on pegs on the wall, and there were a lot of boxes which had been pulled away from the wall, presumably by Harding.

'I found it behind there,' said Harding. 'Not so much hidden as concealed from casual eyes. I knew it must be somewhere around because of the punt.'

Denison had not the faintest idea of what Harding was talking about but he obligingly stepped forward and looked behind the boxes. At first he did not realize what he was looking at; Harding had said something about a gun for a punt and that was what he expected to find – a shotgun to kill ducks. What he saw was something unexpected. True, it *was* a shotgun, as he realized as soon as his mind had shifted gear, but it was a shotgun of Brobdingnagian proportions.

'What the devil . . . ?'

Harding chuckled. 'I thought you'd be surprised.'

'Surprised isn't the word,' said Denison. 'Confounded is more like it. How long is this thing?'

'A bit over nine feet, taking in the stock. The barrel is about seven feet.'

Denison looked down at the monstrous object and bent to peer at the bore. He measured it with his thumb and found it to be over an inch and a half. He put his hand under the muzzle and lifted. 'It's damned heavy. How the hell can you shoot a thing like this? You couldn't get it to your shoulder.'

'You certainly couldn't,' agreed Harding. 'I estimate the weight as something over a hundred and twenty pounds. It'll fire about a pound and a half of shot.'

'Well, how *do* you shoot it?'

'It's a punt gun,' said Harding. 'It lies on the foredeck of that punt. You can see that the breech ropes are attached – they run through the ring bolts on the punt and take up the recoil. The stock is merely for aiming it; if you put your shoulder to it when firing you'd end up with a broken shoulder.'

Denison scratched his jaw. 'An impressive piece of artillery. I've never heard of anything like this.'

'It was developed early in the nineteenth century,' said Harding. 'The idea is that you lie flat in the punt and propel yourself with paddles rather like ping-pong bats. It's quite easy because once all the weight is in the punt it has a free-board of only about four inches. You stalk the birds on the water – going among the reeds – and you aim by pointing the whole punt. When you're in range you fire and, God willing, get yourself a dozen birds.'

'Not very sporting,' commented Denison.

'Oh, it isn't as easy as you'd think. Birds aren't as easy to stalk as all that; they have more chance of escaping than you have of killing them.'

'What kind of cartridge does it use?'

'It doesn't.' Harding grinned. 'Try going to a gunsmith some time and asking for quarter-bore cartridges – he'd think you'd gone mad. If you want cartridges you make up your own. You use ordinary black powder well rammed and with your shot on top with some wadding; you put a detonator on this nipple – I won't now because it makes quite a noise even without a charge in the barrel – and you pull the trigger. Down goes the hammer on the nipple, the detonator explodes, flame shoots down the hole in the centre of the nipple and ignites the main charge. Bang!'

'And the whole punt recoils a few feet.'

'You've got the idea,' said Harding. 'The detonator is a modern touch. The originals used flint and steel – very unreliable – but with detonators you shouldn't have one misfire in a hundred.'

'Interesting,' said Denison.

'But no use without powder.' Harding patted the heavy barrel. 'I'd have liked to try it out. Like Mannermaa, I'm not averse to roast duck.'

'Are you averse to sleep?' Denison checked his watch. 'I'm going to wake you in two hours for the second guard duty. You'd better get your head down.'

THIRTY-TWO

Denison woke up because someone was shaking him. He moaned in protest and opened his eyes to see Diana bending over him. 'Wake up – we've got a visitor.'

He sat up and rubbed bis eyes. 'Who?'

'Come and see.'

McCready was at the window, binoculars to his eyes. As Denison joined him he said, 'It's one of the characters from Kevo – not the Yanks, the other crowd.'

Denison saw the man walking along the edge of the marsh towards the hut. He was about four hundred yards away. 'Alone?'

'I haven't seen anyone else,' said McCready. 'This boy has his nerve, I must say.'

'Perhaps he doesn't know we're here.'

'Then he's a damned fool,' said McCready. 'And they don't send fools on jobs like this. Diana, stand behind the door with your gun.'

The man tramped stolidly towards the hut. If it were not for his pack he would have looked like any holidaymaker on any beach. Within ten minutes he was within hailing distance and he put up his hands showing empty palms. Holding them up he came to a stop ten yards from the door and waited.

'He knows we're here,' said McCready. He took a pistol from his pack and worked the action to put a round into the breech. He went to the door and held the pistol behind his back. 'If he comes in you'll be behind him,' he said to Diana, and opened the door.

The man still had, his hands raised as McCready said, 'What do you want?'

'I want to talk to Dr Harold Meyrick.' The man's English was good but heavily accented. Denison tried to identify the accent but made nothing of it.

'What if Dr Meyrick doesn't want to talk to you?'

'Why not let him make up his own mind?' asked the man.

'Whom shall I announce?' asked McCready suavely.

'Shall we say . . . Herr Schmidt?'

McCready had no trouble with the accent. 'I'd prefer Pan Schmidt – and even then I don't like it. Schmidt isn't a Czech name.'

The man shrugged. 'Many people in Czechoslovakia have German names.' When McCready did not respond he said, 'My arms are getting tired.'

'You put them up, you pull them down – but not just yet.' McCready made up his mind. 'All right, Mr Smith; step into my parlour.' He opened the door wide and stepped back. The man smiled as he came forward, his hands still high.

He walked into the hut and came to a dead stop four feet inside as McCready brought up the hand holding a gun. Diana closed the door behind him. 'Search him,' said McCready.

Schmidt half-turned and smiled as he saw the pistol in Diana's hand. 'So many guns,' he said. 'I am unarmed, of course.'

'There's no of course about it,' said McCready as Diana checked. When she had finished and found nothing McCready wagged the gun. 'Now take off your pack – slowly.'

Schmidt eased the pack from his shoulders and lowered it to the floor. 'That's better,' he said, flexing his arms. 'You people use guns too easily. That's why I came with my hands up – I didn't want to be shot by accident. Why did you shoot at me at Kevo?'

'We didn't,' said McCready. 'You ran into another crowd.'

'You expect me to believe that?'

'I don't give a damn if you believe it or not – but you started a war with the United States. I was watching it – three of you against four Yanks. One of your chaps had a broken arm and an American had a bullet in his leg. I had a ringside seat on the other side of the river.'

'So?' said Schmidt. 'The Americans also.' He smiled pleasantly at Denison and then turned back to McCready. 'What Dr Meyrick carries must be very important,'

'And what is it to you?'

'I've come to get it,' said Schmidt composedly.

'Just like that?'

'Just like that, Mr McCready.' He grinned. 'You see that I know your name. In fact, I know the names of everyone here. Mrs Hansen, Dr Harding, Dr Meyrick and, of course, Miss Meyrick. It wasn't hard.'

'No doubt it wasn't,' said McCready. 'But what makes you think that Dr Meyrick will give you anything?'

Schmidt looked Denison in the eye. 'I should think he values the safety of his daughter. It is unwise to go treasure hunting while in possession of a greater treasure, Dr Meyrick.'

Denison glanced at Lyn, then cleared his throat. 'But we have you, Mr Schmidt – if that's your name.'

Schmidt smiled and shook his head. 'I can see you're no tactician, doctor. You see, I am no treasure. I am sure Mr McCready is ahead of you in his thinking.'

'You've got the place surrounded, then?' said McCready.

'Of course. There are more than three of us this time.' Schmidt looked at his watch. 'The time is up in twenty-five – no, twenty-four – minutes.'

From the window Harding said, 'He could be pulling a bluff. I've seen no one.'

'The answer to that is easy,' said Schmidt. 'Call my bluff. I'm prepared to wait – if I can sit down.' He took a very slow step sideways and hooked a chair forward with his foot, never taking his eyes off McCready's pistol.

McCready leaned against the table. 'All right,' he said. 'Tell me what Meyrick has that interests you Czechs so much.'

A pained look appeared on Schmidt's face. 'Don't be stupid, McCready.' He jerked his thumb at Denison. 'He babbled about it in Stockholm. He discovered what was in his father's papers and where they were, and he talked about it to some Swedish friends. You ought to know scientists can't keep secrets. But then he realized exactly what he was talking about so he shut up and went back to England.'

He stopped. McCready's face was blank. 'Go on.'

'Why?' asked Schmidt. 'You know the answers. By then it was too late; the secret was out. Nothing travels faster than the news of a scientific breakthrough. Scientists like to believe in what they call the community of ideas, so the news got around Sweden, to Germany and to Czechoslovakia.'

'And to the United States,' commented McCready.

Schmidt hunched his shoulders. 'Everyone knows the reputation of old Merikken and everyone knows his history. The guess is that he put his papers somewhere for safe keeping. The way you're behaving leads us to think he buried them – or had them buried – somewhere in northern Finland. So it's a treasure hunt, as I said, and you've got a map with a cross on it. That or the equivalent.' He straightened. 'I want it.'

McCready slanted his eyes towards Denison. 'You see what comes of talking too much.' They were going to give in – that was the plan – but they must not collapse too easily because that would lead to suspicion. 'Let's be democratic,' he said. 'We'll vote on it. Harding?'

'I think he's bluffing,' said Harding flatly. 'I don't think there is anyone out there. Tell him to go to hell.'

Schmidt smiled but said nothing. McCready looked at Denison. 'What about you, Meyrick? You know the importance of this more than anyone.'

'I'm not the only one to be considered,' said Denison. 'Let him have what he wants.'

'Very wise,' said Schmidt.

'Shut up,' said McCready unemotionally. 'Diana?'

'I'm against.'

McCready turned his head. His face was away from Schmidt and he winked at Lyn. 'What do you say?'

'I vote with my father.'

McCready turned back to Schmidt. 'It seems I have the casting vote – yours doesn't count.'

'It will.' Schmidt nodded towards the window. 'My votes are out there.'

'I think you're going to have to prove that,' said McCready. 'You might be bluffing and you might not, but I'm going to call you regardless.'

'This is more dangerous than a game of poker.'

McCready smiled. 'When you came in here you said you didn't want to be shot by accident, so my guess is that if you do have a loaded vote outside you won't use it too forcibly against this hut. You see, you're inside it, too.'

'It's your guess,' said Schmidt.

'And it's your life.' McCready raised his pistol. 'If one bullet comes into this hut you're dead. If I don't kill you Diana will. And there's always Harding in reserve.'

Schmidt looked around at Diana who had a gun trained on him. He glanced at Harding who had also produced a pistol. His hand went to the pocket of his anorak. 'Do you mind if I smoke?'

McCready said nothing. Schmidt shrugged and lit a cigarette. He blew a perfect smoke ring. There was a crackling silence in the hut that went on and on and on.

THIRTY-THREE

Armstrong's hands sweated as he gripped the handles of the wheelbarrow and trundled it along the pavement at a speed that was positively dangerous to the pedestrian population of Enso. Beside him Carey walked quickly to keep pace, every now and then breaking into a little trot. Armstrong came to a halt at a street corner, stopped by the traffic flow.

'Damn Boris Ivanevitch!' said Carey. 'God save us all from talkative coppers. I hope he gets hell for being late on duty.'

'Not far now,' said Armstrong. 'Only another block. You can see the paper mill from here.'

Carey craned his neck and suddenly groaned. 'And I can see that bloody bus – it's just leaving.'

'Is it coming this way? Perhaps we can flag it down.'

'No, damn it! It's going away from us.' Carey checked his watch. 'Dead on time. Huovinen is chicken-livered; he could have delayed it somehow.'

There came a gap in the traffic and Armstrong jolted the barrow over the kerb. 'What now?' he asked as they crossed the street.

'I don't know,' said Carey heavily. 'Let's find a place where we're not too conspicuous.'

'The mill is as good a place as any.'

'No; there'll be a watchman. Go around the next corner and we'll see what we can find.'

They were lucky. A trench was being dug along one side of the street. Carey said, 'Just the thing; we'll stop here.'

Armstrong stopped and lowered the barrow. 'Why here?'

Carey sighed and plucked at his jacket. 'Don't be dim. This uniform and those exposed pipes go together. We look natural'

Armstrong glanced around. 'A good thing the gang's knocked off work for the day.'

'Yes,' said Carey. 'Jump in the hole and you'll look natural.' Armstrong dropped into the trench and Carey squatted on his heels. 'Got any bright ideas?'

'There's the empty house where I found the barrow. We could lie low in the cellar.'

'Until tomorrow?' Carey pondered and shook his head. 'The problem is the head count at the frontier post. They'll be two short and that might make it a bit unhealthy around here before long.'

Armstrong snapped his fingers. 'There's a railway goes from here to Imatra. Maybe we could get a ride.'

'Nothing doing. Railway police are notoriously efficient – especially at frontiers. All it needs is a telephone call from that frontier post to say there are two Finns missing and they'll be doubly efficient.'

'There's a copper coming up just behind you,' said Armstrong.

Carey did not turn. 'Not Boris Ivanevitch, I hope.'

'No.'

'Then have a look at that pipe and tell me what you see.'

Armstrong ducked down into the trench. His voice floated up. 'It's not cracked.'

'It must be cracked somewhere,' said Carey loudly. He heard the crunch of boots on road gravel behind him. 'We'll have to do a smoke test.' He looked up and saw the policeman. 'Good evening, comrade.'

The policeman's face was expressionless. 'Working late?'

'I always have to work late when something goes wrong,' said Carey in a grumbling voice. 'If it isn't one thing it's another, and they always pick on me. Now it's a pipe that's sprung a leak which no one can find.'

The policeman looked into the trench. 'What's this for?'

'Drainage for the new paper mill over there.'

The policeman looked at Carey. His eyes were like stones. 'You won't drain a paper mill through a pipe that size.'

'Not the main drainage for the mill,' said Carey. This is what you might call the domestic drainage for the lavatories and the canteen and so on.' An idea suddenly came into his mind, the brilliance of which astounded him. 'Perhaps the leak is in the mill. I might have to go in and see if I can find it there.' He stood up. 'You never can tell what a bad leak will do underground – undermine walls, anything.' He frowned. 'There's some heavy machinery in there.'

'So they tell me,' said the policeman. 'Imported from Finland.'

'I don't know why we can't use our own Russian stuff,' said Carey disgustedly. 'But Russian or Finnish, it will collapse if the foundations are washed from under it. I'd better go and have a look.'

'You're keen on your job,' said the policeman.

'That's how I got to where I am,' said Carey. He jerked his thumb at Armstrong. 'Now, take that young chap; he'll never rise to be an inspector if he lives a hundred years. He never raises a finger unless someone tells him to.' He turned to the trench. 'Come on, useless; we're going into the mill. Bring your barrow with your spade – we might need them.'

He walked away as Armstrong climbed out of the trench and the policeman fell into step beside him. 'You're right,' said the policeman. 'Some of these young chaps *are* useless.'

'Do you have many like that in your lot?' asked Carey.

The policeman laughed. 'They wouldn't last long with us. No, it's the layabouts I come across in the course of duty who grate on my nerves. Youngsters of fifteen and sixteen with hair half-way down their backs and swilling vodka until they're rotten drunk. I don't know how they can afford it. I can't – not on my pay.'

Carey nodded. 'I'm having something of the same trouble with my own son. This generation is as soft as putty, but what can you do, comrade? What can you do?'

'Well, I'll tell you,' said the policeman. 'Just tell that son of yours to keep out of my way. I'm getting a bit heavy-handed these days.'

They stopped at the mill entrance. 'Perhaps you're right,' said Carey. 'Maybe that's what's needed.'

'It is,' said the policeman. He flicked a hand in farewell. 'I hope you find your leak, comrade.'

'Just a minute,' said Carey. 'I've just thought of something. The watchman might not let us in.'

The policeman grinned. 'I'll have a word with him; it'll be all right.'

He walked into the mill and Carey winked at Armstrong. 'Not bad chaps, these Russian coppers, when you get to know them – in spite of Boris Ivanevitch. Come on.'

'Thanks for the testimonial,' said Armstrong. 'It's just the thing I need to get a job around here. Why are we going in?'

'You park the barrow near the temporary office in the corner. Then you go away and keep the watchman busy while I do a spot of burglary.'

'You can't burgle in front of a copper.'

'He won't stay around,' said Carey. 'He has his beat to cover.'

'All right; you do your burglary – then what?'

Carey grinned. 'Then we get ourselves booted out of Russia.'

Half an hour later, when they were walking up to the frontier post, Carey said, 'It was the papers that bothered me.

Leaving Russia is easy, but not with Merikken's papers. Then I started talking to the copper about the mill and it gave me the idea. I'd seen those blueprints in that office this morning.'

Armstrong trundled the wheelbarrow. 'I hope it works. There's the frontier post.'

'Remember you don't know any Russian,' said Carey. 'It would be uncharacteristic in a Finn of your class.'

'I don't know any Finnish either,' said Armstrong. 'And that's bloody uncharacteristic.'

'Then keep your mouth shut,' said Carey. 'If you have to talk at all use Swedish; but don't talk if you can help it. Leave the talking to me. And hope that none of these guards are studying engineering or mathematics.'

They bore down on the frontier post at a steady three miles an hour. Armstrong was still wearing working overalls but Carey had covered his uniform. He had stopped being a Russian and was now a Finn. The guard regarded them with mild surprise as they approached. 'This is as far as you go,' he said in Russian, and accompanied the statement with a smile.

Carey answered in fast Finnish. 'Did the bus driver tell you we were coming? The fool left us behind. We've had to walk from the paper mill.'

The smile left the guard's face as he heard the Finnish. 'Where the devil have you come from?' he asked in Russian.

'I don't speak Russian,' said Carey. 'Don't you know Finnish?'

'Sergeant!' yelled the guard, passing the buck.

A sergeant came out of the guard house, leisurely fastening his belt. 'What's the matter?'

'These two Finns popped up. They came from back there.'

'Oh, they did, did they?' The sergeant stepped over and inspected them critically, his eyes dwelling for a time on the barrow. In exceedingly bad Finnish he asked, 'Where did you come from?'

'The paper mill,' said Carey, speaking slowly. 'The bus driver left us behind.' He indicated the barrow. 'We had to collect these papers to take to the boss in Imatra. It took us a while to find them and when we came out the bus had gone.'

'What are the papers?'

'Machine drawings and calculations. See for yourself.' Carey threw aside the sacking on top of the barrow and picked up the top document. He unfolded it to reveal a blue-print which he gave to the sergeant. 'That's one of the draw-ings.'

The sergeant studied the complexity of lines with uncomprehending eyes. 'Why take them back to Imatra?'

'For revision,' said Carey. 'It happens all the time. When you build a complicated machine it doesn't always fit together right, usually because some fool of a draughtsman has made a mistake. So the drawings have to be amended.'

The sergeant raised his head and eyed Carey and then looked at the blueprint again. 'How do I know this is what you say it is? I know nothing about paper machinery.'

'In the bottom righthand corner there's the name of our company and a description of the drawing. Can you read that much Finnish?'

The sergeant did not reply. He handed the blueprint back to Carey. 'Are they all like this?'

'Help yourself,' said Carey generously.

The sergeant bent and rooted about in the wheelbarrow. When he straightened he was holding a hardbound exercise book. He opened it and glanced at a solid block of mathe-matical equations. 'And this?'

'I wouldn't know until I saw it,' said Carey. 'It could be about the chemistry or it could be mechanical. Let me see.' He leaned over to look at the page the sergeant was examining. 'Ah, yes; those are the calculations for the roller speeds. This machine is very advanced – very technical. Do you know that the paper goes through at seventy kilometres an hour? You have to be very exact when you're working at those speeds.'

The sergeant flicked through the pages and then dropped the book into the barrow. 'What do you mean – chemical?'

Carey was enthusiastic. 'Papermaking is as much a chemical process as mechanical. There's the sulphite and the sulphate and the clay-all have to be worked out in exact formulae for the making of different kinds of paper. I'll show you what I mean.' He dug into the wheelbarrow and brought up a roll of papers. 'These are the calculations for that kind of thing. Look; these are the equations for making tissue paper of cosmetic quality – and here – the calculations for ordinary newsprint.'

The sergeant waved away the papers from under his nose. 'I'm sorry,' he said. 'I have no authority to let you pass. I will have to consult my captain.' He turned to go back into the guard house.

'Perrrkele!' swore Carey, giving the 'r' its full Finnish value. 'You know damned well by the head count that thirty-six came in and only thirty-four went out.'

The sergeant halted in mid-stride. Slowly he turned and looked at the guard who shrugged helplessly. 'Well?' he asked acidly.

The guard was out of luck. 'I haven't put it in the book yet.'

'How many went out tonight?'

'Thirty-four, plus the driver.'

'How many came in this morning?'

'I don't know. I wasn't on duty this morning.'

'You don't know!' The sergeant was apoplectic. 'Then what's the use of doing a head count?' He took a deep breath. 'Bring me the book,' he said arctically.

The guard bobbed his head and went into the guard house at the double. He emerged in less than fifteen seconds and handed the sergeant a small record book. The sergeant turned the pages and then gave the guard a look that ought to have frozen the blood in his veins. 'Thirty-six came in,' he said softly. 'And you didn't know.'

The luckless guard had the sense to keep his mouth shut. The sergeant checked his watch. 'When did the bus go through?'

'About three-quarters of an hour ago.'

'*About!*' the sergeant screamed. 'You're supposed to know to the second.' He slapped the page. 'You're supposed to record it in here.' He snapped his mouth shut into a straight line and the temperature fell. 'For *about* three-quarters of an hour two foreign nationals have been wandering on the wrong side of the frontier without anyone knowing about it. Am I supposed to tell that to the captain?' His voice was low.

The guard was silent. 'Well, speak up!' the sergeant yelled.

'I . . . I don't know,' said the guard miserably.

'You don't know,' repeated the sergeant in freezing tones. 'Well, do you know this? Do you know what would happen to me – ' he slapped himself on the chest – 'to me if I told him that? Within a week I'd be serving on the Chinese frontier – and so would you, you little turd, but that wouldn't make me any happier.'

Carey tried to look unconcerned; he was not supposed to know Russian. He saw the beginnings of a grin appear on Armstrong's face and kicked him on the ankle.

'Stand to attention!' roared the sergeant, and the guard snapped straight, his back like a ramrod. The sergeant went very close to him and peered at him from a range of six inches. 'I have no intention of serving on the Chinese frontier,' he said. 'But I will guarantee one thing. Within a week you'll be wishing you were on the Chinese frontier – and on the Chinese side of it.'

He withdrew. 'You'll stay there until I tell you to move,' he said quietly, and came over to Carey. 'What's your name?' he asked in Finnish.

'Mäenpää,' said Carey. 'Rauno Mäenpää. He's Simo Velling.'

'Your passes?'

Carey and Armstrong produced their passes and the sergeant scrutinized them. He handed them back. 'Report here when you come in tomorrow. Report to me and no one else.'

Carey nodded. 'We can go?'

'You can go,' said the sergeant tiredly. He swung around and yelled at the unfortunate guard, 'Well, what are you waiting for? The grass to grow between your toes? Raise that barrier.'

The guard was electrified into sudden action. He raised the barrier and Armstrong pushed the wheelbarrow to the other side. Carey was about to follow when he paused. He turned to the sergeant and said, 'Papermaking is very interesting, you know. When the factory is working you ought to go and see it. Very spectacular.'

'I might do that,' said the sergeant.

Carey nodded pleasantly and followed Armstrong. He took a deep breath as though it was a different kind of air.

THIRTY-FOUR

Schmidt consulted his watch. 'One minute.' He dropped a cigarette stub on the floor and put his foot on it.

'We'll wait,' said McCready. He nodded to Denison. 'Check the windows – see if there's anyone out there. You too, Harding.'

Denison went to the window. All was quiet and nothing moved except water ripples in the distance and the reeds which swayed stiffly in the light breeze. 'All quiet.'

'Here, too,' said Harding, who was at the back window. 'Not a thing stirring on the mountain.'

'I think you're trying to pull a fast one,' said McCready. 'It would be a hell of a joke if there was just one man out there.'

Schmidt shrugged. 'Wait for it.'

Denison saw a movement in the reed bed at the edge of the marsh. 'There's something – or someone out there. It's a man. He's . . .'

His words were cut off by staccato explosions. In front of the hut the ground danced and soil fountained under the impact of bullets. An upthrown stone hit the pane of glass in front of Denison and the glass fractured and starred. He ducked hastily.

The noise stopped, chopping off into a dead silence.

McCready let out his breath. 'Automatic weapons. At least three.'

'Five,' said Schmidt. 'Seven men – eight including me.' His hand dipped into his pocket and came back out with the packet of cigarettes. 'I've just cast my vote.'

McCready casually laid down his pistol on the table. 'Power grows out of the barrel of a gun. Your guns are bigger.'

'I thought you'd see sense,' said Schmidt approvingly. 'Where's the map, or whatever it is?'

'Give it to him,' said McCready.

Denison took a folded sheet of paper from his pocket and held it out to Schmidt who examined it with interest. His interest turned to bafflement. 'Is this all?'

'That's all,' said Denison.

'This word – ' Schmidt stumblingly pronounced It – '*Luonnonpuisto*. What does it mean?'

'A literal translation would be "nature park",' said McCready. 'The other three words mean lake, hill and gap. The numbers are co-ordinates in degrees of a circle. If you can find a lake, a hill and a gap in that exact relationship, all in a nature park, then you've solved the problem.' He smiled at Schmidt. 'I can't say I wish you better luck than we've had.'

'Not much to go on,' said Schmidt. 'And this is a photocopy.'

'Someone snatched the original at Kevo. Our friend there got a bump on the head. So it wasn't you, then?'

'Obviously it wasn't,' said Schmidt. 'The Americans?'

'I don't think so.'

'I do think so,' stated Schmidt. 'Because they aren't here. Perhaps they're back at Kevo measuring angles with a theodolite like he was doing.' He pointed at Denison.

'Maybe,' said McCready non-committally.

Schmidt stared at the paper. 'This is foolishness. Why didn't he give the name of the nature park?'

'Why should he?' asked McCready. 'He knew it. That is just an *aide-mémoire* – just for the figures. You see, Merikken *knew* where the papers were and expected to dig them up himself – he didn't expect to be killed in an air raid. But since one bit of rough country looked very much like another he took the precaution of measuring those angles.' He offered Schmidt a derisory smile. 'Those papers will be a hell of a job to find – especially with interference.'

Schmidt had a sour expression on his face as he folded the paper and put it into his pocket. 'Where's your theodolite?'

'Over there in the corner.'

'You don't mind if I borrow it?' His voice was heavily ironic.

'Go ahead; we can get another.'

Schmidt stood up, went to the door and opened it. He shouted something in Czech and came back into the room. 'Put your guns on the table.'

McCready hesitated, then said, 'All right, everybody; put your guns with mine.'

'You're showing sense,' said Schmidt. 'Neither of us can afford a shooting incident – especially if people are killed.' He laughed. 'If only I have the guns we'll both be safe.'

Diana reluctantly laid down her gun and Harding followed suit. When the door opened to admit another man there were five pistols laid out. The man was carrying an automatic rifle and when Schmidt saw that McCready was looking at it with wary interest he laughed, and said, 'We borrowed some of your NATO weapons. They're not bad.' He spoke to the man and pointed at the back packs, then he picked up the pistols, put three of them into his pockets and held the other two in his hands.

'You spoke of interference,' he said to McCready. 'You will not interfere. You are out of the game.'

The other man was dumping the contents of the packs on the floor. He gave a startled exclamation as he came upon McCready's collapsible rifle. Schmidt smiled, and said,

'Always trying, Mr McCready – but that I expect. You will stay in this hut. If you attempt to leave it there is a grave danger of being shot dead.'

'How long for?'

Schmidt shrugged. 'For as long as I consider necessary.'

Diana spoke up. 'We'll need water.'

Schmidt regarded her speculatively, then nodded abruptly. 'I am not an inhumane man.' He pointed to Harding and Denison. 'You and you will bring water now. The rest will stay here.'

Denison picked up the two empty buckets, and Harding said, 'We'll need as much as possible. I'll take the bowls.'

The man with the automatic rifle slung it over his shoulder together with McCready's rifle. He picked up the theodolite and its tripod and left the hut followed by Denison and Harding, and Schmidt brought up the rear, a gun in each hand.

McCready watched them go down to the edge of the marsh, and cocked an eye at Diana. 'They seem to have bought it,' he said softly. 'For the next few weeks all the nature parks in Finland will be crawling with Czechs wielding theodolites. That ought to make the Finns properly suspicious.'

Denison walked down to the marsh acutely aware that the man behind him was holding a pair of pistols. He bent down and began to fill the buckets. Schmidt lobbed the pistols one at a time into the marsh, using an over arm throw like a cricketer. He spaced them well out and Denison knew they would be irrecoverable. He straightened his back and said, 'How will we know when it's safe to come out of the hut?'

There was a grim smile on Schmidt's face. 'You won't,' he said uncompromisingly. 'You'll have to take your chances.'

Denison stared at him and then looked down at Harding who shrugged helplessly. 'Let's go back to the hut,' he said.

Schmidt stood with his hands on his hips and kept his eyes on them all the way to the hut. The door closed behind them and he hitched his pack into a more comfortable position, spoke briefly to his companion, and set off along the edge of the marsh in the same direction from which he had come, keeping up the same stolid pace as when he had arrived.

THIRTY-FIVE

It seemed to Denison that of all the episodes he had gone through since being flung into this hodge-podge of adventures the time he spent in the hut at Sompio was characterized by a single quality – the quality of pure irritation. The five of them were pent up – 'cribbed, cabined and confined', as Harding ironically quoted – and there was nothing that any of them could do about it, especially after McCready tested the temperature of the water.

After two hours had gone by he said, 'I think we ought to do something about this. I'll just stick my toe in and see what it's like.'

'Be careful,' said Harding. 'I was wrong about Schmidt – he doesn't bluff.'

'He can't leave his men around here for ever,' said McCready. 'And we'd look damned foolish if there's no one out there.'

He opened the door and stepped outside and took one pace before a rifle cracked and a bullet knocked splinters from a log by the side of his head so that white wood showed. He came in very fast and slammed the door. 'It's a bit warm outside,' he said.

'How many do you think there are?' asked Harding.

'How the hell would I know?' demanded McCready irritably. He put his hand to his cheek and pulled out a wood splinter, then looked at the blood on his fingertips.

'I saw the man who fired,' said Denison from the window. 'He was just down there in the reeds.' He turned to McCready. 'I don't think he meant to kill. It was just a warning shot.'

'How do you make that out?' McCready displayed the blood on his hand. 'It was close.'

'He has an automatic rifle,' said Denison. 'If he wanted to kill you he'd have cut you down with a burst.'

McCready was on the receiving end for the first time of the hard competency which Carey had found so baffling in Denison. He nodded reluctantly. 'I suppose you're right.'

'As for how many there are, that's not easy to say,' said Denison. 'All it needs is one at the front and one at the back, but it depends on how long Schmidt wants to keep us here. If it's longer than twenty-four hours there'll be more than two because they'll have to sleep.'

'And we can't get away under cover of darkness because there isn't any,' said Harding.

'So we might as well relax,' said Denison with finality. He left the window and sat at the table.

'Well, I'm damned!' said McCready. 'You've got it all worked out, haven't you?'

Denison looked at him with a half-smile. 'Have you anything to add?'

'No,' said McCready disgustedly. He went over to Diana and talked to her in a low voice.

Harding joined Denison at the table. 'So we're stuck here.'

'But quite safe,' said Denison mildly. 'As long as we don't do anything bloody foolish, such as walking through that door.' He unfolded a map of the Sompio Nature Park and began to study it.

'How are you feeling?' asked Harding.

'Fine.' Denison looked up. 'Why?'

'As your personal head-shrinker I don't think you'll be needing me much longer. How's the memory?'

'It's coming back in bits and pieces. Sometimes I feel I'm putting together a jigsaw puzzle.'

'It's not that I want to probe into a delicate area,' said Harding. 'But do you remember your wife?'

'Beth?' Denison nodded. 'Yes, I remember her.'

'She's dead, you know,' said Harding in an even uninflected voice. 'Do you remember much about that?'

Denison pushed away the map and sighed. 'That bloody car crash – I remember it.'

'And how do you feel about it?'

'How the he'll would you expect me to feel about it?' said Denison with suppressed violence. 'Sorrow, anger – but it was over three years ago and you can't feel angry for ever. I'll always miss Beth; she was a fine woman.'

'Sorrow and anger,' repeated Harding. 'Nothing wrong with that. Quite normal.' He marvelled again at the mysteries of the human mind. Denison had apparently rejected his previous feelings of guilt; the irrational component of his life had vanished. Harding wondered what would happen if he wrote up Denison's experiences and presented them in a paper for the journals – 'The Role of Multiple Psychic Trauma in the Suppression of Irrational Guilt'. He doubted if it would be accepted as a serious course of treatment.

Denison said, 'Don't resign yet, Doctor, I'd still like to retain your services.'

'Something else wrong?'

'Not with me. I'm worried about Lyn. Look at her.' He nodded towards Lyn who was lying on her back on a bunk, her hands clasped behind her head and staring at the ceiling. 'I've hardly been able to get a word out of her. She's avoiding me – wherever I am, she's not. It's becoming conspicuous.'

Harding took out a packet of cigarettes and examined the contents. 'I might have to ration these,' he said glumly. 'I've also been wondering about Lyn. She is a bit withdrawn – not surprisingly, of course, because she has a problem to solve.'

'Oh? What's her problem? Apart from the problems we all have here?'

Harding lit a cigarette. 'It's personal. She talked to me about it – hypothetically and in veiled terms. She'll get over it one way or another.' He drummed his fingers on the table. 'What do you think of her?'

'She's a fine person. A bit mixed up, but that's due to her upbringing. I suppose the problem has to do with her father.'

'In a manner of speaking,' said Harding. 'Tell me; what was the difference in age between your wife and yourself?'

'Ten years,' said Denison. He frowned. 'Why?'

'Nothing,' said Harding lightly. 'It's just that it could make things a lot easier – your having had a wife so much younger than yourself, I mean. You used to wear a beard, didn't you?'

'Yes,' said Denison. 'What the he'll are you getting at?'

'I'd grow it again if I were you,' advised Harding. 'The face you're wearing tends to confuse her. It might be better to hide it behind a bush.'

Denison's jaw dropped. 'You mean . . . Diana said something . . . she can't . . . it's imposs . . .'

'You damned fool!' said Harding in a low voice. 'She's fallen for Denison but the face she sees is Meyrick's – her father's face. It's enough to tear any girl in half, so do something about it.' He pushed back his chair and stood up. 'Talk to her, but go easy.' He went to the other end of the room and joined McCready and Diana, leaving Denison staring at Lyn.

McCready organized watches. 'Not that anything is likely to happen,' he said. 'But I'd like advance notice if it does.

Those not on watch can do what they like. My advice is sleep.' He lay on a bunk and followed his own advice.

Harding wandered off into the storeroom and Denison resumed his study of the map of Sompio. From time to time he heard scrapings and bangings as Harding moved boxes about. Diana was on watch at a window and she and Lyn conversed in low tones.

After a couple of hours Harding came back looking rumpled and dishevelled. In his hand he carried what Denison took to be a gallon paint can. 'I've found it.'

'Found what?'

Harding put the can on the table. 'The powder.' He prised the lid off the can. 'Look.'

Denison inspected the grainy black powder. 'So what?'

'So we can shoot the punt gun. I've found some shot, too.'

McCready's eyes flickered open and he sat up. 'What gun?'

'The punt gun I was telling you about. You didn't seem interested in it at the time.'

'That was when we had guns of our own,' said McCready. 'What is it? A shotgun?'

'You could call it that,' said Harding, and Denison smiled.

'I think I'd better look at it,' said McCready, and swung his legs over the side of the bunk. 'Where is it?'

'I'll show you.' Harding and McCready went out, and Denison folded the map and went to the window. He looked out at the unchanging scene and sighed.

'What's the matter?' asked Diana; 'Bored?'

'I was wondering if our friends are still around.'

'The only way to find out is to stick your head outside.'

'I know,' said Denison. 'One of us will have to do it sooner or later. I think I'll have a crack at it. It's three hours since McCready tried.'

'No,' said Lyn. The word seemed to be torn out of her involuntarily. 'No,' she said again. 'Leave that to the . . . the professionals.'

Diana smiled. 'Meaning me? I'm willing.'

'Let's not argue about it,' said Denison peaceably. 'We're all in this together. Anyway, it's a sure cure for boredom. Keep your eye on those reeds, Diana.'

'All right,' she said as he walked to the door. Lyn looked at him dumbly.

He swung open the door slowly and waited a full minute before going outside, and when he did so his hands were above his head. He waited, immobile, for another minute and, when nothing happened, he took another step forward. Diana shouted and simultaneously he saw a movement in the reeds on the edge of the marsh. The flat report of the rifle shot coincided with a clatter of stones six feet in front of him and there was a shrill *spaaang* as the bullent ricocheted over his head.

He waved both his hands, keeping them over his head, and cautiously backed into the hut. He was closing the door when McCready came back at a dead run. 'What happened?'

'Just testing the temperature.' said Denison. 'Somebody has to do it.'

'Don't do it when I'm not here.' McCready went to the window. 'So they're still there.'

Denison smiled at Lyn. 'Nothing to worry about,' he assured her. 'They're just keeping us in a pen.' She turned away and said nothing. Denison looked at McCready. 'What do you think of Harding's gun?'

'He doesn't think much of it,' said Harding.

'For God's sake!' said McCready. 'It's not a shotgun – it's a light artillery piece. Even if you could lift it – which you can't – you couldn't shoot it. The recoil would break your shoulder. It's bloody useless.'

'It's not meant for waving about,' said Harding. 'It's designed for use on the punt, like a 16-inch gun on a battleship. You don't find many of those on land because of the difficulty of absorbing the recoil – but you can put half a dozen on a ship because the recoil is absorbed by the water.'

'Just my point,' said McCready. 'It's as useless as a 16-inch gun would be if we had one. The powder is something else; maybe we can do something with that.'

'Like making hand grenades?' queried Denison sardonically. 'What do you want to do? Start a war?'

'We have to find a way of leaving here.'

'We'll leave when the Czechs let us,' said Denison. 'And nobody will get hurt. They've fallen for your fake treasure map, so what's the hurry now?' There was a cutting edge to his voice. 'Any fighting you do now will be for fighting's sake, and that's just plain stupid.'

'You're right, of course,' said McCready, but there was an undercurrent of exasperation in his voice. 'Your watch, Harding; then Denison and then me.'

'You don't mind if I mess about with the gun while I keep watch?' asked Harding. 'It's of personal interest,' he added apologetically. 'I *am* a wildfowler.'

'Just don't cause any sudden bangs,' said McCready. 'I don't think my heart could stand it. And no one goes outside that door except on my say-so.'

Denison stretched his arms. 'I think I'll try to sleep for a while. Wake me when it's my watch.' He lay on his side on the bunk and for a while regarded Harding who had struggled in with the punt gun. He had some paper and appeared to be making small paper bags.

Denison's eyelids drooped and presently he slept.

He was awakened by Harding shaking his shoulder. 'Wake up, Giles; your watch.'

Denison yawned. 'Anything happening?'

'Not a thing to be seen.'

Denison got up and went to the window. Harding said, 'I think I've figured out the gun. I've even made up some cartridges. I wish I could try it.' There was a wistful note in his voice.

Denison looked about the room. The others were asleep which was not surprising because it was midnight. 'You'd better rest. When we move we'll probably move quickly.'

Harding lay on his bunk and Denison inspected the view from the window. The sun shone in his eyes, just dipping over the horizon far over the marsh; that was the lowest it would set and from then on it would be rising. He shaded his eyes. The sun seemed to be slightly veiled as though there was a thickening in the air over the marsh, the slightest of hazes. Probably a forest fire somewhere, he thought, and turned to the table to find the results of Harding's handiwork.

Harding had made up six cartridges, crude cylindrical paper bags tied at the top with cotton thread. Denison picked one up and could feel the small shot through the paper. The cartridges were very heavy; he bounced one in his hand and thought its weight was not far short of two pounds. A pity Harding could not get his wish but, as McCready had pointed out, firing the gun was impossible.

He bent down and picked up the punt gun, straining his back and staggering under the weight. He cradled it in his arms and attempted to bring the butt to his shoulder. The muzzle swung erratically in a wild arc. It was impossible to aim and the recoil as two pounds of shot left the barrel would flatten the man who fired it. He shook his head and laid it down.

An hour later the view from the window was quite different. The sunshine had gone to be replaced by a diffuse light and the haze over the marsh had thickened into a light mist. He could still see the boathouse where the punt lay, and the reeds at the marsh edge, but farther out the light was gone from the water and beyond that was a pearly greyness.

He woke McCready. 'Come and look at this.' McCready looked at the mist thoughtfully, and Denison said, 'It's been thickening steadily. If it keeps to the same schedule visibility will be down to ten yards in another hour.'

'You think we ought to make a break?'

'I think we ought to get ready,' said Denison carefully. 'And I think we ought to find out if our friends are still there before the mist gets any thicker.'

'We meaning me,' said McCready sourly.

Denison grinned. 'It's your turn – unless you think Harding ought to have a go. Or Diana.'

'I suppose I volunteer – but let's wake up the others first.'

Ten minutes later it was established beyond doubt that the besiegers were still there. McCready slammed the door. 'That bastard doesn't like me; I felt the wind of that one.'

'I saw him,' said Denison. 'The range is a hundred yards – not more. He could have killed you, but he didn't.'

'The mist has thickened,' said Diana. 'Even in the last ten minutes.'

'Let's get everything packed,' said McCready.

They started to repack their gear, all except Denison who went to the window to stare out over the marsh. Fifteen minutes later McCready joined him. 'Aren't you coming?'

'Visibility down to fifty yards,' said Denison. 'I wonder what would happen if someone went outside now.'

'If Johnny is still in those reeds he wouldn't see.'

'What makes you think he's still in the reeds? If he has any sense he'll have closed in. So will the others.'

'Others?'

'Logic says there are at least four-two to watch back and front, and two to sleep.'

'I'm not so sure of that,' said McCready. 'It's only theory.'

'Try climbing out of the back window,' said Denison drily. He rubbed his jaw. 'But you're right in a way; it doesn't make sense, does it? Not when Schmidt could have put two men right here in the hut with us. He'd have saved two men.'

McCready shook his head. 'He's too wise a bird to fall for that. When you have a rifle that'll kill at a quarter mile you don't guard at a range of three yards. Guards that close can be talked to and conned into making a false move. We can't talk to these jokers outside and they talk to us with bullets.'

He tapped on the glass. 'But Schmidt didn't reckon on this mist. It's thickening rapidly and when the visibility gets down to ten yards I think we'll take a chance.'

'Then you take it on your own,' said Denison flatly. 'If you think I'm going to go stumbling around out there when there are four men armed with automatic rifles you're crazy. They might not want to kill us by design but they could sure as hell kill us by accident. I don't go – nor does Lyn. Nor does Harding, if I have any say.'

'A chance like this and you won't take it,' said McCready disgustedly.

'I'm not in the chance-taking business, and in this case it doesn't make sense. Tell me; suppose you leave this hut – what would you do?'

'Head back to Vuotso,' said McCready. 'We couldn't miss it if we skirted the edge of the marsh.'

'No, you couldn't,' agreed Denison. 'And neither could the Czechs miss you. You'd be doing the obvious. Come over here.' He walked over to the table and spread out the map, using Harding's cartridges to hold down the corners. 'I'm not recommending leaving the hut at all – not the way things are now – but if it's necessary that's the way to go.'

McCready looked at the way Denison's finger pointed. 'Over the marsh! You're crazy.'

'What's so crazy about it? It's the unexpected direction. They wouldn't think of following us across there.'

'You're still out of your mind,' said McCready. 'I had a good look at that marsh from up on the mountain. You can't tell where the land begins and the water ends, and where there's water you don't know how deep it is. You'd stand a damned good chance of drowning, especially if you couldn't see ten yards ahead.'

'Not if you took the punt,' said Denison. 'The two girls and one man in the punt – two men alongside pushing. Where the water becomes deep they hang on and are towed while the people in the punt paddle.' He tapped the map. 'The marsh is two miles across; even in pitch darkness you could get through in under four hours. Once you're across you head west and you can't help but hit the main road north from Rovaniemi.' He bent over the map. 'You'd strike it somewhere between Vuotso and Tankapirtti, and the whole journey wouldn't take you more than seven or eight hours.'

'Well, I'll be damned!' said McCready. 'You've really been working all this out, haven't you?'

'Just in case of emergency,' said Denison. He straightened. 'The emergency hasn't happened yet. We're a bloody sight safer here than we would be out there. If there was a life and death reason for getting out of here I'd be in favour of it, but right now I don't see it.'

'You're a really cool logical bastard,' said McCready. 'I wonder what it takes to make you angry. Don't you feel even annoyed that we're being made fools of by those Czechs out there?'

'Not so annoyed as to relish stopping a bullet,' said Denison with a grin. 'Tell you what – you were so keen on the democratic process when you were stringing Schmidt along, so I'll settle for a vote.'

'Balls!' said McCready. 'It's either the right thing to do or it isn't. You don't make it right just by voting. I think you're right but I don't . . .'

He was interrupted by a single shot from outside the hut and then there was a sustained rapid chatter of automatic fire. It stopped, and McCready and Denison stared at each other wordlessly. There was another report, a lighter sound than the rifle fire, and a window of the hut smashed in.

'Down!' yelled McCready, and flung himself flat. He lay on the floor of the hut and then twisted around until he could see Denison. 'I think your emergency has arrived.'

THIRTY-SIX

All was silent.

Denison lay on the floor and looked at McCready who said, 'I think that was a pistol shot; it sounded different. I hope it was.'

'For God's sake, why?'

McCready was grim. 'Just pray they don't start shooting at this hut with those bloody rifles. They're NATO issue and they pack a hell of a wallop. In Northern Ireland the army found they were shooting through houses – through one wall and out the other.'

Denison turned his head. 'Are you all right, Lyn?'

She was flat on the floor by her bunk: 'I . . . I think so.' Her voice was tremulous.

'I'm not,' said Harding. 'I think I was hit. My arm is numb.'

Diana crossed the hut at a low run and flopped down beside Harding. 'Your face is bleeding.'

'I think that was the flying glass,' he said. 'It's my arm that's worrying me. Can you have a look at it?'

'Christ!' said McCready savagely. 'One lousy bullet and he has to get in the way. What do you think now, Denison? Still think it's not time to leave?'

'I haven't heard anything more.' Denison crawled over to the window and cautiously raised himself. 'The mist is much thicker. Can't see a damned thing.'

'Get down from there,' snapped McCready. Denison pulled down his head but stayed in a crouch below the window. 'How's Harding?'

Harding answered. 'The bone is broken,' he said. 'Can someone get my black box? It's in my pack.'

'I'll get it,' said Lyn.

McCready crawled over to Harding and inspected his arm. Diana had torn away the shirt sleeve to get at the wound, a small puncture. Harding's arm was a curious shape; it seemed to have developed an extra joint. 'It was a pistol shot,' said McCready. 'If you'd have been hit by one of those rifle bullets at that range you'd have no arm left.'

Again came the sound of automatic fire but from a greater distance. It sounded like a noisy sewing machine and was interspersed with other single shots. It stopped as quickly as it had begun.

'Sounds like a battle,' said McCready. 'What do you think, Denison?'

'I think it's time to leave,' said Denison. 'We've had one bullet in here – we might get more. You and I will go down to the punt; Diana and Lyn can help Harding along as soon as we've made sure it's safe. We leave the packs and travel light. Bring a compass, if you have one.'

'I've got one in my pocket.' McCready looked down at Harding and saw he had filled a syringe and was injecting himself in the arm. 'How are you, Doctor?'

'That will keep it quiet,' said Harding, taking out the needle. 'If someone can slap a bandage around it.'

'I can do better than that,' said Diana. 'I can make splints.'

'Good,' said Harding. 'I have a broken arm – not a broken leg. I can walk and I'll be ready to move in five minutes. Did you say something about going by punt?'

'Denison's idea.'

'Then why don't we take the gun?'

'Haul that bloody great . . . !' McCready stopped and glanced at Denison. 'What about it?'

Denison thought of two pounds of birdshot. 'Might give someone a fright.'

'Tie that tighter,' said Harding to Lyn. 'Then bring me those cartridges from the table.' He raised his head. 'If you are going scouting we'll have the gun loaded when you get back.'

'All right,' said McCready. 'Let's go.' All the frustration had dropped from him now that he had something to do. 'When we go out of the door we go flat on our bellies.'

He opened the door and wreaths of mist drifted into the hut. When he put his head around the corner of the door at floor level he found the visibility to be ten to fifteen yards, shifting in density as the mist drifted in from the marsh. He wriggled out and waited until Denison joined him, then put his mouth to Denison's ear and whispered, 'We separate but keep in sight of each other – ten yards should do it. We go one at a time in ten yard runs.'

At Denison's nod he went forward, then dropped to the ground ten yards ahead and, after a moment, waved Denison on. Denison angled away until he was parallel with McCready; he lay and stared into the mist but could see nothing. McCready went ahead again and dropped and then Denison followed, and so on until Denison put his hand wrist-deep in cold water. They were at the edge of the marsh.

He lay there, turning his head from side to side, trying to penetrate the pearly mist, his ears strained for the slightest sound. When he looked up he could see the tops of the stiff reeds, and all he could hear was a rustling as the lightest of airs brushed through them. From the marsh came the occasional call of a bird.

McCready edged up next to him. 'Where's the punt?'

'To the left – a hundred yards.'

They went slowly and separately, McCready leading because of his experience. At last he stopped and when Denison drew up with him he saw the loom of the boathouse through the mist. McCready put his lips next to Denison's ear. 'There could be someone in there. I'll take it from the other side. Give me exactly four minutes then close in from this side.' He wriggled away and was lost to sight.

Denison lay there watching the sweep second hand on his watch. Four minutes seemed a hell of a long time. At exactly two minutes there was a renewed burst of firing which made him start; it seemed to come from the direction of the hut but he could not be sure. He found he was sweating despite the cool clamminess of the mist.

At four minutes he went forward carefully and looked into the dimness under the roof of the boathouse. He saw no one until a movement on the other side made his stomach roll over until he realized it was McCready. 'All safe,' said McCready.

'We'd better take the punt out and ran it up on to the beach,' said Denison in a low voice. He waded into the water, trying not to splash, and floated out the punt. Between them they ran it up on to the shingle which crunched loudly. 'For Christ's sake, be quiet!' whispered McCready. 'Did you hear that last lot of shooting?'

'I thought it came from behind me.'

'I thought it came from the marsh,' said McCready. 'You can't tell with mist, though. It distorts sounds. Let's go back and get the others.'

They made it back to the hut uneventfully. McCready closed the door and said, 'There doesn't seem to be anyone out there – not towards the marsh, anyway. That idea of yours might be a good one.'

'I wouldn't go in any other direction,' said Denison briefly. 'Ready to move, Lyn?'

Her face was pale but her chin came up in the resolute gesture he had come to know. 'I'm ready.'

'McCready and I will go first. You follow and help Harding if he needs it. We won't be going too fast if we're carrying the gun.'

'It's loaded – but quite safe,' said Harding. His face was drawn. 'It can't be fired until it's cocked and a detonator cap put on the nipple.'

'We'd better know what we're going to do,' said McCready. 'Are you sure this gun will shoot, Doctor? I don't want us to be lumbered with a load of old iron.'

'It'll shoot,' said Harding. 'I tested the powder and it burns well; and I tested a detonator while they were shooting out there.'

Denison did not know what sound a detonator would make but that might account for his impression that a shot had come from the direction of the hut. He said, 'I think we ought to play safe until we get well into the marsh. Harding ought to go in the punt from the beginning because of his wound – and you, too, George, in case there's shooting. The girls and I will tag on behind.'

McCready nodded, but Harding said, 'I want Denison in the punt with me.'

McCready stared at him. 'Why?'

'Put it down to crankiness or, maybe, loss of blood,' said Harding. 'But that's the way I want it. Believe me, I know what I'm doing.'

McCready looked blankly at Denison. 'What do you say?'

'All right with me. If that's what he wants, that's what he gets.'

'Good,' said Harding. 'Come over here.' He took Denison to where the gun lay. 'It's all ready for going on to the punt. There'll be no difficulty in fixing it – it just drops into place and I have the breech ropes all ready to reeve through the eye-bolts.' He paused. 'There are two important items to remember when you shoot one of these things.'

'Go on.'

'First; keep your head well back when you pull the trigger. There'll be a blowback from the touch-hole which could make a nasty burn on your face. Secondly; you'll be lying flat on your belly when you shoot, and you've got a limited amount of lateral aim by shifting the butt – there's enough play in the breech ropes to allow for that. But just before you pull the trigger raise your knees from the bottom of the punt. That's important.'

'Why?'

Harding shook his head. 'I don't think you realize yet what sort of gun this is. If your knees are in contact with the punt when the recoil comes you're likely to have a couple of shattered kneecaps. Watch it.'

'God Almighty!' said Denison. He looked at Harding curiously. 'Why did you pick me instead of McCready?'

'McCready knows too much about guns,' said Harding. 'He might fall into the error that he knows about this one. I want somebody who'll do exactly as I say without contaminating it with what he thinks.' He smiled wryly. 'I don't know whether we're going to fire this gun – under the circumstances I hope not – but, believe me – when you pull that trigger you'll probably be just as surprised as the man you're shooting at.'

'Let's hope it never happens,' said Denison. 'How's your arm?'

Harding looked down at the improvised sling. 'It'll be fine as long as the drug holds out. I'm leaving my kit but I have a syringe loaded with pain-killer in my pocket. Just one more thing. If we shoot in the marsh it's going to be difficult to reload the gun. It will have to be done in shallow water with McCready at the front of the punt with a ramrod. I'll have a word with him about that.'

He went to McCready and Denison bent to examine the gun. It was suddenly much more real, no longer looking like an old piece of iron piping but a weapon deadly of purpose. He straightened to find Lyn at his side. 'An extra sweater,' she said, holding it out. 'It's always cold on the water.'

'Thanks,' he said, and took it from her. 'It'll be even colder in it. You shouldn't have come, Lyn; this is no place for you. Will you promise me something?'

'That depends.'

'If we get into trouble out there – shooting, perhaps – promise to duck out of it. Get down among the reeds and out of sight. Don't take any chances you don't have to.'

She nodded towards Harding. 'And what about him?'

'Leave him to the professionals. They'll look after him.'

'If it weren't for me he wouldn't be here,' she said sombrely. 'And you're a fine one to talk about not taking chances.'

He shrugged. 'All right – but there is something you can do for me. Find a ball of string. Harding might know where there is some.'

McCready came over. 'We're ready to move. Help me with the gun.' As they lifted it they heard several single shots. 'What the hell's going on out there?' said McCready. 'We're not being shot at – so who is?'

Denison took the strain at the butt end of the gun. 'Who cares? Let's take advantage.'

It was better this second time despite the hampering weight of the gun; they had a better sense of direction and knew where to go. Within five minutes they were lowering the gun on to the foredeck of the punt; it slotted neatly into place and Harding, hovering over it, wordlessly indicated how to fit the breech ropes.

Denison uncoiled the thirty-foot length of string that Lyn had found. He gave one end to McCready. 'Keep at the end of that,' he whispered. 'If you get into trouble tug and I'll stop. Two tugs and I'll back water.'

'Bloody good idea.'

Denison tapped Harding on the shoulder. 'Get in before we launch her.' Harding obeyed and Denison and McCready pushed the punt forward until it was afloat. Again there was the crunch of shingle and they waited with held breath to see if they had attracted attention. Denison climbed aboard over the stern and settled behind the gun. He gave the other end of the string to Harding. 'If you feel a tug let me know. Where are the paddles?'

'On the bottom boards next to the gun butt.'

He scrabbled and found them, short-handled and broad-bladed. Before he put them into the water he stared ahead. He was lying prone with his eyes not more than a foot above the level of the water. Ahead of him, on the fore-deck, stretched nine feet of gun. It looked less clumsy on the punt, more as if it belonged. The weapons system was complete.

'Wait!' whispered Harding. 'Take this needle and push it down the touch-hole.'

Denison stretched out his hand and drew back the hammer. It clicked into place at full cock and he jabbed the needle into the hole in the nipple and felt it pierce the paper cartridge. He waggled it about to enlarge the hole which would allow the flame to reach the powder, and then passed it back to Harding who gave him a detonator cap. Harding whispered, 'I'd keep that in your hand until you're ready to shoot. It's safer.'

He nodded and picked up the paddles and took a short, easy stroke as quickly as he could. The punt moved forward, more quickly than he had expected. Ripples ran backwards vee-shaped from the bow as the punt glided into the mist.

Denison had already determined to stay close to the banks of reeds. From the point of view of paddling the punt he would have been better in mid-channel but there he would be more exposed. Besides, he had the others to think of; they were wading and the water was more likely to be shallow by the reeds.

Harding whispered, 'McCready gave me his compass. What's the course?'

'North-west,' said Denison. 'If we have to make any course changes try to make them north rather than west.'

'Then steady as you go.'

It was an awkward position in which to paddle and he quickly developed aches, particularly at the back of his shoulders. And his breastbone ground against the bottom boards until he thought he was rubbing the skin off his chest. Whoever used the punt must have had a cushion there.

When he estimated they had travelled about two hundred yards he stopped and rested. From behind he could hear faint splashes and, when he looked back, he saw the faint figures of the other three. Beyond there was nothing but greyness. McCready came alongside, water up to his waist. 'What have you stopped for?'

'It's bloody hard work. Unnatural position. I'll be all right.'

From the land came a series of rapid shots, the stammer of an automatic rifle. McCready breathed, 'They're still at it. I'd like to know what . . .'

There was another shot, so shockingly close that McCready instinctively ducked and Denison flattened himself even closer to the bottom of the punt. There was a splashing noise to the left as though someone was running in shallow water; the sound receded and everything was quiet again.

McCready eased himself up. 'That was right here in the marsh. Let's move.'

Denison pushed off again quietly and the punt ghosted into the mist. He was aware that Harding had not said anything, so he turned his head. 'Are you okay?'

'Carry on,' said Harding. 'A bit more to the left.'

As they penetrated the marsh there were flaws in the mist – sudden thinnings and thickenings of the vapour apparently caused by a light air which stroked Denison's cheek with a delicate touch. Visibility would be no more than five yards and then, ten seconds later, the mist would swirl aside so that he could see, perhaps, forty yards. He did not like it; it was unpredictable and could not be relied on.

Behind, McCready plodded thigh-deep in the water. The footing was treacherous – mostly rotting vegetation but with the occasional ankle-twisting stone or, sometimes, an unexpected hole. He cast a glance over his shoulder and saw that Lyn, much shorter than he, had the water to her waist. He grinned at her and she smiled back at him weakly. Diana brought up the rear, turning her head constantly to look back.

They went on for fifteen minutes and then there was a choked cry from behind McCready. He looked back and saw that Lyn was neck-deep and already beginning to swim. Since he himself was in the water to his armpits this was not surprising so he gave two sharp tugs on the string. The punt ahead drifted back silently as Denison back-paddled gently, and came to a halt alongside McCready.

'You'll have to change course. We're getting out of our depth.'

Denison nodded and silently pointed the way he intended to go, keeping close to the reeds and heading towards what seemed to be a promontory about fifty yards away. As the mist closed in again to blot it out he commenced paddling again.

Once more the gentle, vagrant wind parted the mist and Denison, peering forward along the barrel of the gun, saw a movement and dug both paddles into the water as quietly as he could. The punt slowed to a halt. Again the mist closed in but he waited, hoping that McCready would have the sense not to come forward again to find out what was wrong.

When he felt the slight air pressure on his cheek increase he was ready for the diminution of the mist and the suddenly increased visibility. There was a man standing on the promontory which was just a shingle bank outthrust into the channel. Another man was walking towards him, splashing through water, and they waved to each other.

Denison put forth his hand and slipped the detonator cap on the nipple below the hammer, and with his other hand wielded a paddle gently. The punt came around slowly and with it the gun barrel. As the primitive foresight drifted across the target he back-paddled one stroke to arrest the movement.

His finger was on the trigger but he was hesitant about firing. For all he knew these men were innocent Finns caught up in a fortuitous battle with those gun-happy, crazy Czechs. One of the men turned and there was a sharp cry and Denison knew the punt had been seen. The other man brought up his arm stiffly and he saw two brief flashes just as the mist began to close in again.

That did it – no innocent Finn would shoot on sight. He squeezed the trigger, only remembering at the last moment to pull back his head and jerk up his knees from the bottom boards.

There was a pause of a single heart beat and then the gun went off. Flame flared from the touch-hole under the hammer and dazzled him but not so much that he could not see the monstrous flame that bloomed from the muzzle of the gun. Orange and yellow with white at its heart, it shot out twelve feet ahead of the punt, blinding him, and was accompanied by a deep-throated *booom.* The punt shivered and jerked back violently in the water and the bottom boards leaped convulsively under him. Then it was gone and a cloud of black smoke lazily ascended and there was the acrid stink of burnt powder in the air.

Although deafened by the concussion he thought he heard a shriek from ahead. Retinal images danced before his eyes as he tried to penetrate the suddenly dense mist and he could see nothing. An automatic rifle hammered from behind and suddenly the water ahead fountained in spurts right across the channel as someone traversed in a blind burst. There was a whipping sound overhead and bits of reed dropped on to his face as he looked up.

The rifle fire stopped.

After a moment Harding said weakly, 'What about reloading?'

'How long?'

'Five minutes.'

'Christ, no!' Denison burst into activity. 'We've got to move and bloody fast.' He brought up his legs and sat on his haunches so as to give the paddles a better grip in the water. This was no time to hang around and dead silence was not as important as getting clear. He jabbed the paddles into the water and made the punt move. As he skirted the promontory he kept a careful watch, not wanting to run aground, and still less wanting to meet whoever had been there.

The violence of that single shot was seared into him. What, in God's name, could it have been like at the receiving end? He looked sideways but there was only the drifting mist, and all he could hear was the quickened splashing of the others as they increased their pace to his speed.

He paddled until he was thoroughly weary, occasionally changing course as the channel wound among marshy islands or as Harding dictated from the compass. After half an hour at top speed he was exhausted and stopped with his shoulders bowed and paddles trailing in the water. His breath rasped in his throat and his chest felt sore.

Harding touched him on the shoulder. 'Rest,' he said. 'You've done enough.'

McCready came up, half wading and half swimming. 'Jesus!' he said. 'You set a pace.'

Denison grinned weakly. 'It was that last rifle burst. A bit too much for me. All I wanted to do was to get away.'

McCready held on to the side of the punt and surveyed the gun. 'When this thing went off I was sure the barrel had burst. I've never seen anything like it.'

'How far have we come?' asked Denison.

Harding used his good hand to fish in the bottom of the punt. He came up with the map, soggy and running with water, and gave it to Denison who unfolded it. He pointed over Denison's shoulder. 'I think we've just crossed that wide bit of water.'

'It was deep as well as wide,' said McCready. 'We had to swim.'

'That's much more than half-way,' said Denison. 'Dry land not far ahead.'

Diana and Lyn splashed up along the reeds in the shallower water. They were soaked and bedraggled. Denison pushed with a paddle and eased the punt towards them. 'You all right?' he asked quietly.

Diana nodded wearily and Lyn said, 'How much more of this?'

'Not far,' said Denison. 'You can travel the rest of the way in the punt.'

McCready nodded. 'I think we've got clear. I haven't heard any shooting for quite a while.'

Harding was still doing something at the bottom of the punt. 'I'm afraid we're in trouble,' he said. 'I thought this water was the accumulated drips from the paddles, but I think we have a leak. The punt is sinking.'

'Oh, hell!' said McCready.

'My fault,' said Harding unhappily. 'I think I overloaded the gun. The strain on the punt was too much.'

Denison blew out his breath. McCready could have been right; the barrel *could* have burst. He said, 'It seems you'll have to walk the rest of the way, Doctor. Do you think you can make it?'

'I'll be all right when I've given myself another injection.'

'We'll jam the boat into the reeds,' said McCready. 'And then get going. I think the mist is lifting and I want to be out of this swamp by then.'

THIRTY-SEVEN

Carey strolled through a stand of tall timber and looked towards the house. It was not the sort of house you'd expect to see in Britain because the architecture was all wrong, mainly in matters of detail, but he supposed that if it had been in England it would have been called a manor house – one of the lesser stately homes.

He stopped and lit his pipe, ruminating on history. In the days when Finland was a Grand Duchy and part of Imperial Russia the house would have been the residence of one of the minor nobility or, possibly, a bourgeois Swedish Finn of the merchant class. More recently it had belonged to a company in Helsinki who used it as a holiday home for top staff and as a venue for executive conferences. Now it was rented by British Intelligence for their own undisclosed purposes.

Certainly Carey, as he strolled in the grounds clad in Harris tweed and puffing contemplatively on his pipe, looked every inch – or centimetre – the squire or whatever was the Finnish equivalent. He struck another match and, shielding it with his hand, applied it to his recalcitrant pipe. If he was worried it did not show in his manner. With the back of his mind he worried about McCready and his party who had not yet shown up, but with the forefront he worried about what was happening back in London. Apparently his boss, Sir William Lyng, had been unable to do much about Thornton and the in-fighting in Whitehall was becoming severe.

He achieved satisfaction with the drawing of his pipe and glanced towards the house again to see Armstrong approaching. He waited until he was within easy conversational reach, then said, 'Is that boffin still fiddling with those equations?'

'He's finished.'

'About time. Has he found it?'

'No one tells me anything,' said Armstrong. 'But he wants to see you. Another thing – George McCready phoned in. He couldn't say much on the phone but I gather he has a tale to tell. He wants medical supplies for a bullet in the arm.'

'Who?'

'Dr Harding.'

Carey grunted. 'Any other casualties?'

'None that George mentioned.'

'Good! Let's go to see the boffin.'

Armstrong fell in step with him. 'And there's a man to see you – a chap called Thornton.'

Carey's pace faltered. 'He's here now?'

'I put him in the library.'

'Has he seen the boffin?'

'I don't think so.'

'He mustn't.' Carey looked sideways at Armstrong. 'Do you know anything about Thornton?'

'I've seen him around,' said Armstrong. 'But not to speak to. He's a bit above my level on the totem pole.'

'Yes,' said Carey. 'One of the Whitehall manipulators and as tricky as they come. These are my specific instructions regarding Thornton. You're to go back to the library and offer him tea – he'll like that. You're to keep him busy until I see him. I don't want him prowling around; he makes me nervous. Got that?'

'Yes,' said Armstrong. 'What's the trouble?'

'There's a bit of an argument about policy going on back home and Thornton is pushing a bit too hard. It's nothing that should concern you as long as you obey orders – my orders. If Thornton tries to order you around refer him to me.'

'All right,' said Armstrong.

'I'll tell you something about Thornton,' said Carey candidly. 'He's a bastrich – that's a word worthy of Lewis Carroll. It means a combination of a bastard and a son of a bitch. So you don't say a word about this operation in Thornton's presence. That's another order from me.'

'Not even if he asks me directly?'

'Refer him to me,' said Carey. 'And you won't get into trouble. I know he's high-powered and you are but an underling, but you are in a different department. If he tries anything on just tell him to go to hell in a polite way, and I'll back you up.' He smiled. 'And Lyng will back me so you have support all the way to the top.'

Armstrong looked relieved. 'That's clear enough.'

Carey nodded shortly. 'Good. You attend to Thornton. I'll see the boffin.'

The man whom Carey called the boffin was Sir Charles Hastings, F.R.S., a physicist not without eminence. Carey, whose opinion of scientists was low, treated him robustly and with a lack of deference which Sir Charles, who had a sense of humour, found refreshing. Carey now, on entering the room, said, "What's the score?'

Sir Charles picked up a set of papers. 'The answer is unequivocal. This is the crucial document. In it Dr Merikken outlines the germ of an idea, and develops it in a most interesting way. As you may know, the concept of the grazing angle has been utilized in the X-ray telescopes we now use, but Merikken took the idea much farther – which is strange considering he worked so many years ago.'

Sir Charles paused, contemplating a vision of genius. 'Merikken not only worked out the theory but subjected it to tests in the laboratory – the only way, of course. Here is a list of his tests, the results of which are frankly astounding. In his first test he was able to obtain an X-ray reflectance of nearly 25 per cent of the incident illumination.'

'Hold on a minute,' said Carey. 'How does that compare with what we've been able to do up to now?'

Sir Charles laughed shortly. 'There's absolutely no comparison. Apart from anything else, this is going to revolutionize X-ray astronomy; it makes possible an X-ray lens of considerable resolution. But that was just the first of Merikken's tests; in his final test before he ended the series he'd done considerably better than that – and his apparatus was not up to modern standards.'

Carey felt his hands empty and took out his pipe. 'So if we put a team on to this, gave it a hell of a lot of money and a reasonable amount of time, we could improve on what Merikken did. Would you agree with that, Sir Charles?'

'Indeed I would. There's nothing in here that offends any of the laws of physics. It reduces itself to a matter of engineering – advanced engineering, mark you, but nothing more than that.' He spread his hands. 'The X-ray laser has now moved from the barely possible to the probable.'

Carey gestured with his pipe. 'Anything else of value in those papers?'

Sir Charles shook his head. 'Nothing at all. This, for instance – ' he picked up the hardbound exercise book – '. . . this is a series of calculations of nuclear cross-sections. Quite primitive and totally useless.' His voice was a trifle disparaging. 'All the rest is the same.'

'Thank you, Sir Charles.' Carey hesitated. 'I'd be obliged if you would stay in this room until I return. I don't think I'll be more than a few minutes.' He ignored Sir Charles's expression of polite surprise and left the room.

Outside the library he paused and squared his shoulders before opening the door. Thornton was lounging in a leather chair and Armstrong stood at the window. Armstrong looked harassed and was visibly relieved when he saw Carey. 'Good morning,' said Thornton. His voice was cheerful. 'I must say you have your staff well trained, Carey. Mr Armstrong is a positive oyster.'

'Morning,' said Carey curtly.

'I just popped in to find out how Sir Charles Hastings is doing. You must know we're all very keen to see the results of your labours.'

Carey sat down, wondering how Thornton knew about Sir Charles. More and more he was certain there was a leak in Lyng's office. He said blandly, 'You'll have to get that from Sir William Lyng.'

Thornton's cheerfulness diminished a shade. 'Well, I'm sure we can excuse Mr Armstrong while we have a discussion on that matter.' He turned to Armstrong. 'If you don't mind.'

Armstrong made as though to move to the door but stopped as Carey snapped, 'Stay where you are, Ian.'

Thornton frowned. 'As you know, there are certain . . . er . . . details which Mr Armstrong is not entitled to know.'

'He stays,' said Carey flatly. 'I want a witness.'

'A witness!' Thornton's eyebrows rose.

'Come off it,' said Carey. 'When this operation is finished I make out a final report – including what I hear in this room. So does Armstrong – independently. Got the picture?'

'I can't agree to that,' said Thornton stiffly.

'Then you don't have to talk. What you don't say Armstrong can't hear.' Carey smiled pleasantly. 'What time is your plane back to London?'

'I must say you're not making things easy,' said Thornton querulously.

Carey was blunt. 'It's not my intention to make things easy. You've been getting underfoot all through this operation. I haven't liked that and neither has Lyng.'

All cheerfulness had deserted Thornton. 'I think you misunderstood your position, Carey,' he said. 'You're not yet so big that you can't be knocked over. When the Minister reads my report I think you'll be in for a shock.'

Carey shrugged. 'You make your report and I'll make mine. As for the Minister I wouldn't know. I don't rub shoulders with the Cabinet – I leave that to Lyng.'

Thornton stood up. 'After this is over Lyng may not be around. I wouldn't rely on him to protect you.'

'Lyng can fight his own battles,' said Carey. 'He's been very good at it so far. Ian, will you escort Mr Thornton to his car. I don't think he has anything more to say.'

'Just one small item,' said Thornton. 'There are, of course, people other than those in your department who have been involved. You had better make sure that Denison and the Meyrick girl are silenced. That's all I have to say.'

He stalked out, followed by Armstrong. Carey sighed and took out his matches to light his pipe but stared at it in disgust and put it down unlit. Presently he heard a car door slam and the sound of tyres on gravel. When Armstrong came back he said, 'He's gone?'

'Yes.'

'Then give me a cigarette, for God's sake!'

Armstrong looked surprised but produced a packet of cigarettes. As he held a match for Carey, he said, 'You were a bit rough on Thornton, weren't you?'

Carey puffed inexpertly, and coughed. 'It's the only way to handle a bastard like that. He's the biggest con man in Whitehall, but if you hit him over the head hard enough he gets the message.'

'I'm surprised he took it from you. Aren't you afraid he'll jerk the rug from under you? I thought he was a big boy in the corridors of power.'

'Corridors of power!' Carey looked as though he was about to spit. 'I wonder if C. P. Snow knew he was coining *the* cliché of the twentieth century. I'm not afraid of Thornton; he can't get at me directly. Anyway, I'm coming up to retirement and I'll spit in his eye any time I feel like it.'

He drew on the cigarette and expelled smoke without inhaling. 'It's nothing to do with you, Ian. You just soldier on and don't worry your head about policy.'

'I don't even know what it's all about,' said Armstrong with a smile.

'You're better off that way.' Carey stood up and stared out of the window. 'Did you notice anything odd about that conversation?'

Armstrong thought back. 'I can't say that I did.'

'I did. Thornton got so mad at me that he slipped.' Carey drew on the cigarette and blew a plume of smoke. 'How did he know about Denison? You tell me that, my son, and you'll win a big cigar.' He held out the cigarette and looked at it distastefully, then stubbed it out in an ashtray with unnecessary violence. He said curtly, 'Let me know when Denison and McCready arrive.'

THIRTY-EIGHT

Denison lay in the old-fashioned bath with steaming water up to his ears. He lay passively letting the hot water untie all the knots. His shoulders still ached abominably because of the paddling in the marsh of Sompio. He opened his eyes and stared at the elaborately moulded ceiling and then looked at the ceramic stove in the corner, a massive contraption big enough to heat a ballroom let alone a bathroom. He deduced from that that winters in Finland could be chilly.

When the water turned tepid he got out of the bath, dried himself and put on his – or Meyrick's – bath robe. He looked down at it and fingered the fabric. From what Carey had said in the few brief remarks he had offered his days of high living were over. That suited Denison. In the past few days there had been less chance of high living than of low dying.

He left the bathroom and walked along the panelled corridor towards the bedroom he had been given. It seemed that British Intelligence were not averse to a spot of high life; this country house reminded him of those old-fashioned detective plays in which the earl was found dead in the study and, in the last act, it was the butler what done it. Playwrights in those days seemed to think that everybody but butlers had butlers.

He was about to go into his room when the door opposite opened and he saw Lyn. 'Giles, do you have a moment?'

'Of course.' She held the door open in invitation and he went into her bedroom. 'How is Harding?'

'He's quite a man,' she said. 'He took out the bullet and set the arm himself. He said it wasn't as bad as taking out his own appendix, as some doctors have had to do. Diana and I helped to bandage him.'

'I don't think he'll encounter any more bullets,' said Denison. 'From what I gathered from Carey this job is just about over. He said something about us flying back to England tomorrow.'

'So it was successful – he got what he wanted?'

'Apparently so. There was a scientist here who checked the stuff. Diana and Ian Armstrong went back with him to England.'

She sat on the bed. 'So it's all over. What will you do now?'

'Go back into films, I suppose.' He rubbed his jaw and felt the unshaven stubble. 'Carey said he wanted to talk to me about that because it might not be too easy, not with someone else's face.' He waved his arm largely. 'All this Scandinavian stuff is supposed to be kept secret, so I can't very well go back to Fortescue as I am. He'd ask too many questions which I can't answer. The trouble is that the film world is small and if it isn't Fortescue asking awkward questions it will be someone else.'

'So what's the answer?'

'A man called Iredale, I suppose,' he said morosely. 'He's a plastic surgeon. I can't say I fancy the idea; I've always had a horror of hospitals.'

'Do it, Giles,' she said. 'Please do it. I can't . . .'

He waited for her to go on but she was silent, her head averted. He sat next to her and took her hand. 'I'm sorry, Lyn. I'd have given anything for this not to have happened. I didn't like the deception I played on you, and I told Carey so. I was about to insist that it be put to an end when you. . . you found out. I wish to hell we could have met under different circumstances.'

She still said nothing and he bit his lip. 'What will you do?'

'You know what I'll do. I've got a not very good degree so I'll teach – as I told my father.' Her voice was bitter.

'When will you start?'

'I don't know. There's a lot to be straightened out about Daddy's death. Carey said he'll pull strings and make it easy from the legal angle, but there'll still be a lot to do – his will and things like that. There's a lot of money involved – shares in his companies – and there's his house. He once told me that the house would be mine if he died. That was just like him, you know – he said "if" instead of "when".'

Arrogant bastard, thought Denison. He said, 'So you won't start teaching for a long time.'

'Those different circumstances,' said Lyn. 'Perhaps they could be arranged.'

'Would you like that?'

'Oh, yes; to start again.'

'To start again,' mused Denison. 'I suppose it's a wish we all have from time to time. Usually it's impossible.'

'Not for us,' she said. 'After you've had the operation you'll be convalescent for a while. Come to the house and stay with me for that time.' Her hand tightened on his. 'If I could see Giles Denison's face in my father's house perhaps we could start again.'

'A sort of exorcism. It might work.'

'We can try.' She brought her hand up to his face and touched the scar on his cheek. 'Who did this to you, Giles? And who kidnapped my father to let him drown in the sea?'

'I don't know,' said Denison. 'And I don't think Carey knows, either.'

* * *

In the room directly below McCready was giving his report to Carey. He had nearly finished. 'It was a right shambles,' he said. 'The Czechs were shooting up everything in sight.' He stopped and considered. 'Except us.'

'Who were the opposition?'

'I don't know. They were armed with pistols, nothing bigger. We only saw them once in the marsh when Denison tickled them up with that overgrown shotgun. Remarkable man, Denison.'

'I agree,' said Carey.

'He keeps his cool in an emergency and he's a good tactician. It was his idea that we cross the marsh. It was a good idea because we didn't run into the Czechs at all. When the punt sank he led us out.' McCready grinned. 'He had us all lined up on a thirty-foot length of string. And his estimation of speed was accurate; we hit the main road just seven hours after leaving the hut.'

'Did you have any trouble in Vuotso?'

McCready shook his head. 'We nipped in quietly, got into the cars, and drove out. Not far from Rovaniemi we changed into decent clothing to make ourselves presentable for the flight south.' He grinned. 'There's a Dr Mannermaa in Vuotso – a bird watcher. He's going to be a bit peeved about losing his punt and his gun.'

'I'll straighten that out,' said Carey. 'You said the Czechs were also at Kevo.'

'Czechs, Americans – and a crowd of Germans hovering on the outskirts. I didn't tell the others about them because they never really came into the game.'

'East Germans or West Germans?' asked Carey sharply.

'I don't know,' said McCready. 'They all speak the same lingo.'

'And then there was the chap who knocked Denison on the head and took the original map.'

'I never spotted him from start to finish,' said McCready. 'I think he was a singleton – working on his own.'

'Four groups,' said Carey thoughtfully. 'And we can't identify any Russians for certain.'

'Five,' said McCready. 'There's the gang that substituted Denison for Meyrick. They wouldn't have come chasing after us to Kevo and Sompio. They knew better.'

Carey grunted. 'I have my own ideas about who did the dirty on Denison and Meyrick – and I don't think the Russians came into it.'

'You said Thornton was here. What did he want?'

'I didn't find out,' said Carey. 'I wouldn't let him speak to me except in front of a witness and he turned chicken. He's too fly to be caught that way. But he knew about Sir Charles Hastings, and he knew about Denison.'

'Did he, by God? We'll have to seal that leak when we get back to London. What did Hastings say?'

'Oh, we've got the goods all right. He's taken photocopies back to London. Now we can prepare for the next stage of the operation. I hope nothing happens tonight because I'd like to get Denison and the girl out of it. They're leaving tomorrow on the ten o'clock flight from Helsinki.'

'Where are the original papers now?'

'In the safe in the library.'

'In that antique? I could open it with my grandmother's hat-pin.'

Carey smiled blandly. 'Does it matter – under the circumstances?'

'No, I don't suppose it does,' said McCready.

THIRTY-NINE

Denison went to bed early that night because he had a lot of sleep to catch up on and because he had to get up fairly early to catch the flight to London. He said good night to Lyn and then went into his bedroom where he undressed slowly. Before getting into bed he drew the curtains to darken the room. Even though he was now below the Arctic Circle there was still enough light in the sky to make falling asleep annoyingly difficult. It would get darker towards midnight but never more than a deep twilight.

He woke up because someone was prodding him, and came swimming up to the surface out of a deep sleep. 'Giles; wake up!'

'Mmmm. Who's that?'

The room was in darkness but someone looked over him. 'Lyn,' she whispered.

He elbowed himself up. 'What's the matter? Turn on the light.'

'No!' she said. 'There's something funny going on.'

Denison sat up and rubbed his eyes. 'What sort of funny?'

'I don't really know. There are some people in the house – down in the library. Americans. You know the man you introduced me to – the man you said was a bore.'

'Kidder?'

'Yes. I think he's down there. I heard his voice.'

Kidder! The man who had interrogated him in the hotel in Helsinki after he had been kidnapped from the sauna. The man who had led the American party at Kevo. The over-jovial and deadly boring Jack Kidder.

'Christ!' said Denison. 'Hand me my trousers – they're on a chair somewhere.' He heard a noise in the darkness and the trousers were thrust into his groping hand. 'What were you doing prowling in the middle of the night?'

'I couldn't sleep,' said Lyn. 'I was standing at my bedroom window when I saw these men in the grounds – there's still just enough light to see. They didn't seem to be up to any good – they were dodging about a bit. Then they all disappeared and I wondered what to do. I wanted to find Carey or McCready but I don't know where their rooms are. Anyway, I looked down the stairs and there was a light in the library, and when I got to the door I heard Kidder's voice.'

'What was he saying?'

'I don't know. It was just a rumble – but I recognized the voice. I didn't know what to do so I came and woke you.'

Denison thrust his bare feet into shoes. 'There's a sweater on the back of the chair.' Lyn found it and he put it on. 'I don't know where Carey's room is, either. I think I'll just nip downstairs.'

'Be careful,' said Lyn. 'I've heard enough shooting already.'

'I'll just listen,' he said. 'But you be ready to scream the place down.'

He opened the bedroom door gently and went into the dimness of the corridor. He trod carefully on his way to the stairs to avoid creaking boards, and tiptoed down, his hand running along the balustrade. The door to the library was closed but illumination leaked out from under the door. He paused by the door and listened and heard the deep sound of male voices.

He could make nothing of it until he bent and put his ear to the keyhole and then he immediately recognized the gravelly voice of Kidder. He could not distinguish the words but he recognized the voice. Another man spoke in lighter tones and Denison knew it was Carey.

He straightened up and wondered what to do. Lyn had spoken of men in the plural which would mean there were others about besides Kidder. He could cause a disturbance and arouse the house but if Kidder was holding up Carey at gunpoint that might not be good for Carey. He thought he had better find out what was really going on before doing anything drastic. He turned and saw Lyn standing by the staircase and he put his finger to his lips. Then he took hold of the door knob and eased it around very gently.

The door opened a crack and the voices immediately became clearer. Carey was speaking. '. . . and you ran into trouble again at Sompio?'

'Jesus!' said Kidder. 'I thought we'd run into the Finnish army but it turned out they were goddamn Czechs – we wounded one and he was cussing fit to bust. Who the hell would expect to find Czechs in the middle of Finland? Especially carrying automatic rifles and some sort of crazy flame-thrower. That's why I'm bandaged up like this.'

Carey laughed. 'That was our crowd.'

Denison swung the door open half an inch and put his eye to the crack. He saw Carey standing by the safe in the corner but Kidder was not in sight. Carey said, 'It wasn't a flame-thrower – it was a bloody big shotgun operated by no less than the eminent Dr Meyrick.'

'Now, there's a slippery guy,' said Kidder.

'You shouldn't have snatched him from the hotel in Helsinki,' said Carey. 'I thought you trusted me.'

'I trust nobody,' said Kidder. 'I still wasn't sure you weren't going to cross me up. You were playing your cards close to your chest – I still didn't know where the papers were. Anyway, I got nothing out of Meyrick; he gave me a lot of bull which I nearly fell for, then he neatly busted my larynx. You breed athletic physicists in Britain, Carey.'

'He's a remarkable man,' Carey agreed.

Kidder's voice changed and took on a more incisive quality. 'I reckon that's enough of the light conversation. Where are Merikken's papers?'

'In the safe.' Carey's voice sharpened. 'And I wish you'd put that gun away.'

'It's just window dressing in case anyone snoops in,' said Kidder. 'It's for your protection. You wouldn't want it getting around that you're . . . shall we say . . . co-operating with us, would you? What's with you, Carey? When the word came that you were willing to do a deal no one would believe it. Not such an upright guy like the respected Mr Carey.'

Carey shrugged. 'I'm coming up to retirement and what have I got? All my life I've lived on a thin edge and my nerves are so tight I've got a flaming big ulcer. I've shot men and I've been shot at; during the war the Gestapo did things to me I don't care to remember. And all for what? When I retire I get a pension that'll do little more than keep me in tobacco and whisky.'

'Cast away like an old glove,' said Kidder mockingly.

'You can laugh,' said Carey with asperity. 'But wait until you're my age.'

'Okay, okay!' said Kidder soothingly. 'I believe you. You're an old guy and you deserve a break. I know your British Treasury is penny-pinching. You should have worked our side of the fence – do you know what the CIA appropriation is?'

'Now who is making light conversation?' said Carey acidly. 'But now that we're talking of money you'd better make sure that the sum agreed goes into that Swiss bank account.'

'You know us,' said Kidder. 'You know we'll play fair – if you do. Now how about opening that safe?'

Denison could not believe what he was hearing. All the mental and physical anguish he had suffered was going for nothing because Carey – Carey, of all people – was selling out. It would have been unbelievable had he not heard it from Carey's own lips. Selling out to the bloody Americans.

He considered the situation. From what he had heard there were only the two of them in the library. Carey was where he could be seen, over by the safe. Kidder faced him and had his back to the door – presumably. It was a good presumption because nobody conducts a lengthy conversation with his back to the person he is talking to. But Kidder had a gun and, window dressing or not, it could still shoot.

Denison looked around. Lyn was still standing in the same position but he could not ask for her help. He saw a large vase on the hall table, took one step, and scooped it up. When he got back to the door he saw that Carey had opened the safe and was taking out papers and stacking them on top.

Kidder was saying, '. . . I know we agreed to chase Meyrick and McCready just to make it look good but I didn't expect all those goddamn fireworks. Hell, I might have been killed.' He sounded aggrieved.

Carey stooped to pull out more papers. 'But you weren't.'

Denison eased open the door. Kidder was standing with his back to him, a pistol held negligently by his side, and Carey had his head half-way inside the safe. Denison took one quick pace and brought down the vase hard on Kidder's head. It smashed into fragments and Kidder, buckling at the knees, collapsed to the floor.

Carey was taken by surprise. He jerked his head and cracked it on top of the safe. That gave Denison time to pick up the pistol which had dropped from Kidder's hand.

When Carey had recovered he found Denison pointing it at him.

Denison was breathing heavily. 'You lousy bastard! I didn't go through that little bit of hell just for you to make a monkey of me.'

Before Carey could say anything McCready skidded into the room at top speed. He saw the gun in Denison's hand and where it was pointing, and came to a sudden halt. 'Have you gone m . . .'

'Shut up!' said Denison savagely. 'I suppose you're in it, too. I thought it strange that Carey should have got rid of Diana and Armstrong so fast. Just what's so bloody important in London that Diana should have been put on a plane without even time to change her clothes, Carey?'

Carey took a step forward. 'Give me that gun,' he said authoritatively.

'Stay where you are.'

From the doorway Lyn said, 'Giles, what is all this?'

'These bloody patriots are selling out,' said Denison. 'Just for money in a Swiss bank account.' He jerked the gun at Carey who had taken another pace. 'I told you to stay still.'

Carey ignored him. 'You young idiot!' he said. 'Give me that gun and we'll talk about it more calmly.' He went nearer to Denison.

Denison involuntarily took a step backwards. 'Carey, I'm warning you.' He held out the gun at arm's length. 'Come any closer and I'll shoot.'

'No, you won't,' said Carey with certainty, and took another step.

Denison's finger tightened on the trigger and Carey's arm shot out, the hand held palm outwards like a policeman giving a stop sign. He pressed his hand on the muzzle of the pistol as Denison squeezed the trigger.

There was no shot.

Denison found his arm being forced back under the steady pressure of Carey's hand against the muzzle of the gun. He pulled the trigger again and again but nothing happened. And then it was too late because Carey's other hand came around edge on and chopped savagely at his neck. His vision blurred and, at the last, he was aware of but two things; one was Carey's fist growing larger as it approached, and the other was Lyn's scream.

McCready's face was pale as he looked at the sprawled figure of Denison. He let out his breath in a long whistle. 'You're lucky he had the safety catch on.'

Carey picked up the pistol. 'He didn't,' he said sharply.

Lyn ran over to where Denison lay and bent over his face. She turned her head. 'You've hurt him, damn you!'

Carey's voice was mild. 'He tried to kill me.'

McCready said, 'You mean the safety catch *wasn't* on. Then how . . .'

Carey bounced the pistol in his hand. 'Kidder went shopping for this locally,' he said. 'On the principle of "patronize your local gunsmith", I suppose. It's a Husqvarna, Model 40 – Swedish army issue. A nice gun with but one fault – there's about a sixteenth of an inch play in the barrel. If the barrel is forced back, the trigger won't pull.' He pressed the muzzle with the palm of his left hand and pulled the trigger. Nothing happened. 'See!'

'I wouldn't want to stake my life on it,' said McCready fervently. 'Apart from that will it shoot normally?'

Carey cocked an eye at him. 'I suppose Kidder has friends outside. Let's invite them in.' He looked about. 'I never did like that style of vase, anyway.' He raised the gun and aimed it at a vase at the other end of the room, a companion to the one Denison had broken over Kidder's head. He fired and the vase exploded into pieces.

Carey held the gun by his side. 'That ought to bring them.'

They waited quietly in an odd tableau. Lyn was too busy trying to revive Denison to pay much attention to what was happening. She had started at the shot and then resolutely ignored Carey. Kidder lay unconscious. The bandages around his lower jaw had come adrift revealing what seemed to be bloody pockmarks from the birdshot he had received in the marsh of Sompio. Carey and McCready stood in the middle of the room, silent and attentive.

The drawn curtain in front of the french window billowed as though blown by a sudden breeze. A woman's voice said, 'Drop the gun, Mr Carey.'

Carey laid down the pistol on the table and stepped aside from it. The curtains parted and Mrs Kidder stepped into the room. She was still the same mousy, insignificant little woman but what was shockingly incongruous was the pistol she held in her hand. There were two large men behind her.

'What happened?' Her voice was different; it was uncharacteristically incisive.

Carey gestured towards Denison. 'Our friend butted in unexpectedly. He crowned your husband – if that's what he is.'

Mrs Kidder lowered the gun and muttered over her shoulder. One of the men crossed the room and bent over Kidder. 'And the papers?' she asked.

'On top of the safe,' said Carey. 'No problems.'

'No?' she asked. 'What about the girl?' The gun came up and pointed at Lyn's back.

'I said it and meant it,' said Carey in a hard voice. 'No problems.'

She shrugged. 'You're carrying the can.'

The other man crossed to the safe and began shovelling papers into a canvas bag. Carey glanced at McCready and then his eyes slid away to Kidder who was just coming round. He muttered something, not loudly but loud enough for Carey to hear.

He was speaking in Russian.

The mumbling stopped suddenly as the man who was bending over Kidder picked him up. He carried him to the french window and, although Carey could not see properly, he had the strong impression that a big hand was clamped over Kidder's mouth.

The man at the safe finished filling the bag and went back to the window. Mrs Kidder said, 'If this is what we want you'll get your money as arranged.'

'Don't make any mistake about that,' said Carey. 'I'm saving up for my old age.'

She looked at him contemptuously and stepped back through the window without answering, and the man with the canvas bag followed her. Carey waited in silence for a moment and then walked over and closed the window and shot the bolts. He came back into the middle of the room and began to fill his pipe.

'You know that Kidder tried to con me into believing he was with the CIA. I always thought that American accent of his was too good to be true. It was idiomatic, all right, but he used too much idiom – no American speaks with a constant stream of American clichés.' He struck a match. 'It seems the Russians were with us, after all.'

'Sometimes you get a bit too sneaky for me,' said McCready.

'And me,' said Lyn. 'Giles was right – you're a thoroughgoing bastard.'

Carey puffed his pipe into life. 'George: our friend, Giles, has had a rough day. Let's put him to bed.'

FORTY

Denison walked across St James's Park enjoying the bland, late October sunshine. He crossed the road at the Guards Memorial and strolled across Horse Guards Parade and through the Palace arch into Whitehall itself, neatly avoiding a guardsman who clinked a sabre at him. At this time of the year the tourists were thin on the ground and there was not much of a crowd.

He crossed Whitehall and went into the big stone building opposite, wondering for the thousandth time who it was wanted to see him. It could only have to do with what had happened in Scandinavia. He gave his name to the porter and stroked his beard while the porter consulted the appointment book. Not a bad growth in the time, he thought somewhat vaingloriously.

The porter looked up. 'Yes, Mr Denison; Room 541. I'll get someone to take you up. Just sign this form, if you please, sir.'

Denison scribbled his signature and followed an acned youth along dusty corridors, into an ancient lift, and along more corridors. 'This is it,' said the youth, and opened a door. 'Mr Denison.'

Denison walked in and the door closed behind him. He looked at the desk but there was no one behind it and then he turned as he saw a movement by the window. 'I saw you crossing Whitehall,' said Carey. 'I only recognized you by your movements. God, how you've changed.'

Denison stood immobile. 'Is it you I've come to see?'

'No,' said Carey. 'I'm just here to do the preparatory bit. Don't just stand there. Come in and sit down. That's a comfortable chair.'

Denison walked forward and sat in the leather club chair. Carey leaned against the desk. 'I hope your stay in hospital wasn't too uncomfortable.'

'No,' said Denison shortly. It had been damned uncomfortable but he was not going to give Carey even that much.

'I know,' said Carey. 'You were annoyed and worried. Even more worried than annoyed. You're worried because I'm still with my department; you would like to lay a complaint, but you don't know who to complain to. You are frightened that the Official Secrets Act might get in the way and that you'll find yourself in trouble. At the same time you don't want me to get away with it – whatever it is you think I'm getting away with.' He took out his pipe. 'My guess is that you and Lyn Meyrick have been doing a lot of serious talking during the last fortnight. Am I correct?

Carey could be a frightening man. It was as though he had been reading Denison's mind. 'We have been thinking something like that,' he said unwillingly.

'Quite understandable. Our problem is to stop you talking. Of course, if you did talk we could crucify you, but by then it would be too late. In some other countries it would be simple – we'd make sure that you never talked again, to anyone, at any time, about anything – but we don't do things that way here.' He frowned. 'At least, not if I can help it. So we have to convince you that talking would be *wrong*. That's why Sir William Lyng is coming here to convince you of that.'

Even Denison had heard of Lyng; he was somebody in the Department of Defence. 'He'll have his work cut out.'

Carey grinned and glanced at his watch. 'He's a bit late so you'd better read this. It's secret, but not all that much. It represents a line of thought that's in the air these days.' He took a folder from the desk and tossed it into Denison's lap. 'I'll be back in a few minutes.'

He left the office and Denison opened the folder. As he read a baffled look came over his face, and the more he read the more bewildered he became. He came to the end of the few pages in the folder and then started to read from the beginning again. It had begun to make a weird kind of sense.

Carey came back half an hour later; with him was a short, dapper man, almost birdlike in the quickness and precision of his movements. 'Giles Denison – Sir William Lyng.'

Denison got up as Lyng advanced. They shook hands and Lyng said chirpily, 'So you're Denison. We have a lot to thank you for, Mr Denison. Please sit down.' He went behind the desk and cocked his head at Carey. 'Has he . . .?'

'Yes, he's read his homework,' said Carey.

Lyng sat down. 'Well, what do you think of what you've just read?'

'I don't really know,' said Denison, shaking his head.

Lyng looked at the ceiling. 'Well, what would you call it?'

'An essay on naval strategy, I suppose.'

Lyng smiled. 'Not an essay. It's an appreciation of naval strategy from quite a high level in the Department of Defence. It deals with naval policy should the Warsaw Pact and NATO come into conflict in a *conventional* war. What struck you about it? What was the main problem outlined?'

'How to tell the difference between one kind of submarine and other. How to differentiate between them so that you can sink one and not the other. The subs you'd want to sink would be those that attack shipping and other submarines.'

Lyng's voice was sharp. 'Assuming this country is at war with Russia, what conceivable reason can there be for *not* wanting to sink certain of their submarines?'

Denison lifted the folder. 'According to this we wouldn't want to sink their missile-carrying submarines – the Russian equivalent of the Polaris.'

'Why not?' snapped Lyng.

'Because if we sink too many of them while fighting a conventional war the Russians might find themselves losing their atomic edge. If that happened they might feel tempted to escalate into atomic warfare before they lost it all.'

Lyng looked pleased and glanced at Carey. 'He's learned the lesson well.'

'I told you he's a bright boy,' said Carey.

Denison stirred in the chair. He did not like being discussed as though he were absent.

Lyng said, 'A pretty problem, isn't it? If we don't sink their conventional submarines we stand a chance of losing the conventional war. If we sink too many of their missile-carriers the war might escalate to atomic catastrophe. How do you distinguish one submarine from another in the middle of a battle?' He snapped his fingers. 'Not our problem – that's for the scientists and the technologists – but do you accept the validity of the argument?'

'Well, yes,' said Denison. 'I see the point, but I don't see what it's got to do with what happened in Finland. I suppose that's why I'm here.'

'Yes, that's why you're here,' said Lyng. He pointed to the folder in Denison's hand. 'That is just an example of a type of thought. Do you have anything to say, Carey?'

Carey leaned forward. 'Ever since the atomic bomb was invented the human race has been walking a tightrope. Bertrand Russell once said, "You may reasonably expect a man to walk a tightrope safely for ten minutes; it would be unreasonable to do so without accident for two hundred years." ' He hunched his shoulders. 'Well, we've walked that tightrope for thirty years. Now, I want you to imagine that tightrope walker; he carries a long balancing pole.

What would happen if you suddenly dropped a heavy weight so that it hung on one end of the pole?'

'He'd probably fall off,' said Denison. He began to get a glimmer of what these two were getting at.

Lyng leaned his elbows on the desk. 'A man called Merikken invented something which had no application when he invented it. Now it turns out to be something capable of carving up missiles in mid-flight. Mr Denison, supposing Russia developed this weapon – and no one else. What do you think might happen?'

'That depends on the ratio of hawks to doves in the Russian government, but if they were sure they could stop an American strike they might just chance their arm at an atomic war.'

'Meyrick blabbed in Stockholm before he came to us,' said Carey. 'And the news got around fast. Our problem was that the papers were in Russia, and if the Russians got to them first they'd hold on tight. Well, the Russians *have* got the papers – but so have we, in photocopy.'

Denison was suspicious. 'But you sold them to the Americans.'

'Kidder was a Russian,' said Carey. 'I let it be known that I was willing to be bought, but the Russians knew I'd never sell myself to them. After all, I do have certain standards,' he said modestly. 'So they tried to pull a fast one. I didn't mind.'

'I don't quite understand,' said Denison.

'All right,' said Carey. 'The Russians have the secret and they'll know, when we tell them, that we have it, too, and that we'll pass it on to the Yanks. And we'll let the Yanks know the Russians have it. We drop the heavy weight on *both* ends of the balancing pole.'

Lyng spread his hands. 'Result – stalemate. The man remains balanced on the tightrope.'

'There were a lot of others involved but they were small fry,' said Carey. 'The Czechs and the West Germans.' He smiled. 'I have reason to believe that the man who bopped you on the head at Kevo was an Israeli. The Israelis would dearly like to have a defence against the SAM III missiles that the Syrians are playing around with. But, really, only America and Russia matter. And maybe China.' He glanced at Lyng.

'Later, perhaps.' Lyng stared at Denison. 'This country has just lost an Empire but many of its inhabitants, especially the older ones, still retain the old Imperial habits of thought. These modes of thought are not compatible with the atomic era but, unfortunately, they are still with us. If it became public knowledge that we have handed over to the Russians what the newspapers would undoubtedly describe as a super-weapon then I think that one of the minor consequences would be the fall of the government.'

Denison raised his eyebrows. 'Minor!'

Lyng smiled wintrily. 'The political complexion of the government of the day is of little interest. You must differentiate between the government and the state; governments may come and go but the state remains, and the real power is to be found in the apparatus of state, in the offices of Whitehall, in what Lord Snow has so aptly described as the corridors of power.'

Carey snorted. 'Any day I'm expecting a journalist to write that the winds of change are blowing through the corridors of power.'

'That could very well happen,' said Lyng. 'The control of power in the state is not monolithic; there are checks and balances, tensions and resistances. Many of the people I work with still hold on to the old ideas, especially in the War Office.' He looked sour for a moment. 'Some of the senior officers in the Navy, for instance, were destroyer commanders during World War II.'

His hand shot forward, his finger pointing to the folder in Denison's lap. 'Can you imagine the attitude of such men, steeped in the old ideas, when they are expected to issue orders to young officers to sink one type of enemy submarine and not another?' He shook his head. 'Old habits die hard. They're more likely to say, in the old tradition, "Full speed ahead, and damn the torpedoes." They fight to win, forgetting that no one will win a nuclear war. They forget balance, and balance is all, Mr Denison. They forget the man on the tightrope.'

He sighed. 'If the news of what has been done in Finland were to be disclosed not only would the present government fall, a minor matter, but there would be a drastic shift of power in the state. We, who strive to hold the balance, would lose to those who hold a narrower view of what is good for this country and, believe me, the country and the world would not be the safer for it. Do you understand what I am saying, Mr Denison?'

'Yes,' said Denison. He found that his voice was hoarse, and he coughed to clear it. He had not expected to be involved in matters of high policy.

Abruptly the tone of Lyng's voice changed from that of a judge reviewing a case to something more matter-of-fact. 'Miss Meyrick made a specific threat. She derided the efficacy of "D" notices and said that the students of twenty universities would not be bound by them. I regret to say that this is probably quite true. As you know, our student population – or some sections of it – is not noted for its coolheadedness. Any move towards implementing her threat would be potentially disastrous.'

'Why don't you talk to her about it?' said Denison.

'We will – but we believe you have some influence with her. It would be a pity if Miss Meyrick's anger and compassion were to cause the disruption I have described.'

Denison was silent for a long time then he sighed, and said, 'I see your point. I'll talk to her.'

'When will you see her?' asked Carey.

'I'm meeting her at the Horse Guards at twelve o'clock.'

'That's in ten minutes. You talk to her, and I'll have a word with her later.' Carey stood up and held out his hand. 'Am I forgiven?'

'I wanted to kill you,' said Denison. 'I very nearly did.'

'No hard feelings,' said Carey. 'I seem to remember hitting *you* pretty hard.'

Denison got up and shook Carey's hand. 'No hard feelings.'

Lyng smiled and busied himself with the contents of a slim briefcase, trying to efface himself. Carey stood back and looked at Denison critically. 'I wouldn't have believed it – the change in you, I mean.'

Denison put his hand to his face. 'Iredale unstuck the eyelid – that was easy – and took away the scar. He had a go at the nose and that's still a bit tender. We decided to leave the rest – getting the silicone polymer out would amount to a flaying operation so we gave it a miss. But the beard covers up a lot.' He paused. 'Who did it, Carey?'

'I don't know,' said Carey. 'We never did find out.' He looked at Denison quizzically. 'Has Iredale's handiwork made much difference with Lyn?'

'Er . . . why, yes . . . I think . . .' Denison was unaccountably shy.

Carey smiled and took out a notebook. 'I'll need your address.' He looked up, 'At the moment it's Lippscott House, near Brackley, Buckinghamshire. Can I take it that will be your address until further notice?'

'Until further notice,' said Denison. 'Yes.'

'Invite me to the wedding,' said Carey. He put away his notebook and glanced through the window down into Whitehall. 'There's Lyn,' he said. 'Admiring the horses. I don't think there's any more, Giles. I'll keep in touch. If you ever need a job, come and see me. I mean it.'

'Never again,' said Denison. 'I've had enough.'

Lyng came forward. 'We all do what we think is best.' They shook hands. 'I'm glad to have met you, Mr Denison.'

When he had gone Lyng put his papers back into his briefcase and Carey stood at the window and lit his pipe. It took him some time to get it going to his satisfaction. Lyng waited patiently, and then said, 'Well?'

Carey looked down into Whitehall and saw Denison crossing the street. Lyn ran towards him and they kissed, then linked arms and walked past the mounted guards and under the arch. 'They're sensible people; there'll be no trouble.'

'Good!' said Lyng, and picked up the folder from where Denison had left it.

Carey swung around. 'But Thornton is a different matter.'

'I agree,' said Lyng. 'He's got the Minister's ear. We're going to have a rough ride with this one regardless of whether Denison keeps silent.'

Carey's voice was acid. 'I don't mind if Thornton plays the Whitehall warrior as long as the only weapon he shoots is a memorandum. But when it comes to a deliberate interference in operations then we have to draw a line.'

'Only a suspicion – no proof.'

'Meyrick's death was bad enough – although it was accidental. But what he did to Denison was abominable and unforgivable. And if he'd got hold of Merikken's papers his bloody secret laboratories would be working overtime.'

'Forget it,' said Lyng. 'No proof.'

Carey grinned. 'I told a lie just now – the only lie I've told to Denison since I've known him. I've got the proof, all right. I've got a direct link between Thornton and his crooked plastic surgeon – Iredale was able to put me on to that one – and it won't be long before I find the sewer of a psychologist who diddled around with Denison's mind. I'm going to take great pleasure in peeling the skin off Thornton in strips.'

Lyng was alert. 'This is certain? Real proof?'

'Cast iron.'

'Then you won't touch Thornton,' said Lyng sharply. 'Let me have your proof and I'll deal with him. Don't you see what this means? We can neutralize Thornton – he's out of the game. If I can hold that over him I can keep him in line for ever.'

'But . . .' Carey held himself in. 'And where does justice come in?' he asked heavily.

'Oh, justice,' said Lyng indifferently. 'That's something else again. No man can expect justice in this world; if he does then he's a fool.' He took Carey by the elbow and said gently, 'Come; let us enjoy the sunshine while we may.'

THE ENEMY

To all the DASTards

especially

Iwan and Inga
Jan and Anita
Hemming and Annette

'We have met the enemy, and he is ours.'

OLIVER HAZARD PERRY
Heroic American Commodore

'We have met the enemy, and he is us.'

WALT KELLY
Subversive Sociological Cartoonist

ONE

I met Penelope Ashton at a party thrown by Tom Packer. That may be a bit misleading because it wasn't the kind of party that gets thrown very far; no spiked punch or pot, and no wife-swapping or indiscriminate necking in the bedrooms at two in the morning. Just a few people who got together over a civilized dinner with a fair amount of laughter and a hell of a lot of talk. But it did tend to go on and what with Tom's liberal hand with his after-dinner scotches I didn't feel up to driving, so when I left I took a taxi.

Penny Ashton came with Dinah and Mike Huxham; Dinah was Tom's sister. I still haven't worked out whether I was invited as a makeweight for the odd girl or whether she was brought to counterbalance me. At any rate when we sat at table the sexes were even and I was sitting next to her. She was a tall, dark woman, quiet and composed in manner and not very forthcoming. She was no raving beauty, but few women are; Helen of Troy may have launched a thousand ships but no one was going to push the boat out for Penny Ashton, at least not at first sight. Not that she was ugly or anything like that. She had a reasonably good figure and a reasonably good face, and she dressed well. I think the word to describe her would be average. I put her age at about twenty-seven and I wasn't far out. She was twenty-eight.

As was usual with Tom's friends, the talk ranged far and wide; Tom was a rising star in the upper reaches of the medical establishment and he was eclectic in his choice of dining companions and so the talk was good. Penny joined in but she tended to listen rather than talk and her interjections were infrequent. Gradually I became aware that when she did speak her comments were acute, and there was a sardonic cast to her eye when she was listening to something she didn't agree with. I found her spikiness of mind very agreeable.

After dinner the talk went on in the living-room over coffee and brandy. I opted for scotch because brandy doesn't agree with me, a circumstance Tom knew very well because he poured one of his measures big enough to paralyse an elephant and left the jug of iced water convenient to my elbow.

As is common on these occasions, while the dinner-table conversation is general and involves everybody, after dinner the party tended to split into small groups, each pursuing their congenial arguments and riding their hobby-horses hard and on a loose rein. To my mild surprise I found myself opting for a group of two – myself and Penny Ashton. I suppose there were a dozen of us there, but I settled in a corner and monopolized Penny Ashton. Or did she monopolize me? It could have been six of one and half-a-dozen of the other; it usually is in cases like that.

I forget what we talked about at first but gradually our conversation became more personal. I discovered she was a research biologist specializing in genetics and that she worked with Professor Lumsden at University College, London. Genetics is the hottest and most controversial subject in science today and Lumsden was in the forefront of the battle. Anyone working with him would have to be very bright indeed and I was suitably impressed. There was a lot more to Penny Ashton than met the casual eye.

Some time during the evening she asked, 'And what do you do?'

'Oh, I'm someone in the City,' I said lightly.

She got that sardonic look in her eye and said reprovingly, 'Satire doesn't become you.'

'It's true!' I protested. 'Someone's got to make the wheels of commerce turn.' She didn't pursue the subject.

Inevitably someone checked his watch and discovered with horror the lateness of the hour, and the party began to break up. Usually the more congenial the party the later the hour, and it was pretty late. Penny said, 'My God – my train!'

'Which station?'

'Victoria.'

'I'll drop you,' I said and stood up, swaying slightly as I felt Tom's scotch. 'From a taxi.'

I borrowed the telephone and rang for a taxi, and then we stood around making party noises until it arrived. As we were driven through the brightly-lit London streets I reflected that it had been a good evening; it had been quite a while since I'd felt so good. And it wasn't because of the quality of Tom's booze, either.

I turned to Penny. 'Known the Packers long?'

'A few years. I was at Cambridge with Dinah Huxham–Dinah Packer she was then.'

'Nice people. It's been a good evening.'

'I enjoyed it.'

I said, 'How about repeating it – just the two of us? Say, the theatre and supper afterward.'

She was silent for a moment, then said, 'All right.' So we fixed a time for the following Wednesday and I felt even better.

She wouldn't let me come into the station with her so I kept the taxi and redirected it to my flat. It was only then I realized I didn't know if she was married or not, and I tried to remember the fingers of her left hand. Then I thought

I was a damned fool; I hardly knew the woman so what did it matter if she was married or not? I wasn't going to marry her myself, was I?

On the Wednesday I picked her up at University College at seven-fifteen in the evening and we had a drink in a pub near the theatre before seeing the show. I don't like theatre crush bars; they're too well named. 'Do you always work as late as this?' I asked.

She shook her head. 'It varies. It's not a nine-to-five job, you know. When we're doing something big we could be there all night, but that doesn't happen often. I laboured tonight because I was staying in town.' She smiled. 'It helped me catch up on some of the paperwork.'

'Ah; the paperwork is always with us.'

'You ought to know; your job is all paperwork, isn't it?'

I grinned. 'Yes; shuffling all those fivers around.'

So we saw the show and I took her to supper in Soho and then to Victoria Station. And made another date for the Saturday.

And, as they say, one thing led to another and soon I was squiring her around regularly. We took in more theatres, an opera, a couple of ballets, a special exhibition at the National Gallery, Regent's Park Zoo, something she wanted to see at the Natural History Museum, and a trip down the river to Greenwich. We could have been a couple of Americans doing the tourist bit.

After six weeks of this I think we both thought that things were becoming pretty serious. I, at least, took it seriously enough to go to Cambridge to see my father. He smiled when I told him about Penny, and said, 'You know, Malcolm, you've been worrying me. It's about time you settled down. Do you know anything about the girl's family?'

'Not much,' I admitted. 'From what I can gather he's some sort of minor industrialist. I haven't met him yet.'

'Not that it matters,' said my father. 'I hope we've gone beyond snobberies like that. Have you bedded the girl yet?'

'No,' I said slowly. 'We've come pretty close, though.'

'Um!' he said obscurely, and began to fill his pipe. 'It's been my experience here at the college that the rising generation isn't as swinging and uninhibited as it likes to think it is. Couples don't jump bare-skinned into a bed at the first opportunity – not if they're taking each other seriously and have respect for each other. Is it like that with you?'

I nodded. 'I've had my moments in the past, but somehow it's different with Penny. Anyway, I've known her only a few weeks.'

'You remember Joe Patterson?'

'Yes.' Patterson was head of one of the departments of psychology.

'He reckons the ordinary man is mixed up about the qualities he wants in a permanent partner. He once told me that the average man's ideal wife-to-be is a virgin in the terminal stages of nymphomania. A witticism, but with truth in it.'

'Joe is a cynic.'

'Most wise men are. Anyway, I'd like to see Penny as soon as you can screw up your courage. Your mother would have been happy to see you married; it's a pity about that.'

'How are you getting on, Dad?'

'Oh, I rub along. The chief danger is of becoming a university eccentric; I'm trying to avoid that.'

We talked of family matters for some time and then I went back to London.

It was at this time that Penny made a constructive move. We were in my flat talking over coffee and liqueurs; she had complimented me on the Chinese dinner and I had modestly replied that I had sent out for it myself. It was then that she invited me to her home for the weekend. To meet the family.

TWO

She lived with her father and sister in a country house near Marlow in Buckinghamshire, a short hour's spin from London up the M4. George Ashton was a widower in his mid-fifties who lived with his daughters in a brick-built Queen Anne house of the type you see advertised in a full-page spread in *Country Life*. It had just about everything. There were two tennis-courts and one swimming-pool; there was a stable block converted into garages filled with expensive bodies on wheels, and there was a stable block that was still a stable block and filled with expensive bodies on legs – one at each corner. It was a Let's-have-tea-on-the-lawn sort of place; The-master-will-see-you-in-the-library sort of place. The good, rich, upper-middle-class life.

George Ashton stood six feet tall and was thatched with a strong growth of iron-grey hair. He was very fit, as I found out on the tennis-court. He played an aggressive, hard-driving game and I was hard put to cope with him even though he had a handicap of about twenty-five years. He beat me 5–7, 7–5, 6–3, which shows his stamina was better than mine. I came off the court out of puff but Ashton trotted down to the swimming-pool, dived in clothed as he was, and swam a length before going into the house to change.

I flopped down beside Penny. 'Is he always like that?'

'Always,' she assured me.

I groaned. 'I'll be exhausted just watching him.'

Penny's sister, Gillian, was as different from Penny as could be. She was the domestic type and ran the house. I don't mean she acted as lady of the house and merely gave the orders. She *ran* it. The Ashtons didn't have much staff; there were a couple of gardeners and a stable girl, a houseman-cum-chauffeur called Benson, a full-time maid and a daily help who came in for a couple of hours each morning. Not much staff for a house of that size.

Gillian was a couple of years younger than Penny and there was a Martha and Mary relationship between them which struck me as a little odd. Penny didn't do much about the house as far as I could see, apart from keeping her own room tidy, cleaning her own car and grooming her own horse. Gillian was the Martha who did all the drudgery, but she didn't seem to mind and appeared to be quite content. Of course, it was a weekend and it might have been different during the week. All the same, I thought Ashton would get a shock should Gillian marry and leave to make a home of her own.

It was a good weekend although I felt a bit awkward at first, conscious of being on show; but I was soon put at ease in that relaxed household. Dinner that evening, cooked by Gillian, was simple and well served, and afterwards we played bridge. I partnered Penny and Ashton partnered Gillian, and soon I found that Gillian and I were the rabbits. Penny played a strong, exact and carefully calculated game, while Ashton played bridge as he played tennis, agressively and taking chances at times. I observed that the chances he took came off more often than not, but Penny and I came slightly ahead at the end, although it was nip and tuck.

We talked for a while until the girls decided to go to bed, then Ashton suggested a nightcap. The scotch he poured was not in the same class as Tom Packer's but not far short, and we settled down for a talk. Not unexpectedly he wanted to know something about me and was willing to trade information, so I learned how he earned his pennies among other things. He ran a couple of manufacturing firms in Slough producing something abstruse in the chemical line and another which specialized in high-impact plastics. He employed about a thousand men and was the sole owner, which impressed me. There are not too many organizations like that around which are still in the hands of one man.

Then he enquired, very politely, what I did to earn my bread, and I said, 'I'm an analyst.'

He smiled slightly. 'Psycho?'

I grinned. 'No – economic. I'm a junior partner with McCulloch and Ross; we're economic consultants.'

'Yes, I've heard of your crowd. What exactly is it that you do?'

'Advisory work of all sorts-market surveys, spotting opportunities for new products, or new areas for existing products, and so on. Also general economic and financial advice. We do the general dogsbodying for firms which are not big enough to support their own research group. ICI wouldn't need us but a chap like you might.'

He seemed interested in that. 'I've been thinking of going public,' he said. 'I'm not all that old, but one never knows what may happen. I'd like to leave things tidy for the girls.'

'It might be very profitable for you personally,' I said. 'And, as you say, it would tidy up the estate in the event of your death – make the death duties bit less messy.' I thought about it for a minute. 'But I don't know if this is the time to float a new issue. You'd do better to wait for an upturn in the economy.'

'I've not entirely decided yet,' he said. 'But if I do decide to go public then perhaps you can advise me.'

'Of course. It's exactly our line of work.'

He said no more about it and the conversation drifted to other topics. Soon thereafter we went to bed.

Next morning after breakfast – cooked by Gillian – I declined Penny's invitation to go riding with her, the horse being an animal I despise and distrust. So instead we walked where she would have ridden and went over a forested hill along a broad ride, and descended the other side into a sheltered valley where we lunched in a pub on bread, cheese, pickles and beer, and where Penny demonstrated her skill at playing darts with the locals. Then back to the house where we lazed away the rest of the sunny day on the lawn.

I left the house that evening armed with an invitation to return the following weekend, not from Penny but from Ashton. 'Do you play croquet?' he asked.

'No, I don't.'

He smiled. 'Come next weekend and I'll show you how. I'll have Benson set up the hoops during the week.'

So it was that I drove back to London well contented.

I have given the events of that first weekend in some detail in order to convey the atmosphere of the place and the family. Ashton, the minor industrialist, richer than others of his type because he ran his own show; Gillian, his younger daughter, content to be dutifully domestic and to act as hostess and surrogate wife without the sex bit; and Penny the bright elder daughter, carving out a career in science. And she *was* bright; it was only casually that weekend I learned she was an MD although she didn't practise.

And there was the money. The Rolls, the Jensen and the Aston Martin in the garages, the sleek-bodied horses, the manicured lawns, the furnishings of that beautiful house – all these reeked of money and the good life. Not that I envied Ashton – I have a bit of money myself although not in the same class. I mention it only as a fact because it was there.

The only incongruity in the whole scene was Benson, the general factotum, who did not look like anyone's idea of a servant in a rich household. Rather, he looked like a retired pugilist and an unsuccessful one at that. His nose had been broken more than once in my judgement, and his ears were swollen with battering. Also he had a scar on his right cheek. He would have made a good heavy in a Hammer film. His voice clashed unexpectedly with his appearance, being soft and with an educated accent better than Ashton's own. I didn't know what to make of him at all.

Something big was apparently happening in Penny's line of work that week, and she rang to say she would be in the laboratory all Friday night, and would I pick her up on Saturday morning to take her home. When she got into the car outside University College she looked very tired, with dark smudges under her eyes. 'I'm sorry, Malcolm,' she said. 'This won't be much of a weekend for you. I'm going to bed as soon as I get home.'

I was sorry, too, because this was the weekend I intended to ask her to marry me. However, this wasn't the time, so I grinned and said, 'I'm not coming to see you – I'm coming for the croquet.' Not that I knew much about it – just the bit from Alice and an association with vicars and maiden ladies.

Penny smiled, and said, 'I don't suppose I should tell you this, but Daddy says he can measure a man by the way he plays croquet.'

I said, 'What were you doing all night?'

'Working hard.'

'Doing what? Is it a state secret?'

'No secret. We transferred genetic material from a virus to a bacterium.'

'Sounds finicky,' I remarked. 'With success, I hope.'

'We won't know until we test the resulting strain. We should know something in a couple of weeks; this stuff breeds fast. We hope it will breed true.'

What I knew about genetics could be measured with an eye-dropper. I said curiously, 'What good does all this do?'

'Cancer research,' she said shortly, and laid her head back, closing her eyes. I left her alone after that.

When we got to the house she went to bed immediately. Other than that the weekend was much the same as before. Until the end, that is – then it changed for the worse. I played tennis with Ashton, then swam in the pool, and we had lunch on the lawn in the shade of a chestnut tree, just the three of us, Ashton, Gillian and me. Penny was still asleep.

After lunch I was introduced to the intricacies of match-play croquet and, by God, there *was* a vicar! Croquet, I found, is not a game for the faint-hearted, and the way the Reverend Hawthorne played made Machiavelli look like a Boy Scout. Fortunately he was on my side, but all his tortuous plotting was of no avail against Gillian and Ashton. Gillian played a surprisingly vicious game. Towards the end, when I discovered it's not a game for gentlemen, I quite enjoyed it.

Penny came down for afternoon tea, refreshed and more animated than she had been, and from then on the weekend took its normal course. Put down baldly on paper, as I have done here, such a life may be considered pointless and boring, but it wasn't really; it was a relief from the stresses of the working week.

Apparently Ashton did not get even that relief because after tea he retired to his study, pleading that he had to attend to paperwork. I commented that Penny had complained of the same problem, and he agreed that putting unnecessary words on paper was the besetting sin of the twentieth century. As he walked away I reflected that

Ashton could not have got where he was by idling his time away playing tennis and croquet.

And so the weekend drifted by until it was nearly time for me to leave. It was a pleasant summer Sunday evening. Gillian had gone to church but was expected back at any moment; she was the religious member of the family – neither Ashton nor Penny showed any interest in received religion. Ashton, Penny and I were sitting in lawn chairs arguing a particularly knotty point in scientific ethics which had arisen out of an article in the morning newspaper. Rather, it was Penny and her father doing the arguing; I was contemplating how to get her alone so I could propose to her. Somehow we had never been alone that weekend.

Penny was becoming a little heated when we heard a piercing scream and then another. The three of us froze, Penny in mid-sentence, and Ashton said sharply, 'What the devil was that?'

A third scream came. It was nearer this time and seemed to be coming from the other side of the house. By this time we were on our feet and moving, but then Gillian came into sight, stumbling around the corner of the house, her hands to her face. She screamed again, a bubbling, wordless screech, and collapsed on the lawn.

Ashton got to her first. He bent over her and tried to pull her hands from her face, but Gillian resisted him with all her strength. 'What's the matter?' he yelled, but all he got was a shuddering moan.

Penny said quickly, 'Let me,' and gently pulled him away. She bent over Gillian who was now lying on her side curled in a foetal position, her hands still at her face with the fingers extended like claws. The screams had stopped and were replaced by an extended moaning, and once she said, 'My eyes! Oh, my eyes!'

Penny forced her hand to Gillian's face and touched it with her forefinger, rubbing gently. She frowned and put the tip of her finger to her nose, then hastily wiped it on the grass. She turned to her father. 'Take her into the house quickly – into the kitchen.'

She stood up and whirled towards me in one smooth motion. 'Ring for an ambulance. Tell them it's an acid burn.'

Ashton had already scooped up Gillian in his arms as I ran to the house, brushing past Benson as I entered the hall. I picked up the telephone and rang 999 and then watched Ashton carry his daughter through a doorway I had never entered, with Penny close behind him.

A voice said in my ear, 'Emergency services.'

'Ambulance.'

There was a click and another voice said immediately, 'Ambulance service.' I gave him the address and the telephone number. 'And your name, sir?'

'Malcolm Jaggard. It's a bad facial acid burn.'

'Right, sir; we'll be as quick, as we can.'

As I put down the phone I was aware that Benson was staring at me with a startled expression. Abruptly he turned on his heel and walked out of the house. I opened the door to the kitchen and saw Gillian stretched on a table with Penny applying something to her face. Her legs were kicking convulsively and she was still moaning. Ashton was standing by and I have never seen on any man's face such an expression of helpless rage. There wasn't much I could do there and I'd only be in the way so I closed the door gently.

Looking through the big window at the far end of the hall, I saw Benson walking along the drive. He stopped and bent down, looking at something not on the drive but on the wide grass verge. I went out to join him and saw what had attracted his attention; a car had turned there, driving on the grass, and it had done so at speed because the immaculate lawn had been chewed up and the wheels had gouged right down to the soil.

Benson said in his unexpectedly gentle voice, 'As I see it, sir, the car came into the grounds and was parked about there, facing the house. When Miss Gillian walked up someone threw acid in her face here.' He pointed to where a few blades of grass were already turning brown. 'Then the car turned on the grass and drove away.'

'But you didn't see it.'

'No, sir.'

I bent and looked at the wheel marks. 'I think this should be protected until the police get here.'

Benson thought for a moment. 'The gardener made some hurdles for the new paddock. I'll get those.'

'That should do it,' I agreed.

I helped him bring them and we covered the marks. I straightened as I heard the faint hee-haw of an ambulance, becoming louder as it approached. That was quick – under six minutes. I walked back to the house and rang 999 again.

'Emergency services.'

'The police, please.'

Click. 'Police here.'

'I want to report a criminal assault.'

THREE

They got Gillian into the ambulance very quickly. Penny used her authority as a doctor and went into the ambulance with her, while Ashton followed in a car. I judged he was in no condition to drive and was pleased to see Benson behind the wheel when he left.

Before he went I took him on one side. 'I think you ought to know I've sent for the police.'

He turned a ravaged face towards me and blinked stupidly. 'What's that?' He seemed to have aged ten years in a quarter of an hour.

I repeated what I'd said, and added, 'They'll probably come while you're still at the hospital. I can tell them what they need to know. Don't worry about it. I'll stay here until you get back.'

'Thanks, Malcolm.'

I watched them drive away and then I was alone in the house. The maid lived in, but Sunday was her day off, and now Benson had gone there was no one in the house but me. I went into the living-room, poured myself a drink and lit a cigarette, and sat down to think of just what the hell had happened.

Nothing made sense. Gillian Ashton was a plain, ordinary woman who lived a placid and unadventurous life. She was a homebody who one day might marry an equally unadventurous man who liked his home comforts. Acid-throwing wasn't in that picture; it was something that might happen in Soho or the murkier recesses of the East End of London – it was incongruous in the Buckinghamshire countryside.

I thought about it for a long time and got nowhere. Presently I heard a car drive up and a few minutes later I was talking to a couple of uniformed policemen. I couldn't tell them much; I knew little about Gillian and not much more about Ashton and, although the policemen were polite, I sensed an increasing dissatisfaction. I showed them the tracks and one of them stayed to guard them while the other used his car radio. When I looked from the window a few minutes later I saw he had moved the police car so he could survey the back of the house.

Twenty minutes later a bigger police gun arrived in the person of a plain clothes man. He talked for a while with the constable in the car, then walked towards the house and I opened the door at his knock. 'Detective-Inspector Honnister,' he said briskly. 'Are you Mr Jaggard?'

'That's right. Won't you come in?'

He walked into the hall and stood looking around. As I closed the door he swung on me. 'Are you alone in the house?'

The constable had been punctilious about his 'sirs' but not Honnister. I said, 'Inspector, I'm going to show you something which I shouldn't but which, in all fairness to yourself, I think you ought to see. I'm quite aware my answers didn't satisfy your constable. I'm alone in Ashton's house, admit to knowing hardly anything about the Ashtons, and he thinks I might run away with the spoons.'

Honnister's eyes crinkled. 'From the look of it there's a lot more to run away with here than spoons. What have you to show me?'

'This.' I dug the card out of the pocket which my tailor builds into all my jackets and gave it to him.

Honnister's eyebrows rose as he looked at it. 'We don't get many of these,' he commented. 'This is only the third I've seen.' He flicked at the plastic with his thumbnail as he compared me with the photograph. 'You realize I'll have to test the authenticity of this.'

'Of course. I'm only showing it to you so you don't waste time on me. You can use this telephone or the one in Ashton's study.'

'Will I get an answer this time on Sunday?'

I smiled. 'We're like the police, Inspector; we never close.'

I showed him into the study and it didn't take long. He came out within five minutes and gave me back the card. 'Well, Mr Jaggard; got any notions on this?'

I shook my head. 'It beats me. I'm not here in a professional capacity, if that's what you mean.' From his shrewd glance I could see he didn't believe me, so I told of my relationship with the Ashtons and all I knew of the attack on Gillian which wasn't much.

He said wryly, 'This is one we'll have to do the hard way, then – starting with those tracks. Thank you for your co-operation, Mr Jaggard. I'd better be getting on with it.'

I went with him to the door. 'One thing, Inspector; you never saw that card.'

He nodded abruptly and left.

Ashton and Penny came back more than two hours later. Penny looked as tired as she had the previous morning, but Ashton had recovered some of his colour and springiness. 'Good of you to stay, Malcolm,' he said. 'Stay a little longer – I want to talk to you. Not now, but later.' His voice was brusque and he spoke with authority; what he had issued was not a request but an order. He strode across the hall and went into the study. The door slammed behind him. I turned to Penny. 'How's Gillian?'

'Not very good,' she said sombrely. 'It was strong acid, undiluted. Who would do such a barbarous thing?'

'That's what the police want to know.' I told her something of my conversation with Honnister. 'He thinks your father might know something about this. Does he have any enemies?'

'Daddy!' She frowned. 'He's very strong-minded and single-minded, and people like that don't go through life without treading on a few toes. But I can't think he'd make the kind of enemy who would throw acid into his daughter's face.'

Somehow I couldn't, either. God knows some funny things go on in the economic and industrial jungles, but they rarely include acts of gratuitous violence. I turned as Benson came out of the kitchen carrying a tray on which were a jug of water, an unopened bottle of whisky and two glasses. I watched him go into the study then said, 'What about Gillian?'

Penny stared at me. 'Gillian!' She shook her head in disbelief. 'You're not suggesting Gillian could make that kind of enemy? It's preposterous.'

It was certainly unlikely but not as impossible as Penny thought. Quiet homebodies have been known to lead exotic and secret lives, and I wondered if Gillian had done anything else on her shopping trips into Marlow besides buying the odd pound of tea. But I said tactfully, 'Yes, it's unlikely.'

As I helped Penny get together a scratch meal she said, 'I tried to neutralize the acid with a soda solution, and in the ambulance they had better stuff than that. But she's in the intensive care unit at the hospital.'

We had rather an uncomfortable meal, just the two of us because Ashton wouldn't come out of the study, saying he wasn't hungry. An hour later, when I was wondering if he'd forgotten I was there, Benson came into the room. 'Mr Ashton would like to see you, sir.'

'Thank you.' I made my excuses to Penny and went into the study. Ashton was sitting behind a large desk but rose as I entered. I said, 'I can't tell you how sorry I am that this awful thing should have happened.'

He nodded. 'I know, Malcolm.' His hand grasped the whisky bottle which I noted was now only half full. He glanced at the tray, and said, 'Be a good chap and get yourself a clean glass.'

'I'd rather not drink any more this evening. I still have to drive back to town.'

He put down the bottle gently and came from behind the desk. 'Sit down,' he said, and thus began one of the weirdest interviews of my life. He paused for a moment. 'How are things with you and Penny?'

I looked at him consideringly. 'Are you asking if my intentions are honourable?'

'More or less. Have you slept with her yet?'

That was direct enough. 'No.' I grinned at him. 'You brought her up too well.'

He grunted. 'Well, what are your intentions – if any?'

'I thought it might be a good idea if I asked her to marry me.'

He didn't seemed displeased at that. 'And have you?'

'Not yet.'

He rubbed the side of his jaw reflectively. 'This job of yours – what sort of income do you make out of it?'

That was a fair question if I was going to marry his daughter. 'Last year it was a fraction over £8000; this year will be better.' Aware that a man like Ashton would regard that as chickenfeed I added, 'And I have private investments which bring in a further £11,000.'

He raised his eyebrows. 'You still work with a private income?'

'That £11.000 is *before* tax,' I said wryly, and shrugged. 'And a man must do something with his life.'

'How old are you?'

Thirty-four.'

He leaned back in his chair and said musingly, '£8000 year isn't bad – so far. Any prospects of advancement in the firm?'

'I'm bucking for it.'

He then asked me a couple of questions which were a damned sight more personal than digging into my finances but, again, in the circumstances they were fair and my answers seemed to satisfy him.

He was silent for a while, then he said, 'You could do better by changing your job. I have an opening which is ideal for a man like yourself. Initially you'd have to spend at least one year in Australia getting things off the ground, but that wouldn't hurt a couple of youngsters like you and Penny. The only trouble is that it must be now – almost immediately.'

He was going too fast for me. 'Hold on a moment,' I protested. 'I don't even know if she'll marry me.'

'She will,' he said positively. 'I know my daughter.'

He evidently knew her better than I did because I wasn't nearly so certain. 'Even so,' I said. 'There's Penny to consider. Her work is important to her. I can't see her throwing it up and going to Australia for a year just like that. And that's apart from anything I might think about the advisability of making a change.'

'She could take a sabbatical. Scientists do that all the time.'

'Maybe. Frankly, I'd need to know a lot more about it before making a decision.'

For the first time Ashton showed annoyance. He managed to choke it down and disguise it, but it was there. He thought for a moment, then said in conciliatory tones, 'Well, a decision on that might wait a month. I think you'd better pop the question, Malcolm. I can fix a special licence and you can get married towards the end of the week.' He tried to smile genially but the smile got nowhere near his eyes which still had a hurt look in them. 'I'll give you a house for a dowry – somewhere in the South Midlands, north of London.'

It was a time for plain speaking. 'I think you're going a bit too fast. I don't see the necessity for a special licence. In fact, it's my guess that Penny wouldn't hear of it, even if she does agree to marry me. I rather think she'd like to have Gillian at the wedding.'

Ashton's face crumpled and he seemed about to lose what little composure he had. I said evenly. 'It was always in my mind to buy a house when I married. Your offer of a house is very generous, but I think the kind of house it should be – and where it should be – are matters for Penny and me to decide between us.'

He stood up, walked to the desk, and poured himself a drink. With his back to me he said indistinctly, 'You're right, of course. I shouldn't interfere. But will you ask her to marry you – now?'

'Now! Tonight?'

'Yes.'

I stood up. 'Under the circumstances I consider that entirely inappropriate, and I won't do it. Now, if you'll forgive me, I have to go back to town.'

He neither turned nor made an answer. I left him there and closed the study door quietly behind me. I was at a loss to understand his driving insistence that Penny and I should marry quickly. That, and the offer of the job in Australia, had me worried. If this was the way he engaged his staff, not to mention picking a son-in-law, I was surprised how he'd got to where he was.

Penny was telephoning when I entered the hall. She replaced the receiver and said, 'I've been talking to the hospital; they say she's resting easier.'

'Good! I'll be back tomorrow evening and we'll go to see her. It might make her feel better to have someone else around, even a comparative stranger like me.'

'I don't know if that's a good idea,' said Penny, doubtfully. 'She might be . . . well, self-conscious about her appearance.'

'I'll come anyway and we can decide then. I have to go now – it's late.' She saw me to my car and I kissed her and left, wondering what kind of bee was buzzing in Ashton's bonnet.

FOUR

Next morning, when I walked into the office I shared with Larry Godwin, he looked up from the Czechoslovakian trade magazine he was reading and said, 'Harrison wants to see you.' Harrison was our immediate boss.

'Okay.' I walked straight out again and into Harrison's office, sat in the chair before the desk, and said, 'Morning, Joe. Larry said you wanted to see me.'

Harrison was a bit of a stuffed shirt, very keen on formality, protocol and the line of authority. He didn't like me calling him Joe, so I always did it just to needle him. He said stiffly, 'On checking the weekend telephone log I found you had disclosed yourself to a police officer. Why?'

'I was at a house-party over the weekend. There was a nasty incident – one of the daughters of the house had acid thrown in her face. She was taken to hospital and, when the police pitched up, I was alone in the house and they started to get off on the wrong foot. I didn't want them wasting time on me, so I disclosed myself to the officer in charge.'

He shook his head disapprovingly and tried to hold me in what he supposed to be an eagle-like stare. 'His name?'

'Detective-Inspector Honnister. You'll find him at the cop-shop in Marlow.' Harrison scribbled in his desk book, and I leaned forward. 'What's the matter, Joe? We're *supposed* to co-operate with the police.'

He didn't look up. 'You're not supposed to disclose yourself to all and sundry.'

'He wasn't all and sundry. He was a middle-ranking copper doing his job and getting off to a bad start.'

Harrison raised his head. 'You needn't have done it. He would never seriously suspect you of anything.'

I grinned at him. The way you tell it co-operation is a one-way street, Joe. The cops co-operate with us when we need them, but we don't co-operate with them when all they need is a little setting straight.'

'It will be noted in your record.' he said coldly.

'Stuff the record,' I said, and stood up. 'Now, if you'll excuse me I have work to do.' I didn't wait for his permission to leave and went back to my office.

Larry had switched to something in Polish. 'Have a good weekend?'

'A bit fraught. Who's pinched our *Who's Who?*'

He grinned. 'What's the matter? Wouldn't she play?' He fished out *Who's Who* from among the piles of books which cluttered his desk and tossed it to me. Our job called for a lot of reading; when I retired I'd be entitled to a disability pension due to failing eyesight incurred in the line of duty.

I sat at my desk and ran through the 'A's and found that Ashton was not listed. There are not many men running three or more factories employing over a thousand men who are not listed in *Who's Who*. It seemed rather odd. On impulse I took the telephone directory and checked that, and he was not listed there, either. Why should Ashton have an ex-directory number?

I said, 'Know anything about high-impact plastics, Larry?'

'What do you want to know?'

'A chap called Ashton runs a factory in Slough making the stuff. I could bear to know a little more about him.'

'Haven't heard of him. What's the name of the firm?'

'I don't know.'

'You don't know much. There might be a trade association.'

'Great thinking.' I went to our library and an hour later knew there were more associations of plastics manufacturers than I wotted of – there was even one devoted to high-impact plastics – but none of them had heard of George Ashton. It seemed unnatural.

Gloomily I went back to my office. It's a hard world where a man can't check up on his prospective father-in-law. Ashton, as of that moment, knew a hell of a lot more about me than I knew about him. Larry saw my face and said, 'No luck?'

'The man keeps a bloody low profile.'

He laughed and waved his hand across the room. 'You could ask Nellie.'

I looked at Nellie and grinned. 'Why not?' I said lightly, and sat at the console.

You don't have to cuddle up to a computer to ask it questions – all you need is a terminal, and we called ours Nellie for no reason I've ever been able to determine. If you crossed an oversized typewriter with a television set you'd get something like Nellie, and if you go to Heathrow you'll see dozens of them in the booking hall.

Where the computer actually was no one had bothered to tell me. Knowing the organization that employed me, and knowing a little of what was in the monster's guts, I'd say it was tended by white-coated acolytes in a limestone cavern in Derbyshire, or at the bottom of a Mendip mine-shaft; anywhere reasonably safe from an atomic burst. But, as I say, I didn't really know. My crowd worked strictly on the 'need to know' principle.

I snapped a couple of switches, pushed a button, and was rewarded by a small green question mark on the screen. Another button push made it ask:

IDENTIFICATION?

I identified myself – a bit of a complicated process – and Nellie asked:

CODE?

I answered:

GREEN

Nellie thought about that for a millionth of a second, then came up with:

INPUT GREEN CODING

That took about two minutes to put in. We were strict about security and not only did I have to identify myself but I had to know the requisite code for the level of information I wanted.

Nellie said:

INFORMATION REQUIRED?

I replied with:

IDENTITY

MALE

ENGLAND

The lines flicked out as Nellie came back with:

NAME?

I typed in:

ASHTON, GEORGE

It didn't seem to make much difference to Nellie how you put a name in. I'd experimented a bit and whether you put in Percy Bysshe Shelley – Shelley, Percy Bysshe – or even Percy Shelley, Bysshe – didn't seem to matter. Nellie still came up with the right answer, always assuming that Bysshe Shelley, Percy was under our eagle eye. But I always put the surname first because I thought it would be easier on Nellie's overworked little brain.

This time she came up with:

ASHTON, GEORGE – 3 KNOWN

PRESENT ADDRESS – IF KNOWN?

There could have been two hundred George Ashtons in the country or maybe two thousand. It's a common name and not surprising that three should be known to the department. As I typed in the address I reflected that I was being a bit silly about this. I tapped the execute key and Nellie hesitated uncharacteristically. Then I had a shock because the cursor scrolled out:

THIS INFORMATION NOT AVAILABLE ON CODE GREEN

TRY CODE YELLOW

I looked pensively at the screen and tapped out:

HOLD QUERY

Dancing electronically in the guts of a computer was a whole lot of information about one George Ashton, my future father-in-law. And it was secret information because it was in Code Yellow. I had picked up Larry Godwin on a joke and it had backfired on me; I hadn't expected Nellie to find him at all – there was no reason to suppose the department was interested in him. But if he had been found I would have expected him to be listed under Code Green, a not particularly secretive batch of information. Practically anything listed under Code Green could have been picked up by an assiduous reading of the world press. Code Yellow was definitely different.

I dug into the recesses of my mind for the coding of yellow, then addressed myself to Nellie. 'Right, you bitch; try again!' I loaded in the coding which took four minutes, then I typed out:

RELEASE HOLD

Nellie's screen flickered a bit and the cursor spelled out:

THIS INFORMATION NOT AVAILABLE ON CODE YELLOW

TRY CODE RED

I took a deep breath, told Nellie to hold the query, then sat back to think about it. I was cleared for Code Red and

I knew the information there was pretty much the same as the code colour – redhot! Who the hell was Ashton, and what was I getting into? I stood up and said to Larry, 'I'll be back in a minute. Don't interfere with Nellie.'

I took a lift which went down deep into the guts of the building where there lived a race of troglodytes, the guardians of the vaults. I presented my card at a tungsten-steel grille, and said, 'I'd like to check the computer coding for red. I've forgotten the incantation.'

The hard-faced man behind the grille didn't smile. He merely took the card and dropped it into a slot. A machine chewed on it for a moment, tasted it electronically, and liked the flavour but, even so, spat it out. I don't know what would have happened if it hadn't liked the flavour; probably I'd have been struck down by a bolt of lightning. Strange how the real world is catching up with James Bond.

The guard glanced at a small screen. 'Yes, you're cleared for red, Mr Jaggard,' he said, agreeing with the machine. The grille swung open and I passed through, hearing it slam and lock behind me. 'The coding will be brought to you in Room Three.'

Half an hour later I walked into my office, hoping I could remember it all. I found Larry peering at Nellie. 'Do you have red clearance?' I asked.

He shook his head. 'Yellow is my top.'

'Then hop it. Go to the library and study *Playboy* or something elevating like that. I'll give you a ring when I'm finished.'

He didn't argue; he merely nodded and walked out. I sat at the console and loaded Code Red into Nellie and it took nearly ten minutes of doing the right things in the right order. I wasn't entirely joking when I called it an incantation. When faced with Nellie I was always reminded of the medieval sorcerers who sought to conjure up spirits; everything had to be done in the right order and all the right words spoken or the spirit wouldn't appear. We haven't made much progress since then, or not too much. But at least our incantations seem to work and we do get answers from the vasty deep, but whether they're worth anything or not I don't know.

Nellie accepted Code Red or, at least, she didn't hiccough over it.

I keyed in:

RELEASE HOLD

and waited with great interest to see what would come out. The screen flickered again, and Nellie said:

THIS INFORMATION NOT AVAILABLE ON CODE RED

TRY CODE PURPLE

Purple! The colour of royalty and, possibly, of my face at that moment. This was where I was stopped – I was not cleared for Code Purple. I was aware it existed but that's about all. And beyond purple there could have been a whole rainbow of colours visible and invisible, from infra-red to ultra-violet. As I said, we worked on the 'need to know' principle.

I picked up the telephone and rang Larry. 'You can come back now; the secret bit is over.' Then I wiped Nellie's screen clean and sat down to think of what to do next.

FIVE

A couple of hours later I was having a mild ding-dong with Larry. He wasn't a bad chap but his ideals tended to get in the way of his job. His view of the world didn't exactly coincide with things as they are, which can be a bit hampering because a man can make mistakes that way. A spell of field work would have straightened him out but he'd never been given the chance.

My telephone rang and I picked it up. 'Jaggard here.'

It was Harrison. His voice entered my ear like a blast of polar air. 'I want you in my office immediately.'

I put down the phone. 'Joe's in one of his more frigid moods. I wonder how he gets on with his wife.' I went to see what he wanted.

Harrison was a bit more than frigid – he could have been used to liquefy helium. He said chillily, 'What the devil have you been doing with the computer?'

'Nothing much. Has it blown a fuse?'

'What's all this about a man called Ashton?'

I was startled. 'Oh, Christ!' I said. 'Nellie *is* a tattle-tale, isn't she? Too bloody gossipy by half.'

'What's that?'

'Just talking to myself.'

'Well, now you can talk to Ogilvie. He wants to see us both.'

I think I gaped a bit. I'd been with the department for six years and I'd seen Ogilvie precisely that number of times; that's to talk with seriously. I sometimes bumped into him in the lift and he'd exchange pleasantries courteously enough and always asked to be remembered to my father. My monkeying with Nellie must have touched a nerve so sore that the whole firm was going into a spasm.

'Well, don't just stand there,' snapped Harrison. 'He's waiting.'

Waiting with Ogilvie was a short, chubby man who had twinkling eyes, rosy cheeks and a sunny smile. Ogilvie didn't introduce him. He waved Harrison and me into chairs and plunged *in medias res*. 'Now, Malcolm; what's your interest in Ashton?'

I said, 'I'm going to marry his daughter.'

If I'd said I was going to cohabit with the Prince of Wales I couldn't have had a more rewarding reaction. The clouds came over Mr Nameless; his smile disappeared and his eyes looked like gimlets. Ogilvie goggled for a moment, then barked, *'What's that?'*

'I'm going to marry his daughter,' I repeated. 'What's the matter? Is it illegal?'

'No, it's not illegal,' said Ogilvie in a strangled voice. He glanced at Mr Nameless as though uncertain of what to do next. Mr Nameless said, 'What reason did you have for thinking there'd be a file on Ashton?'

'No reason. It was suggested jokingly that I try asking Nellie, so I did. No one was more surprised than I when Ashton popped up.'

I swear Ogilvie thought I was going round the twist. 'Nellie!' he said faintly.

'Sorry, the computer.'

'Was this enquiry in the course of your work?' he asked.

'No,' I said. 'It was personal and private. I'm sorry about that and I apologize for it. But some odd things have been going on around Ashton over the weekend and I wanted to check him out.'

'What sort of things?'

'Someone threw acid into his daughter's face and . . .'

Mr Nameless cut in. 'The girl you intend to marry?'

'No – the younger girl, Gillian. Later on Ashton behaved a bit strangely.'

'I'm not surprised,' said Ogilvie. 'When did this happen?'

'Last night.' I paused. 'I had to disclose myself to a copper, so it came through on the weekend telephone log. Joe and I discussed it this morning.'

Ogilvie switched to Harrison. 'You *knew* about this?'

'Only about the acid. Ashton wasn't mentioned.'

'You didn't ask me,' I said. 'And I didn't know Ashton was so bloody important until Nellie told me afterwards.'

Ogilvie said, 'Now let me get this quite right.' He stared at Harrison. 'A member of your staff in this department reported to you that he'd been involved in police enquiries into an acid-throwing attack, and you didn't even ask who was attacked. Is that it?'

Harrison twitched nervously. Mr Nameless paused in the act of lighting a cigarette and said smoothly. 'I think this is irrelevant. Let us get on with it.'

Ogilvie stabbed Harrison with a glance which told him that he'd hear more later. 'Of course. Do you think this is serious?'

'It could be very serious,' said Mr Nameless. 'But I think we're very lucky. We already have an inside man.' He pointed the cigarette at me just as Leonard Bernstein points his baton at the second violins to tell them to get scraping.

I said, 'Now, hold on a minute. I don't know what this is about, but Ashton is going to be my father-in-law. That's bringing things very close to home. You can't be seriously asking me to . . .'

'You're not being asked,' said Mr Nameless coolly. 'You're being told.'

'The hell with that,' I said roundly.

Momentarily he looked startled, and if ever I thought those eyes had twinkled it was then I changed my mind. He glanced at Ogilvie, and said, 'I know this man has a good record, but right now I fail to see how he achieved it.'

'I've said it once this morning, but I'll say it again,' I said. 'Stuff my record.'

'Be quiet, Malcolm,' said Ogilvie irritably. He turned to Harrison. 'I don't think we need you any more, Joe.'

Harrison's expression managed to mirror simultaneously shock, outrage, curiosity and regret at having to leave. As the door closed behind him Ogilvie said, 'I think a valid point has been made. It's not good for an agent to be emotionally involved. Malcolm, what do you think of Ashton?'

'I like him – what I know of him. He's not an easy man to get to know, but then I haven't had much chance yet; just a couple of weekends' acquaintanceship.'

'A point has been made,' conceded Mr Nameless. He twinkled at me as though we were suddenly bosom friends. 'And in rather unparliamentary language. But the fact remains that Mr Jaggard, here, is on the inside. We can't just toss away that advantage.'

Ogilvie said smoothly, 'I think that Malcolm will investigate the circumstances around Ashton as soon as it is properly explained to him why he should.'

'As to that,' said Mr Nameless, 'you mustn't overstep the limits. You know the problem.'

'I think it can be coped with.'

Mr Nameless stood up. 'Then that's what I'll report.'

When he had gone Ogilvie looked at me for a long moment, then shook his head. 'Malcolm, you really can't go about telling high-ranking civil servants to get stuffed.'

'I didn't,' I said reasonably. 'I told him to stuff my record. I didn't even tell him where to stuff it.'

'The trouble with people like you who have private incomes is that it makes you altogether too bloody independent-minded. Now that, while being an asset to the department, as I told his lordship before you came in, can make things difficult for your colleagues.'

His lordship! I didn't know if Ogilvie was being facetious or not.

He said, 'Will you take things a bit easier in future?'

That wasn't asking too much, so I said, 'Of course.'

'Good. How's your father these days?'

'I think he's a bit lonely now that Mother's dead, but he bears up well. He sends you his regards.'

He nodded and checked his watch. 'Now you'll lunch with me and tell me everything you know about Ashton.'

SIX

We lunched in a private room above a restaurant at which Ogilvie seemed to be well known. He made me begin right from the beginning, from the time I met Penny, and I ended my tale with the abortive checking out of Ashton and my confrontation with Nellie. It took a long time to tell.

When I had finished we were over the coffee cups. Ogilvie lit a cigar and said, 'All right; you're supposed to be a trained man. Can you put your finger on anything unusual?'

I thought a bit before answering. 'Ashton has a man called Benson. I think there's something peculiar there.'

'Sexually, you mean?'

'Not necessarily. Ashton certainly doesn't strike me as being double-gaited. I mean it's not the normal master-and-servant relationship. When they came back from the hospital last night they were closeted in Ashton's study for an hour and a half, and between them they sank half a bottle of whisky.'

'Um,' said Ogilvie obscurely. 'Anything else?'

'The way he was pressuring me into marrying Penny was bloody strange. I thought at one time he'd bring out the traditional shotgun.' I grinned. 'A Purdy, of course – for formal weddings.'

'You know what I think,' said Ogilvie. 'I think Ashton is scared to death; not on his own behalf but on account of his girls. He seems to think that if he can get your Penny away from him she'll be all right. What do you think?'

'It fits all right,' I said. 'And I don't like one damned bit of it.'

'Poor Ashton. He didn't have the time to polish up a scheme which showed no cracks, and he sprang it on you too baldly. I'll bet he pulled that Australian job out of thin air.'

'Who *is* Ashton?' I asked.

'Sorry; I can't tell you that.' Ogilvie blew a plume of smoke. 'I talked very high-handedly to that chap this morning. I told him you'd take on the job as soon as you knew what was involved, but he knew damned well that I can't tell you a thing. That's what he was objecting to in an oblique way.'

'This is bloody silly,' I said.

'Not really. You'll only be doing what you'd be doing anyway, knowing what you know now.'

'Which is?'

'Bodyguarding the girl. Of course, I'll ask you to bodyguard Ashton, too. It's a package deal, you see; one automatically includes the other.'

'And without knowing the reason why?'

'You know the reason why. You'll be guarding Penelope Ashton because you don't want her to get a faceful of sulphuric acid, and that should be reason enough for any tender lover. As for Ashton – well, our friend this morning was right. A commander can't tell his private soldiers his plans when he sends them into battle. He just tells them where to go and they pick up their feet.'

'The analogy is false, and you know it,' I said. 'How can I guard a man if I don't know who or what I'm guarding him against? That's like sending a soldier into battle not only without telling him where the enemy is, but *who* the enemy is.'

'Well, then,' said Ogilvie tranquilly. 'It looks as though you'll have to do it for the sake of my bright blue eyes.'

He had me there and I think he knew it. I had an idea that Mr Nameless, whoever he was, could be quite formidable and Ogilvie had defused what might have been a nasty situation that morning. I owed him something for it. Besides, the cunning old devil's eyes were green.

'All right,' I said. 'But it isn't a one-man job.'

'I'm aware of that. Spend this afternoon thinking out your requirements – I want them on my desk early tomorrow morning. Oh, by the way – you don't disclose yourself.'

I opened my mouth and then closed it again slowly before I swore at him. Then I said, 'You must be joking. I have to guard a man without telling him I'm guarding him?'

'I'm sure you'll do it very well,' he said suavely, and rang for the waiter.

'Then you'll be astonished at what I'll need,' I said acidly.

He nodded, then asked curiously, 'Hasn't it disturbed you that you'll be marrying into a rather mysterious family?'

'It's Penny I'm marrying, not Ashton.' I grinned at him. 'Aren't you disturbed for the same reason?'

'Don't think I'm not,' he said seriously, and left me to make of that what I could.

SEVEN

When I got back to the office Larry Godwin looked me up and down critically. 'I was just about to send out a search party. The griffin is that you've been given a real bollocking. I was just about to go down to the cellar to see if they really do use thumbscrews.'

'Nothing to it,' I said airily. 'I was given the RSPCA medal for being kind to Joe Harrison – that's all.'

'Very funny,' he said acidly, and flapped open a day-old copy of *Pravda*. 'The only time you'll get a medal is when you come with me when I get my knighthood.' He watched me putting a few things in a bag. 'Going somewhere?'

'I won't be around for a couple of days or so.'

'Lucky devil. I never get out of this bloody office.'

'You will one day,' I said consolingly. 'You have to go to Buck House to get a knighthood.' I leaned against the desk. 'You really should be in Slav Section. Why did you opt for General Duties?'

'I thought it would be more exciting,' he said, and added sourly, 'I was wrong.'

'With you around, the phrase "as happy as Larry" takes on an entirely new meaning.' I thought he was going to throw something at me so I ducked out fast.

I drove to Marlow and found the police station. My name presented to the desk sergeant got me Honnister in jig time. He shared an office with another inspector and when I indicated a desire for privacy Honnister shrugged and said, 'Oh, well; we can use an interview room. It's not as comfortable as here, though.'

'That's all right.'

The other copper closed a file and stood up. 'I'm going, anyway. I don't want to pry into your girlish secrets, Charlie.' He gave me a keen glance as he went out. He'd know me again if he saw me.

Honnister sat at his desk and scowled. 'Secretive crowd, your lot.'

I grinned. 'I don't see you wearing a copper's uniform.'

'I had one of your blokes on the blower this morning – chap by the name of Harrison – threatening me with the Tower of London and unnameable tortures if I talk about you.'

I sat down. 'Joe Harrison is a silly bastard, but he means well.'

'If anyone knows how to keep secrets it's a copper,' said Honnister. 'Especially one in the plain clothes branch. I know enough local secrets to blow Marlow apart. Your chap ought to know that.' He sounded aggrieved.

I cursed Harrison and his ham-fisted approach; if he'd queered my pitch with the local law I'd string him up by the thumbs when I got back. I said, 'Inspector, I told you last night I had no official connection with Ashton. It was true then, but it is no longer true. My people now have a definite interest.'

He grunted. 'I know. I've been asked to make an extra copy of all my reports on the Ashton case. As though I don't have enough to do without producing a lot of bloody bumf for people who won't even give me the time of day without consulting the Official Secrets Act.' His resentment was growing.

I said quickly, 'Oh, hell; you can forget that nonsense – just as long as I can see your file copies.'

'You got authority for that?'

I smiled at him. 'A man has all the authority he can take. I'll carry the can if there's a comeback.'

He stared at me and then his lips curved in amusement. 'You and me will get on all right,' he said. 'What do you want to know?'

'First, how's the girl?'

'We haven't been allowed to talk to her so she must be pretty bad. And I need a description. I don't even know the sex of the assailant.'

'So that means no visitors.'

'None except the family. Her sister has been at the hospital most of the day.'

I said, 'I think I might be able to help you there. Suppose I got Penny to ask Gillian for a description. That would do to be going on with until you can ask her yourself.' He nodded. 'I won't be seeing her until later. Where will you be tonight?'

'Theoretically off duty. But I'll be sinking a couple of pints in the Coach and Horses between nine and ten. I'm meeting someone who might give me a lead on another case. You can ring me there. Doyle, the landlord, knows me.'

'Okay. Now, how have you got on with the acid?'

Honnister shrugged. 'About as far as you'd expect. It's battery acid, and the stuff's too common. There are filling stations all around here, and then it might have come from somewhere else.' He leaned back in his chair. 'To me this has the smell of a London job.'

'Have you seen Ashton?'

'Oh, yes, I've seen Ashton. He says he can think of absolutely no reason why his daughter should be attacked in such a manner. No reason whatsoever. It was like talking to a bloody stone wall.'

'I'll be talking to him myself tonight. Maybe I'll get something.'

'Does he know who – and what – you are?'

'No, he doesn't; and he mustn't find out, either.'

'You blokes lead interesting lives,' said Honnister, and grinned crookedly. 'And you wanting to marry his daughter, too.'

I smiled. 'Where did you get that?'

'Just pieced it together from what you told me last night, and from what one of the uniformed boys picked up when talking over a cuppa with the Ashtons' maid. I told you I hear secrets – and I'm not a bad jack, even though I say it myself.'

'All right,' I said. 'Tell me a few secrets about Ashton.'

'Not known to the police. Not criminally. The CPO had a few words with him.'

'CPO?'

'Crime Prevention Officer. There are a lot of big houses around here full of expensive loot worth nicking. The CPO calls in to check on the burglar-proofing. You'd be surprised how stupid some of these rich twits can be. A man will fill his house with a quarter of a million quids' worth of paintings and antiques and balk at spending a couple of thousand on keeping the stuff safe.'

'How is Ashton's burglar-proofing?'

Honnister grinned. 'It might rank second to the Bank of England,' he conceded.

That interested me. 'Anything more on Ashton?'

'Nothing relevant. But he wasn't the one who was attacked, was he?' He leaned forward. 'Have you thought of the possibility that Gillian Ashton might have been sleeping in the wrong bed? There are two things I think of when I hear of an acid attack on a woman; the first is that it could be a gangland punishment, and the other is that it's one woman taking revenge on another.'

'I've thought of it. Penny discounts it, and I don't go much for it myself. I don't think she's the kind.'

'Maybe, but I've been doing a bit of nosing around. I haven't come up with anything yet, but I can't discount it.'

'Of course you can't.'

I stood up, and Honnister said, 'Don't expect too much too quickly. In fact, don't expect anything at all. I've no great hopes of this case. Anyway, we've not gone twenty-four hours yet.'

That was so, and it surprised me. So much had happened that day that it seemed longer. 'Okay,' I said. 'I'll be in touch tonight.'

EIGHT

I drove in the direction of Ashton's house and cruised around slowly, making circuits on the country roads and looking for anything out of the ordinary such as cars parked on the verge with people in them doing nothing in particular. There was nothing like that so after an hour of futility I gave up and drove directly to the house.

The gates were locked but there was a bell-push which I pressed. While I waited I studied the gates in the light of what Honnister had said about Ashton's burglar-proofing. They were of ornamental wrought-iron, about ten feet high, very spiky on top, and hung on two massive stone pillars. They barred an opening in an equally high chain-mesh fence, unobtrusive because concealed by trees, which evidently circled the estate. All very good, but the gates hadn't been closed the day before.

Presently a man came down the drive, dressed in rough country clothes. I hadn't seen him before. He looked at me through the gates and said curtly, 'Yes?'

'My name is Malcolm Jaggard. I'd like to see Mr Ashton.'

'He's not in.'

'Miss Ashton?'

'They're not in, either.'

I tugged thoughtfully at my ear. 'What about Benson?'

He looked at me for a moment, then said, 'I'll see.' He stepped to one side behind one of the stone pillars and I heard a click and then the whirr of a telephone dial. There's a phrase for what was happening; it's known as closing the stable door after the horse has gone.

The man came back into sight and wordlessly began to unlock the gate, so I got back into the car and drove up to the house. Benson, in his courtly Boris Karloff manner, ushered me into the living-room, and said, 'I don't expect Miss Penelope will be long, sir. She rang to say she would be back at five.'

'Did she say how Gillian is?'

'No, sir.' He paused, then shook his head slowly. 'This is a bad business, sir. Disgracefully bad.'

'Yes.' I had always been taught that it is bad form to question servants about their masters, but I had no compunction now. Benson had never struck me as being one of your run-of-the-mill house servants, least of all at that very moment because, unless he'd developed a fast-growing tumour under his left armpit, he was wearing a gun. 'I see you have a guard on the gate.'

'Yes; that's Willis. I'll give him your name so he will let you in.'

'How is Mr Ashton taking all this?'

'Remarkably well. He went to his office as usual this morning. Would you care for a drink, sir?'

'Thank you. I'll have a scotch.'

He crossed the room, opened a cabinet, and shortly came back with a tray which he put on a small table next to my elbow. 'If you will excuse me, sir.'

'Thank you, Benson.' He was not staying around to be questioned, but even if he had I doubted if I could have got much out of him. He tended to speak in clichés and bland generalities, but whether he thought that way was quite another matter.

I had not long to wait for Penny and was barely half way through the drink when she came into the room. 'Oh, Malcolm; how good to see you. What a blessed man you are.' She looked tired and drawn.

'I said I'd come. How's Gillian?'

'A little better, I think. She's getting over the shock.'

'I'm very glad to hear it. I had a talk with Honnister, the police inspector in charge of the case. He wants to interview her.'

'Oh, Malcolm; she's not ready for that. Not yet.' She came to me and I took her in my arms. 'Is it that bad?'

She laid her head on my chest for a moment, and then looked up at me. 'I don't think you know how bad this sort of thing is for a woman. Women seem to care more for their appearance than men – I suppose we have to because we're in the man-catching business, most of us. It's not just the physical shock that's hit Gillian; there's the psychological shock, too.'

'Don't think I'm not aware of it,' I said. 'But put yourself in Honnister's place. He's in a jam – he needs a description. Right now he doesn't even know if he's looking for a man or a woman.'

Penny looked startled. 'I hadn't even thought of that. I assumed it would be a man.'

'Honnister hasn't made that assumption. He hasn't made any assumptions at all because he has damn-all to go on. Is Gillian talking to you?'

'A little, this afternoon.' Penny made a wry face. 'I've kept off the subject of acid-throwing.'

'Could you go to the hospital tonight and see what you can get out of her? Honnister is really at his wits' end about this. Your father couldn't help him and he's stuck.'

'I suppose I could try.'

'Better you than Honnister; he might not have your understanding. I'll come with you; not into the ward, but I'll come along.'

'Will eight o'clock be all right for you? Not too late?'

'All my time is at your disposal.' I didn't tell her that was literally true, by courtesy of one Ogilvie and paid for by the taxpayer. 'You look as though you could do with a drink.'

'I could stand a gin and tonic. Bring it into the kitchen, will you? I have to do something about dinner – Daddy will be home soon.'

She went away and I fixed the drink and took it into the kitchen, I offered to help but she laughed, and said. 'You'd just be in the way. Mary is coming down to help.'

'Mary who?'

'The maid – Mary Cope. You find yourself something to do.'

I went away reflecting that what I really wanted to do was to give Ashton's study a good shake-down. But if it's bad form to question the servants I don't know what the devil it would be called to be found searching through your host's private papers in his *sanctum sanctorum*. Moodily I walked out into the garden.

I was knocking croquet balls about on the lawn when Ashton pitched up. There was a worn and honed look about him as though he was being fined down on some spiritual grindstone. His skin had not lost its tan but he looked paler than usual, and there was still that hurt look in his eyes. It was the look of a little boy who had been punished for something he hadn't done; the anguished look of the injustice of the world. It's hard to explain to a small boy that the world isn't necessarily a just place, but Ashton had been around long enough to know it.

I said, 'Penny's in the kitchen, if you want her.'

'I've seen her,' he said shortly.

'She tells me Gillian's better this evening.'

He looked down, kicking the turf with the toe of his shoe. He didn't speak for some time and I began to think he'd misheard me. But then he looked up and said abruptly, 'She's blind.'

'Christ; I'm sorry to hear that.'

He nodded. 'I had a specialist in this afternoon.'

'Does she know? Does Penny know?'

'Neither of them know. I had it kept from them.'

'I can understand not telling Gillian, but why keep it from Penny?'

'Unlike many sisters they've always been very close even though they are so unalike in temperament – perhaps because of it. I think if Penny knew, Gillian would get it out of her, and she couldn't stand the shock now.' He looked me in the eye. 'Don't tell her.'

Now that was all very logical and carefully thought out, and he had just given me a direct order, there was no doubt about that. 'I won't tell her,' I said. 'But she might find out anyway. She's medically trained and nobody's fool.'

'Just so that it comes later rather than sooner,' he said.

I thought I'd better start to earn my pay. 'I saw Honnister this afternoon. He tells me he didn't get much change out of you this morning. Don't you have any idea why Gillian should be attacked?'

'No,' he said colourlessly.

I studied him carefully. His jacket was much better cut than Benson's but no amount of fine tailoring could hide the slight bulge under his arm. 'You haven't had threatening letters or anything like that?'

'Nothing like that,' he said impatiently. 'I'm at a loss to understand it.'

I felt like asking him, 'Then why carry a gun?" My problem was that I didn't know why he was on our files. Men were listed for many reasons, and to be listed did not make them villains – far from it. The trouble was that no one would tell me which class Ashton came into, and that made this job damned difficult. Difficult to know how to push at him; difficult to identify the cranny into which to push the wedge that would crack him.

But I tried. I said practically. 'Then the reason must lie somewhere in Gillian's own life. Some crowd she's been mixed up with, perhaps.'

He became instantly angry. 'Nonsense!' he said sharply. 'That's a monstrous suggestion. How could she get mixed up with types like that without me knowing? The type who could do such a dreadful thing?'

I was acting the part of the impartial onlooker. 'Oh, I don't know,' I said judiciously. 'It happens all the time judging by what we read in the newspapers. The police arrest a kid and uncover a whole series of offences, from mainlining on heroin to theft to get the cash to feed the habit. The parents are shocked and plead ignorance; they had no idea that little Johnny or little Mary was involved. I believe them, too.'

He took a deep breath. 'For one thing, Gillian isn't a kid; she's a grown woman of twenty-six. And for another, I know my family very well. You paid me a compliment last night: you said I'd brought up Penny too well. That goes for Gillian, too.' He drove his toe viciously into the turf. 'Would you think that of Penny?'

'No, I don't think I would.'

'Then why should you think it of Gillian? It's bloody ridiculous.'

'Because Penny didn't have acid thrown in her face,' I reminded him. 'Gillian did.'

'This is a nightmare,' he muttered.

'I'm sorry; I didn't mean to hurt you. I hope you'll accept my apology.'

He put his hands to his face, rubbing at closed eyelids. 'Oh, that's all right, Malcolm.' His hand dropped to his side. 'It's just that she was always such a good little girl. Not like

Penny; Penny could be difficult at times. She still can. She can be very wilful, as you'll find out if you marry her. But Gillian . . .' He shook his head. 'Gillian was never any trouble at all.'

What Ashton said brought home to me some of the anguish parents must feel when things go wrong with the kids. But I was not so concerned with his agony that I didn't note his reference to *if* I married Penny, not *when* I married her. Evidently the fixation of the previous night had left him.

He disillusioned me immediately. 'Have you given any thought to what we discussed last night?'

'Some.'

'With what conclusion?'

'I'm still pretty much of the same mind,' I said. 'I don't think this is the time to present Penny with new problems, especially if the girls are as close as you say. She's very unhappy, too, you know.'

'I suppose you're right,' he said dispiritedly, and kicked at the grass again. He was doing that shoe no good at all, and it was a pity to treat Lobb's craftsmanship so cavalierly. 'Are you staying to dinner?'

'With your permission,' I said formally. 'I'm taking Penny to the hospital afterwards.'

He nodded. 'Don't tell her about Gillian's eyes. Promise me that.'

'I already have.'

He didn't answer that, but turned on his heel and walked away towards the house. As I watched him go I felt desperately sorry for him. It didn't matter to me then if Nellie had him listed as a hero or a villain; I still felt sorry for him as a simple human being in the deepest of distress.

Penny and I got to the hospital at about half past eight. I didn't go in with her but waited in the car. She was away quite a long time, more than an hour, and I became restive because I had promised to call Honnister. When she came out she said quietly, 'I've got what you wanted.'

I said, 'Will you tell it to Honnister? I have an appointment with him.'

'All right.'

We found Honnister standing at the bar of the Coach and Horses looking broodily into a glass of beer. When we joined him he said, 'My man's been and gone. I've been hanging on waiting for your call.'

'Inspecter Honnister – this is Penny Ashton. She has something to tell you.'

He regarded her with gravity. 'Thank you. Miss Ashton. I don't think you need me to tell you that we're doing the best we can on this case, but it's rather difficult, and we appreciate all the help we can get.'

'I understand,' she said.

He turned to me. 'What'll you have?'

'A scotch and . . .' I glanced at Penny.

'A gin and tonic.'

Honnister called to the man behind the bar. 'Monte, a large scotch and a gin and tonic.' He turned and surveyed the room. 'We'd better grab that table before the last-minute crowd comes in.'

I took Penny over to the table and presently Honnister joined us with the drinks. He wasted no time and even before he was seated, he said, 'Well, Miss Ashton, what can you tell me?'

'Gillian says it was a man.'

'Aah!' said Honnister in satisfaction. He had just eliminated a little more than half the population of Britain. 'What sort of man? Young? Old? Anything you tell me will be of value.'

He led her through the story several times and each time elicited a further nugget of information. What it boiled down to was this: Gillian had walked back from church and, coming up the drive towards the house, had seen a car parked with the bonnet open and a man peering at the engine. She thought he was someone who had broken down so she approached with the intention of offering assistance. As she drew near the man turned and smiled at her. He was no one she knew. She was about to speak when he slammed down the bonnet with one hand and simultaneously threw the acid into her face with the other. The man didn't speak at any time; he was about forty, with a sallow complexion and sunken eyes. She did not know the make of car but it was darkish in colour.

'Let's go back a bit,' said Honnister yet again. 'Your sister saw the man looking at the engine with the bonnet open. Did she mention his hands?'

'No, I don't think so. Is it important?'

'It might be,' said Honnister noncommittally. He *was* a good jack; he didn't put his own ideas into the mouths of his witnesses.

Penny frowned, staring at the bubbles rising in her glass, and her lips moved slightly as she rehearsed her thoughts. Suddenly she said, 'That's it, Inspector. Gillian said she walked up and the man turned and smiled at her, then he took his hands out of his jacket pockets.'

'Good!' said Honnister heartily. 'Very good, indeed!'

'I don't see the importance,' said Penny.

Honnister turned to me. 'Some cars have a rod on a hinge to hold up the bonnet; others have a spring-loaded gadget. Now, if he had his hands in his pockets he couldn't have been holding the bonnet open manually; and if he took them out of his pockets to close the bonnet and throw the acid at the same time then that bonnet was spring-loaded. He wouldn't have time to unhook a rod. It cuts down considerably on the makes of car we have to look for.' He drained his glass. 'Anything more to tell me?'

'I can think of nothing else, Inspector.'

'You and your sister have done very well,' he said as he stood up. 'Now I have to see a man about a dog.' He grinned at me. 'I really mean that – someone pinched a greyhound.'

Penny said, 'You'll let us know if . . .'

'You'll be first to know when something breaks,' promised Honnister. 'This is one villain I really want to get my hands on.'

As he walked out I said, 'He's a good copper.'

'It seems so,' said Penny. 'I wouldn't have thought of the significance of the way a car bonnet is held open.'

I stared into my glass. I was thinking that if I got hold of that acid-throwing bastard first there wouldn't be much left of him for Honnister to deal with. Presently Penny said, 'I can't say, "A penny for your thoughts", or you might get the wrong idea; but what are you thinking?'

I said it automatically; I said it without moving my mind. I said, 'I'm thinking it would be a good idea if we got married.'

'Malcolm!'

I'm pretty good at detecting nuances but there were too damn many in that single two-syllable word to cope with. There was something of surprise and something of shock; something, I was afraid, of displeasure and something, I hoped, of delight. All mixed up together.

'Don't *you* think it's a good idea?' I watched her hunt for words. 'But don't say, "This is so sudden!"'

'But it *is* so damned sudden,' she said, and waved her hand at the room. 'Here, of all places.'

'It seems a good pub to me,' I said. 'Does the place matter?'

'I don't suppose it does,' she said quietly. 'But the time – and the timing – does.'

'I suppose I could have picked a better time,' I agreed. 'But it just popped out. I'm not the only one who thinks it's a good idea. Your father does, too; he wanted me to ask you last night.'

'So you two have been discussing me behind my back. I don't know that I like that.'

'Be reasonable. It's traditional – and courteous, too – for a man to inform his prospective father-in-law of his intentions.' I refrained from saying that it had been Ashton who had brought up the subject.

'What would you have done if he had been against it?'

'I'd have asked you just the same,' I said equably. 'I'm marrying you, not your father.'

'You're not marrying anyone – yet.' I was thankful for the saving grace of that final monosyllable. She laid her hand on mine. 'You idiot – I thought you'd never ask.'

'I had it all laid on, but circumstances got in the way.'

'I know.' There was melancholy in her voice. 'Oh, Malcolm; I don't know what to say. I've been so unhappy today, thinking about Gillian, and seeing her in such pain. And then there was that awful task you laid on me tonight of questioning her. I saw it had to be done, so I did it – but I don't like one bit of it. And then there's Daddy – he doesn't say much but I think he's going through hell, and I'm worried about him. And now you come and give me more problems.'

'I'm sorry, Penny; I truly am. Let's put the question back in the deep freeze for a while. Consider yourself unasked.'

'No,' she said. 'You can't unask a question. In a way that's what my work is all about.' She was silent for a while. I didn't know what she meant by that but I had sense enough to keep my mouth shut. At last she said, 'I will marry you, Malcolm – I'd marry you tomorrow. I'm not one for non-essentials, and I don't want a white wedding with all the trimmings or anything like that. I want to marry you but it can't be now, and I can't tell you when it will be. We've got to get this matter of Gillian sorted out first.'

I took her hand. 'That's good enough for me.'

She gave me a crooked smile. 'It won't be the usual kind of engagement, I'm afraid, I'm in no mood for romantic frivolities. Later, perhaps; but not now.' She squeezed my hand. 'Do you remember when I asked you to come here and meet Daddy? It was the night we had the Chinese dinner in your flat.'

'I remember.'

'It was a diversion. I had to stop myself from doing something.'

'Doing what, for God's sake?'

'Marching into your bedroom and getting into your bed.' She disengaged her hand and finished her drink. 'And now you'd better take me home before I change my mind and we start behaving badly.'

As I escorted her to the car my heart was like a singing bird and all the other guff poets used to write about. They don't any more; they leave it to the writers of pop songs, which is a pity. I drove her home and stopped the car before the gates, and we had five minutes' worth of love before she got out. She had no key and had to press the button for someone to come.

I said, 'We won't announce the engagement, but I think your father ought to know. It seems to be on his mind.'

'I'll tell him now.'

'Are you going to London tomorrow?'

She shook her head. 'Lumsden has given me a few days off. He's very understanding.'

'I'll pop out to see you.'

'But what about your job?'

I grinned. 'I have an understanding boss, too.'

There was a rattle at the gate and it swung open, pushed by Wills, the dour and unfriendly type who had let me in that afternoon. Penny kissed me and then slipped inside and the gate clanged shut. I stepped up to it, and said to Willis, 'Escort Miss Ashton up to the house, see her safe inside, and make sure the house door is locked.'

He looked at me for a moment in silence, then smiled, and it was like an ice floe breaking up. 'I'll do that, sir.'

NINE

I was in the office early next morning and first I had an extended chat with Nellie. I had just moved to the typewriter when Larry came in with a pile of newspapers which he dumped on his desk. 'Thought you were out on a job.'

'I am,' I said. 'I'm not here. I'm a figment of your imagination.'

I finished my list and took it in to Ogilvie, and wasted no time in getting down to the bones of it. I said, 'I don't mind fighting with one hand tied behind my back but I object to having both hands tied. I'll need a list of Ashton's present overt activities and affiliations.'

Ogilvie smiled and pushed a file across the desk. 'I anticipated you.'

In return he got my sheet of paper. 'That's more of what I need.'

He scanned it. 'Six men, six cars, telephone ta . . .' He broke off. 'Who do you think we are – the CIA?'

I looked studiously at the back of my hands. 'Have you ever been in the field, sir?'

'Of course I've . . .' I looked up and found him smiling sheepishly. The smile disappeared as he said irritably, 'I know; you people think we desk-bound types have lost touch. You could be right.' He tapped the paper. 'Justify this.'

'I have to do a twenty-four hour secret surveillance of three – perhaps four – people. It'll be . . .'

He caught me up on that. 'Which three or four?'

'First Ashton and Penny Ashton. Then Gillian Ashton. Just because she's been attacked once doesn't give her a lifelong exemption. I might be able to arrange with Honnister to have one of his chaps at the hospital if I ask him nicely enough. That'll take some of the load off us.'

'And the fourth?'

'Benson. I pushed the lot of them through the computer until I lost them in Code Purple.'

'Benson, too?' Ogilvie thought about it. 'You know, the computer might be going by the address only. Anyone living there might be classed with Ashton.'

'I thought of that and it won't wash. Mary Cope, the maid, lives in and I put her through as a control. Nellie has never heard of her. If Ashton is so damned important then he's six-man-important.'

'I agree – but you can't keep an eye on four people with six men. I'll let you have eight.' He smiled slightly. 'I must be going soft-headed. If Harrison was handling this he'd cut you down to four.'

I was taken aback but rallied enough to discuss who we were going to use on the operation. I said, 'I'd like to take Laurence Godwin.'

'You think he's ready?'

'Yes. If we don't use him soon he'll go sour on us. I've been keeping an eye on him lately; he's been right more times than he's been wrong, which is not bad going in this trade.'

'Very well.' Ogilvie returned to my list. 'I agree that Ashton's telephones should be tapped. If he's being threatened we want to know about it. I'll have to get authorization from upstairs, though; but I'll be as quick as I can. As for the postal surveillance, that's trickier but I'll see what

I can do.' He put his finger down. 'This last item worries me. You'll have to have a damned good reason for wanting a pistol.'

'Benson's carrying a gun in his oxter, and Ashton is carrying another. If they are expecting that sort of action I think we should be prepared.'

'You're sure of this?'

'Dead certain. I'd like to know if they have gun permits.'

Ogilvie considered it. 'Under the circumstances Ashton might. I don't know about Benson. I'll check.' I'd have given a lot to know what those circumstances were but I didn't ask because I knew he wouldn't tell me.

We settled a few more minor details, then Ogilvie said, 'Right, that's it. Round up your boys and brief them. I want a recording made of the briefing, the tape to be given to me personally before you leave. Get on with it, Malcolm.' As I was leaving he added, 'I'll authorize two pistols.'

I went back, and gave Larry a list of names. 'Get on the blower. I want those men in my office ten minutes ago.' I paused. 'And put yourself on the bottom of the list.'

His expression was a study in pure delight. 'You mean . . .'

I grinned. 'I mean. Now get busy.' I sat at my desk and opened the file on Ashton. It was very thin. The names and addresses of his firms were given, but his other associations were few, mostly professional men – lawyers, accountants and the like. He was a member of no club, whether social, sporting or intellectual. A millionaire hermit.

The team assembled and I switched on the tape-recorder. The brieling didn't take long. I outlined the problem and then told how we were going to handle it, then allocated jobs and shifts. One pistol would be carried by the man over-seeing Ashton, whoever he happened to be at the time; the other I reserved for myself.

I said, 'Now we have radios so we use them. Stay on net and report often so everyone is clued up all the time. Those off-shift to be findable and near a telephone. You might be needed in a hurry.'

Simpson asked, 'Do off-shift men go home?' He'd just got back from his honeymoon.

'No. Everyone books into hotels in or near Marlow.' There was an audible groan. 'As soon as you've done it report which hotel together with its phone number so we can find you. I'm at the Compleat Angler.'

Brent said, 'Living it up on the expense account.'

I grinned, then said soberly, 'I don't think we'll have much time for that on this exercise. I might add that this is an important one. You can judge its importance by the fact that Ogilvie raised the team from six to eight on his own initiative and without me having to needle him. In the light of our staff position that says a lot. So don't lose any of these people – and keep your own heads down. Right; that's all.' I switched off the recorder and rewound the tape.

Larry said, 'You haven't given me a job.'

'You stick with me. I'll be back in a minute – I'm going to see Ogilvie.'

As I walked into his outer office his secretary said, 'I was about to ring you, Mr Jaggard. Mr Ogilvie wants to see you.'

'Thanks.' I went on in, and said, 'Here's the tape of the briefing.'

He was frowning and said directly, 'Did you cancel a request given to Inspector Honnister for copies of his reports on the Ashton case?'

I put the cassette on his desk. 'Yes.'

'Why?'

'Because I thought it was a lot of bull,' I said bluntly. 'It was getting in the way of good relations. What Harrison did was bad enough.'

'Harrison! What did Joe do?'

I related Harrison's flat-footed approach and Honnister's reaction to it, and then his views on providing extra copies of his reports. I added, 'If we're going to ask Honnister to provide a guard at the hospital we need to keep in his good books.'

'Very good thinking,' said Ogilvie heavily. 'But for one thing. This department did not request those copies. It came from elsewhere, and someone has just been chewing my ear off by telephone.'

'Oh,' I said, rather inadequately, and then, 'Who?'

'Need you ask?' said Ogilvie acidly. 'The gentleman you met yesterday is sticking his oar in – which, I might add, he is perfectly entitled to do.' He rubbed his jaw and amended the statement. 'As long as he restricts himself to requests for information and does not initiate any action.'

He pondered for a moment, then said, 'All right, Malcolm, you can go. But don't take any precipitate action without referring back to me.'

'Yes. I'm sorry, sir.'

He waved me away.

TEN

There was nearly an hour of bureaucracy to get through before Larry and I could drive to Marlow. On the way I gave him the score up to that point, and his reaction was emphatic. 'This is downright stupid! You mean Ogilvie won't tell you what's behind all this?'

'I think his hands are tied,' I said. 'This is real top-level stuff. He has a character from Whitehall like a monkey on his back.'

'You mean Cregar?'

I glanced sideways at Larry. 'Who?'

'Lord Cregar. Short, chubby little chap.'

'Could be. How did you get on to him? Did you bug Ogilvie's office?'

He grinned. 'I went to the loo yesterday and saw him coming out of Ogilvie's room while you were in there.'

I said musingly, 'Ogilvie did refer to him as "his lordship" but I thought he was joking. How did you know he was Cregar?'

'He got divorced last week,' said Larry. 'His photograph was splashed on the middle inside page of the *Telegraph*.'

I nodded. The *Daily Telegraph* takes a keen interest in the marital ups-and-downs of the upper crust. 'Do you know anything more about him, other than that he's wifeless?'

'Yes,' said Larry. 'He's not womanless – *that* came out very strongly in the court case. But beyond that, nothing.'

We crossed the Thames at Marlow, and I said, 'We'll check the hospital first, then go to the police station and I'll introduce you to a good copper. How good are you at grovelling? I might need a few lessons.'

The hospital car park was full so I put the car illicitly into a doctor's slot. I saw Jack Brent, who was trailing Penny, so that meant she was in the hospital; he was talking to someone over his radio. I was about to go over to him when someone hailed me, and I turned to find Honnister at my elbow.

He seemed quite cheerful as I introduced Larry. I said, 'I got some wires crossed yesterday. My people didn't ask for reports; the request came from elsewhere.'

He smiled. 'I thought the Super was a bit narky this morning. Not to worry, Mr Jaggard. A man can't do more than his best.'

'Any progress?'

'I think we have the make of car. A witness saw a Hillman Sceptre close to Ashton's place on Saturday afternoon. The driver fits the description of the suspect. A dark blue car and spring-loaded bonnet, so it fits.' He rubbed his hands. 'I'm beginning to think we stand a chance on this one. I want to get this man before Miss Ashton for a firm identification.'

I shook my head. 'You won't get it. She's blind.'

Honnister looked stricken. 'Christ!' he said savagely. 'Wait till I lay hands on this whoreson!'

'Stand in line. There's a queue.'

'I'm just going up to see her. The doctor says she's fit to talk.'

'Don't tell her she's blind – she doesn't know yet. And don't tell her sister.' I pondered for a moment. 'We have reason to believe another attack may be made on her. Can you put a man in the hospital?'

'That's asking something,' said Honnister. He paused, then asked, 'Do you know what's wrong with the bloody force? Too many chiefs and not enough Indians. If there's a multiple smash on the M4 we'd be hard put to it to find four uniformed men for crowd control. But go into the nick in Slough and you can't toss a pebble in any direction without it ricocheting off three coppers of the rank of chief inspector or higher.' He seemed bitter. 'But I'll see what I can do.'

I said, 'Failing that, give the hospital staff a good briefing. No stranger to get near Gillian Ashton without authority from you, me or the Ashton family. Pitch it to them strong.'

Brent left his car and joined us and I introduced him to Honnister. 'Everything okay?'

'She's inside now; that's her car over there. But this town is hell on wheels. She went shopping before she came here and led me a devil of a dance. There's nowhere to park – I got two tickets in half an hour.'

'Hell, we can't have that.' I could imagine Penny being abducted while my man argued the toss with a traffic warden. I said to Larry, 'I want CD plates put on all our cars fast.'

'Oh, very tricky!' said Honnister admiringly.

Larry grinned. 'The Foreign Office won't like it.'

'Nothing to do with the Foreign Office,' observed Honnister. 'It's just a convention with no legal significance. A copper once stopped a car with CD plates and found a Cockney driver, so he asked him what CD stood for. The bloke said, "Cake Deliverer". And he was, too.' He shrugged. There was nothing he could do about it.' He nudged me. 'Coming in?'

'I'll join you inside.'

Jack Brent waited until Honnister was well out of earshot before saying, 'I thought it best not to talk in front of him, but Ashton and Benson haven't been found.'

'Ashton isn't at his office?'

'No, and he isn't at home, either.'

I thought about it. In the course of his business Ashton might be anywhere in the Home Counties; he might even have gone to London. And there was nothing to say that Benson was a prisoner in the house; he had to go out some time. All the same, I didn't like it.

I said, 'I'm going to the house. Come on, Larry.' I turned to Brent. 'And you stick close to Penny Ashton. For Christ's sake, don't lose her.'

I drove a little faster than I should on the way to Ashton's place, and when I got there I leaned on the bell-push until Willis arrived wearing an annoyed expression. 'There's no one in,' he said abruptly.

'I want to make sure of that. Let me in.' He hesitated and then opened the gate reluctantly and I drove up to the house.

Larry said, 'He's a surly devil.'

'But reliable, I'd say.' I stopped before the front door, got out, and rang the bell. It was a fair time before the door opened and I was confronted by the maid who looked surprised to see me. 'Oh, Mr Jaggard, Miss Penny's not here. She's at the hospital.'

'I know. Mr Ashton's not in?'

'No, he's out, too.'

'What about Benson?'

'I haven't seen him all morning.'

I said, 'Mind if we come in? I'd like to use the telephone.'

In response she opened the door wider. Larry and I walked into the hall, and I said, 'You're Mary Cope, aren't you?'

'Yes, sir.'

'Have you seen either Mr Ashton or Benson at all today?'

'No, sir.'

'When was the last time you saw them?'

'Well, not really to see,' she said. 'But they were in the study last night; I heard them talking. That would be about nine o'clock. Just before, really, because I was going up to my room to catch the nine o'clock news and I switched on five minutes early.' She paused, wondering if she was right in talking of the doings of the family. After all, I hadn't been around all that long. She said nervously, 'Is this anything to do with what happened to Miss Gillian?'

'It could be.'

'Mr Ashton's bed wasn't slept in,' she volunteered.

I glanced at Larry who raised his eyebrows. 'What about Benson's bed?'

'I haven't looked – but he always makes up his own bed.'

'I see. I'll use the telephone if I may.'

I rang the hospital, asking for Penny, and told the operator she'd be in or near the intensive care unit. It was a long time before she came on the line. 'I hope you haven't waited long,' she said. 'I slipped away for a cup of tea. Gillian's much better, Malcolm; she's talking to Honnister now, and she doesn't mind a bit.'

I said, 'Did you tell your father about us last night?'

'No. He'd gone to bed when I got in.'

'Did you tell him this morning?'

'No. I slept late and he'd gone out when I got up. I expect Mary made breakfast for him.'

I didn't comment on that. 'When did you last see Benson?'

Her voice was suddenly wary. 'What's the matter, Malcolm? What's going on?'

I said, 'Look, Penny, I'm at your house. I'd like you to come home because I want to talk to you about something. I expect Honnister will be at the hospital for quite some time, and there's nothing you can do there.'

'There's something wrong, isn't there?' she said.

'Not really. I'll tell you when I see you.'

'I'm coming now.' She rang off.

I put down the receiver and looked around, to see Mary Cope regarding me curiously from the other end of the hall. I jerked my head at Larry and gave him my keys. 'In the special compartment of my car you'll find a file on Ashton. There's a list of the cars he owns – on page five, I think. Nip-round to the garage and see what's missing. Then go down to the gate and ask Willis what time Ashton and Benson left here.'

He went quickly and I walked into Ashton's study. On his desk were two envelopes; one addressed to Penny and the other to me. I picked up mine and broke the seal.

The note might have been enigmatic to anyone else, but to me it was as clear as crystal. It read:

My dear Malcolm,

You are far too intelligent a man not to have seen what I was driving at in our more recent conversations. You may be acquainted with the French proverb: *Celui qui a trouvé un bon gendre a gagné un fils; mais celui qui en a recontré un mauvais a perdu une fille.*

Marry Penny with my blessing and make her happy – but, for her sake, be a bad son-in-law.

Yours,
George Ashton.

I sat down heavily and had a queasy feeling in the pit of my stomach because I knew we'd botched the job. I picked up the telephone to ring Ogilivie.

ELEVEN

I didn't wrap it up for him. 'Our pigeons have flown the coop,' I said baldly.

He was incredulous. 'What! All of them?'

'Just the two cock birds.'

He was silent for a moment, then said slowly, 'My fault, I'm afraid. I ought to have given you your team yesterday. How certain are you?'

'He left me a note.' I read it out.

Ogilvie put the French into English. '"He who has found a good son-in-law has gained a son, but he who has picked up a bad one has lost a daughter." What the hell is that supposed to mean?'

I said, 'It may be my fault that he's cut and run. He tackled me again last evening about marrying Penny, and I gave him another refusal. I think that since he couldn't get her to cut loose from him, he has cut loose from her. If you read the note in that context you'll see what I mean.'

'Um. What was his attitude last evening?'

'He was a walking disaster,' I said flatly.

'How much start have they had?'

I sorted through the details I had picked up, then checked the time. 'I don't know about Benson, but for Ashton say fifteen hours maximum. I might get to know a bit more in the next few minutes.'

'We don't know that he went,' said Ogilvie objectively. 'He might have been taken. That note to you may be a fraud. Either case is serious, of course.'

'I don't think he was taken. The note is too accurately pointed, and this house is well protected.'

'Yes, it would be.' Ogilvie knew enough of the background to make a statement like that. 'How's the girl taking it?'

'She doesn't know yet. Ashton left her a note, too. I haven't opened it – I'll let her do that. I'll let you know anything that's relevant.'

'Think she'll tell you?'

'Yes. It's a funny thing, sir, but I did ask her to marry me last night and she accepted. She was going to tell Ashton when she got home but she said he'd gone to bed. I think he'd already left. If he'd waited another couple of hours he might have decided not to go.'

'Yes,' said Ogilvie meditatively. 'But don't blame yourself for that.' I looked up as Larry came into the study. Ogilvie said, 'Did you disclose yourself to her?'

'No.'

There was a pause. 'You take your duties very seriously, don't you, Malcolm?'

'I try to. Hang on a minute.' I looked up at Larry. 'Well?'

'There's an Aston Martin short, and both Benson and Ashton left last night at about half past nine, and didn't come back.'

The Aston Martin was Penny's car. I said to Ogilvie, 'We've got a pretty firm time. They left together at nine-thirty last night, probably in a hired car.' He seemed to be a long time digesting that, so I said, 'What's the next step?'

'There's going to be a row, of course,' he said, not sounding too perturbed. 'But I'll handle that. What you do is to go through that house like a dose of salts. See if you can find anything to indicate where Ashton has gone. Anything you don't understand bring here for evaluation.'

I said, 'That will blow my cover with Penny. I can't search the house without giving her an explanation.'

'I know.'

'Hold on.' I turned to Larry. 'Get on the radio – I want everyone here as soon as possible.'

'Off-shift boys included?'

'Yes. And go to the gate to make sure they can get in.'

Before speaking to Ogilvie again I glumly contemplated the explanation I'd have to give Penny. It was a hell of a thing to tell a girl you've just proposed to, and I had the feeling that our relationship was about to alter for the worse.

I pushed it out of my mind, and said, 'Do we bring the police in on this?'

I could almost hear Ogilvie's brains creaking as he thought that one out. At last he said, 'Not at this stage. I'll have to push it upstairs for a ruling. Police security is not too good on this sort of thing – they have too many reporters watching them. How long do you think you'll be there?'

'I don't know. It's a big house and I can see at least one safe from here. If we can't find keys we may have to take extreme measures. I'll give you a ring in an hour. I'll have a better idea by then.'

'I can't hold this for an hour. If you look towards London in fifteen minutes you'll see flames rising from Whitehall. Do your best.' He rang off.

I put down the telephone and looked thoughtfully at the letter addressed to Penny, then crossed to the safe. It had a combination lock and the door didn't open when I turned the handle. I went back to the desk and gave it a quick once-over lightly in the hope of finding something useful immediately. There was nothing. Five minutes later I heard a car draw up outside and, thinking it might be Penny, I went outside.

It was Peter Michaelis, one of the team. He came over with an enquiring look on his face, and I said, 'Stick around.' He had given Larry a lift from the gate, so I called him over. 'Take Ashton's file and start ringing around – his office, factories, every address you find in there. If Ashton is seen he's to ring his home immediately.' I shrugged. 'It won't work but we must cover it.'

'Okay.'

An Aston Martin was coming up the drive so I braced myself. 'Use the telephone in the hall. I want to use the study.'

Larry walked towards the house as Penny's car came to a fast halt, braked hard. She tumbled out, looking uncertainly at Michaelis, then ran towards me. 'I'm being followed,' she said, and whirled around, pointing at the car coming up the drive. 'He followed me into the grounds.'

'It's all right,' I said, as Brent's car stopped. 'I know who he is.'

'What's happening?' she demanded. 'Who are these men?' Her voice caught. 'What's happened to Daddy?'

'As far as I know he's all right.' I took her elbow. 'I want you to come with me.'

I took her into the house and she paused in the hall as she saw Larry at the telephone, then quickened her pace again. We went into the study and I picked up the letter from the desk. 'You'd better read this.'

She looked at me uncertainly before glancing at the superscription. 'It's from Daddy,' she said, and ripped open the envelope. As she read the note she frowned and her face paled. 'But I don't . . . I don't understand. I don't . . .'

'What does he say?'

Wordlessly she handed the letter to me, then walked over to the window and looked out. I watched her for a moment, then bent my head and read:

My dearest Penny,

For reasons I cannot disclose I must go away for a while. The reasons are not disreputable, nor am I a criminal, although that imputation may be made. My affairs are all in order and my absence should not cause you any trouble financially. I have made all the necessary arrangements: for legal advice consult Mr Veasey of Michelmore, Veasey and Templeton; for financial advice go to Mr Howard of Howard and Page. They have been well briefed for this eventuality.

I do not know for how long I shall have to be away. You will be doing me a great service if you make no attempt at all to find me and, above all, I do not wish the police to be brought into this matter if that can be avoided. I assure you again that my reasons for leaving in this manner are purely private and personal. I will come to no harm because my old friend, Benson, will be looking after me.

It would give me the greatest peace of mind if you would marry your Malcolm as soon as is practically possible. I know that you love him and I know that he wants to marry you very much, and I have a great respect for the intelligence and character of the man you have chosen. Please do not let the matter of poor Gillian impede your plans to marry and, on the occasion, please put a notice in *The Times*.

I have the greatest confidence that the two of you will be very happy together, and I am equally sure that you will both look after Gillian. Forgive me for the abrupt manner of my departure but it is in the best interests of all of us.

Your loving father,
George.

I looked up. 'I'm sorry, Penny.'

'But I don't understand,' she cried desolately. 'Oh, Malcolm, what's *happened* to him?'

She came into my arms and I held her close. 'I don't know – but we'll find out.'

She was still for a while, but pushed herself away as two cars arrived in quick succession. She stared from the window at the gathering knot of men. 'Malcolm, who are all those men? Have you told the police? Daddy said not to.'

'No, I haven't told the police,' I said quietly. 'Sit down, Penny; I have a lot to tell you.' She looked at me wonderingly, and hesitated, but sat in the chair behind the desk. I hesitated, too, not knowing where to begin, then thought it best to give it to her straight and fast.

'I work for the firm of McCulloch and Ross, and I've told no lies about what the firm does. It does everything I've said it does, and does it very well, too. Our clients are most satisfied, and they ought to be because of the amount of public money going into their service.'

'What are you getting at?'

'McCulloch and Ross is a cover for a sort of discreet government department dealing mainly with economic and industrial affairs in so far as they impinge on state security.'

'State security! You mean you're some sort of secret agent. A spy?'

I laughed and held up my hands. 'Not a spy. We're not romantic types with double-o numbers and a licence to kill – no nonsense like that.'

'But you were watching and investigating my father like a common spy.' Anger flamed in her. 'And was I just a means to an end? Did you snuggle up to me just to get to know him better?'

I lost the smile fast – this was where the crunch came. 'Christ, no! I didn't know a damned thing about him until yesterday, and I don't know much more now. Believe me when I say it was something I stumbled into by accident.'

She was disbelieving and contemptuous. 'And just what did you *stumble* into?'

'I can't tell you that because I don't know myself.'

She shook her head as though momentarily dizzy. 'That man in the hall – those men outside: are they in your department, too?'

'Yes.'

'Then I'd like to talk to the man in charge.' She stood up. 'I'd like to tell him just what I think of all this. I knew Daddy was under pressure. Now I know where it was coming from.'

I said deliberately, 'You're talking to the man in charge, and you're dead wrong.'

That stopped her. She sat down with a bump. '*You* are in charge?'

'That's right.'

'And you don't know what you're doing?' she laughed hysterically.

'I know what I'm doing, but I don't know why. There's a hierarchy of levels. Penny – wheels within wheels. Let me tell you how I got into this.'

So I told her. I told her everything, holding nothing back. I told her about Nellie and the colour codes; I told her about Ogilvie and Lord Cregar. I told her a damned sight more than I ought to have done, and to hell with the Official Secrets Act.

She heard me out, then said thoughtfully, 'Your people aren't very trusting, are they?'

'They're not in the trust business.' I lit a cigarette. 'The pressure didn't come from us, Penny. We threw no acid. We came into it after that, and my brief was to watch over your father and protect him – your father, you and Gillian, and Benson, too, if I thought it necessary.' I walked over to the window and looked at the cars. The gang had all arrived. 'I've not done a very good job so far.'

'It's not your fault that Daddy went away.' Her words hung heavily in the air, and she seemed to take another look at her father. 'That he *ran* away.'

I turned to her. 'Don't start blaming him without knowing what you're blaming him for.'

She said pensively, 'I wonder if he'd still want me to marry you, if he knew what I know now?'

'I'll ask him as soon as I catch up with him,' I said grimly.

'You're not going after him?' She picked up her letter. 'He said . . .'

'I know what he said. I also know he's regarded by my people as a very important man, and he may be going into danger without knowing it. I still have my job to do.'

'But he doesn't want . . .'

I said impatiently, 'What he wants or doesn't want is immaterial.' I plucked the letter from her fingers and scanned it. 'He says he doesn't want you to go looking for him. Well, you won't – I will. He says not to involve the police. Right; they haven't been told. He says, "I will come to no harm because my old friend, Benson, will be looking after me." Good God, Penny, how old is Benson? He must be pushing sixty-five. He's in no position to protect himself, let alone anyone else.'

She started to weep. She didn't sob or make an outcry, but the tears welled in her eyes and ran down her cheeks. She cried silently and helplessly, and she was shivering as though suddenly very cold. I put my arm around her and she clung to me with a fierce grip. One of the worst things that can happen is when a hitherto cosy and secure world falls apart. An icy wind seemed to be blowing through that pleasant panelled study from the greater and more vicious world outside.

'Oh, Malcolm, what am I to do?'

I said very quietly, 'You must do what you think is best. If you trust me you will help me find him, but I wouldn't – I couldn't – blame you if you refuse. I haven't been open with you – I should have told you about this yesterday.'

'But you were under orders.'

'A common plea,' I said. 'All the Nazis made it.'

'Malcolm, don't make it harder for yourself than you have to.' She put my arm aside, stood up, and went to the window. 'What are your men waiting for?'

I took a deep breath. 'For your decision. I want to search the house, and I can't do that without your permission.'

She came back to the desk and read her father's letter again. I said, 'He wrote to me, too,' and produced the letter. 'You can read it if you like.'

She read it, then gave it back to me. 'Bring in your men,' she said tonelessly.

TWELVE

We found a number of surprising things in that house but nothing that did us much good, at least, not then. In the basement there was a remarkably well-equipped workshop and chemical laboratory, way beyond amateur standard. There was also a small computer with a variety of input and output peripherals including an X – Y plotter. Still on the plotter was a sketch which had been drawn under computer control; it seemed to be a schematic of a complicated molecule and it made no sense to me, but then I'm no expert. For bigger problems with which the little computer couldn't cope there was a modem and an acoustic coupler so that the little chap could be used as a terminal to control a big computer by way of the post office land lines.

In the workshop was a bench on which a thingamajig was under construction. Whatever it was intended to do it was going to do under computer control because there were no fewer than fifteen integrated-circuit microelectronic chips built into it, and that's a fair amount of computing power. Also coupled into it was a laser, a cathode ray tube, a lot of laboratory glassware and a couple of gadgets I didn't recognize.

I didn't snap any switches or push any of the unlabelled buttons because I didn't know what would happen if I did.

Instead I said to Larry, 'Any of Ashton's firms connected with electronics or computers?'

'No, just chemicals and plastics moulding. Some of the chemical processes might be computer-controlled, though.'

I grunted and had the entire basement sealed. The boffins from the department would have to check it out, and I wasn't going to touch anything until they had done so.

Penny had the combination for the safe in the study, and I knew by that we were unlikely to find anything of conesquence in it. I was right. There was a bit of money, less than £50, which was not much considering Ashton's resources – I suppose it was emergency pocket money. There were some account books on which I wasted some time until I discovered they related to the running of the household, the stables and the cars. All very orderly. There was a whole sheaf of balance sheets headed with the name of the firm of accountants, Howard and Page. A quick glance at the bottom lines told me that George Ashton was doing very nicely, thank you, in spite of the economic recession.

And that was all.

Ashton's own quarters were a bit more productive. He had a suite-bedroom, bathroom, dressing-room and sitting-room which were as clean as a whistle. He seemed to live somewhat spartanly; there was less than the usual amount of junk which a man tends to accumulate and it was all very clean and tidy. There was nothing at all in any of the pockets of the clothes hanging in the wardrobes; whoever did his valeting – Benson probably – did a good job.

But a considerable amount of panel-tapping discovered a tambour which, when slid aside after a complicated procedure involving switching on certain lights in all four rooms thus releasing an electrically-controlled lock, revealed a massive metal door of armour-plated steel. The way I've described that might make you think we were lucky to find it, but it wasn't luck. The boys were good at their jobs.

Not good enough to open that vault door, though. After Simpson had done some architectural measuring with a tape I knew that beyond that door was not merely a safe but a sizeable room, big enough to swing a kitten in, if not a cat. Now, any man who would put a door like that as entrance to a room would be sure to take other precautions. The walls, floor and ceiling would be very thick concrete, well reinforced with toughened steel, and the whole package would weigh a lot even when empty. It was on the second floor which meant that a special underpinning structure must have been built to support it. I made a note to look up Ashton's architect.

When the vault door was shown to Penny she was as surprised as anyone. She had never suspected its existence.

All this doesn't mean that I was prowling about the house personally knocking on walls. I left that to the boys and only inspected the results when they came in. I supervised the search of Ashton's study in Penny's presence, then settled down to talk to her because I assumed she would know more about her father than anyone else.

'Benson,' I said. 'How long have you known Benson?'

She looked surprised. 'He's always been around.'

'That's a long time. How long is always?'

'Always is always, Malcolm. I can't remember a time when there wasn't Benson.'

'As long as that? Twenty-five or twenty-six years?'

Penny smiled. 'Longer than that. He was with Daddy before I was born.'

'Always is a long time,' I agreed. 'He does the faithful family retainer bit very well, I must say. But he's more than that, isn't he?'

She crinkled her brow. 'I don't know. That's difficult to assess. When a man had been with a family as long as

Benson he tends to become regarded as more of a friend than a servant.'

'To the extent that your father would share a bottle of whisky with him?'

'I don't think he ever did that.'

'He did on Sunday night,' I observed. 'Has Benson always been a personal servant to your father?'

She thought for a moment. 'We moved into the house in 1961 – I was twelve then. It was then Benson moved in here as Daddy's valet and dogsbody. Before that we had a house in Slough; just a little one, nothing as grand as this. Benson worked in one of Daddy's factories, but he visited the house quite often – at least once a week.' She smiled. 'He was one of our favourites. He used to bring us sweets – forbidden fruit because Daddy didn't like us to eat too many sweets. Benson used to smuggle them to us.'

'What was Benson doing in the factory?'

'I don't know. I was only a little girl.'

'When did your mother die, Penny?'

'When I was four.'

I thought that was bad luck on Ashton, having to bring up two small daughters. Still, he hadn't made a bad job of it. It seemed he didn't make a bad job of anything. I said, 'Do you know how your father got started? I mean, how did he start in business? Did he have inherited money, for instance?'

She shook her head vigorously. 'Daddy never talked much about his early life but I know he didn't inherit anything because he was an orphan brought up in a foundling home. He was in the army during the war and when he came out he met my grandfather and they set up in business together. They didn't have much money at the time, so my grandfather said before he died. He said Daddy's brains made it a success.'

'What was he in the army?' I asked idly.

'Just a private.'

That surprised me. Ashton would have been twenty-six or twenty-seven when he was demobbed and it was strange that a man of his drive and character should still have been a private soldier. Perhaps his army record would bear looking into.

'Did your father ever carry a gun?'

She misunderstood me. 'He did rough shooting at times, but not often.'

'I don't mean a shotgun. I mean a revolver or automatic pistol.'

'Lord, no! He hasn't got such a thing.'

'Would you know?'

'Of course I would.'

'You didn't know about that strong room upstairs.'

She was silent and bit her lip, then said, 'You think he's armed?'

I was saved from answering that because Larry popped his head around the door. 'Can I have a word, Malcolm?' I nodded and joined him in the hall. He said, 'Gillian Ashton's rooms are clean, nothing there of consequence. I read her diaries; she seems to live a quiet, upper-middle-class life – theatre, ballet, opera and so on. She reads a lot, too.'

'Not any more. Any liaisons?'

'Nothing very strong; a string of men who appeared one at a time and then petered out after a while.' He grinned. 'No mysterious assignations with people referred to by only their initials, nothing like that.'

'What about Penny's rooms? Have you checked there?'

Larry looked at me a bit queerly. 'But I thought . . .'

'I don't care what you thought,' I said evenly. 'Do it.'

'Okay.' He went downstairs again, and I thought that young Larry still had a lot to learn.

I was about to return to the study when Michaelis came through the hall. I said, 'Found anything?'

'Nothing for us. But in an attic there's the damnedest thing – the biggest model railway set-up I've seen in my life.'

'Model railway!' I said incredulously.

'It's a real enthusiast's job,' he said. 'I'm a bit keen, myself, but I've never seen anything like this. There must be over a mile of HO-gauge track up there – it's like a bloody spider web. You'd have to do some smart scheduling to keep that lot running smoothly.'

It was a facet of Ashton I wouldn't have dreamed of, but it didn't have a thing to do with the matter at hand. I dismissed it. 'Where's Jack Brent?'

'Giving the out-buildings a going-over – the garages and stables.'

'Tell him I want to see him when he's finished.' I went back into the study and thought it was time to try to find Ogilvie again. I'd been ringing every hour on the hour but each time he'd been out of the office so I'd passed my stuff on to Harrison. I put my hand out to dial again but the telephone shrilled before I got there.

It was Ogilvie. 'What have you got?' he said abruptly.

'I've passed it all to Harrison. Have you spoken to him?'

'No. As you may have gathered the balloon went up on schedule and I've been busy the last few hours. Give me the gist of it.'

'We've got a bloody big vault here,' I said. 'Not a safe, but a professional bank vault. We'll need experts to open it, and it'll probably take *them* a week.'

'It had better not,' said Ogilvie. 'You'll have them within the hour. What else?'

'I'd like some boffins – electronic and chemical. There's a cellar full of scientific stuff to look at. And you'd better send someone competent in computers.' I grinned. 'And maybe a model railway expert.'

'What's that?' he barked.

'Ashton has a model railway lay-out in his attic. I haven't seen it but I'm told it's quite something.'

'This is no time to be funny,' said Ogilvie acidly. 'What else?'

'Damn all. Nothing of use to us.'

'Keep looking,' he said sharply. 'A man can't live fifteen years in a house and not leave something of his personality lying around. There'll be *some* indication of where he's gone.' He thought for a moment. 'But I want you back here. Put someone else in charge.'

'That'll be Gregory,' I said. 'I still have a few things to wrap up – I'll be back in two hours.' I rang off and said to Penny, 'Well, that's it, love. The boss wants me back.'

She said, 'Just before you went out you said something about Daddy having a gun. What did you mean?'

'He's armed,' I said.

She shook her head disbelievingly but, since so many strange things had occurred that day, she could not combat my statement. 'And will you find him?'

'Oh. we'll find him. What's worrying me is that perhaps someone else is looking for him who will find him first. And the hell of it is we aren't sure, one way or another.'

Brent came in. 'You want me?'

I waved him out and joined him in the hall. As I stripped off my jacket I said, 'Find anything?'

'Nothing.'

I unhitched the shoulder-holster from under my left armpit. Take this; you might need it.' I waited until he'd put it on, then took him into the study. 'Penny, this is Jack Brent; he's your guardian angel from now on. He sticks with you everywhere you go, excepting the loo and the bedroom – and he inspects those first.'

Penny looked at me as though she suspected me of joking. 'Are you serious?'

'You'll have to find a room for Jack – he'll be living here as long as you do.' I turned to Brent. 'Make yourself acquainted with the burglar precautions here, and make sure the damn things work.'

He nodded, and said, 'Sorry about this. Miss Ashton; I have to do as I'm told.'

'Another man under orders,' she said tightly. There were pink anger spots in her cheeks. 'Do you really mean that this man goes everywhere I go?'

'As long as you want to keep your schoolgirl complexion.'

Maybe I was a bit brutal about it, but the force of what I said hit her hard. She went very pale. 'My God, Malcolm. What *is* my father?'

'I don't know; but I'm going to wring it out of Ogilvie if it's the last thing I do.'

Jack Brent gave me a look as though he thought it would be the last thing I did. Twisting the boss's arm in any organization is not the way to promotion and that indexed pension.

I said, 'I have things to do. I'll see you before I go, Penny.' I went to brief Gregory on the latest developments and to hand over to him. I found him with Simpson going over Benson's quarters which were a bit more opulent than you'd expect of a house servant – a three-roomed suite. Gregory and Simpson had torn the place apart on my instructions because I was particularly interested in Benson. 'Any luck?'

Gregory grunted. 'Not much. There's this.' He pointed to a small can of oil. 'Recommended for gun actions. And we found a single round of ammunition – unfired. It had rolled under the bed and dropped into a crack near the wall.'

It was a 9 mm parabellum round, popular with the military and the police. 'We know he was armed,' I said. 'Now we know what with – not that it helps. Anything else?'

'Not yet.'

I told Gregory the score and then went to check the activities of the rest of the team. I had to find *something* to take to Ogilvie. In the attic I found two of the boys playing trains. 'Oh, Jesus!' I said. 'Cut it out. We're here on business.'

Michaelis grinned. 'This is business – all in the line of duty. If you want this place searched thoroughly we'll have to look inside every engine, carriage and truck in this lay-out. The only way to do it is to bring them to this central control point a trainload at a time.'

I examined the lay-out and saw he had a point. You might have found a more complicated system in an international model engineering exhibition but I doubted it. There were about ten levels of track and a complexity of points and sidings which was baffling, and the whole lot was controlled from a central console which looked like the flight deck of Concorde. Michaelis seemed to have got the hang of it; maybe he was a budding genius.

'How many trucks and carriages are there?'

'We've looked at about three hundred so far,' he said. 'I reckon that's about a quarter. We're lucky there's an automatic coupling and uncoupling system. See those trucks in the siding over there?' He pointed to a spot about eight yards inside the spider web of rails. 'We'd never be able to get in there without smashing the lot up – so we sent an engine in to pull them out. Like this.'

He flicked switches and an engine about five inches long moved into the siding and attached itself to a line of trucks with a slight click. It reversed slowly, drawing out the train of trucks, and Michaelis smiled with pleasure. 'Now the problem is – how do we get it from there to here?'

My God! I thought. What we have to do in the line of duty.

I snorted and left them to it, and went in search of Penny to make my farewells. Somebody said she was in her bedroom. She answered when I tapped on the door, and she was as angry as I'd ever seen her. 'Come in,' she said impatiently, so I did and she slammed the door behind me with a crash. 'Someone has been searching my room.'

'I know. *All* rooms in the house have been searched.'

'On your instructions?'

'Yes.'

'Oh, no! I thought I deserved better of you than that. You were right when you said you people don't deal in trust. Last night you asked me to marry you, and less than twenty-four hours later you show just how much you trust me. What sort of a man are you that you would send someone in here to paw over my things?'

'It's not a question of trusting or not trusting,' I said. 'I do my job in the way I was taught.'

'So you go by the book! It's not the kind of book I'd want to read.'

And so we had a flaming row – our first. I got so boiling mad that in the end I stormed out of the house and jumped into my car. I left a bit of rubber on the drive and got to the office in record time, being lucky not to be picked up by the police for speeding.

I wasn't in the best of moods when I confronted Ogilvie. He said immediately, 'Got anything more?'

I dropped the round of ammunition on his desk. 'Benson has something which shoots those.'

'All right, Malcolm,' he said. 'Let's begin at the beginning.'

So we talked. I told him in detail everything that had happened and we discussed the implications. Or rather, Ogilvie did. I didn't know enough about Ashton to see any implications. At one point in the discussion I said, 'It's obvious that Ashton had been prepared for this a long time. He told Penny that his lawyer and accountant had been well briefed, and he couldn't have done that in a day. I don't know if he expected acid-throwing, but he was certainly ready to jump. Someone has put the frighteners on him.'

Ogilvie made no comment on that. He said, 'You may know – or not know – that there's an inter-departmental committee for organizations like ours which sits to straighten out any demarcation disputes.'

'I don't know, but it sounds a good idea.'

'There was a special meeting called for this afternoon, and I had to talk very hard and very fast. There was considerable opposition.'

'From Lord Cregar?'

Ogilvie's eyebrows rose. 'How did you identify him?'

'He gets his picture in the papers,' I said sardonically.

'I see. Do you know anything of the early history of this department?'

'Not much.'

He leaned forward and tented his fingers. 'The British way of intelligence and security is rather strange. Over the years we've acquired a reputation for being good at it, good and rather subtle. That is the considered assessment of our American and Russian rivals. They're wrong, of course. What they mistake for subtlety is merely that our right hand hardly ever knows what our left hand is doing.'

He took out a case and offered me a cigarette. 'The politicians are deathly afraid of a centralized intelligence outfit; they don't want anything monolithic like the CIA or the KGB because they've seen what happens when such a group becomes too big and too powerful. And so, in the classic way of divide and rule, intelligence work in Britain is broken down among relatively small groups.'

He accepted a light. 'That has its drawbacks, too. It leads to amateurism, rivalry between departments, overlapping functions, the building of empires and private armies, lack of co-operation, a breakdown of the lines of communication – a whole litany of petty vices. And it makes my job damned difficult.'

His tone was a mixture of bitterness and resignation. I said, 'I can imagine.'

'In the early 1950s the risks of industrial espionage became noticeable. We weren't really bothered about one firm stealing secrets from another, and we're still not, unless it affects state security. The whole problem was that our friends to the east have no private firms, so any industrial espionage from that direction was *ipso facto* state inspired, and that we couldn't have. In our inimitable British fashion a new department was set up to cope. This department.'

'I know what we're doing, but I didn't know how we got started.'

Ogilvie drew on his cigarette. 'There's an important point. In an attempt to cut down on duplication of effort, several other departments had to hand over large chunks of their interests to us. In fact, a couple of them lost entirely their *raison d'être* and were closed down completely. They were only small fry, though. But it all led to jealousy and bad blood which exists in a dilute form to this day. And that's how we inherited the problem of Ashton.'

I said, 'Who did we pinch Ashton from?'

'Lord Cregar's department.' Ogilvie leaned forward. 'This afternoon the Minister came down on our side. Ashton is still our baby and we have to find him. You are still inside man, and that means *you* find him. Any help you need just ask for.'

'That suits me,' I said. 'I want clearance for Code Purple.'

Ogilvie shook his head. 'Not that.'

I blew up. 'For Christ's sake! How can I look for a man when I don't know anything about him? Back in Marlow I had an interesting lecture on trust which has soured me to the belly, and this job has already interfered too much with my private life. Now you either trust me or you don't – and the crunch comes here. I get clearance for Code Purple or my resignation will be on your desk at nine tomorrow morning.'

He said sadly, 'I have warned you about being impetuous. To begin with, I couldn't get you clearance in that time, and even if you did you wouldn't find what you're looking for because Ashton is in Code Black.' His voice was grim. 'And you couldn't be cleared for Code Black inside three months – if ever.'

Code Black sounded as though it was the end of the rainbow and Ashton was the pot of gold. There was a silence which I broke by saying diffidently, 'That's it, then. I'd better go along to my office and type my resignation.'

'Don't be a young fool!' snapped Ogilvie. He drummed on the desk, then said, 'I've come to a decision. If it gets out I could be fired. Wait here.'

He got up and went to an unobtrusive door behind his desk and disappeared. I waited a long time and wondered what I'd done. I knew I'd laid my career on the line. Well, I was prepared for that and with my financial backing I could stand it. Maybe I wouldn't have done it if I had only my pay to depend on. I don't know. And I'd pushed Ogilvie into doing something he might be sorry for, and that was bad because I liked him.

Presently he opened the door, and said, 'Come in here.' I followed him into a small room where there was one of the ubiquitous computer terminals. 'I'm cleared for Code Black,' he said. 'The information on Ashton is coming on line. If you sit there you'll know what you need to know. The computer won't know who is pushing the buttons.' He checked the time. 'I'll be back in two hours.'

I was a bit subdued. 'All right, sir.'

'I want your word,' be said. 'I don't want you roving at random in Code Black. I want to know that you'll stick to Ashton and only to Ashton. There are other matters in Code

Black that are better for you not to know for your own peace of mind.'

I said, 'You can make sure of that just by sitting in here with me.'

He smiled. 'You made a point just now about trust. Either I trust you or I don't, and there's an end to it.'

'You have my word.'

He nodded abruptly and left, closing the door behind him.

I glanced at Nellie who was staring at me with an interrogative bright green question mark and then glanced around the small room which was really more of a cubicle. On one side of the terminal was a small plotter, very much like the one in Ashton's cellar; on the other side was a line printer.

I sat at the console and reflected that if Ashton was so important and had been around and of interest since before the department had started then there was probably reams of stuff about him in Nellie's guts. This idea was reinforced by the two hours Ogilvie had allowed for reviewing the information, so I switched on the printer, and typed:

OUTPUT MODE – PRINTER

Nellie had an attack of verbal diarrhoea. She came back at me with:

PRINTER OUTPUT NEGATIVED UNDER CODE BLACK
NOTE WELL: NO WRITTEN RECORD TO BE MADE
UNDER CODE BLACK
NOTE WELL: NO TAPE-RECORDED TRANSCRIPTIONS
TO BE MADE UNDER CODE BLACK
NOTE WELL: NO PHOTOGRAPHS TO BE TAKEN OF
THE CRT UNDER CODE BLACK

I sighed and switched off the printer.

I've described before how one juggles with Nellie so there's no point in going into that again. What I haven't said is that Nellie is accommodating; if she's going too fast you can slow her down, and if she's producing something of no interest you can speed her up. You can also skip about in the record, going back to items forgotten or neglected. She's quite a toy.

I did quite a bit of skipping when swanning around in Ashton's life. He'd lived quite a bit.

THIRTEEN

Aleksandr Dmitrovitch Chelyuskin was born to poorish, but respectable, parents in the small town of Tesevo-Netyl'skiy, just to the north of Novgorod in Russia. The year was 1919. Both parents were schoolteachers; his mother taught in an infants' school and his father taught mathematics and allied subjects to older boys.

These were the years of revolution, and whether the Whites or the Reds were to come on top had not yet been decided in 1919. Armies of foreigners – British, French, American – were on Russian soil, and it was a time of turmoil and conflagration. Little Aleksandr was very nearly snuffed out just after birth as the waves of war swept over the country. In fact, his elder brother and his two sisters did die during this period as the family was buffeted in the storm; the record did not disclose just how they died.

Eventually, in 1923, the family Chelyuskin came to haven in the town of Aprelevka, just outside Moscow. The family had been reduced to three and, since Aleksandr had been a late child and his mother was now apparently barren, there were to be no more children and he was brought up as an only child. His father found a job teaching mathematics and they settled down to a life of relative security.

Although Dmitri Ivanovitch Chelyuskin was a teacher of mathematics he was not a good mathematician himself in the sense that he produced original work. His role in life was to teach small boys the elements of arithmetic, algebra and geometry, which he did largely by rote, a sarcastic tongue and a heavy hand. But he was good enough at his job to notice that he did not have to tell young Aleksandr anything twice, and when the time came that he found he did not have to tell the boy once and that his son was beginning to ask unanswerable questions it was then that he thought he might have an infant prodigy on his hands.

Aleksandr was about ten years old at the time.

He played chess very well and joined the chess club in Aprelevka where he proceeded to lick the pants off his elders and betters. The elder Chelyuskin forgot about the mathematics and thought of the possibility of having a Grand Master in the family, a great honour in Russia.

One Suslov, a member of the chess club, disagreed. He persuaded Chelyuskin *père* to write to a friend of his in Moscow, a member of the Board of Education. Letters and months passed, and eventually, after a series of supposedly gruelling examinations which Aleksandr went through without so much as a qualm, he was admitted to a Lycée in Moscow at the hitherto unheard-of age of twelve years and ten months. Whether the fact that Suslov had been the undisputed chess champion of Aprelevka, until the appearance of Aleksandr had anything to do with that, is not known. At least, Suslov said nothing for the record but went on to win the club championship the following year.

In Britain the left wing decries elitism; in Russia the communists foster it. When a bright youngster is found he is whisked away to a special school where his mind is stretched. He can no longer count on having an easy time walking nonchalantly through the school subjects without effort, coming out on top while his duller brethren work like hell plodding along behind. Aleksandr was subjected to a forced draught of education.

He liked it. He had the cast of mind which loves grappling with the abstruse and difficult, and he found much to his liking in pure mathematics. Now, mathematics at its purest is a game for adults and need have no relationship at all to the real physical world, and the fact that it sometimes does is a bit of luck. The pure mathematician is concerned with the concept of number at its most abstract, and Aleksandr played happily among the abstractions for quite a while. At the age of sixteen he wrote a paper, 'Some Observations on the Relationship between Mathieu Functions and Weierstrass Elliptic Functions'. It consisted of three paragraphs of written text and ten pages of mathematical formulae, and was rather well received. He followed it up with another paper the following year, and that brought him under the eye of Peter Kapitza and led to the second great change in his life.

It was 1936 and Kapitza was the white hope of Russian physics. He was born in Kronstadt and studied in Kronstadt and Petrograd, as it was then. But in 1925 he made a change which was rather odd for a Russian at the time. He went to Cambridge, then the leading university dealing with physics. He became a fellow of Trinity College, and assistant director of research at the Cavendish Laboratory under Rutherford. He was elected a Fellow of the Royal Society in 1929, and managed to pick up about every scientific honour that was not absolutely screwed down except the Nobel Prize which he missed. In 1936 he went back to Russia, supposedly on a sabbatical, and never left again. Stalin is reputed to have lowered the portcullis on him.

This, then, is the man who extended his influence over Aleksandr Chelyuskin. Perhaps he looked at the youth and was reminded of himself at the age of seventeen. At any rate, he diverted Aleksandr from his playground of pure mathematics and showed him that there were real problems to be solved in the world. Kapitza introduced him to theoretical physics.

Physics is an experimental science, and most physicists are good mechanics and have broken fingernails caused by putting bits and pieces of equipment together. But there are a few – a very few – who do nothing but think. They tend to sit around, gazing into space, and their favourite weapons are blackboard and chalk. After a few hours, days or years of thought they diffidently suggest that an experiment should be made.

The realm of the theoretical physicist is the totality of the universe, and there are very few good ones around at any one time. Aleksandr Chelyuskin was one of them.

He studied magnetism and low temperature physics under Peter Kapitza and, applying quantum theory to the earlier work of Kamerlingh Onnes, did important work relating to phase II of liquid helium, and the new field of superconductivity got under way. But this was just one of the many things he thought about. His work was astonishingly wide-ranging and eclectic, and he published profusely. He did not publish everything he thought because he liked to have things wrapped up tidily, but some of his work, reproduced in the record from his notebooks written at this time, clearly anticipated the cosmological theories of Fred Hoyie in the '50s and '60s. Other work from his notebooks included thoughts on the nature of catalyctic action and a brief sketch extending these thoughts into the organic field of enzymes.

In 1941 the war came to Russia, but the brain the state had so carefully nurtured was considered too valuable to risk having a bullet put through it, and Chelyuskin never saw a shot fired in anger. For most of the war he sat behind the Urals and thought his thoughts. One of the many things he thought about was the fine structure of metals. The resultant improvement in Russian tank armour was quite noticeable.

In March 1945 he was visited by a high official and told to give careful consideration to the atomic structure of certain rare metals. Stalin had just come back from the Yalta Conference where he had been informed of the existence of the atomic bomb.

In the period immediately following the war Chelyuskin became increasingly dissatisfied, mainly because, although the war was over, he was still constrained to involve himself in weapons research. He did not like what he was doing and deliberately slowed his pace. But a mind cannot stop thinking and he turned to other things than physics – to sociology, for example. In short, he stopped thinking about things and began to think about people.

He looked at the world immediately about him and did not like what he saw. This was the time when Stalin was conducting an extended post-mortem on the mistakes made during the war. Returning Russians who had been taken prisoner were hardly given time to sneeze before being whisked into Siberian camps, and hundreds of former officers mysteriously dropped out of sight. He reflected that continuous purging is as bad for a society as it is for a body, and he knew that the infamous army purge of 1936 had so weakened the army that it had contributed largely to the startling defeats at the beginning of the war. And yet the process was continuing.

He was determined, on moral grounds, not to continue with atomic research, and beyond that he was sure he did not want to put such weapons into the hands of a man like Stalin. But he was equally determined not to end up in a forced labour camp as some of his colleagues had done, so he was presented with quite a problem which he solved with characteristic neatness and economy.

He killed himself.

It took him three months to plan his death and he was ruthless in the way he went about it. He needed the body of a man about his own age and with the same physical characteristics. More complicatedly, he needed the body before it had died so that certain surgical and dental work could be done and given time to age. This could not be done on a corpse.

He found what he wanted on a visit to Aprelevka. A boyhood friend of his own age was afflicted with leukaemia and there was much doubt about his survival. Chelyuskin visited the hospital and chatted to his friend, at first in generalities and then, more directly and dangerously, about politics. He was fortunate in that he found his friend to have much the same convictions as himself, and so he was encouraged to ask the crucial question. Would his friend, in the terminal stages of a killing illness, donate his body for Chelyuskin's survival?

The record does not disclose the name of Chelyuskin's friend but, in my opinion, he was a very brave man. Chelyuskin pulled strings and had him transferred to another hospital where he had the co-operation of a doctor. File entries were fudged, papers were lost and bureaucracy was baffled; it was all very efficiently inefficient and ended up with the fact that Chelyuskin's friend was effectively dead as far as anyone knew.

Then the poor man had his leg broken under surgical and aseptic conditions and suffered a considerable amount of dental work. The fracture in the leg corresponded exactly with a similar fracture in Chelyuskin's leg and the dental structure duplicated Chelyuskin's mouth exactly. The bone knitted together, and all he had to do was to wait for his friend to die.

Meanwhile, going through underground channels, he had contacted British intelligence and requested political asylum. We were only too glad to oblige, even on his terms. To wave a defecting Russian scientist like a flag is not necessarily a good ploy, and we were quite happy to respect his terms of secrecy as long as we got him. The necessary arrangements were made.

It took a long time for Chelyuskin's friend to die. In fact, for a period there was a marked improvement in his condition which must have infuriated my masters. I doubt if it worried Chelyuskin very much. He went about his work as usual, attending the committees which were an increasing and aggravating part of his life, and soldiered on. But his friends did comment that he appeared to be doing his best to drown himself in the vodka bottle.

Seven months later the Russian scientific community was saddened to learn that Academician A. D. Chelyuskin had been burnt to death when his *dacha*, to which he had retired for a short period of relaxation, had caught fire. There was a post-mortem examination and an enquiry. The rumour got around that Chelyuskin had been smoking in bed when in his cups and that vodka added to the flames had not helped him much. That was a story everybody could believe.

A month later Chelyuskin slipped over the Iranian border. Three days later he was in Teheran and the following day he was put down at RAF Northolt by courtesy of Transport Command. He was given an enthusiastic welcome by a select group who turned out to welcome this genius who was then at the ripe age of twenty-eight. There would be a lot of mileage left in him.

The powers-that-be were somewhat baffled by Chelyuskin's comparative youth. They tended to forget that creative abstract thought, especially in mathematics, is a young man's game, and that Einstein had published his Special Theory of Relativity when only nineteen. Even the politicians among them forgot that Pitt was Prime Minister at twenty-four.

They were even more baffled and irritated by Chelyuskin's attitude. He soon made it clear that he was a

Russian patriot and no traitor, and that he had no intention of disclosing secrets, atomic or otherwise. He said he had left Russia because he did not want to work on atomics, and that to communicate his knowledge would be to negate the action he had taken. Conversations on atomic theory were barred.

The irritation grew and pressure was applied, but authority found that it could neither bend nor break this man. The more pressure was applied the more stubborn he became, until finally he refused to discuss *any* of his work. Even the ultimate threat did not move him. When told that he could be disclosed to the Russians even at that late stage he merely shrugged and indicated that it was the privilege of the British to do so if they wished, but he thought it would be unworthy of them.

Authority changed its tack. Someone asked him what he wanted to do. Did he want a laboratory put at his disposal, for instance? By now Chelyuskin was wary of the British and their motives. I suppose, in a way, he had been naïve to expect any other treatment, but naïvety in a genius is comparatively normal. He found himself surrounded, not by scientists whom he understood, but by calculating men, the power brokers of Whitehall. Mutual incomprehensibility was total.

He rejected the offer of a laboratory curtly. He saw quite clearly that he was in danger of exchanging one intellectual prison for another. When they asked him again what it was he wanted, he said something interesting, 'I want to live as an ordinary citizen,' he said. 'I want to sink and lose myself in the sea of Western capitalism.'

Authority shrugged its shoulders and gave up. Who could understand these funny foreigners, anyway? A dog-in-the-manger attitude was adopted; if we couldn't get at the man's brain then the Russians didn't have it, either, and that was good enough. He could always be watched and, who knows, he might even declare a dividend in the future.

So Chelyuskin got exactly what he asked for.

A REME soldier called George Ashton had been killed in a traffic accident in Germany. He was twenty-seven and had been brought up in a foundling home. Unmarried and with neither kith nor kin to mourn him, he was the perfect answer. Chelyuskin was flown to Germany, put in the uniform of a private in the British Army, and brought back to England by train and sea, accompanied discreetly at all times. He went through a demobilization centre where he was given a cheap suit, a small amount of back pay and a handshake from a sombre unrecruiting sergeant.

He was also given an honorarium of £2000.

He asked for, and was given, something else before he was cast adrift. Because of the necessity for scientific study he had learned English in his youth and read it fluently. But he never had occasion to speak it, which might have been an advantage when he was put through a six months' total immersion course in conversational English, because he had no bad habits to unlearn. He came out of it with a cultured generalized Home Counties accent, and set out to sink or swim in the capitalist world.

£2000 may not seem much now, but it was quite a sizeable piece of change back in 1947. Even so, George Ashton knew he must conserve his resources; he put most of it in a bank deposit account, and lived very simply while he explored this strange new world. He was no longer an honoured man, an Academician with a car and a *dacha* at his disposal, and he had to find a way of earning a living. Any position requiring written qualifications was barred to him because he did not have the papers. It was a preposterous situation.

He took a job as a book-keeper in the stores department of a small engineering firm in Luton. This was in the days before computers when book-keeping was done by hand as in the days of Dickens, and a good book-keeper could add a triple column of pounds, shillings and pence in one practised sweep of the eye. But there weren't many of those around and Ashton found himself welcome because, unlike the popular myth, he was an egghead who could add and *always* got his change right. He found the job ridiculously easy if monotonous, and it left him time to think.

He struck up an acquaintanceship with the foreman of the toolroom, a man called John Franklin who was about 50 years of age. They got on very well together and formed the habit of having a drink together in the local pub after work. Presently Ashton was invited *chez* Franklin for Sunday dinner where he met Franklin's wife, Jane, and his daughter, Mary. Mary Franklin was 25 then, and as yet unmarried because her fiancé had been shot down over Dortmund in the final days of the war.

All this time Ashton was being watched. If he was aware of it he gave no sign. Other people were watched, too, and the Franklin family came in for a thorough rummaging on the grounds that those interested in Ashton were *per se* interesting in themselves. Nothing was discovered except the truth; that Jack Franklin was a damned good artisan with his brains in his fingertips, Jane Franklin was a comfortable, maternal woman, and Mary Franklin had suffered a tragedy in her life.

Six months after they met, Ashton and Franklin left the engineering firm to strike out on their own. Ashton put up £1500 and his brains while Franklin contributed £500 and his capable hands. The idea was to set up a small plastics moulding shop; Franklin to make the moulds and the relatively simple machines needed, and Ashton to do the designing and to run the business.

The small firm wobbled along for a while without overmuch success until Ashton, becoming dissatisfied with the moulding powders he was getting from a big chemical company, devised a concoction of his own, patented it, and started another company to make it. After that they never looked back.

Ashton married Mary Franklin and I dare say a member of some department or other was unobtrusively present at the wedding. A year later she gave him a daughter whom they christened Penelope, and two years later another girl whom they called Gillian. Mary Ashton died a couple of years later in 1953, from childbirth complications. The baby died, too.

All his life Ashton kept a low profile. He joined no clubs or trade associations; he steered clear of politics, national or local, although he voted regularly, and generally divided his life between his work and his home. This gave him time to look after his two small girls with the help of a nanny whom he brought into the small suburban house in Slough, where he then lived. From the record he was devoted to them.

About 1953 he must have opened his old notebooks and started to think again. As Chelyuskin he had never published any of his work on catalysts and I suppose he thought it was safe to enter the field. A catalyst is a substance which speeds up the chemical reactions between other substances, sometimes by many thousands of times. They are used extensively in chemical processing, particularly in the oil industry.

Ashton put his old work to good use. He devised a whole series of new catalysts tailored to specialized uses. Some he manufactured and sold himself, others he allowed to be made under licence. All were patented and the money began to roll in. It seemed as though this odd fish was swimming quite well in the capitalist sea.

In 1960 he bought his present house and, after fifteen months of extensive internal remodelling, he moved in with his family. After that nothing much seemed to happen except that he saw the portent of North Sea oil, opened another factory in 1970, took out a lot more patents and became steadily richer. He also extended his interest to those natural catalysts, the enzymes, and presumably the sketchy theory presented in the early notebook became filled out.

After 1962 the record became particularly flat and perfunctory, and I knew why. Authority had lost interest in him and he would exist only in a tickler file to remind someone to give an annual check. It was only when I set the bells jangling by my inadvertent enquiry that someone had woken up.

And that was the life of George Ashton, once Aleksandr Dmitrovitch Chelyuskin – my future father-in-law.

FOURTEEN

What I have set down about Ashton-Chelyuskin is a mere condensation of what was in the computer together with a couple of added minor assumptions used as links to make a sustained narrative. Had I been able to use the printer it would have churned out enough typescript to make a book the size of a family bible. To set down in print the details of a man's life needs a lot of paper. Yet I think I have presented the relevant facts.

When I finished I had a headache. To stare at a cathode ray screen for two and a half hours is not good for the eyes, and I had been smoking heavily so that the little room was very stuffy. It was with relief that I emerged into Ogilvie's office.

He was sitting at his desk reading a book. He looked up and smiled. 'You look as though you need a drink.'

'It would go down very well,' I agreed.

He got up and opened a cabinet from which he took a bottle of whisky and two glasses; then he produced a jug of iced water from a small built-in refrigerator. The perquisites of office. 'What do you think?'

'I think Ashton is one hell of a man. I'm proud to have known him.'

'Anything else?'

'There's one fact that's so damned obvious it may be overlooked.'

'I doubt it,' said Ogilvie, and handed me a glass. 'A lot of good men have checked that file.'

I diluted the whisky and sat down. 'Do you have all of Ashton in there?'

'All that we know is there.'

'Exactly. Now, I've gone through Ashton's work in some detail and it's all in the field of applied science – technology, if you like. All the things he's been doing with catalysts is derived from his earlier unpublished work; there's nothing fundamentally new there. Correct me if I'm wrong.'

'You're quite right, although it took a man with Ashton's brains to do it. We've given our own top chemists photocopies of those notebooks and their attitude was that the stuff was all right from a theoretical point of view but it didn't seem to lead anywhere. Ashton made it lead somewhere and it's made him rich. But, in general, your point is good; it's all derivative of earlier work-even his later interest in enzymes.'

I nodded. 'But Chelyuskin was a theoretician. The point is this – did he stop theorizing and, if not, what the hell has he been thinking about? I can understand why you want that bloody vault opened.'

'You're not too stupid,' said Ogilvie. 'You've hit the nail smack on the head. You're right; you can't stop a man thinking, but what he's been thinking about is difficult to figure. It won't be atomic theory.'

'Why not?'

'We know what he reads; the magazines he subscribes to, the books he buys. We know he's not been keeping up with the scientific literature in any field except catalytic chemistry, and no one thinks in a vacuum. Atomic theory has made great strides since Ashton came out of Russia. To do any original work a man would have to work hard to keep ahead of the pack – attend seminars and so on. Ashton hasn't been doing it.' He tasted his whisky. 'What would you have done in Ashton's position and with a mind like his?'

'Survival would come first,' I said. 'I'd find a niche in society and look for security. Once I'd got that perhaps I'd start thinking again – theorizing.'

'What about? In your struggle for survival the world of thought has passed you by; you've lost touch. And you daren't try to regain touch, either. So what would you think about?'

'I don't know,' I said slowly. 'Perhaps, with a mind like his, I'd think about things other people haven't been thinking about. A new field.'

'Yes,' said Ogilvie thoughtfully. 'It makes one wonder, doesn't it?'

We sat for a few moments in silence. It was late – the light was ebbing from the summer sky over the City – and I was tired. I sipped the whisky appreciatively and thought about Ashton. Presently Ogilvie asked, 'Did you find anything in the file to give you a clue about where he's gone?'

'Nothing springs to mind. I'd like to sleep on it – let the unconscious have a go.' I finished the whisky. 'Where does Cregar fit into this?'

'It was his crowd Ashton approached when he wanted to leave Russia. Cregar went into Russia himself to get him out. He was a young man then, of course, and not yet Lord Cregar – he was the Honourable James Pallton. Now he heads his department.'

I'd come across the name Pallton in reading the file, but I hadn't connected it with Cregar. I said, 'He mishandled Ashton right from the start. He approached him with all the sensitivity of a fifty-pence whore. First he threatened, then he tried to bribe. He didn't understand the type of man he'd come across, and he put Ashton's back up.'

Ogilvie nodded. 'That's one element in the mixture of his resentment. He always thought he could retrieve Ashton;

that's why he was so annoyed when the Ashton case was transferred to us. That's why he's sticking his oar in now.'

'What steps have already been taken to find Ashton?'

'The usual. The Special Branch are on the watch at sea ports and airports, and they're checking passenger lists for the past twenty-four hours. You'd better liaise with Scotland Yard on that tomorrow.'

'I'll do that. And I'll have a go from the other end. There's one thing I'd like to know.'

'What's that?'

'Who threw such a scare into Ashton? Who threw that bloody acid?'

I was overtired that night and couldn't get to sleep. As I tossed restlessly Penny was very much on my mind. It was evident from what she had said that she knew nothing of Ashton in the larval stage, before he changed from Chelyuskin. Her account of his early life fitted that of the REME soldier killed in Germany.

I wondered how it would be with Penny and me. I had been damned insensitive that afternoon. Her room had to be searched, but if anyone had done it then it ought to have been me, preferably in her presence. I didn't blame her for blowing her top and I wondered how I could retrieve the situation. I felt very bad about it.

Most people, when they have had a burglary, are not so much concerned about the articles stolen as about the intrusion into the heart of their lives, the home which is so peculiarly their own. It is the thought that strange hands have been delving among their innermost secrets, rummaging in drawers, opening doors in the private parts of the house – all this is profoundly shocking. I knew all that and ought to have applied it to Penny.

At last I sat up in bed, checked the time, then stretched for the telephone. Although it was late I was going to talk to her. Mary Cope answered my call. 'Malcolm Jaggard here; I'd like to talk to Miss Ashton.'

'Just a moment, sir,' she said. She wasn't away long. 'Miss Ashton isn't in, sir.' There was a hint of nervousness in her voice as though she thought I wouldn't believe her. I didn't, but there was nothing I could do about it.

It was early morning when I finally slept.

I spent most of the forenoon at Scotland Yard with a Special Branch officer. I had no great hope of success and neither had he but we went through the motions. His crowd had been busy but even so the reports were slow to come in. A lot of people leave from Heathrow in twenty-four hours and that is only one exit from the country.

'Ashton and Benson,' he said morosely, as he ticked off a name. 'Bloody near as bad as Smith and Robinson. Why the hell do people we're interested in never have names like Moneypenny or Gotobed?'

Six Bensons and four Ashtons had left from Heathrow. Half could be eliminated because of sex and the Ashtons were a family of four. But two of the Bensons would have to be followed up; one had gone to Paris and the other to New York. I got busy on the telephone.

Heathrow may be large but it is still only one place and there are other airports, more than the average person realizes. And there were the sea ports of which islanded Britain has a plentitude. It was going to be a long job with nothing but uncertainty guaranteed.

The Special Branch man said philosophically, 'And, of course, they may have left under other names. Getting a spare passport is dead easy.'

'They may not have left at all,' I said. 'Tell your chaps to keep their eyes open.'

I lunched in a commissary at the Yard and then went back prepared for a slogging afternoon. At three o'clock

Ogilvie rang me. 'They'll be opening that vault later today. I want you there.'

A drive to Marlow would be a lot more refreshing than checking passenger lists. 'All right.'

'Now, these are my exact instructions. When that door is opened you will be present, and the head of the safe-cracking team. No one else. Is that clear?'

'Perfectly clear.'

'Then you send him out of the room and check the contents. If they are removeable you bring them here under guard. If not, you close and lock the door again, first making sure we can open it again more easily.'

'How long are you staying at the office?'

'All night, if necessary.' He hung up.

So I drove to Marlow and to Ashton's place. I was wearing grooves in that road. Simpson was the gate man and he let me in and I drove up to the house. I met Gregory in the hall. 'Found anything useful?'

He shrugged. 'Not a thing.'

'Where's Miss Ashton?'

'At the hospital. Jack Brent is with her.'

'Good enough.' I went up to Ashton's quarters and found the safe-cracking team at work. I don't know where the department kept its experts when not in use, but they were always available when needed. The chief safe-cracker was a man I'd met before by the name of Frank Lillywhite. 'Afternoon, Frank,' I said. 'How much longer?'

He grunted. 'An hour.' He paused. 'Or two.' There was a longer pause as he did something intricate with a tool he held. 'Or three.'

I grinned. 'Or four. Is this a tricky one?'

'They're all tricky. This is a twenty-four hour safe, that's all.'

I was curious. 'What do you mean?'

Lillywhite stepped away from the vault door and an underling moved in. 'Safe manufacturers don't sell security – they sell time. Any safe made can be cracked; all the manufacturer guarantees is the length of time needed to crack it. They reckon this is a twenty-four hour job; I'm going to do it in twenty – with a bit of luck. The tricky part comes in circumventing the booby traps.'

'What booby traps?'

'If I do the wrong thing here, twelve bloody big tungsten steel bars will shoot out all round the door. Then only the maker will be able to open it.'

'Then why didn't we get the maker on the job in the first place?'

Lillywhite sighed, and said patiently, 'The whole vault would have to be ripped out and taken to the factory. They've got a bloody big tin-opener there that weighs a thousand tons. Of course the vault wouldn't be good for much after that.'

I contemplated the awful possibility of taking the whole vault out. 'Neither would this house. I'll stop asking silly questions. Don't open the door unless I'm here.'

'Message received and understood.'

I went down to the cellar where I found a couple of studious-looking types being baffled by Ashton's contraption. Their conversation, if you could call it that, was in English, but that's to use the word loosely; it was technical, jargon-ridden and way over my head, so I left them to it. Another man was packing tape cassettes into a box ready to take away. I said, 'What are those?'

He indicated the little computer. 'Program and data tapes for this thing. We're taking them to the lab for analysis.'

'You're listing everything, I hope. You'll have to give a receipt to Miss Ashton.' He frowned at that, and I said acidly, 'We're not thieves or burglars, you know, It's only by courtesy of Miss Ashton that we're here at all.' As I left the cellar he was taking cassettes out of the box and stacking them on a table.

An hour and a half later Gregory found me in Ashton's study. 'They'll be opening the vault in about fifteen minutes.'

'Let's go up.'

We left the study and encountered Lord Cregar in the hall; with him was a big man with the build of a heavy-weight boxer. Cregar looked brisk and cheerful but his cheerfulness, if not his briskness, evaporated when he saw me. 'Ah, Mr Jaggard,' he said. 'A fine mess has been made of things, I must say.'

I shrugged. 'Events moved faster than we anticipated.'

'No doubt. I understand there's a vault here which is being opened this afternoon. Has it been opened yet?'

I wondered where he'd got his information. 'No.'

'Good. Then I'm in time.'

I said, 'Am I to understand that you wish to be present when the vault is opened?'

'That's correct.'

'I'm sorry,' I said. 'But I'll have to take that under advisement.'

He looked at me thoughtfully. 'Do you know who I am?'

'Yes, my lord.'

'Very well,' he said. 'Make your telephone call.'

I jerked my head at Gregory and we went back into the study. 'There's no need for a call,' I said. 'Ogilvie's instructions were very precise, and they didn't include Cregar.'

'I know that big chap,' said Gregory. 'His name is Martins. A bad chap to tangle with.' He paused. 'Maybe you'd better check with Ogilvie.'

'No. He's told me what to do and I'm going to do it.'

'So what if Cregar won't take it? A bout of fisticuffs with a member of the House of Lords could have its repercussions.'

I smiled. 'I doubt if it will come to that. Let's tell his lordship the bad news.'

We went back into the hall to find that Cregar and Martins had vanished. 'They'll be upstairs,' said Gregory.

'Come on.' We ran upstairs and found them in Ashton's room. Cregar was tapping his foot impatiently as I stepped forward and said formally, 'My lord, I regret to inform you that you will not be permitted to be present when the vault is opened.'

Cregar's eyes bulged. 'Did Ogilvie say that?'

'I have not spoken to Mr Ogilvie recently. I am merely following instructions.'

'You take a lot upon yourself,' he commented.

I turned to Lillywhite. 'How much longer, Frank?'

'Give me ten minutes.'

'No – stop work now. Don't start again until I tell you.' I turned back to Cregar. 'If you would like to speak to Mr Ogilvie yourself you may use the telephone here or in the study.'

Cregar actually smiled. 'You know when to pass the buck. You're quite right; it's better if I speak to Ogilvie. I'll use the study.'

'Show his lordship where it is,' I said to Gregory, and the three of them left the room.

Lillywhite said, 'What was all that about?'

'A bit of inter-departmental nonsense; nothing to do with humble servants like ourselves. You can carry on, Frank. That vault must be opened come what may.'

He went back to his job and I strolled over to the window and looked down at the drive. Presently Cregar and Martins came out of the house, got into a car, and drove away. Gregory came into the room. 'Cregar was a bit sour when he came out of the study,' he remarked. 'Ogilvie wants to talk to you.'

I walked over and picked up the telephone next to Ashton's bed. 'Jaggard here.'

Ogilvie said quickly: 'On no account must Cregar know what's in that vault. Don't let him pull rank on you – it's got nothing to do with him.'

'He won't,' I said. 'He's gone.'

'Good. When will you open it?'

'Another five minutes.'

'Keep me informed.' He rang off.

Gregory held out a packet of cigarettes and we smoked while Lillywhite and his two assistants fiddled with the door. At last there was a sharp click and Lillywhite said, 'That's it.'

I stood up. 'All right. Everybody out except me and Frank.' I waited until they left then went to the vault. 'Let's get at it.'

'Right.' Lillywhite put his hand to a lever and pulled it down. Nothing happened. 'There you are.'

'You mean it's open now?'

'That's right. Look.' He pulled and the door began to open. It was nearly a foot thick.

'Hold it,' I said quickly. 'Now, can it be locked again and opened easily?'

'Sure. Nothing to it now.'

'That's all I need to know. Sorry, Frank, but I'll have to ask you to leave now.'

He gave a crooked smile. 'If what's in here can't even be seen by a member of the House of Lords it's certainly not for Frank Lillywhite.'

He went out and closed the door emphatically.

I opened the vault.

FIFTEEN

Ogilvie gaped. 'Empty!'

'As bare as Mother Hubbard's cupboard.' I considered that. 'Except for a layer of fine dust on the floor.'

'You checked all the shelves and cabinets?'

'There were no cabinets. There were no shelves. It was just an empty cube. I didn't even go inside; I just stuck my head in and looked around. Then I closed the door again and had it relocked. I thought I'd better leave it as it was in case you want the forensic chaps to have a look at it. My bet is that it's never been used since it was built fifteen years ago.'

'Well, my God!' Ogilvie stopped then. He seemed at a total loss for words, but he was thinking furiously. I stepped over to the window and looked down into the empty street. It was late and the bowler-hatted tide had receded from the City leaving it deserted except for a few stragglers. There is no other urban area in the world that can look so empty as the City of London.

Ogilvie said thoughtfully, 'So only you, the chief of the safe-opening team, and now me, know about this.'

I turned. 'Even your Chief Burglar doesn't know. I sent Lillywhite out of the room before I opened the vault.'

'So it's only you and me. Damn!'

He swore so explosively that I said, 'What's wrong?'

'It's backfired on me. Cregar will never believe me now when I tell him the truth about that damned vault. I wish now he'd been there.'

Personally I didn't care what Cregar believed or didn't believe. I took a sheet of paper from my wallet, unfolded it, and laid it on the desk. 'This is the new combination for opening the vault. Lillywhite reset it.'

'This is the only copy?'

'Lillywhite must have a record of it.'

Ogilvie wagged his head. 'This will bear a lot of thinking about. In the meantime you carry on looking for Ashton and Benson, and don't forget they might have split up. Made any progress?'

'Only by elimination, if you call that progress.'

'All right,' said Ogilvie tiredly. 'Carry on.' I had my hand on the doorknob when he said, 'Malcolm.'

'Yes.'

'Watch out for Cregar. He makes a bad enemy.'

'I'm not fighting Cregar,' I said. 'He's nothing to do with me. What's between you and him is way over my head.'

'He didn't like the way you stood up to him this afternoon.'

'He didn't show it – he was pleasant enough.'

'That's his way, but he'll only pat you on the back to find a place to stick a knife. Watch him.'

'He is nothing to do with me,' I repeated.

'Maybe,' said Ogilvie. 'But Cregar may not share your view.'

After that nothing happened for a while. The Special Branch investigation petered out with no result although their men at the exits were still keeping a sharp watch in case our pair made a late dash for it. Honnister had nothing to offer. On my third enquiry he said tartly, 'Don't ring us – we'll ring you.'

I spent two and a half days reading every word of the bushel or so of miscellaneous papers Gregory had brought back from Ashton's house – appointment books, financial records, business diaries, letters and so on. As a result of that many enquiries were made but nothing of interest turned up. Ashton's companies were given a thorough going-over with like result.

A week after Ashton's disappearance my team was cut in half. I kept Brent with Penny and Michaelis looked after Gillian, leaving two to do the legwork. I was doing a lot of legwork myself, going sixteen hours a day, running like hell like the Red Queen to stay in the same place. Larry Godwin was back at his desk reading the East European journals. His fling at freedom had been brutally brief.

The boffins had nothing much to report. The computer tapes showed nothing out of the ordinary except some very clever program designing, but what the programs did was nothing special. The prototype whatsit Ashton had been tinkering with caused a flood of speculation which left a thin sediment of hard fact. The consensus of opinion was that it was a pilot plant of a process designed to synthesize insulin; very ingenious and highly patentable but still in an early stage of design. It told me nothing to my purpose.

The day after we opened the empty vault I had telephoned Penny. 'Is this to tell me you've found Daddy?' she asked.

'No, I've nothing to tell you about that. I'm sorry.'

'Then I don't think we've much to talk about, Malcolm,' she said, and rang off before I could get in another word. Right at that moment I didn't know whether we were still engaged or not.

After that I kept in touch with her movements through Brent. She went back to doing her work at University College, London, but tended to use her car more instead of the train. She didn't seem to resent Brent; he was her passenger in her daily journeys to and from London, and she always kept him informed of her proposed movements. He was enjoying his assignment and thought she was a very nice person. He didn't think she knew he was armed. And, no, she never talked of me.

Gillian was moved to Moorfields Eye Hospital and I went to see her. After checking with Michaelis I had a few words with her doctor, a specialist called Jarvis. 'She's still heavily bandaged,' he said. 'And she'll need cosmetic plastic surgery, but that will be later and in another place. Here we are concerned only with her eyes.'

'What are the odds, Doctor?'

He said carefully, 'There may be a chance of restoring some measure of sight to the left eye. There's no hope for the right eye at all.' He looked straight at me. 'Miss Ashton doesn't know that yet. Please don't tell her.'

'Of course not. Does she know that her father has – er – gone away?'

'She does, and it's not making my job any easier,' said Jarvis waspishly. 'She's very depressed, and between us we have enough problems without having to cope with a psychologically depressed patient. It's most insensitive of the man to go on a business trip at this time.'

So that's what Penny had told Gillian. I suppose it was marginally better than telling her that Daddy had done a bolt. I said, 'Perhaps I can cheer her up.'

'I wish you would,' Jarvis said warmly. 'It would help her quite a lot.'

So I went to talk to Gillian and found her flat on her back on a bed with no pillow and totally faceless because she was bandaged up like Claude Rains in the film. *The Invisible Man*. The nursing sister gently told her I was there, and went away. I steered clear of the reasons she was there, and asked no questions about it. Honnister was probably a better interrogator than I and would have sucked her dry. Instead

I stuck to trivialities and told her a couple of funny items I had read in the papers that morning, and brought her up-to-date on the news of the day.

She was very grateful. 'I miss reading the papers. Penny comes in every day and reads to me.'

Brent had told me of that. 'I know.'

'What's gone wrong between you and Penny?'

'Why, nothing,' I said lightly. 'Did she say there was anything wrong?'

'No, but she stopped talking about you, and when I asked, she said she hadn't seen you.'

'We've both been busy,' I said.

'I suppose that's it,' said Gillian. 'But it's the way she said it.'

I changed the subject and we chatted some more and when I left I think she was a little better in outlook.

Michaelis found his job boring, which indeed it was. As far as the hospital staff were concerned, he was a policeman set to guard a girl who had been violently attacked once. He sat on a chair outside the ward and spent his time reading paperbacks and magazines.

'I read to Miss Ashton for an hour every afternoon,' he said.

'That's good of you.'

He shrugged. 'Nothing much else to do. There's plenty of time to think on this job, too. I've been thinking about that model railway in Ashton's attic. I've never seen anything to beat it. He was a schedules man, of course.'

'What's that?'

'There's a lot of variety in the people who are interested in model railways. There are the scenic men who are bent on getting all the details right in miniature. I'm one of those. There are the engineering types who insist their stuff should be exact from the engineering aspect; that's expensive. I know a chap who has modelled Paddington Station; and all he's interested in is getting the trains in and out according to the timetable. He's a schedules man like Ashton. The only difference is that Ashton was doing it on a really big scale.'

Hobbies are something that people really do become fanatical about, but Ashton hadn't struck me as the type. Still, I hadn't known that Michaelis was a model railwayman, either. I said, 'How big a scale?'

'Bloody big. I found a stack of schedules up there which made me blink. He could duplicate damn nearly the whole of the British railway system – not all at once, but in sections. He seemed to be specializing in pre-war stuff; he had schedules for the old LMS system, for instance; and the Great Western and the LNER. Now that takes a hell of a lot of juggling, so you know what he'd done?'

Michaelis looked at me expectantly, so I said, 'What?'

'He's installed a scad of microprocessors in that control board. You know – the things that have been called a computer on a chip. He could program his timetables into them.'

That sounded like Ashton, all right; very efficient. But it wasn't helping me to find him. 'Better keep your mind on the job,' I advised. 'We don't want anything happening to the girl.'

Two weeks after Ashton bolted Honnister rang me. Without preamble he said, 'We've got a line on our man.'

'Good. When are you seeing him?' I wanted to be there.

'I'm not,' said Honnister. 'He's not in my parish. He's a London boy so he's the Met's meat. A chap from the Yard will be seeing him tonight; Inspector Crammond. He's expecting you to ring him.'

'I'll do that. What's this character's name, and how did you get on to him?'

'His name is Peter Mayberry, aged about forty-five to fifty, and he lives in Finsbury. Apart from that I know damn-all. Crammond will pick it up from there. Mayberry hired the car for the weekend – not from one of the big hire-car firms, but from a garage in Slough. The bobbies over there came across it as a matter of routine and asked a few questions. The garage owner was bloody annoyed; he said someone had spilled battery acid on the back seat, so that made us perk up a bit.'

I thought about that. 'But would Mayberry give his real name when he hired the car?'

'The bloody fool did,' said Honnister. 'Anyway, he'd have to show his driving licence. This one strikes me as an amateur; I don't think he's a pro. Anyway, Crammond tells me there's a Peter Mayberry living at that address.'

'I'll get on to Crammond immediately. Thanks, Charlie. You've done very well.'

He said earnestly, 'You'll thank me by leaning bloody hard on this bastard.' I was about to ring off, but he chipped in again. 'Seen anything of Ashton lately?'

It was the sort of innocuous question he might be expected to ask, but I thought I knew Honnister better than that by now; he wasn't a man to waste his time on idle chitchat. 'Not much,' I said. 'Why?'

'I thought he'd like to know. Every time I ring him he's out, and the beat bobby tells me there's been some funny things going on at the house. A lot of coming and going and to-ing and fro-ing.'

'I believe he went away on a business trip. As for the house I wouldn't know – I haven't been there lately.'

'I suppose that's your story and you're sticking to it,' he said. 'Who's going to tell the Ashton sisters – you or me?'

'I will,' I said. 'After I've made sure of Mayberry.'

'All right. Any time you're down this way pop in and see me. We can have another noggin at the Coach and Horses. I'll be very interested in anything you can tell me.' He rang off.

I smiled. I was sure Honnister would be interested. Something funny was going on in his parish which he didn't know about, and it irked him.

I dialled Scotland Yard and got hold of Crammond. 'Oh yes. Mr Jaggard: it's about this acid-throwing attack. I'll be seeing Mayberry tonight – he doesn't get home until about six-thirty, so his landlady tells us. I suggest you meet me here at six and we'll drive out.'

'That's fine.'

'There's just one thing,' Crammond said. 'Whose jurisdiction applies here – ours or yours?'

I said slowly, 'That depends on what Mayberry says. The acid-throwing is straightforward criminal assault, so as far as that's concerned he's your man and you can have him and welcome. But there are other matters I'm not at liberty to go into, and we might like to question him further before you charge him. Informally, of course.'

'I understand,' said Crammond. 'It's just that it's best to get these things straight first. See you at six, Mr Jaggard.'

Crammond was properly cautious. The police were not very comfortable when mixing with people like us. They knew that some of the things we did, if strictly interpreted, could be construed as law-breaking, and it went against the grain with them to turn a blind eye. Also they tended to think of themselves as the only professionals in the business and looked down on us as amateurs and, in their view, they were not there to help amateurs break the law of the land.

I phoned Ogilvie and told him. All he said was, 'Ah well, we'll see what comes of it.'

I met Crammond as arranged. He was a middling-sized thickset man of nondescript appearance, very useful in a plain clothes officer. We went out to Finsbury in his car, with a uniformed copper in the back seat, and he told me what he knew.

'When Honnister passed the word to us I had Mayberry checked out. That was this morning so he wasn't at home. He lives on the top floor of a house that's been broken up into flats. At least, that's what they call them: most of them are single rooms. His landlady described him as a quiet type – a bit bookish.'

'Married?'

'No. She thinks he never has been, either. He has a job as some kind of clerk working for a City firm. She wasn't too clear about that.'

'He doesn't sound the type,' I complained.

'He does have a police record,' said Crammond.

'That's better.'

'Wait until you hear it. One charge of assaulting a police officer, that's all. I went into it and the charge should never have been brought, even though he was found guilty. He got into a brawl during one of the Aldermaston marches a few years ago and was lugged in with a few others.'

'A protester,' I said thoughtfully. 'Amateur or professional?'

'Amateur, I'd say. He's not on our list of known rabble-rousers and, in any case, he has the wrong job for it. He's not mobile enough. But his appearance fits the description given by Honnister's witness. We'll see. Who does the asking?'

'You do,' I said. 'I'll hang about in the background. He'll think I'm just another copper.'

Mayberry had not arrived home when we got there so his landlady accommodated us in her front parlour. She was plainly curious and said archly, 'Has Mr Mayberry been doing anything naughty?'

'We just want him to help us in our enquiries.' said Crammond blandly. 'Is he a good tenant, Mrs Jackson?'

'He pays his rent regularly, and he's quiet. That's good enough for me.'

'Lived here long?'

'Five years – or is it six?' After much thought she decided it was six.

'Has he any hobbies? What does he do with his spare time?'

'He reads a lot; always got his head in a book. And he's religious – he goes to church twice every Sunday.'

I was depressed. This sounded less and less like our man.

'Did he go to church on the Sunday two weekends ago?' asked Crammond.

'Very likely,' she said. 'But I was away that weekend.' She held her head on one side. 'That sounds like him now.'

Someone walked along the passage outside the room and began to ascend the stairs. We gave him time to get settled then went after him. On the first landing Crammond said to the uniformed man, 'Wait outside the door, Shaw. If he makes a break grab him. It's not likely to happen, but if he is an acid-throwing bastard he can be dangerous.'

I stood behind Crammond as he tapped on Mayberry's door and noted that Shaw was flat against the wall so Mayberry couldn't see him. It's nice to see professionals at work. Mayberry was a man in his late forties and had a sallow complexion as though he did not eat well. His eyes were sunk deep into his skull.

'Mr Peter Mayberry?'

'Yes.'

'We're police officers,' said Crammond pleasantly. 'And we think you can help us. Do you mind if we come in?'

I saw Mayberry's knuckles whiten a little as he gripped the edge of the door. 'How can I help you?'

'Just by answering a few questions. Can we come in?'

'I suppose so.' Mayberry held open the door.

It wasn't much of a place; the carpet was threadbare and the furniture was of painted whitewood and very cheap;

but it was clean and tidy. Along one wall was a shelf containing perhaps forty or fifty books; anyone with so many would doubtless be a great reader to Mrs Jackson who probably got through one book a year, if that.

I glanced at the titles. Some were religious and of a decidedly fundamentalist slant: there was a collection of environmental stuff including some pamphlets issued by Friends of the Earth. For the rest they were novels, all classics and none modern. Most of the books were paperbacks.

There were no pictures in the room except for one poster which was stuck on the wall by sticky tape at the corners. It depicted the earth from space, a photograph taken by an astronaut. Printed at the bottom were the words: I'M ALL YOU'VE GOT; LOOK, AFTER ME.

Crammond started by saying, 'Can I see your driving licence, Mr Mayberry?'

'I don't have a car.'

'That wasn't what I asked,' said Crammond. 'Your driving licence, please.'

Mayberry had taken off his jacket which was hanging on the back of a chair. He bent down and took his wallet from the inside breast pocket, took out his licence and gave it to Crammond who examined it gravely and in silence. At last Crammond said approvingly, 'Clean; no endorsements.' He handed it to me.

'I always drive carefully,' said Mayberry.

'I'm sure you do. Do you drive often?'

'I told you – I don't have a car.'

'And I heard you. Do you drive often?'

'Not very. What's all this about?'

'When did you last drive a car?'

Mayberry said, 'Look, if anyone says I've been in an accident they're wrong because I haven't.' He seemed very nervous, but many people are in the presence of authority, even if innocent. It's the villain who brazens it out.

I put the licence on the table and picked up the book Mayberry had been reading. It was on so-called alternative technology and was turned to a chapter telling how to make a digester to produced methane from manure. It seemed an unlikely subject for Finsbury.

Crammond said, 'When did you last drive a car?'

'Oh, I don't know – several months ago.'

'Whose car was it?'

'I forget. It was a long time ago.'

'Whose car do you usually drive?'

There was a pause while Mayberry sorted that one out. 'I don't *usually* drive.' He had begun to sweat.

'Do you ever hire a car?'

'I have.' Mayberry swallowed. 'Yes. I have hired cars.'

'Recently?'

'No.'

'Supposing I said that you hired a car in Slough two weekends ago, what would you say?'

'I'd say you were wrong,' said Mayberry sullenly.

'Yes, you might say that,' said Crammond. 'But would I be wrong. Mr Mayberry?'

Mayberry straightened his shoulders. 'Yes,' he said defiantly.

'Where were you that weekend?'

'Here as usual. You can ask Mrs Jackson, my landlady.'

Crammond regarded him for a moment in silence. 'But Mrs Jackson was away that weekend, wasn't she? So you were here all weekend. In this room? Didn't you go out?'

'No.'

'Not at all? Not even to church as usual?'

Mayberry was beginning to curl up at the edges. 'I didn't feel well,' he muttered.

'When was the last time you missed church on Sunday, Mr Mayberry?'

'I don't remember.'

'Can you produce one person to testify to your presence here in this room on the whole of that Sunday?'

'How can I? I didn't go out.'

'Didn't you eat?'

'I didn't feel well, I tell you. I wasn't hungry.'

'What about the Saturday? Didn't you go out then?'

'No.'

'And didn't you eat on the Saturday, either?'

Mayberry shifted his feet nervously; the unending stream of questions was getting to him. 'I had some apples.'

'You had some apples,' said Crammond flatly. 'Where and when did you buy the apples?'

'On the Friday afternoon at a supermarket.'

Crammond let that go. He said, 'Mr Mayberry, I suggest that all you've told me is a pack of lies. I suggest that on the Saturday morning you went to Slough by train where you hired a Chrysler Sceptre from Joliffe's garage. Mr Joliffe was very upset by the acid damage to the back seat of the car. Where did you buy the acid?'

'I bought no acid.'

'But you hired the car?'

'No.'

'Then how do you account for the fact that the name and address taken from a driving licence – this driving licence – ' Crammond picked it up and waved it under Mayberry's nose – 'is your name and your address?'

'I can't account for it. I don't have to account for it. Perhaps someone impersonated me.'

'Why should anyone want to impersonate you, Mr Mayberry?'

'How would I know?'

'I don't think anyone would know,' observed Crammond. 'However, the matter can be settled very easily. We have the fingerprints from the car and they can be compared with yours quite easily. I'm sure you wouldn't mind coming to the station and giving us your prints, sir.'

It was the first I'd heard of fingerprints and I guessed Crammond was bluffing. Mayberry said, 'I'm . . . I'm not coming. Not to the police station.'

'I see,' said Crammond softly. 'Do you regard yourself as a public-spirited citizen?'

'As much as anybody.'

'But you object to coming to the police station.'

'I've had a hard day,' said Mayberry. 'I'm not feeling well. I was about to go to bed when you came in.'

'Oh,' said Crammond, as though illuminated with insight. 'Well, if that's your only objection I have a fingerprint kit in the car. We can settle the matter here and now.'

'You're not taking my fingerprints. I don't have to give them to you. And now I want you to leave.'

'Ah, so that's your true objection.'

'I want you to leave or I'll –' Mayberry stopped short.

'Send for the police?' said Crammond ironically. 'When did you first meet Miss Ashton?'

'I've never met her,' said Mayberry quickly. Too quickly.

'But you know of her.'

Mayberry took a step backwards and banged into the table. The book fell to the floor. 'I know nobody of that name.'

'Not personally, perhaps-but you do know of her?'

I stopped to pick up the book. A thin pamphlet had fallen from the pages and I glanced at it before putting the book on the table. Mayberry repeated, 'I know nobody of that name.'

The pamphlet was a Parliamentary Report issued by the Stationery Office. Beneath the Royal coat-of-arms was the title: *Report of the Working Party on the Experimental Manipulation of the Genetic Composition of Micro-organisms.*

A whole lot of apparently unrelated facts suddenly slotted into place: Mayberry's fundamentalist religion, his environmental interests, and the work Penny Ashton was doing. I said, 'Mr Mayberry, what do you think of the state of modern biological science?'

Crammond, his mouth opened to ask another question, gaped at me in astonishment. Mayberry jerked his head around to look at me. 'Bad,' he said. 'Very bad.'

'In what way?'

'The biologists are breaking the laws of God,' he said. 'Defiling life itself.'

'In what way?'

'By mixing like with unlike – by creating monsters.' Mayberry's voice rose. '"And God said, 'Let the earth bring forth the living creature after his kind.'" "That's what He said – *after his kind*. "Cattle, and creeping thing, and beast of the earth after his kind." *After his kind!* That is on the very first page of the Holy Bible.'

Crammond glanced at me with a mystified expression, and then looked again at Mayberry. 'I'm not sure I know what you mean, sir.'

Mayberry was exalted. 'And God said unto Noah. "Of fowls after their kind" – *after their kind* – "and of cattle after their kind" – *after their kind* – "of every creeping thing of the earth after his kind" – *after his kind* – "two of every sort shall come unto thee, to keep them alive." She's godless; she would destroy God's own work as is set down in the Book.'

I doubted if Crammond knew what Mayberry was saying, but I did. I said, 'How?'

'She would break down the seed which God has made, and mingle one kind with another kind, and so create monsters – chimaeras and abominations.'

I had difficulty in keeping my voice even. 'I take it by "she" you mean Dr Penelope Ashton?'

Crammond's head jerked. Mayberry, still caught up in religious fervour, said thoughtlessly, 'Among others.'

'Such as Professor Lumsden,' I suggested.

'Her master in devilry.'

'If you thought she was doing wrong why didn't you talk to her about it? Perhaps you could have led her to see her error.'

'I wouldn't foul my ears with her voice,' he said contemptuously.

I said, 'Doesn't it say in the Bible that God gave Adam dominion over the fish of the sea, the fowls of the air, and every beast or thing that creeps on the earth? Perhaps she's in the right.'

'The Devil can quote scripture,' said Mayberry, and turned away from me. I felt sick.

Crammond woke up to what was happening. 'Mr Mayberry, are you admitting to having thrown acid into the face of a woman called Ashton?'

Mayberry had a hunted look, conscious of having said too much. 'I haven't said that.'

'You've said enough.' Crammond turned to me. 'I think we have enough to take him.'

I nodded, then said to Mayberry, 'You're a religious man. You go to church every Sunday – twice, so I'm told. Do you think it was a Christian act to throw battery acid into the face of a young woman?'

'I am not responsible to you for my actions,' said Mayberry. 'I am responsible to God.'

Crammond nodded gravely. 'Nevertheless, I believe someone said, "Render unto Caesar the things that are Caesar's." I think you'll have to come along with us, Mr Mayberry.'

'And may God help you,' I said. 'Because you got the wrong girl. You threw the acid in the face of Dr Ashton's sister who was coming back from church.'

Mayberry stared at me. As he had spoken of being responsible to God he had worn a lofty expression but now his face crumpled and horror crept into his eyes. He whispered. 'The wrong . . . wrong . . .' Suddenly he jerked convulsively and screamed at the top of his voice.

'Oh, Christ!' said Crammond as Shaw burst into the room.

Mayberry collapsed to the floor, babbling a string of obscenities in a low and monotonous voice. When Crammond turned to speak to me he was sweating. 'This one's not for the slammer. He'll go to Broadmoor for sure. Do you want any more out of him?'

'Not a thing,' I said. 'Not now.'

Crammond turned to Shaw. 'Phone for an ambulance. Tell them it's religious mania and they might need a restraining jacket.'

SIXTEEN

By the time we'd got Mayberry into an ambulance Ogilvie had left the office and gone home. I didn't bother ringing his home, but I did ring Penny because I thought she ought to know about Mayberry. Mary Cope answered again and said that Penny wasn't in, but this time I pushed it harder. She said Penny had gone to Oxford to attend a lecture and wouldn't be back until late. I rang off, satisfied I wasn't being given another brush-off.

Before seeing Ogilvie next morning I rang Crammond. 'What's new on Mayberry?'

'He's at King's College Hospital – under guard in a private ward.'

'Did he recover?'

'Not so you'd notice. It seems like a complete breakdown to me, but I'm no specialist.'

'A pity. I'll have to talk to him again, you know.'

'You'll have to get through a platoon of assorted doctors first,' warned Crammond. 'It seems he's suffering from everything from ingrowing toenails to psychoceramica.'

'What the hell's that?'

'It means he's a crack-pot,' said Crammond sourly. 'The head-shrinkers are keeping him isolated.'

I thanked him for his help and went to see Ogilvie. I told him about Mayberry and his face was a study in perplexity. 'Are you sure Mayberry isn't pulling a fast one?'

I shook my head. 'He's a nutter. But we've got him, and a psychiatrist will sort him out for us.'

'I'll buy that – for the moment.' Ogilvie shook his head. 'But I wouldn't call psychiatry an exact science. Have you noticed in court cases that for every psychiatrist called for the defence there's another called for the prosecution who'll give an opposing opinion? Still, supposing Mayberry is established as a religious maniac without doubt, there are a few questions which need asking.'

'I know. Why did he pick on Penny or the girl he thought was Penny? Did he act of his own volition or was he pointed in the right direction and pushed? I'll see he gets filleted as soon as he can be talked to. But you're avoiding the big problem.'

Ogilvie grunted, and ticked points off on his fingers. 'Supposing Mayberry *is* crazy; and supposing he *wasn't* pushed – that he did it off his own bat, and that Penelope Ashton was a more or less random choice among the geneticists. That leaves us up a gum tree, doesn't it?'

'Yes.' I put the big question into words. 'In that case why did Ashton do a bunk?'

I was beginning to develop another headache.

I'd had second thoughts about ringing Penny: it wasn't the sort of thing to tell her on the telephone. But before going to University College I rang Honnister and told him the score. He took it rather badly. His voice rose. 'The wrong girl! The inefficient, crazy bastard picked the wrong girl!' He broke into a stream of profanity.

'I thought you ought to know. I'll keep you informed on future developments.'

I went to University College and was about to enquire at the reception desk when I saw Jack Brent standing at the end of a corridor. I went up to him. 'Any problems?'

'Nary a one.'

'Where's Penny Ashton?'

He jerked his thumb at a door. 'With her boss. That's Lumsden's office.'

I nodded and went in. Penny and Professor Lumsden looked very professional in white laboratory coats, like the chaps who sell toothpaste in TV ads. They were sitting at a desk, drinking coffee and examining papers which looked like computer print-outs. Lumsden was much younger than I expected, not as old as I was; pioneering on the frontiers of science is a young man's game.

Penny looked up. A look of astonishment chased across her face and then she became expressionless, but I noted the tightening of muscles at the angle of her jaw and the firmly compressed lips. I said, 'Good morning, Dr Ashton – Professor Lumsden. Could I have a word with you, Penny?'

'Well?' she said coolly.

I glanced at Lumsden. 'It's official, I'm afraid. In your office, perhaps?'

She said shortly, 'If it is official . . .' and regarded me distrustfully.

'It is,' I said, matching her curtness.

She made her excuses to Lumsden and we left his office. I said to Brent, 'Stick around,' then followed Penny who led me along another corridor and into her office. I looked around. 'Where's the microscope?'

Unsmilingly she said, 'We're working on things you can't see through microscopes. What do you want? Have you found Daddy?'

I shook my head. 'We've found the man who threw the acid.'

'Oh.' She sat at her desk. 'Who is he?'

'A man called Peter Mayberry. Ever heard of him?'

She thought for a moment. 'No, I can't say that I have. What is he?'

'A clerk in a City office – and a religious maniac.'

She frowned, then said questioningly, 'A religious maniac? But what would he have to do with Gillian? She's an Anglican – and you can't get more unmaniacal than that.'

I sat down. 'Brace yourself. Penny. The acid wasn't intended for Gillian. It was intended for you.'

'For me!' Her forehead creased and then she shook her head as though she wasn't hearing aright. 'You did say . . . for me?'

'Yes. Are you sure you haven't heard of this man?'

She ignored my question. 'But why would a religious maniac . . .?' She choked on the words. 'Why me?'

'He seemed to think you are tampering with the laws of God.'

'Oh.' Then: 'Seemed? He's not dead?'

'No, but he's not doing much thinking right now. He's gone off into some kind of fugue.'

She shook her head. 'There have been objections to what we've been doing, but they've been scientific. Paul Berg, Brenner, Singer and a few others objected very strongly to . . .' Suddenly it hit her. 'Oh, my God!' she said. 'Poor Gillian!'

She sat rigidly for a moment, her hands clasped together tightly, and then she began to shake, the tremors sweeping across her body. She moaned – a sort of keening sound – and then fell forward across her desk, her head pillowed on her arms. Her shoulders shook convulsively and she sobbed stormily. I located a hand basin in the corner of the office and filled a glass with water and returned quickly to the desk, but there wasn't much I could do until the first shock had abated.

Her sobbing lessened in intensity and I put my arm around her. 'Steady on. Drink this.'

She raised her head, still sobbing, and showed a tear-stained face. 'Oh, Gillian! She'd be . . . all right . . . if I . . . if I hadn't . . .'

'Hush,' I said. 'And stop that. Drink this.'

She gulped down some water, then said, 'Oh, Malcolm; what am I to do?'

'Do? There's nothing to do. You just carry on as usual.'

'Oh, no. How can I do that?'

I said deliberately, 'You can't possibly blame yourself for what happened to Gillian. You'll tear yourself apart if you try. You can't hold yourself responsible for the act of an unbalanced man.'

'Oh, I wish it had been me,' she cried.

'No, you don't,' I said sharply. 'Don't ever say that again.'

'How can I tell her?'

'You don't tell her. Not until she's well – if then.' She began to cry again, and I said, 'Penny, pull yourself together – I need your help.'

'What can *I* do?'

'You can tidy yourself up,' I said. 'Then you can get Lumsden in here, because I want to ask you both some questions.'

She sniffled a bit, then said, 'What sort of questions?'

'You'll hear them when Lumsden comes in. I don't want to go through it all twice. We still don't know why your father went away, but it seemed to be triggered by that acid attack, so we want to find out as much about it as we can.'

She went to the hand basin and washed her face. When she was more presentable she rang Lumsden. I said, 'I'd rather you don't say anything about your father before Lumsden.' She said nothing to that, and sat at the desk.

When Lumsden came in he took one glance at Penny's reddened eyes and white face, then looked at me. 'What's happened here? And who are you?'

'I'm Malcolm Jaggard and I'm a sort of police officer, Professor.' To divert him from asking for my warrant card I added, 'I'm also Penny's fiancé.'

Penny made no objection to that flat statement, but Lumsden showed astonishment. 'Oh. I didn't know . . .'

'A recent development,' I said. 'You know, of course, of the acid attack on Penny's sister.'

'Yes, a most shocking thing.'

I told him about Mayberry and he became very grave. 'This is bad,' he said. 'I'm deeply sorry, Penny.' She nodded without saying anything.

'I want to know if you or anyone in your department has been threatened – anonymous letters, telephone calls, or anything like that.'

He shrugged. 'There are always the cranks. We tend to ignore them.'

'Perhaps that's a mistake,' I said. 'I'd like some specifics. Do you keep any such letters? If so, I want them.'

'No,' he said regretfully. 'They are usually thrown away. You see . . . er . . . Inspector?'

'Mister.'

'Well, Mr Jaggard, most of the crank letters aren't threatening – they just tend to ramble, that's all.'

'About what?'

'About supposed offences against God. Lots of biblical quotations, usually from *Genesis*. Just what you might expect.'

I said to Penny, 'Have you had any of these letters?'

'A couple,' she said quietly. 'No threats. I threw them away.'

'Any telephone calls? Heavy breathers?'

'One about six months ago. He stopped after a month.'

'What did he say?'

'What Lummy has described. Just what you might expect.'

'Did you get the calls here or at home?'

'Here. The telephone at home is unlisted.'

I turned to Lumsden. 'You've both used the same phrase – "Just what you might expect". What might I expect, Professor Lumsden?'

'Well, in view of our work here . . .' He threw out his hands expressively.

We were still standing. I said, 'Sit down. Professor, and tell me of your work, or about as much as you can without breaking the Official Secrets Act.'

'Breaking the Official Secrets Act! There's no question of that – not here.'

'In that case, you won't object to telling me, will you?'

'I don't suppose so,' he said doubtfully, and sat down.

He was silent for a moment, marshalling his thoughts, and I knew what was happening. He was hunting for unaccustomed simple words to explain complex ideas to an unscientific clod. I said, 'I can understand words of three syllables – even four syllables if they're spoken slowly. Let me help you. The basis of inheritance is the chromosome; inside the chromosome is an acid called DNA. A thing called a gene is the ultimate factor and is very specific; there are distinct genes for producing the different chemicals needed by the organism. The genes can be thought of as being strung along a strand of DNA like beads on a spiral string. At least, that's how I visualize them. That's where I get lost so you'd better go on from there.'

Lumsden smiled. 'Not bad, Mr Jaggard; not bad at all.' He began to talk, at first hesitantly, and then more fluently. He ranged quite widely and sometimes I had to interrupt and bring him back on to the main track. At other times I had him explain what he meant in simpler terms. The basic concepts were rather simple but I gathered that execution in the laboratory was not as easy as all that.

What it boiled down to was this. A strand of DNA contains many thousands of genes, each gene doing its own particular job such as, for instance, controlling the production of cholinesterase, a chemical which mediates electrical action in the nervous system. There are thousands of chemicals like this and each has its own gene.

The molecular biologist had discovered certain enzymes which could cut up a strand of DNA into short lengths, and other enzymes which could weld the short lengths together again. They also found they could weld a short length of DNA on to a bacteriophage, which is a minute organism capable of penetrating the wall of a cell. Once inside, the genes would be uncoupled and incorporated into the DNA of the host cell.

Put like that it sounds rather simple but the implications are fantastic, and Lumsden was very emphatic about this. 'You see, the genes you incorporate into a cell need not come from the same kind of animal. In this laboratory we have bacterial cultures which contain genetic material from mice. Now a bacterium is a bacterium and a mouse is a mammal, but our little chaps are part bacterium and part mammal.'

'Breaking down the seed, mingling one kind with another, creating chimaeras,' I mused.

'I suppose you could put it that way,' said Lumsden.

'I didn't put it that way,' I said. 'Mayberry did.' At that stage I didn't get the point. 'But what's the use of this?'

Lumsden frowned as though I was being thick-witted, as I suppose I was. Penny spoke up. 'Lummy, what about *Rhizobium*?'

His brow cleared. 'Yes, that's a good example.'

He said that although plants need nitrogen for their growth they cannot take it from the air, even though air is 78 per cent nitrogen. They need it in the form of nitrates which, in man-planted cash crops, are usually spread as artificial fertilizer. However, there is a range of plants, notably the legumes – peas, beans and so on – which harbours in its roots the *Rhizobium* bacterium. This organism has the power of transforming atmospheric nitrogen into a form the plant can use.

'Now,' said Lumsden. 'All plants have bacteria in their roots and some are very specific. Supposing we take the *Rhizobium* bacterium, isolate the gene that controls this nitrogen-changing property, and transfer it into a bacterium that is specific to wheat. Then, if it bred true, we'd have self-fertilizing wheat. In these days of world food shortages that seems to me to be a good thing to have around.'

I thought so, too, but Penny said, 'It can be pretty dangerous. You have to be damned sure you've selected the right gene. Some of the *Rhizobium* genes are tumour-causing. If you get one of those you might find the world wheat crop dying of cancer.'

'Yes,' said Lumsden. 'We must be very sure before we let loose our laboratory-changed organisms. There was a hell of a row about that not long ago.' He stood up. 'Well, Mr Jaggard, have you got what you wanted?'

'I think so,' I said. 'But I don't know if it's going to do me a damned bit of good. Thanks for your time, Professor.'

He smiled. 'If you need more information I suggest you ask Penny.' He glanced at her. 'I suggest you take the day off, Penny. You've had a nasty shock – you don't look too well.'

She shivered. 'The thought that there are people in the world who'd want to do that to you is unnerving.'

'I'll take you home,' I said quietly. 'Jack Brent can follow in your car.' She made no objection, and I turned to Lumsden. 'I suggest that any crank letters – no matter how apparently innocuous – should be forwarded to the police. And telephone calls should be reported.'

'I agree,' he said. 'I'll see to it.'

So I took Penny home.

SEVENTEEN

My relationship with Penny improved although neither of us referred to marriage. The shock of Mayberry's error had been shattering and I stuck around and helped her pick up the pieces; from then on propinquity did the rest. She was persuaded by Lumsden to stay with her work and her life took a triangular course – her home, her work, and whatever hospital Gillian happened to be in at the time.

Mayberry was thoroughly investigated, by a band of psychiatrists and by Mansell, the department's best interrogator, a soft-spoken man who could charm the birds from the trees. They all came to the same conclusion: Mayberry was exactly what he appeared to be – a nut case. 'And a bit of a coward, too,' said Mansell. 'He was going for Lumsden at first, but thought a woman would be easier to handle.'

'Why did he pick on Lumsden's crowd?' I asked.

'A natural choice. Firstly, Lumsden is very well known – he's not as averse to talking to newspaper reporters as a lot of scientists are. He gets his name in the papers. Secondly, he hasn't been reticent about what he's been doing. If you wanted a handy geneticist Lumsden would be the first to spring to mind.'

Mayberry was the deadest of dead ends.

Which caused the problem Ogilvie and I had anticipated. If the acid attack had been fortuitous why should Ashton have bolted? It made no sense.

Once Mayberry had been shaken down the guards were taken from Penny and Gillian, and my legmen were put to other work. Ogilvie had little enough manpower to waste and the team investigating the Ashton case was cut down to one – me, and I wasted a lot of time investigating mistaken identities. Ashton's bolt-hole was well concealed.

And so the weeks – and then the months – went by. Gillian was in and out of hospital and finally was able to live at home, managing on a quarter of her normal eyesight. She and Penny were making plans to go to the United States where she would undergo plastic surgery to repair her ravaged face.

Once, when I persuaded Penny to dine with me, she asked, 'What did you find in that big vault of Daddy's?'

It was the first time she had shown any interest. 'Nothing.'

'You're lying.' There was an edge of anger.

'I've never lied to you. Penny,' I said soberly. 'Never once. My sins have been those of omission, not commission. I may have been guilty of *suppressio veri* but never *suggestio falsi.*'

'Your classical education is showing,' she said tartly, but she smiled as she said it, her anger appeased. 'Strange. Why should Daddy build such a thing and not use it? Perhaps he did and found it too much trouble.'

'As far as we can make out it was never used,' I said. 'All it contained was stale air and a little dust. My boss is baffled and boggled.'

'Oh, Malcolm. I wish I knew why he disappeared. It's been over three months now.'

I made the usual comforting sounds and diverted her attention. Presently she said, 'Do you remember when you told me of what you really do? You mentioned someone called Lord Cregar.'

'That's right.'

'He's been seeing Lumsden.'

That drew my interest. 'Has he? What about?'

She shook her head. 'Lummy didn't say.'

'Was it about Mayberry?'

'Oh, no. The first time he came was before you told us about Mayberry.' She wrinkled her brow. 'It was two or three days after you opened the vault.'

'Not two or three weeks?'

'No – it was a matter of days. Who is Lord Cregar?'

'He's pretty high in government, I believe.' I could have told her that Cregar had smuggled her father out of Russia a quarter of a century earlier, but I didn't. If Ashton had wanted his daughters to know of his Russian past he would have told them, and it wasn't up to me to blow the gaff. Besides, I couldn't blab about anything listed under Code Black: it would be dangerous for me, for Ogilvie and, possibly, Penny herself. I wasn't supposed to know about that.

All the same it was curious that Cregar had been seeing Lumsden before we knew about Mayberry. Was there a connection between Ashton and Lumsden – apart from Penny – that we hadn't spotted?

I caught the eye of a passing waiter and asked for the bill. As I drained my coffee cup I said, 'It's probably not important. Let's go and keep Gillian company.'

Ogilvie sent for me next morning. He took an envelope, extracted a photograph, and tossed it across the desk. 'Who's that?'

He wore a heavy coat and a round fur hat, the type with flaps which can be tied down to cover the ears but which never are. Wherever he was it was snowing; there were white streaks in the picture which was obviously a time exposure.

I said, 'That's George Ashton.'

'No, he isn't,' said Ogilvie. 'His name is Fyodr Koslov, and he lives in Stockholm. He has a servant, an elderly bruiser called Howell Williams.' Another photograph skimmed across the desk.

I took one look at it, and said, 'That be damned for a tale. This is Benson. Where did you get these?'

'I want you to make quite sure,' said Ogilvie. He took a sheaf of photographs and fanned them out. 'As you know, we had a couple of bad pictures of Ashton and none at all of Benson. You are the only person in the department who can identify them.'

Every one of the photographs showed either Ashton or Benson, and in two of them they were together. 'Positive identification,' I said flatly. 'Ashton and Benson.'

Ogilvie was pleased. 'Some of our associated departments are more co-operative than others,' he remarked. 'I had the pictures of Ashton circulated. These came back from a chap called Henty in Stockholm. He seems to be quite good with a camera.'

'He's very good.' The pictures were unposed – candid camera stuff – and very sharp. 'I hope he's been circumspect. We don't want them to bolt again.'

'You'll go to Stockholm and take up where Henty left off. He has instructions to co-operate.'

I looked out at the bleak London sky and shivered. I didn't fancy Stockholm at that time of year. 'Do I contact Ashton? Tell him about Mayberry and persuade him to come back?'

Ogilvie deliberated. 'No. He's too near Russia. It might startle him to know that British Intelligence is still taking an interest in him – startle him into doing something foolish. He had a low opinion of us thirty years ago which may not have improved. No, you just watch him and find out what the hell he's doing.'

I took the sheet of paper with Henty's address in Stockholm and his telephone number, then said, 'Can you think of any connection between Cregar and Professor Lumsden?' I told him Penny's story.

Ogilvie looked at the ceiling. 'I hear backstairs gossip from time to time. There could be a connection, but it's nothing to do with Ashton. It *can't* have anything to do with Ashton.'

'What is it?'

He abandoned his apparent fascination with the electric fittings and looked at me. 'Malcolm, you're getting to know too damned much – more than is good for you. However, I'll humour you because, as I say, this is only servants' hall rumour. When this department was set up we took a sizeable chunk from Cregar which diminished his outfit considerably, so he began to empire-build in a different direction. The story is that he's heavily involved in CBW – that would explain any interest he has in Lumsden.'

By God it would! Chemical and bacteriological warfare and what Lumsden was doing fitted together like hand in glove. 'Is he still in security?'

'No, he's executive. He mediates between the Minister and the scientists. Of course, with his experience he also handles the security side.'

I could just imagine Cregar happily contemplating some previously inoffensive microbe now armed for death and destruction by genetic engineering. 'Is he in with the Porton Down crowd?'

'The Ministry of Defence is closing down Porton Down,' said Ogilvie. 'I don't know where Cregar does his juggling with life and death. Microbiology isn't like atomics; you don't need a particle accelerator costing a hundred million and a power plant capable of supplying energy for a fair-sized city.

The physical plant and investment are both relatively small, and Cregar may have a dozen laboratories scattered about for all I know. He doesn't talk about it – not to me.'

I contemplated this, trying to find a link with Ashton, and failed. There was only Penny, and I said so. Ogilvie asked, 'Has Cregar talked to her?'

'No.'

'I told you it can't have anything to do with Ashton,' he said. 'Off you go to Sweden.'

There was something else I wanted to bring up. 'I'd like to know more about Benson. He's probably filed away in Code Black.'

Ogilvie looked at me thoughtfully then, without speaking, got up and went into the room behind his desk. When he came back he was shaking his head. 'You must be mistaken. Benson isn't listed – not even under Code Green.'

'But I took him up as far as Code Purple,' I said. 'Someone is monkeying around with that bloody computer.'

Ogilvie's tips tightened. 'Unlikely,' he said shortly.

'How unlikely?'

'It's not easy to suborn a computer. It would need an expert.'

'Experts are ten a penny – and they can be bought.'

Ogilvie was palpably uneasy. He said slowly, 'We aren't the only department on line with this computer. I've been pressing for our own computer for several years but without success. Some other department . . .' He stopped and sat down.

'Who determines what material is added to the files – or removed?'

'There's an inter-departmental review committee which meets monthly. No one is authorized to add or subtract without its approval.'

'Someone has subtracted Benson,' I said. 'Or, more likely, he's been blocked off. I'll bet someone has added a tiny subprogram which would be difficult to find – if Benson is asked for say there's no one here of that name.'

'Well, it's for me to deal with,' said Ogilvie. 'There's a meeting of the review committee on Friday at which I'll raise a little bit of hell.' He stuck his finger out at me. 'But you know nothing about this. Now, go away. Go to Sweden.'

I got up to leave but paused at the door. 'I'll leave you with a thought. I got into the Ashton case by asking Nellie about Ashton. Two hours later I was on the carpet in your office with you and Cregar asking awkward questions. Did Cregar come to you with it?'

'Yes.'

'In two hours? How did he know who was asking questions about Ashton unless the computer tipped him off? I don't think you have far to look for the chap who is monkeying around with it.'

I left leaving Ogilvie distinctly worried.

EIGHTEEN

It was dark and cold in Stockholm at that time of year. All the time I was in Sweden it didn't stop snowing; not heavily most of the time, but there was a continual fall of fine powder from leaden-grey clouds as though God up there was operating a giant flour sifter. I was booked into the Grand, which was warm enough, and after I had made my call to Henty I looked out over the frozen Strömmen to the Royal Palace. Edward VII didn't like Buckingham Palace, and called it 'that damned factory'. It's not on record if he said anything about the Palace in Stockholm, but that afternoon it looked like a dark satanic mill.

There were swans on the Strömmen, walking uneasily on the ice and cuddling in clusters as though to keep warm. One was on an ice floe and drifting towards Riddarfjärden; I watched it until it went out of sight under the Ström bridge, then turned away feeling suddenly cold in spite of the central heating. Sweden in winter has that effect on me.

Henty arrived and we swapped credentials. 'We don't have much to do with your mob,' he commented as he handed back my card. He had a raw colonial accent.

'We don't move out of the UK much,' I said. 'Most of our work is counter-espionage. This one is a bit different. If you can take me to George Ashton I'll buy you a case of Foster's.'

Henty blinked. 'Good beer, that. How did you know I'm Australian? I've not been back for twenty years. Must have lost the accent by now.'

I grinned. 'Yes, you've learned to speak English very well. Where's Ashton?'

He went to the window and pointed at the Royal Palace. 'On the other side of that. In Gamla Stan.'

Gamla Stan – the Old Town. A warren of narrow streets threading between ancient buildings and the 'in' place to live in Stockholm. Cabinet ministers live there, and film directors – if they can afford it. The Royal Palace is No. 1, Gamla Stan. I said, 'How did you find him?'

'I got a couple of crummy pictures from London, and the day I got them I walked slam-bang into this character on the Vasabron.' Henty shrugged. 'So it's a coincidence.'

'By the laws of statistics we've got to get lucky some time,' I observed.

'He has a flat just off Västerlånggatan. He's passing himself off as a Russian called Fyodr Koslov – which is a mistake.'

'Why?'

Henty frowned. 'It's a tip-off – enough to make me take the pictures and send them back. There's something funny about the way he speaks Russian – doesn't sound natural.'

I thought about that. After thirty years of non-use Ashton's Russian would be rusty; it's been known for men to forget completely their native language. 'And Benson is with him in the flat?'

'Benson? Is that who he is? He calls himself Williams here. An older man; looks a bit of a thug. He's definitely British.'

'How can I get a look at them?'

Henty shrugged. 'Go to Gamla Stan and hang around outside the flat until they come out – or go in.'

I shook my head. 'Not good enough. They know me and I don't want to be seen. What's your status here?'

'Low man on the bloody totem,' said Henty wryly. 'I'm junior partner in an import-export firm. I have a line into the Embassy, but that's for emergency use only. The diplomats here don't like boys like us, they reckon we cause trouble.'

'They could be right,' I said drily. 'Who do I see at the Embassy?'

'A Second Secretary called Cutler. A toffee-nosed bastard.' The iron seemed to have entered Henty's soul.

'What resources can you draw on apart from the Embassy?'

'Resources!' Henty grinned. 'You're looking at the resources – me. I just have a watching brief – we're not geared for action.'

'Then it will have to be the Embassy.'

He coughed, then said, 'Exactly who is Ashton?' I looked at him in silence until he said, 'If it's going to be like that . . .'

'It always is like that, isn't it?'

'I suppose so,' he said despondently. 'But I wish, just for once, that I knew why I'm doing what I'm doing.'

I looked at my watch. 'There's just time to see Cutler. In the meantime you pin down Ashton and Benson. Report to me here or at the Embassy. And there's one very important thing – don't scare them.'

'Okay – but I don't think you'll get very much change out of Cutler.'

I smiled. 'I wouldn't want either you or Cutler to bet on that one.'

The Embassy was on Skarpögatan, and Cutler turned out to be a tall, slim, fair-haired man of about my age, very English and Old School Tie. His manner was courteous but rather distant as though his mind was occupied by other, and more important, considerations which a non-diplomat could not possibly understand. This minor Metternich reminded me strongly of a shop assistant in one of the more snob London establishments.

When I gave him my card – the special one – his lips tightened and he said coolly, 'You seem to be off your beat, Mr Jaggard. What can we do for you?' He sounded as though he believed there was nothing he could possibly do for me.

I said pleasantly, 'We've mislaid a bit of property and we'd like it back – with your help. But tact is the watch-word.' I told him the bare and minimum facts about Ashton and Benson.

When I'd finished he was a shade bewildered. 'But I don't see how . . .' He stopped and began again. 'Look, Mr Jaggard, if this man decides to leave England with his man-servant to come to Sweden and live under an assumed name I don't see what we can do about it. I don't think it's a crime in Swedish law to live under another name; it certainly isn't in England. What exactly is it that you want?'

'A bit of manpower,' I said. 'I want Ashton watched. I want to know what he does and why he does it.'

'That's out of the question,' said Cutler. 'We can't spare men for police work of that nature. I really fail to see what your interest is in the man on the basis of what you've told me.'

'You're not entitled to know more,' I said bluntly. 'But take it from me – Ashton is a hot one.'

'I'm afraid I can't do that,' he said coldly. 'Do you really think we jump when any stranger walks in off the street with an improbable story like this?'

I pointed to my card which was still on the blotter in front of him. 'In spite of that?'

'In spite of that,' he said, but I think he really meant because of it. 'You people amaze me. You think you're

James Bonds, the lot of you Well, I don't think I'm living in the middle of a highly coloured film, even if you do.'

I wasn't going to argue with him. 'May I use your telephone?' He frowned, trying to think of a good reason for denial, so I added, 'I'll pay for the call.'

'That won't be necessary,' he said shortly, and pushed his telephone across the desk.

One of our boffins once asked me what was the biggest machine in the world. After several abortive answers I gave up, and he said, 'The international telephone system. There are 450 million telephones in the world, and 250 million of them are connected by direct dialling – untouched by hand in the exchanges.' We may grouse about the faults of local systems, but in under ninety seconds I was talking to Ogilvie.

I said, 'We have Ashton but there's a small problem. There's only one of Henty, and I can't push in too close myself.'

'Good. Get on to the Embassy for support. We want him watched. Don't approach him yourself.'

'I'm at the Embassy now. No support forthcoming.'

'What's the name of the obstruction?'

'Cutler – Second Secretary.'

'Wait a moment.' There was a clatter and I heard the rustle of papers in distant London. Presently Ogilvie said, 'This will take about half an hour. I'll dynamite the obstruction. For God's sake, don't lose Ashton now.'

'I won't,' I said, and hung up. I stood up and picked my card from Cutler's blotter. 'I'm at the Grand. You can get me there.'

'I can't think of any circumstances in which I should do so,' he said distantly.

I smiled. 'You will.' Suddenly I was tired of him. 'Unless you want to spend the next ten years counting paper clips in Samoa.'

Back at the hotel there was a curt note from Henty: 'Meet me at the Moderna Museet on Skeppsholmen.' I grabbed a taxi and was there in five minutes. Henty was standing outside the main entrance, his hands thrust deep into his pockets and the tip of his nose blue with cold. He jerked his head at the gallery. 'Your man is getting a bit of culture.'

This had to be handled carefully. I didn't want to bump into Ashton face to face. 'Benson there too?'

'Just Ashton.'

'Right. Nip in and locate him – then come back here.'

Henty went inside, no doubt glad to be in the warm. He was back in five minutes. 'He's studying blue period Picassos.' He gave me a plan of the halls and marked the Picasso Gallery.

I went into the Museum, moving carefully. There were not many people in the halls on the cold winter's afternoon, which was a pity because there was no crowd to get lost in. On the other hand there were long unobstructed views. I took out my handkerchief, ready to muffle my face in case of emergency, turned a corner and saw Ashton in the distance. He was contemplating a canvas with interest and, as he turned to move on to the next one, I had a good sight of his face.

To my relief this *was* Ashton. There would have been a blazing row if I had goosed Cutler to no purpose.

NINETEEN

Cutler jumped like a startled frog. An hour later, when I was unfreezing my bones in a hot bath and feeling sorry for Henty who was still tagging Ashton, the telephone rang to announce that he was waiting in the hotel foyer. 'Ask him to come up.' I dried myself quickly and put on a dressing-gown.

He brought two men whom he introduced as Askrigg and Debenham. He made no apologies for his previous attitude and neither of us referred to it. All the time I knew him he maintained his icily well-bred air of disapproval; that I could stand so long as he did what he was told and did it fast, and I had no complaints about that. The only trouble was that he and his people were lacking in professionalism.

We got down to business immediately. I outlined the problem, and Askrigg said, 'A full-time surveillance of two men is a six-man job.'

'At least,' I agreed. 'And that's excluding me and Henty. Ashton and Benson know me, so I'm out. As for Henty, he's done enough. He spotted Ashton for us and has been freezing his balls off ever since keeping an eye on him. I'm pulling him out for a rest and then he'll be in reserve.'

'Six men,' said Cutler doubtfully. 'Oh, well, I suppose we can find them. What are we looking for?'

'I want to know everything about them. Where they go, what they eat, who they see, do they have a routine, what happens when they break that routine, who they write to – you name it, I want to know.'

'It seems a lot of fuss over a relatively minor industrialist,' sniffed Cutler.

I grinned at him, and quoted, ' "Yours not to reason why, Yours but to do or die." 'Which could happen because they're probably armed.'

That brought a moment of silence during which Cutler twitched a bit. In his book diplomacy and guns didn't go together. I said, 'Another thing: I want to have a look inside Ashton's apartment, but we'll check their routine first so we can pick the right moment.'

'Burglary!' said Cutler hollowly. 'The Embassy mustn't be involved in that.'

'It won't be,' I said shortly. 'Leave that to me. All right; let's get organized.'

And so Ashton and Benson were watched, every movement noted. It was both wearisome and frustrating as most operations of this nature are. The two men led an exemplary life. Ashton's was the life of a gentleman of leisure; he visited museums and art galleries, attended the theatre and cinemas, and spent a lot of time in bookshops where he spent heavily, purchasing fiction and non-fiction, the non-fiction being mostly biographies. The books were over a spread of languages, English, German and Russian predominating. And all the time he did not do a stroke of what could reasonably be called work. It was baffling.

Benson was the perfect manservant. He did the household shopping, attended to the laundry and dry-cleaning, and did a spot of cooking on those occasions when Ashton did not eat out. He had found himself a favourite drinking-hole which he attended three or four times a week, an *ölstuga* more intellectual than most because it had a chess circle. Benson would play a couple of games and leave relatively early.

Neither of them wrote or received any letters.

Neither appeared to have any associates other than the small-change encounters of everyday life.

Neither did a single damned thing out of the ordinary with one large and overriding exception. Their very presence in Stockholm was out of the ordinary.

At the beginning of the third week, when their routine had been established, Henty and I cracked the apartment. Ashton had gone to the cinema and Benson was doing his Bobby Fischer bit over a half-litre of Carlsberg and we would have an hour or longer. We searched that flat from top to bottom and did not find much.

The main prize was Ashton's passport. It was of Israeli issue, three years old, and made out in the name of Fyodr Antonovitch Koslov who had been born in Odessa in 1914. I photographed every page. including the blank ones, and put it back where I found it. A secondary catch was the counterfoil stub of a cheque-book. I photographed that thoroughly, too. Ashton was spending money quite freely; his casual expenses were running to nearly £500 a week.

The telephone rang. Henty picked it up and said cautiously, *'Vilket nummer vill ni ha?'* There was a pause. 'Okay.' he put down the receiver. 'Benson's left the pub; he's on his way back.'

I looked around the room. 'Everything in order?'

'I reckon so.'

'Then let's go.' We left the building and sat in Henty's car until Benson arrived. We saw him safely inside, checked his escort, then went away.

* * *

Early next morning I gave Cutler the spools of film and requested negatives and two sets of prints. I got them within the hour and spent quite a time checking them before my prearranged telephone call from Ogilvie. It had to be prearranged because he had to have a scrambler compatible with that at the Embassy.

Briefly I summarized the position up to that point, then said, 'Any breakthrough will come by something unusual – an oddity – and there are not many of those. There's the Israeli passport – I'd like to know if that's kosher. I'll send you the photographs in the diplomatic bag.'

'Issued three years ago, you say.'

'That's right. That would be about the time a bank account was opened here in the name of Koslov. The apartment was rented a year later, also in the name of Koslov; it was sublet until four months ago when Ashton moved in. Our friend had everything prepared. I've gone through cheque stubs covering nearly two months. Ashton isn't stinting himself.'

'How is he behaving? Psychologically, I mean.'

'I've seen him only three times, and then at a distance.' I thought for a moment. 'My impression is that he's more relaxed than when I saw him last in England; under less of a strain.' There didn't seem much else to say. 'What do I do now?'

'Carry on,' said Ogilvie succinctly.

I sighed. 'This could go on for weeks – months. What if I tackled him myself? There's no need to blow my cover. I can get myself accredited to an international trade conference that's coming up next week.'

'Don't do that,' said Ogilvie. 'He's sharper than anyone realizes. Just keep watching; something will turn up.'

Yes, Mr Micawber, I thought, but didn't say it. What I said was, 'I'll put the negatives and prints into the diplomatic bag immediately.'

Two more weeks went by and nothing happened. Ashton went on his way serenely, doing nothing in particular. I had another, more extended, look at him and he seemed to be enjoying himself in a left-handed fashion. This was possibly the first holiday he'd ever had free from the cares of the business he had created. Benson pottered about in the shops and markets of Gamla Stan most mornings, doing his none-too-frugai shopping, and we began to build up quite a picture of the culinary tastes of the *ménage* Ashton. It didn't do us one damned bit of good.

Henty went about his own mysterious business into which I didn't enquire too closely. I do know that he was in some form of military intelligence because he left for a week and went north to Lapland where the Swedish Army was holding winter manoeuvres. When he came back I saw him briefly and he said he'd be busy writing a report.

Four days later he came to see me with disturbing information. 'Do you know there's another crowd in on the act?'

I stared at him. 'What do you mean?'

'I've got a bump of curiosity,' he said. 'Last night, in my copious spare time, I checked to see whether Cutler's boys were up to snuff. Ashton is leading quite a train – our chap follows Ashton and someone else follows him.' I was about to speak but he held up his hand. 'So I checked on Benson and the same is happening there.'

'Cutler's said nothing about this.'

'How would he know?' said Henty scathingly. 'Or any of them. They're amateurs.'

I asked the crucial question. 'Who?'

Henty shrugged. 'My guess is Swedish Intelligence. Those boys are good. They'd be interested in anyone with a

Russian name and even more interested to find out he's under surveillance. They'll have made the connection with the British Embassy by now.'

'Damn!' I said. 'Better not let Cutler know or he'll have diplomatic kittens. I think this is where we join in.'

Next morning, when Ashton took his morning constitutional, we were on the job. Ashton appeared and collected the first segment of his tail who happened to be Askrigg. Henty nudged me and pointed out the stranger who fell in behind. 'That's our joker. I'll cross the road and follow him. You stay on this side and walk parallel, keeping an eye on both of us.'

By God, but Henty was good! I tried to watch both him and the man he was following but Henty was invisible half the time, even though I knew he was there. He bobbed back and forth, letting the distance lengthen and then closing up, disappearing into shop entrances and reappearing in unexpected places and, in general, doing his best not to be there at all. Two or three times he was even in front of the man he was shadowing.

It was one of Ashton's book mornings. He visited two bookshops and spent about three-quarters of an hour in each, then he retired with his plunder to a coffee-house and inspected his purchases over coffee and Danish pastries. It was pretty funny. The coffee-house was on the corner of a block. Askrigg waited outside while, kitty-corner across the street, his follower stamped his feet to keep warm while ostensibly looking into a shop window. The third corner held Henty, doing pretty much the same, while I occupied the fourth corner. My own wait was made risible by the nature of the shop in which I was taking an intent interest. Henty was outside a camera shop. Mine sold frilly lingerie of the type known pungently as passion fashion.

Out came Ashton and the train chugged off again, and he led us back to where we had started, but going home by the

Vasabron just to make a variation. So far the whole thing was a bust, but better times were coming. Our man went into a tobacconist's shop and I followed. As I bought a packet of cigarettes I heard him speaking in low tones on the telephone. I couldn't hear what he said but the intonation was neither English nor Swedish.

He left the shop and walked up the street while I followed on the other side. A hundred yards up the street he crossed, so I did the same; then he reversed direction. He was doing what he hoped was an unobtrusive patrol outside Ashton's flat.

Fifteen minutes later came the event we'd waited for – his relief arrived. The two men stood and talked for a few moments, their breath steaming and mingling in the cold air, then my man set off at a smart pace and I followed. He turned the corner which led around the back of the Royal Palace, and when I had him in sight he was dickering with a taxi-driver.

I was figuring out how to say, 'Follow that car!' in Swedish when Henty pulled up alongside in his car. I scrambled in, and Henty said in satisfaction, 'I thought he might do that. We've all had enough walking for the day.' I've said he was good.

So we followed the taxi through Stockholm, which was not particularly difficult, nor did he take us very far. The taxi pulled up outside a building and was paid off, and our man disappeared inside. Henty carried on without slackening speed. 'That does it!' he said expressively.

I twisted in my seat and looked back. 'Why? What is that place?'

'The bloody Russian Embassy.'

TWENTY

I expected my report on that to bring action but I didn't expect it to bring Ogilvie. I telephoned him at three in the afternoon and he was in my room just before midnight, and four other men from the department were scattered about the hotel. Ogilvie drained me dry, and I ended up by saying, 'Henty and I did the same this evening with the man following Benson. He went back to a flat on Upplandsgatan. On checking, he proved to be a commercial attaché at the Russian Embassy.'

Ogilvie was uncharacteristically nervous and indecisive. He paced the room as a tiger paces its cage, his hands clasped behind his back; then he sat in a chair with a thump. 'Damn it all to hell!' he said explosively. 'I'm in two minds about this.'

I waited, but Ogilvie did not enlarge on what was on either of his minds, so I said diffidently, 'What's the problem?'

'Look, Ashton hasn't given us what we expected when we sprung him from Russia. Oh, he's done a lot, but in a purely commercial way – not the advanced scientific thought we wanted. So why the hell should we care if he plays silly buggers in Stockholm and attracts the attention of the Russians?'

Looked at in a cold and calculating way that was a good question. Ogilvie said, 'I'd wash my hands of him – let the

Russians take him – but for two things. The first is that I don't *know* why he ran, and the hell of it is that the answer might be quite unimportant. It's probably mere intellectual curiosity on my part, and the taxpayer shouldn't be expected to finance that. This operation is costing a packet.'

He stood up and began to pace again. 'The second thing is that I can't get that empty vault out of my mind. Why did he build it if he didn't intend to use it? Have you thought of that, Malcolm?'

'Yes, but I haven't got very far.'

Ogilvie sighed. 'Over the past months I've read and reread Ashton's file until I've become cross-eyed. I've been trying to get into the mind of the man. Did you know it was he who suggested taking over the persona of a dead English soldier?'

'No. I thought it was Cregar's idea.'

'It was Chelyuskin. As I read the file I began to see that he works by misdirection like a conjuror. Look at how he got out of Russia. I'm more and more convinced that the vault is another bit of misdirection.'

'An expensive bit,' I said.

'That wouldn't worry Ashton – he's rolling in money. If he's got something, he's got it somewhere else.'

I was exasperated. 'So why did he build the safe in the first place?'

'To tell whoever opened it that they'd reached the end of the line. That there are no secrets. As I say – misdirection.'

'It's all a bit fanciful,' I said. I was tired because it was late and I'd been working hard all day. Hammering the ice-slippery streets of Stockholm with my feet wasn't my idea of pleasure, and I was past the point of coping with Ogilvie's fantasies about Ashton. I tried to bring him to the point by saying, 'What do we do about Ashton now?' He was the boss and he had to make up his mind.

'How did the Russians get on to Ashton here?'

'How would I know?' I shrugged. 'My guess is that they got wind of a free-spending fellow-countryman unknown to Moscow, so they decided to take a closer look at him. To their surprise they found he's of great interest to British Intelligence. That would make them perk up immediately.'

'Or, being the suspicious lot they are, they may have been keeping tabs on the British Embassy as a matter of routine and been alerted by the unaccustomed activity of Cutler and his mob, who're not the brightest crowd of chaps.' Ogilvie shrugged. 'I don't suppose it matters how they found out; the fact is that they have. They're on to Koslov but have not, I think, made the transition to Ashton – and certainly not to Chelyuskin.'

'That's about it. They'll never get to Chelyuskin. Who'd think of going back thirty years?'

'Their files go back further, and they'll have Chelyuskin's fingerprints. If they ever do a comparison with Koslov's prints they'll know it wasn't Chelyuskin who died in that fire. They'd be interested in that.'

'But is it likely?'

'I don't know.' He scowled in my direction but I don't think he saw me; he was looking through me. 'That Israeli passport is quite genuine,' he said. 'But stolen three years ago. The real Koslov is a Professor of Languages at the University of Tel Aviv. He's there right now, deciphering some scrolls in Aramaic.'

'Do the Israelis know about Koslov? That might be tricky.'

'I shouldn't think so,' he said absently. Then he shook his head irritatedly. 'You don't think, much of my theories about Ashton, do you?'

'Not much.'

The scowl deepened. 'Neither do I,' he admitted. 'It's just one big area of uncertainty. Right. We can do one of two things. We can pull out and leave Ashton to sink or swim on his own; or we can get him out ourselves.' Ogilvie looked at me expectantly.

I said, 'That's a policy decision I'm not equipped to make. But I do have a couple of comments. First, any interest the Russians have in Ashton has been exacerbated by ourselves, and I consider we have a responsibility towards him because of that. For the rest – what I've seen of Ashton I've liked and, God willing, I'm going to marry his daughter. I have a personal reason for wanting to get him out which has nothing to do with guessing what he's been doing with his peculiar mind.'

Ogilvie nodded soberly. 'Fair enough. That leaves it up to me. If he really has something and we leave him for the Russians then I'll have made a big mistake. If we bring him out, risking an international incident because of the methods we may have to use, and he has nothing, then I'll have made a big mistake. But the first mistake would be bigger than the second, so the answer is that we bring him out. The decision is made.'

TWENTY-ONE

Ogilvie had brought with him Brent, Gregory, Michaelis and, to my surprise, Larry Godwin, who looked very chipper because not only had he got away from his desk but he'd gone foreign. We had an early morning conference to discuss the nuts and bolts of the operation.

Earlier I had again tackled Ogilvie. 'Why don't I approach Ashton and tell him the Russians are on to him? That would move him.'

'In which direction?' asked Ogilvie. 'If he thought for one moment that British Intelligence was trying to manipulate him I wouldn't care to predict his actions. He might even think it better to go back to Russia. Homesickness is a Russian neurosis.'

'Even after thirty years?'

Ogilvie shrugged. 'The Russians are a strange people. And have you thought of his attitude to you? He'd immediately jump to wrong conclusions – I won't risk the explosion. No, it will have to be some other way.'

Ogilvie brought the meeting to order and outlined the problem, then looked about expectantly. There was a lengthy pause while everyone thought about it. Gregory said, 'We have to separate him from the Russians before we can do anything at all.'

'Are we to assume he might defect to Russia?' asked Brent.

'Not if we're careful,' said Ogilvie. 'But it's a possibility. My own view is that he might even be scared of the Russians if he knew they were watching him.'

Brent threw one in my direction. 'How good are the Russians here?'

'Not bad at all,' I said. 'A hell of a lot better than Cutler's crowd.'

'Then it's unlikely they'll make a mistake,' he said glumly. 'I thought if he knew the Russians were on to him he might cut and run. That would give us the opportunity for a spoiling action.'

Ogilvie said, 'Malcolm and I have discussed that and decided against it.'

'Wait a minute,' I said, and turned to Larry. 'How good is your conversational Russian?'

'Not bad,' he said modestly.

'It will have to be better than not bad,' I warned. 'You might have to fool a native Russian.' I didn't tell him Ashton *was* a Russian.

He grinned. 'Which regional accent do you want?'

Ogilvie caught on. 'I see,' he said thoughtfully. 'If the Russians don't make a mistake we make it for them. I'll buy that.'

We discussed it for a while, then Michaelis said, 'We'll need a back-up scheme. If we're going to take him out against his will we'll need transport, a safe house and possibly a doctor.'

That led to another long discussion in which plans were hammered out and roles allocated. Kidnapping a man can be complicated. 'What about Benson?' asked Gregory. 'Is he included in the deal?'

'I rather think so,' said Ogilvie. 'I'm becoming interested in Benson. But the primary target is Ashton. If it ever comes to a choice between taking Ashton or Benson, then drop Benson.' He turned to Michaelis. 'How long do you need?'

'If we use Plan Three we don't need a house, and the closed van I can hire inside an hour. But I'll have to go to Helsingborg or Malmo to arrange for the boat and that will take time. Say three days.'

'How long to cross the strait to Denmark?'

'Less than an hour; you can nearly spit across it. But someone will have to organize a receiving committee in Denmark.'

'I'll do that.' Ogilvie stood up and said with finality, 'Three days, then; and we don't tell Cutler anything about it.'

Three days later the operation began as planned and started well. The situation in Gamla Stan was becoming positively ridiculous: two of Cutler's men were idling away their time in antique shops ready for the emergence of Ashton and Benson and unaware that they were being watched by a couple of Russians who, in their turn, were not aware of being under the surveillance of the department. It could have been a Peter Sellers comedy.

Each of our men was issued with a miniature walkie-talkie with strict instructions to stay off the air unless it was absolutely necessary to pass on the word. We didn't want to alert the Swedes that an undercover operation was under way: if they joined in there'd be so many secret agents in those narrow streets there'd be no room for tourists.

I sat in my car, strategically placed to cover the bridges leading from Gamla Stan to the central city area, and kept a listening watch. Ogilvie stayed in his room in the hotel next to the telephone.

At ten-thirty someone came on the air. 'Bluebird Two. Redbird walking north along Västerlånggatan.' Ashton was coming my way so I twisted in my seat to look for him.

Presently he rounded the corner and walked up the road next to the Royal Palace. He passed within ten feet of me, striding out briskly. I watched him until he turned to go over Helgeandsholmen by way of Norrbro, then switched on the car engine. Ahead I saw Larry slide out of his parking place and roll along to turn on to Norrbro. His job was to get ahead of Ashton.

I followed behind, passing Ashton who was already carrying a tail like a comet, crossed Norrbro and did a couple of turns around Gustav Adolfs Torg, making sure that everything was in order. I saw Gregory leave his parking place to make room for Larry; it was important that Larry should be in the right place at the right time. Michaelis was reserving a place further west should Ashton have decided to go into town via the Vasabron. I switched on my transmitter and said to him, 'Bluebird Four to Bluebird Three; you may quit.'

At that point I quit myself because there was nothing left to do – everything now depended on Larry. I drove the short distance to the Grand Hotel, parked the car, and went to Ogilvie's room. He was nervous under his apparent placidity. After a few minutes' chat he said abruptly, 'Do you think Godwin is up to it? He's not very experienced.'

'And he never will be if he's not given the chance.' I smiled. 'He'll be all right. Any moment from now he'll be giving his celebrated imitation of an inexperienced KGB man. From that point of view his inexperience is an asset.'

Time wore on. At twelve-thirty Ogilvie had smörgåsbord sent up to the room. 'We might as well eat. If anything breaks you'll be eating on the run from now on.'

At five to one the telephone rang. Ogilvie handed me a pair of earphones before he picked up the receiver. It was Brent, who said, 'Redbird is lunching at the Opera – so am I and so is everyone else concerned. He's looking a bit jumpy.'

'How did Godwin handle first contact?'

'Redbird went into that corner bookshop on the Nybroplan. Godwin was standing next to him when he barked his shin on a shelf; Larry swore a blue streak in Russian and Redbird jumped a foot. Then Larry faded out as planned.'

'And then?'

'Redbird wandered around for a bit and then came here. I saw him get settled, then signalled Larry to come in. He took a table right in front of Redbird who looked worried when he saw him. Larry has just had a hell of a row with a waiter in very bad, Russian-accented Swedish – all very noisy. Redbird is definitely becoming uncomfortable.'

'How are the others taking it?'

'The real Russians look bloody surprised. Cutler's chap . . . wait a minute.' After a pause Brent chuckled. 'Cutler's chap is heading for the telephones right now. I think he wants to report that the Russians have arrived. I think I'll let him have this telephone.'

'Stay with it,' said Ogilvie. 'Stick to Ashton.' He replaced the receiver and looked up. 'It's starting.'

'Everything is ready,' I said soothingly. I picked up the telephone and asked the hotel operator to transfer my calls to Ogilvie's room.

We had not long to wait. The telephone rang and I answered. Cutler said, 'Jaggard, there may be an important development.'

'Oh,' I said seriously. 'What's that?'

'My man with Ashton seems to think the Russians are interested.'

'In Ashton?'

'That's right.'

'Oh. That's bad! Where is Ashton now?'

'Lunching at the Opera. Shall I put someone on to the Russian? There may be time.'

Ogilvie had the earphone to his ear and shook his head violently. I grinned, and said, 'I think not. In fact I think you'd better pull out all your men as soon as you can get word to them. You don't want the Russians to know you're on to Ashton, do you?'

'My God, no!' said Cutler quickly. 'We can't have the Embassy involved. I'll do as you say at once.' He rang off, seemingly relieved.

Ogilvie grunted. 'The man's an idiot. He's well out of it.'

'It does clear the field,' I said, and put on my jacket. 'I'm going over to Gamla Stan for the beginning of the second act. If Larry does his stuff we should get a firm reaction from Ashton,' I paused. 'I don't like doing it this way, you know. I'd much prefer we talk to him.'

'I know,' said Ogilvie sombrely. 'But your preferences don't count. Get on with it, Malcolm.'

So I got on with it. I went to Gamla Stan and met Henty in a bar-restaurant in Västerlånggatan, joining him in a snack of herring and aquavit. He had been watching the flat, so I said, 'Where's Benson?'

'Safe at home. His Russian is still with him but Cutler's boy has vanished. Maybe Benson lost him.'

'No. Cutler is no longer with us.' I described what had happened.

Henty grinned. 'Something should break any moment then.' He finished his beer and stood up. 'I'd better get back.'

'I'll come with you.' As we left I said, 'You're our Swedish expert. Supposing Ashton makes a break – how can he do it?'

'By air from Bromma or Arlanda, depending on where he's going. He can also take a train. He doesn't have a car.'

'Not that we know of. He could also leave by sea.'

Henty shook his head. At this time of year I doubt it. There's a lot of ice in the Baltic this year – the Saltsjön was frozen over this morning. It plays hell with their schedules.

If I were Ashton I wouldn't risk it; he could get stuck on a ship which didn't move for hours.'

The bone-conduction contraption behind my ear came to life. 'Bluebird Two. Redbird by Palace heading for Västerlånggatan and moving fast.' Bluebird Two was Brent.

I said to Henty, 'He's coming now. You go on ahead, spot him and tag that bloody Russian. I don't want Ashton to see me.'

He quickened his pace while I slowed down, strolling from one shop window to the next. Presently there came the news that Ashton was safely back home, and then Henty came back with Larry Godwin. Both were grinning, and Henty remarked, 'Ashton's in a muck-sweat.'

I said to Larry, 'What happened?'

'I followed Ashton from the Opera – very obviously. He tried to shake me; in fact, he did shake me twice, but Brent was able to steer me back on course.'

Henty chuckled. 'Ashton came along Västerlånggatan doing heel-and-toe as though he was in a walking race, with Godwin trying hard for second place. He went through his doorway like a rabbit going down a hole.'

'Did you speak to him, Larry?'

'Well, towards the end I called out, "*Grazhdaninu* Ashton – *ostanovites!*" as though I wanted him to stop. It just made him go faster.'

I smiled slightly. I doubt if Ashton relished being called 'citizen' in Russian, especially when coupled with his English name. 'The ball is now in Ashton's court, but I doubt he'll move before nightfall. Larry, go and do an ostentatious patrol before Ashton's flat. Be a bit haphazard – reappear at irregular intervals.'

I had a last word with Henty, and then did the rounds, checking that every man was in his place and the Russians were covered. After that I reported by telephone to Ogilvie.

Larry caught up with me in about an hour. 'One of those bloody Russians tackled me,' he said. 'He asked me what the hell I thought I was doing.'

'In Russian?'

'Yes. I asked him for his authority and he referred me to a Comrade Latiev in the Russian Embassy. So I got a bit shirty and told him that Latiev's authority had been superseded, and if Latiev didn't know that himself he was even more stupid than Moscow thought. Then I said I didn't have time to waste and did a quick disappearing act.'

'Not bad,' I said. 'It ought to hold Comrade Latiev for a while. Any reaction from the flat?'

'A curtain did twitch a bit.'

'Okay. Now, if Ashton makes his break I don't want him to see you – we don't want to panic him more than necessary. Take over Gregory's car, ask him what the score is, and send him to me.'

It was a long wait and a cold wait. The snow came down steadily and, as darkness fell, a raw mist swept over Gamla Stan from the Riddarfjärden, haloing the street lights and cutting down visibility. I spent the time running over and over in my mind the avenues of escape open to Ashton and wondering if my contingency planning was good enough. With Henty there were six of us, surely enough to take out the two Russians and still keep up with Ashton wherever he went. As the mist thickened I thought of the possibility of taking Ashton there and then, but thought better of it. A quiet kidnapping in a major city is hard enough at the best of times and certainly not the subject for improvization. Better to follow the plan and isolate Ashton.

It happened at ten to nine. Gregory reported Ashton and Benson on Lilla Nygatan moving south, and both had bags. Michaelis chipped in and said that both Russians were also on the move. I summoned up my mental map of Gamla

Stan and concluded that our targets were heading for the taxi rank on the Centralbron, so I ordered the cars south ready to follow. More interestingly, on the other side of the Centralbron, in the main city, was Stockholm's Central Railway Station.

Then I ordered Michaelis and Henty, our best strong-arm men, to take the Russians out of the game. They reported that, because of the mist, it was easy and that two Russians would have sore heads the following morning.

After that things became a bit confused. When Ashton and Benson reached the taxi rank they took separate cabs, Benson going over the Centralbron towards the railway station, and Ashton going in the dead opposite direction towards Södermalm. Larry followed Benson, and Brent went after Ashton. I got busy and ordered the rest of the team to assemble at the railway station which seemed the best bet under the circumstances.

At the station I stayed in the car and sent in Henty to find out if Larry was around. He came back with Larry who got into the car, and said, 'Benson bought two tickets for Göteborg.'

They were heading west. From my point of view that was a relief; better west than east. I said, 'When does the train leave?'

Larry checked his watch. 'In a little over half an hour. I bought us four tickets – and I got a timetable.'

I studied the timetable and thought out loud. 'First stop – Södertälje; next stop – Eskilstuna. Right.' I gave a ticket each to Gregory and Henty. 'You two get on that train: spot Ashton and Benson and report back by radio. Then stick with them.'

They went into the station, and Larry said, 'What do we do?'

'You and I lie as low as Br'er Rabbit,' I turned to Michaelis. 'Scout around in the station and see if you can spot Ashton. Make sure he's on that train when it leaves, then come back here.'

He went away and I wondered how Brent was getting on. Presently Gregory radioed in. 'We're on the train – spotted Redbird Two – but no Redbird One.'

We'd lost Ashton. 'Stay with it.'

The time ticked by. At five minutes to train-time I became uneasy, wondering what had happened to Ashton. At two minutes to train-time Brent pitched up. 'I lost him,' he said hollowly.

'Where did he go?'

'He went bloody island-hopping – Södermalm – Långholmen – Kungsholmen; that's where I lost him. He seemed to be heading in this general direction at the time so I took a chance and came here.'

'We haven't seen him and he's not on the train so far. Benson is, though; with two tickets to Göteborg.'

'When does it leave?'

I looked over his shoulder and saw Michaelis coming towards the car. He was shaking his head. I said, 'It's just left – and Ashton wasn't on it.'

'Oh, Christ! What do we do now?'

'The only thing we can do – stick with Benson and pray. And this is how we do it. Get yourself a timetable like this one, and check the stops of that train. You and Michaelis take the first stop – that's Södertälje, you check with Gregory and Henty on the train and you team up if Benson gets off. You also report to Ogilvie. In the meantime Larry and I will be heading for the next stop at Eskilstuna – same procedure. And we leapfrog up the line until the train arrives at Göteborg or anything else happens. Got that?'

'Okay.'

'Reporting to Ogilvie is very important because he can keep us all tied in. I'm going to ring him now.'

Ogilvie wasn't at all pleased but he didn't say much – not then. I told him how I was handling it and he just grunted. 'Carry on – and keep me posted.'

I went back to the car, slumped into the passenger's seat, and said to Larry, 'Drive to Eskilstuna – and beat that train.'

TWENTY-TWO

From Stockholm to Eskilstuna is about 100 kilometres. The first 40 kilometres are of motorway standard and we were able to make good time, but after that it became more of an ordinary road with opposing traffic and our average speed dropped. It was very dark – a moonless night – but even if there had been a moon it wouldn't have helped because there was a thick layer of cloud from which descended a heavy and continuous fall of snow.

Like all modern Swedish cars ours was well equipped for this kind of weather. The tyres had tungsten-steel studs for traction and the headlights had wipers to clear the encrusting snow, but that didn't mean fast driving and I suppose we didn't average more than 70 KPH and that was a shade fast for the conditions. Neither Larry nor I could be classed as rally drivers, and I was very much afraid the train would be faster. Fortunately, I saw by the map that it had further to go, the track sweeping round in a loop. Also it would stop at Södertälje.

After an hour I told Larry to pull into a filling station where he refuelled while I phoned Ogilvie. When I got back to the car I was smiling, and Larry said, 'Good news?'

'The best. I'll drive.' As we pulled away I said, 'Ashton tried to pull a fast one. When Brent lost him he wasn't on his way to the railway station in Stockholm; he took a taxi ride to the Södertälje station and got on the train there. We've got them both now.'

Thus it was that I was quite happy when we pulled up outside the railway station at Eskilstuna to find the train standing on the platform. I switched on my transmitter, and said, 'Any Bluebirds there? Come in, Bluebirds.'

A voice in my ear. 'Redbird and friend jumped train.'

'What the hell?'

Henty said, 'What do you want me to do?'

'Get off that bloody train and come here. We're parked outside the station.' Even as I spoke the train clanked and began to move slowly. I was beginning to wonder if Henty had made it when I saw him running towards the car. I wound down the side window. 'Get in and tell me what, for Christ's sake, happened.'

Henty got into the back seat. 'The train pulled up at some bloody whistle-stop called Åkers-styckebruk, and don't ask me why. Nothing happened until it began to move out, then Ashton and Benson jumped for it. Gregory went after them but it was too late for me – and the way he went he was like to break a leg.'

I got out the road map and studied it. 'Åkers-styckebruk! The place isn't even on the map. Have you reported to Ogilvie?'

'No. I was just going to when you called me.'

'Then I suppose I have to.'

I went into the station and rang Stockholm, and Ogilvie said testily, 'What the devil's going on? I've just had a call from Gregory in some God-forsaken place. He's either broken or sprained his ankle and he's lost Ashton. He thinks they've gone to somewhere called Strängnäs.'

Strängnäs was back along the road; we'd skirted around the edges. I said, 'We'll be there in an hour.'

'An hour may be too late,' he snapped. 'But get on with it.'

I ran back to the car. 'Get weaving, Larry – back where we came from.' He moved over into the driving seat and I hadn't closed the door before he took off. I twisted around and said to Henty, 'What can you tell me about Strängnäs? Anything there we ought to know about?'

He snapped his fingers. 'Of course! There's a spur-line going into Strängnäs from Åkers-styckebruk – no passenger trains, just the occasional *räslbuss.*'

'What's that?'

'A single coach on the railway – diesel driven.'

'You say it's a spur-line. You mean the rail stops at Strängnäs?'

'It has to, or it would run into Lake Mälaren,'

I contemplated that. 'So it's a dead end.'

'For the railway, but not for cars. There's a road which goes by way of the islands to the north shore of Mälaren. But it's late; I wouldn't bet they'll be able to hire a car at this time of night.'

True,' I said. 'But step on it, Larry.' I watched the road unwinding out of the darkness against the hypnotic beat of the wipers as they cleared snow from the windscreen. The headlights brightened as Larry operated the light wipers. 'Anything else about Strängnäs?'

'It's not much of a place.' said Henty. 'Population about twelve thousand; a bit of light industry – pharmaceuticals, penicillin. X-ray film – stuff like that. It's also a garrison town for a training regiment, and it's HQ, East Military Command.' His interest sharpened. 'Is Ashton connected with the soldier boys?'

'No,' I said.

Henty persisted. 'You'd tell me if he is? That's my line of country, and I've helped you enough.'

'Definitely not,' I said. 'His interests aren't military, and neither are mine. We're not poaching on your patch.'

'Just as long as I know.' He seemed satisfied.

We didn't bother going back all the way to Åkersstyckebruk; finding Ashton was more important than finding the state of Gregory's ankle. We came to the outskirts of Strängnäs and coasted gently through snow-covered streets towards the lake edge and the centre of town. A few turns around the town centre proved one thing – there was only one hotel – so we pulled up on the other side of the street from the Hotel Rogge and I sent Henty in to find out the form.

He was away about five minutes and when he came back he said. 'They're both there-booked under the names of Ashton and Williams.'

'So he's reverted,' I said. 'Using his own passport. Koslov has suddenly become too hot.'

'I booked in for the three of us.'

'No; you stay, but Larry and I are going to find Gregory. I'll ring Ogilvie now and ask him to retrieve Brent and Michaelis from wherever the hell they are now – they can have the other two beds here. We'll be back at six tomorrow morning and I want a concentration inside and outside the hotel. Where are Ashton and Benson now?'

'Not in any of the public rooms,' said Henty. 'I'd say they're in bed.'

'Yes, they're getting pretty old for this sort of thing,' I said pensively. 'Come to think of it, so am I.'

TWENTY-THREE

Gregory had sensibly waited at the railway station at Åkers-styckebruk for someone to pick him up. He said he was stiff, cold, tired, and that his ankle hurt like hell, so we all booked into a hotel. At five next morning Larry and I were on our way back to Strängnäs, but Gregory was able to sleep in because I decided to send him back to Stockholm. He'd be no good to us because his ankle really was bad, but he had the satisfaction of knowing that, because of him, we'd pinned down Ashton and Benson.

Just before six I parked the car around the corner from the Hotel Rogge, and at six on the button I went on the air. 'Hello,' I said brightly. 'Any Bluebirds awake?'

Henty said disgruntedly into my ear, 'Don't be so bloody cheerful.'

'Did the other two arrive?'

'Yes; at two this morning. They're still asleep.'

'And Redbird and his friend?'

'They're definitely here – I made sure of that – they're asleep, too.' He paused. 'And I wish to Christ I was.'

'Come out here. We're just around the corner on – ' I craned my neck to find a street sign – 'on Källgatan.'

He said nothing but the transmission hum stopped so I switched off. He did not appear for a quarter of an hour so Larry and I made small talk. There was nothing much to say because we'd talked the subject to death already. When Henty did arrive he was newly shaven and looked in reasonably good shape even though his manner was still a little shaggy. 'Morning,' he said shortly, as he got into the car.

I passed a vacuum flask over my shoulder. 'Be gruntled.'

He unscrewed the top and sniffed appreciatively. 'Ah, scotch coffee!' He poured a cupful and was silent for a moment before he said, 'That's better. What's the drill?'

'What time is breakfast?'

'I don't know. Say, from seven o'clock – maybe seven-thirty. These country hotels all differ.'

'I want the three of you in the breakfast room as soon as it opens; you at one table, Michaelis and Brent at another. They are to talk to each other and one of them has to give a running commentary over the air about Ashton and Benson as soon as they come in to breakfast. I want to know exactly how Ashton is acting – and reacting.'

'We can do that,' said Henty. 'But I don't get the reason.'

I said, 'Half way through breakfast I'm going to send Larry in to do a replay of his Russian act.'

'Jesus! You'll give Ashton a heart attack.'

'We've got to keep the pressure on,' I said. 'I don't want to give them time to hire a car, and I want to herd them out of town pretty early. Where's the closed van Michaelis has been driving?'

Henty pointed across the darkened street. 'In the hotel car park.'

'Good enough. I want him inside it and ready to go as soon as Ashton moves. I want this whole bloody thing cleaned up before eight o'clock if possible. Now you can go in and wake the sleeping beauties.'

When Henty had gone Larry regarded me curiously. 'I know you've been keeping out of sight,' he said. 'But if what you're doing ever comes out you're not going to be popular with the Ashton family.'

'I know,' I said shortly. 'But this is the way Ogilvie wants it done. And I'm making bloody sure I do stay out of sight, not for Ogilvie's reasons but my own.' Christ! I thought. If Penny ever got to know about this she'd never forgive me in a thousand years.

The time passed and we shared the flask of scotch coffee between us. Strängnäs began to wake up and there was movement in the streets, and we occasioned a couple of curious glances from passers-by. I suppose it was strange for a couple of men to be sitting in a parked car so early in the morning so I told Larry to drive into the hotel car park which was more secluded.

The hotel breakfast started at seven-thirty. I knew that because Jack Brent came on the air with a description of the breakfast he was eating. He described the herring and the boiled eggs and the cheese and the coffee and all the trimmings until I began to salivate. He was doing it deliberately, the bastard.

Because I made no response he tired of the game and switched off, but at seven-fifty he said, 'They're here now – Ashton and Benson. Just sitting down – two tables away. Benson looks dour but Ashton seems cheerful enough.'

No one would know Brent was broadcasting; apparently he would be chatting animatedly to Michaelis. but every word was picked up by the throat microphone concealed beneath the knot of his tie. The throat microphone gave a peculiarly dead quality to the broadcast; there was no background noise – no clatter of cutlery or coffee cups to be heard – just Brent's voice and the rasp of his breathing greatly magnified. Even if he spoke in a whisper every word would come across clearly.

I listened to his description and felt increasingly uneasy. Not about Ashton who, according to Brent, seemed fairly relaxed; I was uneasy about myself and my role in this charade. I would have given a lot to be able to walk into the

Hotel Rogge, sit down at Ashton's table, and have a down-to-earth chat with him. I was convinced I could get him back to England just by talking to him, but Ogilvie wouldn't have that. He didn't want our cover blown.

I was depressed when I turned to Larry, and said quietly, 'All right. Go in and have your breakfast.' He got out of the car and walked into the hotel.

Brent said, 'Ashton's just poured himself another cup of coffee. He hasn't lost his appetite, that's for certain. Ho ho! Larry Godwin has just walked in. Ashton hasn't seen him yet, nor has Benson. Larry's talking to the waitress by the door. God, how he's mangling his Swedish – can hear him from here. So can Ashton. He's turned and he's looking at Larry. I can't see his face. He's turned back again and now he's nudging Benson. He's as white as a sheet. The waitress is coming forward with Larry now – showing him to a table. Larry is passing Ashton's table – he turns and speaks to him. Ashton has knocked over his coffee cup. Benson is looking bloody grim; if ever I saw a man capable of murder it's Benson right now. He's no oil painting at the best of times but you should see him now. Ashton wants to get up and leave, but Benson is holding him back.'

I switched channels on my transmitter and Brent's voice abruptly stopped. I said, 'Henty, finish your breakfast and leave. Cover the front of the hotel. Michaelis, same for you, but get in your van and cover the back.'

I reversed out of the hotel car park and drove a little way up Källgatan and parked where I could see the front entrance of the hotel. When I switched back to Brent he was saying '. . . looks pretty shattered and Benson is talking to him urgently. I think he's having a hard job keeping control. You'd think it would be the other way round because Benson is only Ashton's servant. Anyway, that's what it looks like from here – Ashton wants to make a break and Benson is stopping him. Larry isn't doing much – just eating his breakfast – but every now and then he looks across at Ashton and smiles. I don't think Ashton can take much more of it. I'll have to stop now because Michaelis is leaving and I'll look bloody funny talking to myself.'

He stopped speaking and the transmission hum ceased. I keyed my transmitter. 'Larry, when Ashton and Benson leave follow them from behind with Brent.' I saw Henty come out of the hotel and walk across the street. Michaelis came next and walked around to the car park where he disappeared from sight.

Ten minutes later Ashton and Benson appeared, each carrying a bag. They stepped out on to the pavement and Ashton looked up and down the street uncertainly. He said something to Benson who shook his head, and it looked as though there was a difference of opinion. Behind them Larry appeared in the hotel entrance.

I said, 'Larry, go and talk to Ashton. Ask him to follow you. If he agrees, take him to the van and put him in the back.'

'And Benson?'

'Him, too – if possible.'

Ashton became aware that Larry was watching him and pulled at Benson's arm. Benson nodded and they began to walk away but stopped at Larry's call. Larry hurried over to them and began talking and, as he did so, Brent came out and stood close to them.

I heard the one-way conversation. Larry talked fast in Russian and twice Ashton nodded, but Benson made interjections, each time accompanied by a headshake, and tried to get Ashton away. At last he succeeded and the pair of them walked off, leaving Larry flat. They were coming straight towards me so I ducked out of sight.

While I was down on the car floor I spoke to Larry. 'What happened?'

'Ashton nearly came, but Benson wouldn't have it. He spoiled it.'

'Did Benson speak Russian?'

'No, English; but he understood my Russian well enough.'

'Where are they now?'

'Going up the street – about thirty yards past your car.'

I emerged from hiding and looked in the mirror. Ashton and Benson were walking away quickly in the direction of the railway station.

After that it all became a little sick because we literally herded them out of town. They found the railway station blocked by Brent, and when they tried to duck back to the town centre they were confronted by Larry and Henty. They soon became aware they had a quartet of opponents and, twist and turn as they might, they found themselves being driven to the edge of town. And all the time I orchestrated the bizarre dance, manipulating them like puppets. I didn't like myself at all.

At last we got to the main Stockholm-Eskilstuna road and they plunged across, Benson nearly being hit by a speeding car which went by with a wailing blast of horn. There were no more streets or houses on the other side – just an infinity of pine trees. I had Michaelis go back and pick up the van, and sent the other three into the forest while I parked my car before following. It seemed as though the chase was nearly over – you can't be more private than in a Swedish forest.

They made better time over rough country than I would have expected of two elderly men. Ashton had already proved his fitness to me, but I hadn't expected Benson to have the stamina because he was a few years older than Ashton. Once in the trees you couldn't see far and they kept foxing us by changing direction. Twice we lost them; the first time we picked them up by sheer luck, and the second time, by finding their abandoned bags. And all the time I was leading from the rear, directing the operation by radio.

We had gone perhaps three kilometres into the forest and the going was becoming rougher. Where the ground was not slippery with snow and ice it was even more slippery with pine needles. The ground rose and fell, not much but enough to take your breath away on the uphill slopes. I paused at the top of one such slope just as Brent said in my ear, 'What the hell was that?'

'What?'

'Listen!'

I listened, trying to control my heavy breathing, and heard a rattle of shots in the distance. They seemed to come from somewhere ahead, deeper in the forest.

'Someone hunting,' said Larry.

Brent said incredulously, 'With a machine-gun!'

'Quiet!' I said. 'Is Ashton spotted?'

'I'm standing looking into a little valley,' said Henty. 'Very few trees. I can see both Ashton and Benson – they're about four hundred yards away.'

'That's all very well, but where the hell are you?'

'Just keep coming ahead,' said Henty. 'It's a long valley – you can't miss it.'

'Everybody move,' I said. Again came the sound of firing, this time a sporadic rattling of badly-spaced single shots. Certainly not a machine-gun as Brent had suggested. It could have been the shoot-out at the OK Corral, and I wondered what was happening. Hunters certainly didn't pop off like that.

I pressed on and presently came to a crest where I looked down into the valley. Henty was right; it was relatively treeless and the snow was thicker. In the distance I saw Ashton and Benson moving very slowly; perhaps they were hampered by the snow, but I thought the chase was telling on them. Henty was at the valley bottom below me, and Brent and Larry were together, bounding down the hillside, closing in on our quarry from an angle.

Again came firing and, by God, this time it was machine-gun fire, and from more than one machine-gun. Then there came some deeper coughs, followed by thumping explosions. In the distance, not too far ahead, I saw a haze of smoke drifting above the trees on the far side of the valley.

Henty had stopped. He looked back at me and waved, and said over the radio, 'I know what it is. This is an army exercise area. They're having war games.'

'Live ammunition?'

'Sounds like it. Those were mortars.'

I began to run, bouncing and slithering down the slope. When I got to the bottom I saw that Brent and Larry were within fifty yards of Ashton and gaining on him fast. Ashton switched direction, and I yelled, 'Brent – Larry – fall back!'

They hesitated momentarily but then went on, caught in the lust of the chase. I shouted again. 'Fall back! Don't drive him into the guns.'

They checked, but I ran on. I was going to speak to Ashton myself, regardless of what Ogilvie had said. This was a sick game which had to be stopped before somebody was killed. Ashton was climbing the other side of the valley, heading towards the trees on the crest, but going very slowly. Benson was nowhere to be seen. I ran until I thought my chest would burst, and gained on Ashton.

At last I was close enough, and I shouted, 'Ashton – George Ashton – stop!'

He turned his head and looked back at me as a further burst of firing came, and more explosions of mortar bombs. I took off the fur hat I was wearing and threw it away so that he could get a good look at me. His eyes widened in surprise and he hesitated in his upward climb, then stopped and turned around. Brent and Larry were coming in on my left and Henty on the right.

I was about to call out to him again when there was another single shot, this time from quite close, and Ashton stumbled forward as though he had tripped. I was within ten yards of him and heard him gasp. Then there was another shot and he whirled around and fell and came rolling down the slope towards me to stop at my feet.

I was aware that Henty had passed me and momentarily saw a gun in his fist, then I bent over Ashton. He coughed once and blood trickled from the corner of his mouth. His eyes still held surprise at the sight of me, and he said, 'Mal . . . colm . . . what . . .'

I said, 'Take it easy, George,' and put my hand inside his coat. I felt a warm wetness.

He scrabbled in his pocket for something, and said, 'The . . . the . . .' His hand came up before my face with the fist clenched. 'The . . . the . . .' Then he fell back, his eyes still open and looking at the sky with deeper surprise. A snowflake fell and settled on his left eyeball, but he didn't blink.

In the distance mortars thumped and machine-guns rattled, and there were more single shots, again from quite close. I looked down at Ashton and cursed quietly. Brent crunched over the snow. 'Dead?'

I withdrew my hand and looked at the blood. Before wiping it clean on the snow I said, 'You try his pulse.'

I stood up as Brent knelt and thought of the unholy mess we – *I* – had made of the operation. The snow around Ashton's body was changing colour from white to red. Brent looked up at me. 'Yes, he's dead. From the amount of blood here the aorta must have been cut. That's why he went so fast.'

I had never felt so bad in all my life. We had driven Ashton towards the guns as beaters drive an animal. It was so stupid a thing to do. I didn't feel very human at that moment.

Henty came crunching down the slope, carrying a pistol negligently in his right hand. 'I got him,' he said matter-of-factly.

I could smell the faint reek of cordite as he came closer. 'Got who, for Christ's sake?'

'Benson.'

I stared at him. *'You shot Benson!'*

He looked at me in surprise. 'Well, he shot Ashton, didn't he?'

I was stupefied. 'Did he?'

'Of course he did. I saw him do it.' Henty turned and looked up the slope. 'Maybe you couldn't see him from this angle – but I did.'

I was unable to take it in. *'Benson* shot Ashton!'

'He bloody nearly shot me,' said Henty. 'He took a crack at me as soon as I showed myself up there. And if anyone shoots at me I shoot back.'

It had never occurred to me to ask Henty if he was armed. Nobody else was on Ogilvie's instructions, but Henty was from another department. I was still gaping at him when there was a grinding rattle from above and a tank pointed its nose over the crest and began to come down into the valley. Its nose was a 105 mm high-velocity tank gun which looked like a 16-incher as the turret swivelled to cover our small group. They wouldn't have bothered to use that, though; the machine-gun in the turret of that Centurion was capable of taking care of us much more economically.

As the tank stopped I dropped to my knees next to Ashton's body. The turret opened and a head popped out, followed by a torso. The officer raised his anti-flash goggles and surveyed us with slightly popping eyes. Henty moved, and the officer barked, *'Stopp!'* With a sigh Henty tossed his pistol aside in the snow.

I opened Ashton's clenched fist to look at what he had taken from his pocket. It was a crumpled railway timetable of the route from Stockholm to Göteborg.

TWENTY-FOUR

I don't know what sort of heat was generated at a higher level but the Swedes never treated me with anything less than politeness – icy politeness. If I had thought about it at all that cold correctitude would have been more frightening than anything else, but I wasn't thinking during that period – I was dead inside and my brains were frozen solid.

The Swedes had found two dead men and four live men on army territory. One of the dead men had two passports, one stolen and the other genuine; the other had three passports, all false. The passports of the four live men were all genuine. It was claimed that one of the dead men had shot the other and, in turn, was shot and killed by one of the live men, an Australian living and working in Sweden. He had no permit for a gun.

It was all very messy.

Ogilvie was out of it, of course, and so were Michaelis and Gregory. Michaelis had waited with the van at the road, but when a squad of infantry in full battle order debouched from the forest and systematically began to take my car to pieces he had tactfully departed. He drove back into Strängnäs and rang Ogilvie who pulled him back to Stockholm. And what Ogilvie heard from the Embassy made him decide that the climate of London was more favourable than the chilliness of Stockholm. The three of them were back in London that night and Cutler was saying, 'I told you so.'

The four of us were taken to the army barracks in Strängnäs, HQ the Royal Södermanland Regiment and HQ East Military Command. Here we were searched and eyebrows were lifted at the sight of our communication equipment. No doubt conclusions were duly drawn. We weren't treated badly; they fed us, and if what we ate was representative of army rations then the Swedish Army does a damned sight better than the British Army. But we were not allowed to talk; a stricture reinforced by two hefty Swedes armed with sub-machine-guns.

After that I was led into an empty room and, just as I thought the interrogation was about to begin, a civilian arrived and began being nasty to the military. At least, that's the impression I had judging by the rumble of voices from the office next door. Then an army colonel and a civilian came in to see me and, having seen me, went away without saying a word, and I was transferred into a cell in which I spent the next three weeks apart from an hour's exercise each day. During that time I didn't see the others at all, and the Swedes wouldn't give me the time of day, so I ought to have been pretty lonely, but I wasn't. I wasn't anything at all.

I was awakened one morning at three a.m., taken into an ablutions block and told to take a shower. When I came out I found my own clothes – the army fatigues I had been wearing had disappeared. I dressed, checked my wallet and found everything there, and put on my watch. The only things missing were my passport and the radio.

I was marched smartly across the dark and snow-covered parade ground and shown into an office where a man dressed in civilian clothes awaited me. He wasn't a civilian, though, because he said, 'I am Captain Morelius.' He had watchful grey eyes and a gun in a holster under his jacket. 'You will come with me.'

We went outside again to a chauffeur-driven Volvo, and Captain Morelius didn't say another word until we were standing on the apron of Arlanda Airport over three hours later. Then he pointed to a British Airways Trident, and said, 'There is your aircraft, Mr Jaggard. You realize you are no longer welcome in Sweden.' And that is all he said.

We walked to the gangway and he handed a ticket to a steward who took me inside and installed me in a first-class scat. Then they let on the common herd and twenty minutes later we were in the air. I had good service from that steward who must have thought I was a VIP, and I appreciated the first drink I had had for nearly a month.

When we landed at Heathrow I wondered how I was going to get by without a passport; I certainly didn't feel like going into tedious explanations. But Ogilvie was waiting for me and we walked around Passport Control and Customs. Once in his car he asked, 'Are you all right, Malcolm?'

'Yes.' I paused. 'I'm sorry.'

'Not to worry,' he said. 'We'll leave the explanations for later.'

Going into town he talked about everything except what had happened in Sweden. He brought me up-to-date on the news, talked about a new show that had opened, and generally indulged in light chit-chat. When he pulled up outside my flat he said, 'Get some sleep. I'll see you in my office tomorrow.'

I got out of the car. 'Wait! How's Penny?'

'Quite well, I believe. She's in Scotland.'

'Does she know?'

He nodded, took out his wallet, and extracted a newspaper cutting. 'You can keep that,' he said, and put the car into gear and drove away.

I went up to the flat and its very familiarity seemed strange. I stood looking around and then realized I was holding the newspaper cutting. It was from *The Times*, and read:

> KILLED IN SWEDEN
>
> Two Englishmen, George Ashton (56) and Howard Greatorex Benson (64) were killed near Strängnäs, Sweden, yesterday when they wandered on to a firing range used by the Swedish army. Both men died instantaneously when they were caught in a shell explosion.
>
> A Swedish army spokesman said that the area was adequately cordoned and that all roads leading into it were signposted. Announcements of the proposed firing of live ammunition were routinely made in the local newspapers and on the radio.

The dateline of the story was five days after Ashton and Benson died.

TWENTY-FIVE

When I walked into my office Larry Godwin was sitting at his desk reading *Pravda* and looking as though he had never left it. He looked up. 'Hello, Malcolm.' He didn't smile and neither did I. We both knew there was nothing to smile about.

'When did you get back?'

'Three days ago – the day after Jack Brent.'

'Henty?'

He shook his head. 'Haven't seen him.'

'How did they treat you?'

'Not bad. I felt a bit isolated, though.

'Has Ogilvie debriefed you?'

Larry grimaced. 'He emptied me as you'd empty a bottle of beer. I still feel gutted. It'll be your turn now.'

I nodded, picked up the telephone, and told Ogilvie's sceretary I was available. Then I sat down to contemplate my future and couldn't see a damned thing in the fog. Larry said, 'Someone knew the right strings to pull. I tell you, I wasn't looking forward to a stretch in a Swedish jail. They'd have put us in their version of Siberia – up in the frozen north.'

'Yes,' I said abstractedly. I wondered what *quid pro quo* the Swedes had claimed for our release and their silence.

Ogilvie called me in twenty minutes later. 'Sit down, Malcolm.' He bent to his intercom. 'No more calls for the rest of the morning, please,' he said ominously, then looked at me. 'I think we have a lot to talk about. How are you feeling?'

I felt he really wanted to know, so I said, 'A bit drained.'

'The Swedes treat you all right?'

'No complaints.'

'Right. Let's get to the crux. Who killed Ashton?'

'Of my own knowledge I don't know. At the time I thought he'd caught a couple from the Swedes – there was a lot of shooting going on. Then Henty told me Benson had shot him.'

'But you didn't see Benson shoot him.'

'That's correct.'

Ogilvie nodded. 'That fits with what Godwin and Brent told me. Now, who killed Benson?'

'Henty said he did it. He said he saw Benson shooting at Ashton so he drew his own gun and went after him. Apparently Benson was at the top of the slope in the trees. He said that Benson shot at him, too, so he shot back and killed him. I didn't even know Henty was armed.'

'Have you thought why Benson should have killed Ashton? It's not the normal thing for an old family retainer to do to his master.'

A humourless thought crossed my mind: in the less inventive early British detective stories it was always the butler who committed the murder. I said, 'I can think of a reason but it doesn't depend on Benson's status as a servant.'

'Well?'

'Henty was coming up on my right, and Brent and Godwin angling in from the left. Ashton was just above, but there was a big boulder screening me from the top of the slope. I didn't see Benson and I don't think he saw me. But he did see Larry, and Larry was a Russian, remember. When Ashton stopped and turned, and showed signs of coming down, then Benson shot him.'

'To prevent him falling into the hands of the Russians. I see.'

I said, 'And that makes him something more than a family servant.'

'Possibly,' said Ogilvie. 'But I've been going into the history of Howard Greatorex Benson and the man is as pure as the driven snow. Born in Exeter in 1912, son of a solicitor; normal schooling but flunked university entrance to his father's disappointment. Did clerical work for a firm in Plymouth and rose to be the boss of a rather small department. Joined the army in 1940 – rose to be a sergeant in the RASC – he was an ideal quarter-master type. Demobilized in 1946, he went to work for Ashton, running the firm's office. There he ran into the Peter Principle; he was all right as long as the firm remained small but, with expansion, it became too much for him. Remember he never rose to be more than a sergeant – he was a small-scale man. So Ashton converted him into a general factotum which would seem to be ideal for Benson. There'd be nothing too big for him to handle, and he was glad to be of service. Ashton probably got his money's worth out of him. He never married. What do you think of all that?'

'Did you get that from the computer?'

'No. The brains are still baffled. They're telling me now Benson can't be in the data bank.'

'They're wrong,' I said flatly. 'He popped up when I asked Nellie.'

Ogilvie looked at me doubtfully, then said, 'But what do you think of his history as I've related it?'

'There's nothing there to say why he should kill Ashton. There's nothing there to say why he should be carrying a gun in the first place. Did he have a pistol permit?'

'No.'

'Have you traced the gun?'

Ogilvie shrugged. 'How can we? The Swedes have it.' He pondered for a moment, then opened a quarto-sized, hard-backed notebook and took the cap off his pen. 'I wanted to go for the main point first, but now you'll tell me, in detail, everything that happened right from the time Ashton and Benson left their flat in Stockholm.'

That took the rest of the morning. At quarter to one Ogilvie recapped his pen. 'That's it, then. Now you can go home.'

'Am I suspended from duty?'

He looked at me from lowered eyebrows. 'There are a few people around who would like to see you fired. Others favour a transfer to the Outer Hebrides so you can counter industrial espionage into the production of Harris Tweed; they're talking about a twenty year tour of duty. Have you any idea of the trouble this enterprise of ours has caused?'

'I have a good imagination.'

He snorted. 'Have you? Well, imagine how the Swedes felt about it, and imagine their reaction when we began to put on the pressure at a high level. It got up to the Cabinet, you know, and the Ministers aren't at all happy. They're talking about bungling amateurs.'

I opened my mouth to speak, but he held up his hand. 'No, you're not suspended from duty. What you did was under my instruction, and I can't see that you could have done differently given the circumstances. Neither of us expected Benson to kill Ashton, so if anyone carries the can it's me, as head of the department. But this department is now under extreme pressure. There's an inter-departmental meeting tomorrow morning at eleven at which the screws will begin to turn. You will be required to attend. So you will go away now and come back here at ten-fifteen tomorrow, rested and refreshed, and prepared to have a hard time. Do you understand?'

'Yes.'

'And I would be obliged if you do not disclose to the committee that you are aware of the Ashton file in Code Black. We're in enough trouble already.'

I stood up. 'All right, but I'd like to know one thing – what happened to the bodies?'

'Ashton and Benson? They were brought back to England two weeks ago. There was a funeral service in Marlow and they are buried in adjoining graves in the cemetery there.'

'How did Penny take it?'

'As you might expect. Both the daughters were hit rather badly. I wasn't there myself, of course, but I was informed of the circumstances. I managed to have word passed to Miss Ashton that you were in America but were expected back in the near future. I thought that advisable.'

Advisable and tactful. 'Thanks,' I said.

'Now go away and prepare your thoughts for tomorrow.' I walked towards the door, and he added, 'And Malcolm: regardless of how the meeting goes, I want you to know there is much still to be explained about the Ashton case – and it will be explained. I am becoming very angry about this.'

As I left I thought that Ogilvie angry might be formidable indeed.

I was left to my own thoughts for a long time while the committee meeting was in progress; it was twelve-fifteen before an usher entered the ante-room and said, 'Will you come this way, Mr Jaggard.' I followed him and was shown into a large, airy room overlooking an inner courtyard somewhere in Westminster.

There was a long, walnut table around which sat a group of men, all well-dressed and well-fed, and all in late middle-age. It could have been the annual meeting of the directors of a City bank but for the fact that one of them wore the uniform of a Commander of the Metropolitan Police and another was a red-tabbed colonel from the General Staff. Ogilvie twisted in his chair as I entered and indicated I should take the empty seat next to him.

Chairing the meeting was a Cabinet Minister whose politics I didn't agree with and whose personality I had always thought of as vacillating in the extreme. He showed no trace of vacillation that morning, and ran the meeting like a company sergeant-major. He said, 'Mr Jaggard, we have been discussing the recent Swedish operation in which you were involved, and in view of certain differences of opinion Mr Ogilvie has suggested that you appear to answer our questions yourself.'

I nodded, but the colonel snorted. 'Differences of opinion is putting it mildly.'

'That has nothing to do with Mr Jaggard, Colonel Morton,' said the Minister.

'Hasn't it?' Morton addressed me directly. 'Are you aware, young man, that you've lost me my best man in Scandinavia? His cover is blown completely.'

I concluded that Morton was Henty's boss.

The Minister tapped the table with his pen and Morton subsided. 'The questions we shall ask are very simple and we expect clear-cut, unequivocal answers. Is that understood?'

'Yes.'

'Very well. Who killed Ashton?'

'I didn't see who shot him. Henty told me it was Benson.'

There was a stir from lower down the table. 'But you don't know that he did, other than that you have been told so.'

I turned and looked at Lord Cregar. 'That is correct. But I have, and still have, no reason to disbelieve Henty. He told me immediately after the event.'

'After he had killed Benson?'

'That's right.'

Cregar regarded me and smiled thinly. 'Now, from what you know of Benson, and I'm assuming you had the man investigated, can you give me one reason why Benson should kill the man he had so faithfully served for thirty years?'

'I can think of no sound reason,' I said.

His lip curled a little contemptuously. 'Can you think of any unsound reasons?'

Ogilvie said tartly, 'Mr Jaggard is not here to answer stupid questions.'

The Minister said sharply, 'We shall do better if the questions are kept simple, as I suggested.'

'Very well,' said Cregar. 'Here is a simple question. Why did you order Henty to kill Benson?'

'I didn't,' I said. 'I didn't even know he was armed. The rest of us weren't; those were Mr Ogilvie's instructions. Henty was in a different department.'

Colonel Morton said, 'You mean Henty acted on his own initiative?'

'I do. It all happened within a matter of, say, twenty seconds. At the time Benson was killed I was trying to help Ashton.'

Morton leaned forward. 'Now, think carefully, Mr Jaggard. My men are not in the habit of leaving bodies carelessly strewn about the landscape. What reason did Henty give for shooting Benson?'

'Self-defence. He said Benson was shooting at him, so he shot back.'

Colonel Morton leaned back and appeared satisfied, but Cregar said to the company at large, 'This man, Benson,

Cregar overrode him. '. . . all the events since have ·oved my point. He let Ashton slip from under his nose at time when he had free access to Ashton's home. That :cessitated the Swedish operation which he has also ›tched, and botched for good, if I may say so, because ;hton is now dead. As for claiming that all he did was on ›ur direct instructions, you have just heard him admit to sobeying your orders.'

'He used his initiative at a critical time.'

'And with what result? The death of Ashton,' said Cregar :vastatingly. 'You have expounded before on the initiative ' this man. I wasn't impressed then, and I'm still less ıpressed now.'

'That will be enough,' said the Minister chillily. 'We will ave no more of this. Are there any more questions for Mr ıggard? Questions that are both simple and relevant, ease.' No one spoke, so he said, 'Very well, Mr Jaggard. ıat will be all.'

Ogilvie said in an undertone, 'Wait for me outside.'

As I walked to the door Cregar was saying, 'Well, that's ıe end of the Ashton case – after thirty long years. He was failure, of course; never did come up to expectations. I ıggest we drop it and get on to something more productive. I think . . .'

What Cregar thought was cut off by the door closing :hind me.

ıey came out of committee twenty minutes later. Ogilvie uck his head into the ante-room. 'Let's have lunch,' he :oposed. He didn't seem too depressed at what had happened, but he never did show much emotion.

As we were walking along Whitehall he said, 'What do ›u think?'

I summoned a hard-fought-for smile. 'I think Cregar ›esn't like me.'

seems to be acting more and more out of character. Here we have an old age pensioner behaving like Billy the Kid. I find it unbelievable.'

Ogilvie dipped his fingers into a waistcoat pocket and put something on the table with a click. 'This is a round of 9 mm parabellum found in Benson's room in Marlow. It would fit the pistol found with Benson's body. And we know that the bullet recovered from Ashton's body came from that pistol. We got that from the Swedes.'

'Precisely,' said Cregar. 'All you know is what the Swedes told you. How much is that really worth?'

'Are you suggesting that Benson did not kill Ashton?' asked Morton. There was a note of sourness in his voice.

'I consider it highly unlikely,' said Cregar.

'I don't employ men who are stupid enough to lie to me,' said Morton, in a voice that could cut diamonds. 'Henty said he saw Benson kill Ashton, and I believe him. All the evidence we have heard so far does not contradict that.'

Ogilvie said, 'Unless Lord Cregar is suggesting that my department, Colonel Morton's department and Swedish Army Intelligence are in a conspiracy to put the blame for Ashton's death on Benson and so shield the killer.' His voice was filled with incredulity.

The uniformed commander guffawed and Cregar flushed. 'No,' he snapped. 'I'm just trying to get to the bottom of something damned mysterious. Why, for instance, *should* Benson shoot Ashton?'

'He is not here to be asked,' said the Minister coolly. 'I suggest we stop this chasing of hares and address ourselves to Mr Jaggard.'

The Commander leaned forward and talked to me around Ogilvie. 'I'm Pearson – Special Branch. This Swedish operation isn't my bailiwick but I'm interested for professional reasons. As I take it, Mr Ogilvie did not want Ashton to become aware that British Intelligence was taking note of him. Do you know why?'

That was a tricky one because I wasn't supposed to know who Ashton really was. I said, 'I suggest you refer that question to Mr Ogilvie.'

'Quite so,' said the Minister. 'It involves information to which Mr Jaggard is not privy.'

'Very well,' said Pearson. 'At the same time he wanted Ashton out of Sweden because the Russians had become attracted, so he put pressure on Ashton by having a man pretend to be Russian and thus "explode Ashton out of Sweden", as he has put it. What I don't understand is why this kidnapping attempt in Strängnäs was necessary. Why did you try it?'

I said, 'They took tickets from Stockholm to Göteborg. That was all right with me. I intended to shepherd them along and, if they took ship from Göteborg to find out where they were going. The important thing was to get them out from under the Russians in Sweden. But when they gave us the slip and went to Strängnäs it became something more complex than a discreet escort operation. Stronger measures were necessary as sanctioned by Mr Ogilvie.'

'I see,' said Pearson. 'That was the point I misunderstood.'

'I misunderstood something, too,' said Cregar. 'Are we to assume that your instructions precluded the disclosure of yourself to Ashton?'

'Yes.'

'Yet according to what I've been told you did so. We have been informed by Mr Ogilvie this morning that you showed yourself to him deliberately. It was only when he saw you that he turned back. Is that not so?'

'That's correct.'

'So you disobeyed orders.'

I said nothing because he hadn't asked a questi
barked, 'Well, didn't you?'

'Yes.'

'I see. You admit it. Now, with all respect t
Morton's trust in the truthfulness of his staff, I'm
fied by the somewhat misty evidence presented
Benson shot Ashton; but the fact remains that As
shot by someone, and it is highly likely that he
because he turned back. In other words, he died beca
disobeyed an order not to disclose yourself.' His v
scathing. 'Why did you disobey the order?'

I was seething with rage but managed to keep m
even. 'The idea was not to kill Ashton but to bring
alive. At that time he was going into grave danger.
was heavy fire in that part of the forest where h
heading – machine-guns and mortars, together wi
fire. Just what was going on I didn't know. It seemed i
ative to stop him and he did stop and started to come
That he was shot by Benson came as a complete shock

'But *you* don't know he was shot by Benson,' obje
Cregar.

The Minister tapped with his pen. 'We have already
over that ground. Lord Cregar.'

'Very well.' Cregar regarded me and said si
'Wouldn't you say that your conduct of this whole o
tion, right from the beginning, has been characteriz
shall we say, a lack of expertise?'

Ogilvie bristled. 'What Mr Jaggard has done ha
on my direct instruction. You have no right or au
to criticize my staff like this. Address your critic
me, sir.'

'Very well, I will,' said Cregar. 'Right at the be
I objected to your putting Jaggard on this case,
the . . .'

'That's not my recollection,' snapped Ogilvie.

'Did you hear what he said as you were leaving?'

'Something about the Ashton case being over, wasn't it?'

'Yes. Ashton is buried and that buries the Ashton case. He's wrong, you know.'

'Why?'

'Because from now on until everything is accounted for and wrapped up you are going to work full time on the Ashton case.' He paused, then said meditatively, 'I wonder what we'll find.'

TWENTY-SIX

In view of what had been said at the meeting Ogilvie's decision came as a profound surprise. The worst possibility that had come to mind was that I would be fired; drummed out of the department after my special card had been put through the office shredding machine. The best that occurred to me was a downgrading or a sideways promotion. I had the idea that Ogilvie had not been entirely joking when he had spoken of the Hebrides. That he was carrying on with the Ashton case, and putting me in charge, gave me a jolt. I wondered how he was going to make it stick with the Minister.

He told me. 'The Minister won't know a damned thing about it.' He gave me a wintry smile. 'The advantage of organizations like ours is that we really are equipped to work in secret.'

This conversation took place in the privacy of his office. He had refused to speak of the case at all after dropping his bombshell and the luncheon conversation had been innocuous. Back at the office he plunged into the heart of it.

'What I am about to do is unethical and possibly mutinous,' he said. 'But, in this case, I think I'm justified.'

'Why?' I asked directly. If I was going to be involved I wanted to know the true issues.

'Because someone has done a conjuring trick. This department has been deceived and swindled. Who organized the deception is for you to find out – it may have been Ashton himself, for all we know. But I want to know who organized it, and why.'

'Why pick me? As Cregar made plain, I've not done too well up to now.'

Ogilvie raised his eyebrows. 'You think not? You've satisfied me, and I'm the only man who matters. There are several reasons why I've picked you. First, you're the totally unexpected choice. Secondly, you are still the inside man in the Ashton family. Thirdly, I have complete confidence in you.'

I stood up and went to the window. A couple of pigeons were engaged in amorous play on the window ledge but flew away as I approached. I turned and said, 'I'm grateful for your thirdly, but not too happy about your secondly. As you know, I dropped into the middle of the Ashton case sheerly by chance and ever since then my private life has been intolerably disturbed. I have just harried a man to his death and you expect me to be *persona grata* with his daughters?'

'Penelope Ashton doesn't know of your involvement. I made sure of that.'

'That's not the point, and you know it,' I said sharply. 'You're too intelligent a man not to know what I mean. You're asking me to live a lie with the woman I want to marry – if she still wants to marry me, that is.'

'I appreciate the difficulty,' said Ogilvie quietly. 'You mustn't think I don't. But . . .'

'And don't ask me to do it for the good of the department,' I said. 'I hope I have higher loyalties than that.'

Ogilvie quirked his eyebrows. 'Your country, perhaps?'

'Even than that.'

'So you believe with E. M. Forster that if you had to choose between betraying your country and betraying your friend you would hope to have the guts to betray your country. Is that it?'

'I'm not aware that betraying my country comes into this,' I said stiffly.

'Oh, I don't know,' said Ogilvie musingly. 'Betrayal takes many forms. Inaction can be as much betrayal as action, especially for a man who has chosen your work of his own will. If you see a man walking on a bridge which you know to be unsafe, and you do not warn him so that he falls to his death, you are guilty in law of culpable homicide. So with betrayal.'

'Those are mere words,' I said coolly. 'You talk about betrayal of the country when all I see is an interdepartmental squabble in which your *amour propre* has been dented. You loathe Cregar as much as he loathes you.'

Ogilvie looked up. 'How does Cregar come into this? Do you know something definite?'

'He's been trying to poke his nose in, hasn't he? Right from the beginning.'

'Oh, is that all,' said Ogilvie tiredly. 'It's just the nature of the beast. He's a natural scorer of points; it feeds his enormous ego. I wouldn't jump to conclusions about Cregar.' He stood up and faced me. 'But I really am sorry about your opinion of me. I thought I deserved better than that.'

'Oh, Christ!' I said. 'I'm sorry; I didn't really mean that. It's just that this thing with Penny has me all mixed up. The thought of talking to her – lying to her – makes me cringe inside.'

'Unfortunately it goes with the job. We're liars by profession, you and I. We say to the world we work for McCulloch and Ross, economic and industrial consultants, and that's a lie. Do you think my wife and daughters really know what I do? I lie to them every minute of every day merely by existing. At least Penny Ashton knows what you are.'

'Not all of it,' I said bitterly.

'You're not to blame for Ashton's death.'

I raised my voice. 'No? I drove him to it.'

'But you didn't kill him. Who did?'

'Benson did, damn it!'

Ogilvie raised his voice to a shout. 'Then find out why, for God's sake! Don't do it for me, or even for yourself. All her life that girl of yours has been living in the same house as the man who eventually murdered her father. Find out why he did it – you might even be doing it for her sake.'

We both stopped short suddenly and there was silence in the room. I said quietly, 'You might have made your point – at last.'

He sat down. 'You're a hard man to convince. You mean I've done it?'

'I suppose so.'

He sighed. 'Then sit down and listen to me.' I obliged him, and he said, 'You're going to be in disgrace for a while. Everybody will expect that, including the Minister. Some sort of downgrading is indicated, so I'm going to make you a courier. That gives you freedom of action to move around in this country, and even out of it.' He smiled. 'But I'd hesitate about going back to Sweden.'

So would I. Captain Morelius would become positively voluble, even to the extent of speaking three consecutive sentences. And I knew what he'd say.

'We've been making quite a noise in here,' said Ogilvie. 'Had a real shouting match. Well, that will add verisimilitude to an otherwise bald and unconvincing narrative. There's one thing about being in an organization of spies – news gets around fast. You may expect some comments from your colleagues; can you stand that?'

I shrugged. 'I've never worried much about what people think of me.'

'Yes,' he agreed. 'Cregar discovered that when he first met you. All right; you'll have complete autonomy on this job. You'll do it in the way you want to do it, but it will be a solo operation; you'll have all the assistance I can give you short of men. You'll report your results to me and to no one else. And I do expect results.'

He opened a drawer and took out a slim file. 'Now, as for Penny Ashton, I laid some groundwork which will possibly help you. As far as she knows you have been in America for the past few weeks. I hope you didn't write from Sweden.'

'I didn't.'

'Good. She has been tactfully informed that you have been away on some mysterious job that has debarred you from writing to her. Knowing what she thinks she knows about your work it should seem feasible to her. However, you were informed of her father's death through the department, and you sent this cable.'

He passed the slip of paper across the desk. It was a genuine Western Union carbon copy emanating from Los Angeles. The content was trite and conventional, but it would have to do.

Ogilvie said, 'You also arranged for wreaths at the funeral through a Los Angeles flower shop and Interflora. The receipt from the flower shop is in this file together with other bits and pieces which a man might expect to pick up on a visit and still retain. There are theatre ticket stubs for current shows in Los Angeles, some small denomination American bills, book matches from hotels, and so on. Empty your pockets.'

The request took me by surprise and I hesitated. 'Come now,' he said. 'Dump everything on the desk.'

I stripped my pockets. As I took out my wallet Ogilvie delved in the small change I had produced. 'You see,' he said in triumph, and held up a coin. 'A Swedish crown mixed with your English money. It could have been a dead giveaway. I'll bet you have a couple of Swedish items in your wallet. Get rid of them.'

He was right. There was a duplicate bar bill from the Grand which had yet to be transferred to my expense account, and a list of pound-kroner exchange rates made when I was trying to keep up with the vagaries of the falling pound sterling. I exchanged them for the Americana, and said, 'You were sure of me, after all.'

'Pretty sure,' he said drily. 'You got back from the States yesterday. Here is your air ticket – you can leave it lying around conspicuously somewhere. Penny Ashton, to the best of my knowledge, is coming back from Scotland tomorrow. You didn't buy any Swedish clothing?'

'No.'

'There are a couple of shirts and some socks in that small case over there. Also some packets of cigarettes. All genuine American. Now, leave here, go back to your office and mope disconsolately. You've just been through the meat grinder and you can still feel the teeth. I expect Harrison will want to see you in about half an hour. Don't try to score any points off him; let him have his little triumph. Remember you're a beaten man, Malcolm – and good luck.'

So I went back to the office and slumped behind my desk. Larry rustled his paper and avoided my eyes, but presently he said, 'I hear you were with the top brass all morning.'

'Yes,' I said shortly.

'Was Cregar there?'

'Yes.'

'Bad?'

'You'll know all about it soon,' I said gloomily. 'I don't think I'll be around here much longer.'

'Oh.' Larry fell silent for a while, then he turned a page and said, 'I'm sorry, Malcolm. It wasn't your fault.'

'Somebody has to get the axe.'

'Mmm. No, what I meant is I'm sorry about you and Penny. It's going to be difficult.'

I smiled at him. 'Thanks, Larry. You're right, but I think I'll make out.'

Ogilvie was right in his prediction. Within the hour Harrison rang and told me to report to his office. I went in trying to appear subdued and for once did not address him as Joe, neither did I sit down.

He kept me standing. 'I understand from Mr Ogilvie that you are leaving this section.'

'I understand so, too.'

'You are to report to Mr Kerr tomorrow.' His eyes glinted with ill-suppressed joy. He had always thought me too big for my britches and now I was demoted to messenger-boy – thus are the mighty fallen. 'This is really very difficult, you know,' he said fretfully. 'I'm afraid I'll have to ask you to clean out your desk before you leave today. There'll be another man coming in, of course.'

'Of course,' I said colourlessly. 'I'll do that.'

'Right,' he said, and paused. I thought for a moment he was going to give me a homily on the subject of mending my ways, but all he said was, 'You may leave, Jaggard.'

I went and cleared out my desk.

TWENTY-SEVEN

I trotted in to see Kerr next morning. He was one of several Section heads, but his Section was the only one to make a financial profit because, among other things, it ran the legitimate side of McCulloch and Ross, the bit the public knew about. It made a good profit, too, and so it ought; if it made a loss with all the professional expertise of the other sections behind it then Kerr ought to have been fired. Under Kerr also came several other miscellaneous bits and pieces including the couriers – the messenger-boys.

He seemed somewhat at a loss as to how to deal with me. 'Ah, yes – Jaggard. I think I have something here for you.' He handed me a large, thick envelope, heavily sealed. 'I'm told you know where to deliver that. It appears that . . . er . . . delivery may take some time, so you may be absent for a period.'

'That's so.'

'I see,' he said blankly. 'Will you be needing desk space – an office?'

'No, I don't think so.'

'I'm glad. We're tight for space.' He smiled. 'Glad to have you . . . er . . . with us,' he said uncertainly. I don't know what Ogilvie had told him but evidently he was baffled by my precise status.

In my car I opened the envelope and found £1000 in used fivers. That was thoughtful of Ogilvie but, after all, I could hardly claim expenses in the normal way on this operation. I put the money in the special locker built under the front passenger seat and drove to the police station in Marlow where I asked for Honnister. He came out front to meet me. 'You haven't been around for a while,' he said, almost accusingly. 'I've been trying to get you.'

'I've been in the States for a few weeks. What did you want me for?'

'Oh, just a chat,' he said vaguely. 'You must have been away when Ashton and Benson were killed in Sweden.'

'Yes, but I was told of it.'

'Funny thing, Ashton going away like that.' There was a glint in his eye. 'And then getting messily killed. Makes a man wonder.'

I took out a packet of cigarettes and offered it. 'Wonder what?'

'Well, a man like Ashton makes his pile by working hard and then, when he's still not too old to enjoy it, he suddenly gets dead.' He looked at the packet in my hand. 'No, I don't like American coffin nails. They take good Virginia tobacco, mix it with Turkish, then roast it and toast it and ultraviolet-ray it until it tastes like nothing on God's earth.'

I shrugged. 'Everybody dies. And you can't take it with you, although they tell me Howard Hughes tried.'

'Seen Penelope Ashton?'

'Not yet.' I lit a cigarette although I didn't like them, either. 'I'll be going to the house. I hear she's expected back today. If she's not there I'll see Gillian anyway.'

'And she'll see you,' said Honnister. 'But only barely. I had a talk with Crammond. He tells me Mayberry hasn't been brought to trial, and it's not likely that he will. He's unfit to plead.'

'Yes, I know about that.'

Honnister eyed the desk sergeant and then pushed himself upright from the counter. 'Let's have a noggin,' he proposed. I agreed quickly because it meant he wanted to talk confidentially and I was short of information. On the way to the pub he said, 'You didn't come to chat for old times' sake. What are you after?'

I said, 'When we started investigating we concentrated on Ashton and didn't look too closely at Benson, although at one point it did cross my mind that he might have chucked the acid.'

'Not the act of an old family servant.'

Neither was drilling his master full of holes – but I didn't say that aloud. 'Did you check on him?'

We turned into the Coach and Horses. 'A bit; enough to put him in the clear.' Honnister addressed the landlord. 'Hi, Monte; a large scotch and a pint of Director's.'

'My shout,' I said.

'It's okay – I'm on an expense account.'

I smiled. 'So am I.' I paid for the drinks and we took them to a table. It happened to be the same table at which I'd proposed marriage to Penny; it seemed a lifetime ago. It was early, just before midday, and the pub was quiet. I said, 'I've developed an interest in Benson.'

Honnister sank his nose into his beer. When he came up for air he said, 'There's been something funny going on in the Ashton family. This will have to be tit-for-tat, you know.'

'I'll tell you as much as I'm allowed to.'

He grunted. 'A fat lot of good that'll do me.' He held up his hand. 'All right, I know your lips are sealed and all that bull, and that I'm just a bumbling country copper who doesn't know which end is up – but tell me one thing: was Ashton kidnapped?'

I smiled at Honnister's description of himself which was a downright lie. 'No, he went under his own steam. He specifically asked that the police not be involved.'

'So he thought we might be. That's interesting in itself. And Benson went with him. What do you want to know about him?'

'Anything you can tell me that I don't know already. I'm scraping the bottom of the barrel.'

'Bachelor – never married. Worked for Ashton since the dark ages – butler, valet, handyman, chauffeur – you name it. Age at death, sixty-four, if you can believe *The Times*.'

'Any family – brothers or sisters?'

'No family at all.' Honnister grinned at me. 'As soon as I saw that bit in *The Times* I got busy. The itch in my bump of curiosity was driving me mad. Benson had a bit of money, about fifteen thousand quid, which he left to Dr Barnardo's Homes for Boys.'

'Anything else?' I asked, feeling depressed.

'Ever been in a war?' asked Honnister unexpectedly,

'No.'

'Seen any deaths by violence?'

'A few.'

'So have I, in my professional capacity. I've also seen the results of bombs and shellfire. It was a bit difficult to tell after a pathologist had been at them but I'd say Ashton had been shot in the back twice, and Benson shot through the head from the front. Caught in a shell blast, my arse!'

'You've seen the bodies!'

'I made it my business to – unofficially, of course. I went to the mortuary here. I told you my bump of curiosity was itching.'

'Charlie, you keep that under your bloody hat or you'll find yourself in dead trouble. I really mean that.'

'I told you before I can keep secrets,' he said equably. 'Anyway, Sweden isn't in my parish, so there's nothing I can do about it. If they were killed in Sweden,' he added as an afterthought.

'They were killed in Sweden,' I said. 'That's genuine. And they *were* killed in a Swedish battle practice area while manoeuvres were going on.' I paused. 'Probably *The Times* got the report wrong.'

'In a pig's eye,' said Honnister pointedly.

I shrugged. 'Anyone else here seen the bodies?'

'Not that I know of. The coffins arrived here sealed and complete with death certificates, probably signed by one of your department's tame doctors. Christ, talk about medical ethics! Anyway, they're underground now.'

'Any more about Benson?'

'Not much. He lived a quiet life. He had a woman in Slough but he gave that up about five years ago.'

'What's her name?'

'It won't do you any good,' he said. 'She died of cancer eighteen months ago. Benson paid for her treatment in a private ward – for old times' sake, I suppose. Other than that there's nothing I can tell you. There was nothing much to Benson; he was just a sort of old-maid bachelor with nothing remarkable about him. Except one thing.'

'What was that?'

'His face. He'd taken a hell of a beating at one time or other. Nature didn't make him like that – man did.'

'Yes,' I said. I was bloody tired of coming up against dead ends. I thought about it and decided that my best bet would be to look into Benson's army career but I wasn't sanguine that anything would come of that.

'Another drink?'

'No, thanks, Charlie. I want to see the Ashtons.'

'Give them my regards,' he said.

I drove to the Ashton house and, to my surprise, bumped into Michaelis who was just leaving. Under his arm he carried a loose-leaf ledger about as big as two bibles. 'What the devil are you doing here?'

He grinned. 'Playing puff-puffs. You know I'm interested and Miss Ashton gave me permission to mess about in the attic pretty nearly any time I like. It really is a fascinating set-up.'

I suppose it wasn't too weird that a counter-espionage agent should be nuts on model railways. I indicated the big book. 'What's that?'

'Now this is really interesting,' he said. 'Let me show you.' He rested the book on the bonnet of my car. The letters 'LMS' were inscribed on the leather-bound cover in gilt. 'This is a set of timetables for the old LMS – the London, Midland and Scottish railway that was before nationalization. Effectively speaking, the railways were nationalized in 1939 and all the trains were steam in those days.'

He opened the book and I saw column after column of figures. 'Ashton was duplicating the LMS timetable, but I haven't figured out which year he was using so I'm taking this home to check against some old Bradshaws I have. Ashton's system up there in the attic isn't what you'd call standard practice in the model world – most of us can't afford what he'd got. I told you about those microprocessors he can program. These figures give the settings needed to the control panel to duplicate parts of the LMS timetable. He'd also got similar books for other pre-war railway companies – the London and North-Eastern, the Great Western and so on. It's bloody remarkable.'

'Indeed it is,' I said. 'Which Miss Ashton gave you permission?'

'Gillian. I talked to her a lot in hospital, about her father at the beginning, but one thing led to another. She was lonely, you know, being all bandaged up like that. I used to read books and newspapers for her. Anyway, I talked about the model railway and she found I was interested so she said I could come and play.'

'I see.'

'Gillian's a very nice girl,' he said. 'We get on very well.' He paused. 'I don't spend all my time in the attic'

I studied Michaelis in a new light. It occurred to me that he was unmarried like myself and, if all went well with both of us, I was probably talking to my future brother-in-law. 'Is Gillian home now?'

'Yes – and she's expecting Penny for lunch.' He slammed the ledger closed. 'I heard on the grapevine what's happened to you. I think it's a bloody disgrace. Who the hell was to know . . .'

I interrupted. 'The less said about it the better, even in private. Don't talk about it at all – ever. That way nothing will slip out accidentally.' I consulted my watch. 'If you're so chummy with Gillian I thought you might be staying for lunch.'

He shook his head. 'I don't feel like facing Penny so I made an excuse. You see. Penny hasn't told Gillian about us – the department, I mean. She doesn't know anything about it and that makes it easier. But I haven't seen Penny since we came back from Sweden and I haven't the guts to face her yet – not after what happened. I have a weird feeling she might read my mind.'

'Yes,' I agreed. 'It is bloody difficult.'

'You're more involved than I am,' he said. 'How do you feel about it?'

'Pretty much the same as you, but maybe a bit more so. Well, I'll go in and see Gillian. See you around.'

'Yes,' said Michaelis. 'I hope so.'

TWENTY-EIGHT

I had forgotten that Gillian was not very pretty to look at and she came as a renewed shock. Her face was puckered and drawn with scar tissue and her right eyelid was pulled almost closed. The first few moments were not at all easy; there was the double embarrassment of condoling on the death of her father and coping with her dreadful appearance, and I hoped my face did not reflect what I felt. But she put me at my ease, gave me a scotch and had a sherry herself.

Of her father she had little to say beyond expressing a puzzled sadness and a total lack of knowledge of his motives. 'What can I say? There *is* nothing to be said, except that I'm deeply sorry and totally bewildered.'

Of herself she had come to terms with her affliction and was prepared to talk about it. 'Of course, it will be better after the plastic surgery. I'm told the best man for that is in America, and Penny wants me to go over. But my face is not so nice now, and I don't go out much.' She smiled lopsidedly. 'I saw you talking to Peter Michaelis outside. Do you know him?'

I said carefully, 'I met him at the hospital.'

'Oh, yes; you would, of course.' She smiled again, and there was a happy sparkle in her good eye. 'One never thinks of policemen as ordinary human beings – just shadows dashing about on television arresting people. Peter is such a delightful man.'

I agreed that a policeman's lot, etc., 'Must cramp their social lives.'

'He just told me about Mayberry. It appears the man is quite insane. Penny told me about . . . about the mistake.'

'So you know.'

'She waited until I'd been home a few days. I suppose she was right to withhold it until then. I wasn't in any condition to take more shocks. But how awful for her. It took a great deal of straight talking from me to make her carry on with Professor Lumsden.'

'I'm glad you did.'

Gillian looked at me closely. 'There's something wrong between you and Penny, isn't there? I think she's unhappy about it. What is it, Malcolm?'

'I don't know if the trouble altogether concerns me,' I said. 'I rather think she's unhappy about what happened to you, and then to your father.'

'No,' she said pensively. 'She appears to involve you in it, and I don't know why. She won't talk about it, and that's unlike her.' She turned her head to the window as a car drew up. 'Here she is now. You'll stay for lunch, of course.'

'Glad to.'

I was pleased to find that Penny was pleased to see me. 'Oh, Malcolm!' she cried, and hurried to meet me. I met her half way across the room, took her in my arms, and kissed her.

'I was very sorry to hear about your father.'

She looked beyond me to where Gillian sat, and said quietly, 'I want to talk to you about that afterwards.'

I nodded. 'Very well.'

'A sherry,' she said. 'A sherry, to save my life. Lummy and I have talked our throats dry this morning.'

So we had lunch, at which we chatted amiably and kept away from controversial subjects. We discussed Gillian's forthcoming trip to the United States, and Penny asked about my experiences there. 'I was told where you were,' she said obliquely.

Later she said, 'Gillian and I have decided to sell the house. It's much too big for the two of us, so we've decided to set ourselves up in a decent flat in town. Gillian will be closer to the theatres and concert halls, and I won't have to commute to the lab.'

'That sounds sensible,' I said. 'When do you move?'

'I'll be going to America with Gillian,' she said. 'We're selecting some of the best pieces from here and the rest will be auctioned, the antiques at Sotheby's and the rest of the stuff from the house. But we'll be in America then. I couldn't bear to stay and see the place sold up. So I suppose the auction will be in about three weeks. I'm making the final arrangements this afternoon.'

And that would put paid to Michaelis's fun and games with the model railway. I wondered if he was preparing to put in a bid.

After lunch Gillian pleaded tiredness and went to rest in her room, but I rather think she wanted to leave us alone together. Penny and I sat before the blazing fire with a pot of coffee and I could tell she was getting set for a serious discussion. 'Malcolm,' she said, 'what's the truth about Daddy?'

I offered her one of my American cigarettes which she took. 'I don't think anyone will ever know.'

'Did he die the way they said? You must know, being who you are, even though you were in America at the time. You were investigating him, after all.'

'My information is that he was in a Swedish army proving ground where they were using live ammunition when he was killed.'

'And that's the truth?' she said steadily. 'You wouldn't he to me?'

'That's the truth.' But not the whole truth, Jaggard, you bastard!

She was silent for a while, gazing into the flames. 'I don't understand,' she said at last. 'I don't understand any of it. What was he doing in Sweden?'

'Apparently nothing very much, from what I can gather. He was living quietly in Stockholm with Benson to look after him. He read a lot and went to the occasional concert. A quiet and placid life.'

'How do you know this?'

'The department checked, of course.'

'Of course,' she said colourlessly. 'I'm going to Sweden. I want to find out for myself. Will you come with me?'

That was a poser! I could imagine the expression on the face of the colonel of the Royal Södermanland Regiment if I poked my nose into Strängnäs again. I needed no imagination at all to picture the cold grey eyes of Captain Morelius of Swedish Army Intelligence.

'That may not be easy,' I said. 'I've just been transferred and my time isn't my own.'

'Transferred from your department?'

'No, just within the department, but I may be office-bound from now on. Still, I'll see what I can do.' Which would be precisely nothing. 'Look, Penny, how would it be if I arranged for you to talk with my chief? He can tell you all that's known about your father in Sweden.' And he can tell my damned lies for me, I thought savagely.

She thought about it, then said, 'Very well. But that doesn't mean I'm not going to Sweden.'

'I'll arrange it.' I rose to pour us some more coffee. 'Penny, what's happening to us? I still want to marry you, but every time I get near the subject you edge away. I'm very much in love with you and it's becoming damned frustrating. Have you turned off?'

She cried, 'Oh, Malcolm, I'm sorry; I really am. Everything turned topsy-turvy so suddenly. First there was Gillian, then Daddy – and then you. I've been going about looking at people I know and wondering if what I think I know is really so. Even Lummy has come under scrutiny – I'm beginning to worry him, I think. He imagines I'm going paranoid.'

'It's not been too easy for me, either,' I said. 'I didn't want to have anything to do with the Ashton case.'

'The Ashton case,' she repeated. 'Is that what they call it?' When I nodded, she said, 'That takes the humanity out of it, doesn't it? When it's a "case" it's easy to forget the flesh and blood because a case is mostly dockets and paperwork. How would you like to be referred to as the Jaggard case?'

'Not much,' I said sombrely.

Penny took my hand. 'Malcolm, you'll have to give me time. I think – no – I *know* I love you, but I'm still a bit mixed up; and I don't know that I'm too happy about what you do with your life. That's something else which needs thinking about.'

'My God!' I said. 'You make it sound as though I go about eating live babies. I'm just a dreary counter-espionage man specializing in industry and making sure too many secrets don't get pinched.'

'You mean weapons?'

I shook my head. 'Not necessarily. That's not our pigeon – and we're not interested in the latest toothpaste additive, either. But if an engineering firm has ploughed a couple of millions into research and come up with something revolutionary, then we don't want some foreign Johnny nicking it and going into competition with a head start And, don't forget, the foreign Johnnies from the East are state supported.'

'But these things are patented, aren't they?'

'Patents are a dead giveaway. The really big stuff isn't patented, especially in electronics. If you produce a new electronic chip which does the work of eleventy thousand transistors the opposition can put the thing under a microscope and see what you've done, but how the hell you've done it is quite another thing, and our boys aren't telling. They're certainly not going to disclose the process in a published patent.'

'I see,' she said. 'But that means you're just another sort of policeman.'

'Most of the time,' I said. 'Our problem is that the theft of information, as such, is not illegal in this country. Suppose I stole a sheet of paper from your lab, say, and I was caught. I'd be found guilty of the theft of a piece of paper worth one penny, and I'd suffer the appropriate penalty. The fact that written on that paper was some formula worth a million quid wouldn't count'

Her voice rose. 'But that's silly.'

'I agree,' I said. 'Do you want to hear something really silly? A few years ago a chap was caught tapping a post office line. The only charge they could get him on was the theft of a quantity of electricity, the property of the Postmaster-General. It was about a millionth of a watt.' Penny laughed, and I said, 'Anyway, that's my job, and it doesn't seem all that heinous to me.'

'Nor to me, now you've explained it. But where did Daddy come into this?'

I said, 'You may not realize how important a man your father was. The catalysts he was developing were revolutionizing the economics of the oil industry and helping the economics of the country. When a man like that goes missing we want to know if anyone has been putting pressure on him, and why. Of course, if he's just running away from a shrewish wife then it's his affair, and we drop it. That's happened before,'

'And what conclusions did you come to about Daddy?'

'At first we tied it in with the attack on Gillian,' I said. 'But that's a dead end; we know Mayberry was a loner. As it is, as far as the department could make out, your father was living quietly in Stockholm and apparently taking an extended holiday. There's nothing we could do about that.'

'No,' said Penny. 'We're not yet a police state. What's being done now?'

I shrugged. 'The committee of brains at the top has decided to drop the matter.'

'I see.' She stared into the fire for a long time, then shook her head. 'But you'll have to give me time, Malcolm. Let me go to America. I'd like to get away from here and think. I'd like to . . .'

I held up my hand. 'Point taken – no further argument. Change of subject. What were you doing in Scotland?' I was damned glad to change the subject; I'd been shaving the truth a bit too finely.

'Oh, that. Acting as adviser in the reconstruction of a laboratory. It's been worrying me because they're only willing to go up to P3 and I'm recommending P4. I was arguing it out with Lumsden this morning and he thinks I'm a bit . . . well, paranoiac about it.'

'You've lost me,' I said. 'What's P3? To say nothing of P4.'

'Oh, I forgot.' She waved her hand at the room. 'I was so used to talking things out here with Daddy that I'd forgotten you're a layman.' She looked at me doubtfully. 'It's a bit technical,' she warned.

'That's all right. Mine is a technical job.'

'I suppose I'd better start with the big row,' she said. 'An American geneticist called Paul Berg . . .'

It seemed that Berg blew the whistle. He thought the geneticists were diddling around with the gene in the same way the physicist had diddled around with the atom in the

'20s and '30s, and the potential hazards were even more horrendous. He pointed out some of them.

It seems that the favourite laboratory animal of the geneticists is a bacterium called *Escherichia coli* and it is the most studied organism on earth – more is known about *E.coli* than about any other living thing. It was natural that this creature be used for genetic experimentation.

'There's only one snag about that,' said Penny. '*E.coli* is a natural inhabitant of the human gut, and I don't mean by ones and twos – I mean by the million. So if you start tinkering around with *E.coli* you're doing something potentially dangerous.'

'For example?' I asked.

'You remember Lummy's example of genetic transfer from *Rhizobium* to make an improved wheat. I said we'd have to be careful not to transfer another, more dangerous, gene. Now, consider this. Supposing you incorporated into *E.coli*, accidentally or on purpose, the gene specifying the male hormone, testosterone. And supposing that strain of *E.coli* escaped from the laboratory and entered the human population. It would inhabit the digestive tracts of women, too, you know. They might start growing beards and stop having babies.'

'Christ!' I said. 'It would be a catastrophe.'

'Berg and some of his concerned friends called an international conference at Asilomar in California in 1975. It was well attended by the world's geneticists but there was much controversy. Gradually a policy was hammered out involving the concept of biological containment. Certain dangerous experiments were to be banned pending the development of a strain of *E.coli* unable to survive outside the laboratory and unable to colonize the human gut. The specification laid down was that the survival rate of the new strain should not be more than one in a thousand million.'

I smiled. 'That sounds like certainty.'

'It's not,' said Penny soberly, 'considering the numbers of *E.coli* around, but it's close. I think that was the most important conference in the history of science. For the first time scientists had got together to police themselves without having restrictions thrust upon them. I think at the back of all our minds was the bad example set by the atomic physicists.'

Fifteen months later the development of the new strain was announced by the University of Alabama. Penny laughed. 'A writer in *New Scientist* put it very well. He called it "the world's first creature designed to choose death over liberty".'

I said slowly, 'The first creature *designed* . . . That's a frightening concept.'

'In a way – but we've been designing creatures for a long time. You don't suppose the modern dairy cow is as nature intended it to be?'

'Maybe, but this strikes me as being qualitatively different. It's one thing to guide evolution and quite another to bypass it.'

'You're right,' she said. 'Sooner or later there'll be some hack or graduate student who will go ahead with a bright idea without taking the time to study the consequences of what he's doing. There'll be a bad mistake made one day – but not if I can help it. And that brings us to Scotland.'

'How?'

'What I've just described is biological containment. There's also physical containment to keep the bugs from escaping. Laboratories are classified from P1 to P4. P1 is the standard microbiological lab; P4 is the other extreme – the whole of the lab is under negative air pressure, there are air locks, showers inside and out, changes of clothing, special pressurized suits – all that kind of thing.'

'And you're running into trouble with your recommendations in Scotland?'

'They're upranking an existing P2 lab. In view of what they want to do I'm recommending P4, but they'll only go to P3. The trouble is that a P4 lab is dreadfully expensive, not only in the building, but in the running and maintenance.'

'Are there no statutory regulations?'

'Not in this field; it's too new. If they were working with recognized pathogens then, yes – there are regulations. But they'll be working with good old *E.coli*, a harmless bacterium. You have about a couple of hundred million of them in your digestive tract right now. They'll stay harmless, too, until some fool transfers the wrong gene.' She sighed. 'All we have are guidelines, not laws.'

'Sounds a bit like my job – not enough laws.'

She ruefully agreed, and our talk turned to other things. Just before I left she said, 'Malcolm; I want you to know that I think you're being very patient with me – patient and thoughtful. I'm not the vapouring sort of female, and I usually don't have much trouble in making up my mind; but events have been getting on top of me recently.'

'Not to worry,' I said lightly. 'I can wait.'

'And then there's Gillian,' she said. 'It may have been silly of me but I was worrying about her even before all this happened. She's never been too attractive to men and she looked like turning into an old maid; which would have been a pity because she'd make someone a marvellous wife. But now – ' she shook her head – 'I don't think there's a chance for her with that face.'

'I wouldn't worry about that, either,' I advised. 'Michaelis has a fond eye for her.' I laughed. 'With a bit of luck you'll not have one, but two, spies in the family.'

And with that startling thought I left her.

TWENTY-NINE

The British weekend being what it is I didn't get to the War Office until Monday. Anyone invading these islands would be advised to begin not earlier than four p.m. on a Friday; he'd have a walkover. I filled in the necessary form at the desk and was escorted by a porter to the wrong office. Two attempts later I found the man I needed, an elderly major called Gardner who was sitting on his bottom awaiting his pension. He heard what I had to say and looked at me with mournful eyes. 'Do you realize the war has been over for thirty years?'

I disliked people who ask self-evident questions. 'Yes, I'm aware of it; and I still want the information.'

He sighed, drew a sheet of paper towards him, and picked up a ball point pen. 'It's not going to be easy. Do you know how many millions of men were in the army? I suppose I'd better have the names.'

'I suppose you had.' I began to see why Gardner was still a grey-haired major. 'George Ashton, private in the Royal Electrical and Mechanical Engineers; demobilized 4 January, 1947.'

'In London?'

'Probably.'

'Could have been at Earl's Court; that was used as a demob centre. The other man?'

'Howard Greatorex Benson, sergeant in the Royal Army Service Corps. I don't know where he was demobilized.'

'Is that all you know of these men?'

'That's it.'

Gardner laid down his pen and looked at me glumly. 'Very well, I'll institute a search. You'd better give me your address or a phone number where I can find you.' He sniffed lugubriously. 'It'll take about a month, I should say.'

'That's not good enough. I need the information a damned sight faster than that.'

He waved a languid hand. 'So many records,' he said weakly. 'Millions of them.'

'Don't you have a system?'

'System? Oh, yes; we have a system – when it works.'

I set out to jolly him along and by a combination of sweet talk, name-dropping and unspoken threats got him out of his chair and into action, if one could dignify his speed by such a name. He stood up, regarding me owlishly, and said, 'You don't suppose we keep five million army records here, do you?'

I smiled. 'Shall we take your car or mine?'

I had what I wanted four hours later. At the time I thought I'd been lucky but later decided that luck had nothing to do with it because it had been planned that way thirty years earlier.

We started with the records of Earl's Court, now an exhibition hall devoted to such things as cars and boats, but then a vast emporium for the processing of soldiers into civilians. There they exchanged their uniforms for civilian clothing from the skin out – underwear, shirt, socks, shoes, suit, overcoat and the inevitable trilby or fedora hat of the 1940s. There was also the equivalent of a bank which took in no money but which lashed it out by the million; the serviceman's gratuity, a small – very small – donation from a grateful nation. At its peak the throughput of Earl's Court was

5000 men a day but by early 1947 it had dropped to a mere 2000.

The ledgers for 4 January were comparatively small; they had coped with only 1897 men – it had been a slack day. Infuriatingly, the ledgers were not listed in alphabetical order but by army number, which meant that every name and page had to be scanned. 'What was the name again?' said Gardner,

'Ashton.'

'Ashton,' he muttered, as he started on the first page of a ledger. 'Ashton . . . Ashton . . . Ashton.' I think he had to repeat the name to himself because he had the attention span of a retarded five-year-old.

I took another ledger and started to check it. It was like reading a war memorial with the difference that these were the survivors; a long list of Anglo-Saxon names with the odd quirky foreigner for spice, and even more boring than checking Heathrow passenger lists. Half an hour later Gardner said, 'What was that name again?'

I sighed. 'Ashton. George Ashton.'

'No – the other one.'

'Benson, Howard Greatorex.'

'He's here,' said Gardner placidly.

'Benson!' I went to the other side of the table and leaned over Gardner's shoulder. Sure enough, his finger rested under Benson's name, and the rest of the information fitted. Sergeant H. G. Benson, RASC, had been discharged on the same day, and from the same place, as Private G. Ashton, REME. I didn't think coincidence could stretch that far.

'That's a piece of luck,' said Gardner with smug satisfaction. 'Now we have his army number we shall find his file easily.'

'We haven't got Ashton yet,' I said, and we both applied ourselves to the ledgers. Ashton came up three-quarters of an hour later. Gardner scribbled on a piece of paper and drifted away in his somnambulistic manner to organize the search for the files, while I sat down and began to sort out what we'd found.

I tried to figure out the odds against two specific men in the British Army being demobilized on the same day and from the same place, but the mathematics were too much for me – I couldn't keep count of the zeroes, so I gave up. It was stretching the long arm a bit too far to suggest that it had happened by chance to two men who subsequently lived together as master and servant for the next quarter of a century. So if it wasn't coincidence it must have been by arrangement.

So who arranged it?

I was still torturing my brain cells when Gardner came back an hour later with the files. There was a sticky moment when I said I wanted to take them away; he clung to them as though I was trying to kidnap his infant children. At last he agreed to accept my receipt and I left in triumph.

I studied the files at home, paying little attention to Ashton's file because it had nothing to do with the Ashton I knew, but I went over Benson's file in detail. His career was exactly as Ogilvie had described. He joined the army in 1940 and after his primary training and square-bashing he was transferred to the RASC and his promotions came pretty quickly at first – to lance-corporal, to corporal, and then to sergeant where he stuck for the rest of the war. All his service was in England and he never went overseas. Most of his duties were concerned with storekeeping, and from the comments of his superiors written in the file, he was quite efficient, although there were a few complaints of lack of initiative and willingness to pass the buck. Not many, but enough to block his further promotion.

His pay-book showed that he was unmarried but was contributing to the upkeep of his mother. The payments ceased in 1943 when she died. From that time until his discharge his savings showed a marked increase. I thought that anyone who could save out of army pay in those days must have lived a quiet life.

His medical record was similarly uneventful. Looked at *en masse* it appeared alarming, but closer inspection revealed just the normal ailments which might plague a man over a period of years. There were a couple of tooth extractions, two periods of hospitalization – one for a bout of influenza and the other when he dropped a six-inch shell on his left foot. Luckily the shell was defused.

My attention was caught by the last entry. Benson had complained of aches in his left arm which had been preliminarily diagnosed as twinges of rheumatism and he had been given the appropriate treatment. He was thirty-three then, and rheumatism seemed a bit odd to me, especially since Benson had a cushy billet for a soldier in wartime. Not for him route marches in the pouring rain or splashing about joyfully in the mud; he worked in a warm office and slept every night in a warm bed.

Evidently the medical officer had thought it odd, too, when the treatment didn't work. In a different coloured ink he had appended a question mark after the previous diagnosis of rheumatism, and had scribbled beneath, 'Suggest cardiogram.' The amendment was dated 19 December, 1946.

I went back to the general service file where I struck another oddity, because his immediate superior had written as the last entry, 'Suggested date of discharge – 21 March, 1947,' Underneath another hand had written, 'Confirmed', and followed it with an indecipherable signature.

I sat back and wondered why, if it had been suggested and confirmed that Benson should be discharged in March, 1947, he should have been discharged three months earlier. I consulted the medical record again and then rang Tom Packer.

This account started with Tom Packer because it was at his place I first met Penny. I rang him now because he was a doctor and I wanted confirmation of the idea that was burgeoning. If he didn't know what I wanted he'd be certain to know who could tell me.

After a brief exchange of courtesies, I said, 'Tom, I want a bit of free medical advice.'

He chuckled. 'You and the rest of the population. What is it?'

'Supposing a man complains of a pain in his left arm. What would you diagnose?'

'Hell, it could be anything. Have you got such a pain?'

'This is hypothetical.'

'I see. Could be rheumatism. What's the hypothetical age of this hypothetical chap?'

'Thirty-three.'

'Then it's unlikely to be rheumatism if he's lived a normal civilized life. I say unlikely, but it could happen. Did he say pain or ache?'

I consulted the medical file. 'Actually, he said ache.'

'Um. Not much to go on. Doctors usually have real patients to examine, not wraiths of your imagination.'

I said, 'Supposing the man was treated for rheumatism and it didn't work, and then his doctor thought a cardiogram was indicated. What would you think then?'

'How long has the man been treated for rheumatism?'

'Hang on.' I checked the file. 'Three months.'

Tom's breath hissed in my ear. 'I'm inclined to think the doctor should be struck off. Do you mean to say it took him three months to recognize a classic symptom of ischæmia?'

'What's that?'

'Ischæmic heart disease – *angina pectoris.*'

I suddenly felt much happier. 'Would the man survive?'

'That's an imponderable question – very iffy. *If* he's had that ache in his arm for three months and *if* it is ischæmic and *if* he hasn't had treatment for his heart then he'll be in pretty bad shape. His future depends on the life he's been living, whether he smokes a lot, and whether he's been active or sedentary.'

I thought of Sergeant Benson in an army stores office. 'Let's say he's been sedentary and we'll assume he smokes.'

'Then I wouldn't be surprised to hear he's dropped dead of a coronary one morning. This *is* hypothetical, isn't it? Nobody I know?'

'No one you know,' I assured him. 'But not quite hypothetical. There was a man in that condition back in 1946. He died about a month ago. What do you think of that?'

'I think that I think I'm surprised, but then, medicine isn't a predictive sport and the damnedest things can happen. I wouldn't have thought it likely he'd make old bones.'

'Neither would I,' I said. 'Thanks for your trouble, Tom.'

'You'll get my bill,' he promised, and rang off.

I depressed the telephone rest, rang Penny, and asked her the name of Benson's doctor. She was faintly surprised but gave it to me when I said my boss wanted to tidy up a few loose ends before I was transferred. 'It's just a matter of firm identification.'

The doctor's name was Hutchins and he was a shade reserved. 'Medical files are confidential, you know, Mr Jaggard.'

'I don't want you to break any confidences, Dr Hutchins,' I said. 'But the man is dead after all. All I want to know is when Benson last had a heart attack.'

'Heart attack!' echoed Hutchins in surprise. 'I can certainly tell you all about that. It's no breach of confidentiality on a doctor's part if he says a man is perfectly well. There was absolutely nothing wrong with Benson's heart; it was in better condition than my own, and I'm a much younger man. He was as fit as a flea.'

'Thank you, Doctor,' I said warmly. 'That's all I wanted to know.' As I put down the telephone I thought I'd handled that rather well.

I sat back and checked off all the points.

ITEM: Sergeant Benson was suffering from heart disease at the end of 1946. His condition, according to Tom Packer, was grave enough so that no one would be surprised if he dropped dead.

HYPOTHESIS: Sergeant Benson had died of heart disease some time after 18 December, 1946 and before 4 January, 1947.

ITEM: Civilian Benson was discharged at Earl's Court on 4 January, 1947 and subsequently showed no trace of a bad heart condition.

HYPOTHESIS: Civilian Benson was a planted substitute for Sergeant Benson, exactly as Chelyuskin was a substitute for Private Ashton. The method was exactly the same and it happened on the same day and in the same place, so the likelihood of a connection was very high, particularly as Benson worked for Ashton for the rest of his life.

COROLLARY: Because the methods used were identical the likelihood was high that both substitutions were planned by the same mind. But Ogilvie had told me that the idea was Chelyuskin's own. Was Benson another Russian? Had two men been smuggled out?

It all hung together very prettily, but it still didn't tell me who Benson was and why he had shot Ashton.

THIRTY

Ogilvie was pleased about all that even though it got us no further into cracking the problem of why Benson should kill Ashton. At least we had seen the common linkage and he was confident that by probing hard enough and long enough we – or rather I – would come up with the truth. All the same he coppered his bet by having me do an intensive investigation into the life of Sergeant Benson before he joined the army. Ogilvie was a belt-and-braces man.

So I spent a long time in the West Country looking at school records in Exeter and work records in Plymouth. At Benson's school I found an old sepia class photograph with Benson in the third row; at least, I was assured it was Benson. The unformed young face of that thirteen-year-old gazing solemnly at the camera told me nothing. Some time in the ensuing years Benson had had his features considerably rearranged.

There were no photographs of an older Benson to be found in Plymouth, but I did talk to a couple of people who knew him before the war. The opinion was that he wasn't a bad chap, reasonably good at his job, but not very ambitious. All according to the record. No, he hadn't been back since the war; he had no family and it was assumed there was nothing for him to go back for.

All this took time and I got back to London just as Penny and Gillian were about to leave for America. I drove them to Heathrow myself and we had a drink in the bar, toasting surgical success. 'How long will you be away?' I asked Gillian. She wore a broad-brimmed straw hat with a scarf tied wimple-fashion and large dark glasses; style coming to the aid of concealment.

'I don't know; it depends how the operations go, I suppose.' She sketched a mock shiver. 'I'm not looking forward to it. But Penny will be back next week.'

Penny said, 'I just want to see Gillian settled and to make sure everything is all right, then I'll be back. Lummy wants to go to Scotland with me.'

'So you undermined his certainty.'

'Perhaps,' she said noncommittally.

'Did you arrange for the auction?'

'It's on Wednesday – viewing day on Tuesday. We already have a flat in town.' She took a notebook and scribbled the address. 'That's where you'll find me when I come back, if I'm not in Scotland.'

Gillian excused herself and wandered in the direction of the ladies' room. I took the opportunity of asking, 'How did you get on with Ogilvie?' I had arranged the meeting with Ogilvie as promised. He hadn't liked it but I'd twisted his arm.

Penny's brow furrowed. 'Well enough, I suppose. He told me pretty much what you have. But there was something . . .'

'Something what?'

'I don't know. It was like speaking in a great empty hall. You expect an echo to come back and you're a bit surprised when there isn't one. There seemed to be something missing when Ogilvie talked. I can't explain it any better than that.'

Penny was right – there was a hell of a lot missing. Her psychic antennae were all a-quiver and she perceived a wrongness but had no way of identifying it. Below the level of consciousness her intelligence was telling her there was something wrong but she didn't have enough facts to prove it.

Ogilvie and I *knew* there was something wrong because we had more facts, but even we were blocked at that moment.

I saw them into the departure lounge, then went home and proceeded to draw up an elaborate chart containing everything I knew about the Ashton case. Lines (ruled) were drawn to connect the *dramatis personae* and representing factual knowledge; lines (dashed) were drawn representing hypotheses.

The whole silly exercise got me nowhere.

About this time I started to develop an itch in my mind. Perhaps it had been the drawing of the chart with its many connections which started it, but I had something buried within me which wanted to come to the surface. Someone had said something and someone else had said something else, apparently quite unrelated and the little man Hunch who lived in the back of my skull was beginning to turn over in his sleep. I jabbed at him deliberately but he refused to wake up. He would do so in his own good time and with that I had to be content.

On the Tuesday I went to the Ashton house for the public viewing. It was crowded with hard-eyed dealers and hopeful innocents looking for bargains and not finding much because all the good stuff had gone to the London flat or to Sotheby's. Still, there was enough to keep them happy; the accumulated possessions of a happy family life of fifteen years. I could see why Penny didn't want to be there.

I wasn't there to buy anything, nor was I there out of mere curiosity. We had assumed Ashton had hidden something and, although we hadn't found it, that didn't mean it wasn't there. When I say 'we' I really mean Ogilvie, because I didn't wholly go along with him on that. But he could have been right, and I was on hand to see if any suspicious-looking characters were taking an undue interest. Of course, it was as futile an exercise as drawing the chart because the normal dealer looks furtive and suspicious to begin with.

During the morning I bumped into Mary Cope. 'Hello, Mary,' I said. 'Still here, then.'

'Yes, sir. I'm to live in the house until it's been sold. I still have my flat upstairs.' She surveyed the throng of inquisitive folk as they probed among the Ashtons' possessions. 'It's a shame, sir, it really is. Everything was so beautiful before . . . before . . .'

She was on the verge of tears. I said, 'A pity, Mary, but there it is. Any offers for the house yet?'

'Not that I know of, sir.'

'What will you do when it's sold?'

'I'm to go to London when Miss Penny and Miss Gillian come back from America. I don't know that I'll like London, though. Still, perhaps it will grow on me.'

'I'm sure it will.'

She looked up at me. 'I wish I knew what was in God's mind when he does a thing like this to a family like the Ashtons. You couldn't wish for better people, sir.'

God had nothing to do with it, I thought grimly; what happened to the Ashtons had been strictly man-made. But there was nothing I could say to answer such a question of simple faith.

'It's not only Mr Ashton, though,' said Mary wistfully. 'I miss Benson. He was such a funny man – always joking and light-hearted; and he never had a wrong word for anyone. He did make us laugh, sir; and to think that he and Mr Ashton should die like that, and in a foreign country.'

'Did Benson ever talk about himself, Mary?'

'About himself, sir? How do you mean?'

'Did he ever tell anecdotes – stories – about his early life, or when he was in the army?'

She thought about it, then shook her head. 'No, Benson was a man who lived in the present. He'd joke about politicians, and what he'd read in the papers or seen on telly. A real comedian, Benson was; had us in stitches a lot of the time. I used to tell him he should have been on the stage, but he always said he was too old.'

A real comedian! What an epitaph for a man whose last macabre joke was to shoot his master. I said, 'You'd better look sharp, Mary, or some of these people will be stealing the spoons.'

She laughed. 'Not much chance of that, sir. The auctioneer has Securicor men all over the place.' She hesitated. 'Would you like a cup of tea? I can make it in my flat.'

I smiled. 'No, thank you, Mary. I don't think I'll be staying long this morning.'

All the same, I was there next day for the actual auction, and why I was there I didn't really know. Perhaps it was the feeling that with the dispersal of the contents of the house the truth about the Ashton case was slipping away, perhaps to be lost forever. At any rate I was there, impotent with ignorance, but on the spot.

And there, to my surprise, was also Michaelis. I didn't see him until late morning and was only aware of him when he nudged me in the ribs. The auctioneer was nattering about a particularly fine specimen of something or other so we withdrew to Ashton's study, now stripped rather bare. 'What a bloody shame this is,' he said. '*I'm* glad Gillian isn't here to see it. Have you heard anything yet?'

'No.'

'Neither have I,' he said broodily. 'I wrote to her but she hasn't replied.'

'She's only been gone four days,' I pointed out gently. 'The postal services weren't that good even in their palmy days.'

He grinned and seemed oddly shy. 'I suppose you think I'm making a damned fool of myself.'

'Not at all,' I said. 'No more than me. I wish you luck.'

'Think I have a chance?'

'I don't see why not. In fact, I think you have everything going for you, so cheer up. What are you doing here anyway?'

'That model railway still interests me. I thought that if it's broken up for sale I might put in a bid or two. Of course, in model railway terms to break up that system would be like cutting up the Mona Lisa and selling bits of it. But it won't be broken up and I won't have a chance. Lucas Hartman is here.'

'Who's he?'

'Oh, everybody in the model railway world knows Hartman. He's a real model railway buff, but he calls it railroad because he's an American. He's also quite rich.'

'And you think he'll buy it as it stands?'

'He's sure to. He's up in the attic gloating over it now.'

'How much do you think it will bring?' I asked curiously.

Michaelis shrugged. 'That's hard to say. It's not exactly standard stuff – there's so much extra built in that it's hard to put a price on it.'

'Have a try.'

'For the rail and rolling stock and normal control instrumentation, all of which is there, it would cost about £15,000 to build from scratch, so let's say it might bring between £7000 and £10,000 at auction. As for the other stuff built in, that's more difficult to assess. I'd say it'll double the price.'

'So you think it will bring somewhere between £15,000 and £20,000.'

'Something like that. Of course, the auctioneer will have a reserve price on it. Any way you look at it, Hartman will get it. He'll outbid the dealers.'

'Ah, well,' I said philosophically. 'It will fall into good hands – someone who appreciates it.'

'I suppose so,' said Michaelis gloomily. 'The bloody thing beat me in the end, you know.'

'What do you mean?'

'Well, you know those schedules I talked about – I showed you one of them.'

'The London, Midland and Scottish, I think it was.'

'That's right. I compared them against old Bradshaws and got nowhere. I even went right back to mid-1800s and nothing made sense. The system doesn't seem to compare with any normal railway scheduling.'

'Not even when those schedules were clearly labelled "LMS" and so on,' I said slowly.

'They don't fit at any point,' said Michaelis. 'It beats me.'

There was a picture in my mind's eye of Ashton's clenched fist opening to reveal a railway timetable – Stockholm to Göteborg, and it was like a bomb going off in my skull. 'Jesus!'

Michaelis stared at me. 'What's wrong?'

'Come on. We're going to talk to that bloody auctioneer.'

I left the study at a fast stride and went into the crowded hall where the auction was taking place. The auctioneer had set up a portable rostrum at the foot of the stairs and, as I elbowed my way through the throng towards it, I took a business card from my wallet. Behind me Michaelis said, 'What's the rush?'

I flattened myself against the wall and scribbled on the card. 'Can't explain now.' I pushed the card at him. 'See the auctioneer gets this.'

Michaelis shrugged and fought his way through to the rostrum where he gave the card to one of the auctioneer's assistants. I walked up the stairs and stood where I could easily be seen. The auctioneer was in mid-spate, selling an eighteen-place Crown Derby dinner service; he took the card which was thrust under his nose, turned it over, looked up at me and nodded, and then continued with hardly a break in his chant.

Michaelis came back. 'What's the panic?'

'We must stop the sale of that railway.'

'I'm all for that,' he said. 'But what's your interest?'

The auctioneer's hammer came down with a sharp crack. 'Sold!'

'It's too complicated to tell you now.' The auctioneer had handed over to his assistant and was coming towards the stairs. 'It'll have to keep.'

The auctioneer came up the stairs. 'What can I do for you – er – ' He glanced at the card – 'Mr Jaggard.'

'I represent Penelope and Gillian Ashton. The model railway in the attic mustn't be sold.'

He frowned. 'Well, I don't know about that.'

I said, 'Can't we go somewhere a bit more quiet while I explain?'

He nodded and pointed up the stairs, so we went into one of the bedrooms. He said, 'You say you represent the Ashton sisters?'

'That's right.'

'Can you prove that?'

'Not with anything I carry with me. But I can give you written authority if you need it.'

'On your signature?'

'Yes.'

He shook his head. 'Sorry, Mr Jaggard, but that's not good enough. I was engaged by Penelope Ashton to sell the contents of this house. I can't vary that agreement without her authority. If you can give me a letter from her, that's different.'

'She's not easy to get hold of at short notice. She's in the United States.'

'I see. Then there's nothing to be done.' Something in my expression caused him to add quickly, 'Mr Jaggard, I don't know you. Now, I'm a professional man, engaged to conduct this sale. I can't possibly take instructions from any Tom, Dick or Harry who comes here telling me what to do or what not to do. I really don't conduct my business that way. Besides, the railway is one of the plums of the sale. The press is very interested; it makes a nice filler for a columnist.'

'Then what do you suggest? Would you take instruction from Miss Ashton's legal adviser?'

'Her solicitor? Yes, I might do that.' He frowned perplexedly. 'This all appears very odd to me. It seems, from what you say, that Miss Ashton knows nothing about this and it is something you are taking upon yourself. But if I have written instructions from her solicitor, then I'll withdraw the railway.'

'Thank you,' I said. 'I'll get in touch with him. Oh, by the way, what's the reserve price?'

He was affronted. 'I really can't tell you that,' he said coldly. 'And now you must excuse me. There are some important pieces coming up which I must handle myself.'

He turned to walk away, and I said desperately, 'Can you tell me when the railway will come up for sale?'

'Things are going briskly.' He looked at his watch. 'I'd say about three this afternoon.' He walked out.

'A telephone,' I said. 'My kingdom for a telephone.'

'There's one next door in Ashton's bedroom.' Michaelis looked at me a little oddly. 'This sudden interest in model railways doesn't seem kosher to me.'

I had a sudden thought. 'Where are those schedules?'

'In the attic; on a shelf under the control console. There are a dozen.'

'I want you in the attic on the double. Keep an eye on that railway and especially on those schedules. I don't want anything removed and I want note taken of anyone who takes a special interest. Now move.'

I went into Ashton's room and attacked the telephone. For the first time Ogilvie let me down; he wasn't in the office and no one knew where he was or when he'd be back. Neither was he at home. I left messages to say he should ring me at the Ashton house as soon as possible.

There were more frustrations. Mr Veasey of Michelmore, Veasey and Templeton, was away in the fastness of Wales talking to a valued but bedridden client. His clerk would not make a decision in the matter, and neither would any of the partners. They did say they would try to get hold of Veasey by telephone and I had to be satisfied with that. I had no great hopes of success – Veasey didn't know me and I had no standing.

I went up to the attic and found Michaelis brooding over the railway. Several small boys were larking about and being chased off by a Securicor guard. 'Any suspects?'

'Only Hartman. He's been checking through those schedules all morning.' He nodded in the direction of the control console. There he is.'

Hartman was a broad-shouldered man of less than average height with a shock of white hair and a nut-brown lined face. He looked rather like Einstein might have looked if Einstein had been an American businessman. At that moment he was poring over one of the schedules and frowning.

I said, 'You're sure that *is* Hartman?'

'Oh, yes. I met him three years ago at a Model Railway Exhibition. What the hell are you really up to, Malcolm?'

I looked at the railway. 'You're the expert. Are there any other peculiarities about this other than the schedules?'

Michaelis stared at the spider web of rails. 'It did occur to me that there's an excessive number of sidings and marshalling yards.'

'Yes,' I said thoughtfully. 'There would be.'

'Why would there be?' Michaelis was baffled.

'Ashton was a clever bastard,' I said. 'He wanted to hide something so he stuck it right under our noses. Do you know how a computer works?'

'In a vague sort of way.'

I said, 'Supposing you instruct a computer that A=5. That tells the computer to take that number five and put it in a location marked A. Suppose you gave the instruction C=A+B. That tells the computer to take whatever number is in A, add it to whatever number is in B, and put the result in C.' I jerked my head towards the railway. 'I think that's what this contraption is doing.'

Michaelis gasped. 'A *mechanical* computer!'

'Yes. And those schedules are the programs which run it – but God knows what they're about. Tell me, how many different kinds of rolling stock are there in the system? I'd say ten.'

'You'd be wrong. I counted sixty-three.'

'Hell!' I thought about it a little more. 'No, by God, I'm right! Ten for the numbers 0 to 9; twenty-six for the letters of the alphabet, and the rest for mathematical signs and punctuation. This bloody thing can probably talk English.'

'I think you're nuts,' said Michaelis.

I said, 'When Ashton was shot he couldn't talk but he was trying to tell me something. He pulled something from his pocket and tried to give it to me. It was a railway timetable.'

'That's pretty thin,' said Michaelis. 'Larry had one, too.'

'But why should a man in his last extremity try to give me, of all things, a railway timetable? I think he was trying to tell me something.'

'I can see why you want the sale stopped,' admitted Michaelis. 'It's a nutty idea, but you may be right.'

'I haven't got very far,' I said gloomily. 'Ashton's law firm won't play and Ogilvie's gone missing. I'd better try him again.'

So I did, but with no joy. I tried every place I thought he might be – his clubs, the restaurant he had once taken me to, then back to the office and his home again. No Ogilvie.

At half past two Michaelis sought me out. 'They're about to start bidding on the railway. What are you going to do?'

'Make another call.'

I rang my bank manager, who said, 'And what can I do for you this afternoon, Mr Jaggard?'

'Later today I'm going to write a largish cheque. There won't be enough funds to cover it, either in my current account or in the deposit account I don't want it to bounce.'

'I see. How much will the cheque be for?'

'Perhaps £20,000.' I thought of Hartman, 'Maybe as much as £25,000.1 don't quite know.'

'That's a lot of money, Mr Jaggard.'

I said, 'You know the state of my financial health, and you know I can cover it, not immediately but in a few weeks.'

'In effect, what you're asking for is a bridging loan for, say, a month.'

'That's it.'

'I don't see any difficulty there. We'll accept your cheque, but try to keep it down; and come in tomorrow – we'll need your signature.'

'Thanks.' I put down the telephone knowing that if I was wrong about the railway I was about to lose a lot of money. I couldn't see Ogilvie dipping into the department's funds to buy an elaborate toy, and the only person who might be happy about it would be Michaelis.

I went into the hall to see a small crowd gathered by the rostrum listening to a man talking. Michaelis whispered,

'They've got old Hempson from *Model Railway News* to give a pep-talk. I suppose they think that'll drive up the price.'

Hempson was saying, '. . . core of the system is the most remarkable console I have ever seen, using the ultimate in modern technology. It is this which makes this example of the art unique and it is to be hoped that the system will be sold as a complete unit. It would be a disaster if such a fine example should be broken up. Thank you.'

He stepped down to a low murmur of agreement, and I saw Hartman nodding in approval. The auctioneer stepped up and lifted his gavel. 'Ladies and gentlemen: you have just heard Mr Hempson who is an acknowledged expert, and his opinion counts. So I am about to ask for bids for the complete system. It would be normal to do this on site, as it were, but even in so large a house the attic is not big enough to hold both the exhibit and the crowd gathered here. However, you have all had the opportunity of examining this fine example of the model-maker's art, and on the table over there is a representative collection of the rolling stock.'

He raised his gavel. 'Now what am I bid for the complete system? Who will start the bidding at £20,000?'

There was a sigh – a collective exhalation of breath. 'Come,' said the auctioneer cajolingly. 'You just heard Mr Hempson. Who will bid £20,000? No one? Who will bid £18.000?'

He had no takers at that, and gradually his starting price came down until he had a bid of £8000. '£8000 I am bid – who will say nine? Eight-five I am bid – thank you, sir – who will say nine? Nine I am bid – who will say ten?'

Michaelis said, 'The dealers are coming in, but they won't stand a chance. Hartman will freeze them out.'

I had been watching Hartman who hadn't moved a muscle. The bidding crept up by 500s, hesitated at the £13,500 mark, and then went up by 250s to £15,000 where it stuck.

'Fifteen I am bid; fifteen I am bid,' chanted the auctioneer. 'Any advance on fifteen?'

Hartman flicked a finger. 'Sixteen I am bid,' said the auctioneer. '£16,000. Any advance on sixteen?' The dealers were frozen out.

I held up a finger. 'Seventeen I am bid. Any advance on seventeen? Eighteen I am bid – and nineteen – and twenty. I have a bid of £20,000. Any advance on twenty?'

There was a growing rustle of interest as Hartman and I battled it out. At £25,000 he hesitated for the first time and raised his bid by £500. Then I knew I had him. I raised a single finger and the auctioneer said, 'Twenty-six and a half – any advance . . . twenty-seven, thank you, sir – twenty-eight I am bid.'

And so it went. Hartman lost his nerve at thirty and gave up. The auctioneer said, 'Any advance on thirty-one? Any advance on thirty-one? Going once.' *Crack!* 'Going twice.' *Crack!* 'Sold to Mr Jaggard for £31,000.'

Crack!

I was now the proud owner of a railway. Maybe it wasn't British Rail but perhaps it might show more profit. I said to Michaelis, 'I wonder if Ogilvie has that much in the petty cash box?'

Hartman came over. 'I guess you wanted that very much, sir.'

'I did.'

'Perhaps you would be so kind as to let me study the layout some time. I am particularly interested in those schedules.'

I said, 'I'm sorry. I acted as agent in this matter. However, if you give me your address I'll pass it to the owner for his decision.'

He nodded. 'I suppose that will have to do.'

Then I was surrounded by pressmen wanting to know who, in his right mind, would pay that much money for a toy. I was rescued by Mary Cope. 'You're wanted on the telephone, Mr Jaggard.'

I made my escape into Ashton's study. It was Ogilvie. 'I understand you wanted me.'

'Yes,' I said, wishing he had rung half an hour earlier. 'The department owes me £31,000 plus bank charges.'

'What's that?'

'You now own a model railway.'

His language was unprintable.

THIRTY-ONE

I saw Ogilvie at his home that night. His welcome was somewhat cool and unenthusiastic and he looked curiously at the big ledger I carried as he ushered me into his study. I dumped it on his desk and sat down. Ogilvie warmed his coat tails at the fire, and said, 'Did you really spend £31,000 on a toy train set?'

I smiled. 'Yes, I did.'

'You're a damned lunatic,' he said. 'And if you think the department will reimburse you, then I'll get the quacks in and have you certified. No bloody model railway can be worth that much.'

'An American called Hartman thought it worth £30,000,' I observed. 'Because that's how much he bid. You haven't seen it. This is no toy you buy your kid for Christmas and assemble on the floor before the living-room fire to watch the chuff-chuff go round in circles. This is big and complex.'

'I don't care how big and complex it is. Where the hell do you think I'm going to put it in the department budget? The accountants would have *me* certified. And what makes you think the department wants it?'

'Because it holds what we've been looking for all the time. It's a computer.' I tapped the ledger. 'And this is the programing for it. One of the programs. There are eleven more which I put in the office vaults.'

I told him how Michaelis had unavailingly tried to sort out the schedules and how I'd made an intuitive jump based on the timetable in Ashton's hand. I said, 'It would be natural these days for a theoretician to use a computer, but Ashton knew we'd look into all his computer files and programs. So he built his own and disguised it.'

'It's the most improbable idea I've ever heard,' said Ogilvie. 'Michaelis is the train expert. What does he think?'

'He thinks I'm crazy.'

'He's not far wrong.' Ogilvie began to pace the room. 'I tell you what I think. If you're right then the thing is cheap at the price and the department will pay. If you're wrong then it costs *you* £31,000.'

'Plus bank charges.' I shrugged. 'I stuck out my neck, so I'll take the chance.'

'I'll get the computer experts on it tomorrow.' He wagged his head sadly. 'But where are we to put it? If I have it installed in the department offices it'll only accelerate my retirement. Should the Minister hear of it he'll think I've gone senile – well into second childhood.'

'It will need a big room,' I said. 'Best to rent a warehouse.'

'I'll authorize that. You can get on with it. Where is it now?'

'Still in the Ashtons' attic. Michaelis is locked in with it for the night.'

'Enthusiastically playing trains, I suppose.' Ogilvie shook his head in sheer wonderment at the things his staff got up to. He joined me at the desk and tapped the schedule. 'Now tell me what you think this is all about.'

It took four days to dismantle the railway and reassemble it in a warehouse in South London. The computer boys thought my idea hilarious and to them the whole thing was a big giggle, but they went about the job competently enough. Ogilvie gave me Michaelis to assist. The department had never found the need for a model railway technician and Michaelis found himself suddenly elevated into the rank of expert, first class. He quite liked it.

The chief computer man was a systems analyst called Harrington. He took the job more seriously than most of the others but even that was only half-serious. He installed a computer terminal in the warehouse and had it connected to a computer by post office land lines; not the big chap Nellie was hooked up to, but an ordinary commercial time-sharing computer in the City. Then we were ready to go.

About this time I got a letter from Penny. She wrote that Gillian was well and had just had the operation for the first of the skin grafts. She herself was not coming back immediately; Lumsden had suggested that she attend a seminar at Berkeley in California, so she wouldn't be back for a further week or ten days.

I showed the letter to Michaelis and he said he'd had one from Gillian, written just before the operation. 'She seemed a bit blue.'

'Not to worry; probably just pre-operation nerves.'

The itch at the back of my mind was still there, and so the buried connection was nothing to do with the railway. Little man Hunch was sitting up and rubbing his eyes but was still not yet awake. I badly needed to talk to Penny because I thought it was something she had said that had caused the itch. I was sorry she wasn't coming home for that reason among many.

One morning at ten o'clock Harrington opened the LNER schedule. 'The first few pages are concerned with the placement of the engines and the rolling stock,' he said. 'Now, let's get this right if we can. This is silly enough as it is without us putting our own bugs into the system.'

It took over an hour to get everything in the right place – checked and double checked. Harrington said, 'Page eleven to page twenty-three are concerned with the console settings.' He turned to me. 'If there's anything to your idea at all these Roms will have to be analysed to a fare-thee-well.'

'What's a Rom?'

'A read-only module – this row of boxes plugged in here. Your man, Michaelis, calls them microprocessors. They are pre-programed electronic chips – we'll have to analyse what they're programed to do. All right; let's get on with the setting.'

He began to call out numbers and an acolyte pressed buttons and turned knobs. When he had finished he started again from the beginning and another acolyte checked what the first had done. He caught three errors. 'See what I mean,' said Harrington. 'One bug is enough to make a program unworkable.'

'Are you ready to go now?'

'I think so – for the first stage.' He put his hand on the ledger. 'There are over two hundred pages here, so *if* this thing really is a computer and *if* this represents one program, then after a while everything should come to a stop and the console will have to be readjusted for the next part of the program. It's going to take a long time.'

'It will take even longer if we don't start,' I said tartly.

Harrington grinned and leaned over to snap a single switch. Things began to happen. Trains whizzed about the system, twenty or thirty on the move at once. Some travelled faster than others, and once I thought there was going to be a collision as two trains headed simultaneously for a junction; but one slowed just enough to let the other through and then picked up speed again.

Sidings and marshalling yards that had been empty began to fill up as engines pushed in rolling stock and then uncoupled to shoot off somewhere else. I watched one marshalling yard fill up and then begin to empty, the trains being broken up and reassembled into other patterns.

Harrington grunted. 'This is no good; it's too damned busy. Too much happening at once. If this is a computer it isn't working sequentially like an ordinary digital job; it's working in parallel. It's going to be hell to analyse.'

The system worked busily for nearly two hours. Trains shot back and forth, trucks were pushed here and there, abandoned temporarily and then picked up again in what seemed an arbitrary manner. To me it was bloody monotonous but Michaelis was enthralled and even Harrington appeared to be mildly interested. Then everything came to a dead stop.

Harrington said, 'I'll want a video-camera up there.' He pointed to the ceiling. 'I want to be able to focus on any marshalling yard and record it on tape. And I want it in colour because I have a feeling colour comes into this. And we can slow down a tape for study. Can you fix that?'

'You'll have it tomorrow morning,' I promised. 'But what do you think now?'

'It's an ingenious toy, but there may be something more to it,' he said, noncommittally. 'We have a long way to go yet.'

I didn't spend all my time in the warehouse but went back three days later because Harrington wanted to see me. I found him at a desk flanked by a video-recorder and a TV set. 'We may have something,' he said, and pointed to a collection of miniature rolling stock on the desk. 'There *is* a number characterization.'

I didn't know what he meant by that, and said so. He smiled. 'I'm saying you were right. This railway is a computer. I think that any of this rolling stock which has red trim on it represents a digit.' He picked up a tank car which had ESSO lettered on the side in red. 'This one, for instance, I think represents a zero.'

He put down the tank car and I counted the trucks; there were nine, but one had no red on it. 'Shouldn't there be ten?'

'Eight,' he said. This gadget is working in octal instead of decimal. That's no problem – many computers work in octal internally.' He picked up a small black truck. 'And I think this little chap is an octal point – the equivalent of a decimal point.'

'Well, I'm damned! Can I tell Ogilvie?'

Harrington sighed. 'I'd rather you didn't – not yet. We haven't worked out to our satisfaction which number goes with which truck. Apart from that there is a total of sixty-three types of rolling stock; I rather think some of those represent letters of the alphabet to give the system alphanumeric capability. Identification may be difficult. It should be reasonably easy to work out the numbers; all that it takes is logic. But letters are different. I'll show you what I mean.'

He switched on the video-recorder and the TV set, then punched a button. An empty marshalling yard appeared on the screen, viewed from above. A train came into view and the engine stopped and uncoupled, then trundled off. Another train came in and the same thing happened; and yet again until the marshalling yard was nearly full. Harrington pressed a button and froze the picture.

'This marshalling yard is typical of a dozen in the system, all built to the same specification – to hold a maximum of eighty trucks. You'll notice there are no numbers in there – no red trucks.' With his pen he pointed out something else. 'And scattered at pretty regular intervals are these blue trucks.'

'Which are?'

Harrington leaned back. 'If I were to talk in normal computer terms – which may be jargon to you – I'd say I was looking at an alphameric character string with a maximum capacity of eighty characters, and the blue trucks represent the spaces between words.' He jabbed his finger at the screen. 'That is saying something to us, but we don't know what.'

I bent down and counted the blue trucks; there were thirteen. 'Thirteen words,' I said.

'Fourteen,' said Harrington. 'There's no blue truck at the end. Now, there are twelve marshalling yards like this, so the system has a capacity of holding at any one time about a hundred and sixty words in plain, straightforward English – about half a typed quarto sheet. I know it's not much, but it keeps changing all the time as the system runs; that's the equivalent of putting a new page in the typewriter and doing some more.' He smiled. 'I don't know who designed this contraption, but maybe it's a new way of writing a novel.'

'So all you have to do is to find out which truck equals which letter.'

'All!' said Harrington hollowly. He picked up a thick sheaf of colour photographs. 'We've been recording the strings as they form and I have a chap on the computer doing a statistical analysis. So far he's making heavy weather of it. But we'll get it, it's just another problem in cryptanalysis. Anyway, I just thought I'd let you know your hare-brained idea turned out to be right, after all.'

'Thanks,' I said, glad not to be £31,000 out of pocket. Plus bank charges.

Two days later Harrington rang me again. 'We've licked the numbers,' he said. 'And we're coming up with mathematical formulae now. But the alphabet is a dead loss. The statistical distribution of the letters is impossible for English, French, German, Spanish and Latin. That's as far as we've gone. It's a bit rum – there are too many letters.'

I thought about that. 'Try Russian; there are thirty-two letters in the Russian alphabet.' And the man who had designed the railway was a Russian, although I didn't say that to Harrington.

'That's a thought. I'll ring you back.'

Four hours later he rang again. 'It's Russian,' he said. 'But we'll need a linguist; we don't know enough about it here.'

'Now is the time to tell Ogilvie. We'll be down there in an hour.'

So I told Ogilvie. He said incredulously, 'You mean that bloody model railway speaks Russian?'

I grinned. 'Why not? It was built by a Russian.'

'You come up with the weirdest things,' he complained.

'I didn't,' I said soberly. 'Ashton did. Now you can make my bank manager happy by paying £35,000 into my account.'

Ogilvie narrowed his eyes. 'It cost you only £31,000.'

'"Thou shalt not muzzle the ox that treadeth the corn",' I quoted. 'It was a risky investment – I reckon I deserve a profit.'

He nodded. 'Very well. But it's going to look damned funny in the books – for one model railway, paid to M. Jaggard, £35,000.'

'Why don't you call it by its real name? A computing system.'

His brow cleared. 'That's it. Now let's take a look at this incredible thing.' We collected Larry Godwin as an interpreter and went to the warehouse.

The first thing I noticed was that the system wasn't running and I asked Harrington why. 'No need,' he said cheerfully. 'Now we've got the character list sorted out we've duplicated the system in a computer – put it where it really belongs. We weren't running the entire program, you know; just small bits of it. To run through it all would have been impossible.'

I stared at him. 'Why?'

'Well, not really impossible. But look.' He opened the LNER schedule and flipped through. 'Take these five pages here. They contain reiterative loops. I estimate that to run these five pages on the system would take six days, at twenty-four hours a day. To run through the whole program would take about a month and a half – and this is one of the smaller programs. To put all twelve of them through would take about two years.'

He closed the schedule. 'I think the original programs were written on, and for, a real computer, and then transferred on to this system. But don't ask me why. Anyway, now we've put the system back into a computer we're geared to work at the speed of electrons and not on how fast a model railway engine can turn its wheels.'

Ogilvie said, 'Which computer?'

'One in the City; a time-sharing system.'

Ogilvie looked at me. 'Oh, we can't have that. I want everything you've put into that computer cleared out. We'll put it in our own computer.'

I said quickly, 'I wouldn't do that. I don't trust it. It lost Benson.'

Although Harrington could not know what we were talking about he caught the general drift. 'That's no problem.' He pointed to the railway. 'As a model railway that thing is very elaborate and complex, but as a computer it's relatively simple. There's nothing there that can't be duplicated in the Hewlett-Packard desk-top job I have in my own office. But I'll need a printer to handle Russian characters and, perhaps, a modified keyboard.'

Ogilvie said, 'That's a most satisfactory solution.' He walked over to the railway and looked at it. 'You're right; it is complex. Now show me how it works.'

Harrington smiled. 'I thought you'd ask that. Can you read Russian?'

Ogilvie indicated Larry. 'We've brought an interpreter.'

'I'm going to run through the program from the beginning; it's set up ready. I want you to keep an eye on that marshalling yard there. When it's full you can read it off because I've labelled each truck with the character it represents. I'll stop the system at the right time.'

He switched on and the trains began to scurry about, and the marshalling yard, which was empty, began to fill up. Harrington stopped the system. 'There you are.'

Ogilvie leaned forward and looked. 'All right, Godwin, What does it say?'

Harrington handed Larry a small pair of opera glasses. 'You'll find these useful.'

Larry took them and focused on the trains. His lips moved silently but he said nothing, and Ogilvie demanded impatiently, 'Well?'

'As near as I can make out it says something like this: "First approximation using toroidal Legendre function of the first kind."'

'Well, I'll be damned!' said Ogilvie.

Later, back at the office, I said, 'So they're not going to use the railway.'

'And better not,' said Ogilvie. 'We can't wait two years to find out what this is all about.'

'What will you do with it? According to Harrington it's a pretty simple-minded computer. Without the schedules – the programs – it's just an elaborate rich man's toy.'

'I don't know what to do with it,' said Ogilvie. 'I'll have to think about that.'

'Do me a favour,' I said. 'Give it to Michaelis. It was he who figured those schedules were fakes. It'll make his day.'

THIRTY-TWO

So Harrington put the programs on tape acceptable to his own computer and the Russian character printer began to spew out yards of Russian text and international figures. When Larry translated the Russian it proved to be oddly uninformative – brief notes on what the computer was doing at the time, but not why it was doing it. I mean, if you read a knitting pattern and find 'knit 2, purl 1', that doesn't tell you if you're knitting a body-belt for a midget or a sweater for your hulking Rugby-playing boy-friend. And that's not really such a good analogy because if you're knitting you know you're knitting, while a computer program could be doing damned nearly anything from analysing the use of the subjunctive in Shakespeare's *Titus Andronicus* to designing a trajectory for a space shot to Pluto. The field was wide open so a selection of assorted boffins was brought in.

All this was beyond me so I left them to it. I had other things on my mind, the principal one being that Penny had cabled me, saying that she was returning and giving her flight number and time of arrival at Heathrow. I felt a lot better immediately because it meant she expected me to meet her, and she wouldn't have done it if her decision had not been in my favour.

When I met her she was tired. She had flown from Los Angeles to New York, stopped for a few hours only to see

Gillian, and then flown the Atlantic. She was suffering from jet lag and her stomach and glands were about nine hours out of kilter. I took her to the hotel where I had booked her a room; she appreciated that, not wanting to move into an empty flat with nothing in the refrigerator.

I joined her in a coffee before she retired to her room, and she told me that the operation on Gillian was going well and would I pass that message on to Michaelis. She smiled. 'Gillian particularly wants him to know.'

I grinned. 'We mustn't hinder the marriage of true minds.'

She talked briefly about what she had been doing in California and of a visit to the Harvard School of Medical Studies. 'They're doing good work there with PV40,' she said.

'What's that?'

'A virus – harmless to human beings.' She laughed. 'I keep forgetting you're not acquainted with the field.'

I said nothing to her about the model railway, although she would have to be told eventually. We couldn't just expropriate the knowledge to be found there – whatever it was – although the legal position would seem to be confused. The department had bought it, but whether the information it held came under the Copyright Act or not was something to keep the lawyers happy for years. In any case it was for Ogilvie to make the decision.

But she had just said something that had jerked little man Hunch out of bed and he was yelling his head off. I said, 'Did you talk over your work much with your father?'

'All the time,' she said.

'It doesn't seem a subject that would interest a man primarily versed in catalysts,' I said casually. 'Did he know much about it?'

'Quite a lot,' she said. 'Daddy was a man with a wide range of interests. He made one or two suggestions which really surprised Lummy when they worked in the laboratory.' She finished her coffee. 'I'm for bed. I feel I could sleep the clock around.'

I saw her to the lift, kissed her before she went up, then went back to the office at speed. Ogilvie wasn't in, so I went to see Harrington and found him short-tempered and tending to be querulous. 'The man who put these programs together was either quite mad or a genius. Either way we can't make sense out of them.'

Harrington knew nothing about Ashton and I didn't enlighten him beyond saying, 'I think you can discount insanity. What can you tell me about the programs – as a whole?'

'As a whole?' He frowned. 'Well, they seem to fall into two groups – a group of five and a group of seven. The group of seven is the later group.'

'Later! How do you know?'

'When we put them through the computer the last thing that comes out is a date. The first five seem to be totally unrelated to each other, but the group of seven appear to be linked in some way. They all use the same weird system of mathematics.'

I thought hard for some minutes and made a few calculations. 'Let me guess. The first of the group of seven begins about 1971, and the whole lot covers a period finishing, say, about six months ago.'

'Not bad,' said Harrington. 'You must know something I don't.'

'Yes,' I said. 'I rather think I do.'

I sought Ogilvie again and found he had returned. He took one look at my face, and said, 'You look like the cat that swallowed the canary. Why so smug?'

I grinned and sat down. 'Do you remember the time we had a late night session trying to figure what Ashton would have been working on? We agreed he would keep on theorizing, but we couldn't see what he could theorize about.'

'I remember,' said Ogilvie. 'And I still can't. What's more, neither can Harrington and he's actually working on the material itself.'

'You said he wouldn't be working in atomics because he hadn't kept up with the field.'

'He didn't keep up in any field with the exception of catalytic chemistry, and there he was mainly reworking his old ideas – nothing new.'

'You're wrong,' I said flatly.

'I don't see what he could have kept up in. We know the books he bought and read, and there was nothing.'

I said softly, 'What about the books Penny bought?'

Ogilvie went quite still. 'What are you getting at?'

'Penny said something just before she went to the States which slipped right past me. We were talking about some of the complications of her work and most of it was over my head. We were in her home at the time, and she said she was so used to talking with her father in that room she'd forgotten I was a layman.'

'The implication being that Ashton wasn't?'

'That's it. It came up again just now and this time it clicked. I've just been talking to Harrington, and he tells me there's a group of seven linked programs. I made an educated guess at the period they covered and I got it right first time. They started when Penny first began her graduate work in genetics. I think Ashton educated himself in genetics alongside his daughter. This morning Penny said he'd made suggestions which surprised Lumsden when they worked in the laboratory. Now, Penny works with Lumsden, one of the top men in the field. Everything he knew and learned she could pass on to Ashton. She read the relevant journals – and so did Ashton; she attended seminars and visited other laboratories – and passed everything back to Ashton. She could have been doing it quite unconsciously, glad to have someone near to her with whom she could discuss her work. He was right in the middle of some of the most exciting developments in science this century, and I'm not discounting atomic physics. What's more likely than that a man like Ashton should think and theorize about genetics?'

'You've made your point,' said Ogilvie. 'But what to do about it?'

'Penny must be brought in, of course.'

He shook his head. 'Not immediately. I can't make that decision off the cuff. The problem lies in the very fact that she *is* Ashton's daughter. She's intelligent enough to ask why her father should have considered it necessary to hide what he's doing, and that, as the Americans say, opens up a can of worms, including his early history and how and why he died. I doubt if the Minister would relish an angry young woman laying siege to his office or, much worse, talking to newspaper reporters. I'll have to ask him for a decision on this one.'

I said, 'You can't possibly suppress a thing like this.'

'Who is talking about suppressing it?' he said irritably. 'I'm merely saying we'll have to use tact in handling it. You'd better leave it with me. You haven't said anything to her about it, have you?'

'No.'

'Good. You've done well on this, Malcolm. You'll get the credit for it when the time comes.'

I wasn't looking for credit, and I had an uneasy feeling that Ogilvie wasn't being quite straight with me. It was the first time I had ever felt that about him, and I didn't like it.

I saw Penny the following afternoon, by arrangement, at University College. As I walked down the corridor towards her office the door of Lumsden's office opened and Cregar came out so that I had to sidestep smartly to avoid barging into him. He looked at me in astonishment and demanded, 'What are you doing here?'

Apart from the fact that it wasn't any of his business, I still felt sore enough at the roasting he had given me at the committee meeting to be inclined to give him a sharp answer. Instead I said, mildly enough, 'Just visiting.'

'That's no answer.'

'Perhaps that's because I neither liked the question nor the way it was put.'

He boggled a bit then said, 'You're aware the Ashton case is closed?'

'Yes.'

'Then I'll have to ask you again – what are you doing here?'

I said deliberately, 'The moon will turn into green cheese the day I have to ask your permission to visit my fiancée.'

'Oh!' he said inadequately. 'I'd forgotten.' I really think it had slipped his memory. Something in his eyes changed; belligerence gave way to speculation. 'Sorry about that. Yes, you're going to marry Dr Ashton, aren't you?'

At that moment I didn't know whether I was or not, but I wouldn't give Cregar that satisfaction. 'Yes, I am.'

'When is the wedding to be?'

'Soon, I hope.'

'Ah, yes.' He lowered his voice. 'A word to the wise. You are aware, of course, that it would be most undesirable if Miss Ashton should ever know what happened in Sweden.'

'Under the circumstances I'm the last person likely to tell her,' I said bitterly.

'Yes. A sad and strange business – very strange. I hope you'll accept my apology for my rather abrupt manner just now. And I hope you'll accept my good wishes for your future married life.'

'Of course – and thank you.'

'And now you must excuse me.' He turned and went back into Lumsden's office.

As I walked up the corridor I speculated on Cregar's immediate assumption that my presence in University College was linked to the Ashton case. Granted that he had genuinely forgotten I was to marry Penny, then what possible link could there be?

I escorted Penny to Fortnum's where she restocked her depleted larder. Most of the order was to be sent, but we took enough so that she could prepare a simple dinner for two. That evening, in the flat, as we started on the soup she said, 'I'm going to Scotland tomorrow.'

'With Lumsden?'

'He's busy and can't come. The extra time I spent in America has thrown our schedule out a bit.'

'When will you be back?'

'I don't think I'll be away as much as a week. Why?'

'There's a new play starting at the Haymarket next Tuesday which I thought you might like to see. Alec Guinness. Shall I book seats?'

She thought for a moment. 'I'll be back by then. Yes, I'd like that I haven't been in a theatre for God knows how long.'

'Still having trouble in Scotland?'

'It's not really trouble. Just a difference of opinion.'

After dinner she made coffee, and said, 'I know you don't like brandy. There's a bottle of scotch in the cabinet.'

I smiled. 'That's thoughtful of you.'

'But I'll have a brandy.'

I poured the drinks and took them over to the coffee table. She brought in the coffee, and then we sat together on the settee. She poured two black coffees, and said quietly, 'When would you like us to get married, Malcolm?'

That was the night the new carpet became badly coffee-stained, and it was the night we went to bed together for the first time.

It had been quite long enough.

THIRTY-THREE

The rest of the week went slowly. Penny went to Scotland and I booked a couple of seats at the Haymarket Theatre. I also made enquiries into exactly how one gets married; it hadn't come up before. I felt pretty good.

Ogilvie was uncommunicative. He wasn't around the office much during the next few days and, even when he was, he didn't want to see me. He asked how I was getting on with the investigation of Benson and made no comment when I said I was stuck. Twice thereafter he refused to see me when I requested an audience. That worried me a little.

I checked with Harrington to find how he was doing and to see if any genetics experts had been brought in – not by asking outright but by tactful skating around the edges. No new boffins were on the job and certainly no biologists of any kind. That worried me, too, and I wondered why Ogilvie was dragging his heels.

Harrington's temper was becoming worse. 'Do you know what I've found?' he asked rhetorically. 'This joker is using Hamiltonian quaternions!' He made it sound like a heinous offence of the worst kind.

'Is that bad?'

He stared at me and echoed, 'Bad! No one, I repeat – *no one* – has used Hamiltonian quaternions since 1915 when tensor analysis was invented. It's like using a pick and shovel when you have a bulldozer available.'

I shrugged. 'If he used these Hamilton's whatsits he'd have a sound reason.'

Harrington stared at a print-out of the computer program with an angry and baffled expression. 'Then I wish I knew what the hell it is.' He went back to work.

And so did I, but my trouble was that I didn't know what to do. Benson was a dead issue – there seemed to be no possible way of getting a line on him. Ogilvie seemed to have lost interest, and since I didn't want to twiddle my thumbs in Kerr's section, I spent a lot of time in my flat catching up on my reading and waiting for Tuesday.

At the weekend I rang Penny hoping she'd be back but got no answer. I spent a stale weekend and on the Monday morning I rang Lumsden and asked if he'd heard from her. 'I spoke to her on Thursday,' he said. 'She hoped to be back in London for the weekend.'

'She wasn't.'

'Well, perhaps she'll be back today. If she comes in is there a message for her?'

'Not really. Just tell her I'll meet her at home at seven tomorrow evening.'

'I'll tell her,' said Lumsden, and rang off.

I went to the office feeling faintly dissatisfied and was lucky to catch Ogilvie at the lift. As we went up I asked bluntly, 'Why haven't you given Harrington a geneticist to work with him?'

'The situation is still under review,' he said blandly.

'I don't think that's good enough.'

He gave me a sideways glance. 'I shouldn't have to remind you that you don't make policy here,' he said sharply. He added in a more placatory tone, 'The truth is that a lot of pressure is being brought to bear on us.'

I was tired of framing my words in a diplomatic mode. 'Who from – and why?' I asked shortly.

'I'm being asked to give up the computer programs to another department.'

'Before being interpreted?'

He nodded. 'The pressure is quite strong. The Minister may accede to the request.'

'Who the devil would want . . .?' I stopped and remembered something Ogilvie had let drop. 'Don't tell me it's Cregar again?'

'Why should you think . . .' He paused and reconsidered. 'Yes, it's Cregar. A persistent devil, isn't he?'

'Jesus!' I said. 'You know how he'll use it. You said he was into bacteriological warfare techniques. If there's anything important in there he'll use it himself and hush it up.'

The lift stopped and someone got in. Ogilvie said, 'I don't think we should discuss this further.' On arrival at our floor he strode away smartly.

Tuesday came and at seven in the evening I was at Penny's flat ringing the bell. There was no answer. I sat in my car outside the building for over an hour but she didn't arrive. She had stood me up without so much as a word. I didn't use the tickets for the show but went home feeling unhappy and depressed. I think even then I had an inkling that there was something terribly wrong. Little bits of a complicated jigsaw were fitting themselves together at the back of my mind but still out of reach of conscious reasoning power. The mental itch was intolerable.

The next morning, as early as was decent, I rang Lumsden again. He answered my questions good-humouredly enough at first, but I think he thought I was being rather a pest. No, Penny had not yet returned. No, he had not spoken to her since Thursday. No, it wasn't at all unusual; her work could be more difficult than she expected.

I said, 'Can you give me her telephone number in Scotland?'

There was a silence at my ear, then Lumsden said, 'Er . . . no – I don't think I can do that.'

'Why? Haven't you got it?'

'I have it, but I'm afraid it isn't available to you.'

I blinked at that curious statement, and filed it away for future reference. 'Then can you ring her and give her a message?'

Lumsden paused again, then said reluctantly, 'I suppose I can do that. What's the message?'

'It'll need an answer. Ask her where she put the letters from her father. I need to know.' As far as I knew that would be perfectly meaningless.

'All right,' he said. 'I'll pass it on.'

'Immediately,' I persisted. 'I'll wait here until you ring me back.' I gave him my number.

When I sorted the morning's post I found a slip from British Road Services; they had tried to deliver a package but to no avail because I was out – would I collect said package from the depot at Paddington? I put the slip in my wallet.

Lumsden rang nearly an hour later. 'She says she doesn't know which particular letters you mean.'

'Does she? That's curious. How did she sound?'

'I didn't speak to her myself; she wasn't available on an outside line. But the message was passed to her.'

I said, 'Professor Lumsden, I'd like you to ring again and speak to her personally this time. I . . .'

He interrupted. 'I'll do no such thing. I haven't the time to waste acting as messenger-boy.' There was a clatter and he was cut off.

I sat for a quarter of an hour wondering if I was making something out of nothing, chasing after insubstantial wisps as a puppy might chase an imaginary rabbit. Then I drove to Paddington to collect the package and was rather shattered to find that it was my own suitcase. Captain Morelius had taken his time in sending my possessions from Sweden.

I put it in the boot of my car and opened it. There seemed to be nothing missing although after such a length of time I couldn't be sure. What was certain was that Swedish Intelligence would have gone over everything with a microscope. But it gave me an idea. I went into Paddington Station and rang the Ashton house.

Mary Cope answered, and I said, 'This is Malcolm Jaggard. How are you, Mary?'

'I'm very well, sir.'

'Mary, has anything arrived at the house from Sweden? Suitcases or anything like that?'

'Why, yes, sir. Two suitcases came on Monday. I've been trying to ring Miss Penny to ask her what to do with them, but she hasn't been at home – I mean in the flat in London.'

'What did you do with them?'

'I put them in a box-room.'

There were traffic jams on the way to Marlow. The congestion on the Hammersmith By-Pass drove me to a distraction of impatience, but after that the road was open and I had my foot on the floor as I drove down the M4. The gates of the house stood open. Who would think Mary Cope might need protection?

She answered the door at my ring, and I said immediately, 'Has anyone else asked about those cases?'

'Why, no, sir.'

'Where are they?'

'I'll show you.' She led me upstairs by the main staircase and up another flight and along a corridor. The house was bare and empty and our footsteps echoed. She opened a door. 'I put them in here out of the way.'

I regarded the two suitcases standing in the middle of the empty room, then turned to her and smiled. 'You may congratulate me, Mary. Penny and I are getting married.'

'Oh, I wish you all the best in the world,' she said.

'So I don't think you'll have to stay in London, after all. We'll probably have a house in the country somewhere. Not as big as this one, though.'

'Would you want me to stay?'

'Of course,' I said. 'Now, I'd like to look at this stuff alone. Do you mind?'

She looked at me a shade doubtfully, then made up her mind. So many strange things had happened in that house that one more wouldn't make any difference. She nodded and went out, closing the door behind her.

Both cases were locked. I didn't trouble with lock-picking but sprung open the catches with a knife. The first case was Ashton's and contained the little he had taken with him on the run from Stockholm. It also contained the clothes he had been wearing; the overcoat, jacket and shirt were torn – bullet holes – but there was no trace of blood. Everything had been cleaned.

It was Benson's case I was really interested in. In this two-cubic-foot space was all we had left of Howard Greatorex Benson, and if I couldn't find anything here then it was probable that the Ashton case would never be truly solved.

I emptied the case and spread everything on the floor. Overcoat, suit, fur hat, underwear, shirt, socks, shoes – everything he had died with. The fur hat had a hole in the back big enough to put my fist through. I gave everything a thorough going-over, aware that Captain Morelius would have done the same, and found nothing – no microfilm, beloved of the thriller writers, no hidden pockets in the clothing, nothing at all out of the usual.

There was a handful of Swedish coins and a slim sheaf of currency in a wallet. Also in the wallet were some stamps, British and Swedish; two newspaper cuttings, both of book reviews in English, and a scribbled shopping-list. Nothing there for me unless smoked salmon, water biscuits and Mocha coffee held a hidden meaning, which I doubted.

I was about to drop the wallet when I saw the silk lining was torn. Closer inspection showed it was not a tear but a cut, probably made by a razor blade. Captain Morelius left nothing to chance at all. I inserted my finger between the lining and the outer case and encountered a piece of paper. Gently I teased it out, then took my find to the window.

It was a letter:

TO WHOM IT MAY CONCERN

Howard Greatorex Benson is the bearer of this letter. Should his *bona fides* be doubted in any way the undersigned should be consulted immediately before further action is taken with regard to the bearer.

Stapled to the letter was a passport-type photograph of Benson, a much younger man than the Benson I remembered but still with the damaged features and the scar on the cheek. He looked to be in his early thirties. Confirmation of this came from the date of the letter – 4 January, 1947. At the bottom of the letter was an address and a telephone number; the address was in Mayfair and the number was in the old style with both letters and digits, long since defunct. The letter was signed by James Pallson.

The itch at the back of my mind was now assuaged, the jigsaw puzzle was almost complete. Although a few minor pieces were missing, enough pieces were assembled to show the picture, and I didn't like what I saw. I scanned the letter again and wondered what Morelius had made of it, then put it into my wallet and went downstairs.

I telephoned Ogilvie but he was out, so after making my farewell to Mary Cope I drove back to London, going immediately to University College. Aware that Lumsden might refuse to see me, I avoided the receptionist and went straight to his office and went in without knocking.

He looked up and frowned in annoyance as he saw me. 'What the devil . . . I won't be badgered like this.'

'Just a few words, Professor.'

'Now look here,' he snapped, 'I have work to do, and I haven't time to play post office between two love-birds.'

I strode to his desk and pushed the telephone towards him. 'Ring Penny.'

'I will not.' He picked up the card I flicked on to the desk, then said, 'I see. Not just a simple policeman, after all. But I can't see this makes any difference.'

I said, 'Where's the laboratory?'

'In Scotland.'

'Where in Scotland?'

'I'm sorry. I'm not at liberty to say.'

'Who runs it?'

He shrugged. 'Some government department, I believe.'

'What's being done there?'

'I really don't know. Something to do with agriculture, so I was told.'

'Who told you?'

'I can't say.'

'Can't or won't?' I held his eye for a moment and he twitched irritably. 'You don't really believe that guff about agriculture, do you? That wouldn't account for the secretive way you're behaving. What's so bloody secret about agricultural research? Cregar told you it was agriculture and you accepted it as a sop to your conscience, but you never really believed it. You're not as naïve as that.'

'We'll leave my conscience to me,' he snapped.

'And you're welcome to it. What's Penny doing there?'

'Giving general technical assistance.'

'Laboratory design for the handling of pathogens,' I suggested.

'That kind of thing.'

'Does she know Cregar is behind it?'

'You're the one who brought up Cregar,' said Lumsden. 'I didn't.'

'What did Cregar do to twist your arm? Did he threaten to cut off your research funds? Or was there a subtly-worded letter from a Cabinet Minister suggesting much the same thing? Co-operate with Cregar or else.' I studied him in silence for a moment. 'That doesn't really matter – but did Penny know of Cregar's involvement?'

'No,' he said sullenly.

'And she didn't know what the laboratory was for, but she was beginning to have suspicions. She had a row with you.'

'You seem to know it all,' said Lumsden tiredly, and shrugged. 'You're right in most of what you say.'

I said, 'Where is she?'

He looked surprised. 'At the laboratory. I thought we'd established that.'

'She was very worried about safety up there, wasn't she?'

'She was being emotional about it. And Cregar was pushing Carter hard. He wants results.'

'Who is Carter?'

'The Chief Scientific Officer.'

I pointed to the telephone. 'I'll lay you a hundred pounds to a bent farthing that you won't be able to talk to her.'

He hesitated for a long time before he picked up the telephone and began to dial. Although he was being niggly on secrecy, on security he was lousy. As he dialled I watched his finger and memorized the number. 'Professor Lumsden here. I'd like to speak to Dr Ashton. Yes, I'll hang on.'

He put his hand over the mouthpiece. 'They've gone to call her. They think she's in her room.'

'Don't bet on it.'

Lumsden hung on to the telephone for a long time, then suddenly said, 'Yes? . . . I see . . . the mainland. Well, ask her to ring me as soon as she comes back. I'll be in my office.' He put down the telephone and said dully, 'They say she's gone to the mainland.'

'So it's on an island.'

'Yes.' He looked up and his eyes were haunted. 'They could be right, you know.'

'Not a chance,' I said. 'Something has happened up there. You referred to your conscience; I'll leave you with it. Good day, Professor Lumsden.'

I strode into Ogilvie's outer office, said to his secretary, 'Is the boss in?' and breezed on through without waiting for an answer. There were going to be no more closed doors as far as I was concerned.

Ogilvie was just as annoyed as Lumsden at having his office invaded. 'I didn't send for you,' he said coldly.

'I've cracked Benson,' I said. 'He was Cregar's man.'

Ogilvie's eyes opened wide. 'I don't believe it.'

I tossed the letter before him. 'Signed, sealed and delivered. That was written on the fourth of January, 1947, the day Benson was discharged from the army, and signed by the Honourable James Pallson who is now Lord Cregar. Christ, the man has no honour in him. Do you realize, that when Ashton and Benson skipped to Sweden and Cregar was doing his holier-than-thou bit, he knew where they were all the time. The bastard has been laughing at us.'

Ogilvie shook his head. 'No, it's too incredible.'

'What's so incredible about it? That letter says Benson has been Cregar's man for the past thirty years. I'd say

Cregar made a deal with Ashton. Ashton was free to do as he wanted – to sink or swim in the capitalist sea – but only on condition he had a watchdog attached: Benson. And when the reorganization came and Cregar lost responsibility for Ashton he conveniently forgot to tell you about Benson. It also explains why Benson was lost from the computer files.'

Ogilvie drew in his breath. 'It fits,' he admitted. 'But it leaves a lot still to be explained.'

'You'll get your explanation from Cregar,' I said savagely. 'Just before I skin him and nail his hide to the barn door.'

'You'll stay away from Cregar,' he said curtly. 'I'll handle him.'

'That be damned for a tale. You don't understand. Penny Ashton has gone missing and Cregar has something to do with it. It will take more than you to keep me off Cregar's back.'

'What's all this?' He was bewildered.

I told him, then said, 'Do you know where this laboratory is?'

'No.'

I took a card from my wallet and dropped it on the desk. 'A telephone number. The post office won't tell me anything about it because it's unlisted. Do something.'

He glanced at the card but didn't pick it up. He said slowly, 'I don't know . . .'

I cut in. 'I know something. That letter is enough to ruin Cregar, but I can't wait. Don't stop me. Just give me what I need and I'll give you more than that letter – I'll give you Cregar's head on a platter. But I'm not going to wait too long.'

He looked at me thoughtfully, then picked up the card and the telephone simultaneously. Five minutes later he said two words. 'Cladach Duillich.'

THIRTY-FOUR

Cladach Duillich was a hard place to get to. It was one of the Summer Isles, a scattering of rocks in an indentation of the North Minch into Ross and Cromarty. The area is a popular haunt of biological dicers with death. Six miles to the south of Cladach Duillich lies Gruinard Island, uninhabited and uninhabitable. In 1942 the biological warfare boys made a trifling mistake and Gruinard was soaked with anthrax – a hundred years' danger. No wonder the Scots want devolution with that sort of foolishness emanating from the south.

I flew to Dalcross, the airport for Inverness, and there hired a car in which I drove the width of Scotland to Ullapool at the head of Loch Broom. It was a fine day; the sun was shining; the birds singing and the scenery magnificent – all of which left me cold because I was trying to make good speed on a road which is called in Scotland, 'Narrow, Class 1 (with passing places)'. I felt with a depressing certainty that time was a commodity which was running out fast.

It was latish in the day when I arrived in Ullapool. Cladach Duillich lay twelve miles further, out in the bay; say a four hour round trip for a local fishing boat. I dickered with a couple of fishermen but none was willing to take me out at that time. The sun was an hour from setting, clouds were building up in the west, and a raw wind blew down the narrow loch, ruffling water which had turned iron grey. I made a tentative deal with a man called Robbie Ferguson to take me out to the island at eight the next morning, weather permitting.

It was not yet the tourist season so I found a room in a pub quite easily. That evening I sat in the bar listening to the local gossip and putting in a word or two myself, not often but often enough to stake a conversational claim when I decided to do a small quiz on Cladach Duillich.

It was evident that the rising tide of Scottish nationalism was in full rip in the West Highlands. There was talk of English absentee landlords and of 'Scottish' oil and of the ambivalent attitude of the Scottish Labour Party, all uttered in tones of amused and rather tired cynicism as though these people had lost faith in the promises of politicians. There was not much of it, just enough to spice the talk of fishing and the weather, but if I had been a bland habitué of the Westminster corridors of power it would have been enough to scare the hell out of me. Ullapool, it seemed, was further removed from London than Kalgoorlie, Australia.

I finished my half-pint of beer and switched to scotch, asking the barman which he recommended. The man next to me turned. 'The Talisker's not so bad,' he offered. He was a tall, lean man in his mid-fifties with a craggy face and the soft-set mouth found in Highlanders. He spoke in that soft West Highland accent which is about as far from Harry Lauder as you can get.

'Then that's what I'll have. Will you join me?'

He gave me a speculative look, then smiled. 'I don't see why not. You'll be from the south, I take it. It's early for folk like you.'

I ordered two large Taliskers. 'What sort am I, then?'

'A tourist, maybe?'

'Not a tourist – a journalist.'

'Is it so? Which paper?'

'Any that'll publish me. I'm a freelance. Can you tell me anything about Gruinard Island?'

He chuckled, and shook his head. 'Och, not again? Every year we get someone asking about Gruinard; the Island of Death they used to call it. It's all been written, man; written into the ground. There's nothing new in that.'

I shrugged. 'A good story is still a good story to anyone who hasn't heard it. There's a rising generation which thinks of 1942 as being in the Dark Ages. I've met kids who think Hitler was a British general. But perhaps you're right. Anything else of interest around here?'

'What would interest an English newspaper in Ullapool? There's no oil here; that's on the east coast.' He looked into his whisky glass thoughtfully. 'There's the helicopter which comes and goes and no one knowing why. Would that interest you?'

'It might,' I said. 'An oil company chopper?'

'Could be, could be. But it lands on one of the islands. I've seen it myself.'

'Which island?'

'Out in the bay – Cladach Duillich. It's just a wee rock with nothing much on it. I doubt if the oil is there. They put up a few buildings but no drilling rig.'

'Who put up the buildings?'

'They say the government rented the island from an English lord. Wattie Stevenson went over in his boat once, just to pass the time of day, you know, and to say that when the trouble came there'd always be someone in Ullapool to help. But they wouldn't as much as let him set foot on the rock. Not friendly neighbours at all.'

'What sort of trouble was your friend expecting?'

'The weather, you understand. The winter storms are very bad. It's said the waves pass right over Cladach Duillich. That's how it got its name.'

I frowned. 'I don't understand that.'

'Ah, you haven't the Gaelic. Well, long ago there was a fisherman out of Coigach and his boat sank in a storm on the other side of the island out there. So he swam and he swam and he finally got ashore and thought he was safe. But he was drowned all the same, poor man, because the shore was Cladach Duillich. The water came right over. Cladach Duillich in the English would be the Sad Shore.'

If what I thought was correct it was well named. 'Do the people on Cladach Duillich ever come ashore here?'

'Not at all. I haven't seen a one of them. They fly south in the helicopter and no one knows where it goes or where it comes from. Not a penny piece do they spend in Ullapool. Very secret folk they are. There's just one landing place on Cladach Duillich and they've put up a big notice about trespassers and what will be done to them.'

I noticed that his glass was empty and wondered when he'd sunk the whisky. He must have done it when I blinked. I said, 'Have another, Mr . . . er . . .'

'You'll have one with me.' He signalled to the barman, then said, 'My name is Archie Ferguson and it's my brother who'll be taking you out to Cladach Duillich tomorrow morn.' He smiled sardonically at my evident discomfiture, and added, 'But I doubt if you'll set foot there.'

'I'm Malcolm Jaggard,' I said. 'And I think I will.'

'Malcolm's a good Scots name,' said Ferguson. 'I'll drink to your success, anyway; whatever it may be.'

'There's certainly something odd about the place,' I said, 'Do you think it's another Gruinard?'

Ferguson's face altered and for a moment he looked like the wrath of Almighty God. 'It had better not be so,' he said sternly. 'If we thought it was we would take the fire to it.'

I chewed that over together with my dinner, then made a telephone call – to Cladach Duillich. A voice said, 'How can I help you?'

'I'd like to speak to Dr Ashton. My name is Malcolm Jaggard.'

'Just a moment. I'll see if she's available.'

There was a four minute silence, then another voice said, 'I'm sorry, Mr Jaggard, but I'm told Dr Ashton went to the mainland and is not yet back.'

'Where on the mainland?'

There was a pause. 'Where are you speaking from, Mr Jaggard?'

'From London. Why?'

He didn't answer the question. 'She went to Ullapool – that's our local metropolis. She said she'd like to stretch her legs; there's not much scope for walking where we are. And she wanted to shop for a few things. May I ask how you got our number?'

'Dr Ashton gave it to me. When do you expect her back?'

'Oh, I don't know. The weather has closed in, so I don't think shell be back until tomorrow morning. You could speak to her then.'

'Where would she stay in Ullapool? I don't know the place.'

'I really couldn't say, Mr Jaggard. But she'll be back tomorrow with the boat.'

'I see. May I ask who I'm speaking to?'

'I'm Dr Carter.'

'Thank you, Dr Carter. I'll ring tomorrow.'

As I put down the telephone I reflected that someone was lying – other than myself – and I didn't think it was Archie Ferguson. But to make sure I went into the bar and found him talking to Robbie, his brother. I joined them. 'Excuse me for butting in.'

'That's all right,' said Ferguson. 'I was just talking over with Robbie your chances of getting out to Cladach Duillich the morrow's morn.'

I looked at Robbie. 'Is there any doubt of it?'

'I think there'll be a wee blow,' he said. 'The glass is dropping as the weather forecast said. Have you a strong stomach, Mr Jaggard?'

'Strong enough.'

Archie Ferguson laughed. 'You'll need one of cast iron.'

I said, 'The people on Cladach Duillich also said the weather is closing in.'

Archie raised his eyebrows. 'You've been talking to them! How?'

'By telephone – how else?'

'Aye,' said Robbie. 'They had the cable laid.' He shook his head. 'Awful expensive.'

'A man there told me a woman came ashore today from Cladach Duillich – here in Ullapool. She's about five feet eight inches, dark hair, age twent . . .'

Robbie interrupted. 'How did she come?'

'By boat.'

'Then she didn't come,' he said positively. 'All the comings and goings are by that bluidy helicopter. There's no boat on Cladach Duillich.'

'Are you sure?'

'O' course I'm sure. I pass the place twice a day, most days. You can take my word – there's no boat.'

I had to make sure of it. 'Well, supposing she came anyway. Where would she stay in Ullapool?'

'Ullapool's not all that big,' said Archie. 'If she's here at all we can put our hands on her – in a manner o' speaking, that is. What would be the lassie's name?'

'Ashton – Penelope Ashton.'

'Rest easy, Mr Jaggard. You'll know within the hour.' He smiled genially at his brother. 'Do you not smell something awful romantic, Robbie?'

THIRTY-FIVE

The wind whistled about my ears as I stood on the pier at eight next morning. The sky was slate-grey and so was the loch, stippled with whitecaps whipped up by the wind. Below me Robbie Ferguson's boat pitched violently, the rubber tyre fenders squealing as they were compressed and rubbed on the stone wall. It looked much too fragile to be taken out on such a day, but Robbie seemed unconcerned, He had taken the cover off the engine and was swinging on a crank.

Beside me, Archie Ferguson said, 'So you think the young lady is still on Cladach Duillich?'

'I do.'

He pulled his coat closer about him. 'Maybe we're wrong about the government,' he said. 'Could this be one of those queer religious groups we're importing from America these days? Moonies or some such? I've heard some remarkably funny things about them.'

'No, it's not that.' I looked at my watch. 'Mr Ferguson, could you do me a favour?'

'If I can.'

I estimated times. 'If I'm not back in eight hours – that's by four this afternoon – I want you to get the police and come looking for me.'

He thought about it for a moment. 'No harm in that. What if Robbie comes back and you don't?'

'Same thing applies. They might spin Robbie a yarn, tell him I've decided to stay. They'll be lying, but he's to accept the lie, come back here, and raise the alarm.'

Below, the diesel engine spluttered into life and settled down into a slow and steady thumping. Archie said, 'You know, Malcolm Jaggard, I don't believe you're a journalist at all.'

I took a card from my wallet and gave it to him. 'If I don't come back ring that number. Get hold of a man called Ogilvie and tell him about it.'

He studied the card. 'McCulloch and Ross – and Ogilvie. It seems we Scots have taken over the City of London.' He looked up. 'But you look less like a financier than you do a journalist. What's really going on out there on Cladach Duillich?'

'We spoke about it last night,' I said. 'And you talked of fire.'

A bleakness came over him. 'The government would do that again?'

'Governments are made of men. Some men would do that.'

'Aye, and some men can pay for it.' He looked at me closely. 'Malcolm Jaggard, when you come back you and I are going to have a bit of a talk. And you can tell yon laddies on Cladach Duillich that if you don't come back we'll be bringing the fire to them. A great cleanser is fire.'

'Stay out of it,' I said. 'It's a job for the police.'

'Don't be daft, man. Would the police go against the government? You leave this to me.' He looked down into the boat. 'Away with you; Robbie is waiting. And I'll away and have a talk with a few of my friends.'

I didn't argue with him. I climbed down the iron ladder which was slippery with water and seaweed and tried to time my drop into the boat to coincide with its erratic pitching. I fumbled it but was saved from sprawling full length by Robbie's strong arm.

He looked me up and down, then shook his head. 'You'll freeze, Mr Jaggard.' He turned and rummaged in a locker and brought out a seaman's guernsey. 'This'll keep you warm, and this –' he gave me a pair of trousers and an anorak, both waterproof – 'this'll keep you dry.'

When I had put them on he said, 'Now sit you down and be easy.' He went forward, walking as easily in that tossing boat as another man would walk a city pavement. He cast off the forward line, then walked back, seemingly unconcerned that the bow was swinging in a great arc. As he passed the engine he pushed over a lever with his boot, then dexterously cast off the stern line. The throbbing note of the engine deepened and we began to move away from the pier wall. Robbie was standing with the tiller between his knees, looking forward and steering by swaying motions of his body while he coiled the stern line into a neat skein.

The wind strengthened as we got out into the loch and the waves were bigger. The wind was from the north-west and we plunged into the teeth of it. As the bow dipped downwards sheets of spray were blown aft and I appreciated the waterproofing. As it was, I knew I'd be thoroughly drenched by the time we got to Cladach Duillich.

Presently Robbie sat down, controlling the tiller with one booted foot. He pointed, and said, 'The Coigach shore.'

I ducked a lump of spray. 'What sort of man is your brother?'

'Archie?' Robbie thought a bit and then shrugged. 'He's my brother.'

'Would you call him a hot-headed man?'

'Archie hot-headed!' Robbie laughed 'Why, the man's as cold as an iceberg. I'm the laddie in the family to take the chances. Archie weighs everything in a balance before he does anything. Why do you ask?'

'He was talking about what he'd do if I didn't come back from Cladach Duillich.'

'There's one thing certain about my brother – he does what he says he'll do. He's as reliable as death and taxes.'

That was comforting to know. I didn't know what lay ahead on Cladach Duillich, but I knew I wasn't going to get an easy answer. The knowledge that I had a reliable backstop gave me a warm feeling.

I said, 'If I go missing on that bloody bit of rock you'll take no for an answer. You'll swallow what they tell you, then go back and see your brother.'

He looked at me curiously. 'Are you expecting to disappear?'

'I wouldn't be surprised.'

He wiped the spray from his face. 'I don't ken what this is about, but Archie seems to like you, and that's enough for me. He's a thinker.'

It was a long haul across Annat Bay towards the Summer Isles. The waves were short and deep, and the pitching was combined with rolling, giving a corkscrew motion which was nauseating. Robbie looked at me and grinned. 'We'd better talk; it'll take your mind off your belly. Look, there's Cam nan Sgeir, with Eilean Dubh beyond. That's Black Island in the English.'

'Where's Cladach Duillich?'

'Away the other side of Eilean Dubh. We've a way to go yet.'

'Why don't they keep a boat there? If I lived on an island it's the first thing I'd think of.'

Robbie chuckled. 'You'll see when we get there – but I'll tell you anyway, just for the talking. There's but one place to land and a chancy place it is. There's no protection for boat or man. You can't just tie up as you can at Ullapool Pier. There'd be no boat when you got back if there was anything of a blow. It would be crushed on the rocks. I won't be waiting there for you, you know.'

'Oh? Where will you be?'

'Lying off somewhere within easy reach. There are more boats wrecked on land than at sea. It's the land that kills boats. I'll be doing a wee bit of fishing.'

I looked at the jumbled sea. 'In this!'

'Och, I'm used to it. You give me a time and I'll be there.'

'I'll tell you now. I want exactly two hours ashore.'

'Two hours you'll get,' he said. 'About the boat they haven't got on Cladach Duillich. When those folk first came they had a boat but it got smashed, so they got another and that was smashed. After they lost the third they began to get the idea. Then they thought that if they could take the boat ashore it would be all right, but it's an awful weary job pulling a boat ashore on Cladach Duillich because there's no beach. So they rigged davits just like on a ship and they could take the boat straight up a cliff and out of the water. Then a wave came one night and took the boat and the davits and they were never seen again. After that they gave up.'

'It sounds a grim place.'

'It is – in bad weather. It won't be too bad today.' I looked at the reefing seas and wondered what Robbie called bad weather. He pointed. 'There it is – Cladach Duillich.'

It was just as Archie Ferguson had described it – a wee bit of rock. There were cliffs all around, not high but precipitous, and the sea boiled white underneath them. Off the island was a scattering of rocks like black fangs and I thought the people on Cladach Duillich had been right when they decided this was no place for a boat.

As we drew nearer Robbie said, 'See that ravine? The landing place is at the bottom.'

There was a narrow crack in the cliff face at the bottom of which the sea seemed to be calmer – relatively speaking.

Robbie swung the tiller over sharply to avoid a rock which slid astern three feet off the port quarter, then he swung hard the other way to avoid another. He grinned. 'This is when you hope the engine doesn't pack in. You'd better get right forrard – you'll have to jump for it, and I won't be able to hold her there long.'

I scrambled forward and stood right in the bows as he brought the boat in. Now I saw that the crack in the rock was wider than at first glance and there was a concrete platform built at the bottom. The engine note changed as Robbie throttled back for the final approach. It was an amazing feat, but in that swirling sea with its cross-currents he brought her in so the bow kissed the concrete with a touch as light as a feather. At his shout I jumped and went sprawling as my feet skidded from under me on the weed-covered surface. When I picked myself up the boat was thirty yards off-shore and moving away fast. Robbie waved and I waved back, and then he applied himself to the task of avoiding rocks.

I looked at my surroundings. The first thing I saw was the notice board Archie Ferguson had mentioned. It was weather beaten and the paint was peeling and faded but it was still readable.

GOVERNMENT ESTABLISHMENT
Landing is Absolutely Prohibited
By Order

It did not say who had issued the order.

A path led from the concrete platform up the ravine, so I followed it. It climbed steeply and led to a plateau, sparsely grassed, in the centre of which was a group of buildings. They were low concrete structures which had the appearance of military blockhouses, probably because they were windowless. From what had been said about Cladach

Duillich they were the only type of building which could survive there.

I had no more time to study the place because a man was approaching at a run. He slowed as he came closer, and said abruptly, 'Can't you read?'

'I can read.'

'Then clear off.'

'The age of miracles is past, friend. Walking on the water has gone out of fashion. The boat's gone.'

'Well, you can't stay here. What do you want?'

'I want to talk to Dr Carter.'

He seemed slightly taken aback, and I studied him as he thought about it. He was big and he had hard eyes and a stubborn jaw. He said, 'What do you want to talk to Dr Carter about?'

'If Dr Carter wants you to know he'll tell you,' I said pleasantly.

He didn't like that but there wasn't much he could do about it. 'Who are you?'

'Same thing applies. You're out of your depth, friend. Let's go and see Carter.'

'No,' he said curtly. 'You stay here.'

I looked at him coldly. 'Not a chance. I'm wet through and I want to dry out.' I nodded to the buildings. 'Those look as bloody inhospitable as you behave, but I'm willing to bet they're warm and dry inside. Take me to Carter.'

His problem was that he didn't know me or my authority, but I was behaving as though I had a right to be there and making demands. He did as I thought he would and passed the buck. 'All right, follow me. You see Carter and you go nowhere else.'

THIRTY-SIX

As we walked towards the buildings I looked around at Cladach Duillich. It was not very big – about a third of a mile long and a quarter-mile across. Life had a poor existence on this rock. What grass had managed to gain a roothold was salt resistant marram, growing in crannies where a poor soil had gathered, and even the dandelions were wizened and sickly growths. The seabirds appeared to like it, though; the rocks were white with their droppings and they wheeled overhead screaming at our movements below.

There were three buildings, all identical, and I noted they were connected by enclosed passages. To one side, on a level bit of ground, was a helicopter pad, empty. I was conducted around the corner to one of the buildings and ushered through the doorway, bidden to wait, and then taken through another doorway. I looked back and realized I had gone through an air lock.

We turned sharply left and into a room where a man in a white coat was sitting at a desk and writing on a pad. He was slightly bald, had a thin face and wore bifocals. He looked up and frowned as he saw me, then said to my escort, 'What's this, Max?'

'I found him wandering about loose. He says he wants to see you.'

Carter's attention switched to me. 'Who are you?'

I glanced sideways at Max, and said smoothly, 'Who I am is for your ears only, Dr Carter.'

Carter sniffed. 'More cloak and dagger stuff. All right, Max. I'll take care of this.'

Max nodded and left, and I stripped off the anorak. 'I hope you don't mind me getting out of this stuff,' I said, as I began to take off the waterproof trousers. 'Too warm for indoors.'

Carter tapped on the desk with his pen. 'All right. Who are you, and what do you want?'

I tossed the trousers aside and sat down. 'I'm Malcolm Jaggard. I've come to see Dr Ashton.'

'Didn't you ring me last night? I told you she wasn't here – she's on the mainland.'

'I know what you told me,' I said evenly. 'You said she'd be back this morning, so I came to see her.'

He gestured. 'You've seen the weather. She wouldn't come over in this.'

'Why not? I did.'

'Well, she hasn't. She's still in Ullapool.'

I shook my head, 'She's not in Ullapool, and she wasn't there last night, either.'

He frowned. 'Look here, when I asked last night you said you were ringing from London.'

'Did I? Must have been force of habit,' I said blandly. 'Does it make a difference where I rang from?'

'Er . . . no.' Carter straightened and squared his shoulders. 'Now, you're not supposed to be here. This establishment is, shall we say, rather hush-hush. If it became known you were here you could be in trouble. Come to that, so could I, so I'll have to ask you to leave.'

'Not without seeing Penny Ashton. She's supposed to be here. Now isn't that a funny thing. I'm where I'm supposed not to be, and she's not where she's supposed to be. How do you account for it?'

'I don't have to account for anything to you.'

'You'll have to account for a lot, Dr Carter, if Penny Ashton doesn't turn up pretty damn quick. How did she get to Ullapool?'

'By boat, of course.'

'But this establishment doesn't have a boat. All journeys are by helicopter.'

He moistened his lips. 'You appear to be taking an unhealthy interest in this place, Mr Jaggard. I warn you that could be dangerous.'

'Are you threatening me, Dr Carter?'

'For any purpose prejudicial to the safety of the State, to approach, inspect or enter any prohibited place, or to . . .'

'Don't quote the Official Secrets Act at me,' I snapped. 'I probably know it better than you do.'

'I could have you arrested,' he said. 'No warrant is needed.'

'For a simple scientist you appear to know the Act very well,' I observed. 'So you'll know that to arrest me automatically brings in the Director of Public Prosecutions.' I leaned back. 'I doubt if your masters would relish that, seeing that Penny Ashton is missing from here. I told you, you'll have to account for a lot, Dr Carter.'

'But not to you,' he said, and put his hand on the telephone.

'I hope that's to give instructions to have Dr Ashton brought in here.'

A cool and amused voice behind me said, 'But Dr Carter really can't have her brought in here.' I turned my head and saw Cregar standing at the door with Max. Cregar said, 'Doctor, I'll trouble you for the use of your office for a moment. Max, see to Mr Jaggard.'

Carter was palpably relieved and scurried out. Max came over to me and searched me with quick, practised movements. 'No gun.'

'No?' said Cregar. 'Well, that can be rectified if necessary. What could happen to an armed man who breaks into a government establishment, Max?'

'He could get shot,' said Max unemotionally.

'So he could, but that would lead to an official enquiry which might be undesirable. Any other suggestions?'

'There are plenty of cliffs around here,' said Max. 'And the sea's big.'

It was a conversation I could do without. I said, 'Where's Penny Ashton?'

'Oh, she's here – you were quite right about that. You'll see her presently.' Cregar waved his hands as though dismissing a minor problem. 'You're a persistent devil. I almost find it in me to admire you. I could do with a few men of your calibre in my organization. As it is, I'm wondering what to do with you.'

'You'd better not compound your offences,' I said. 'Whatever you do about me, you've already done for yourself. We've linked you with Benson. I wouldn't be surprised if the Minister hasn't already been informed of it.'

The corners of his mouth turned down. 'How could I be linked with Benson? What possible evidence could there be?'

'A letter dated the fourth of January, 1947, carried by Benson and signed by you.'

'A letter,' said Cregar blankly, and looked through me into the past. Comprehension came into his eyes. 'Are you telling me that Benson still carried that damned letter after thirty years?'

'He'd probably forgotten about it – just as you had,' I said. 'It was hidden in the lining of his wallet.'

'A brown calf wallet with a red silk lining?' I nodded and Cregar groaned. 'I gave Benson that wallet thirty years ago. It would seem I tripped myself.'

He bent his head, apparently studying the liver spots on the backs of his hands. 'Where is the letter?' he asked colourlessly.

'The original? Or the twenty photocopies Ogilvie will have already made?'

'I see,' he said softly, and raised his head. 'What were your first thoughts on seeing the letter?'

'I knew you were linked with Ashton because you brought him out of Russia. Now you were linked with Benson, too. I thought of all the odd things that had happened, such as why a gentleman's gentleman should carry a gun, and why you tried to discount the fact he had shot Ashton when we had the meeting on my return from Sweden. It seemed hard to believe he was still your man after thirty years, but I was forced into it.'

Cregar lounged back in his chair and crossed his legs. 'Benson was a good man once, before the Germans got him.'

He paused. 'Of course he wasn't Benson then, he was Jimmy Carlisle and my comrade in British Intelligence during the war. But he lived and died as Benson, so let him remain so. He was captured in a Gestapo round-up in '44 and they sent him to Sachsenhausen, where he stayed until the end of the war. That's where he got his broken nose and his other brutalized features. They beat him with clubs. I'd say they beat his brains out because he was never the same man afterwards.'

He leaned forward, elbows on the desk. 'He was in a mess after the war. He had no family – his father, mother and sister were killed in an air raid – and he had no money apart from a disability pension. His brains were addled and his earning capacity limited. He'd never be any good in our line of work after that, but he deserved well of us, and by 1947 I pulled enough weight to help him, so I offered him the job of shepherd to Chelyuskin – Ashton as he became. It was a sinecure, of course, but he was pathetically grateful. You see, he thought it meant he wasn't finished in his job.'

Cregar took out a packet of cigarettes. 'Are you finding this ancient history interesting?' He held out the packet.

I took a cigarette. 'Very interesting,' I assured him.

'Very well. We switched him into the person of Benson at the same time we switched Chelyuskin to Ashton, then he hung around for a while. When Ashton got going Benson had a job in Ashton's office, and then later he became Ashton's factotum.'

'And Ashton knew what he was?'

'Oh, yes. Benson was the price Ashton had to pay for freedom. I knew that a man with that calibre of mind would not long be content to fiddle around in industry and I wanted to keep tabs on what he was doing.' He smiled. 'Benson was on to quite a good thing. We paid him a retainer and Ashton paid him, too.'

He leaned forward and snapped a gold lighter into flame under my nose. 'When the reorganization came and I lost Ashton to Ogilvie I kept quiet about Benson. In fact, I paid his retainer out of my own pocket. He didn't cost much; the retainer wasn't raised and the erosion in the value of money made Benson dirt cheap. It was an investment for the future which would have paid off but for you.'

I said, 'Did you know Ashton was into genetics?'

'Of course. Benson caught on to that as soon as it started happening. His job was to *know* what Ashton was doing at all times and, being permanently in the house, he could hardly miss. It was an incredible stroke of luck – Ashton becoming interested in genetics, I mean – because after the reorganization I had moved into the biological field myself.' He waved his hand. 'As you have discovered.'

'Ogilvie told me.'

'Ogilvie appears to have told you too much. From what you have let fall he appears to have given you the run of

Code Black. Very naughty of him, and something he may regret. I was fortunate enough to be able to put a block on the computer to cover Benson, but evidently it wasn't enough.' He stopped suddenly, and stared at me. 'Even I appear to be telling you too much. You have an ingratiating way with you.'

'I'm a good listener.'

'And I become garrulous as I grow old, a grave failing in a man of our profession.' He looked at his half-smoked cigarette distastefully, stubbed it out, and put his hands flat on the desk. 'I'm at a loss to know how to dispose of you, young Jaggard. Your revelation that Ogilvie has that letter makes my situation most difficult.'

'Yes, he's in a position to blast hell out of you,' I agreed. 'I don't think the Minister will be pleased. I rather think you've put yourself on the retirement list.'

'Very succinctly put. Nevertheless, I will find a way out of the difficulty. I have surmounted difficulties before and I see no reason why I should fail this time. All it takes is applied thought to the study of men's weaknesses.' He slapped his hands together. 'And that is what I must do immediately. Put him somewhere safe, Max.'

I ignored the hand on my shoulder. 'What about Penny Ashton?'

'You will see her in my good time,' said Cregar coldly. 'And only if I think it advisable.'

In my rage I wanted to lash out at him but I couldn't ignore that tightening hand. Max leaned over me. 'No tricks,' he advised. 'I have a gun. You won't see it but it's there.'

So I rose from the chair and went with him. He took me from the office and along a corridor. Because the place was windowless it was almost like being in a submarine; everything was quiet except that the air shivered with the distant rumble of a generator. At the other end of the corridor I saw movement on the other side of a glass partition as a man walked across. He was wearing totally enveloping overalls and his head was hooded.

I had no time to see more because Max stopped and opened a heavy door. 'In there,' he said curtly, so I walked through and he slammed the door, leaving me in total darkness because he had not seen fit to turn on a light. The first thing I did was to explore my prison and arrived at the conclusion that it was an unused refrigerated room. The walls were thick and solid, as was the door, and I soon came to the conclusion that the only way out was to be let out. I sat on the floor in a corner and contemplated possibilities.

It appeared to have been wise to tell Cregar of the letter. Up to then he had primarily been interested in discussing ways and means of transforming me into a corpse safely, but my disclosure that Ogilvie had the letter had put a stopper on that line of thought. But what a ruthless bastard he had turned out to be.

I don't know what makes men like Cregar tick, but there seem to be enough of the bastards around just as there are many Carters eager to help them. Somewhere in the world, I suppose, is the chemist who lovingly mixed a petroleum derivative with a palm oil derivative to produce napthenic acid palmetate, better known as napalm. To do that required a deliberate intellectual effort and a high degree of technical training, and why a man should put his brain to such a use is beyond me. Supervising that chemist would be an American Cregar whose motives are equally baffling, and at the top are the politicians ultimately responsible. Their motive is quite clear, of course: the ruthless grasp of sheer power. But why so many others should be willing to help them is beyond me.

It's hard to know who to blame. Is it the Lumsdens of the world who know what is going on but turn a blind eye, or is it the rest of us who don't know and don't take the trouble to find out? Sometimes I think the world is like a huge ant heap full of insects all busily manufacturing insecticide.

I was in the black room for a long time. The only light came from the luminous dial of my watch which told me of hours ticking away. I was oppressed by the darkness and became claustrophobic and suffered strange fears. I got up and began to walk around the room, keeping to the walls; it was one way of taking exercise. The silence was solid except for the sound of my own movements and a new fear came upon me. What if Cladach Duillich had been abandoned – evacuated? I could stay in that room until the flesh rotted from my bones.

I stopped walking and sat in the corner again. I may have fallen asleep for a while, I don't remember. The hours I spent there are pretty much blanked out in my memory. But I was aware when the door opened to let in a flood of light as glaring as from arc lamps. I put my hands to my eyes and saw Cregar at the door. He tut-tutted, and said, 'You didn't leave him a light, Max.'

'Must have forgotten,' said Max indifferently.

The light was quite ordinary light shed from fluorescent tubes in the ceiling of the corridor. I got up and went to the door. 'God damn you!' I said to Max.

He stood back a pace and lifted the pistol he held. Cregar said, 'Calm down. It wasn't intentional.' He saw me looking at the pistol. 'That's to warn you not to do anything silly, as well you might. You wanted to see the girl, didn't you? Well, you can see her now. Come with me.'

We walked along the corridor side by side with Max bringing up the rear. Cregar said conversationally, 'You won't see any of the staff because I've had them cleared out of this block. They're scientific types and a bit lily-livered. The sight of guns makes them nervous.'

I said nothing.

We walked a few more paces. 'I think I've found a way of confounding Ogilvie – there'll be no problem there – but that still leaves you. After we've seen Dr Ashton we'll have a talk.' He stopped at a door. 'In here,' he said, and let me precede him.

It was a strange room because one wall was almost entirely glass but the window looked, not upon the outside, but into another room. At first I didn't know what I was looking at, but Cregar said, 'There's Dr Ashton.' He pointed to a bed in the next room.

Penny was in bed, seemingly asleep. Her face was pale and ravaged, she could have been a woman twice her age. Around the bed were various bits of hospital equipment among which I recognized two drip feeds, one of which appeared to contain blood. I said, 'In God's name, what happened?'

Cregar said, almost apologetically, 'We had . . . er . . . an accident here last week in which Dr Ashton was involved. I'm afraid she's rather ill. She's been in a coma for the last two days.' He picked up a microphone and snapped a switch. 'Dr Ashton, can you hear me?'

His voice came amplified and distorted from a loudspeaker in the next room. Penny made no movement.

I said tightly, 'What's she got?'

'That's rather hard to say. It's something nobody has ever had before. Something new. Carter has been trying to run it down but without much success.'

I was frightened and angry simultaneously. Frightened for Penny and angry at Cregar. 'It's something you brewed up here, isn't it? Something that got loose because you were too tight-fisted to have a P4 laboratory as she wanted.'

'I see that Dr Ashton has been chattering about my business.' Cregar gestured. 'That's not a proper hospital ward of course; it's one of our laboratories. She had to be put somewhere safe.'

'Not safe for her,' I said bitterly. 'Safe for you.'

'Of course,' said Cregar. 'Whatever she's got we can't have spread about. Carter thinks it's most infectious.'

'Is Carter a medical doctor?'

'His degree is in biology not medicine, but he's a very capable man. She's getting the best of attention. We're transfusing whole blood and glucose, as you see.'

I turned to him. 'She should be in a hospital. This amateur lash-up is no good, and you know it. If she dies you'll be a murderer, and so will Carter and everybody else here.'

'You're probably right,' he said indifferently. 'About the hospital, I mean. But it's difficult to see how we could put her in a hospital and still maintain security.' His voice was remote and objective. 'I pride myself on my ability to solve problems but I haven't been able to solve that one.'

'Damn your security!'

'Coming from a man in your profession that smacks of heresy.' Cregar stepped back as he saw my expression, and gestured to Max who lifted the pistol warningly. 'She's having the best attention we can give her. Dr Carter is assiduous in his duties.'

'Carter is using her as a guinea pig and you damned well know it. She must be taken to a hospital – better still, to Porton. They understand high-risk pathogens there.'

'You're in no position to make demands,' he said. 'Come with me.' He turned his back and walked out.

I took a last look at Penny, then followed him with Max close behind. He walked up the corridor and opened a door on the other side. We entered a small vestibule and Cregar waited until Max had closed the outer door before proceeding. 'We do take precautions, in spite of anything you've been told,' he said. 'This is an air lock. The laboratory through there is under low pressure. Do you know why?'

'If there's a leak air goes in and not out.'

He nodded in satisfaction as though I'd passed a test, and opened the inner door. My ears popped as the pressure changed. 'This is Carter's own laboratory. I'd like to show it to you.'

'Why?'

'You'll see.' He began a tour, behaving for all the world like a guide in one of those model factories where they show you what they're proud of and hide the bad bits. 'This is a centrifuge. You'll notice it's in an air-tight cabinet; that's to prevent anything escaping while it's in operation. No aerosols – microbes floating in the air.'

We passed on, and he indicated an array of glass-fronted cabinets covering one wall. 'The incubating cabinets, each containing its own petri dish and each petri dish isolated. Nothing can escape from there.'

'Something escaped from somewhere.'

He ignored that. 'Each cabinet can be removed in its entirety and the contents transferred elsewhere without coming into contact even with the air in the laboratory.'

I looked into a cabinet at the circular growth of a culture on a petri dish. 'What's the organism?'

'*Escherichia coli*, I believe. It's Carter's favourite.'

'The genetically weakened strain.'

Cregar raised his eyebrows. 'You seem well informed for a layman. I don't know; that's Carter's affair. I'm not the expert.'

I turned to face him. 'What's this all about?'

'I'm trying to show you that we do take all possible precautions. What happened to Dr Ashton was purely accidental – a million to one chance. It's very important to me that you believe that.'

'If you'd listened to her it wouldn't have happened, but I believe you,' I said. 'I don't think you did it on purpose. What's so important about it?'

'I can come to an accommodation with Ogilvie,' he said. 'I'll lose some advantage but not all. That leaves you.'

'Have you spoken with Ogilvie?'

'Yes.'

I felt sick. If Cregar could corrupt Ogilvie I wouldn't want to work with him again. I said steadily, 'What about me?'

'This. I can do a deal with Ogilvie all right, but I don't think I could make it stick if anything happened to you. He always was squeamish. That means you have to be around and able to talk for some time to come which, as you will appreciate, presents me with a problem.'

'How to keep my mouth shut without killing me.'

'Precisely. You are a man like myself – we cut to the heart of a problem. When you appeared in the Ashton case I had you investigated most thoroughly. To my surprise you had no handle I could get hold of, no peccadilloes to be exploited. You seem to be that rarity, the honest man.'

'I won't take compliments from you, damn it!'

'No compliment, I assure you, Just a damnable nuisance. I wanted something to hold over you, something with which to blackmail you. There was nothing. So I have to find something else to close your mouth. I think I've found it.'

'Well?'

'It will mean my giving up more of the advantage I have achieved over the years, but I'll retain the most of it. I'll trade the young lady in the next laboratory for your silence.'

I looked at him with disgust. He had said the solution to his problem would lie in the study of men's weaknesses and he had found mine. He said, 'As soon as you agree, the girl can be taken to hospital, in carefully controlled conditions, of course. Perhaps your suggestion that she be taken to Porton is best. I could arrange that.'

I said, 'What guarantee would you have that I won't talk when she's well? I can't think of anything but no doubt you can.'

'Indeed I can – and I have. In Carter's office there's a document I want you to sign. I should say it's a carefully constructed document which took all my ingenuity to concoct. Quite a literary gem.'

'About what?'

'You'll see. Well, do you agree?'

'I'll need to read it first.'

Cregar smiled. 'Of course you may read it, but I think you'll sign it anyway. It's not much to ask – your signature for the life of your future wife.'

'You sicken me,' I said.

A telephone rang, startlingly loud. Cregar frowned, and said to Max, 'Answer it.' He held out his hand. 'I'll have the pistol. I don't trust him yet.'

Max gave him the gun and walked to the other end of the laboratory. Cregar said, 'Sticks and stones, etcetera. I don't care what you think of me as long as I get my way.'

'Show me what you want me to sign.'

'We'll wait for Max.'

Max talked in monosyllables in a low voice, then hung up and came back. 'Carter's got his knickers in a twist. He says a lot of men are landing. He reckons there are twenty boats out there.'

Cregar frowned. 'Who the hell are they?'

'He reckons they're local fishermen.'

'Damned Scots peasants! Go and shoo them away, Max. Put the fear of God into them with the Official Secrets Act. Get rid of them any way you can. Threaten them with the police if you have to.'

'Just threaten or actually send for them?'

'You can send for them if you think the situation warrants it.'

Max nodded towards me. 'That may not be entirely safe.'

'Don't worry about Jaggard,' said Cregar. 'We've reached an agreement.' As Max left he turned to me. 'Is this your doing?'

'How could I start a popular uprising?' I asked. 'They've probably got wind of what you're doing here, and remembering Gruinard, are determined not to let it happen again.'

'Ignorant bastards,' he muttered. 'Max will put them in their place.'

I said, 'I want Penny in hospital fast. How do we get off here?'

'A phone call will bring the helicopter in two hours.'

'You'd better make the call, then.'

He looked down at the floor, rubbing the side of his jaw while he thought about it. It was then I hit him in the belly, knocking the wind out of him. The gun went off and a bullet ricocheted from the wall and there was a smash of glass. I grabbed his wrist as he tried to bring up the gun and chopped him across the neck with the edge of my hand. He sagged to the floor.

When he painfully picked himself up I had the pistol. He glanced at it, then raised his eyes to mine. 'Where do you think this will get you?'

'I don't know about me, but it'll put you in prison.'

'You're a stupid, romantic fool,' he said.

'What's the number to ring for the helicopter?'

He shook his head. 'You don't know how government works, damn it. I'll never go to prison, but you'll be in water so hot you'll wish you'd never heard of Ashton or me.'

I said, 'I don't like hitting old men but I'll hammer hell out of you if I don't get that number.'

He turned his head and froze, then a weird bubbling cry came from him. 'Oh, Christ! Look what you've done!' His hand quivered as he pointed to the wall.

I looked, being careful to step behind him. At first I didn't see it. 'No tricks. What am I supposed to see?'

'The cabinets. Two are broken.' He whirled on me. 'I'm getting out of here.'

Blindly he tried to push past me, ignoring the gun. He was in a frenzy of terror, his face working convulsively. I stiff-armed him but his panic gave him added strength and he got past me and headed for the door. I went after him, reversed the pistol and clubbed him over the head. He went down like a falling tree.

I dragged him away from the door and went back to see the damage. Two of the panes in the incubating cabinets were broken and fragments of the petri dishes were scattered on the floor as were slimy particles of the cultures they had contained.

I whirled round as the door of the laboratory burst open. There stood Archie Ferguson. 'You're right, Mr laggard,' he said. 'It's another damned Gruinard.'

'Get out!' I yelled. 'For your life, get out!' He looked at me with startled eyes, and I pointed to the glass wall at the end of the room. 'Go next door – I'll talk to you there. Move, man!'

The door slammed shut.

THIRTY-SEVEN

When I picked up the microphone my hand was shaking almost uncontrollably. I pushed the transmit button and heard a click. 'Can you hear me, Archie?' Ferguson, on the other side of the glass, nodded and spoke but I heard nothing. 'There's a microphone in front of you.'

He looked about him, then picked it up. 'What happened here, Malcolm?'

'This place is bloody dangerous. Tell your men not to enter any of the laboratories – especially this one and the one across the corridor. Do that now.'

'I'll have guards on the doors.' He dropped the microphone and left on the run.

I went across to Cregar who was breathing stertorously. His head was twisted in an awkward position so I straightened him out and he breathed easier but showed no signs of coming awake.

'Mr Jaggard – are you there?'

I went back to the window to find Archie and Robbie Ferguson and a third man, one of the biggest I've seen, who was introduced as Wattle Stevenson. Archie said, 'It would seem you have problems. Is the lassie across the corridor the one you looked for?'

'Yes. You haven't been in there, have you?'

'No. I saw her by this arrangement we have here.'

'Good. Keep out of there. What size of an army did you bring? I heard of twenty boats.'

'Who told you that? There's only the six.'

'Have any trouble?'

'Not much. A man has a broken jaw.'

I said, 'How many people are there in this place?'

'Not as many as I would have thought. Maybe a dozen.'

Ogilvie had been right. It didn't take much to run a microbiological laboratory; perhaps half a dozen technical staff and the same number of domestics and bottlewashers. 'Put the lot under arrest. You have my authority for it.'

Archie looked at me speculatively. 'And what authority would that be?' I took out my departmental card and held it against the glass. He said, 'It doesn't mean much to me, but it looks official.'

'It takes you off the hook for invading government property. You did it on my instructions and you're covered. Oh, if you find a character called Max I don't care how roughly he's handled.'

Robbie Ferguson laughed. 'He's the one with the broken jaw. Wattie, here, hit him.'

'Och, it wasna' more than a wee tap,' said Wattie. 'The man has a glass jaw.'

'Wattie won the hammer throwing at the last Highland Games,' said Archie, with a grim smile. 'Besides, it was the man, Max, who sent Wattie away with a flea in his ear when he offered to help. What's to do now?'

'Did you ring Ogilvie as I asked?'

'Aye. He said he already knew about it.'

I nodded. He would have talked with Cregar. 'I want you to ring him again and the call put through to this telephone in here. You'll find a switchboard somewhere.'

'You can't come out?'

'No. You have my permission to listen in when I talk.' There was a groan behind me and I turned to see Cregar stirring. I said, 'Tell your men guarding the laboratories it's just as important that no one comes out. In fact, it's more important. This place being what it is there's probably some guns somewhere. In emergency use them.'

Archie looked grave. 'Is it so fearsome a thing?'

'I don't know,' I said wearily. 'I'm just taking prophylactic measures. Get busy, will you?'

I went back to Cregar, helped him to get up, and sat him in a chair where he slumped flaccidly. He was dazed and in shock; too old to cope with the rough stuff any more. I said, 'Cregar, can you hear me?' He muttered something indistinguishable, and I slapped his cheek. 'Can you hear me?'

'Yes,' he whispered.

'Don't try to leave. There's a man outside with orders to shoot. Do you understand?'

He looked at me with glazed eyes, and nodded. 'Doesn't matter,' he muttered. 'I'm dead anyway. So are you.'

'We'll all be dead in a hundred years,' I said, and went to look again at the cultures in the broken petri dishes. The stuff looked harmless enough but I was careful not to touch it. Penny had described the elaborate precautions which were taken to prevent the escape of dangerous organisms from laboratories and, according to her, the lab I was now in wasn't up to snuff for what Carter had been doing.

The cultures could have been ordinary *E.coli* and, as such, perfectly harmless. But if they were cultures of *E.coli* which Carter had diddled around with then they could be dangerous in totally unpredictable ways. Cregar wasn't a scientist but he knew what Carter was up to, and the broken dishes had been enough to scare him half to death. From now on no chances would be taken and I hoped there had not been an escape already when Archie had opened the door.

I didn't think so – the laboratory had low air pressure and I'd got him out fast.

Twenty minutes later I had Ogilvie on the phone. I wasted no time on politeness and answered none of the questions he shot at me. I said, 'This is a matter for urgency, so get it right the first time. Have you something to write with?'

'I'll record.' I heard a click.

'Cregar's laboratory on Cladach Duillich has run wild. There's one serious case of infection and two suspected. The organism causing it is new to medicine and probably man-made; it's also highly infectious. I don't know if it's a killer but it's highly likely. You'll have to set the alarm ringing and probably Lumsden, Penny's boss, is the best man to do it. Tell him hospitalization for three is needed in P4 – repeat – P4 conditions. He'll know what that means. Tell him I suggest Porton Down, but he might have a better idea.'

'I'll get on to it immediately,' said Ogilvie. 'Who are the three?'

'The serious case is Penny Ashton.'

There was a sharp withdrawal of breath. 'Oh, Christ! I'm sorry, Malcolm.'

I went on, 'The suspected cases are Cregar and myself.'

'For the love of God!' said Ogilvie. 'What's been going on up there?'

I ignored him. 'There's a helicopter pad on Cladach Duillich so Lumsden had better use a chopper. Tell him the man to see here is a Dr Carter. He's the chap who cooked up whatever hellbrew has got loose.'

'I've got that.'

'Then make it quick. I think Penny is dying,' I said bleakly.

THIRTY-EIGHT

Cregar and I were in an odd position. Loathing each other beyond all belief, we were condemned to each other's company for an unspecified period. The next few hours were to be extremely uncomfortable, but I tried to make them as comfortable as possible.

Archie Ferguson came back as soon as I had spoken to Ogilvie and the expression on his face was terrifying. He looked like one of the Old Testament prophets might look after inditing one of the more dire chapters of the Bible. 'May their souls rot forever in hell!' he burst out.

'Take it easy,' I said. 'There are practical things to do.' I thought of Ogilvie recording my telephone conversation and it gave me an idea. 'See if you can find a tape-recorder. I'll need it.'

Archie simmered down. 'Aye, I'll see what I can do.'

'And we'll need food in here, but you can give us food once and once only. What you do is this. You open the outer door of the laboratory and put the food on the floor just inside. Tell me when you've closed the door and I'll come out and get it. It can be done once only because I can't risk contamination through the air lock, so you'd better give us enough for three meals. If you can find vacuum flasks for coffee that would be a help.'

Ferguson looked past me. 'Is yon man the Cregar you spoke of?'

'Yes.'

'Then he gets nothing from me.'

'You'll do as I say,' I said sharply. 'We both eat or neither of us eats.'

He took a deep breath, nodded curtly, then laid down the microphone and went away. Half an hour later he came back. 'Your food's there. I did better than flasks; there's a coffee percolator to make your own.'

'Thanks.' I had another idea. 'Archie, this laboratory is maintained at a lower air pressure than the outside. That means pumps, and pumps mean electricity. Put someone to watch the generator; I don't want it stopping, either by breakdown or lack of fuel. Will you see to that?'

'Aye. It won't stop.'

I went into the air lock and got the food – a pile of sandwiches – and also found a small battery-powered cassette tape-recorder. I put everything on the table next to the telephone. Cregar was apathetic and looked at the sandwiches without interest. I filled the percolator from a tap on one of the benches and got the coffee going. Cregar accepted coffee but he wouldn't eat.

Unobtrusively I switched on the recorder; I wanted Cregar condemned out of his own mouth. I said, 'We've a lot to talk about.'

'Have we?' he said without interest. 'Nothing matters any more.'

'You're not dead yet, and you may not be if Ogilvie does his stuff. When did Benson learn of Ashton's interest in genetics?'

He was silent for a moment, then said, 'Must have been 1971. He saw that Ashton was keeping up with the girl's studies, and then starting to do a lot of work on his own, usually at the weekends – a lot of calculating. He tried to get a look at it, but Ashton kept it locked away.' Cregar brooded. 'Ashton never did like me. I've often wondered if he knew what I was doing.' He waved his hand at the laboratory. 'This, I mean. It's supposed to be secret, but a man with money can usually find out what he wants to know.' He shrugged. 'Anyway, he made damned certain that Benson didn't lay an eye on his work.'

'That empty vault must have come as a shock.'

He nodded. 'Benson knew about the vault but never managed to get inside. And when Ogilvie told me it was empty I didn't believe him. It was only when he offered to let one of my forensic chaps look at the vault that I accepted the fact.' He looked up. 'You're a clever man. I never thought of the railway. I ought to have done. Ashton wasn't the man to fool about with toy trains.'

Now Cregar had started to talk he positively flowed. I suppose he thought there was no reason to keep his silence. It was a sort of deathbed confession.

I said, 'What I can't understand was how you engineered Mayberry's acid attack – and why. That's the bit that seems senseless.'

'It was senseless,' said Cregar. 'I had nothing to do with it. I didn't even know Mayberry existed until the police tracked him down. Do you remember when you appeared before the inter-departmental committee, Ogilvie said something about you "exploding Ashton out of Stockholm"? Well, I exploded him out of England.'

'How?'

He shrugged. 'Opportunism combined with planning. I'd been wanting to have a dig at Ashton for a long time. I wanted to get him out of that house so I could get into that vault. I thought whatever he had would be ripe. I'd already made preparations – rented the flat and opened the bank account in Stockholm, got the Israeli passport, and so on. All I needed was a trigger. Then along came that maniac,

Mayberry – most opportunely. I got Benson to panic Ashton, talking of threats to the other girl, and so on. Benson told him my department couldn't cope with that sort of thing unless Ashton got out, that we were prepared to help and that we had a safe hideaway for him, which of course we had. And after all that the damned vault was empty.'

'But why did Benson kill Ashton?'

'Standing orders from thirty years ago,' said Cregar simply. 'Ashton wasn't to be allowed to go back to the Russians. If there was a chance of him falling into Russian hands Benson was to kill him. Benson had every reason to think you were Russians.'

'Jesus!' I said. 'What sort of man was Benson to kill Ashton after being with him thirty years?'

Cregar gave me a lopsided smile. 'He had gratitude, I suppose; and personal loyalty – to me.'

I remembered my musings in the dark room and, out of curiosity, said, 'Cregar, why did you do all this?'

He looked at me in surprise. 'A man must leave his mark on the world.'

I felt chilled.

There wasn't much I wanted to know after that, but, the dam now broken, Cregar rambled on interminably, and I was glad when the telephone rang. It was Ogilvie. 'There'll be an RAF helicopter on its way with a medical team. Lumsden thinks you're right about Porton and he's made the arrangements.' He paused. 'He also wants me to pass on his apologies – I don't know why.'

'I do. Thank him for me. When will the chopper get here?'

'They're assembling the team now. I'd say six hours. How's Miss Ashton?'

'I don't know,' I said bitterly. 'I can't get to her. She's in a coma. You can tell that to Lumsden, too.'

Ogilvie was inclined to talk but I cut him off. I wasn't in the mood for that. Half an hour later the phone rang again and I found Archie Ferguson on the line. 'There's someone called Starkie wants to talk to the man Carter. Shall I let him?'

'Let me talk to Starkie.' The earphone crackled and a deep voice said, 'Richard Starkie here – is that Dr Carter?'

'Malcolm Jaggard here. Who are you?'

'I'm a doctor speaking from Porton Down. Are you one of the infected men?'

'Yes.'

'Any symptoms starting to show?'

'Not yet.'

'If Carter manufactured this bug he'll know more about it than anyone. I need the information.'

'Right,' I said. 'If you don't get satisfaction from him let me know. Are you on the line, Archie?'

'Aye.'

'Let them talk. If Carter wants persuading I'm sure you know what to do.'

They came for us seven hours later, dressed like spacemen in plastic clothing with self-contained breathing apparatus. They put us in plastic envelopes whole and entire, plugged in an air supply and sealed us up. We stopped in the air lock and the envelopes and themselves were drenched with a liquid, then we were carried out to the helicopter where I found Penny already installed in her own envelope. She was still unconscious.

THIRTY-NINE

A month later I was feeling pretty chipper because Starkie had given me a clean bill of health. 'For three weeks now we've inspected every damned *E.coli* bug that's come out of you and they're all normal. I don't know why you're still lying around here. What do you think this is, a doss house?'

He hadn't always been as cheerful as that. At the beginning I was placed in a sterile room and untouched by human hand for the next two weeks. Everything that was done to me was done by remote control. Later they told me that a team of thirty doctors and nurses was working on me alone.

Penny did better. For her they apparently mobilized the entire medical resources of the United Kingdom, plus sizeable chunks from the United States and the Continent, with a little bit from Australia. The bug she had was different from the one I'd caught, and it was a real frightener. It got the medical world into a dizzy tizzy and, although they were able to cure her, they wanted to make sure that the bug, whatever it was, was completely eradicated. So I came out of Porton Down a month before her.

Starkie once said soberly, 'If she'd have been left another day with the minimal attention she was getting I don't think we could have done it.' That made me think of Carter and I wondered what was being done about him. I never found out.

When I came out of purdah but before I was discharged I went to see her. I couldn't kiss her, or even touch her, but we could speak separated by a pane of glass, and she seemed cheerful enough. I told her something of what had happened, but not everything. Time enough for that when she was better. Then I said, 'I want you out of here pretty damned quick. I want to get married.'

She smiled brilliantly. 'Oh, yes, Malcolm.'

'I can't fix a day because of that bloody man Starkie,' I complained. 'He's likely to keep you in here forever, investigating the contents of your beautiful bowels.'

She said, 'How would you like a double wedding? I had a letter from Gillian in New York. Peter Michaelis flew over and proposed to her. She was lying in bed with her left arm strapped to her right cheek and swaddled in bandages when he asked her. She thought it was very funny.'

'I'll be damned!'

'It will be a little time yet. We all have to get out of our hospitals. Is four months too long to wait?'

'Yes,' I said promptly. 'But I'll wait.'

I didn't ask anyone how Cregar was doing because I didn't care.

On the day I came out of the sterile room Ogilvie came to see me, bearing the obligatory pound of grapes. I received him with some reserve. He asked after my health and I referred him to Starkie, then he said, 'We got the tape cassette after it had been decontaminated. Cregar won't be able to wriggle out of this one.'

I said, 'Had any success with Ashton's computer programs?'

'Oh, my God, they're fantastic. Everyone has claimed the man was a genius and he's proved it.'

'How?'

Ogilvie scratched his head. 'I don't know if I can explain – I'm no scientist – but it seems that Ashton has done for genetics what Einstein did for physics. He analysed the DNA molecule in a theoretical way and came up with a series of rather complicated equations. By applying these you can predict exactly which genes go where and why, and which genetic configurations are possible or not possible. It's a startling breakthrough; it's put genetics on a firm and mathematical grounding.'

'That should make Lumsden happy,' I said.

Ogilvie ate a grape. 'He doesn't know. It's still confidential. It hasn't been released publicly yet.'

'Why not?'

'The Minister seems to feel . . . well, there are reasons why it shouldn't be released yet. Or so he says.'

That saddened me. The bloody politicians with their bloody reasons made me sick to the stomach. The Minister was another Cregar. He had found a power lever and wanted to stick to it.

Ogilvie took another grape. 'I asked Starkie when you'd be coming out but he isn't prepared to say. However, when you do I've a new job for you. As you may know, Kerr is retiring in two years. I want to groom you for his job.' Kerr was Ogilvie's second-in-command. He smiled. 'In seven years, when I go, you could be running the department.'

I said bluntly, 'Get lost.'

He was not a man who showed astonishment easily, but he did then. '*What did you say?*'

'You heard me. Get lost. You can take Kerr's job and your job and stuff them wherever you like. The Minister's backside might be a good place.'

'What the devil's got into you?' he demanded.

'I'll tell you,' I said. 'You were going to do a deal with Cregar.'

'Who said that?'

'Cregar.'

'And you believed him? The man lies as naturally as he breathes.'

'Yes, I believed him because at that point he had no reason to lie. He did proposition you, didn't he?'

'Well, we talked – yes.'

I nodded. 'That's why you won't get me back in the department. I'm tired of lies and evasions; I'm tired of self-interest masquerading as patriotism. It came to me when Cregar called me an honest man, not as a compliment but as someone to corrupt. I realized then that he was wrong. How could an honest man do what I did to Ashton?'

'I think you're being over-emotional about this,' Ogilvie said stiffly.

'I'm emotional because I'm a man with feelings and not a bloody robot,' I retorted. 'And now you can take your bloody grapes and get the hell out of here.'

He went away moderately unhappy.

FORTY

And they all lived happily ever after. The hero married the principal girl, the second hero got the second girl, and they moved out of the poor woodcutter's cottage into the east wing of the king's palace.

But this is not a fairy tale.

On the day Penny came out of hospital she, Peter Michaelis and I went on a wing-ding in the East End and the three of us became moderately alcoholic and distinctly merry. On the day Gillian arrived back from New York the four of us went on another wing-ding with similar effects. That American plastic surgeon must have been a genius because Gillian's new face was an improvement on the one she had before the acid was thrown. I was very glad for Peter.

The clanging of wedding bells could be heard in the near future. Penny and Gillian were dashing about London denuding the better stores of dresses and frillies for their trousseaux, while I scouted around for a house, introduced it to Penny, and then secured it with a cash deposit against the time the lawyers had finished their expensive wrangling over the deeds. It was all very exhilarating.

Ten days before the wedding I felt it incumbent on me to go back to see Starkie. He heard what I had to say and frowned, then took me into a laboratory where I was subjected to a battery of tests. He told me to go away and return in a week.

On the day I went back I read of Cregar's death in *The Times*. The obituary was sickening. Described as a faithful public servant who had served his country with no thought of self for many years, he was lauded as an example for coming generations to follow. I threw the paper out of the train window and was immediately sorry; that sort of stuff could pollute the countryside very seriously.

Starkie was serious, too, when I saw him, and I said, 'It's bad news.'

'Yes, it is,' he said directly. 'It's cancer.'

It was a blow, but I had half-expected it. 'How long do I have?'

He shrugged. 'Six months to a year, I'd say. Could be longer, but not much.'

I walked to his office window and looked out. I can't remember what I saw there. 'Cregar's dead,' I said. 'Same thing?'

'Yes.'

'How?'

Starkie sighed. 'That damned fool, Carter, was doing shotgun experiments. That means he was chopping up DNA molecules into short lengths, putting them into *E.coli*, and standing back to see what happened. It's not a bad technique if you know what you're doing and take the proper precautions.'

'He was taking precautions,' I said. 'The stuff got loose because of my own damned foolishness.'

'He wasn't,' snapped Starkie. 'Cregar was putting pressure on him – wanting fast results. He couldn't wait for a consignment of genetically weakened *E.coli* from the States so he used the normal bug. There was no biological containment at all. The stuff went straight into your gut and started to breed happily.'

'To cause cancer?' It didn't seem likely.

'I'll try to explain this as simply as possible,' said Starkie. 'We believe that in the genetic material of all normal cells there are genes which can produce tumour-forming chemicals, but they are normally repressed by other genes. Now, if you do a shotgun experiment and introduce a short length of DNA into *E.coli* you're in danger of introducing a tumour gene without the one that represses it. That's what's happened to you. The *E.coli* in your gut was producing tumour-forming chemicals.'

'But you said the *E.coli* coming out of me was normal,' I objected.

'I know I did, and so it was. One of the most difficult things to do in these experiments is to get a new strain to breed true. They're very unstable. What happened was that this strain began to breed back to normal *E.coli* almost immediately. But it was in your gut long enough to do the damage.'

'I see.' I felt a sudden chill. 'What about Penny?'

'She's all right. That was a different bug entirely. We made sure of that.'

I said, 'Thank you, Dr Starkie. You've been very direct and I appreciate it. What's the next step?'

He rubbed his jaw. 'If you hadn't come to see me I'd have sent for you – on the basis of what happened to Lord Cregar. This is a type of cancer we haven't come across before; at least it hasn't been reported in the literature in this particular form. Cregar went very fast, but that may have been because of his age. Older cellular structures are more susceptible to cancers. I think you have a better chance.'

But not much better, I thought. Starkie spoke in the flat, even tone used by doctors when they want to break the bad news slowly. He scribbled on a sheet of paper. 'Go to this man. He's very good and knows about your case. He'll probably put you on tumour-reducing drugs and, possibly, radiation therapy.' He paused. 'And put your affairs in order as any sensible man should.'

I thanked him again, took the address, and went back to London where I heard another instalment of bad news. Then I told Penny. I had no need to give her Starkie's explanation because she grasped that immediately. It was her job, after all. I said, 'Of course, the marriage is off.'

'Oh, no; Malcolm!'

And so we had another row – which I won. I said, 'I have no objection to living in sin. Come live with me and be my love. I know a place in the south of Ireland where the mountains are green and the sea is blue when the sun shines, which it does quite often, and green when it's cloudy and the rollers come in from the Atlantic. I could do with six months of that if you're with me.'

We went to Ireland immediately after Peter and Gillian were married. It was not the happy occasion one would have wished; the men were sombre and the women weepy, but it had to be gone through.

At one time I thought of suicide; taking the Hemingway out, to perpetrate a bad pun. But then I thought I had a job to do, which was to write an account of the Ashton case, leaving nothing out and making it as truthful as possible, and certainly not putting any cosmetics on my own blemishes. God knows I'm not proud of my own part in it. Penny has read the manuscript; parts of it have amused her, other parts have shattered her. She has typed it all herself.

We live here very simply if you discount the resident medical staff of a doctor and three nurses which Penny insisted upon. The doctor is a mild young American who plays bad chess and the nurses are pretty which Penny doesn't mind. It helps to have a wealthy woman for a mistress. For the first few months I used to go to Dublin once a fortnight where they'd prod and probe and shoot atoms into me. But I stopped that because it wasn't doing any good.

Now time is becoming short. This account and myself are coming to an end. I have written it for publication, partly because I think people ought to know what is done in their names, and partly because the work of Ashton on genetics has not yet been released. It would be a pity if his work, which could do so much good in the right hands, should be withheld and perhaps diverted to malignant uses in the hands of another Cregar. There are many Cregars about in high office.

Whether publication will be possible at all I don't know. The wrath of the Establishment can be mighty and its instruments of suppression strong and subtle. Nevertheless Penny and I have been plotting our campaign to ensure that these words are not lost.

A wise one-legged American, in adapting the words of a naval hero, once said, 'We have met the enemy, and he is us.'

God help you all if he is right.

'DESMOND BAGLEY'

This illuminating pen portrait of the author was written by Desmond Bagley himself for the original release of *The Tightrope Men*. It is the first time it has appeared in any of his books.

'I want to write – Galsworthy's dead and there's only Maugham left, so there's a chance for me,' fourteen-year old Desmond Bagley told his mother when she enquired about his future career. Today, slight, bearded, bespectacled Bagley is among the biggest-selling novelists of the 'sixties – and 'seventies.

'Desmond Bagley must be just about the fastest developing writer in the thriller business,' said Gavin Lyall in 1966 reviewing Bagley's third successive best-seller, *Wyatt's Hurricane*. Then by November 1971, *Vogue* reviewing his last novel, *The Freedom Trap*, wrote: 'The most exciting to date of the tough, literate, fast-paced spy thrillers which have become the unchallenged territory of Desmond Bagley.'

Since the publication in 1963 of his first novel, *The Golden Keel*, Bagley has not only built up a reputation which puts him in the top bracket of thriller writers, but he has notched up sales of over two and a half million copies: all nine of his titles have been Book Club choices; editions of his books have appeared in ten European countries and in the United States; and his first eight titles have been published in paperback by Fontana.

Desmond Bagley was a freelance journalist living in South Africa when he sat down to write his first novel. Like many readers, he had often felt as he laid a book aside that he could do as well – but he did not leave it there. With the help of his wife, director of a bookshop in Johannesburg, he set to work systematically to see what kind of book sold well and who published it. The result was that he decided to write a thriller for Collins (he thinks a would-be writer should always choose his publisher first and write to suit that publisher's list). He then analysed many thrillers to isolate what seemed to him the ingredients of success, and produced *The Golden Keel*. Collins accepted it at once.

An American publisher who saw the manuscript immediately gave Bagley a three-book contract and a five-figure advance. Since then, Desmond Bagley has averaged a novel a year – his latest being *The Tightrope Men*, which was published on 19th March 1973. He makes almost no notes, writes his first draft straight on to an electric typewriter, and carries his vast store of technical and geographical information in his head. But query his facts and he is likely to come up with an article from some obscure mining journal; ask him how he gets his plots and he will produce a newspaper cutting or the notebook, no bigger than a pocket diary, in which he occasionally jots down an idea.

The plot of *The Golden Keel*, his first novel now in its tenth reprint, which deals with an attempt to smuggle Mussolini's hidden gold out of Italy, dates back to 1949, soon after Bagley arrived in South Africa. He was working in an office in Natal and struck up a friendship with the man at the next desk. This man, a South African who had been captured at Tobruk, had joined a band of Italian partisans after the Germans invaded Italy and had helped to ambush a German convoy which turned out to be full of gold. The South African was the last survivor who knew where the gold lay hidden. He and Bagley discussed returning to fetch it, but when Bagley moved to Johannesburg, the two men lost touch.

'Over the years,' says Bagley, 'the story kept coming back to me and, as an imaginative exercise, I mulled over the problems of smuggling treasure from Italy. The problem seemed insurmountable until I hit on the idea that finally formed the basis of *The Golden Keel*. By this time I was a journalist writing extensively for the South African press as a freelance, and during a slack period in 1962 I sat down to put my imaginings on paper.'

Normally, Desmond Bagley's meticulous research is very necessary, for he does not usually visit the areas where his novels are set. For instance, before writing *Landslide*, set in British Columbia, Bagley took out a three months' subscription to the *Vancouver Sun* and soaked himself in the Canadian atmosphere for three months before he even started to write.

However, in 1972, Desmond Bagley went to Finland to see if he could find a book there. He did. In fact he fell in love with the place; the gay, volatile people with a high regard for individuality, which is reflected in their politics by a new government every year, and the country itself, with its beautiful lakes and trees, and its freedom. Now the book has come, where action, pace and suspense dominate the story of a man who wakes up to find he is somebody else – and Finland is one of the characters. The book is *The Tightrope Men*.

Other elements of success in Bagley's novels are his plots, which are strong action stories with their full share of violence (but without the sadism that too often accompanies it) and his characters, who are human and sharply differentiated, yet fitted neatly to their allotted tasks.

Born in 1923 in Kendal, Westmorland, where his parents kept a theatrical boarding house, Bagley can recall being dangled on Basil Rathbone's knee when that actor was on tour. This early contact with the stage had no lasting effect on him, and when he was four the family moved first to Bolton, and then to Blackpool. On leaving school, Bagley became a printer's devil. He hated it, so he took a job in a factory making plastic electrical fittings, transferring when war broke out to one making aircraft components instead.

In 1946, tired of austerity England and fired by the tales of Air Force friends who had trained overseas, he decided to emigrate to South Africa. The problem was that in 1946 shipping and airlines were booked up for two years solid. Bagley's solution was to journey to South Africa by road. He prepared with his usual systematic thoroughness, and on 7th January 1947 left Blackpool in a blizzard, accompanied by the good wishes of the Mayor and Corporation.

Crossing the Sahara so soon after the war was a risky business, since it did not then have the roads and safety precautions it does today, but Bagley reached Kampala, Uganda, took a job, went down at once with malaria – and left hastily for a better climate. He worked his way down Africa, taking jobs in asbestos and gold mines, mainly in store-keeping and store accounts, and in 1957 decided to try his hand at freelance journalism.

In 1964, following the success of his first two books, he and his wife Joan (whom he married in 1960) returned to England, where they now live in Totnes, Devon. As a full-time writer, Desmond Bagley now has time to indulge his hobbies of sailing, motor-boating, reading and what he calls 'just plain loafing'.

A friend of Bagley's once said that his books read like fictionalised versions of the *National Geographic Magazine*. Bagley believes he meant this in praise and not in disapproval. He says: 'For myself, I am an entertainer and not a pedagogue. I don't know if my readers are instructed while reading my books – that is not my aim. I do know that while doing research in odd corners of the world I am giving myself a liberal education.'

March 1973

DESMOND BAGLEY

'Unbeatable for sheer gripping excitement.'
Daily Telegraph

RUNNING BLIND

The assignment begins with a simple errand – a parcel to deliver. But to Alan Stewart, standing on a deserted road in Iceland with a murdered man at his feet, it looks anything but simple. The desolate terrain is obstacle enough. But when Stewart realises he has been double-crossed and that the opposition is gaining ground, his simple mission seems impossible . . .

THE FREEDOM TRAP

The Scarperers, a brilliantly organised gang which gets long-term inmates out of prison, spring a notorious Russian double agent. The trail leads Owen Stannard to Malta, and to the suave killer masterminding the gang. Face to face at last with his opponents, Stannard must try to outwit both men – who have nothing to lose and everything to gain by his death . . .

'Literate, exciting, knowledgeable adventure stories – Desmond Bagley is incomparable.' *Sunday Mirror*

978-0-00-730474-5

DESMOND BAGLEY

'Compulsively readable.' *Guardian*

FLYAWAY

Why is Max Stafford, security consultant, beaten up in his own office? What is the secret of the famous 1930s aircraft, the Lockheed Lodestar? And why has accountant Paul Bilson disappeared in North Africa? The journey to the Sahara desert becomes a race to save Paul Bilson, a race to find the buried aircraft, and – above all – a race to return alive . . .

WINDFALL

When a legacy of £40 million is left to a small college in Kenya, investigations begin about the true identities of the heirs – the South African, Dirk Hendriks, and his namesake, Henry Hendrix from California. Suspicion that Hendrix is an impostor leads Max Stafford to the Rift Valley, where a violent reaction to his arrival points to a sinister and far-reaching conspiracy far beyond mere greed . . .

'From word one, you're off. Bagley's one of the best.'
The Times

978-0-00-730476-9

DESMOND BAGLEY

'The best adventure stories I have read for years.'

Daily Mirror

THE GOLDEN KEEL

When the Allies invaded southern Italy in 1943, Mussolini's personal treasure was moved north to safety under heavily armed guard. It was never seen again. Now, an expedition plans to unearth the treasure and smuggle it out of Italy. But their reckless mission is being followed – by enemies who are as powerful and ruthless as they are deadly . . .

THE VIVERO LETTER

Jeremy Wheale's well-ordered life is blasted apart when his brother is murdered. The killer was after a family heirloom – an antique gold tray – which sets Wheale on a trail from Devon to the tropical rainforest of Yucatan. There he joins the hunt for a lost Mayan city. But in the dense cover of the jungle a band of vicious convict mercenaries are waiting to strike . . .

'Bagley has no equal at this sort of thing.'

Sunday Mirror

978-0-00-730477-6

DESMOND BAGLEY

'Tense, heroic, chastening . . . a thumping good story.'
Sunday Express

THE SNOW TIGER

Fifty-four people died in the avalanche that ripped apart a small New Zealand mining town. But the enquiry which follows unleashes more destructive power than the snow-fall. As the survivors tell their stories, they reveal a community so divided that all warnings of danger went unheeded. At the centre of the storm is Ian Ballard, whose life depends upon being able to clear his name . . .

NIGHT OF ERROR

When Mark Trevelyan dies on a journey to a remote Pacific atoll, the verdict that it was natural causes doesn't convince his brother, Mike. The series of violent attacks that follows only adds to his suspicions. Just two clues – a notebook in code and a lump of rock – are enough to trigger off a hazardous expedition, and a violent confrontation far from civilization . . .

'The detail is immaculately researched – the action has the skill to grab your heart or your bowels.' *Daily Mirror*

978-0-00-730481-3

DESMOND BAGLEY

'Bagley in top form.' *Evening Standard*

THE SPOILERS

When film tycoon Robert Hellier loses his daughter to heroin, he declares war on the drug pedlars, the faceless overlords whose greed supplies the world with its deadly pleasures. London drug specialist Nicholas Warren is called upon to organise an expedition to the Middle East to track down and destroy them – but with a hundred million dollars' worth of heroin at stake, Warren knows he will have to use methods as deadly as his prey . . .

JUGGERNAUT

It is no ordinary juggernaut. Longer than a football pitch, weighing 550 tons, and moving at just five miles per hour, its job – and that of troubleshooter Neil Mannix – is to move a giant transformer across an oil-rich African state. But when Nyala erupts in civil war, Mannix's juggernaut is at the centre of the conflict – a target of ambush and threat, with no way to run and nowhere to hide . . .

'Bagley is a master story-teller.' *Daily Mirror*

978-0-00-730480-6

DESMOND BAGLEY

'Bagley is one of the best.' *The Times*

HIGH CITADEL

When Tim O'Hara's plane is hijacked and forced to crash land in the middle of the Andes, his troubles are only beginning. A heavily armed group of communist soldiers intent on killing one of his passengers – an influential political figure – have orders to leave no survivors. Isolated in the biting cold of the Andes, O'Hara's party must fight for their lives with only the most primitive weapons . . .

LANDSLIDE

Bob Boyd is a geologist, as resilient as the British Columbia timber country where he works for the powerful Matterson Corporation. But his real name and his past are mysteries – wiped out by the accident that nearly killed him. Then Boyd reads a name that opens a door in his memory: Trinavant – and discovers that Bull Matterson and his son will do almost anything to keep the Trinavant family forgotten forever . . .

'Very much of the moment. The characters are sympathetic and believable' *Sunday Times*

978-0-00-730479-0

DESMOND BAGLEY

'Stories charged with suspense.' *Financial Times*

WYATT'S HURRICANE

Ferocious Hurricane Mabel is predicted to pass harmlessly amongst the islands of the Caribbean. But David Wyatt has developed a sixth sense about hurricanes. He is convinced that Mabel will change course to strike the island of San Fernandez and its capital, St Pierre. But nobody believes him, and the hurricane is only one of the problems that threaten San Fernandez . . .

BAHAMA CRISIS

Tom Mangan was a sharply successful entrepreneur who lured the super-rich to his luxury hotels in the sun-soaked Bahamas. Then violent tragedy struck: his own family disappeared, and a series of misfortunes, accidents and mysterious epidemics began to drive the tourists away and wreck Mangan's livelihood. Fatally, he becomes determined to confront his enemy – and the hunt is on . . .

'Tautly written adventure, packed with exhaustive detail. You will be out of breath when you finish.'

Books And Bookmen

978-0-00-730478-3

LEN DEIGHTON

'A stunning spy story' *Guardian*

XPD

June 11, 1940 – where is Winston Churchill?

A private aircraft takes off from a small town in central France, while Adolf Hitler, the would-be conqueror of Europe, prepares for a clandestine meeting near the Belgian border.

For more than forty years the events of this day have been Britain's most closely guarded secret. Anyone who learns of them must die – with their file stamped: *XPD – expedient demise*

'Exciting and well made.' *Daily Telegraph*

'Deighton in top form . . . the best kind of action entertainment.' *Publishers Weekly*

'Deliciously sharp and flawlessly accurate dialogue, breathtakingly clever plotting, confident character drawing . . . a splendidly strongly told story.' *The Times*

978-0-586-05447-5

LEN DEIGHTON

'A brilliant picture of Britain under German rule.'

Sunday Telegraph

SS-GB

In February 1941 British Command surrendered to the Nazis. Churchill has been executed, the King is in the Tower and the SS are in Whitehall. For nine months Britain has been occupied – a blitzed, depressed and dingy country. However, it's 'business as usual' at Scotland Yard run by the SS when Detective Inspector Archer is assigned to a routine murder case. Life must go on.

But when SS Standartenführer Huth arrives from Berlin with orders from the great Himmler himself to supervise the investigation, the resourceful Archer finds himself caught up in a high level, all action, espionage battle.

'One of Deighton's best. Apart from his virtues as a story-teller, his passion for researching his backgrounds gives his work a remarkable factual authority.'

Anthony Burgess, *Observer*

'Len Deighton is the Flaubert of the contemporary thriller writers . . . there can be little doubt that this is much the way things would have turned out if the Germans had won the war.'

Michael Howard, *Times Literary Supplement*

978-0-586-05002-6

LEN DEIGHTON

'A massively different novel . . . the effect is – quite literally – devastating.'

Sunday Times

BOMBER

Bomber follows the progress of an Allied air raid through a period of twenty-four hours in the summer of 1943. It portrays all the participants in a terrifying drama, in the air and on the ground, in Britain and in Germany. In its documentary style, it is unique. In its emotional power, it is overwhelming.

Len Deighton has been hugely acclaimed both as a novelist and as an historian. In *Bomber* he has combined both talents to produce a masterpiece.

'The magnificent *Bomber* is rich with historical detail.'

The Times

'A massive and superbly mobilised tragedy of the machines which men create to destroy themselves . . . masterly and by far Mr Deighton's best.'

Douglas Hurd, *Spectator*

'A magnificent story . . . the characters lean out of the pages.'

Daily Mirror

978-0-586-04544-2

LEN DEIGHTON

'The sheer charge of the writing swept me into another world.' H.R.F. Keating, *The Times*

GOODBYE MICKEY MOUSE

In *Goodbye Mickey Mouse* Len Deighton has written a brilliant, multi-dimensional picture of what it is to be at war . . . and what it was to be in love in the England of 1944.

'It is a novel of memory, satisfying on every imaginable level, but truly astonishing in its recreation of a time and place through minute detail. Deighton has written well of the air before, nonfictionally, and he informs us in an afterword that it took six years of research to do this novel. It shows. The only way you could know more about flying a P-51 Mustang, after reading this book, is to have flown one.' *Washington Post*

'He writes, as usual, with authority and a superb sense of period.' *Daily Telegraph*

978-0-586-05448-2

ALISTAIR MACLEAN
SAM LLEWELLYN

'Compulsively exciting.' *Daily Telegraph*

THE GUNS OF NAVARONE

Mallory, Miller and Andrea are a lethally effective team. Their mission: to silence the impregnable guns set in the tall cliffs of Navarone. On their success or failure rests one of the most critical offensives of the Second World War.

FORCE TEN FROM NAVARONE

The three Navarone heroes are parachuted into war-torn Yugoslavia to rescue a division of partisans on a mission so deadly that it must be hidden even from their own allies.

STORM FORCE FROM NAVARONE

The surviving commandos are sent on a perilous journey through the Pyrenees to disable the greatest threat to the impending D-Day landings: the 'Werwolf' U-boats. But it seems impossible – D-Day is less than six days away.

THUNDERBOLT FROM NAVARONE

Mallory, Miller and Andrea are given a final assignment: to reconnoitre the Greek island of Kynthos and destroy the German facilities developing the lethal V3 weapon. A rocket expert is to accompany them – but can he be trusted not to turn the operation into a suicide mission?

'Could hardly be bettered.' *Sunday Times*

978-0-00-728422-1